I'm in Chengshi sector, between Apogee and Gardens—just over halfway to the drop-off.

I'll have to stop to refill somewhere in Gardens, because there's no chance of getting any water from Darnell. I might be bringing him a package, but asking that guy for water is almost as deadly as jumping off a catwalk blindfolded.

The corridors here are darker than before. I have to pay more attention to the surface as I run towards the next turn, watching for the places where the steel plates are twisted and bent. Surprisingly, there's a working screen here, grimy with dust but still showing a cheery recruitment ad for the space construction corps. A smiling spaceman, clad in a sleek black suit with the visor up, wielding a plasma cutter as he maneuvers himself around a construction ship's arm. The video fills the corridor with soft blue light, and as I turn the corner, I close my eyes for a split second. The light filters through my lids, flickering a warm orange.

I've never been there, but sometimes I like to imagine myself on Earth, running across fields of grass, under a sky so blue that it hurts to look at it. The sun, warm on the back of my neck as I go faster, and faster, and faster. Until I'm no longer running. I'm airborne.

I open my eyes.

Just in time to see the metal pole swing out from behind the corner and slam into my chest.

Praise for the

OUTER EARTH TRILOGY

"The literary equivalent of a base jump: fast, exhilarating, and unforgettable, and once you start it you can't stop. I loved it."

—Sarah Lotz, author of *The Three*, on *Tracer*

"Ludicrously fast-paced, with a brilliant sci-fi setting, *Tracer* is an absolute blast of a read."

—David Owen, author of *Panther*

"A stunning debut by Rob Boffard that never lets up, from the nerve-jangling beginning to the explosive end."

—James Douglas, author of *The Doomsday Machine*, on *Tracer*

"Ambitious and intriguing." —*Kirkus* on *Tracer*

"*Tracer* sets a new standard for all-action SF."

—Ken MacLeod, author of the Second Law trilogy

OUTER EARTH

By Rob Boffard

THE OUTER EARTH TRILOGY

Tracer
Zero-G
Impact

Adrift

OUTER EARTH

ROB BOFFARD

This omnibus edition contains

Tracer

Zero-G

Impact

orbit

www.orbitbooks.net

Author photograph by Nicole Simpson
Cover art by DAS ILLUSTRAT München, using material by ZargonDesign / iStockphoto and Johan Swanepoel / Shutterstock

Orbit
Hachette Book Group
1290 Avenue of the Americas
New York, NY 10104
orbitbooks.net

Originally published in Great Britain by Orbit in 2017
First U.S. Edition: February 2018

Orbit is an imprint of Hachette Book Group.
The Orbit name and logo are trademarks of Little, Brown Book Group Limited.

The publisher is not responsible for websites (or their content) that are not owned by the publisher.

The Hachette Speakers Bureau provides a wide range of authors for speaking events. To find out more, go to

Library of Congress Control Number: 2017954010

ISBNs: 978-0-316-43907-7 (trade paperback), 978-0-316-43906-0 (ebook)

Printed in the United States of America

LSC-C

10 9 8 7 6 5 4 3 2 1

For Johanna

Contents

TRACER

Seven years ago

The ship is breaking up around them.

The hull is twisting and creaking, like it's trying to tear away from the heat of re-entry. The outer panels are snapping off, hurtling past the cockpit viewports, black blurs against a dull orange glow.

The ship's second-in-command, Singh, is tearing at her seat straps, as if getting loose will be enough to save her. She's yelling at the captain, seated beside her, but he pays her no attention. The flight deck below them is a sea of flashing red, the crew spinning in their chairs, hunting for something, *anything* they can use.

They have checklists for these situations. But there's no checklist for when a ship, plunging belly-down through Earth's atmosphere to maximise the drag, gets flipped over by an explosion deep in the guts of the engine, sending it first into a spin and then into a screaming nosedive. Now it's spearing through the atmosphere, the friction tearing it to pieces.

The captain doesn't raise his voice. "We have to eject the rear module," he says.

Singh's eyes go wide. "Captain—"

He ignores her, reaching up to touch the communicator in his ear. "Officer Yamamoto," he says, speaking as clearly as he can. "Cut the rear module loose."

Koji Yamamoto stares up at him. His eyes are huge, his mouth slightly open. He's the youngest crew member, barely eighteen.

The captain has to say his name again before he turns and hammers on the touch-screens.

The loudest bang of all shudders through the ship as its entire rear third explodes away. Now the ship and its crew are tumbling end over end, the movement forcing them back in their seats. The captain's stomach feels like it's broken free of its moorings. He waits for the tumbling to stop, for the ship to right itself. Three seconds. Five.

He sees his wife's face, his daughter's. *No, don't think about them. Think about the ship.*

"Guidance systems are gone," McCallister shouts, her voice distorting over the comms. "The core's down. I got nothing."

"Command's heard our mayday," Dominguez says. "They—"

McCallister's straps snap. She's hurled out of her chair, thudding off the control panel, leaving a dark red spatter of blood across a screen. Yamamoto reaches for her, forgetting that he's still strapped in. Singh is screaming.

"Dominguez," says the captain. "Patch me through."

Dominguez tears his eyes away from the injured McCallister. A second later, his hands are flying across the controls. A burst of static sounds in the captain's comms unit, followed by two quick beeps.

He doesn't bother with radio protocol. "Ship is on a collision path. We're going to try to crash-land. If we—"

"John."

Foster doesn't have to identify himself. His voice is etched into the captain's memory from dozens of flight briefings and planning sessions and quiet conversations in the pilots' bar.

The captain doesn't know if the rest of flight command are listening in, and he doesn't care. "Marshall," he says. "I think I can bring the ship down. We'll activate our emergency beacon; sit tight until you can get to us."

"I'm sorry, John. There's nothing I can do."

"What are you talking about?"

There's another bang, and then a roar, as if the ship is caught in the jaws of an enormous beast. The captain turns to look at Singh, but she's gone. So is the side of the ship. There's nothing but a jagged gash, the edges a mess of torn metal and sputtering wires. The awful orange glow is coming in, its fingers reaching for him, and he can feel the heat baking on his skin.

"Marshall, listen to me," the captain says, but Marshall is gone too. The captain can see the sky beyond the ship, beyond the flames. It's blue, clearer than he could have ever imagined. It fades to black where it reaches the upper atmosphere, and the space beyond that is pinpricked with stars.

One of those stars is Outer Earth.

Maybe I can find it, the captain thinks, if I look hard enough. He can feel the anger, the *disbelief* at Marshall's words, but he refuses to let it take hold. He tells himself that Outer Earth will send help. They have to. He tries to picture the faces of his family, tries to hold them uppermost in his mind, but the roaring and the heat are everywhere and he can't—

1

Riley

My name is Riley Hale, and when I run, the world disappears.

Feet pounding. Heart thudding. Steel plates thundering under my feet as I run, high up on Level 6, keeping a good momentum as I move through the darkened corridors. I focus on the next step, on the in–out, push–pull of my breathing. Stride, land, cushion, spring, repeat. The station is a tight warren of crawlspaces and vents around me, every surface metal etched with ancient graffiti.

"She's over there!"

The shout comes from behind me, down the other end of the corridor. The skittering footsteps that follow it echo off the walls. I thought I'd lost these idiots back at the sector border—now I have to outrun them all over again. I got lost in the rhythm of running—always dangerous when someone's trying to jack your cargo. I refuse to waste a breath on cursing, but one of my exhales turns into a growl of frustration.

The Lieren might not be as fast as I am, but they obviously don't give up.

I go from a jog to a sprint, my pack juddering on my spine as I pump my arms even harder. A tiny bead of sweat touches my eye, sizzling and stinging. I ignore it. No tracer in my crew has ever failed to deliver their cargo, and I am not going to be the first.

I round the corner—and nearly slam into a crush of people. There are five of them, sauntering down the corridor, talking among themselves. But I'm already reacting, pushing off with my right foot, springing in the direction of the wall. I bring my other foot up to meet it, flattening it against the metal and tucking my left knee up to my chest. The momentum keeps me going forwards even as I'm pushing off, exhaling with a whoop as I squeeze through the space between the people and the wall. My right foot comes down, and I'm instantly in motion again. Full momentum. A perfect tic-tac.

The Lieren are close behind, colliding with the group, bowling them over in a mess of confused shouts. But I've got the edge now. Their cries fade into the distance.

There's not a lot you can move between sectors without paying off the gangs. Not unless you know where and how to cross. Tracers do. And that's why we exist. If you need to get something to someone, or if you've got a little package you don't want any gangs knowing about, you come find us. We'll get it there—for a price, of course—and if you come to my crew, the Devil Dancers, we'll get it there *fast*.

The corridor exit looms, and then I'm out, into the gallery. After the corridors, the giant lights illuminating the massive open area are blinding. Corridor becomes catwalk, bordered with rusted metal railings, and the sound of my footfalls fades away, whirling off into the open space.

I catch a glimpse of the diagram on the far wall, still legible a hundred years after it was painted. A scale picture of the station. The Core at the centre, a giant sphere which houses the main fusion reactor. Shooting out from it on either side, two spokes, connected to an enormous ring, the main body. And under it, faded to almost nothing after over a century: Outer Earth Orbit Preservation Module, Founded A.D. 2234.

Ahead of me, more people emerge from the far entrance to the catwalk. A group of teenage girls, packed tight, talking loudly among themselves. I count ten, fifteen—*no*. They haven't seen me. I'm heading full tilt towards them.

Without breaking stride, I grab the right-hand railing of the catwalk and launch myself up and over, into space.

For a second, there's no noise but the air rushing past me. The sound of the girls' conversation vanishes, like someone turned down a volume knob. I can see all the way down to the bottom of the gallery, a hundred feet below, picking out details snatched from the gaps in the web of criss-crossing catwalks.

The floor is a mess of broken benches and circular flowerbeds with nothing in them. There are two young girls, skipping back and forth over a line they've drawn on the floor. One is wearing a faded smock. I can just make out the word Astro on the back as it twirls around her. A light above them is flickering off–on–off, and their shadows flit in and out on the wall behind them, dancing off metal plates. My own shadow is spread out before me, split by the catwalks; a black shape broken on rusted railings. On one of the catwalks lower down, two men are arguing, pushing each other. One man throws a punch, his target dodging back as the group around them scream dull threats.

I jumped off the catwalk without checking my landing zone. I don't even want to think what Amira would do if she found out. Explode, probably. Because if there's someone under me and I hit them from above, it's not just a broken ankle I'm looking at.

Time seems frozen. I flick my eyes towards the Level 5 catwalk rushing towards me.

It's empty. Not a person in sight, not even further along. I pull my legs up, lift my arms and brace for the landing.

Contact. The noise returns, a bang that snaps my head back even as I'm rolling forwards. On instinct, I twist sideways, so the impact can travel across, rather than up, my spine. My right hand hits the ground, the sharp edges of the steel bevelling scraping my palm, and I push upwards, arching my back so my pack can fit into the roll.

Then I'm up and running, heading for the dark catwalk exit on the far side. I can hear the Lieren reach the catwalk above. They've spotted me, but I can tell by their angry howls that it's too late. There's no way they're making that jump. To get to where I am, they'll have to fight their way through the stairwells on the far side. By then, I'll be long gone.

"Never try to outrun a Devil Dancer, boys," I mutter between breaths.

2

Darnell

"So you don't have it?"

The technician is doing his best not to look at Oren Darnell. He frowns down at the tab screen in his hands, flicking through the menu with one trembling finger.

Darnell's nose twitches, and he takes a delicate sniff, tasting the air. He's always had a good sense of smell. He can identify plants by their scent, stripping them down into their component notes. The smell of the bags of fertiliser stacked along the walls is powerful, pungent even, but he can still smell the technician's sweat, hot and tangy with fear. Good.

"I know it was here," the tech says, shaking his head. He's a short man, with a closely shorn head and a barely visible mask of stubble on his face. "Someone must have signed it out."

He glances up at Darnell, just for a second, then looks down again. "But it doesn't make sense. That shipment was marked for your use only."

Darnell says nothing. He reaches up to scratch his neck, glancing back towards the door of the storeroom. His guard Reece is lounging against the frame, looking bored. He catches Darnell's eye, and shrugs.

"Don't worry though, Mr. Darnell," the tech says, snapping the tab screen off and slipping it under his arm. He pushes it too far, and has to catch it before it falls. "I'll find it. Have it sent right up to your office. Bring it myself, actually. You leave it with me."

Darnell smiles at him. It's a warm smile, almost paternal. "That's all right," he says. "It happens."

"I know what you mean, Sir," the tech says, meeting Darnell's smile with one of his own. "But we'll get to the bottom of—"

"Do me a favour," Darnell says. He points to the back of the storeroom. "Grab me a bag of micronutrient, would you?"

The tech's smile gets wider, relieved to have a purpose, a job he can easily accomplish. "You got it," he says, and scampers across the room, already scanning the shelves for the dull orange bag of fertiliser he needs. He sees it on the top shelf, just out of reach, and is standing on his toes to snag the edge when something whistles past his head. The knife bounces off the wall, spinning wildly before coming to a stop on the floor. The tech can see his own expression in the highly polished blade. A thin whine is coming out of his mouth. The tab screen falls, shattering, spraying shimmering fragments.

"I always pull to the right," Darnell says as he strolls towards the tech. "Don't hold it against me, though. Throwing a knife is hard—and that's with a blade that's perfectly balanced."

The tech can't speak. Can't move. Can't even take his eyes off the knife, the one that passed an inch from the back of his neck. The handle is hardwood, shiny with oil, the grain smooth with age.

"It's all in the arm," Darnell says. "You can't release it until your arm is straight. I know, I know, I need to get better. But hey, you don't have anything to do at the moment, right? Why don't you stay and help me out? It's easy. You just have to stand real still."

He points at the knife. "Pick it up."

When the tech still doesn't move, doesn't do anything except stand there shaking, Darnell gives his shoulder a push. It's a light touch, gentle even, but the tech nearly falls over. He squeaks, his hands clenching and unclenching.

"Pick it up."

"Boss." Reece is striding towards them, his hands in his pockets. Darnell glances up, and Reece jerks his head at the door.

Darnell looks back at the tech, flashing him that warm smile again. "Duty calls," he says. "Truth be told, it's hard to find the time to practise. But don't worry—when I get a moment, I'll let you know."

The tech is nodding furiously. He doesn't know what else to do.

Darnell turns to go, but then looks back over his shoulder. "The blade hit the wall pretty hard. Probably blunted it up good. Would you make yourself useful? Get it sharpened for me?"

"Sure," the tech says, in a voice that doesn't seem like his own. "Sure. I can do that."

"Kind of you," Darnell says, striding away. He exchanges a few whispered words with Reece, then raises his voice so the tech can hear. "Good and sharp, remember. You should be able to draw blood if you put a little bit of pressure on the edge."

He sweeps out of the room, Reece trailing a few steps behind.

3

Riley

I slow down slightly as I enter the Level 5 corridor. Drop-off is way up the ring, at the Air Lab in Gardens sector. With each sector in the ring three miles long—and with six sectors in all—it's a long way to go. Unless you're a tracer, with the stamina and skill to get things where they need to be. I don't mind the distance—heading to the Air Lab means I get to see Prakesh.

I smile at the thought, before remembering that he's not there today. It's a rare day off for him, one he was boasting about when I saw him a couple of weeks ago.

The package snuggled next to my spine—the one the Lieren want to jack in the hope it's something good—is going to Oren Darnell, the man who runs the Air Lab. It was given to me by a merchant in the Apogee sector market. The merchant—Gray, I think his name was—paid with six fresh batteries, slapping them down on the rusty countertop of his stall, barely looking at me. Totally fine with that; pay is good, so your package gets delivered.

As I enter the corridor I reach back over my shoulder for the thin plastic nozzle protruding from the top of my pack, jamming it into my mouth and sucking down water from the reservoir. It's warm, and feels viscous in my mouth. There's not much, but it'll keep me going.

I'm in Chengshi sector, between Apogee and Gardens—just over halfway to the drop-off. I'll have to stop to refill somewhere in Gardens, because there's no chance of getting any water from Darnell. I might be bringing him a package, but asking that guy for water is almost as deadly as jumping off a catwalk blindfolded.

The corridors here are darker than before. I have to pay more attention to the surface as I run towards the next turn, watching for the places where the steel plates are twisted and bent. Surprisingly, there's a working screen here, grimy with dust but still showing a cheery recruitment ad for the space construction corps. A smiling spaceman, clad in a sleek black suit with the visor up, wielding a plasma cutter as he manoeuvres himself around a construction ship's arm. The video fills the corridor with soft blue light, and as I turn the corner, I close my eyes for a split second. The light filters through my lids, flickering a warm orange.

I've never been there, but sometimes I like to imagine myself on Earth, running across fields of grass, under a sky so blue that it hurts to look at it. The sun, warm on the back of my neck as I go faster, and faster, and faster. Until I'm no longer running. I'm airborne.

I open my eyes.

Just in time to see the metal pole swing out from behind the corner and slam into my chest.

For a second I really am airborne, lying prone in mid-air. I crash to the ground, my bones feeling like they're going to vibrate out of my skin. I try to scream, but all I can manage are thick, wheezing gasps.

The one with the pole is just a fuzzy black blur; he twirls the weapon in his hand, like he's out for a stroll. Another spasm of pain crackles across my chest, and I begin to cough: a deep, hacking, groaning noise that causes the pain to spread to my abdomen.

"Good hit," says a voice from the left. There's laughter from somewhere else, behind him.

Then there are six of them looking down on me. More Lieren—different from the ones who were chasing me. I cough again, even worse this time, like there's a dagger in my chest.

The one that hit me looks around nervously. I glimpse a dark red wolf tattoo on his neck. "Come on," he says, looking back down the passage. "Get her pack."

Someone wedges a boot under the small of my back and flips me over, forcing another cough out of my body. A foot on the back of my neck slams me into the floor before two others take my arms, yanking them backwards and sliding my backpack off.

My mind is racing. There should have been other people in this corridor by now. I can't be the only person here. Even if they didn't intervene, they might be the distraction I need to get away. And how did the Lieren set this ambush in the first place? They were behind me. I only came this way because the catwalk was blocked, and I had to...

Oh. Oh, that's clever. The group of girls on the catwalk. They were sent directly into my path, either paid or forced to do what the Lieren wanted. They knew they weren't fast enough to catch me, so they funnelled me right to them. I've run cargo to the Air Lab before—they'd know the routes I take, where I'd go and what I'd do when I was chased. Played like a fool, Riley.

"Anything else we can get? Her jacket?" I hear one of them say. Anger shoots through me; if they take my dad's jacket, I'll kill them. Every one of them.

"Nah, it's a piece of shit. The cargo'll be enough."

They yank the pack off and force me back down. Someone reaches into my jacket pockets and grabs the batteries. The boot is lifted off my back. I raise my head and see the kid with the pole tossing a battery up and down, a weird little grin on his face. He has my pack dangling from his other hand, and he and the other five are already moving away.

I push myself to my feet, chest aching with the effort, forcing myself to stay silent. I gain my balance, then start towards them, shifting onto the balls of my feet to lower the noise in the cramped corridor. Quick steps.

It's the one with my pack I'm after, and at the very moment he realises I'm behind him, I bring my right hand up in a lunging strike. I've balled my hand into a fist, with the knuckle of my index finger protruding slightly, and I'm aiming right for the base of his skull. Amira's tried to teach me about pressure points before, but this is the first time I've ever had to put it into practice.

My strike is true, hitting the tiny pocket of flesh where the skull joins the spine, and I feel something under my fist crack. He makes a strangled sound, and flies forward, my pack falling from his hand.

I have about half a second to appreciate my victory. Then one of his friends steps forward and socks me in the eye so hard that I just go somewhere else for a while.

When I come back—seconds later? Minutes?—I'm pushed up against the corridor wall, two of the Lieren holding me in place. My face is numb, and there's blood in my mouth; I can taste the metallic edge, sharp and nasty. The one I attacked is still out on the ground. As I watch, he groans, twitching under the flickering lights.

The Lieren with the wolf tattoo is standing in front of me, rearing back for another hit. If this one connects, it's goodbye Riley.

He throws the punch. I wrench my head to the side, and his fist slams into the metal wall, sending a resonant clang rattling around the corner. He pulls it back with a cry of pain. A flap of skin hangs off his middle finger, blood already welling up around the edges of the wound. His buddies relaxed their grip in surprise for a moment when I dodged, but not enough for me to break free, and now they force me back against the wall. "She's got some fight in her," growls one.

Tattoo is holding his wrist and shaking his hand back and forth. "You missed," I say. "Can't even hit someone standing still, can you?"

"Is that right?" he says, wiping his mouth with his uninjured hand.

"Yeah. Maybe you have these guys let me loose, and we go a few rounds. You and me. See who's faster."

"Think so? You're kind of small for a tracer. What are you, fifteen?"

"Twenty," I spit back, instantly regretting it.

"She's ugly, too," says one of the Lieren holding me. "Like some nuke mutant from back on Earth."

"Maybe she's got some cousins down there right now. New life forms."

There's laughter, cruel and sharp. I try to keep my voice calm. "Listen to me," I say. "That cargo is going to Oren Darnell. I'm under his protection in Gardens. If you take my cargo, you'll have to answer to him."

"The hell is Oren Darnell?" says the one holding my left shoulder.

"Don't you know anything?" says the Lieren with the tattoo. "He's in charge of the Air Lab." But no fear crosses his face—instead, he looks amused, still flicking his wrecked hand. Not good.

"He's got gang connections," I say. "Death's Head. Black Hole Crew. You sure Zhao would want you to jack cargo going in their direction?"

I'm half hoping that mentioning the name of Zhao Zheng, the leader of the Lieren, would have some effect. But Tattoo just laughs. "Rumours, honey. That's all there is to it."

"It's the truth. I…"

And then Tattoo pulls out a knife, and the words die on my lips.

4

Darnell

Darnell marches across the Air Lab, his heavy footfalls ringing out across the metal walkways. He doesn't need to check that Reece is following him; the guard is always close by, always there when Darnell needs him. His footsteps are as silent as his boss's are loud.

There are algae pools lined up along the walkway, each one thirty square feet, with surfaces like murky glass. Darnell leans over one of them, idly running a finger along the slime.

"So what's so urgent you had to pull me away?" he says.

Reece stops a short distance away, his arms folded. He glances left and right. There are plenty of other techs on the floor of the cavernous Air Lab, tending to trees or crossing the floor in tight groups, but there's nobody close to where he and Darnell are.

"Well?" Darnell says, staring intently at the viscous water.

"What's going on, boss?" Reece says.

Darnell says nothing.

Reece unfolds his arms, hooks his thumbs in his belt. "This isn't some gangster who hasn't paid us his water tax," he says. "That was one of your employees. I can cover for you on most things, but even I might struggle to square that one."

Darnell swings himself upright, pointing a finger at Reece. A tiny thread of algae comes with it, swinging back and forth. "You getting scared, Reece?" he says, stepping away from the tank. "You think I'm going too far?"

The guard doesn't flinch, just refolds his arms.

"If I'm going too far," Darnell says, "then maybe you should stop me. How about it, Reece? Want to try?"

Reece's cool eyes look back at him. Despite his anger at the insubordination, a part of Darnell marvels at Reece's refusal to get scared. It's why he's kept him around so long.

"You've been distracted, boss," Reece says. "For like a month now. And I've never seen you flip out on one of your own techs before, not like that. Whatever's going on, you should tell me so I can—"

"Should?"

Reece stops dead.

"You just make sure that shipment gets here," Darnell says. He sweeps his arm around to indicate the rest of the hangar. "Isn't that what you do? I'm in charge of the Air Lab, Reece. I'm responsible for every molecule of oxygen that you suck into your lungs and every molecule of CO_2 that comes out of them. You need to make sure I have everything I need to do it. That's what you need to do."

"I'll handle it," Reece says.

"Excellent," Darnell says, resuming his march towards the control room, his mind already elsewhere. He's got bigger things to worry about, like the other shipment: the little package Arthur Gray is supposed to deliver. If someone diverts that, they'll have a lot more to worry about than his shitty knife-throwing.

5

Riley

It'd be nice to say it's a beautiful blade. It's not. The handle is patched and frayed, and the steel is laced with rust. If the cut doesn't kill you, the infection will.

Tattoo holds it up, the metal catching the edge of the light. "You know," he says, "we just wanted a score. We weren't really planning on killing you."

He rotates the knife, angling the point towards my eyes. "But now, we have to take something back. You can't hurt one of us, and not expect to get it back in return. You understand, right?"

I try to say something, but I can't look away from the blade. He leans in close. The point is now inches away. "What'll it be? Left ear, or right?"

"Let me go," I finally say. It's almost a snarl. But the knife remains steady, its tip hardly wavering at all as it creeps towards my face. He starts flicking it gently back and forth. I can feel sweat soaking my shirt at the small of my back. I yank my body to one side, but the Lieren holding me are too strong. One of them plants a hand on my forehead, pinning me in place. "You might want to stay still," he says.

Left, right, left, right.

There's a yell from behind Tattoo. He straightens up, irritated, and looks back over his shoulder. One of the other Lieren, tall and gangly with sallow skin, is holding my pack. It's open, and he's frantically beckoning his buddies over.

With a sigh, Tattoo drops the knife from my face and walks over to him. "And now? What's the matter with..."

His voice falters as he looks into the pack. He turns, blocking my view, holding a whispered conversation with his partner.

I don't have the first clue about what's in my pack. We never do. It's one of the reasons why my crew gets so much work. You can send whatever you want, and you can trust us to never know about it.

I feel a flicker of hope: for the first time, it looks like it might just save my life.

After a minute of hissed back-and-forth with his friend, Tattoo signals to the ones holding me against the wall. Abruptly, they let me go. I collapse against the wall, try to rise, but my legs have stopped listening to me.

Tattoo is staring at me with an odd look on his face. He walks over, leans close, whispers: "This isn't finished."

He holds up a battery, bringing it as close to my face as he did the knife. "And we're keeping these."

The one who opened the bag lets it fall, and it lands with a thump on the floor. With a gesture from Tattoo, the Lieren set off down the corridor. One of them grabs the man I took down with the pressure-point strike, swinging him over his shoulders like a crop bag.

I don't want to, but I stay down until they're out of sight. I'm shaking, and it takes a minute for me to steady myself. Then it takes me another minute to rise—I nearly lose my balance when I do, and some blood droplets patter onto the floor ahead of me. My face is humming with pain, and my eye socket is on fire. But I can't worry about that now. I've lost too much time already.

As I move to grab my still-open pack and zip it shut, I can't help but see what's inside. It's the box Gray gave me to deliver—barely the size of a fist, like something you'd keep a small machine part in. The top of the box has been opened up by the Lieren. Inside is something wrapped in layers of opaque plastic padding—a blurred shape, vaguely familiar.

And from the bottom right corner of the box, slowly leaching into the protective foam, I can see a thin trickle of blood.

I want to close the bag, to zip it shut and finish the job and not think about the thing in the plastic, but my hands falter. The blood is still there, pooling on the foam. The corridor is deserted.

I have to know.

Slowly, I push a finger into the plastic wrapping. It's thick, clammy-cold against my skin. The wrapping is tight against the cargo, the edges catching as I lift it up. But then my fingers brush against something soft and slick, and the blurred shape in the bag leaps out at me.

I'm staring at it, willing myself to look away, but there's no mistaking it.

It's an eyeball. I've been carrying an eyeball.

6

Darnell

Darnell has a table at the back of the darkened control room, surrounded by battered chairs. Every tech who works there knows not to move them, not even an inch, or to say anything about the suffocating temperature their boss likes to keep the room at.

He's sitting at the table, going through reports, when Reece brings the storage technician in. The man hovers off to one side, a small box under his arm, waiting for Darnell to notice him.

Eventually Darnell waves him over. The tech scurries across the floor, holding the box out in front of him like a shield. The heavy lettering on the front reads AIR LAB CONSIGNMENT 6/00/7-A MOST URGENT.

"Found it, Sir," he says. "Just got misplaced, that's all. Temporarily."

Darnell barely glances at him. "And the knife?"

The man swallows. With a trembling hand, he pulls the knife out of his pocket, careful to hold it by the blade. He places it flat on the table, lined up next to the box.

Darnell tilts his head. "You got fingerprints on the blade."

"I..."

"You sharpen it, like I said?"

"Yes, Sir. Like you said."

An urge takes Darnell then, hot and demanding: the urge to test the knife's sharpness by sliding it into the man's stomach. His fingers twitch. It would take less than a second. In and out.

Instead, he waves the man away. The tech backs off, nodding like his neck is already broken. Darnell returns to his reports, scowling. As much as he hates to admit it, Reece's words have stayed with him. He needs to be more careful. He's worked too hard and waited too long to get distracted now.

He tears the top off the box, wiggling his hand inside. His fingers brush machined glass, and he pulls out a tab screen—smaller than the regular units, with a bulbous antenna poking out the top. He switches it on, flicking through the menu options. A smile creeps across his face like oil moving through water. His connection in Tzevya sector did his job.

The storage tech nearly trips over the door as he leaves the control room, and the thunk of his foot on the metal lip makes Darnell look up. He's pleased with himself for not giving in to his urges. Besides, the tech will get what's coming to him soon enough.

Along with Reece, and the other techs, and everyone else on Outer Earth, if he can just keep it together. Discipline, that's the key. Control.

7

Riley

A dry heave builds in my throat, boiling up from my stomach. My hand jerks, and the box is jolted sideways. It slips out of the pack, and the thing slides out of the plastic and hits the floor with a muffled plop.

It rolls in place, the trailing optic nerve stuck to the floor on a meniscus of blood. It's not looking at me, but I can see the iris, dark blue, surrounding the inky-black dot of the pupil. I have to force myself to look away, and as I do the heave becomes a full-blown retch. Doubling over, I push it back, forcing it down.

You will not throw up. Not here.

Never look at what you carry. It's the one big unbreakable, the one thing Amira has told us over and over again. There's a reason for that: it gets us work. People trust us. We're not going to steal your cargo, or even care what it is.

Plus, not knowing keeps us alive. Tracers, us included, sometimes carry bad things. Weapons, contraband, drugs concocted somewhere in the Caves and destined for sale in a distant sector. Be nice if we could live off doing hospital runs, but we can't. It's better if we don't know. Realistically, I know I could have been carrying severed eyes for years and never known. But actually seeing it, touching it...

Crouching, I use a corner of the plastic to grip the nerve, gently tugging at it. The iris rolls towards me, and I force myself to look away. The retch comes again, and I have to close my eyes and inhale through my nose for a few seconds, before looking back. More details begin to jump out. Tiny, milky-smooth clouds in the pupil that I hadn't noticed before. Thin arteries, running off the iris like fine pen lines.

Movement. Voices. Without thinking, I grab the eyeball. It's soft and pliable in my grip, like putty.

Don't squeeze it too hard or it'll pop.

I have to force back another heave. I shove it back into the box and zip my backpack shut as the owners of the voices come round the corner.

Two stompers. They're officially known as Station Protection Officers, but nobody calls them that any more. I'm surprised to see them; there aren't too many around these days.

A few times a year, you hear stories about gang bosses joining forces, declaring open season on any stomper foolish enough to walk into their territories. It always ends up with plenty dead on both sides—but when it comes to new members, people always seem to be more willing to join up with the gangs. The sector leaders do their best, showing face in the bars and the market and the mess halls, looking for recruits to the stomper corps, but they always have to go back to the council in Apex with bad news.

The stompers walking towards me are dressed in thick grey jumpsuits with the station logo—a stylised ring silhouette—stitched into the top pocket. The noise of their boots is heavy in the cramped space. On their hips rest specially modified pistols: guns with ammunition designed to go through flesh and bone, but not metal. We call them stingers.

I've seen the one on the left before—Royo, I think his name is, a bear-like man with dark skin and a shaved head. His partner is just as big, with a shaggy beard. In different circumstances, he'd probably look jovial, but as he locks me in his gaze I see that his right eye is glass, dead and inert in its socket.

Left, right, left, right.

They take in the scene. A blood-splattered floor, and a tracer who looks like she just had a head-on collision with an asteroid. "What's going on here?" says Royo, but even as the words are out of his mouth I'm bolting past him. His partner makes a grab for me, but I'm too quick, slipping under his arm. "Cargo delivery!" I say over my shoulder.

I'm expecting them to give chase, maybe even draw on me. But they don't follow, and I heave a sigh of relief. Maybe they figure a beat-up tracer isn't worth their time. Good news for me. I have a lot of ground to make up. My collarbone seems OK, but my face is throbbing again, and prickly waves of pain are spreading out from where I got punched.

A million thoughts are crowding for attention. Part of me wants to drop the box somewhere and run, pretend that I'd never taken the job. I turn that option down in seconds—I don't even want to think what will happen if Darnell doesn't get his eyeball. He'll probably use one of mine as a replacement. And if he decides to take revenge on the Devil Dancers…

But can I really deliver the cargo? Pretend I never saw the eyeball, walk away, and hope everything goes back to normal? Is that even possible now? Every time someone hands me cargo, or asks me to turn around so they can put it in my pack, I'm going to be thinking about today.

But it's not a choice. Not really. I have to finish the job. There's a chance that Darnell will find out that I saw my cargo, but it's a lot less risky than abandoning the job completely.

Every time the pack jolts, every time the cargo shifts against my back, a fresh wave of horror rolls through me.

I pass the mining facilities Chengshi is known for. Their kilns and machines are silent, and the rooms that hold them spill no light into the corridors. They won't be up and running again until the next asteroid catcher ship swings into orbit alongside the station. I don't really like running here; I always seem to come out with streaks of grime on my skin and clothes. I tell myself to keep going, that it can't be more than a mile to the Gardens border.

There are more slag rooms, dotted here and there with run-down habs, all locked up tight. Several times I have to react quickly to stop myself smashing into people in the corridors. Some lie sprawled on the ground, their possessions arranged in haphazard piles. With no hab units willing to take them, they have to sleep where they can.

Tracer

I'm struggling to run at full speed after the attack, so I slow back to a jog. As I do so, I turn the corner and nearly collide with a tagger.

He's painting something onto the wall—I catch a glimpse of it as I dodge past, a slogan. "It's the only way." The phrase doesn't make any sense, until I remember where I've heard it before. At a demonstration in one of the galleries, where it was being chanted. But what were they protesting about again?

The tagger catches sight of me. "We need to control the birth rate," he says, his voice on the edge of a shout. "Humans were never meant to keep existing..."

Ah. That was it. Voluntary human extinction.

"Out of the way," I say, all but hurling the words in his direction as I flash past.

I've heard it all before. How we need to stop having children to restore balance to the universe. Voluntary euthanasia. If I let the tagger stop me, he'll end up telling me all about how Outer Earth shouldn't even exist, that it was a pissing contest between Earth governments that got too far along to kill. Population overflow, they called it. I know the story like every person on this station.

Of course, a massive nuclear war a few years later didn't help either.

But that was a long time ago, and I just don't care that much. I turn around, and flip the tagger a raised middle finger. Then I keep running.

Soon, I'm jogging under the sign that marks the border between Gardens and Chengshi. I look up as I pass underneath it. A long time ago, someone took a spray-can, crossed out the words Sector 2 and drew crude pictures of flowers and trees in green paint around it.

You can cross sector borders on nearly all the levels, but for some reason, I always find myself on this one. Gardens is cleaner than Chengshi—better maintained, with much less graffiti and dust. Most of the sector is given over to the Air Lab and the Food Lab, the places which give Gardens its name. They're behind a set of enormous airlock doors at the bottom of the gallery. I can see the two guards on duty today: Dumar and Chang. Chang's new—a couple of weeks ago, he refused me entry, and I had to wait for Prakesh to come out for a break before I could get in—but Dumar's been working there for years. He's a stocky guy with dark eyes and a huge, black, knotted beard. He raises a hand as I approach, less a command to stop than a friendly greeting. But I can see his hand resting, as always, on his stinger holster.

"Back again?" he says.

I force a smile. "Good to see you too, Dumar."

"I swear, one day you're gonna go in there and grow roots, you visit so often."

"Hey, I just visit. You work here."

We've been exchanging the same lines for years. He gives a good-natured grunt as he turns to his control panel. Behind him, Chang sniffs. Prakesh once told me that on his first day he attempted to body-search every tech who came through the door.

Dumar eyes my pack. "You doing a delivery?"

I swallow. "That's right. Up to Mr. Darnell."

He shakes his head. "You want to be careful with that one," he says. He seems about to go on, but Chang flashes him a dark look, and he falls silent.

Dumar presses a few keys, and the outer airlock door hisses open. I step through. "Have fun," he says over his shoulder as the door closes behind me. As I wait for the inner door to open, I run a hand through my hair. As usual, it's greasy, caked with grit, uncomfortably sticky. I try to keep it short, but it doesn't help all that much.

I can see myself in the reflective metal door. My hair frames a face shiny and gleaming with sweat. I try not to look into the reflection's dark-grey eyes. Instead, I focus on the body, stretching my arms out to the sides, shaking my legs out. The jacket is bulky, but the body underneath it is lithe and supple, muscles sculpted from endless running and climbing and jumping.

There's a buzz, then a brief flash of purple light—ultraviolet, designed to zap any surface bacteria. I don't know why they bother. I'm not even sure it works. The door in front of me hisses open, vanishing into the wall.

You get to the Air Lab by going through the Food Lab. I can

dimly see the shapes of the crops through the opaque plastic domes in the hangar: corn, tomato plants, beds of lettuce, beans, all bathed in a soft, green glow from the grower bulbs. There are no main lights in the Food Lab itself; the path ahead is softly lit by the ambient light, and a gentle hum emanates from the large aircon units on the walls. The hangar seems to stretch on for miles, and in the distance I can see the lights of the lab complex where the techs work to make the crops more efficient, easier to grow.

Beyond the greenhouses is the insect colony: what I've heard the lab techs call the buzz box. Tiny beetles and little silkworms can't make much noise on their own, but get millions of them in one place and the hum they generate can shake your stomach. Still, they taste OK. Especially the fried beetles they do in the market sometimes. Crunchy and salty. Much better than the mess hall stuff.

I turn right, by a greenhouse labelled Soja Japonica, and head down the rows. Before long I'm walking through a door and then the space above is filled with a thick green canopy. The trees are a special breed of oak, enormous, designed to suck in carbon dioxide and pump out as much oxygen as possible. And some of them are old—much older than the techs who work on them. Over the years, their roots have broken free of their metal prisons, pushing up through the floor. I have to step over a couple as I move between the trees.

Unlike the Food Lab, the Air Lab is brightly lit, huge lights beaming down from the ceiling. I stop for a moment under a tree with a thick, gnarled trunk, and tilt my head up, watching the rays of light filter through the branches. The air is cool. Were it not for the fact that the floor under my feet was metal grating, and that I was surrounded by huge pools of algae, nestled between the trees, I could be somewhere on Earth. If the nukes hadn't turned most of the planet into a burning wasteland before I was born, maybe I would be.

Of course, by then there weren't many trees left anyway.

The Air Lab is just as big as the cavernous Food Lab—it has to be to provide enough air for the station. I head towards the back, to the control rooms, towering over the trees. It's tempting to just drop the cargo off at an office somewhere, maybe the storerooms, just to avoid Darnell. No chance. I deliver the cargo right into its recipient's hands, or I don't deliver it all.

No matter what's inside.

I climb the clanking metal stairs, wondering how a place in which I can find someone as good as Prakesh is also home to a person like Darnell. As I reach the top, I spot the usual guard outside. He's a short man, wiry, with a grim face and a grubby, knee-length coat. He gives a nod when he sees me, and hauls open the door to the main control room—after so many runs, he's used to me by now.

Stepping through the door, I'm blasted by a wave of heat. The convection fins on the hull keep the station cool—most of the time—but Darnell likes to keep the temperature up. He likes to make visitors uncomfortable.

I can feel the sweat begin to run again, pooling at my waist. I'm dying for water—I burned the last of my pack supply on the final stretch here—but you don't ask Oren Darnell for a drink.

The control units around the walls hum away quietly, attended to by white-coated techs who have shrunk into their chairs like beetles. In the centre of the room are two large drums of water, sloshing gently—just the sight of them makes my tongue jump, like it's touched an electric wire. Darnell is seated at the back, deep in conversation with one of his lieutenants.

The air is thick with dry heat. In the background, a clanging starts—from one of the water pipes somewhere else in Gardens, maybe—but it only lasts a moment before the door swings shut behind me, reducing the sound to a muted boom. Right then, Darnell looks up and sees me.

He's a giant of a man, with thick arms and a chest like the hull of a ship. He dresses well: a tight-fitting black shirt and slim black pants made from a smooth fabric. I don't know what to do with my hands, so I busy myself removing my pack. The straps feel rough and unyielding, my fingers clumsy.

"Riley Hale," he says. His voice is soft and high-pitched, like a child's. It sounds strange, coming from someone so enormous. He moves towards me in long, languid strides, and his eyes rove across my body, passing over my battered face. "A pleasure to see you again. I trust you are well?"

I shrug, trying to avoid his gaze. Instead, I reach into my pack, and pull out the box.

Darnell gestures to a tech, who steps forward and takes the box from me, reaching out to grab it before shrinking away, as if I might bite his arm off. I made sure I sealed the box shut before I got here—there's no evidence that it's been opened.

The tech hands it to Darnell, who quickly breaks the seal, glancing inside. My stomach churns. Darnell nods, reseals the box, and hands it to the tech, who spirits it away to the back of the room.

I'm still watching the box when I realise that Darnell has taken a step closer. Before I can stop him, he runs a finger delicately across my bruises, around the side of my eye. I have to force myself not to flinch.

"These are fresh," he says. "Tell me who did this."

"It's nothing," I say, trying to turn away. He doesn't lift his hand from my face, and the light pressure forces the words out of me. "Just another gang thinking they could jack the cargo."

"But you fought them off."

"Of course," I say, taking a step back. His hand drops from my face. "Cargo this important, it's—"

"Important?"

I keep my expression as neutral as I can. Inside, I'm screaming at myself. The words just tumbled out of me, knocked loose by his touch, the feeling of his smooth fingers on my skin. Darnell is looking at me, his eyes narrowed.

"Yeah, important," I say. Amazingly, I manage a casual shrug. "'Cos it's you, you know. You're not just a regular client." The words sound forced even as I say them, but I keep my voice steady.

Darnell doesn't move. For a good three seconds, he simply stares at me.

Then he smiles. "Well, if you ever decide you'd like some payback, you just let me know. I don't imagine today was the first time you've run into trouble."

I try not to exhale. It's all I can do to shrug a second time, like it's nothing.

Darnell raises his eyebrows in mock alarm. "But I'm being such a terrible host. Something to drink?" He gestures to the water in the drums.

"Thanks," I say, finally meeting his gaze. "I'm good."

He chuckles. It's an odd sound, gravelly and brief, like a bare foot stepping on broken glass. "On the house, Riley. No charge. And look..." He strides over to the drums and draws a handful of liquid to his lips. "It's clean. Didn't even spike this one."

A few drops leak out of his cupped hands, splashing back into the drum. I'm conscious of my tongue, large and dry in my mouth, like a hunk of old resin.

One of Darnell's men appears at his side with a tin cup, and he fills it and hands it to me. I pause, but only for a moment. The water is cool and sweet, with just a faint hint of the metal in the drum. I've raised the cup with both hands, and tilt it to catch every last drop.

I hand back the cup and wipe a hand across my lips. All of a sudden, I want out of there, bad. I nod thanks, taking my pack and turning to leave—job done, cargo delivered, time to go.

Darnell clears his throat behind me. "Riley."

I look back over my shoulder. He goes on: "You really should think about making our arrangement a little more..." He searches for the right words. "More full-time. I could use your talents."

"Sorry," I say. "I like what I do."

"I wasn't suggesting you stop. I could use a tracer in-house. Someone who worked exclusively for the Air Lab. For me."

"You've got crews in Gardens. Hire one of them."

"Them?" That laugh again. His eyes are ice crystals. "No. They don't know what it means to work for something. But you..."

"Like I said. Not interested." I step towards the door, but he clears his throat again, and this time the noise freezes me in my tracks.

"I usually only make an offer once, Riley. But I'll let you think about it. Just let it roll around in that little head of yours. I could give you protection. Imagine: no more black eyes."

I say nothing. His smile doesn't change. "You be safe now."

He turns away, striding back to the table, like he's already forgotten about me. I turn to go, ignoring the eyes of his techs, burning into my back. On the catwalk outside, the guard gives me a lazy mock salute before gently pushing the door shut.

8

Riley

I'm almost at the bottom of the stairs when I collapse.

I don't know whether it's the shock catching up with me, or simply the beating I took from the Lieren, but one second I'm taking the last few steps, and the next I'm lying flat on my stomach. The metal flooring is cool against my cheek. It feels good.

Hands on my back, then around my shoulders, lifting me up. Someone is saying my name, and then I'm looking into the face of Prakesh Kumar.

He's taller than me, his arms strong from digging in the dirt every day, and before I know it he's sat me on the edge of an algae tank. "Gods, Ry, what the hell happened?"

His hands are already reaching towards my face, but I brush them away. His walnut-dark skin is calloused, flecked with grains of dark soil.

"Thought you were off today," I say. I have to focus on each word, form them carefully so I don't slur.

"Cancelled. They needed extra hands. What happened?"

"I'm OK," I say. "Just had a little problem on the run."

"A *little* problem?" He moves his hands up again, and I have to push them away more firmly.

"I said I'm fine," I mutter.

"You don't look fine. You don't even look close to fine." He folds his arms, eyeing my bruises. On the other techs, the white lab coats look bulky, almost baggy, but Prakesh wears his well, square on his shoulders over a rough cotton shirt.

I keep my voice low, in case anyone is listening. "Ambush. Lieren. They were trying to jack my cargo. Managed to fight them off…" I have to stop as a cough bursts up through my throat, doubling me over.

Prakesh's hands are on my back, steadying me. "Easy. Easy. Just sit here, OK? I'll get some water." I try to push him away again, try to tell him that I already had some from his boss, but this time he pushes back, his hand holding steady between my shoulder blades. "No. You're hurt. You can take some water. I'll be right back."

He leaves, and I sit back down heavily on the edge of the tank. After a minute, I'm feeling less woozy, and stumble over to one of the nearby trees. Steadying myself against it, I sink down onto the soft, loamy soil. Prakesh will probably shout at me for sitting on something as precious as his good soil, but I don't care. I'm just happy to be off my feet. I lick my lips. The crust of blood on them cracks just a little, like old glass.

My thoughts drift back to when I met Prakesh. Back when we were in school, we had to file into a cramped room with hard chairs and harsh lights. When you're little, it's kind of fun—you don't spend as much time there, and you're mostly being taught how to read and write and count, and sometimes even draw pictures if the teacher had some coloured pencils.

But when you get older, the classrooms get more packed, and there's less space on the chairs. What you learn doesn't make sense, either: the teachers would show us pictures or videos of life back on Earth: animals in captivity, blue-green oceans, huge collections of buildings called cities. They'd try to teach us how it all worked. I remember looking at something, some animal—a huge, improbable thing with a massive, tentacle-like nose and horrible, wrinkled, grey skin—and trying to picture it in real life, as it would have been back on Earth. I couldn't do it. I just couldn't see it. I knew what it looked like but I couldn't picture it. And the name: elephant, like something out of a scary story. The letters in a weird order, a word light years away from anything I knew.

I got angry and started punching the tab screen in a fit of stupid rage. I remember the thin glass on the screen cracking, the tiny sting as a piece cut me and the elephant vanished. I was seven.

I hadn't really paid much attention to Prakesh up until then. I'd sort of known who he was, sure, but I'd never spoken to him. But for whatever reason, he was sitting next to me that day, and as my hand came down for a fourth time to smash the screen he caught me, grabbing my wrist. I looked at him, startled: I expected to see fear, even anger, but his eyes were kind. He reached across, and gently plucked the piece of glass out of my hand. As I watched, a thin dot of blood appeared, seemingly out of nowhere.

And then the teacher grabbed me by the scruff of my neck. He tossed me out of school right there, ordering me to go home. But as I stood in the corridor, the real pain just starting to creep into my hand, I realised that for the first time, I wanted to get back in.

It didn't last. My mom begged them to let me come back, and after a while they did, but I just couldn't concentrate. Prakesh was friendly, and we started spending more time together, but it wasn't enough. When my mom died, a few days after my fourteenth birthday, I told Prakesh I was finished. Not surprisingly, the school didn't come looking for me.

I didn't see him for a long time. It's funny the way this place works. We're packed in so tight, a million people in this little steel ring that was only designed to hold half that, but you can go years without seeing someone. And then, a few months ago, a woman asked me to deliver a package to her son in Gardens. I almost didn't recognise Prakesh at first, but he remembered who I was. He was just a food tech then, another guy in a white lab coat. But he showed me around, gave me some water and some fresh, crisp beans to eat, told me about his work. I realised how much I'd missed him.

Prakesh comes back, bearing a thick plastic flask. He mutters something under his breath when he sees me sitting against the tree, but doesn't protest. Instead, he drops to one knee and hands me the bottle, and I raise it to my lips, drinking deeply. The water is deliciously cold, so cold it almost stings, and before I know it I've drained the bottle.

"You're not done yet," he says, digging some baby tomatoes out of the pocket of his lab coat. As he passes them to me, our hands touch, the warm skin of his fingers brushing mine.

I eat two tomatoes before I stop suddenly, another halfway to my mouth. "This isn't the genetic stuff, is it?"

"Genetic stuff. I love how your mind works sometimes, Riley," he says, and takes a bite himself. "No, this is good old natural veggie. We won't have results on the genetic stuff for another year at least. But once we do—"

"You'll be able to grow millions of plants in a nanosecond and feed the entire station in a day and use your science skills to give me biological rocket boosters so I can fly away. I know, you've told me before."

He scratches the back of his head. "Well, we did have a breakthrough yesterday. We actually got an entire soybean plant to sprout in twenty-four hours. Of course, it would have killed anyone who ate it, but it's a long way from the kids' stuff they were doing before. And gene work isn't the whole picture—the plants need the right minerals to grow. It's been months since we had an asteroid catcher bring back a haul, and the stuff we got from Mars and the moon isn't doing the job."

"Forget the minerals, then. Start doing the genetics on human beings. We don't need minerals to function." I hold up the last tomato, then pop it into my mouth. "Just give us the odd tomato to eat, and we're good to go."

"Yes, because hominid genetic modification worked out *so* well last time. Or don't you remember school history?"

"I think I missed that class."

He looks down, then back up at me, his eyes clouded.

"What?" I say. And then, annoyed: "What?"

"What really happened, Ry? On the run?"

"What do you mean?"

"So you managed to fight off an entire crew by yourself? In an ambush? Bullshit, Ry. You got your ass kicked, and now you're lying to me about it."

"I'm not."

He raises his eyebrows. Usually, I laugh at him when he does this—it makes him look like someone's just told him a rude joke—but this time, I can see the frustration in his face. His one hand is digging in the soil, and the dark grains are squishing out from between his fingers. I don't even think he realises he's doing it.

"Why do you always do this?" he says. His voice is quiet, but there's no mistaking the anger. I always forget how quickly his mood can change. He may have stopped me from smashing the tab screen, back in that school room, but as we've got older it's like all my anger has slipped into him.

"Do what?"

"I try to help, and you just shut me out."

"I don't need help." The words sound stupid and petulant, even as I say them. "I can take care of myself, thanks."

"Really?" he says, jabbing a finger at my face. "Is this taking care of yourself?"

"Well, what do you want me to do?" I ask, my voice rising. "You want me to stop running? Other gangs are part of the job, Prakesh. You live with it."

"It's not worth it. Not for this. There are other jobs you could do."

"Oh yeah? Like what?" I pull myself to my feet. The ache in my arches wakes up, starts growling.

He rises to meet me, springing off the tree with frustratingly easy grace. "Anything. You're smart, you could get a job anywhere on this station. But running? For what?"

"For your information, I actually like running."

"I know," he says. "But there's nothing else in your life. You run, and that's it. And if you get hurt like this again? What are you going to do?"

I glare at him. "There's plenty of stuff I do when I'm not running."

His laugh is bitter. "Riley, come on. After all this time, I've never seen you do anything else besides run and play cards. Putting your life in danger for what, a few batteries? Some stolen food? It's not worth it."

"Better than working for nothing in a greenhouse all day," I say. The second the words are out of my mouth, I want to pull them back. Prakesh, however, absorbs them without comment, simply staring at me.

After a while, he says, "What we do here keeps people alive. In case you haven't noticed, there aren't a lot of us left. And without air, without food, there'd be a lot less. So you can come in here and drink my water, and if you want to get angry with me for it, that's fine. But don't ever tell me I'm working for nothing."

We stare at each other. Our outburst has attracted the attention of another tech, a timid woman with shocking-red hair who's walking nervously towards us. "Is everything all right, Prakesh?" she says. "I can call security if..."

"No, Suki, we're good here," he responds, but he doesn't look away.

"And I was just going," I say, breaking his gaze and shouldering my pack.

His hand is on my shoulder. "Riley, listen..." But I shrug it off and break into a run, leaving them standing beside the tree. Before long, I'm outside the Forest, dashing past a startled Dumar. Letting the rhythm of my movement calm me as I run back into the galleries. People are waking up, walking from their quarters to the mess, to school, to their jobs. As I run, my own anger fades, like a handprint evaporating from a pane of glass, and I lose myself in the crowds.

9

Darnell

The door to Oren Darnell's office is a slab of thick metal, its hinges ringed with rust. It's half open when he arrives, and he shoves it to one side. The bang when it hits the wall is loud enough to shake the giant window that overlooks the Air Lab. One of the control room techs has followed him, wanting to ask him something, and he has to dodge out of the way as it bounces back.

Darnell doesn't even glance at him. "Get out," he says over his shoulder.

The tech knows better than to persist. He scurries out, pulling the door shut behind him. Just before it closes, Darnell bellows, "And tell Reece I want to see him. Now."

The door wavers, then snicks shut.

Darnell turns back to the window. Despite what the tech might think, he isn't angry. He's excited. So excited that he feels like laughing out loud. He smiles instead, his teeth reflected in the window. He flips open the box, upends it, and rolls the eyeball around in his hands. It leaves his palms slightly sticky, but he barely notices.

It's taken so long. So many years of watching and waiting, of having to associate with the filth that make up most of the station's population. Of having to pretend to the council and the techs and the countless functionaries that he gives a shit about the station's air quality. No more. The eyeball is the final detail—and at long last, he can give this rotten wreck of a station everything it deserves.

He tells himself to stay calm. There are still certain things to take care of. Riley Hale, for example. She hadn't even entered his thoughts as "a thing to take care of" until she walked into the control room. It wasn't just the bruises. Riley Hale had delivered goods to Darnell a dozen times, and he'd never seen her on edge. Not until this particular delivery. Her entire body was tense, like she was plugged into a power socket. So yes, he knew she'd seen inside her pack, even before she made that crack about the cargo being important.

Darnell had wanted to wrap his fingers around that pretty throat right then and there when she turned him down, take care of the problem as soon as it presented itself, but he told himself to hold back. It wouldn't do to kill someone in the Air Lab. Just as it wouldn't do to let her walk free. He's much too close to let things like that cause problems for him.

And he was fair. He gave her a chance to join him. Of course, it won't matter one way or another—she, and he, and everyone else on the station have a lifespan measured in days. But it might have been fun to bring her over. With her speed, she'd have been exceedingly useful. Now, she's just a liability.

He's pleased at the eye's condition—Gray had told him that he'd inject it with a compound he'd developed, some sort of preserving fluid to slow decomposition. He bounces it in his palm. It makes a very soft squidging sound, as if he's handling rotten fruit.

Movement, right at the edge of the Air Lab. It's Hale, sprinting silently down the path between two enormous oaks, heading right for the exit. Darnell can just see the edge of her jacket, flying out behind her.

He seals the eyeball back in its box and sits down at his desk. It's wood, carved from a dead tree—as far as Darnell knows, it's the only piece of wooden furniture on the entire station, maybe even the only piece left in existence. He keeps it polished, shiny with oil.

The desk is dominated by a bonsai tree: a Japanese boxwood, no bigger than his head, with a thin, twisted trunk and puffs of bright green leaves. Darnell keeps a set of shears on his desk, short and stubby, and he reaches for them now. He leans in, grips a twig, and cuts. A single tiny leaf drifts to his desk. He moves, leans forward, cuts again.

Once, there were hundreds of thousands of boxwood trees across Asia. Beautiful trees, with thick, green foliage. All gone. But maybe, Darnell thinks, they might grow again. If no human beings are around to interfere, to cut them down, to destroy their habitats.

The door hinges creak. Reece enters, his long coat sweeping around his legs. Darnell doesn't look up. "You know that tracer, came in earlier?" he says.

"Uh-huh."

"She was ambushed on her way over here. Some gang or other. They'll need a visit. Make her tell you who they were. Be persuasive."

"What about the tracer?"

"Kill her."

10

Riley

I make it as far as the Gardens border before I have to stop. I can feel every muscle in my legs and abdomen, white-hot filaments criss-crossing my body. When I slow to a jog, a stitch springs up in my side, biting deep. My body begs me to bend over, to relieve tension on the muscles, but I force myself to stay upright, breathing long and slow through my nose. My eye socket throbs with pain.

I did it. I finished the job, delivered the cargo, got away clean. I have no idea how the hell I pulled that off, but I did it.

No more jobs today. I am going home, and then I'm going to sleep. Probably forever.

I'm on the bottom level of the sector, and the corridor is blissfully deserted. I let myself lean on the wall. The metal is cold and oily under my palm, so I rest my shoulder on it instead. Then I turn so I've got my back on it. And before I know it, I slide right down the wall. There's a low power box jutting out right where the wall meets the floor, and I sit down on it, my legs splayed out in front of me. My breathing has slowed, and the heat in my muscles has gone from white hot to a sullen red. It'll do. At least until I can get back home.

I can still hear the crowd from the distant corridors behind me. The noise is given a metallic edge by the time it reaches me, twisted and bent by the floor and walls, so that it sounds like a weird alien monster roaming the station.

It takes me a minute to realise that there's another sound too. Footsteps. My eyes fly open, just in time to see a figure stepping towards me, silhouetted by the flickering fluorescents.

The figure stops, raises his hands. "Woah, hey, be cool. I just wanted to ask if you had some food."

I blink. The voice is weirdly familiar. Then my eyes adjust, and I see that it's the tagger I saw earlier. The one I blazed past in the upper-level corridors, just before the border, while I was running to the Air Lab. He's younger than I first thought, little more than a kid, with a bad case of acne and dark hair that sticks to his forehead. His paint can is tucked in his waistband.

If he recognises me from before, he gives no sign, just gives my pack a pleading look. I'm about to tell him to get lost, but then I remember that I already flipped him off once today, and feel kind of bad.

"Sure," I say. I'm almost certain that my bag's empty, but there's always a chance that half a protein bar or something got lost in the bottom. Part of me knows I should stay alert, but surely not even I would be unlucky enough to get jacked twice in one day.

"Thanks," he says, as I zip open my bag and rummage through it. "I haven't had anything to eat all day, and I can't go to the mess hall until I find a job, so—hey, what—"

His words turn into a horrific, bubbling scream. I jerk my head upright just in time to see a flash of metal at his throat, followed by a dark spurt of blood. I bolt to my feet just as the figure behind the tagger shoves him to the side.

I react on instinct, leaning backwards just as the knife flashes out at me. I get a half-second look at my attacker's face—it's Darnell's guard, the one who let me into the control room. What the hell?

He slashes at me again, and I manage to grab his arm, just below the elbow. The tip of the knife nicks my neck, and I hiss in pain. The guard twists away, laughing, then attacks again, driving me back down the corridor. Behind us, the tagger's body twitches as he bleeds out.

I turn to run—there's no way this guy can beat me in a straight sprint. But I barely manage two steps before he grabs the back of my jacket. For a second, it's like we're locked in an insane dance. I'm bending over backwards, leaning into his body. He's dropping his shoulder towards me, the blade close behind it.

I twist to the side, ripping free of his grip, only just managing to stay on my feet. He laughs again. Little needles of terror are shooting through me, but there's something underneath it too: anger. I delivered the cargo clean. *I finished the damn job.* And now

Darnell wants me gone? Like I'm a loose end that needs to be snipped off?

No way. Not today.

The guard reaches out for me. He's a good fighter, and fast, but he's easy to read. He wants to pull me in and drive the knife into my belly. So instead of leaning back, like he expects me to, I drop, swinging my right leg in a wide arc.

He spots the move, dodges back, but not before the edge of my shoe clips his ankle. It's just enough. He stumbles, tries to stay upright, then crashes to the ground. His right foot hits the ground, bounces up, comes to a rest on the power box where the wall meets the floor.

I don't let myself second-guess it. I jump as high as I can, and bring both feet down on his kneecap. There's a thin snap, like someone breaking a stick of celery, and then the guard is screaming.

I stumble off him, grab my pack, and run.

11

Prakesh

The glass beaker smashes against the wall. In the silence that follows, the only sound is the gentle hum of the lab's DNA thermocycler.

Prakesh Kumar looks away from the mess of glass, furious with himself. Glass beakers aren't easy to replace. Still, at least he can clear it up before anyone notices. He's by himself in the mobile lab, on the opposite end of the hangar to the main control room. Not that it bothers him. He likes working alone.

Especially when he decides to vent some anger by smashing things.

He grabs a bucket from a nearby tool shelf and crouches down, picking the big pieces off the floor and dropping them inside.

Damn thermocycler. He couldn't get it to work—the temperature wouldn't rise, and he had to reset the system three times to get it to budge even a little. By the time he got it working, every muscle in his body felt like it was on an electrical circuit. He didn't even realise what he was doing until the glass was in jagged pieces on the floor.

Except it's not the thermocycler Prakesh is angry with. Not really. It's a machine. He can understand machines, just like he can understand trees, or algae. When they stop working there's always a solution that you can use to set the problem right—a system reset, a different kind of fertiliser. They're not like human beings.

When he's filled the bucket, he pushes it under the table, telling himself he'll deal with it later. He stands and rubs his eyes, amazed at how tired he is. It'll take a couple of hours before he can send the results for gel electrolysis. Time for a break.

He steps out of the lab, shutting the door behind him, and walks back to the control room, zig-zagging down the walkways between the trees. There's no one around, not even Suki, who's known to stay way past the shift change. No one interrupts him as he walks down the hangar.

Riley's back in his head. He always ends up on the same image of her: the first time she came back to the Air Lab to visit him, after that first delivery. She was jogging to a stop, her hair flying out behind her, a smile playing across her face. He remembers thinking that he'd never seen anyone so at ease with speed, so in love with movement.

Not that it matters. *She won't let you in*, he thinks. *She won't even let you help her when she gets hurt. You're a friendly face to her, someone who can get her some food when she needs it. Nothing more.*

The locker room is at the back of the main lab. The floor is grimy with tracked soil, the lockers bent and rusty. The one Prakesh uses doesn't even shut properly any more, but the only thing he keeps in there is his lab coat, and anybody who wants to steal that is more than welcome. He slips it off his shoulders and shoves it in, shutting the door with a bang. Then he rests his head on the metal and shuts his eyes, just for a second.

When he turns around, Oren Darnell is standing there.

He's standing with his arms folded, his face expressionless. He's close enough for Prakesh to pick out the pores on his skin.

Prakesh tells himself not to freak out. He knows Mr. Darnell's reputation—everyone does—but he's not in the habit of messing with the techs. Not unless they cross him. He needs them to keep producing results, so he can stay in the top spot at the Air Lab. Prakesh meets his eyes, even though he really doesn't want to.

"Something I can help you with?" he says.

Darnell doesn't answer. Instead, he grabs Prakesh's shoulders, slamming him up against the lockers. They creak and groan, juddering against his back. He's too stunned to speak, caught too tight to move. His shoulders feel like they're trapped in a vice.

"Where is she?" Darnell says quietly. He could be asking for an update on the electrolysis results.

Prakesh swings his arm up, trying to hit Darnell across the side of the face. Darnell knocks it away, his hand swinging back. Prakesh's anger vanishes, replaced by bright terror. He tries to hit Darnell again, but the lab boss grabs his wrist.

"Do that again, and you'll lose the arm. Where is Riley Hale?"

Prakesh tries to answer. He might as well try to make trees grow using his mind. All the stories, all the little rumours he's heard when he's taking a break with the other techs, are popping up one after the other. It feels as if they're clogging his throat, sealing it shut.

Darnell sighs. He jabs his forearm into Prakesh's neck, banging his head back against the lockers.

Prakesh claws at the arm, desperate for air. There's a tiny sting in his neck. It grows and grows, the pain flooding through his body. He has to scream, he has to, but Darnell clamps a hand over his mouth.

"You're not going to like what happens when you wake up," he says. He's at the end of a very long, dark tunnel, and by the time Prakesh figures out what the words mean, he's gone.

12

Riley

Too close. That was way too close.

Every stride brings another image flashing up. The tagger standing above me. The glint of metal. The sound of his scream, like water burbling through a rusted pipe. If he hadn't been there, if I hadn't stopped in that exact spot…

No. I can't think about it like that. Darnell's guard killed the tagger because he was in the way. If it wasn't him, it would have been someone else. I was the target—and since not even Darnell would risk murdering me in the middle of the Air Lab, he sent his goon to do it for him. It's a good thing I left before…

Oh gods—*Prakesh.*

I'm already running through every memory I can think of, trying to remember if Darnell had ever seen us together. I don't think so. But the last words Prakesh and I said to each other are running over and over in my head.

I should go back. No. No way. I can't show my face in Gardens until I've figured this whole mess out. Stompers? Not a chance. They'll throw me in the brig along with Darnell.

Amira. She'll know what to do.

I keep running, fast as I can, doing my best to push everything else away. But the anger I felt when I was attacked is still rolling in my stomach. It's not just anger at Darnell. It's anger at the ugliness of the station. The dirtiness of it. It's like I've ripped back a scab, one so old that I'd almost forgotten it was there. I feel like I've had a look at the raw flesh underneath.

Enough. Focus on running.

Movement helps. It always does. I let my muscle memory take over, and in no time at all, I'm in the upper-level Apogee corridor that leads to the Nest.

For most people, there are only six levels on Outer Earth. But there are things in this place you won't find on any official map. Vents, wiring ducts, sewerage pipes. And storage units that a person can easily stand up in. These are places that the rest of the station has long since forgotten about. But if you know where to look, you can score yourself a very handy base.

I have to look for a moment to spot the hatch in the ceiling. In the dim light, I can just make out the yellow warning label, its Hindi and Chinese script almost illegible. I break into a run, willing my body to go a little further. It's nine miles from the Air Lab to the Nest in Apogee, and I can feel every single one of them in the arches of my feet.

As I run up to the hatch, I jump towards the wall, launching myself back off it in a reverse tic-tac towards the ceiling. I flatten my hand against the hatch as I pass underneath it, and push—it glides silently upwards and away, the hydraulics Carver built into it working perfectly. I land, and then immediately leap towards the opposite wall for another tac, pushing off and backwards in one smooth move.

I fell on my ass hard the first few times I tried this. As I jump, I reach up and behind me, grasping the lip of the opening. I relax into the movement, letting my body rock backwards, and then using the forward momentum of the swing to haul myself up through the hatch.

I roll onto my side as I do so. My body screams at me to stay there, but I ignore it, forcing myself to my feet.

The hatch slips back into place with a tiny hiss. The entranceway is almost completely dark, the only light coming from a tiny digital keypad bolted onto the wall behind me. It's the perfect security system: getting up into the storage unit requires either something to stand on, or the moves of a tracer, and even then you've got to know the access code to the inner door. Whoever designed this part of Outer Earth probably didn't plan on it being used this way, but it's worked out pretty well for us.

I have to fiddle with the 9 for a bit before the number appears on the display: the unit's old, salvaged from a discarded piece of machinery, and although Carver works hard to maintain it, it's slowly wearing down.

The keypad soon gives two welcoming beeps. I push on the door, but instead of swinging open, it remains locked shut. Frowning, I look at the keypad. Right before the display resets itself, I catch sight of the code I entered. It was correct.

I do *not* have time for this.

I punch it in again, but still the metal door refuses to budge. I'm about to enter the code a third time when I realise exactly what the problem is.

"Carver, open this door!" I shout, not caring if there's anybody in the passage below to hear me. I hammer on the metal, and the sound sets my ears ringing.

There's movement from the other side, and then a voice: "That kind of tone won't get you anywhere. Say please."

The attempt to control myself lasts perhaps two seconds. "I swear, Carver, if you don't open this door right now, I will tear it off the wall and make you eat it."

I hear muted laughter, and then the click of the lock being released. The door opens, and as I step through into the Nest I reach for the first thing I can see—in this case, an old battery lying on a nearby chair—and hurl it across the room at Aaron Carver. As much as I wish it wasn't the case, his reflexes are as good as ever. The battery smashes harmlessly into the wall with a clang before bouncing out of sight.

There's a small box in his hand, and I can see the thin wires snaking across the floor to the entrance. He's perched at his workbench, a mess of something black and spiky on the table in front of him. We have him to thank for our super-light backpacks. They're better than the canvas packs we used to use—with those, the cargo would be shaken to pieces inside of ten minutes.

None of which stops him being incredibly annoying.

There's a gasp on my right. Then a voice, high and musical: "Who beat up your *face*?"

I look round to find the Twins: Yao Shen and Kevin O'Connell. Yao is on the right, sitting cross-legged on the floor, staring goggle-eyed at my bruises. She's a wispy, elfin thing, with curious eyes and a tiny bud-shaped mouth. When I first saw her, I thought she was way too young and fragile to be a tracer, but she's got some serious moves: the bigger the jump, the harder she throws herself at it.

Kev is seated next to her. While Yao is tiny, Kev is enormous: a bruiser with upper arms that look like thick steel cables. There's a book next to his knee—*the* book, rather, a copy of *Treasure Island* that we've each read so many times the jacket has disintegrated and most of the pages are torn.

The Twins take jobs together, run together, fight together. From what Amira has told me, they aren't lovers, but sometimes I find it hard to believe. I once referred to them as the Twins for a joke, and the name stuck.

I rub my eye socket absently. "Got in a fight," I say, in answer to Yao's question. "Where's Amira?"

"Out on a job," says Carver. He's also staring at my face, his eyes narrowed. As usual, he's wearing a sleeveless T-shirt—red today—and his blond hair is perfect, the goggles on his forehead positioned just so.

"Who'd you get in a fight with?" Yao asks, squirming to her feet. "Everyone on the station? Did you win?"

"I'm fine." Now that I've stopped running, the anxiety has come rushing back. Does Darnell know which crew I run with? Does he know where we live? If they get here, can we fight our way out? And Prakesh...

"Don't look fine," says Kev, his voice rumbling. He starts to get to his feet. It's like a crane arm on a construction ship unfolding, with heavy joints locking into place.

"We should go find 'em," Yao says. "Who were they, Riley? I'll tear their legs off and play catch with their kneecaps."

"Yao, be still," Kevin says, without looking at her. Yao pouts and subsides, but she's still looking at me, anger and worry on her face.

"Leave her alone, kids," says Carver, turning back to his workbench and picking up a soldering iron. "She's good. What're a few bumps and bruises to someone like Riley Hale? It's all part of the job."

I've put up some pretty thick walls in my mind to keep it together today, but Carver's words go right through them, like they're nothing more than cloth. Without another word, I walk over to his workbench. He's set a bunch of parts to one side, neatly arranged on the scarred surface, and I slam my fist down right in the middle. The parts scatter, jingling as they bounce off the bench.

"The hell—" Carver says.

I get right in his face. "Do you know what I've been carrying all day? An eyeball. Ripped from someone's skull. I've gone through ambushes and assassination attempts, and I'm a little wired right now. So do me a favour, and don't tell me what is and isn't part of the job."

Carver is looking at me like I've gone insane. Kev and Yao are staring, open-mouthed.

"Well," says a voice. "I'm so glad things didn't fall apart while I was gone."

Amira Al-Hassan is standing by the door, her arms folded, her eyes locked on mine.

13

Riley

If she hadn't spoken, none of us would have noticed Amira come in. She's deathly quiet, always has been, and runs as if her feet aren't touching the ground. The jumps that I stumble and crash on, she lands with gentle ease, soft and hushed as a kiss.

She has to bend her head slightly to come through the door. Amira's older than me by a good ten years, and is dressed simply, in a grey tank top and cargo pants. Around her neck is a faded red scarf, the frayed ends falling down her back. Her pack hangs loosely from one hand.

She walks over to Carver's bench, taking in my bruises. "This is a story I have to hear," she says, before reaching inside her pack and pulling out a box of protein bars. "I got these from the job. Let's have some breakfast."

"Yeah," says a dazed Carver, getting to his feet. "Good idea."

I sit down on the pile of mattresses in the corner. It was a little hard to stay standing—my body seems to give up all at once, the strength flowing out of my legs. My dad's flight jacket bunches up around me, the sleeves pushing down over my hands.

The Nest doesn't look like much. It's just two narrow interconnected rooms, low ceilinged, with hissing pipes scaling the walls. The room that houses Carver's workbench is where we tend to hang out—the other one has an air shower and chemical toilet, which he's hooked into the main system. People who come here say the place smells. It probably does, what with five Devil Dancers living right on top of each other—the Nest being the size it is, it's not really up to holding a lot of people. But I don't think I've noticed a smell for years. It's home.

My gaze strays to the colours on the wall by my head. Abstract shapes in shades of red and green and black and gold. Yao's mural. None of us are really sure what she's painting—sometimes, I don't even think she knows. The homemade tattoo ink she traded for might have been too old and toxic to go into skin, but it works great on the walls—even if Carver did complain that he'd been wanting to trade for a new wrench instead.

Amira tosses me a protein bar, and I catch it without thinking. "So, Riley," she says, arranging herself on Carver's chair. "Let's hear why you're carrying body parts. And how you *know* you've been carrying body parts."

The gummy, chewy protein slabs taste faintly sweet and stick to the teeth in stubborn little clumps, but they keep you going forever—after even one, you feel like you've had a full meal. They're hard to come by, so we dig into them, washing them down with gulps of water from our stash. We prefer food we can get ourselves to anything from the mess halls; the food there is barely edible, cooked into mush, and some of the workers won't let you eat if you don't have a sanctioned job. Being a tracer doesn't count.

Between bites, I tell them what happened—the chase, the ambush, Darnell, all of it. Amira doesn't speak while she eats, using her left hand to take large bites of the protein bar. Her right hand rests on the workbench, and I notice that the stumps where her index and middle fingers used to be are raw and red. She's been rubbing them again; most of the time, she doesn't even realise she's doing it. Her little souvenirs from the lower sector riots, years ago. From running the Core without a thermo-suit, going from Apogee to Apex via the sub-zero hell of the fusion reactor, carrying a bomb on a delay timer. Anarchists had set it up, but she managed to pull it free and run.

Frostbite might have taken her fingers, but after she jettisoned the bomb from the dock on the other side, Amira was a hero. She was offered a seat on the council, where her parents before her had sat. But I guess after running the Core, council politics don't do it for you.

Hence the Dancers. Hence, us.

After a hundred years, it's got a lot harder to replace or fix anything on the station, so transporting objects and messages is tougher than it used to be—especially with gangs waiting to snatch them. Tracers are the network that allows it to happen, and the Devil Dancers are among the best crews on Outer Earth. There are plenty of others, but under Amira's leadership, we've developed a pretty solid rep.

When I finish my story, the crew sits in silence for a moment, and then everyone tries to talk at once. Carver and Yao are angrily demanding we bring the fight to Darnell, but Amira raises a hand, and they reluctantly calm themselves. Carver, muttering obscenities, turns back to his bench, grabbing his goggles and pulling them down roughly over his eyes, making his hair stick up in strange directions. Amira just stares at me, and this time there's a flash of reproach in her eyes.

"Not good," Kev says to Amira, giving an uncharacteristic shudder.

Yao agrees, nodding furiously. "There was that woman who went missing a while ago. She worked in the mess. And I did that run to Chengshi and heard about a sewerage tech who went missing. I didn't think about it before, but what if it's the guy who gave you the cargo?"

We all stare at her. She has a damn good point.

"Imagine if we caught the guy," she says, her eyes glittering.

"Are you insane?" The goggles have been yanked off, and Carver is staring at Yao as if she's grown an extra head. "Are we actually talking about going after someone who sends eyeballs by special delivery? No. Hell no. I like breathing. And by the way, nice work, Riley. I always enjoy ending my day with a fight to the death against the minions of a psychotic lab boss."

"I *wasn't* followed," I say. It's almost a snarl, covering up the uncertainty I feel.

Amira has remained silent, her hands clasped before her, tilted back with the fingertips just touching her lips. She looks at me. "We're not supposed to know what we carry," she says. "That's the job. That's the only way we survive, and you know it. You should never have looked in your pack—I trained you better than that."

A hot flush comes to my cheeks, but I hold her gaze.

She shrugs. "You got us into this, Riley. What do you think we should do?"

I take a deep breath, trying to push my thoughts into some sort of order. "Darnell's going to want revenge," I say. "The man he sent after me won't be the last. That means everyone here is at risk."

"So what? We can take 'em," says Carver. Amira raises her hand, silencing him.

"It's more than that though," I say. "We shouldn't have to do this. We shouldn't have to be a part of whatever…sick game this is."

"Mmm," says Amira. "So what do you suggest?"

"Right now, we're the only people outside of Darnell and the guy who gave me the package—"

"Gray."

"Right. Gray. Outside of them, it's just us. So we bring the fight to them. Let them know we don't go down easy—starting with Gray."

"Why not hit the big bad guy first?" says Yao, but Amira interrupts. "No, Riley's right," she says. "This merchant—this Gray—he picked us because he knew that we do not wish to know what we carry. He took advantage of our trust." She shakes her head. "I won't allow that. Attacking Darnell isn't the answer—not right now, anyway—but we can take care of Gray ourselves. Send a message."

Yao is gagging. "I think I ate one of his onions the other day. What if he fertilises them with *human blood*?" Carver rolls his eyes.

Amira glances at me. "We're probably going to have to deal with this head-on at some point. Riley—you've dealt with Darnell more than the rest of us have. Anything we need to know?"

I let out a long breath. "He's nasty. Keeps a low profile, but he practically runs some of the gangs up there. Water points mostly—he's got connections, so he shuts them down until people have something worth trading."

"So it won't just be him we're facing?"

"Probably not."

"Stompers?" says Kevin, echoing my earlier thoughts.

Carver throws his arms up. "Great idea, Kev. Because we have such a great relationship with the stompers anyway."

"No stompers," says Amira. "This is our problem. We'll deal with it." She turns to the Twins. "We'll need as much intelligence as we can get. I want you to go to Gardens and find a way into the Air Lab. Observe Darnell, see what he's doing, and report back. If he really is going to come after us, we need to know about it."

With only the briefest of shared glances, the Twins head out, dropping through the hatch. I can hear their soft footfalls disappearing down the corridor.

Amira turns back to us. Her eyes are cold slits. "We're going back to the market. Time to meet this Arthur Gray."

She jerks her chin at my bruises. "Are those going to be a problem?"

I shake my head. "I'll live."

"Good."

When we drop out the hatch, the corridor is quiet, with no sound save for the rumble of the station. But as we start jogging towards the gallery, there's a shout from the far end of the corridor. Someone yelling my name.

I whirl, bracing myself for the worst—the Lieren, or another attack from Darnell—but then I see it's a tracer, sprinting towards us from the far end. He's an older guy, one I've seen around, with flecks of grey in his shoulder-length hair. Not someone I know.

"You're Riley Hale?" he asks, jogging to a halt.

I nod. "That's right." My fists are curled into tight balls. With an effort of will, I force them apart. Carver and Amira are a little way ahead of me, looking back quizzically at the new arrival.

"Cargo for you," says the tracer, reaching into the pocket of his jacket. He thrusts something at me—it takes me a second to realise what I'm looking at.

"Is that—paper?" says Carver.

Outside of our copy of *Treasure Island*, I don't think I've ever seen a sheet of loose paper. It feels strangely soft in my hands. The tracer gives a curt nod, and takes off in the direction he came from.

"What is it?" Amira asks.

My stomach is doing that long, slow roll again, and the noise as I unfold the paper is too loud in the cramped corridor. I read the message, written in a tiny cursive script, and my heart starts thudding again in my chest.

"Riley?" says Amira.

I thought Darnell would send more people after us. But this is worse. Much, much worse.

Dear Miss Hale,

You will die quickly. Prakesh Kumar will not. I suggest you trade your life for his. And when you come back to the Air Lab, come alone.

Warmest regards,

Oren Darnell

14

Darnell

The foreman tries to tell him that the monorail is full. The man is new, barely a month into the job, and all he's concerned about are the food shipments to Chengshi and Apogee and New Germany.

He doesn't notice the other workers edging away from him, doesn't see the averted eyes or the sudden interest in train schedules and food manifests.

Darnell puts an arm around the foreman. "What's your name?"

"Judd, Sir." The foreman's words come out a little muffled, mostly because his head is buried in Darnell's armpit.

"Judd. OK. Do you know my bodyguard? Goes by the name of Reece?"

Judd tries to shake his head, doesn't quite manage it.

"He got his knee snapped in two a couple of hours ago. Mostly because he didn't do exactly what I asked him to do."

Darnell lets him go. Judd stumbles away, staring at his boss. Darnell points to the crate behind him—a big, sealed metal box on a wheeled pallet, labelled Soja Japonica. "Load my crate, Judd," he says.

He can see the questions in Judd's eyes—like why another crate of soybeans needs to be loaded onto a monorail already full of them. Or why Darnell wants to accompany the shipment personally. But by the time Darnell climbs aboard the back monorail car, his crate is loaded and strapped down. With a rumble, the train pulls out of the loading dock.

It's black inside the tunnels. The big halogen bulb on the train's cabin doesn't reach this far back, and Darnell has to hold on to the crates for balance. There used to be dozens of monorails trundling around the inside of the ring—it was the station's public transport system. But it became impossible to maintain, and now monorail use is restricted to food shipments and council use only.

The train passes an abandoned station, the platform thick with dust. There's evidence of human habitation—pieces of trash, a clean space in the dust where someone might have bedded down—but it's empty now. Just before the darkness swallows them again, Darnell spots the mark on one of the tunnel supports. A rough white cross, spray-painted on the metal.

Darnell gauges the train's speed. Slow enough. Working quickly, he uses his knife to cut through the straps that tie the crate to the train car, then hauls the lid off. Prakesh Kumar is inside, still unconscious, his body twisted awkwardly.

Oren Darnell reaches in, lifting the comatose technician up. Then he hurls him off the train.

Prakesh bounces off the side of the tracks, rolling to a stop. Darnell sees his mouth twitch, form a groan of pain, but he doesn't wake up, and the sound is lost in the rumble of the monorail. Darnell jumps, landing squarely on the side of the tracks.

He nearly falls. Even overloaded and moving slowly, the monorail shakes the tunnel. The surface under his feet vibrates, like it's alive. But he just bends his knees a little more, leans into it, and lands clean.

He reaches down, grabbing Prakesh and swinging him across his shoulder. Arthur Gray calls the stuff quicksleep. Darnell likes to carry some in his pocket, a small pouch filled with tiny capped syringes.

He stills himself for a moment, letting his eyes get used to the darkness again. He quickly spots the door, recessed slightly into the wall of the tunnel. He walks over to it, activates the entry keypad, sending a dull white glow into the tunnel. Gray didn't want to give Darnell the code to what he calls his workroom. Darnell made him change his mind.

He punches it in, and the door locks disengage, the sound echoing around the cramped tunnel. The passage beyond the door is dimly lit, the metal walls pitted and scarred. Hefting his loads, Darnell heads down the passage. After he dumps the idiot tech, he can head back to the Air Lab, and await the return of Riley Hale. He won't even have to dose her. She'll come with him willingly, if she knows what's good for her. He can give her to Arthur Gray as a…

Darnell stops, listening closely.

The door hasn't clicked shut behind him.

He looks over his shoulder. The door is slightly ajar. His eyes move to the bottom, where the toe of a shoe is positioned in the space between the frame and the door.

Darnell charges. He uses the tech's body as a battering ram, slamming into the door. It flies open, sending the owner of the shoe stumbling backwards. Darnell lets go of Prakesh, hurling him outwards, and his pursuer crumples under the dead-weight, crashing onto the track.

Movement. To his right. A figure leaps at him, barrelling out of the darkness. Darnell back-hands the attacker. She cries out, and blood spatters across his hand. He can't see it in the darkness, but he can feel it, hot and sticky, and it brings a smile to his face.

The first one is up. Darnell can't see his features in the darkness, but he's enormous, with arms like tree trunks. For a split second, Darnell hesitates. But as the man gets to his feet, he makes the mistake of glancing down in horror at the tech's body.

Darnell lifts two syringes out of his pocket, flips the caps off. They bounce away across the floor. The first needle only scratches the giant, but it's enough to get some quicksleep into his blood, and in seconds he's stumbling, throwing uncoordinated punches. Darnell dodges, dodges again, then plants the needles right in the giant's chest.

The man collapses almost instantly, dropping first to his knees, and then flat onto his face. There's an incoherent yell of fury, and then the little one is back.

She rushes towards Darnell, her shoulder low, aiming for his legs. He snags her by the neck before she can get close, lifting her up. She kicks out at him, tries to scratch the exposed skin on his arm, but it's no use. His hand goes all the way around her neck, locking her in a vice.

There's some light coming from Gray's passage. Darnell can just make out his attacker. She's a tiny woman, her skin spangled with colourful tattoos. High up on her neck, curving around to her throat, are two words in a delicate, curlicued font. *Devil Dancers*.

Riley Hale's crew. So.

Her struggles are getting more urgent. Darnell's fingers clench. A little more pressure, and her fragile spine will snap. And there's his blade, tucked in his belt. A single short cut will open her throat.

No. Better to keep his options open—for now. Darnell pulls out another syringe. He takes the cap in his mouth, grips it in his teeth, pulls and spits. The girl's eyes go wide, and then he jabs the needle into her neck and they defocus, the irises rolling back.

He drops her, and the tunnel is silent again.

15

Riley

I read the note again. And the horrible sick feeling in my chest begins to grow. Anger blooms like a poisonous flower.

Trembling, I pass the paper to Amira, and she and Carver scan it. When she looks up, her face is grim. "We should stick to the plan," she says quietly.

I stare at her. "Stick to the...no. I have to fix this. I'm going back to the Air Lab."

"He'll kill you if you do."

"He'll kill Prakesh if I don't."

"Slow up, Riley," says Carver. I'm expecting a wisecrack, but his voice is calm. "Amira's right. You don't just rip out someone's eyeball or hold kidnapped techs in the Air Lab—he'll have somewhere quiet and out of the way. And if you show up in the Labs, he'll kill you *and* Prakesh."

"So what do we do?" I say. My voice cracks on the last word.

"We stick to the plan," Amira says again. "We find Gray. We track him. He leads us right to them."

Another burst of guilt as I remember that we sent Kev and Yao over to Darnell's. "What about the Twins?"

"They can handle themselves," Amira says.

She doesn't wait for a response, taking off down the corridor in a run. After a moment, Carver and I join her, running in tight formation. As we turn the corner, we see more people in the corridor ahead, right in our path.

Amira yells over her shoulder, "Riley, point!" and I accelerate, bursting ahead to overtake her.

There's an art to running in a group. You have to move in single file, creating as narrow a profile as possible. Even then, you have to know when to break formation to cut through the crush of people. The fastest tracer sets the pace and the route, and I pick the quickest one I know, heading back past the mess hall and into the maze of corridors on the bottom level.

There are crowds we have to fight through by the habs—the ones in this part of the sector are dorm-style, designed to hold a lot of people. There aren't any mining or factory facilities in Apogee, and over the years more and more people have moved in. There are plenty of families here, which means the corridors are always crowded and noisy—mostly with kids, no matter what the hour is.

As we descend, I come round a corner on a stairwell to find a ball flying right at my head. I have to spin to the side to avoid it, nearly colliding with the wall. Amira knocks the ball back without stopping—it's nothing more than rags held together with tight strips of cloth. The kids are in a tight group at the top of the stairs, and one of them catches the ball above his head, a huge smile on his face. I have to suppress the urge to shout at him. How can he be so happy when Prakesh is…

I fight it off. Let my movements and the rhythm of my breathing take over. Every so often, when the crush forces us to break out of single file, I'll catch a glimpse of the other two Dancers cutting in alongside me.

I might have pure speed on my side, but Amira moves with a devastating economy, each foot placed exactly, perfectly balanced, her shoulders tilted back and her eyes on the horizon. Her scarf billows out behind her, the faded red material catching the light.

Carver's technique is less precise, but his sheer brute strength and long arms mean he can take the biggest of jumps with ease. As we near the market, we reach a small open area, where the passage we're in narrows to a dead end by a bank of terminals. Another walkway runs parallel, above and to the left. Amira and I have to tic-tac off the opposite wall to reach it, but Carver just flings himself upwards in one huge leap, hauling himself over.

Sometimes, the crush of the crowds forces us away from each other, but we always link back up. Just when I think I've got ahead of them, Amira will appear, or Carver, shooting out of a darkened passage where the lights have burned out, or slipping through a crowd. It feels horribly wrong to be running away from where Prakesh is, but Amira's right. The only way is to stick to the plan.

The crush gets thicker the closer we get to the market. More and more often, we're having to spread out to find the gaps. But we've made good time, and we soon reach the huge hangar doors marking the entrance. Merchants have spilled out the doors, their makeshift tables jumbled together. The air is hot, thick with smoke from improvised forges and furnaces. I can smell iron, and spices.

My throat is parched, and I'm grateful when Amira pulls a small flask out of her pocket and passes it over. There's not a lot, but we manage a few gulps between us. We passed a few water points on the way over here, but I didn't think to stop at any of them. They're all over Outer Earth: machines set into the walls of corridors and galleries where you can get clean water, purified from recycled human waste, connected by a nerve system of pipes and filters that extends across the whole station. It's nasty when you think hard about it, but it's also the only source of water we've got.

"What now, boss?" says Carver as he passes the flask back.

Amira takes a final swig and runs a hand across her mouth. "We go in. Riley, stay out of sight, no matter what. Wait a few minutes before you follow us."

"Got it."

Amira and Carver move off, walking slowly through the massive doors. Soon, they're lost in the sprawl. I wait a few moments more, then follow, ducking my way under an awning and cutting to the left.

The hangar is enormous—they used to build ships here. The noise rises to ear-splitting levels as I enter, not only from the bustling crowds but from the merchants trying to shout over each other. Everywhere, people barter vegetables, scrap metal, batteries, machinery, tiny packets of spices haggled over in dark corners. Beetles sizzle on fat-caked metal. There are piles of silkworm larvae, barely cooked, served in dirty cloth bags. I had some once, and I'm glad it was only once.

To the right, a burst of sparks shoots out across the stalls as a man demonstrates a homemade plasma cutter, filthy goggles pulled down over his eyes.

There's at least one market in every sector. People used to rely completely on the mess for food, back when everybody had a job and showing up for work was the only way to get on the food list. They'd go to work at the Gardens, or lifting crates in the ship docks, or on maintenance crews assigned to maintain the pipes and power lines. But when the number of people here grew larger than the amount of available jobs, people started taking care of themselves.

"Riley," someone says, and I turn to find Old Madala grinning at me.

Short and stooped, he's lost most of his teeth, save for the odd fuzzy, yellow stump. The left sleeve of his overalls is tied at the shoulder, flopping loosely in place of his missing arm. He's a regular client, a vegetable grower—our last run for him netted us a thick bunch of sweet, crunchy carrots. I don't even think he has another spot on the station; he just seems to sleep under his table, relying on the other merchants to keep an eye on his goods.

His toothless smile widens. "You not come see me for long time there," he says in his odd patois. "Where you been?"

"Just busy. Around. Thanks for the carrots, by the way."

"You want some more? I got a job for you, if you like." He holds up his hand, and I see he's carrying a small parcel, wrapped in tattered oilcloth.

I shake my head, forcing myself to stay calm. "No, I'm on another run right now, but I'll tell Kev to come find you."

"OK, no problem. But come by soon, eh? You don't want to leave an old man lonely now, do you?"

He gives a lascivious wink. Coming out of anybody else, it would be creepy, but Madala has this way about him that makes it hard to get angry at him.

"I will," I say, and lean close. "Listen, I want to ask you something."

He raises his eyebrows quizzically. "Information? I tell you things? Gonna cost you, you know."

I pout. "Oh come on," I say. "We've been doing business for a long time. You can spot me this one."

He barks a short laugh. "True. True. What you wanna know?"

"Anything you can tell me about the guy who sells onions over by Takashi's. Gray."

His expression is puzzled. "Gray? Nothing here. Not much I know 'bout him. He stay quiet, keep his business his business, you know? I never get any trouble from him. S'good. We need more like that."

"Do you know where he lives?"

Madala rubs his chin, then jerks his finger upwards. "Up on top levels, I think. But thinking now, my friend Indira, she live there too. Take her long time to get up and down every day, not good with her leg."

I interrupt him. "What'd she say?"

He looks me in the eye. "He never there. He never go back. I think he sleep somewhere else maybe."

I grip his hand and squeeze. "Thanks, Madala. We'll come find you when we're done, all right?"

He winks again before turning and moving back into the smoke, ducking under another shower of sparks.

I move along the wall of the hangar. Ahead of me, two musicians have set up: a man carrying an ancient, battered guitar, and a young girl, barely a teen. She's singing, and a small crowd has started to gather, drawn by her voice. Her song is fragile, brittle, but it carries over the wallah of the market.

I want to stay and listen—she's singing in Hindi, a language I can only mutter a few words in, but her voice is haunting, soft. There's no time to stop. Not now. So I push through the group of people who have gathered to listen.

And as I do so, I feel eyes on my back. I turn, expecting danger, but finding no one. It's a moment before I catch sight of a woman, staring at me through the crowd. She's around sixty, her head covered by a blue scarf, and she has the oddest expression on her face; deep sadness mixed with…something else. Before I can react, she vanishes, turning back into the crowd.

Whoever she was, she can wait. I force myself to keep moving, pushing through the crowd, away from the singer.

As I move towards the back of the hangar, I pass under the massive outline of the station spray-painted on the wall. Not for the first time, I wonder how they even conceived this place. It would have been so much easier to build a city on Earth, underground maybe. But Outer Earth is what happens when a bad idea gets a lot of backers. People can be pretty stupid sometimes. Especially if they're in government, and have something to prove.

Split the ring into six sectors, running clockwise from Apex through Gardens, Chengshi, Apogee, New Germany and Tzevya, all the way round the ring. The names are old, given to the sectors by the first people who came here. Some of the names are hangovers from where they lived back on Earth; places that don't even exist any more. I sometimes wonder what old Germany was really like. What it would have been like to live there, or in China, where the word Chengshi came from.

Run a monorail round the inner edge of the ring, and there you go: one space station, three hundred miles above the Earth, fit for habitation until the sheer amount of population growth pops it like a grape.

It's weird to think that the floor below us is really the outer wall of the station. Thanks to its ring shape, the floors of Outer Earth are all slightly curved, although the curve is so imperceptible that you have to concentrate hard to see it, even when you're running around it—that'll happen when the ring itself has an eighteen-mile circumference. The higher you go, the closer you actually get to the centre of the ring, although the distance is relatively so small that you can't feel any change in gravity.

The spokes running out from the Core meet the ring at Apogee and Apex. Enter the path to the Core, through the ceiling of Level 6 in Apogee, and keep running, and pretty soon you'll be in zero-G. The further in you go, the lighter you get.

Through the haze in the market, I see Takashi's Bar, at the far end of the hangar. It used to be a reclaimed office, the only actual building in the hangar. Takashi himself died in the riots years ago, but the bar kept his name, and it's been selling homebrew for as long as I can remember—as well as a regular supply of super-pricey weed, if you know who to talk to.

Takashi's is right up against the wall of the market—right where the escape pods used to be. People have taken them over the years, cutting themselves loose, refusing to believe that there's nothing left on Earth to go back to. Most of the pods had been stripped for parts before they even got there, their fuel tanks drained dry. Didn't stop people from taking them.

The last one was shot out of Outer Earth decades ago. There are ghost stories about them: pods that never made it back home, that are still floating through the void.

I tear my eyes away from the gaps in the wall. And it's then that I see him. Arthur Gray.

I didn't pay a lot of attention to him when I picked up the cargo. He has a face you'd forget instantly if you passed over it in the crush. He's nearly bald, with just a few thin wisps of white hair around his ears. His tunic is stained brown, although the stains are liquid somehow—more sweat than grime.

Gray is leaning over his table, a dirty box of onions behind him, deep in conversation with a buyer. I duck behind a stack of crates, and watch as they talk. He and the buyer reach some kind of agreement, and strike palms. And then, Gray smiles, and it's all I can do not to run screaming towards him, leaping over the table and wrapping my hands around his throat. Because his smile is the most awful thing I've seen.

I'm halfway through calculating my jump distance and working out whether I should skip the chokehold and just kick him in the face when I realise that Gray is packing up. He's closing his boxes, pulling an old, rusty chain over them and clicking a solid padlock shut. He busies himself with securing the boxes to a nearby wall strut.

Amira and Carver. Surely they'll have seen him too. But as I scan the stalls again, I can't pick them out of the throng.

Gray heads off through the crowd, moving with surprising speed. I look around, expecting to see someone slip from their hiding place and give chase, but there's nobody. He's heading for a gap between two stalls piled high with scrap; in seconds, he'll be gone, vanished into the crowd. Amira might have warned me to stay hidden, but I can't let him slip away.

The part of my mind still working properly is screaming at me. There's no proof he even knows Prakesh exists. Following him could be a giant waste of time—and besides, you can't risk getting near him. Let Amira and Carver do it.

I step out from behind the crates, and take off into the market, after Gray.

16

Darnell

By the time he's finished dragging the two tracers and the technician inside, Darnell is dripping with sweat. It sticks his shirt to his back and runs in rivulets down his chest.

The big one was the worst. Darnell couldn't lift him up; he had to grab him under the arms, pull him down the passage. He's in an ugly mood. The joy he felt when he received the eyeball has burned away.

He straightens up, his shoulders aching. Gray's workroom doesn't have a lot in it—a few benches, a couple of mobile storage containers. A big metal table, suspiciously clean. Darnell's gaze falls back on the unconscious trio. Should he restrain them somehow? He knows where the cuffs and the zip ties are, in the storage area at the back. Gray once showed Darnell what he called his toys; the knives and pliers and handheld blowtorches, all arranged on neatly labelled shelves.

He shakes his head. He needn't bother with restraints. He's seen quicksleep in action before—they'll be out for hours, which gives him plenty of time, and even when they wake up, they'll be too groggy to do anything.

Gray. The man is meticulous. Fastidious, even. But even meticulous men make mistakes, and Gray's mistake has made things exceptionally complicated. Darnell is so close to his goal that he feels as if he can reach out and touch it. But he has only got this far by being meticulous himself, by minimising error.

He licks his lips, and looks back at his prisoners.

Even small mistakes can have consequences that spiral out of control. He can't risk those mistakes. And he definitely can't risk someone like Gray making them for him.

He pulls a metal chair off a stack on one side of the room, and sits down heavily. He'll need to get back to the Air Lab soon, to take care of Hale. But first, he's going to have a little talk with Arthur Gray.

17

Riley

The worst thing a tracer can do is run in the dark.

There are parts of the station we call black runs: areas where the lights have burned out and plunged the surroundings into darkness. It's not just about injury; it's the gangs too, lurking in the shadows, just waiting for a rookie tracer to take an easy shortcut.

And the number one place to avoid? The darkest part of Outer Earth? The monorail tracks running around the inside of the ring.

Unless a food train is coming through, the tunnels are black as death—cold and silent. When the station started getting really crowded, people tried sleeping in the tunnels, but after a few got crushed under the monorail, everybody else got the message.

I have a feeling in my gut that the tracks are exactly where Gray is going. I should wait for Amira. But there's no way I'm letting Gray get away. Not when he might be my only link to Prakesh. I keep my distance from him, trying to blend into the stream of people in the market. I've never had to tail someone before; usually, I'm running away from trouble, not towards it.

To get to the tracks, you've got to climb to the top level and enter via one of the old platforms. Gray pauses at the market entrance, and I tense, ready to slip behind a nearby stall if he turns around. But instead, he tilts his face upwards for a moment, then resumes trudging, heading out towards the nearby stairwell. He begins to climb, taking long, purposeful strides.

Still no sign of Amira, or Carver. I swallow hard, and keep on him.

The crush thins out as we ascend, and by the time we reach Level 6, the stairs are all but deserted. As I suspected, he heads straight for the monorail platform, climbing the last set of stairs onto track level. This time, I hang back until he's out of sight.

I count to ten, then quietly climb the stairs to the platform.

I haven't been here in a while, and I'm surprised to find that the digital readouts still work. There are luminous orange holograms above the tracks, meant to indicate when the next train will arrive. They're just flashing gibberish now, endless lines of meaningless code, but they bathe the platform in a warm glow. A couple of the fluorescent lights are working, too—not even flickering. The floor is made of black steel plates, and the walls are lined with dusty benches. Metal columns sprout from the ground beside the tracks.

I close my eyes and listen. There—very faint: the sound of footsteps, heading off down the tunnel to my left. Gently, I lower myself from the platform to the track below. The light from the platform ends where the tunnel begins, cut off, as if it's run up against an invisible barrier. My hand rests on the edge on the platform.

Terror grips tight. I've seen nothing of Carver or Amira since I left the market. I'm breaking every rule we have: never go into the tunnels, never run in the dark, and never go off on your own to tail someone while breaking the above two rules.

I take a deep breath, and step into the darkness of the tunnel.

I have to force myself to pause so my eyes can adjust. In the distance, I can hear Gray's footsteps, getting fainter and fainter. Even so I wait until I can make out the edges of the track, then slowly make my way along it. I've shifted onto the balls of my feet, trying to move as silently as possible. If a train comes along, I'm finished, but I calm myself by thinking that if Gray has a hideout here, then he'll know when it's safe to walk the tracks.

Air whistles down the tunnel. In the darkness, I place a hand on the wall to steady myself. The sound of my fingers on it is dull and faint, the metal slightly greasy to touch. The walls of Outer Earth are several yards thick to protect us from radiation, but it still feels as if the vacuum is sucking at my hand, inches away, scrabbling at the wall. It's so easy to forget that we're in space, that the station is just a tiny metal capsule floating in the void.

The footsteps have stopped. I freeze, listening hard. How long have I been walking? Is he still ahead of me?

But then I hear his breathing, haggard and rough, right next to me, and it's all I can do not to scream. Instead, I quickly flatten myself against the tunnel wall. I can hear him moving now, a faint rustle of cloth, then the tiny glow of a keypad. He's up ahead on the opposite side, his back to me. The beeps as he punches in the code seem as loud as klaxons. There's a click, and suddenly light floods the tunnel. He steps through, and the door shuts behind him with a resounding slam, plunging the tunnel into darkness again. When the echo fades, there's only the sound of my heartbeat, so loud that I'm sure he must be able to hear it behind the door.

I hop the tracks, and run my hands over the keypad, mentally kicking myself for not thinking this far ahead. *Of course* he'd have a lock on the door. He wasn't just going to leave it open for anybody to find. I look around, my eyes searching the gloom for anything that could help, but see nothing. Carver would know how to hack this thing, and if I'd waited for him...I swear under my breath, and I'm about to turn back to the keypad when I glance up, and stop dead.

Surely not even I can be that lucky.

One of the plates in the roof is loose. There's just enough light to see that it's pushed very slightly to one side, with darkness beyond the opening.

I have no idea where it goes, or if I'll even be able to squeeze through, but it's the only option I've got. Getting into it is going to be tricky. I consider tic-taccing off the wall, as I would to enter the Nest, but that's no good. It'll be way too noisy. No, there's got to be another way.

I look around, and see the struts on the wall next to the door. They're old and rusted, but look like they'd support my weight. I brace my hands on the outer lips of the strut closest to the hatch, then lean back experimentally. The rust bites into my palms, and the strut groans slightly, but it holds.

I lift my feet onto the wall, and start to pull myself up, hanging back off the strut, my arm muscles flaring in protest. When I reach the top, I very carefully reach one hand back. My fingers catch the edge of the roof plate, lose it, catch it again and pull it towards me. With a creak of old metal, the loose plate slides across the opening.

I tense, take two quick breaths, then throw myself backwards, grabbing the lip of the opening with both hands. Part of the edge is jagged, slicing into my right palm. Hot blood runs down my wrist, and I have to stifle a howl of pain as I swing backwards. I force myself to use my momentum, and as I begin to swing forwards I pull myself up in one movement.

I'm forced to my stomach almost immediately. The crawlspace above the opening is tiny, enough for me to lie prone but no more. It's thick with wires and cables, and everything has a fine film of dust which tickles my nose. I run my thumb over the wound in my hand, hissing with pain: it's cut deeply in a ragged line, just where the fingers meet the palm.

One more injury to add to the list, I think. *Racking up quite a score there.*

The sound of air rushing down the tracks has vanished. I have no idea if the crawlspace even follows the path Gray took; it could diverge, or swing off in a different direction entirely. Worse, it could split into multiple paths. And—I taste another dose of bitter fear at the thought—there's no way to turn around. The only way out of here is backwards.

I've never had a problem with enclosed spaces—when you live with a million other people in close quarters, you sort of get used to the idea—but the tunnel ahead seems to tighten as I look at it. My throat twinges—the familiar thirst, biting down again. I shake it off, and begin to crawl, using my arms to pull my body forwards. My jacket hisses as it rubs against the side.

My fingers scrape a wall ahead of me that I can't see. I run my hands along it, and discover that the path turns sharply to the right.

There's no way I'm going to turn the corner prone. I push my body up, leaning hard onto my left side. The zipper of my jacket digs into my waist, an unexpectedly sharp pain that I can do nothing about. I concentrate on slowly inching forward, pushing past the turn: first my head, then my shoulders, squeezing through. A skein of dust falls onto my face from the roof of the tunnel, tickling my nostrils.

Something moves under my hand. Something alive.

Forcing back a shriek, I rip my hand away, and in the darkness I hear a tiny flutter, a skittering sound as something crawls along the metal. A bug. A beetle, maybe. One that got lucky and escaped from the buzz box. I shudder as I imagine them breeding, forming colonies in the blackness of the vent systems. The fear is back, fighting for control.

I'm halfway around the turn, about to reach my arms out and pull my legs around, when I feel it. The vibration. It's only slight at first, a tiny tremor in the back of my heels, which are forced into the far wall. But it rapidly grows, and the entire crawlspace begins to rumble and shake. The noise is huge, a low rumble that takes hold of a deep part of me and shakes.

The train. A monorail passing on the tracks behind me. I'm in no danger, but every fibre in my being wants to scream. I try to clamp my hands over my ears and shut off the insane noise, but they're pushed ahead of me, and I can't get them back far enough. I lie, trembling, until the train passes, its behemoth rumbling replaced by a high-pitched whine in my ears.

I remain still, breathing hard for a moment, before reaching out and pulling myself round the corner. The crawlspace is still completely black, and I realise that at some point, if I can't find a way to Gray, I'm going to have to push myself backwards down the tunnel.

I've been crawling way too long. I could be anywhere, maybe even near the outer hull, unprotected by the thick shielding and getting a dose of lethal radiation. I pause for a moment, panting, the exertion of pulling myself along seeming to catch up with me in one awful moment. Thick, sour saliva coats my mouth. I swallow, and as I do, I hear them: voices. Very faint, but there.

I stop, hardly daring to breathe. For a moment, I think I've imagined them, but then they catch the edge of my hearing again. I force myself forwards, pushing on through the blackness. The voices get louder. I can't make out the words. One of the speakers is Gray, I'm sure of it. But who is he talking to?

Around another corner, I see a tiny shaft of light, piercing the darkness of the tunnel and revealing grimy, dirt-blackened walls. The light is coming from a small chink in the tunnel's bottom panels, a gap which looks like it wasn't welded properly and which came loose over time. The voices are louder now; I still can't make out who Gray is talking to, although I have a good idea who it might be. Slowly, I pull myself along to the gap, and look through.

A room. Brightly lit, with the usual plate-metal floor. A storeroom of some kind. Gray is there. He has his back to me, and he's talking to his companion, a blur at the edge of my vision. I can finally hear his words, coming up through the gap in the tiles. "I did what you wanted," he says.

The other person in the room replies, "No, you didn't. You screwed up, Arthur."

I know that voice. It's the same fluty, gentle tone that offered me a job barely hours ago.

Oren Darnell steps forward, into my field of vision. And as he does so, I catch sight of Prakesh.

He's behind Darnell, sprawled on the floor—not bound, but unconscious. My breath catches in my throat. Not just because of him.

Lying next to Prakesh are Yao and Kevin.

18

Prakesh

Prakesh doesn't realise he's awake until he hears the voices. They're muffled, metallic, but as he slowly fights his way out of the darkness, they become clearer.

"I ask you for one very simple thing, and you can't deliver," a man says. "I don't have a lot of respect for people who can't keep their promises."

That's Mr. Darnell, Prakesh thinks. The thought is fuzzy, indistinct. His eyes are closed. He tries to open them, but it's like they've been glued shut. For some reason, he finds this very funny. Not that he can laugh; there's an ache in his throat, a hot ring above his Adam's apple. It doesn't seem important.

"You wanted him dead, he got dead!" says another man. And that's when Prakesh remembers everything. Remembers his boss's hands around his throat. He is suddenly awake, more alert than he's ever been, but his body refuses to obey him. His eyes remain stubbornly shut.

"I also wanted his left eye delivered in such a way that it didn't attract the attention of *every tracer on Outer Earth*," Darnell says. "You should have brought it to me yourself, instead of using a little delivery girl to do it for you. Now I have to kill a lot of people to make this go away."

This is all wrong, Prakesh thinks. With an effort of will, he finds that he can force his eyelids open a crack. Sharp light lances through, and he closes them again. Pain stabs deep into his skull, takes up residence, starts beating out a drum line.

"Don't worry about them," says the other man. He sounds confident, but his voice tremors ever so slightly. "The quicksleep did the trick, didn't it? We can deal with them whenever we want."

"They belong to the same crew as the tracer you hired," Darnell says. "It's not just them. Are you beginning to understand the problems your failure has caused?"

"But you got the eye, didn't you?" A sullen note has crept into Gray's voice. "You can crack the scanner. So what's the problem?"

It's all Prakesh can do to open his eyes again. He focuses every ounce of energy he possesses into the muscles around his eyes. He makes them stay open. Slowly, with every moment bringing agony, Prakesh lets the light in.

He's on his back, staring up at the ceiling. He can just make out Oren Darnell, upside-down above him, and he can see the person he's talking to—a bald man, his skin shiny with sweat.

Darnell's eyes are cold and black, and the face they're set into seems made of steel. "Do you know why you've been left alone for so long? Why the stompers never cottoned on to this nasty little habit of yours?"

The other man moans, sweat dripping down his face.

"We spent a long time recruiting sleepers," Darnell says. "People we could count on. And you—you were the only one who knew about killing."

It's then that Prakesh sees movement. Up in the ceiling. There's a smudge on one of the plates—no, not a smudge, a gap. And there's something behind it. An eye. Someone is watching them. Someone is looking down. The eye isn't focused on him; it's looking away, flicking between Darnell and his accomplice. Prakesh wills his eyes to stay open, wills the other eye to look at him.

The eye shifts. Prakesh gets a quick glimpse of a nose, the edge of a mouth. And at that moment, the person in the ceiling snaps into focus.

No, Riley, Prakesh thinks. *Don't come in here.*

"You could have been very useful in the days to come," Darnell says.

"I still can!"

"I disagree," says Darnell, and whips a knife into the side of the man's neck.

Prakesh can't scream. He can't do anything. As blood spatters onto the floor, dotting his cheek, he feels his grip on his eyelids slipping. Then it fails completely, and the world goes dark.

19

Riley

The move is so quick, so immediate, that it takes a second for me to realise what Darnell's done. Gray gives a horrible, strangled cough, as short and sharp as the blade itself. Darnell pulls it out, with a horrible sucking sound that reaches up into the crawlspace like a long, black tendril. I have to bite my tongue to stop myself from crying out.

He pulls a rag from his pocket and wipes off the knife, running it gently down the blade. His expression is calm, a thin sheen of sweat on his forehead, and with a sickening feeling I understand that the sweat isn't from guilt or apprehension, just exertion. He looks as if he's just hefted a heavy crate.

At his feet, Gray shudders and jerks as he dies. A gout of dark blood is spreading across the floor.

I've got to get in there. I'm the only person who knows where Prakesh and the Twins are. Going back isn't an option; it'll take far too long to squeeze myself backwards in the black crawlspace, and even then I'll be stuck facing the locked door with no other way to enter, while Darnell does to them what he did to Gray. I'll have to keep moving forwards, but even as the thought occurs I realise with a start that I can't do that either. The crawlspace I'm in goes right over the middle of the room, and I can't move along it silently enough. If I make even the slightest noise while pulling myself along, I'm done for. I see the knife rammed upwards through the thin metal and into my stomach. Darnell could do that and walk away, leaving me to bleed out in the duct, with no one to hear my screams.

Through the gap, I see him turn to the Twins, his knife in hand, and my heart leaps up into my throat. But all he does is look at them for a long moment before striding out of view, stepping over Gray's body as he does so. I hear the door below me open, and close again. Faint footsteps echo up into my crawlspace as Darnell heads back towards the tracks.

Very quietly, I take a few deep breaths, and then pull myself forwards through the tunnel. The noise of my elbows and knees banging the metal seems far too loud, but I'm pretty sure that Darnell won't hear them, and before long I've reached the wall at the other end of the room.

I badly want to rest, to lie in the tunnel and let my aching arms and legs take a break. No chance.

Ahead of me, the tunnel splits in a T-junction, and I impulsively take the right fork, bending my body past the turn, my fingers feeling ahead of me for changes in the tunnel floor. And suddenly, my fingers collide with something: a raised knot in the floor, gritty with rust. I pause, and slowly move my hands over the surface. I thought my eyes would adjust to the dark, but after the piercing light of the peephole I'm blind again.

My fingers feel out another knot. It's a hinge. I've happened on a trapdoor, another entry into the crawlspace, and relief floods through me. I hurriedly scratch around, locate the outer edge and pull it up. By now I'm beyond caring about how much noise I make. I just want out.

A little light brightens the tunnel, coming from the room below. I pull myself forwards, past the open trapdoor, then gingerly lower my legs backwards into it. It's still too dark to see where the floor below is, or even what I'm dropping into, so I take it as slowly as I dare.

I quietly move down to a hanging position, and let go. My feet hit metal, and I drop to a crouch, scanning the room. The light is coming from a tiny crack under a door to my left, and I can see that the room I'm in is another storeroom, stashed with old electrical equipment. Puffs of cold air are coming from vents set low in the wall, but there's no way of knowing if it's air conditioning, or just the breathing of the station. Despite that, the room has an odd smell—thin, unpleasant, almost chemical.

There's a row of big lockers lining the back wall, and stray wires and tools lie stacked on shelves around the room, dimly visible in the low light. This place would be a goldmine for the guys in the market.

The pain in my right hand flares, and I clutch it to my chest. Opening it gingerly, I run a finger along the gash. It's already crusted with dried blood and dirt, and even the slightest touch makes me wince. But I can't worry about it now. By my reckoning, the crawlspace has dropped me into a room just off the one where Gray and Darnell were talking. I drop to one knee and lower my head, tilting it sideways and squinting to see under the door. Nothing: just a bar of blinding white light.

Tracer

I don't want to go into that room.

The thought of finding Darnell there causes little electric shocks to rocket up my spine, and as I slowly raise myself up, I have to struggle to control my breathing. I should have waited for Amira and Carver. Three of us against Darnell might even the odds; hell, Carver alone could probably take him down with a little luck. But me?

And that's just it. Right now, there's only me.

Slowly, I pad towards the door. What if it's locked? Sealed by a keypad on the other side? No. Can't think about that now. I have to get to the Twins. I push my ear to the door, listening intently. Unlike a lot of the doors on the station, this one isn't electronic. It has an old-fashioned handle, caked with dust.

For what feels like a whole minute, I listen, but there's not a single sound. Very slowly, I reach towards the edge of the door, grasp the handle, and pull.

With a click that's too loud, way too loud, the door clacks off its lock. Dazzling white light shoots through the crack, blinding me for an instant. I blink several times, and very carefully step into the room.

The place is sparsely furnished, with workbenches pushed up against the far wall. It must have once been used by repair techs working on the monorail. Gray's body is on the other side of the room, and I do my best not to stare at it.

The Twins and Prakesh are on my right. Yao's face is swollen and bloodied. She must have fought when Darnell hit her with the quicksleep.

I scan the room once more, and run to them, sliding to my knees as I reach Prakesh. I'm more terrified than I've ever been in my life. The fear digging into me is like a creature perched on the back of my neck, running its claws along my shoulders.

I reach out a hand, gripping his shoulder. "Prakesh," I hiss.

His eyes flicker open, and at that moment, huge, damp hands close around my throat.

20

Riley

His grip is steel. I claw at his enormous hands, desperately wanting to scream, but all that comes out is a horrified wheeze. How could a man so enormous be so quiet?

His hands tighten, those wet fingers crushing my windpipe. A dull ache starts in my chest, sharpening as he squeezes. He lifts me right off my feet, before spinning me around and slamming me into the wall above the Twins.

His expression is not one of anger, but something even more terrifying: joy. He grins, showing huge teeth. They're pearly-white, dazzling in the fluorescent lights, and it's that fact—that he's somehow managed to keep them clean and pristine—that makes me lose it. I pummel at his arms, try to squirm out of his grip, but his smile just gets bigger. My feet are dancing, trying to kick him, but he's way out of range, holding me at arm's length against the wall.

"You should have taken my offer," he whispers. He flicks his eyes to the ceiling. "I knew you were there the whole time. I didn't even have to come and find you. You came right to me."

He leans in slightly closer, and I take the chance, swinging my hand up and raking my nails across his face. I keep them cut short, but they're still ragged and uneven, and they open up three thin cuts across his forehead. He swings his head to the side, but can't avoid the strike, and when he turns back the childlike joy has been replaced by fury.

In a rage, he hurls me across the room. I wasn't expecting it, and there's no time to drop my shoulder before I hit the ground. The impact knocks what little breath I have right out of me. My head collides with the wall, causing another starburst of pain.

But I can breathe again, and the oxygen rushing into my lungs fuels my anger. I push off the ground and spring up, woozy but alert. I am *through* getting my ass kicked.

Tracer

Darnell crosses the room in a matter of seconds, his footfalls booming on the metal as he breaks into a run. His left arm is pulled back, level with his waist, winding up a gut-punch. But he's coming too fast to control himself: I feint right, then drop into a crouch and throw my left leg out. He sees the move, tries to dodge, but his back foot catches my thigh and he ends up smashing into the wall.

He roars, but he's off balance, and as I spring backwards from my crouch I bring my other foot up and kick hard, aiming right for his crotch.

But for a giant, Darnell is obscenely fast. He grabs my ankle in that tempered-steel grip, and in one movement he regains his balance and yanks me towards him.

My heart is full go, pounding in my ears, and I'm more scared than I've ever been in my life. I see his hands on my throat again, and terror surges through me. If I can get away and get a little head start, I might just be able to find help.

I twist to one side, throw my torso upwards—and sink my teeth into his calf.

The thin fabric of his trouser leg rips under my bite, and he howls in agony. Burning-hot blood explodes in my mouth. Every instinct is to let go, and I can feel my gorge rising, but I force myself to hold on.

He kicks out with his other leg, and connects with my bruised collarbone. He couldn't have had a better hit if he'd planned it. A grinding agony flares in my shoulder, and I let go of his leg, crying out. My face is sticky with blood. I try to get to my feet, but the balance has been knocked out of my legs.

Through eyes blurred and wet, I see the kick coming in, and this time there's no bracing for it. His massive boot connects squarely with my stomach, and every atom of air inside me explodes from between my lips.

I lie there, heaving, and Darnell flips me over. He straddles me, and with a sound like a dying breath, draws a knife from his belt. His breath is hot, ragged with effort. A short laugh crawls out of his mouth.

I summon up every piece of energy I have and spit right in his face. The move costs me, and a fresh wave of heaving rolls through my chest. Darnell flicks the spittle off his cheek. I hear it patter softly on the ground. "That's the spirit," he says. And with that, he flips the shank in one effortless movement, and raises it above his head to stick me.

There's a bang, and Darnell is knocked sideways. I see the hand holding the blade, twisted backwards in the air. And then Darnell's gone, and the world is filled with noise and movement and shouting voices. Hands grip my shoulders, hoist me up. For a moment, the room seems filled with a dazzling white light.

Amira is there, mouthing words I can't quite hear, gripping my shoulders. Behind her, the room swarms with stompers and medics, a buzzing cacophony of grey and white jumpsuits. Darnell is on his stomach, his arms being restrained behind him, blood leaking from a stinger wound below his left shoulder. He's shouting, swearing revenge. A stomper aims a kick at his chest; he curls into a foetal position and falls silent.

Yao is sitting up, and one of the medics—a young woman with blonde hair split by a streak of electric blue—is shining a light in her eyes. Kev and Prakesh are blinking in the light. Nobody seems to be looking at the body of Gray, sprawled in the middle of the room.

"The blood," says Amira. "Riley? Riley, where's it coming from?"

It takes me a moment to realise she's talking about Darnell's blood, splattered on my face. "Not mine," I say. "It's not mine."

"You should have waited, damn you," whispers Amira. I just catch her voice above the chaos. I manage to sit up. Carver is standing by the door, and there's a weird look on his face—pleased and appalled at the same time.

I jump up and run to Prakesh. A medic pushes me back, but I dodge under his grip. I want to look everywhere on Prakesh's body at once, desperate to see if he's been hurt. He pulls me into a hug. I freeze up on instinct, not used to the contact, then I hug him back. It seems crazy not to.

"I'm sorry," I say. "I'm so, so sorry. This was all because of me, I..."

"I'm fine," he whispers in my ear, his voice hoarse. "It's OK. Let them do what they need to do. We're good."

I squeeze him tight, then do as he asks, dropping back. Kev gives me a bleary thumbs-up.

Amira explains how they saw me start tailing Gray in the market; they'd been hidden close to his stall, and when I started the pursuit ahead of them, she decided that rather than try to intercept me, they should hang back and follow me as a fail-safe. "Darnell might have seen us if we'd crossed paths with you," she says.

I stare at her, an unsettling thought occurring. "You used me as bait."

Her gaze is steady. "You left us no choice. You always were impatient."

They'd come up behind me in the tunnels, and when they saw how I'd gained access through the roof, they decided not to follow me—"Three people in the service ducts would've been a bad idea," Amira says—and it was then that they'd decided to find the stompers. It was a gamble that paid off.

A medic comes over and crouches down to my level. He's an older guy with a craggy face, but his eyes are friendly, and Amira steps back so he can look at me. I get the light-in-the-eyes treatment too, and he runs a hand over my collarbone, my stomach. "Bruises and some shock, but nothing major," he says. "You are one lucky kid."

I gesture to the Twins. "They got hit with something. Quicksleep, I heard him call it."

He nods. "We've seen similar things before. It was a powerful strain he was cooking, but it'll wear off."

He lifts up my hand, and mutters something before rummaging in his tattered shoulder bag and taking out an injector. He notices me staring. "Disinfectant," he says. "It'll keep that cut from going bad."

"Does it hurt?"

"Let's find out," he says brightly, and squirts a jet of white foam into my palm. The sting is so sudden and strong that I have to stop myself from lashing out, but after a moment the pain fades, replaced by a throbbing warmth. The foam bubbles, and seems to sink into the cut, forming a hard, white crust. The medic stands, holds out his hand, and, despite the shock, a wave of elation surges through me. I reach out with my good one and grab it, and I'm pulled roughly to my feet.

"Captain," a voice shouts from the storeroom. "We've got bodies back here."

The lockers. That thin smell. I have to work very hard not to ask if one of them is missing an eye.

A stomper steps out from behind the medic, and I'm surprised to see that it's the one I met in the run to Darnell's. Royo. His expression is still gruff, but as he looks me over it softens very slightly.

"You owe these two big time," he says, looking at Amira and Carver. "We wanted to arrest them for going into the tunnels." His voice is rough, as if a statue, heavy with dust and grit, had learned to speak. "Can any one of you tell me how we ended up arresting the chief of the Air Lab instead? Anyone? Not that I wasn't looking for a reason before."

I do most of the talking: I have to tell him the entire story, and then I have to repeat it when his boss—a bigger, uglier version of Royo named Santos—comes over.

I tell him that I've delivered cargo before, but never knew what it was. When he hears that, Royo gives me a long, hard stare—enough to make me trail off for a moment. Finally, he utters a non-committal grunt. He's probably got every right to take us all in for assisting in criminal business, but he says nothing, and I decide not to chance it.

After a few more questions, Royo turns to leave, but turns back to offer his hand. His grip is firm. Carver has sauntered over, and does a double take at the sight of a tracer shaking hands with a stomper. I laugh, despite myself.

"So we're good?" Carver says, looking sideways at Royo. It doesn't look as if he trusts him all the way.

Royo releases my hand, and looks at him. "You just created a massive power vacuum," he says. "Now every gang on Outer Earth is going to try get a piece of the water points. Which means we're going to be working overtime to stop them killing each other."

He pauses—and I swear I see the ghost of a smile slip across his face. "But in my experience, that usually takes a few days to happen. If we can get in there and show some face, maybe we can disrupt things. Anyway. I don't usually trust you tracers, but you did good today."

"And what's that worth, exactly?" asks Amira. Royo shakes his head and turns away, his good humour exhausted.

Behind him, Darnell has been pulled to his feet, and all at once his voice is back. "Your world's going to end!" he screams. More stompers have to rush in to hold him. He strains at his cuffs, muscles standing out on his neck "You're all going to burn! All of you! You're all going to burn!"

His voice fades as he's dragged into the corridor, dwindling to nothingness. A fresh wave of nausea threatens to bend me double again as I realise what I just escaped. Amira's hand is on my shoulder, worry creasing her face, but I wave her off, pulling it together, and stand. Yao walks by, supported by a medic, and reaches out to squeeze my arm.

Soon we're out, into the tunnels, shot through with torchlight from dozens of stompers. Prakesh is holding my hand, gripping it like he never wants to let it go, and then we're onto the tracks by the platforms. Amira jumps up ahead of me, then reaches out for me. I have to let go of Prakesh to climb up, and when I reach back for him, I see that one of the stompers has pulled him aside to ask him something.

For a moment, I want to be down there with him, but then Amira and Carver are hustling me away, and then he's gone.

21

Riley

I was wrong about the Nest. It can hold plenty of people.

The corridor was already heaving when we arrived, and a huge cheer went up as people caught sight of us. Once in a while, gossip moves faster than the tracers—especially when it concerns someone as feared as Oren Darnell. Seems like everybody wanted to shake my hand or pull me into an embrace. I couldn't help smiling, especially when Carver started making loud hooting noises.

He quickly set up a makeshift ladder into the access hatch, ignoring Amira's protests that we had to keep our home a secret ("It's not as if people don't know where we live already," Carver told her, rolling his eyes, and Amira relented).

Soon, even more people started pouring into the Nest, filling it with music, plates of food, buckets of homebrew. Someone brought some extra tattoo ink, which Yao and a couple of her buddies jumped on immediately, splashing it all over the wall. Despite her head injury, and the skanky bits of dried blood still crusted in her hair, she's made a pretty swift recovery. Kev is still a little groggy: he's been given pride of place on the mattresses in the corner, clutching a cup of homebrew and staring blearily about him, a small smile on his face.

I push through the crowd and find a clear space against the wall, relieved to go unnoticed for a moment. Whatever the medic used on my cut, it's amazing stuff: the wound knitted within minutes, and although there's a dull ache in my palm I can almost make a complete fist. Somebody pushes a mug of homebrew into my good hand, and I take a deep drink. For once, the acrid, salty burn of the alcohol is welcome. I haven't been drunk or even tipsy for quite a while, but I'm enjoying the buzz.

As more people climb the ladder into the Nest, they bring more rumours with them. Someone heard that the bodies in Gray's workroom had been identified, and a little while later, someone else arrives with names. Turns out one of them was someone fairly important: a man named Marshall Foster. He used to head up the council, years ago, and moved down to Apogee after his retirement. None of the news coming up through the hatch explains why Gray killed him—or whether he was missing any body parts. In fact, nobody mentions the eyeball at all—it's probably still somewhere in the Air Lab.

Gray might have messed up in a big way when he killed Foster, but he was on a roll. There were two other bodies in the lockers. Gray had snatched a sewerage tech and a mess worker using his quicksleep serum, taken them back to his room by the tracks, and done…things to them. Conspiracy theories are already flying around as to what Darnell and Gray were planning together—and whether it had anything to do with Foster's death.

With an effort, I shake off my dark thoughts. Looking over, I see Amira drop onto the mattresses next to Kev. She's sober, despite having knocked back more homebrew than anyone. She leans close to Kev, tilting her head to his ear and whispering something which makes his smile grow wider. She catches my eye, and winks before raising her glass in my direction. I raise it back, and take a slug of the drink—this time, the burn is too much and I cough.

"That's what I always said about you, Riley," says Carver, clapping a hand on my shoulder. "You never could hold your booze."

He's in a good mood. Before we left, he had a chance to raid Gray's place for spare parts, and even managed to grab a few vials of the quicksleep.

"I think I've earned this drink," I say, laughing.

"Oh, hell yes."

He leans in close. He's drunk, his eyes unfocused and floating in their sockets, but it's a good drunk. "They're going to be talking about this for years. The girl who took down the monster of the market."

"Gray?"

"That's what everybody's calling him. And then there's Darnell—he's locked up in the brig with about fifteen guards. I think half the sector wants to break in and beat him to death."

"You do know it wasn't me who killed Gray, right?"

"Doesn't matter. People believe what they want to. One dead murderer, one corrupt Air Lab boss in jail, two rescued tracers. Not bad for a trouble-magnet like you."

"Careful," I say, but there's a smile in my voice. "Anyway," I continue, "nice work on the party. Who brought the booze? Or did we trade for this one?"

"Suki had some with her," he says, waving back over his shoulder, indicating a girl in the corner with a shocking crop of bright red hair, chatting with Prakesh. I know her, vaguely.

Carver wanders away, tottering towards Yao, who's still working on the wall with her friends. It's a riot of colour, extending upwards to the ceiling, the wet ink still glistening in the lights.

Your world's going to end.

Prakesh catches my eye and gives a questioning thumbs-up. I nod and smile, but Darnell's words cling to the edges of my mind like dust.

Words like *sleepers*. And *in the days to come*.

Almost without realising it, I'm pushing off from the wall and walking across to Prakesh.

"Hey you," he says. "You know Suki, right?"

The red-haired sprite flicks me a small salute.

"Thanks for the drink," I say.

"No problem. My brother and I make it. Beats going to work."

I turn to Prakesh. "Listen, I'm going to take a walk. I'm feeling a little closed in."

"Are you sure? I can always come with you if…"

"No," I interrupt him, forcing myself to smile. "I'm fine. Just need to clear my head."

I'm worried he's going to insist—concern is written on his face—but then he smiles too. "I guess we know you can take care of yourself," he says.

I feel like I have to say something more. "Listen, I'm really sorry. About before."

His smile flickers, but he brings it back, waving me away. "I'm good, Ry. Promise. Get out of here."

I hold his gaze for a moment, matching his smile, then turn to leave, ducking through the door. Behind me, another massive cheer goes up, and I turn to see Carver kissing Yao. She has her hand clasped around his head, his on her ass, and behind her Kev is looking stunned. Amira is laughing. "Aaron, I told you, no work relationships!" she says.

Unbelievable. I drop through the hatch.

The sector is surprisingly quiet, and I slip unseen through the corridors of Outer Earth. I'm taking it easy, walking more often than running, my bruised body grateful for the break.

The brig is on the bottom level, and my mind drifts as I head down towards it, the homebrew giving my thoughts some extra colour. I'm trying to piece everything I've been through together—Gray, Darnell, Foster. I'm dropped so deep into my own world that it takes me a few seconds to realise that I'm walking past the Memorial.

The corridor here is wider than most, and the Memorial takes up a whole wall. Proper paint, not just tattoo ink. Janice Okwembu commissioned it—she runs the station council now. Everybody was allowed to draw something—I must have been the only one in the whole sector who refused—and right in the middle, they let one of the more talented artists paint the ship itself.

I look at it before I can tell myself not to, pulling my jacket closer around me. The painting has faded over the years, but is still recognisable. The huge, tapered body, the swept-back fins, the bulging sections near the back which would have held supplies. And underneath it, in black lettering: Earth Return.

There are religious icons too: dozens of them, stacked on top of each other. Candles, crosses, metal bent into strange shapes. Tributes to Allah, Yahweh, Buddha, Kali, Vishnu, to gods I can't even name.

I try to stay away from the Memorial as much as I can, taking the upper levels when I need to leave Apogee. I've spent too long staring at it in the past, and it brings back too many memories I'd rather leave behind. I walk on, my gaze locked on a point further down the corridor. Before long, I reach the brig. It's small—just a few cells, located near the Chengshi border. As I approach, I can see four stompers standing outside, clad in the usual grey uniforms. They look cold and lonely.

Two of them see me coming, and their hands drop to the holsters on their waists, fingers close around the butts of their stingers. But then one seems to recognise me, and motions his buddies to back off.

"You're the one who found him, aren't you?" he says.

I nod. "That's me."

"I got to admit, that takes spine," says one of the others. "I'm impressed. Have to say though, it's a good thing we got there when we did."

They're more relaxed now—apparently a single tracer isn't a threat. I take a deep breath. "So this sounds weird, but I need to get in to see him. There's something I need to know."

A swift shake of the head from the first guard. "Not a chance."

"Seriously, I'll be two minutes. In and out."

But he stares impassively back at me. His colleague steps forward. He's a man almost as big as Darnell, and his jumpsuit seems ready to burst off him. "You heard what the man said. No one gets in. You did well today, but go home."

The thought of trying to flirt with them crosses my mind, but I push it away, irritated with myself. Bribery might work, and I'm on the verge of offering them a job or two for free when I see Royo walk up to the barred entrance behind them. I shout his name, and he looks up, his face clouding with concern.

There's a metallic buzz. The gate slides open, and he strides towards me. He looks tired, more human somehow. "You shouldn't be here," he says.

I hurriedly explain to him what I want to do. His eyes narrow. "Do you think we haven't talked to him already? You don't just hire someone to kill a council member for fun. But he hasn't said a damn thing."

"He's known me for a long time. I used to run jobs for him, remember? He might let something slip."

"He nearly killed you."

I don't have an answer to that one. But after glowering for a moment, Royo relents. "Fine," he says. "You come in with me, you stay two minutes, then you leave. And if I even get a hint that you're going to do something stupid, I'll have you in a cell of your own so fast your words will still be hanging in the air."

The other guards, bored with the conversation, have gone back to chatting among themselves. We step through into the entranceway—there are two doors, and the inner one doesn't open until the outer one is locked shut. Another ear-splitting buzz, and we're through, into a small corridor lit only by a couple of bare fluorescents.

The corridor opens up into a larger one, with the cells on either side. There's no overhead light in this corridor, but the cells are brightly lit. Each tiny room contains a single hard cot and a toilet, and the front of every cell is covered with thick, transparent plastic, nearly unbreakable, with two thin slits cut in it for food trays. Some are occupied, and the people in them are collapsed on their cots, shivering. It's cold here; there's no point diverting heat to the brig, and I pull my jacket closer around me. Walking next to me, Royo has gone silent.

We stop at the last cell on the right. I follow Royo's gaze, and see Oren Darnell. He's seated on his cot, staring at the wall, seemingly unaware of our presence and looking as if he doesn't feel the cold. He's been given a thin, light-grey prison jumpsuit to wear.

"You have two minutes," says Royo, and at his voice, Darnell swings his huge head towards us. His eyes have lost none of their malice, and as he sees me, his face stretches in another awful grin.

"Riley Hale," he says quietly, his voice given an odd tang by the plastic.

I'm careful to keep my expression neutral. "What did you mean when you said that the world was going to end?"

Darnell points to Royo. "Why don't you speak to him? He's already asked me the exact same thing."

"And what did you say? Why is the world going to end?"

He stands up quickly, his huge bulk rocketing off the bed, at the barrier in an instant. I take a step back.

"Not *the* world," he says. "*Your* world. The world will carry on as it always has."

Royo tries to pull me away. "Same shit. You don't have to listen to this."

I shrug his hand off, and Darnell laughs. The control I worked so hard to keep vanishes. I slam a hand on the plastic. It shudders under my palm. "Tell me!"

"Oh, I don't think so," he says. His voice is innocent, carefree, awful. He looks like a man whose destiny has finally revealed itself. "Why would I? It would spoil the fun. And there is going to be so much fun, you believe that."

"Kind of hard to do from inside the brig, don't you think?"

His eyes are wide, almost beseeching. "We locked ourselves away in this metal box so we could continue to exist, even when everything on the planet was telling us that we'd failed. That's something we're going to fix."

Without wanting to, I think of the tagger, the one Darnell's guard murdered, the one who was spraying up messages for voluntary human extinction. I force the image away. That's not what this is. This is something else entirely.

Without another word, he turns and lies down on his bunk, facing the wall. I bang on the plastic again, yelling at him, but this time Royo's hand on my shoulder is firm.

"I told you you weren't getting anything out of him," mutters Royo, and he leads me away, back towards the gate. The other prisoners haven't stirred. A cold dread has settled on my shoulders like a cloak.

As we walk, I half expect to hear something from the cell at the end, perhaps even laughter, but there's just the silence, and the echoing, rumbling movements of Outer Earth.

22

Prakesh

Prakesh has to yell out Riley's name a few times before the Nest trapdoor slides back and her face appears.

"You wanna keep it down out there?" she says.

He shrugs. "Wasn't even sure you'd be home."

"Amira says I need to rest."

"How's that working out for you?"

Her face vanishes, then a ladder drops through the gap, hitting the floor with a clunk. Prakesh climbs up, clambering into the Nest entrance. The door to the Devil Dancers' home is open, and Prakesh can see that Riley's alone. Detritus from the party is still scattered across the floor, and he's amused to see that some of it has found its way onto Carver's workbench, as if ready to be turned into some new toy.

"How's it working out?" Riley says, striding back into the Nest. "How do you think? Amira told me no jobs, no running, no anything."

"She's right," Prakesh says. Under the Nest lights, he can still see the bruised halo around Riley's eye. She's tried to hide it with her hair, pulling some of her fringe across, but it's not quite enough to cover the bruise. It gives her a faintly lopsided look.

"Doesn't matter if she's *right*," Riley says, turning away. "I'm bored out of my mind."

She sits on the floor and folds her legs under her. Taking a pack of frayed cards out of her jacket pocket, she spreads them across the metal plating.

Prakesh sits down opposite her. "What are we playing?"

"Acey-deucy?"

"Sure."

They play in silence for a while. Prakesh is good at the game—something that Riley always forgets. His family grew up playing it, and he was throwing down twos from an early age. He wins the first few sets easily. Riley is reckless, too quick to throw down a challenge. Her eyes are fixed intently on the cards in front of her.

For once, Prakesh is relieved to be away from the Air Lab. Oren Darnell might have been corrupt, but at least he kept some sort of control. Now that he's gone, some of the techs have already begun pushing for the top spot. Prakesh isn't one of them, but it's made getting things done difficult. He'd never dare mention this to Riley—she's been through enough.

After she loses the third set, Riley throws down her cards in disgust. "Cheater."

"I don't cheat. I'm just that good." Prakesh fans his cards.

She lifts up a king of hearts. "See this card? I will stuff it down your throat, Prakesh Kumar."

"Only you would treat a playing card like a weapon."

"It is when I'm holding it," she says.

He can't help but smile. "Death by card."

She lifts the card like she's about to throw it. "Right between the eyes."

"You could roll one up. Turn it into a blowgun."

"Sharpen up the edges."

Now they're both laughing—the kind of laughter you try to

hold in but which sneaks out anyway. Riley clears her throat, still grinning, and looks away.

The words are out of Prakesh before he can stop them. "You should come stay with me, up in Gardens. It'd be a break from—"

"From what?"

Riley is looking at him expectantly, and suddenly Prakesh isn't sure what he was going to say.

He shuffles his cards absently. "From everything."

They're silent for a moment. Then Riley says, "Did you ever hear about Amira's girlfriend?"

He looks up, confused. "What?"

"Amira's girlfriend."

"Amira the ice-queen has a girlfriend?"

"Had. Shut up and listen. She worked in a hospital up in New Germany. Even came by the Nest a couple of times. She was all right."

"What was her name?"

"Doesn't matter. Amira went to visit her a lot, too, but she wasn't there often enough. She'd be on a job, or back here, or doing gods know what. And after a while, her girlfriend asks Amira to choose. Her or us."

"I would never."

"You'd never what?"

He sighs. "Nothing. Don't worry about it."

For a moment, Riley seems about to pursue it. Instead, she quietly deals out another round.

Prakesh wants to rage at her for being so cruel, for being so short-sighted. The business with Darnell was horrendous, but the one good thing he'd thought might come out of it would be he and Riley becoming closer. He still remembers when she hugged him, right after he woke up in Gray's room, when there was light and noise everywhere and she was the only thing he recognised.

He catches the anger before it can really take hold, consciously neutralising it. For a moment, he briefly wonders if he might not be suffering some sort of post-traumatic stress. It's certainly possible, and he fixes on the idea, keeping it in the front of his mind. It helps. He can feel the anger settling, like ripples in a cup of water, finally fading away.

But the effort has rattled him; he loses the next two games, his usual strategies falling apart. Riley is smirking. She's got the cards up to her face, hiding her mouth, flashing eyes peeking over them. "You might be good, 'Kesh, but I'm better," she says.

Something about the way she says it brings the anger back. Very carefully, he puts his cards down on the floor, face-up, then gets to his feet. "I gotta go."

Riley looks at the cards. "You had double deuce. You don't want to finish the hand, at least?"

"I gotta go," he says again. It's about all he can say, like any other words will mutate into something he'll regret.

Riley jumps up too. "'Kesh, come on, I was just playing. I didn't mean anything by it."

She reaches out to him, and for the first time, he doesn't want her anywhere near him. He pushes his way out, sits with his legs dangling out the trapdoor. The ladder is there, but he feels the need to drop. To let the shockwave from the landing travel through him.

"Don't be like this," Riley says. She's standing in the doorway, arms folded. The look of contrition has left her face. Now she just looks resigned. Like this fight was inevitable.

A burst of air pretending to be a laugh escapes Prakesh. He could say a million things right now, about choice, about him, about her. But he doesn't. He just pushes himself off the edge, and then he's gone.

23

Darnell

Darnell's clothes have been taken away from him. So has his knife, and his remaining vials of quicksleep. By now, his office will have been searched, the eyeball found, logged, then incinerated. The thought of stompers moving around his beloved bonsai, *touching it*, is enough to bring the rage back.

His hands clench involuntarily, knotting the blankets on the thin cot. The standard-issue prison jumpsuit is too short for him, barely reaching his wrists.

He looks around the cell. Bare walls, a single bright light set deep into the ceiling. The fisheye lens of a camera, socketed next to it. The light is reflected in the plastic barrier at the front of the cell. The place smells the same as his family's hab did, back in New Germany: antiseptic mingled with the sour tang of sweat.

He remembers the hab well. His mother never left her bed. When she smiled, spit would leak out of the drooping, immobile side of her face.

His father worked in the mining facilities, and most of his time at home was spent caring for his wife. He and Darnell cleaned her body, tried to feed her. Darnell hated both of them. There was never enough food, never enough water. And *she* got most of it.

He doesn't know where the bean plant came from, but he remembers it clearly: the plastic pot, the thick smell, the dark soil. He loved how its leaves hunted for the light, how its only purpose was to survive. It took so little, and gave so much back.

Darnell was nine years old when his father died. An accident in the refinery. He was angry at first, angry at being left alone, but also strangely happy. It meant space for more plants. His garden grew, every spare inch of hab space stacked with pots and grow-boxes.

Nobody came to check in on Darnell and his mother. Nobody needed to. Darnell did well in school—enjoyed it, even. Sometimes, the teachers would show them pictures of things that used to exist on Earth, like rainforests and botanical gardens. With fierce pride, he'd realised that he was growing some of the same plants: the flowers and vines and fruit. And with the pride came something else: anger. These plants sustained the whole planet. But the teachers kept saying that everything on Earth was gone, and Darnell couldn't understand why.

And no matter how many plants he filled the hab with, he could never get rid of the stench of his mother.

He would bring home food for her from the mess. Instead of wasting away, her body had ballooned, spreading out across the surface of the cot. One night, he found himself staring at her, at the wobbling fat on her legs where the blanket had rucked up. The pale skin, the patch of drool on the pillow. He suddenly couldn't believe how fat she'd become, how useless.

"You're too fat already," Darnell says, the sound echoing around the cell. He hardly realises he's speaking. "You don't need any more food."

Darnell shakes his head, angry with himself for letting his memories get the better of him. It's been happening more and more lately—they'll come at odd times, and he finds himself lost in them before he even realises it's happening.

He tries to tell himself that his being locked in the cell doesn't matter. That Outer Earth is finished no matter what he does. It doesn't help. Instead, it just makes it worse. He wanted to spend the final days tearing the station apart, piece by rotten piece.

It won't make a single bit of difference to the outcome. That was set in play ages ago. But it isn't fair. He can rant and rage all he wants, but no one will listen to him. Not from in here. And if he is tried before it happens, if he is found guilty and executed...

"Prisoner Darnell."

Darnell looks up to see one of the brig guards standing behind the plastic barrier. He's got a tray of food with him—Darnell's lip curls as he remembers the fruit that he'd be eating if he was still in the Air Lab. He gestures to the guard to leave it. If there was no plastic barrier between them, he'd break the tray in half and jam the jagged edge into the guard's face.

"Got a message for you, Sir."

It's the "Sir" that makes Darnell look again. The guard's face is familiar, somehow, but he can't quite place it.

Darnell stands and walks to the barrier, resting his forehead on it. The guard meets his eyes, doesn't look away.

"Prisoner Darnell, your trial has been scheduled for three days' time," the guard says, speaking loudly and slowly. "Your case is to be heard by the full council in a public hearing. If you wish to call witnesses in your defence, you must inform me of their names now. Do you have any questions?"

As it happens, Darnell has plenty of questions, but he doesn't get to ask them, because suddenly the guard says quietly, "Reach through and grab me."

Darnell stares at him.

The guard flicks his eyes down towards the slot in the plastic, the slot holding the food tray with its load of grey slop. Darnell knocks the food tray aside, reaches through, snags the front of the guard's jumpsuit. He yanks him forwards, slamming against the plastic with a dull bang. Somewhere, an alarm begins blaring, but the guard's eyes show no fear. He speaks quickly and calmly.

"I'll be standing next to you during the trial," the guard says. "When the time comes, follow me. Don't ask questions, don't hesitate. Everything is going as planned, Sir."

Darnell smiles, and the guard nods. Then he's being pulled away by the other stompers, and the plastic barrier is whooshing open, and Darnell is being forced to the floor and stomper boots are being driven into his side and his stomach. But even through the pain, even though every kick feels like a red-hot rod being driven into him, Oren Darnell manages to keep smiling.

24

Riley

It's not long before Amira puts me back on the job. Not that I mind. The faster I run, the further I seem to leave the last few days behind. The pain in my collarbone and chest and eye socket dwindle and vanish, replaced by the everyday muscle aches of a tracer.

Tracer

They've scheduled Darnell's trial for a few days' time. That's no surprise—with space at a premium, people don't usually spend all that much time in the brig. They get them up in front of the sector leaders fast—if they're guilty, it's usually a harsh spell of hard labour, working to clean the corridors or helping to maintain the machinery inside the freezing path that leads to the Core. If what they've done is too serious for that, it's the firing squad.

His words keep coming back to me, and more than once I find myself brooding on what he said.

The trial—and the likely outcome—give me chills. They shouldn't, but they do. They used to hold the trials in private, but after a while the clamour to hold them in public got too loud to ignore. Now, they're a form of entertainment, something to keep people happy. Of course, there are plenty of people who don't want it that way, but it's not like anyone listens to them.

When I wake on the day of the trial, the Nest is cold, resonating with the distant hum of the station. Kev is passed out at the workbench, sleeping on his arms, snoring delicately. Carver and Yao are nowhere to be seen. I pulled a blanket around me when I lay down, but I kicked it off during the night. It lies bundled and twisted at my feet, and cold shivers slither up my body.

There's a noise to my right, and I lift my head, eyes blurry with sleep. Amira is there, stretching, her back to me.

I sit up, rubbing my eyes, and as I reach for a nearby canteen she speaks without turning around. "Got a job for you," she says.

"Another one?" I give off a yawn, so big that my jaw clicks.

"That's right," says Amira. "I went down to the market to get us some work. Two jobs. I'll take one, and since you're up first, you can take the other."

"Sure."

"I need you to go to the sector hospital. Nurse at the market was looking for a tracer. Apparently they need something delivered to the hospital in New Germany. Catch and release job."

I nod, and move on to stretching my thighs, bending down into a lunge position. Amira reaches in her pack and tosses me something small and green—I catch it without fumbling, sleep failing to dull my reflexes. It's an apple, smooth and perfect. I flash her a grateful smile. The apple is crisp, and so juicy I have to wipe my chin after I'm done.

It's right then that I remember something. "I used your move," I say to Amira.

She looks over her shoulder. "What?"

"Your move. The pressure point." I quickly tell her about how I took down one of the Lieren using the strike she taught me. As I tell the story, her face breaks into a huge smile.

"Nice," she says when I've finished, turning back to her stretching.

How long has it been since I've seen a smile from Amira? That, too, seems like years. In the time I've known her, I can only think of a few times when I've genuinely pleased her.

We met a year after my dad died. I was thirteen. For a year, my mom struggled on. I had to watch her getting sadder and sadder. And then one day, she just gave up, and I was alone.

That was when I left school. I dropped out for a few months, scavenging food, doing odd jobs, sleeping in storage rooms or under tables in the cold passages.

They came when I was sleeping in a passage on the bottom level of Chengshi, curled up with my head tucked into the crook of my arm. There were at least four of them, hard men with worn faces. I recognised them as soon as they pulled me into the middle of the corridor: merchants. I'd managed to steal some food that day—it was one of the few times I didn't go to sleep on an empty stomach.

I screamed and shouted and cried, but nobody came. And they were silent: lips tight, faces hard, as if I was nothing more than a piece of machinery which had broken down once too often and needed to be fixed with anger and a firm hand. The only sound was my screams as they dragged me down the corridor. I lashed out at them with my feet, but they batted them away, like they were nothing.

And then Amira was there, a whirlwind of fists and elbows and blades, smashing and cutting and breaking. I remember being amazed at how fast she was. The man holding my right arm went down first, a red slash exploding at his throat as Amira whipped her blade across it. The others ran at her, shouting, but in moments they were down, with arms twisted the wrong way and deep cuts already turning the floor a dark red.

When it was over, Amira paused for a moment, silhouetted in the lights above, breathing hard. She tucked the blade back into her pocket, then reached out a hand to me.

We lived together, we trained together, we got hurt together. I was her first Dancer, and she taught me everything: how to run, how to move through crowds, how to land. How to fight. How to find jobs, which ones to take and which ones to refuse. And how to never get caught again. By anyone.

"Get going," she says, gesturing to the door. "Jobs don't wait, you know."

Usually, if I have to take a job right after I wake up, my body feels slow and clumsy. But not today. I'm pulling off flawless moves and hitting the mark on every jump I make, even putting a little flair on a couple of wall passes. At one point, I jump down an entire set of stairs, taking a running leap off the top step and grabbing a roof strut before swinging into space, my head up and my arms thrown above and behind me, and landing so perfectly I don't even have to roll. The move feels so good I burst out laughing, and a man sitting on the steps behind me applauds. I wave and take off again, losing myself in the movement.

The hospital's not too far from the Nest. They're regular clients; while most sectors keep to themselves, hospitals across the entire station tend to share equipment, sending supplies wherever they're needed. A lot of our work comes from them—if we're not ferrying the supplies themselves, then we're delivering requests for them, going back and forth between the sectors.

When I arrive, a doctor is deep in conversation with one of the nurses. They're wearing scrubs that used to be white, and like every doctor I've ever seen, they look barely alive. He looks up and sees me; his black hair, like his tunic, has turned silvery grey, and his face is lined with worry. But he smiles, and beckons me over.

"I'm Doctor Arroway," he says and holds out his hand. I give it a quick shake; the palm of his hand is rough, like old rust.

"You had some cargo you needed delivering?" I say.

The doctor reaches behind him, picking up a squat white box from the table. "That's right. We've got a box of—"

I clear my throat, and he looks up, puzzled. Then he nods. "Of course, sorry—I forget that you prefer not to know. But really, it's nothing bad. Are you sure?"

"Positive."

He sighs. "OK. Just get it there in one piece. There's a doctor at the hospital in New Germany, name of Singh. It's got to get to him fast. He's got some people in the isolation rooms who need it ASAP."

"You're talking to the right person," I say, taking the box and dropping it into my pack. "So. What's in it for us?"

He looks at me, his arms folded. "You know, what you're carrying is going to save lives. Maybe a lot of lives. This doesn't have to be difficult."

I return his stare. "Actually, it does. No fee, no delivery, so make me an offer." I hate negotiating. I'm much more comfortable when the price is set beforehand. But it'd be worse to bring back nothing, or something that wasn't worth the trip.

He sighs irritably. "Fine. I'll give you a box of painkillers. Not the good stuff, by any means, but with your job, they'll probably come in handy."

"Make it the good stuff. It's a long run."

He rolls his eyes. After rummaging in a wall unit behind him, he hands me a small white box. I shake it. It gives a reassuring rattle, and I stuff it into the inside pocket of my jacket.

On the way out, a man seated in a battered chair, who up until now looked like he was unconscious, calls out my name. His beard reaches to his chest like a grey river, and he has a nasty-looking bloody bandage wrapped around his left hand. "Go get 'em," he says, shaking his hand in the air; a couple of blood drops spatter the floor. I dodge back, laughing.

From the chatter I hear in the stairwells, Darnell's trial is in a couple of hours' time, in the Apogee gallery. Better there than in Gardens, where things might get hairy. The gangs Darnell was in with might be reeling a little, like Royo said, but it's not unheard of for people to disrupt trials—sometimes violently. I make a mental note to be as far away as possible. By now, the eyeball is common knowledge, too. It was found in Darnell's office, and was logged and incinerated by the stompers. Apparently, it was already beginning to decay.

By the time I hit the New Germany border, the corridors have become even more crowded. People mill in large groups, leaning up against walls thick with rust and dirt. There's no sign here like there is at the Gardens border—just the supports where one used to hang, jutting down from the ceiling.

Despite the crowds, I make it to the hospital in good time. The doctor, Singh, gives me a brief nod, nothing more, and locks the package away in a heavy steel cabinet. He looks distracted, glancing back towards the exam rooms. His hospital is much busier than the one I was in before, and the low groans of patients fill the air, slipping out of the darkened wards like oil from a worn seal. My good mood feels dampened here, smothered.

As I turn to go, there's a hand on my arm, and I turn to see the grey bulk of a stomper. His face is a perfect blank. Surprised, I try to jerk my arm away, but his grip holds.

"What?" I say. "Did I do something wrong? You got any problems, you can take it up with my crew leader..."

His expression hasn't changed; he looks like he could stand there all day if he had to. It's then that I notice the red patch near his shoulder, in the shape of the station's silhouette, and a little worm of fear coils in my stomach. He's no stomper. Red patches belong to the elite units who guard the council.

His grip gets firmer. "Ms. Hale. Janice Okwembu would like a word." His voice is monotone, as immovable as the walls around us.

The head of the council? I'm too shocked to resist, and he starts to walk me towards the wards. I find my voice: "Then why aren't we going to Apex?" But he ignores me, pulling me down the central corridor between the curtained-off wards.

25

Riley

There are more guards here, not lounging against the walls like a regular stomper might, but standing bolt upright, eyes scanning the corridor.

One of them turns to us: "Is this her?" he says. The other guard nods, and releases me.

By now, the anger I first felt has been replaced by curiosity: what is Janice Okwembu doing here? And why does she want to see me? I've never even seen her in person. She occasionally comes down to the lower sectors, but not when I've been there. And I've never been up to Apex—not once, not even to do a delivery. They keep it pretty secure; when you've got the council chamber and the main station control room there, you try to keep most people out if you can.

The guard beckons me towards one of the curtains, and pulls it aside. In the dim light, I can just make out Janice Okwembu. She's leaning over a bed, whispering to an old man. He's heavily bandaged, with a thick gauze patch over his left eye. He doesn't appear to be conscious, but Okwembu is whispering something to him. I can't make out the words, and the guard motions me to wait, gesturing me back.

After a moment, Okwembu bends down, and plants a kiss on the man's cheek. She turns, and sees us standing in the entrance. "I knew him from long ago," she says, gesturing to the old man in the bed. She moves with a controlled, gentle grace. "I shouldn't really show favouritism to anybody, but I like to know that he's being looked after."

I find my voice. "How did you know I was coming here?"

She just smiles. Glancing at the guard, she says, "I believe the room next door is free. Could you please ask Dr. Singh to turn up the lights there?" He nods, and turns smartly on his heels.

Okwembu comes closer. The grey in her hair is more pronounced than it looks when I see her on the comms screen; she occasionally broadcasts messages, speaking on behalf of the council. It's her eyes, however, that are the most striking: a pale green, almost white, and ringed with a feathered blue on the outer edge.

She's short, perhaps the same height as me, but even a cursory glance shows toned arms under the white jumpsuit. She catches my eye and laughs, an unexpectedly girly sound. "I try to keep in shape," she says, placing a hand on the small of my back and guiding me out of the ward. "I was a computer technician once, and I realised I didn't want to end up like my colleagues—fat and lazy."

She pulls open the curtains on the ward next door. The lights are up, and she gestures to two chairs in the corner, caked with a layer of dust. I take a seat—I half expect her to wipe down the chair, but she simply pauses for a moment before perching on the edge of it, hands clasped in her lap. Above us, the light flickers silently. With a start, I realise how unkempt I must look, with my scarred jacket and greasy hair. I have to force myself not to run a hand through it.

"I wanted to congratulate you personally," she says. I open my mouth to reply, but she raises a hand. "You did a very brave thing. I was horrified when I heard about Marshall Foster."

"Did you know him?"

"Yes," she says. "I joined the council while he was its leader. He was…" She pauses for a moment. "A friend."

"I'm sorry."

"You have nothing to apologise for," she says. "I've been aware of your crew for some time, and of course we've always been grateful to Amira Al-Hassan for what she did." I think of Amira's missing fingers, her run through the Core all those years ago, and a little dark cloud settles on my heart.

"Thanks, I guess," is all I can come out with.

She sits back, her lips pursed, as if deep in thought. "You could have gone to get help instead of going in. Most people would have. But not you."

"I wasn't going to wait. If I'd gone to get help, Prakesh and Yao and Kevin would be dead too." I trip over my words, realising she might not know who they are, but she just nods.

"They're lucky to know you," she says, but there's no warmth in her voice: it's cool, calculating. "But then, you know what it's like to lose someone."

It takes me a moment to form the words. "That was a very long time ago."

"Indeed. Seven years now. But what your father did—what he died doing—was nothing short of remarkable."

I can't look at her. I was hoping that this year I was going to get away with not thinking about Earth Return. But with this, plus my unexpected visit to the Memorial, it doesn't look like that's going to happen.

If she sees my distress, she ignores it. "After your father... after the *Akua Maru* was lost, we struggled for a long time. This station was designed to support a fleet of ships, but the *Akua* was one of our best, and we took a hit when it was destroyed. Keeping morale up has been difficult."

"I know."

Okwembu raises a palm. "Please. Let me finish. People need something to gather around, and as the daughter of someone like John Hale, you might be just what they're looking for. We were hoping you might testify at Darnell's trial today."

"I'm not a political tool," I say, surprising myself with the note of anger in my voice.

She dips her head. "Of course. I wasn't suggesting that."

"You want to make peace with the gangs and keep people happy, find someone else. Patch up the graffiti. Put plants back in the galleries. Do something about the mess food. Don't use me."

Okwembu raises an eyebrow, and I tail off, but she doesn't interrupt me, and doesn't appear angry.

"Well, I hope you'll think about it," she says after a long moment, her voice so soft I have to strain to hear her.

We fall silent. After a few moments, I meet her gaze. "That's not all, is it? You didn't come down here just to ask me to testify."

"Actually, I came down here to visit a friend," she says. "But since you mention it, there is something else."

She leans forward. "I need to know that you told the protection officers everything. If there's something you held back, you need to let me know, and you need to do it now. Nothing will happen to you, but you must tell me. I can't stress how important it is."

I shrug. "We did a job for him, and it didn't feel right. He took my…Prakesh, and two of my crew. We tailed him, we got lucky. That's all."

But she doesn't sit back. "When we found Marshall's body, one of his eyes was missing. We think it has something to do with why he wanted Foster out of the way, and whatever Oren Darnell was planning. I think you know about it too, Riley. And I think you haven't been honest with us." Her voice is still deathly quiet.

I plaster disgust on my face, hoping that I'm not overdoing it. "I didn't know that. His eye, I mean. Why? Why would Gray do that?"

I can feel her pale gaze trying to reach in, as if she wants to dig around in my mind. Eventually, she sits back, her eyes still on me. "I know you and your friends sometimes take on jobs that involve carrying things that…" She pauses, choosing her words. "Well, let's just say that sometimes what you do is not in the best interests of Outer Earth. We let the tracers exist because you perform a valuable service, and we know that by doing that, we risk that you might transport something dangerous. Something which we should perhaps know about."

The sweat on my face has dried to a thin crust, itching gently. I force myself to keep my hands in my lap. Her words aren't a threat, not really, but there's no mistaking the cold intent behind them.

She continues. "I will be watching you, Ms. Hale. You would do well to remember that nothing lasts forever."

Abruptly, she stands up, and gives me a curt nod before drawing the curtain aside. I rise to my feet, and I'm about to follow when she turns back. Her voice is cool, but business-like. "I'd like you to think some more about appearing at the trial."

I want more than anything for her to go, and I nod, which seems to satisfy her. She turns away, motioning for her guard to follow. The sound of their footsteps echoes in the wards as they march off, and I hear her exchanging a few words with Dr. Singh. The warmth in her voice is back, as if she flicked a switch. I remain where I am, unable, for a moment, to move.

I pull my jacket around myself, but the cold that I felt earlier refuses to vanish, running icy fingers up the back of my neck. I can't help but think back to when the man from the council came to see my mother and me in our little room in Apogee. I remember his uniform, a heavy grey tunic with red highlights, tight around the throat. The look of sorrow on his face as he told us about the massive explosion on atmosphere entry, the catastrophic reactor failure. That there would be no new colony on Earth, no terra-forming, no resources to send home. That John Hale and his crew would not be coming back.

26

Darnell

His hands are cuffed first, the thick metal bands ratcheting around his wrists in front of him. He has to put his hands through the slot in the plastic, then step back once he's restrained. Two stompers hold his legs at the knees, a third holds his arms, and a fourth snaps ankle cuffs on. The chain between his wrists and ankles is too long, clattering the floor whenever he moves.

They march Darnell out of his cell, one on each side. The stompers walk fast, and he struggles to match their long strides with his cuffed feet. He keeps his eyes focused on the floor in front of him, careful not to betray his excitement. He doesn't even know which stomper is the guard who promised to free him. They wear full body armour, their faces covered by dark visors and thick, angular helmets.

He can't help grinning when they walk out into the corridors, past the crowds assembled outside the brig. There are dozens of them, and they're all booing and jeering, shouting his name and laughing. Darnell scans the crowd. He's looking for those who aren't booing. Those who are watching intently.

Darnell has been seeding sleepers in Outer Earth for over a year, tapping into the creeping network of the voluntary human extinction movement. The movement itself was a joke, something that was never going to be taken seriously, so it wasn't difficult to find those who had become disillusioned with it.

It was easier than Darnell would have imagined. These people were emotionally vulnerable, sick of waiting, sick of asking nicely. Even the ones who hadn't considered doing what Darnell asked them to do were easily led in that direction. All he had to do was give them a little push.

And the best part? The beliefs, ideas, whatever you called them, were like viruses. Give them the right conditions, and they thrive. They multiply. They make copies of themselves. And the more revolutionary the idea—the more potent the virus—the harder it would be to eradicate. Soon there was a new network, reaching across Outer Earth: a network of people fuelled by the ideas they carried.

Unless…

It's possible—just possible—that the stompers are messing with him. That they found out about his sleepers, and decided to have a little fun, holding out hope and intending to snatch it away. There'll be no signal, no rogue guard leading him to safety.

For the first time, Darnell feels a twinge of fear. If he is found guilty—and he will be—they'll stand him up against a wall right there, in front of everyone.

Oren Darnell isn't afraid of dying. But he is afraid of dying without his revenge.

"Move it," mutters one of the guards. Darnell, lost in his thoughts, has slowed down, and the stompers holding him nearly yank him off his feet. He stumbles, keeping himself going with the thought of the stompers' faces melting off in screaming agony.

And just then, just as he regains his balance, the stomper on his left looks at him and nods. Ever so slightly. His black faceplate reveals nothing, reflecting Darnell's own face back at him. The moment is brief, and then the stomper is eyes front again, dragging Darnell onwards.

He can hear the gallery ahead. The noise is intense, pushed into a concentrated roar by the corridors surrounding the open space. Darnell smiles to himself, and somehow manages to stand a little straighter, his body dwarfing the stompers around him.

Darnell doesn't know what the signal will be, but he'll be ready.

27

Riley

I don't want to go to Darnell's trial, but after a while I find myself heading there anyway. Maybe Okwembu's more persuasive than even she realises. I'm not testifying though, whatever she thinks.

When I left the hospital in New Germany, I toyed with going up to Gardens to see Prakesh—now that Darnell's gone, the water in his sector is probably running freely again, so he'll be in a good mood—but I decided I couldn't face the crush. I began running back towards the market in Apogee, thinking I could maybe go and see Madala and pick up that job he was talking about.

But the joy I'd felt earlier is gone, replaced by a growing unease. My movements feel stilted and slow, and I can't get Okwembu's words out of my head. You have to be pretty ruthless to stay in the council's top spot for ten years, but it's unsettling to see it up close.

I'm wearing an old hoodie under my jacket, and as I hit the Apogee border I pull the hood up. The corridors have become even more crowded, the crush building inside them as people hustle to the gallery for the best spots. Instead, I force my way up the stair-wells, eventually emerging onto the Level 3 catwalk. It's only just filling up with people, and is a lot quieter than the chaos down below. The noise is insane: a roaring mix of laughter, shouts, and calls from merchants taking advantage of a captive audience. They've set up stalls along the walls—one of them has even managed to score a prime spot in the centre. He's a blur behind his table, dishing out what look like cooked beetles, the crates behind him overflowing with traded objects. The smell of frying food drifts up from below in thick clouds. The atmosphere is buoyant, almost like a festival.

The sea of people spread out on the gallery floor stops dead by the far wall, brought up short by a line of waist-high barricades. There are stompers behind it, facing the crowd. They wear black full-face masks, and thick helmets squashed onto their heads. Every one of them is holding a stinger. Behind them, two people are putting the finishing touches on a platform—a dais of some kind, made of steel plates and welded pipes.

A little way down the catwalk, I see Amira and Carver, leaning over the railing. Amira waves me over.

"Didn't expect to see you here," she says, having to raise her voice above the noise. "Everything OK with the job?"

I pull the painkillers out and give them a shake. "Smooth as."

"Good. We've been getting a lot of new work offers after yesterday, so we need to stay focused."

"Relax, boss," says Carver, leaning with his back to the railing and stretching his neck out, gazing up at the ceiling. "We're golden. Or at least, Riley's golden," he adds, jerking a thumb in my direction. "I've never had so many people request a tracer personally."

"Where are the Twins?" I ask.

"Back at the Nest," says Amira. "Although Kevin still isn't too happy about last night." She gives Carver a pointed look. He's suddenly gone very quiet.

There's movement off to one side of the gallery. A roar goes up from the crowd and, at first, I think Darnell is being brought out, but then I see that it's the council, led by Okwembu, walking towards the dais. There are six of them, grey men and women who look nervous facing the people, as if it's them being judged. Only Okwembu, standing out front, looks confident and proud, her chin up, raising a hand to greet the crowd. Her eyes sweep the catwalks above her. It might be my imagination, but I swear that when she looks at the area I'm standing in, she smiles.

"Okwembu came to see me," I mutter, then wish I hadn't.

"What?" Amira yells—the noise has rocketed, a thundering boom in the enclosed space that has my stomach rumbling with its sheer force.

I reluctantly raise my voice a notch, leaning in closer. "Okwembu. When I was at the hospital in New Germany, she was there. She asked to see me."

I see Amira's eyes widen in astonishment, and she's about to say something when Darnell is hustled out of one of the corridors, and the crowd explodes.

He wears the same grey prison jumpsuit, his hands cuffed in front of him, his ankles shackled. His arms are gripped on each side by stompers in full body armour. Darnell dwarfs his escort, and they have to march in double time simply to keep up with his huge strides. The leering grin is back on his face.

I'm half expecting people to throw things, but nothing comes—they don't want to waste anything, I guess. It doesn't stop them from jeering, and loud boos and catcalls are hurled out from all around me.

Amira leans into my field of view, but I can't hear what she's saying, and after a moment of fruitless shouting she gives up. Her eyes hold plenty of unanswered questions, and it's clear we're not done just yet.

Darnell is led to the area in front of the council platform. The stompers don't raise their stingers, but even from the catwalk, I can see them tense.

On the platform, one of the men steps forward, and the crowd noise ebbs slightly. He's surprisingly young—his forties, maybe, which is unusual for a council member. Most of them make their way up the political ranks over time: level chief to deputy sector chief and then representing their home sector on the council. That can take years—spots on the council don't open often.

The man is holding some sort of device to his mouth, which allows him to transmit through the comms.

"Oren Darnell," his voice booms, echoing off the walls. "You are accused by this council of the following crimes..."

As he begins to list the charges, someone grips my shoulder and pulls me backwards.

For a terrible moment, I'm certain it's one of the Lieren, and I'm about to have a blade rammed into the small of my back. I spin around, ready to attack, and find myself staring into the face of an old woman. She's wearing a blue headscarf, and it takes a second for me to place her.

The market. The strange woman in the crowd.

She embraces me, placing her mouth by my right ear. "I can't believe I found you again," she says, her high voice cutting through the noise. I try to say something, to ask who she is, but she cuts me off, squeezing me tighter, her voice urgent and husky in my ear. "My name is Grace Garner. I was Marshall Foster's assistant. I have to talk to you—there's something you need to know."

"Tell me," I say.

Garner pulls back, looks me in the eyes. "Not here. We need to talk in private."

A million questions fly around my head. Why is she telling me? And how does she know who I am? The fear is back, the cold fingers tracing the curve of my neck. Behind me, I can feel Amira and Carver tensing, not knowing who the woman is, or whether I'm in any danger. The people around me are starting to take an interest; I can see a couple straining to hear our conversation, desperate to catch what might be a new piece of gossip. In the background, I can still hear the man from the council rattling off a list of crimes.

I'm about to tell her to go and wait in the Nest, or the market, but an idea suddenly hits.

"Go to Gardens," I say. "The Air Lab. Ask for a man named Prakesh Kumar—*Prakesh Kumar*," I repeat, raising my voice. "Tell him I sent you, and tell him that you're to wait for me there. I'll come and find you."

It's then that I notice how terrified Garner looks, how worn. But she nods again, gives me a final squeeze, and vanishes into the crowd.

Carver leans in. "What was that all about?" he shouts, but before I can answer, I hear the announcer ask Darnell to respond to the charges.

Darnell stands proud, his grin wider than ever, staring around the galleries expectantly. One of the stompers, his stinger up, steps forward and holds one of the speaker devices to Darnell's mouth. He keeps it a fair distance away, as if he's worried Darnell might lunge forwards and bite him.

Looking directly at the council, Darnell says, very clearly, "Guilty as charged."

The roar from the crowd is the loudest yet, a shocked eruption of sound. Amira places her hands over her ears; mine are already gently aching from the noise, and I follow suit.

At that moment, with a sickening click, every fluorescent light in the room dies, plunging us into the darkness.

There's a split second of stunned silence, then the shouting starts again. This time, the noise is fearful, with screams starting to slip into the noise, like daggers through a ribcage. Behind me, I can feel the crowd on the catwalk spinning in place, hands frantically reaching out to try and grab friends, family.

The noise builds to a crescendo, and with a huge flare of light from below, a massive explosion rocks the gallery.

28

Prakesh

Prakesh's footsteps reverberate on the metal as he walks across the labs. There are a few other techs tending to the trees; one of them is suspended from a pulley system, legs akimbo over a branch. He glances down as Prakesh walks underneath him, his face expressionless.

Prakesh ignores him. Truth be told, he hasn't had a lot of time to talk to the other techs. Not since Oren Darnell got caught. All those people hunting for the top spot has left a lot of work unfinished, a lot of soil untended. Prakesh doesn't mind. The extra work means he doesn't have to think. He can take Riley and Mr. Darnell and just ignore them for a while, letting his hands get good and filthy.

He needs a fresh pH monitor—the one he and Suki were using is dead, its batteries drained. The Air Lab and the Food Lab share a single tool-storage unit, which is just inside the Food Lab. Prakesh slips through the door connecting the two. The air changes. It's darker in here, more humid, and he can feel the heat baking off the greenhouses. The bass rumble from the buzz box rattles the back of his skull.

Prakesh stops. He takes a deep breath, inhaling wet air, picking up a dozen different scents. He can smell strawberries, and pumpkins, and the earthy musk of the potatoes in the far corner, hidden under dark covers. He can smell the refrigerant from the air conditioning, sharp and unpleasant.

And there's something else. Something he can't place.

He shakes his head, and keeps walking.

The tool storage is just ahead, a long, thin structure lit from within by glaring lights. It looks as if the building is on fire, like it's containing something white hot. Prakesh pays it no attention, striding up to the counter. He'll talk to Deakin, the guy in charge of storage. Mention the weird smell. Odds are, it's just a new fertiliser someone's using.

But Deakin isn't at the desk. Prakesh leans over it, twisting his head to take in the stores. There's no one there—just the tools, hanging from hooks and balanced precariously on rusted shelves. The seed bank is at the back, a huge walk-in freezer, its door shut tight and sealed with a keypad.

"Deakin?" Prakesh says. Then, louder: "You there?"

No answer. Just the insects in the buzz box, humming away.

Prakesh decides to vault the counter and pick out what he needs. He can see a tab screen off to one side, which means he can leave Deakin a note. But just as he puts his hands on the countertop, he registers movement behind him.

He whirls, thinking only of Darnell, of how close he was before, but there's no one there.

He takes another deep breath, turns back, and that's when he catches sight of Deakin.

The store controller is standing by one of the greenhouses, his back to Prakesh. He's looking up at the ceiling, his arms hanging by his sides. He appears to be taking deep breaths, his shoulders rising and falling.

"Deak," says Prakesh, not understanding the prickles of fear scurrying across his shoulder blades and along the back of his neck. "Need to take out a pH monitor, man. Could you—"

"I never got to see her," Deakin says.

Prakesh freezes. There is something in Deak's voice he doesn't like at all. He takes a step closer.

Deak turns. He's an older man, over fifty, but in the blazing light from the stores he looks thirty years younger. His eyes are wet with tears.

And in that instant, Prakesh realises what the strange smell is. It's the burned-plastic stench of ammonia. Specifically, ammonium nitrate, a compound created from fertiliser.

Deakin's shirt is open. Underneath it, he's wearing a vest of some kind, a mess of plastic and metal and cotton pouches. His fingers are wrapped around a thin cord, leading right to the centre of his chest.

"I never got to see the Earth," Deakin says, and pulls the cord.

29

Riley

The shockwave rips through the catwalk, and I feel the metal buckle as the rivets struggle to hold it in place. The world is filled with a horrible orange light. My hands over my ears saved me from the worst of it, but it's still loud enough to shake my bones.

Someone collides with me, and I'm thrown to the right. I land on someone else, with only a moment to gasp for breath before another body collapses right on top of me. My hands are wrenched from my ears, and the noise swells back into a dying bass note and the terrified roar of the crowd. Underneath us, the catwalk gives another sickening lurch. The overhead lights flash back on. The people around me are on the floor, bodies piling on top of each other, thrashing, yelling, scrambling for grip.

Whoever landed on top of me is heavy, his elbow pushing painfully into my chest. Over my shoulder, I see Amira grab the railing and leap into space.

For a moment, I'm convinced she's been thrown to her death by the twisting catwalk. I push the man off me with strength I didn't know I had, and scramble to the railing. Then I see her hands gripped onto it, and I realise what both she and Carver have done. To escape the crowd, they flipped themselves onto the outside edge of the railing. Bending their legs and arms, they flexed with the catwalk and held on, away from the crush of bodies. If I hadn't been hit, I'd have done the same thing.

Amira grabs my hand, and starts to pull herself over. As she does so, I see what's below us, and for a moment, I just stop breathing.

The bomb detonated right in the middle of the crowd. The black, burned ring around the centre of the blast is scattered with blood and torn clothing. Darnell is gone, the barricades knocked over, the stompers scattered and shouting. Okwembu and the rest of the council are nowhere to be seen. The Level 1 catwalk has been sheared in half, with the broken edges twisted upwards. The Level 2 catwalk just below us is intact, but only just: the metal plates are bulging in the middle, as if a giant hand had pushed them from beneath. People lie sprawled along it; knocked senseless by the blast.

Far below, a man tries to crawl away, pulling himself along the ground with one arm. His other is gone at the shoulder, leaving nothing more than a nub of bone surrounded by pulpy wetness.

Dark blood stains his side. As I watch, he reaches out his remaining arm, as if hunting for something he can no longer see. Then he falls still. Around him lie charred bodies. Some are still smoking.

The scene before me seems too vivid. I can feel it fixing in my mind, its awful roots digging deep and refusing to let go.

I shut my eyes tight and pull, hauling Amira over the railing.

Carver flips himself over too, landing squarely on someone's back. He hops off, a horrified expression on his face, and turns to us. His mouth is moving, but I can't make out the words, and it's only then that I notice the siren blaring from the comms. I'm shaking, and I reach up to block my ears again, but then the siren cuts off abruptly. It's replaced by a voice, female, automated. And far too calm.

"Warning. Fire detected in Apogee sector. Fire detected in Gardens sector. Please move calmly to your nearest evacuation point. Warning..."

And as the message repeats itself, Amira meets my eye, and the same horrifying realisation seems to dawn.

Prakesh. The Air Lab.

He always hated the trials. He's never been to one, always refused, said they were barbaric. He'll still be there, in the Air Lab. And if someone let off a bomb there...

The catwalk under us groans. The left side sags, then jerks downwards, sending shockwaves up through our feet. The shockwave from the bomb has weakened it—all that old metal, some of it a hundred years old. Around us, more panic starts to spread through the crowd: their senses heightened by fear and adrenaline, they begin to push, crushing up against the entrances on either side, a seething mass of flesh.

The man who fell on me barrels past, his face twisted in a rictus of terror. The catwalk gives another terrible noise, and this time I swear I hear the sound of shearing metal. The panic rises, boils over: the crowd is screaming now, forcing up against each other, people clawing others out of the way, desperate to escape. Below us, the floor has completely emptied, the crowd streaming into the corridors surrounding the gallery.

30

Darnell

Free.

Darnell's body is stained with sweat and smoke. His ears are ringing, and he managed to twist his ankle when the explosion knocked him off his feet. It's throbbing painfully, but he doesn't care. He's free.

He doesn't know how they got out of the gallery. He doesn't even know where they are. He's been following the guard, ducking under pipes and threading through deserted rooms and clambering across the monorail tracks. There's a part of him that doesn't want to trust the guard, that doesn't want to trust anyone. But he keeps thinking back to the bomb, how the explosion tore the crowd apart like their bodies were made of paper. He keeps thinking back to how the guard worked quickly, undoing his restraints, pulling him along. No, he can trust his sleepers.

They stop near a ganglia of gurgling pipes. The only light comes from two slits in the wall, no bigger than a man's finger. They must be near one of the corridors; Darnell can hear thundering feet, the sweet sound of panicked shouting.

He collapses against the wall, amazed at how thirsty he is. The guard stays on his feet. He digs behind one of the pipes, and tosses Darnell a canteen. Darnell flips the top off, drinking greedily.

"We did it, Sir," says the guard. Darnell looks at him. He's younger than he thought he was, with a mess of dirty blond hair and a face flushed with excitement. Briefly, Darnell wonders what happened in his past. Why he's so eager. He's not someone Darnell recruited—he's just another node on the network, another flare point on the fuse.

Darnell gets to his feet. "I need to get back to my office. There's a—"

"Way ahead of you, Sir."

The guard produces a tab screen from inside his jacket, and hands it over. Darnell has to hide his surprise; it's the one that he had specially modified. The stubby antenna on the side gives him wireless access to Outer Earth's comms system—with it, he can broadcast at any time. But there's no way the guard could have known about it.

Darnell glances at the man, then back to the screen. "You went into my office?"

"Yeah," the guard says. "I was one of the stompers who got told to search it. Thought a tab screen might come in handy. Got this for you, too." He passes Darnell his knife—the thick-handled wedge of steel that Darnell had previously asked the poor tech to sharpen up for him.

"Nice blade," the guard says.

Darnell stares at him. "You've been busy."

The guard returns his stare. "I'm just trying to help, Sir. We're doing a good thing. Without human beings, the biosphere can recover. You're saving the world, and...and I'm behind you, Sir, you know what I mean? Hundred per cent."

Darnell ignores the rhetoric. But as the man speaks, he glances towards the corridor, to the slits that lead to the outside world. He doesn't see Darnell reach up, doesn't see the hand until it's wrapped around his head.

Darnell slams the guard's head into the wall, again, again. With each hit, the guard's struggles grow weaker, and the red patch on the wall grows bigger and bigger. Blood splatters Darnell's thin prison jumpsuit.

It's over inside ten seconds.

Darnell lets go. He waits a few moments, looking for any sign of life. Nothing.

There, he thinks. Now the only one who knows where he is, is him.

Working quickly, he strips the guard of his hard body armour, then his shirt, jacket and pants. The shirt is long-sleeved, made of a stretchy, artificial fabric, slightly loose on the guard's body but fitting tightly across Darnell's chest and shoulders. The jacket is too small for him, unable to zip closed, and the pants don't quite reach his ankles, but they'll be warmer than a prison jumpsuit. He'll need that where he's going. He tucks the knife in his waistband, behind his back.

He looks down at the tab screen. In a moment, he'll turn it on, accessing the comms. And then he can talk to everyone on Outer Earth, and tell them what's coming next.

31

Riley

Amira grabs me. She's outwardly calm, but her eyes burn with adrenaline. She jerks her head in the direction of the railing, and I realise what she wants us to do. She, Carver and I grab the railing, and in one synchronised movement, hurl ourselves up and over.

For a moment, I flashback to the job where I transported the eye to Darnell, when I threw myself off the Level 5 catwalk to escape the Lieren, and time seemed to stop. It seems like years ago. Decades. This time, there's no silence, no peaceful floating sensation. Just the air rushing in my ears and the screams from the catwalk above.

The Level 2 catwalk is directly below, flying up towards me. There's a body sprawled on the catwalk, someone—man, woman, I don't know—with a long grey coat, their right leg twisted at an impossible angle.

This time, there's no avoiding it. There's no space, nowhere to get a clean landing. Nothing I can do. I bend my knees, throw my arms above my head and make contact, smashing right into the back of the prone body. I feel it spasm under my feet. Whoever it is cries out, and then I'm bouncing forwards, rolling, colliding with the railing and collapsing in an ugly heap of limbs.

Amira has landed a little way along, managing—somehow—to

avoid landing on anyone. Carver is nowhere to be seen, and my heart leaps into my throat. Where is he? Did he miss the catwalk completely? But then there's a yell of pain, and I see a hand clenched onto the railing. Carver overshot the catwalk, and somehow managed to grab the rail and check his fall.

Amira reaches down, grabbing Carver under both arms and hauling him over the railing. Carver falls to the ground. His breathing is too regular, as if he's having to will each breath out of his lungs, and he's clutching his arm. His face is deathly white. Amira crouches down. "Dislocated," he says, spitting the word out through gritted teeth.

At that moment, the Level 3 catwalk that we just jumped from gives one last deep, rending screech, and the side furthest from us sheers off from the wall.

"Oh shit," says Carver.

The far edge of the falling catwalk smashes into ours with a dull boom, throwing us off our feet again. The catwalk collides with the railing, crushing it. It's still attached to the wall at the far side, and people are sliding down it, falling off the sides, screaming, smashing on the burned ground below. Above and behind me, I can see the side still connected to the wall beginning to come away, the rivets beginning to twist and turn, jiggling loose.

Fear surges through me, and I leap to my feet, reaching out and grabbing both Carver and Amira and pulling them forwards. "Move!" I yell. The siren is screaming again. We run.

Carver is swearing in pain. Around us, the gallery destroys itself in a whirlwind of screaming, shredded metal. We're barely feet from the corridor entrance ahead when the near side of the Level 3 catwalk rips free, separating from the wall with one final ear-splitting screech. I grab Carver and Amira, and throw us all forwards into the corridor ahead. I get a split-second glimpse of the people still on the catwalk before the falling slab of metal collapses onto them. It bounces upwards, falls back down with another bone-shattering boom, then slides off and crashes to the floor below.

We tumble to the floor, our chests heaving. I'm soaked in sweat, my mouth too dry, the blood in my ears pumping almost as loud as the siren. Carver has gone silent, his eyes tightly shut, his fingers twisted into half-fists. The lights in the corridor are flickering madly, casting dancing shadows across the wall. The sirens pause, and the emergency message repeats itself. Fire in Gardens sector.

Amira is kneeling next to Carver, gingerly testing his shoulder. I open my mouth to say something, but she cuts me off, pointing down the corridor in the direction of Gardens. "Go!" she screams. I force myself to my feet, and take off, at full speed almost at once, not looking back.

It's the most terrifying run of my life. The panic has become a living thing, coursing through the corridors and catwalks like poison through veins. Stompers are everywhere, shouting over the sirens, yelling at people to keep calm. There's stinger fire, both in the distance and, once, shockingly close, where I come up a level to see a stomper draw a bead on a man in a dirty white vest. I'm just in time to see the man raise his arms, the look of surprise on his face, before the stinger goes off and blood blooms on his chest. The stomper senses movement behind him and swings around, but I'm gone, barely pausing, my arms pumping and that sour taste of fear flooding my mouth. I can't lose Prakesh again.

Several times, I nearly fall, barrelling round a corner too fast or not spotting a group of people until it's almost too late. I manage to keep my balance, flying through Apogee and then through Chengshi, my chest burning, a stitch ripping at my side. Halfway there, it occurs to me that I sent Grace Garner to the Air Lab to meet Prakesh, and I'm speared by a realisation that I may have sent her to her death.

No. She wouldn't have had time to even get out of the sector before the bomb went off, let alone make it to Gardens. She could be anywhere.

Not far now, barely five minutes away, up through the stairwells, cut through the Chengshi mess hall and the schoolrooms, take that shortcut down into the service passage by the Level 2 corridor…

And then I turn the corner, and ahead of me is the Lieren with a red wolf tattooed on his neck.

32

Prakesh

The fire consumes Deakin instantly.

There's no explosion, no concussive blast, but the wave of bitter heat is enough to knock Prakesh backwards. Deakin's entire body lights up, and for a second, Prakesh can see his face, staring out of a corona of flame. The tear-tracks on Deakin's cheeks boil away.

Then he's gone, his body writhing, and the fire is reaching out, sucking up every molecule of oxygen, becoming its own fuel source as it spreads. It moves faster than anything Prakesh has ever seen. Liquid waves of it curl up and over the greenhouses, puddle across the floor.

Prakesh runs.

The greenhouses explode behind him, popping with a sound that echoes around the hangar. The air is filling with smoke—hot, sickening, thick, burning his throat and scratching at his eyes. All he can think of is what they were taught in school: the worst thing that can happen in a space-borne module is fire. In an enclosed area like Outer Earth, it can destroy everything. A little one can be contained, controlled. This is not a little one.

The suppressors activate. He can hear their metallic whine above the roaring fire and screaming techs. The foam is meant to retard the fire and cut off its oxygen, but the burning chemicals slice right through the slick white foam, fizzling it out of existence.

Heat licks at the back of his neck. Techs are streaming past him, running for the main doors. One of them trips ahead of him, sliding across the plate flooring, her hands scrabbling at it. Prakesh reaches down and grabs her under the arm, hauls her to her feet an instant before she gets trampled.

And as he does so, he gets a look at the door between the Air Lab and the Food Lab.

It's supposed to shut if there's a fire. The sensors are meant to seal it automatically. But it's wide open. Maybe Deakin sabotaged the sensors, or maybe they broke down years ago. Prakesh doesn't know, and right then, he doesn't care. He can see the trees through the opening, the air processors arranged in tiered banks on the far wall of the Air Lab. If the fire reaches them…

Prakesh pushes the tech towards the doors. She tries to pull him with her, pleading wordlessly, but he's already moving. He bolts sideways down the greenhouses, the stores to his left—the entire structure nothing more than a burning shell. His throat is stripped raw, slashed to ribbons by the smoke.

There are Air Lab techs running for the doors—they've seen what he's seen, but they're too far away. A jet of fire appears around the edge of a greenhouse, questing like a snake, spitting black smoke. Prakesh dodges to the side, nearly loses his balance, holds it. He can feel his hair singeing, the smell scorching the inside of his skull.

The controls to shut the doors are on a large panel on the right of them. Prakesh slams into it at full speed, hammers on it like he's trying to bust through the wall. Liquid fire is spreading across the floor, heading right for the gap, seeking fresh air.

This isn't just ammonium nitrate, Prakesh thinks. On some level, he's stunned at how rational the thought is. As if the fire were nothing more than an experiment, something that could be quantified by a DNA thermocycler or a pH monitor.

With a groan, the doors judder closed, seconds before the fire reaches them. Prakesh has no way to tell if they'll hold. He's got to get out of here, got to reach the main doors before—

With a giant bang, one of the greenhouses behind him pops open. The shockwave knocks him off his feet, slamming into the wall and peppering him with shards of molten plastic. He's surrounded on all sides by the fire, its tendrils reaching out for him.

The doors, he thinks. *I closed the doors; that's all that—*

33

Riley

There are three Lieren—Tattoo, the lanky one who looked into my pack, and someone else I don't know, a kid so short he's practically a dwarf. They're standing in the middle of the cramped corridor, hands on hips, breathing hard. I catch sight of the white hospital-issue box under the dwarf's arm. They've been busy.

I see a look of startled recognition on Tattoo's face. But I'm not stopping, or even slowing down. Instead, I push my body into a sprint. I jump, taccing off the wall for height, springing right towards them. Tattoo gets out a "Hey—" before my outstretched foot crashes into his face.

His nose shatters. His head snaps backwards, throwing up blood in a fine spray. The other two Lieren are reaching for me, but I'm moving too fast, my momentum carrying me through. As I tuck for landing, Tattoo gives off a strangled, squawking cry, flailing his arms. I land, roll, spring up and run without looking back.

I can hear a thin mewl of pain from Tattoo as he clutches his destroyed nose, and above it, pounding footsteps and angry cries behind me as the others give chase. But they're going from a standing start. I'm already back at full speed, vanishing into the corridors, and after a moment their cries fade into the background.

I tilt my head forwards, and force my screaming muscles to go faster. Scared and exhausted as I am, I feel myself smiling. *Gods*, that felt good.

It doesn't take me much longer to get there. I've come into the gallery on the Level 1 catwalk. It's chaos down below. Dumar, Chang and about ten stompers are trying to hold back a rapidly growing crowd. The huge doors are open—both the main one, and the smaller one inside the decontamination chamber—and what's beyond them is hell: a black, smoking, burning wilderness, scattered with flecks of fire and foam. I can hear a man shouting, yelling about salvaging food. Techs are stumbling out of the doors; Prakesh isn't among them.

I have to get inside. I have to find him. I force myself to calm down, to breathe, sucking in huge gulps of air.

And then I see her: a woman with fiery red hair, bent double with hacking coughs. She's come out of the main doors and is standing off to one side, away from the stompers. Her once-white lab coat is now black and streaky with soot, and her hair is matted and dark. I know her. She's one of Prakesh's colleagues, and she was at the party we had in the Nest. What's her name? I know it... Suki. It's Suki.

The idea is fully formed before I realise it's there. I ignore the stairs at the far end, jumping the rail and dropping to the floor below. The catwalk is no more than a few feet up, and with a quick roll, I'm on my feet again. I can feel my back aching in protest against the rolls I've been forcing it to do, but I ignore it. I can worry about that later.

I skirt the crowd, working my way towards Suki. I can hear Chang shouting in his nasal voice: "Please! We can't let anybody in!"

Nobody notices me. They're all focused on the entrance, which is now billowing thick white smoke. I glance up; the top of the gallery is gone, invisible in a white fog. Suki is still bent double when I reach her, shivering, her arms crossed in front of her. Her face under the streaks of soot is deathly pale.

"Suki," I say, skidding to a halt. She looks up, but shock has wiped her eyes clean. I repeat her name, and after a moment she nods slowly, as if only just realising that I'm talking to her.

"Suki, where is Prakesh?" I say slowly, emphasising every word. When she doesn't respond, I grab her shoulders, arresting her panicked gaze. "Suki, look at me. Where is Prakesh? Did he come out with you? Is he here?"

"Prakesh, he..." She trails off. Her voice is roughly ringed with smoke. I stay silent, looking her in the eyes. Frustration is boiling through me, and it's all I can do not to start shaking her back and forth, screaming in her face.

Her eyes focus, snapping back to life. "Prakesh! He's in there. He's still in there!" She pulls away and begins running towards the doors, but I reach out and snag her back. She gives an incoherent yell, trying to shake me off, but I hold firm.

"Listen to me, Suki," I say. I'm hissing now, holding the terror back at knifepoint. "You need to get me inside."

She doesn't seem to hear me. "But we've got to get Prakesh!" She's screaming now, fear coursing through her voice. "Someone's got to go back in and get Prakesh!" she repeats, as if saying his name will cause him magically to pop into existence.

"I'll go," I say. Maybe it's something in my voice, because she stops yelling and stares at me. Seizing the advantage, I tell her to give me her lab coat. She hesitates for a moment, her pleading eyes now gushing large tears, and then rips her coat off and hands it to me. It's heavy, the rough fabric damp and slimy with soot. But by now there are more techs falling out the doors, and one more white coat won't be noticed.

"They're going to seal it off," says Suki, the manic edge returning to her voice. "It's the only way to fight the fire."

"What about the foam?"

There are no sprinklers or fire hoses on the station—nobody would waste water like that—but there are systems that spray chemical foam if a fire breaks out. They should be suppressing the fire, but Suki shakes her head, flicking it from side to side for a lot longer than normal. "It didn't work. The fire just burned right through it, like it wasn't even there. You have to be quick, or they'll trap you inside."

I'm already running. Leaving behind a babbling Suki, I head towards the doors, hoping that nobody picks out my face. Not one tech or stomper looks in my direction.

I can feel the darting tongues of heat from the fire. They lick at my skin, and I have to force my eyes shut as one sickeningly hot blast washes over me. Beyond me, the Food Lab is a mess of smoke and flame, lit with showers of sparks and the red glow of emergency lights. I can see a few greenhouses still standing, glowing from within like lanterns.

I should be scared. I should be running, away, far away. But I feel none of that. Instead, I'm gripped by a deathly calm, and there's only a single thought in my mind.

Prakesh. I'm coming.

There's an angry shout from behind me. Someone grabs at my arm, yelling for me to stop. In one movement, I shrug off Suki's lab coat, and start running. Straight into hell.

The heat envelops me, so intense that nausea begins to boil in my stomach. The smoke is thick, and I blink rapidly as I run down the rows of greenhouses. Ahead of me, two of them pop, exploding outwards with a bang, showering the ground with flecks of molten plastic. There's too much fire. It's everywhere, blanketing the floor, the walls.

I don't know how long I've got. I scream Prakesh's name, and get a mouthful of hot, stinging smoke. A series of coughs explode out of me, hard enough to bring me crashing to my knees, each one like something ripping its way out of my throat with ragged nails. I haul myself up, and keep running, pushing towards the Air Lab. The white smoke and dull red fire turn the gardens into a swirling wilderness, and I'm not even sure I'm heading in the right direction.

I turn a corner, and reach out a hand to steady myself, then pull it back with a yelp. A thin line of shiny molten plastic has splattered across the back of my hand, and I frantically wipe it on my sleeve. The plastic peels off my hand, taking a thin layer of skin with it. The pain is so sharp and bright that I actually gasp. By now, my eyes are streaming, stinging from the smoke and the heat.

I stagger on, forcing myself forwards, trying to dodge the pools of fire even as my legs threaten to give way. *I have to find him. I have to.*

But even as the thought forms, I know it's hopeless. The entire hangar is a burning coffin, and I'm trapped inside. I haven't come across a single person since I dived in, but with the smoke they could have passed within feet of me and I wouldn't have known. Even if I somehow find Prakesh, there's no way we'll get to the main doors before they seal us in. And they *will* seal us in: the need to starve the fire of oxygen is going to outweigh the lives of a tracer and a lab tech.

I sink to the ground, collapsing onto my side. The air is clearer down here, and I suck in great lungfuls of it, bringing on another bout of coughing. My chest is a taut drum. There's a hum in the air, rumbling under the crackling of the fire, and it takes me a moment to realise that it's coming from the buzz box. The insects. Millions of them must be dying, their enclosure turned into a furnace.

The smoke is heavy now, starting to rest on the floor, and the searing heat scorches my back through my jacket. I should be scared, but the calm has returned, washing over me. I picture Prakesh's face, holding it in the front of my mind, trying to recall every detail. I see him smiling, laughing at a stupid joke, the concern on his face when he saw I'd been ambushed, the relief when he hugged me in Gray's chamber. The look in his eyes when we were alone.

And then, unbidden, the others come to mind: Carver, Amira, the Twins. My mother and father.

Survived an ambush, caught a killer, went through a bombing, then died in a fire trying to save your best friend, I think, closing my eyes. *At least they'll be able to tell one hell of a story.*

This last thought is like something glimpsed only in passing before it vanishes into the distance.

And then strong hands grab me and haul me bodily off the floor. Prakesh's face is streaked with dirt and soot, ringed with the white smoke. For a moment, I'm paralysed, not sure if he's real or the first thing I see in the next world, but then he wraps an arm around me and starts pulling me with him. I force myself to walk, matching his pace.

My voice takes a moment to kick in. "They're sealing it off. All of it!" I shout.

"I know!" he yells back.

Ahead of us, I can see the doors to the labs: the panes of glass in each glow red with the reflected fire, like malevolent eyes. For a second, I'm seized with the idea that we need to get inside there, that they will provide shelter. But Prakesh seems to sense what I'm thinking and shakes his head, pulling us to the right along the wall. We're both coughing again, trying to find tiny pockets of air in the smoke.

A tongue of fire explodes across the passage. The heat jabs out at us, and we both collapse backwards, turning away from it as we crash to the ground. I feel as if I'm being baked alive, but Prakesh hauls me up again. "Don't you *dare* die on me," he says.

And suddenly, ahead of us, the entrance looms. A figure, silhouetted in the spotlights, is running towards us. More hands pulling us out into the dazzling light. And there is no smoke, only clean air, and Prakesh and I collapse onto each other, crashing to the floor. I never knew how delicious air could be, how cool and sweet. I want to bathe in it, roll around in it, stuff great handfuls of it into my mouth.

Behind us, the doors shut with a boom, and the rumble and crackle of the fire vanishes, replaced by the noise of the crowd.

Prakesh rolls away from me. His face is covered in soot. I turn my head to the side to look at him. He sees me, and half smiles. "Don't worry. Your face is as dirty as mine, I promise," he says, his voice edged with smoke, and despite myself, I laugh. It hurts my chest, and soon turns into another coughing fit. Prakesh reaches out his arm across the floor, and grips my hand. I squeeze back.

There's a shadow over Prakesh, and then the worried face of Dumar comes into view. He glances angrily at me, and grabs Prakesh by the shoulder.

"Please tell me you two were the last ones out?" he asks. "Tell me there's no one in there."

Prakesh shakes his head. "No. Just us. We managed to get everyone else out, I think." Anxiety flits across his face. "Did someone get the gene banks out?"

"We did," says a voice behind Dumar. It's Suki, who looks as if she wants to hug Prakesh, or punch him, or faint, all at once.

Prakesh sits up, holds his head. I suck in more crisp, clean air—and suddenly, worry surges through me.

"Prakesh," I say. "Please tell me the fire didn't reach the Air Lab. Tell me the trees didn't catch."

He's silent, and for a moment I'm almost certain that our air is about to be snatched away, but then he turns to me and I can see relief in his eyes. "They're OK. I sealed the Air Lab off." His expression turns grave. "But the Food Lab. The insects..." We all turn to stare at the huge doors that now seal the lab away.

We now have no food.

I hear Darnell's words again. *There is going to be so much fun, you believe that.*

34

Riley

The crowd around is still cut through with panic. Several people have begun to bang on the doors to the Food Lab, demanding that they be opened. Dumar hauls Prakesh to his feet, and then reaches out a hand to me. He seems about to hug me, like he did back in Gray's room, but he stops halfway through the motion, looking me up and down instead.

"You all right?" he says. I can't read his eyes.

"I'm fine," I say. I mean it, too: the tightness in my chest is fading, and every breath still tastes as sweet as ice-cold water. I glance at my hand. The red strip across the back where the molten plastic kissed it is painful, but looks superficial. I won't have to get another blast of that white foam from the medics.

Prakesh chances a smile. "Maybe we shouldn't fight any more," he says.

"You think?"

"I'm just saying. Fires, kidnapping, bombs...maybe the universe is trying to tell us something." He gives a nervous laugh.

"What now?" says Suki. She and Dumar look lost.

Prakesh thinks for a moment. "Suki, we should still have some soil in the upper labs," he says. "We need to get an emergency food op going, and we need to do it now. Tell the guys to start bringing it over, along with the spare UVs—do it right in the Air Lab. The GM plants aren't even close to ready, but we can use those new carbide seeds the lab rats were working on. And while you're at it, we're going to need some sort of hydroponic system. Tell Yoshiro to use whatever he needs, and tell him he'll have to do it double-time."

Suki stares at him, taken aback for a moment, but then nods and runs off, shouting for the techs to follow her.

Prakesh turns to me. "The others? Amira?"

"Safe. Carver hurt his shoulder, but they're OK. The Twins were in the Nest the last I heard."

"The message over the comms said there was a fire in your sector. Was there another bomb?"

I quickly fill him in on what happened back at Darnell's trial in Apogee.

"How many were hurt?"

I avoid his eyes, and his shoulders sag. He wraps an arm around me; his grip is strong, comforting. "Let's get you back," he says.

"I can walk myself," I reply, irritated.

"Walk? Ry, you can barely stand. Come on. Suki has things under control here."

I look at the growing crowd hammering on the doors, calling out in terror to the others. "I doubt that."

"They aren't getting in. Not through those doors, anyway. Let's go."

We move towards the stairwell at the far end of the gallery. The lights far above us have dimmed, as if in sympathy with the chaos below.

The world might not have ended, but it can't be far off. The chaos gets worse as we cross the border into Chengshi. Several times, we pass people fighting over food: men hurling insults at each other over caches of vegetables, held back by their friends. Someone being robbed on the ground as we cross the catwalk above, a knife waved in his face for a box of protein bars. I want to help, but Prakesh pulls me onward. We enter the maze of corridors again, and pass the mess. The door is shut, and two stompers in full armour guard the entrance. I swear I see them tighten their grip on their stingers as we walk past. Prakesh nods to them, but they just stare back.

We're nearing the Apogee border when there's a crackle from a nearby comms screen, set into the corridor wall. The station logo flashes briefly, and then Janice Okwembu is standing there. She's back in the boardroom, standing alone behind a lectern. We stop to watch; even on the crackly monitor, I can see her lips set tight, the steel in her eyes.

She doesn't bother with a greeting. "Today, we suffered two coordinated attacks," she begins. I hear her words echoing down the corridor, repeating themselves through a dozen different speakers. "The first bomb was set off at a criminal trial in Apogee, and a remote device was triggered in our Food Lab. The first explosion claimed the lives of nearly fifty people, and the second, while less deadly, contained an incendiary chemical agent.

"We don't know how they were set, or what their composition was. The damage was great, both human and otherwise. Fortunately, the structural integrity of the station has not been compromised, and the engineers have told me that our orbit has not been disrupted. I would urge everybody to remain calm, to share what food you have, to help each other through this crisis."

"Like that's going to happen," Prakesh says.

Okwembu continues, leaning forward on the lectern, staring straight into the camera. "There is much to be done before..." The picture crackles, then vanishes entirely. Okwembu's voice cuts off abruptly, replaced by a loud burst of static.

And then Darnell is on the screen and my heart freezes solid in my chest.

It's impossible to tell where he is. Whatever is behind him is cloaked in shadow. Prakesh is squeezing my hand tight, and around me I hear people gasp.

"Sorry to interrupt," Darnell says. "I wanted to take this opportunity to thank everyone for coming to my trial. And if you missed it, don't worry—there's plenty more still to come."

The feed glitches, the static ripping Darnell's face in two. The audio cuts out, and when he comes back a moment later, it's horribly distorted, as if he's put the microphone right up to his face.

"...forty-eight hours. That's the time you have left to live. That's all the time we're giving you."

The last word is caught somewhere in the feed and stretches out, mutating into a metallic buzz that seems to take an age to fade.

I've stopped breathing. I have to force myself to suck air into my lungs, and every word of our conversation in the brig is surfacing in my mind.

"Humans don't deserve Outer Earth," Darnell says, his grin glitching in and out as the feed struggles to keep up. "Not after what we did to our planet. We bombed and killed and—"

This time, the screen goes completely black, the audio vanishing. When it comes back, Darnell is walking with the camera. The lights on the ceiling turn his face into a dark silhouette. He laughs, that childish voice becoming a shrieking cackle, which in turn morphs into a horrendous coughing fit.

"We need to go. Now," I say to Prakesh.

But even as we move down the corridor, Darnell's words follow us, turning into a monstrous echo. Wherever he is, he's hacked the entire system.

"And there are more than enough of us," he's saying. "We're living among you, right now. Your best friend. The person across from you in the mess. Your sister. And all of us together? We're the Sons of Earth."

We're at the sector border. Around us, people are staring at the screens in disbelief. Darnell's words are everywhere.

"And when we're gone? Our planet will restore itself. It'll take millennia. But after a while, it'll be as clean and fresh as it was when we first crawled out of the muck. And do you know why? Because we won't be there."

He stops. For a second, I think the audio has cut out again, hope it has, but he's just pausing. He leans close to the microphone—close enough for us to hear his breathing.

"The next two days are going to be so much fun. We—"

Another burst of static rattles through "...cut the signal! Cut it!"

Janice Okwembu's voice is urgent. I catch a glimpse of a screen as we cut through one of the lower corridors. She looks flustered, her veneer of control cracked. But she nods to someone off camera, and stares at the screen. Her eyes are made of steel.

"I heard what you all just heard," she says, and her voice is strong. "Let me make this clear. We will find Oren Darnell. We will bring him down. You have my word on that. For now, please try to stay calm. We will all get through this." She pauses, and the screen reverts to the station logo.

As the broadcast ends, I can hear shouts from behind us. Fear becomes panic in seconds, washing across the crowd. Prakesh and I keep moving. What else is there to do?

Suddenly, I remember the woman on the catwalk. Grace Garner. Whatever she had to tell me looks more important by the second—a possible piece in the puzzle of Gray, Darnell and the Sons of Earth. I should have listened to her then. I should have made her tell me.

I turn to Prakesh, quickly explaining what happened and what Garner looks like, but his expression is puzzled. "A woman? No, sorry, Ry, she didn't show up. Just as well, right?" He barks a laugh and looks away, and it suddenly occurs to me just how much the loss of the Food Lab must hurt him. There are dark circles under his eyes, and it's not just the smoke and the exertion that's made him look so drawn, so tired.

He shakes his head, as if trying to bring himself back. "If she had something to tell you about Darnell, then we need to find her," he says.

I nod. "We should get cleaned up first. Get some water. And we've got some food back at the Nest."

I start down the corridor, but Prakesh shakes his head. "You go. I need to check on my parents."

"Are you—"

"I'll be fine. Go link up with the rest of the Dancers. When you're together, come and find me."

I give his hand a squeeze, and he turns, jogging off down the corridor.

Without his support, my legs feel numb, soft as a wedge of tofu, and I nearly collapse to the ground. My mouth is coated with thick saliva. I realise I'm still wearing my pack, and I reach back for the water tube, but it's dry, without even a single drop left. I shoulder the pack into a more comfortable position, and head down the corridor, distant shouts from the galleries chasing me.

The Dancers are there when I reach the Nest, and as I haul myself up through the trapdoor, Kev sticks his head out the door. There's uncharacteristic anger on his face. "Where you been?"

I cut him off. "I'm OK. The others?"

"Here." He throws open the door, revealing the rest of the crew. Carver is leaning against the wall, flexing his arm, his hand clasped on his shoulder. Yao is at the workbench, rummaging through the drawers. And in the centre of the room stands Amira, hands on hips, anger on her face.

"Tell me you've got some food in that pack," she says. I shake my head, and she grimaces.

It's then that I see the pile of food on the table; they must have raided every corner of the Nest to see what we had left. It's shockingly little, barely enough to last us three days. Some ancient potatoes, tinged with green and already sprouting little nubbly shoots. A few protein bars. Two withered carrots. A small pile of hoarded sugar shots, little jellies in thin cups. Behind the pile, a dirty bottle of homebrew. Yao reaches up, and dumps a small pile of dried fruit on the bench—apples, it looks like.

Carver says, "Well, at least we won't die hungry."

"Oh come on," Yao says. "You don't believe he can actually pull it off?"

We all stare at her. "What?" she says. "He's a guy with a camera, and now everyone on Outer Earth thinks he's a god or something. I ain't scared of him."

"Save it, Yao," snaps Amira. Her patience seems to be exhausted. I want to tell her about Garner, about Prakesh, but before I can say anything she passes me a cup of water. "Have a drink, then I need you back out there. I want you working the market: that goodwill you stored up after we caught Darnell? Time to use it. Yao, Kevin, I want you on the gallery floor. There's got to be some people there who need something transported."

I take a slug of the water; it's warm, but soothes my throat, and I have to force myself not to gulp, to take slow sips.

"Are you going to be OK? Your arm isn't going to fall off, is it?" Yao asks Carver.

"Oh, I thought I'd chill out here for a while, sweetie," Carver replies, flashing a smile which turns into a grimace. "Let you do some work for a change."

Amira glares at him, then turns back to us. "We don't know how long this situation is going to last. Even if the stompers find Darnell, food's going to be hard to come by for a while. So we carry on as normal. Trade runs for food—*only* food. It'll be tough out there, but take whatever you can get."

Nobody says anything, but the glances we share speak volumes. Amira's right. With the Food Lab down, it'll be hard enough even for those who have access to mess food. For tracers like us, who have to find our own food?

I'm about to tell Amira what happened back on the catwalk, but as she glances at me I pause. That can wait. Right now, survival is more important. Wherever Garner is, Prakesh will take care of her.

"Something you want to say, Riley?" Amira's voice is impatient, testy.

I shake my head. "No. Let's do it."

35

Prakesh

Prakesh's parents live on the edge of Gardens, close to the white lights and clean surfaces of Apex. They have their own hab, a comparatively large unit with a double cot and its own bathroom. Ravi Kumar's long-service awards still hang on the wall, strips of black metal engraved with the dates he spent in the space construction corps. His wife has decorated the hab with pot plants—some given to her by Prakesh, some grown by her alone.

"You—inside, now," Achala Kumar barks when she opens the door to Prakesh. He's momentarily stunned, but no sooner is the door shut than she's hugging him tight, her face buried in his shoulder.

"When they said—and then that man..." she manages, and then she's sobbing, her tears soaking through the fabric of his shirt.

Prakesh's father is seated on the edge of the bed. The left leg of his red pants is knotted tight below the knee, his cane resting easily across his lap.

"It's OK," Prakesh says, lifting his mother's face towards him. "We got out all right."

"No, you didn't. Look at you!" She wipes at his face, smearing the soot.

"Achala, leave the boy alone." Ravi Kumar stands up, rising off the bed with an experienced grace. His cane taps as he limps towards them, his eyes boring into his son's. "How bad is it? The damage?"

"Bad." Prakesh reaches around his mother to one of the shelves, snags a canteen. He's more thirsty than he's ever been in his life, and sinks at least half the water in the bottle.

"You two got enough food?" he says to his father.

"Don't ask him," his mother says, jerking a finger at the older Kumar. "He doesn't even know how to fix the chemical toilet when it goes on the fritz."

"Achala."

"Well, you don't. It's just like the plasma cutter all over again, when you were working on the *Shinso Maru*."

"Again, you bring this up?"

Prakesh can't help smiling. It's easy to forget that his mother was his father's boss, a long time ago. He talks over them, his ravaged throat aching. "Someone tell me what your food stocks are like."

"We're fine," his father says. "We have a little stored away."

"How little?"

"Enough. We're fine, Prakesh, and you need to go."

"No, I need to..." Prakesh stops. He has no idea what he needs to do. By now, the Air Lab will be insane: the temporary growth operations will need all the hands they can get, and Suki and company can only keep them going for so long. But Riley sent someone to him—someone she needed to keep safe. And then there are his parents. He doesn't believe that they've got enough food left. Not even close. He should stay, help them keep going.

He shuts his eyes tight. He opens them when he hears the click of his father's crutch, feels his hand on his shoulder.

"Prakesh," says Ravi Kumar. "We're fine. You need to be back out there."

He sighs. "I know."

"And not just in the laboratory," his mother says. "You should be out in the rest of the sector. Making sure this *kutha sala* Darnell doesn't get inside people's heads."

"What?"

"I always said you should be involved in politics," Achala says, folding her arms. "People trust you."

"Only in the Air Lab," Prakesh says. He can feel his cheeks getting hot. "Only when I'm talking about trees."

"Nonsense. People look up to you. You might prefer to ignore it, but they do. And you can't afford to be afraid. Not now."

"But what if—"

"Go," they both say at once, then glance at each other. Achala Kumar has a strange smile on her face. "We can take care of ourselves," she says.

But as Prakesh looks at his parents, all he can see are the things that hold them back. It's not just his father's leg, which keeps him a virtual prisoner in Gardens, which has kept him away from the spacewalks he loved so much. It's the wrinkles around his mother's eyes, the way her neck and upper back are stooped. They were middle-aged when they had him, and the years since then haven't been kind.

His anger at Riley, his frustration, has found another target. He can almost feel it physically moving in his gut, swinging around to focus on Oren Darnell. He's trying to make everyone on the station suffer, and it's people like his parents who will suffer the most.

His mother is right—he does need to get back. But he's not just thinking about the Air Lab. He's thinking about the woman Riley sent to him. The woman who said she knew something.

The Air Lab can wait. If there's even the slightest chance that she could help stop Darnell, he has to find her.

36

Riley

It's amazing how everybody suddenly knows exactly how long we have left. Of course, it's not forty-eight hours any more. It's forty-four hours and thirteen minutes—at least, according to a man I passed on the way to market. His friend disagreed, said it was eleven minutes, waving a homemade watch around like a holy book.

The nervous energy has built up, kettling in the corridors and pushing at the walls of the galleries, thrumming with awful power. Rumours are everywhere, changing and mutating in the space of minutes, stories of possible sightings and citizen watch groups and computer hacks. I've never felt the station like this.

As I approach the market, winding my way through the bottom-level corridors of Apogee, I hear two people talking. They're husband and wife by the look of it, and she's cradling a baby, wrapped in tatty blankets, fast asleep.

"If they've hacked the Apex comms feed, then it won't be long before they take the control room," says the woman. "And when they do…"

The man interrupts her. "I refuse to believe that every single escape pod is gone."

"They are. You know that. But we could always take one of the tugs," the woman replies. There are dark circles under her eyes. "If there are enough of us, we could..."

Her words fade as I slip past. I almost want to go back, tell her not to bother. The tugs, which we use for shipping asteroid slag into the station when the catcher ships come into our orbit, don't have nearly enough range. You'd run out of fuel long before you reached Earth. And it's not as if we can call the asteroid catcher ships for help.

There are only two of them left now: enormous vessels which track the rocks through space, pull them in, drag them back to be processed down into slag. We depend on that slag for our minerals, our building materials. Their missions take years, and right now, both of them are in deep space. If this had happened ten or twenty years ago, they might have been closer, on the moon or on Mars. But the resources that were being brought back weren't good enough, so the catchers were retrofitted to snag asteroids. Even if we sent a distress signal, and they came back for us, they'd never get here in time.

I expect the market to be insane, even to see looters wrecking the stalls, but it's the same as it was yesterday, and the merchants are doing a roaring trade. Food is going for a premium, and several stalls have crowds around them, with impromptu auctions breaking out for mouldy onions or a single protein bar. I cut through a narrow gap between two stalls, earning an angry shout from the merchant. I raise a hand in apology, and as I glance behind me I notice two people in the crowd staring angrily at me, as if memorising my face. Strange.

I find Old Madala near the bar. He's at one of the tables outside, nursing a cup of homebrew. The cup sits on the table in front of him, his hands resting either side of it. I grab a chair, and sit down opposite him. He looks up, surprised.

"Now, about that job you mentioned..." I begin, but he jumps to his feet, knocking over his chair. It clatters on the metal plating as he quickly walks away. I stop, confused, before pushing my chair back and following, cutting in ahead of him.

"Madala, what is it?" I say, but as he turns to me I see fear in his eyes, and it stops me cold.

"Go away. You can't be here," he mutters, and turns away again. Worry coils in the pit of my stomach, and I reach out for him, but he jerks away, the fear turning to anger in his eyes. "Go!" he shouts. "I not talk to you." He moves away into the market, his shoulders hunched, not looking back.

All at once, it feels like the noise of the market intensifies, crowding out my thoughts.

A job from Madala would have scored us some food, some more dried fruit or some green beans. Now, I'm going to have to find someone else, someone who might not be so inclined to trade for something good. I push through a crowd yelling out for what looks like a block of tofu, set on a counter behind a heavily tattooed seller, facing them with his arms folded.

The next three people I speak to act the same as Madala. In one case a merchant I've had a good relationship with in the past tells me angrily to never speak to him again. Nobody tells me why. At first, I think it's just because they don't want to trade away food or don't have anything they need transported, but after a while confusion gives way to fear, and then to a sickening dread.

Darnell said he'd recruited people. What if they think I'm one of them?

I have to get out of here, now. I slip between a pile of crates and a stall piled high with battery cases, heading towards the exit. I'm hoping that something will work out, that I won't have to come back to the Nest empty-handed, but I'm getting more and more glares as I pass by. I keep my head down, and keep walking.

Someone steps into my path, blocking out the light. A bald man, with a nasty, thickened scar on his neck, wearing a soiled T-shirt and old denim pants. His arrival is so sudden that I almost crash into him.

"You," he says, and his voice is tinged with malice. "We know what you're doing."

I stare at him blankly, his words not registering.

He spits angrily, a thick gob of saliva spattering a nearby crate.

"You killed a lot of people today. And you walk in here like we wouldn't notice."

"Hey," I raise my hands, startled. "I don't know what you think I did, but I didn't kill anybody."

"You're one of them," he says. "The Sons of Earth. I heard you got Darnell caught just to keep people occupied while you planted the bombs. That's what I heard." His voice has become a low growl.

"I didn't. I'm not!" I say. "I'm just a tracer. I carry cargo."

His eyes narrow again, and he steps towards me. I move back, and bump into something solid and unyielding. The crowd has closed in around me, trapping me in a narrowing circle.

The man behind me places a hand on my shoulder, and I whirl around, throwing a punch in his direction. He swings his head to the side, and my fist glances off his ear. Then the crowd is on me, hands everywhere, grabbing and pulling and yanking at my pack and screaming obscenities in my face.

I lash out, but it's like fighting air. The crowd is a single being, a hive-mind, a monster with many hands and thousands of fingers. I've seen what happens to people who get taken by a mob. I swing my arms even more wildly, desperately trying to punch my way out, shouting for someone, anyone. But there is no help, and I'm lifted above the crowd, hands gripping my arms and legs. I'm propelled towards the back of the market, and at one point my left leg is pulled down, twisted by a dozen hands. I cry out in agony, and throw my foot out.

The movement causes the crowd ahead of me to sway. They're tightly packed, pushing against each other to try and get a hand on me, and they collapse in a heap of tangled limbs. The bodies carrying me shudder. The hands lose their grip and I'm thrown forwards onto the pile of people. I push frantically against them, trying to force my way up, but then more hands grip me from behind, more people bellow in anger.

Someone grabs me. It's Madala, his face a mask of fear. I'm certain he's with them, that he's trying to hurt me too, but then I see the urgency in his eyes, and then he's hurling me forwards, away from the angry crowd.

"Run!" he yells, and then the monster grabs him, hands pulling him inwards. I bolt, terror pricking at my sides as I jump across a nearby table and smash through a pile of discarded boxes. Behind me, Madala cries out, a horrifying wail which nearly brings me to a halt. I'm desperate to go back for him, but I keep running, and his wails follow me, growing steadily fainter.

Somehow, I come out of the crowd facing the front of the market, and I sprint towards the doors. Behind me, I can hear parts of the beast detaching, giving chase. There are no cries from Madala now. My pack is gone, my jacket hanging on by a single sleeve. I pull my arm into the other as I run, then drop into a roll under a table, coming out the other side as my pursuers crash into it, swearing and screaming. My lungs are burning, and a stitch grips my side in a ring of iron. But I keep sprinting, and then suddenly I'm out of the market, the cries of the monster growing fainter behind me.

How can they possibly believe that I'm a part of it? Someone must have told them. Someone said something, and the people on Outer Earth, desperate for justice, jumped on it.

No time to think about that now. If the people in the market think I'm one of the Sons of Earth, then chances are others will too. I have to get out of the corridors, get somewhere safe. And people know where the Nest is, so I can't go there. I've got to find somewhere else. I look back down the corridor, swearing under my breath.

Movement. I swing round, my fists clenched, ready to fight. Yao steps forward out of the shadows, her hands up. "Easy, Riley. Simmer down a little."

Kev steps in behind her, his face grave.

"Listen, you have to believe me," I say. "I'm not one of them."

"We know," says Kev, his eyes calm.

"Come on," says Yao. "It can't be that bad. How many are we talking here?"

"Everyone. All of them. They all…" I'm breathing too hard, and one of the breaths becomes a half-sob.

Without a word, Kev hands me his pack; his water bag is full, and I suck in the water as fast as I can, slaking the ever-present thirst. "I have to get somewhere safe," I say, wiping my mouth. "Any ideas?"

Kev shakes his head, but then his eyes light up. "Near the Chengshi border."

Yao whirls to face him. "Kev! We were keeping that for emergencies."

"It's an emergency."

She huffs. "Fine. One of the Level 3 corridors, near the habs. The conduits in the floor should be OK, and we stashed some water there a while ago. You should be able to hide out for a while."

"How do I get there?"

"Head down on that level until you come to a power box on the wall. It's the closest to the start of the corridor. A few steps on from that, you'll see a trapdoor in the floor. It's easy to miss, but it's there."

I'm about to thank them, but then something bounces off the floor nearby. It's a chunk of twisted scrap metal, and the man who threw it is at the end of the corridor, yelling behind him: "Found her! She's here!"

"If you want to fight them, we'll stay with you," says Yao quietly, without looking at me. Her eyes are fixed on a point in the distance, her fists clenched.

I want to say yes. More than anything, I don't want to be alone right now. And I'm not just scared. I'm angry. I want fists to meet flesh and nails to tear and scratch, and to show these people that I am *not* who they think I am.

But I can't. Even with three of us, we won't be able to fight them all off. And I can't let the Twins get hurt. Not because of me. Not again.

Almost imperceptibly, I shake my head. Yao catches the gesture, glances in Kev's direction, and dives to the side. Kev grabs me, and he too starts yelling. "Got her! She's over here!" I'm too startled to respond, but then he theatrically hurls himself backwards, as if pushed off. A performance like that from someone like Kev almost makes me laugh out loud, but the laugh dies on my lips when I see his expression. It's the same one that Madala had before he was swallowed up. Kev remains silent, his eyes implore me to do only one thing:

Run.

There are more people at the far end now, running towards me, screaming with mad hatred. With one lingering look back at Kev, I take off, bolting down the corridor, away from the monster.

37

Riley

I don't know how long I run for. The corridors are endless, stretching off into the distance, punctuated by galleries filled with noise and anger. I run, and run, and run.

It's not long before I manage to lose my pursuers. But I can't lose the rumour about me being involved. It's spread through the station like a virus, infecting everyone. Every time I think I've got ahead of it, that I've reached a level or a corridor where people don't know who I am, there's an angry shout from behind me. More people chasing me, more crowds wanting me dead. When I do eventually slow to a halt, my chest heaving, it takes me a moment to figure out where I am.

I've overshot the border somewhere. After a while, the corridors blur into one another, an endlessly unspooling road of black metal and flickering lights. I come to a stop, resting my hands on my hips, head down, sucking in great gasps of air. The run has pushed my body to the limit. Thirst and hunger tear at me. If I don't find Kev's stash soon, I'm finished. I need to get my bearings. Work out which level I'm on.

I force myself to move, pleading with my exhausted body to hold on just a little bit longer. Heading back the way I came, I hit the stairwell; it's crowded, filled with nervous energy, but I keep my head down and this time nobody stops me. It occurs to me that there are other tracer crews who might help me—or at least, who won't attack me on sight. People like the Cossacks or the Area

Boys probably won't be too pleased to see me—they're no fans of the Devil Dancers—but maybe I can find someone from D-Company. They've never really given a damn about anything that didn't have something in it for them, but they know me, and might give me shelter.

I can't waste time hunting for them, though, and it doesn't take long to find the Twins' trapdoor. It's exactly where Yao said it would be, and mercifully, there's nobody around to watch me open it. It's heavy, rusted with age, and it takes some time and a lot of noise to pull upwards. I'm worried that the screeching is going to bring curious onlookers, but in the end nobody comes, and I manage to slip through into the conduit below the passage.

It's tiny, barely big enough for me to crouch in. I can feel thick dust underneath my feet. Spaces below the floor tend to be dirtier and nastier than ones you reach through the ceiling. Darker, too; I have to sit for some time before my eyes become accustomed to the gloom. There are thick electrical cables running along the corners, and one digs uncomfortably into my ass. But I'm not moving. I'm still. My quaking body sends up waves of relief.

I hear footsteps on the floor above me, booming through the tight conduit, but they don't stop, vanishing into the distance. I realise I've been holding my breath, and let it out in a long, slow exhale. The breath causes a puff of dust to burst up. I have to force myself not to cough. But I can see now, and almost immediately I spot the steel canteen propped against the wall. Not for the first time, I send a silent thank you winging in the Twins' direction.

Trying to be as quiet as possible, I drink deeply from the canteen. The water is warm and slightly stale, but it soothes my parched throat. I have to force myself not to drink it all in one go, reminding myself that I might have to be here for a little while.

Amira must be looking for me by now. She would have found out what happened in the market, and hopefully the Twins managed to escape and tell her where I was headed. But she might as well be a million miles away. Her last words to me, the irritation on her face, come hurtling back. What if I never see her again? Or Prakesh? The Twins? I'd probably even be grateful to see Aaron Carver.

For the first time in years, I feel truly alone.

I set the water down slowly, trying to lessen the loud tang of metal on metal. I lean my head back against the side of the conduit, my eyes closed. I have to think. Work something out. There's got to be some way I can convince people I had nothing to do with any of it.

It's some time before I open my eyes. Almost immediately, I start cursing myself for falling asleep—how long was I out?—but then I realise the pain in my legs and sides is almost gone. I can't stretch my legs out too far in the tunnel, but even an experimental flex feels good.

Above me, the station is quiet. There's a distant rumbling as some machine or other kicks into gear, but otherwise it doesn't sound like there's anybody around. I risk a peek, pushing up the trapdoor above me just a fraction, wincing as the metal squeals.

The corridor is deserted. I drop back below, and take another sip of the brackish water.

There's something I'm not seeing here. Every time I try to get a hold of it in my mind it slips away, falling just out of reach. Grace Garner, Marshall Foster, Arthur Gray, Oren Darnell...they're all connected, to be sure, but how? There's some big element of this puzzle missing, and somehow, I can't shake the feeling that Garner has information that could stop this whole thing in its tracks. I don't know if Darnell is after her—or if he even knows she exists yet. All I can do is get to her.

Finding her means going back into Gardens. And walking into Gardens means going right onto what used to be Darnell's turf. But it's the only way to the Air Lab. There's no other option.

I drain the water—with no pack, there's no real way to carry it if I want my hands free—and hoist myself into the corridor above. Fortunately, it's still deserted, and I manage to get a good head of speed heading towards Gardens. I've already got the route I plan to take in my mind, one which sticks to the upper levels, away from the main public areas. I'll cut through the corridors around the furnaces—since the station was thrown into a total panic, there's less chance that there'll be any people there. I can take the topmost catwalk in the galleries—no people walking above me, which means less chance of being spotted.

I've been running for less than five minutes, having just exited the stairwell up into the Level 6 corridor, when another ferocious thirst kicks in. My throat goes dry and lifeless almost instantly, and when I swallow, a sharp pain rips through it. I slow down, try to get some saliva flowing in my mouth, but it just makes it worse.

Damn it, why now?

I keep my speed down, trying to use as little energy as possible in each stride. But the thirst just increases, a burning desire for liquid that wraps lead weights around my feet. The last time I felt anything like it, I'd just finished a multi-stage cargo run which took me through four sectors and lasted about five hours. There's hardly anybody around the furnaces, and those I do see barely glance at me. I'm running past one of the open doors when I hear it: the distinctive gush and spray of a water point as someone fills a bottle or a cup. With a pack and full water tank on my back I'd hardly notice it, but now it's like someone flicking a torch on and off in a dark room.

The furnace chamber where the noise is coming from is dimly lit, but even in the low light I can see it's almost deserted. It's a mess, strewn with discarded boxes, but at the far end, lit by a single light, is a water point. A man in overalls is bent over it, his back to me.

As I watch, I hear another soothing gurgle of water. The sound is a soft hand which reaches deep down into my body and then grips tight. The pain in my dry throat swells and stirs, and then I'm walking into the furnace, hoping and praying that I can get just a little water. The tiniest sip, just the tiniest.

The man stands up as I approach; I expect him to take a drink immediately, but he just places a small bottle in the pocket of his overalls. I sidle in beside him, giving him a big smile and a nod. Last thing I need is more hostility.

Instead of moving, he blocks the water point from me, staring me down.

"Hi," I say. He doesn't respond. My heart falls slightly, but I keep smiling.

"It's still working right?" I continue. "I've been running all day, and I don't have any with me. I'm really thirsty." I force a laugh, hoping to put him at ease, but he does nothing, his hand holding tight onto his pocket. I hear the water inside his bottle slosh ever so gently, and it takes everything I have not to reach for it.

Instead, I spread my arms, trying to be as friendly as possible. "If you're in control of this water point, maybe I can trade for it," I say. "I'm a tracer. I'm with a crew called the Devil Dancers. Fastest on Outer Earth. Maybe there's something you need transporting? Some cargo? A message maybe? I'll take it wherever you need, really, even one of the upper sectors…" I'm babbling now, and he still hasn't uttered a word.

I tail off. This isn't working. I'm torn between pushing my way past him, trying to fight him, and going to look for another water point. In the end, the third option wins out. I'm in no state to fight anyone right now.

"Thanks anyway," I sigh.

"Please don't move," he says quietly.

I've turned around already. There are three stompers, standing in the shadows. Their stingers are out, and every one is pointing right at me.

38

Prakesh

"No ID, no entry," says the stomper.

"Come on, man," says Prakesh. "I *work* here. I'm an Air Lab tech."

"Then where's your ID?"

"Lost it."

"Really."

"Yeah, really. I left it behind in the Air Lab, right before the fire.

Which, coincidentally, I helped contain, so maybe you should cut me a break, move out of the way, and let me in so I can do my job."

"You don't even have a lab coat."

"Did I mention the fire?"

The guard pauses for a moment, then shakes his head. "Don't know you."

"Of course you don't know me. I don't know you either. I've never seen you in my life." Prakesh makes himself stop. This is getting nowhere. The door to the Air Lab—one of the auxiliary entrances, one that he was sure would be unmanned—remains stubbornly shut. And now the stomper has his stinger out, not pointed at Prakesh but not exactly held at ease, either. He jerks his head. "Go somewhere else."

Prakesh mutters under his breath, walking away. Ordinarily, he'd look for someone he knows, someone who could vouch for him. But there's no one around—not Suki, not Dumar, not even bloody Chang. They're probably all inside already.

It doesn't matter. There are other ways to get into the Air Lab, access points this moronic stomper wouldn't even *think* to look for. He quickens his pace as he strides down the corridor, heading back towards the galleries, searching for the storage room which he just *knows* has a loose panel on its back wall.

He stops. If he couldn't get into the Air Lab through the regular channels, what luck is Grace Garner going to have? If he gets in there, they won't let him leave—he'll be pulled in a dozen different directions, asked to oversee everything from soil quality to the UV emitters. For a moment, he's torn—that's what he *should* be doing. But then he sees his parents' faces again, remembers how helpless he felt when he visited them.

He decides to look for Grace Garner in the galleries, in the endless corridors surrounding the Air Lab. He's on edge, waiting for another crackle of static over the comms system, waiting for Oren Darnell to appear. But the only thing he finds in the corridors is very scared people. Habs are locked down, barred and shut. Lights flicker above clusters of young gang members, talking in hushed voices and casting dirty looks at Prakesh as he walks past.

He walks up to one group, a mix of what look like Area Boys and Black Hole Crew. Some of them have ritual scars on their faces, parallel lines cut into the flesh and made to heal badly. The livid red scars look like warpaint.

Prakesh doesn't hesitate. You show fear with these guys, they'll break you. "I'm looking for someone."

They look at him like he's crawled out of the buzz box. He keeps talking anyway. "Old woman, 'bout sixty, blue headscarf. Seen her anywhere?"

Someone yells for them from the other end of the corridor. The gang takes off at a run. One of them looks back and says, "Doesn't matter who you're looking for, man. We're all done. All of us."

He keeps looking. Garner is nowhere. It's maddening—she could be behind any one of the locked doors. She could also be in Apogee, or Chengshi, or in the middle of the Core, for that matter. It's less than an hour before Prakesh gives up, furious with himself. He sits down on one of the benches in the gallery. A dull ache has settled into his limbs, and no matter how much water he drinks, his throat keeps returning to its shredded state. The crowd outside the main doors to the Food Lab has become mad with fear, screaming slogans, arms around each other.

He leans back, closing his eyes, weighing up the options. Option one: sneak into the Air Lab, get to work making food. Option two: go back to Apogee, find Riley, tell her that Garner is gone. For the second time, Prakesh tells himself that he should be in the Air Lab. He should be doing what he's supposed to.

Which is how, hours later, he finds himself crossing the border into Apogee. The further he gets from Gardens, the worse it gets. He avoids the galleries as much as he can—they've become boiling cauldrons of anger, of stompers trying to hold back growing crowds who are demanding to have their sector councillors address them. The Apogee main gallery has been closed off, blocked by lines of stompers. Prakesh can't understand what they're doing there—they're guarding an empty room. And he can smell the aftermath, a sick, sulphurous smell with an edge of burned fat. It's enough to make his gorge rise, and he quickly makes his way upwards, climbing the levels towards the Nest.

He takes the last few steps at a jog, suddenly desperate to find Riley, to know that she's OK. But as he enters the corridor where he can get into the Nest, he sees Aaron Carver and the Twins. They're collapsed against the wall, and the trapdoor above them is wide open.

Carver looks up as he approaches. "P-Man," he says, using Prakesh's least favourite nickname.

The Twins raise their heads towards him. Kev's face is one big, mottled bruise. Yao's shirt is ripped, and there's a grimy crust of blood under her nose.

There's a sick feeling in Prakesh's stomach, made worse by the absence of Riley, or Amira. "What happened?"

"Your friend Riley's pissed a lot of people off," says Carver.

"Riley—why would—"

"They wrecked the Nest."

"I hate 'em," Yao says, her voice small and furious. "All of 'em. Why can't they just leave us alone? What did we do?"

Prakesh takes a deep breath, and asks them to start from the beginning. The Twins fill him in on what happened at the market. When they tell him what happened to Riley, the sick feeling in his stomach swells and rises, threatening to overwhelm him. "Then we got back here, and they were tearing the Nest up," Yao says.

Kev shakes his head. He seems to have gone beyond words.

"Where's Riley?" Prakesh says. His voice is turned into razor blades by his dry throat.

"We don't know," says Carver. "We've lost Amira too."

"We have to go find them."

"Where?" says Kev.

"Where is right," Carver says. He sounds worn out, more tired than Prakesh has ever heard him. It occurs to Prakesh that if the Nest has been destroyed, that means Carver's workbench, and all his experiments, will have been wrecked as well.

"You want to go looking for her, be my guest," Carver goes on. "But right now, Devil Dancers aren't too popular round here. Or anywhere, actually."

He stands, dusts his pants down. "We need to go. Probably best for us to lie low for a while."

"What if Riley and Amira come back?"

"They'll know where to find us," Carver says, glancing at Yao. "Trust me."

39

Riley

The cell I'm in is six paces long, five across. I've counted them out. Twice.

There's a camera in the ceiling, enclosed behind tough plastic. The white light from the thin fluorescent strips on either side of the camera captures and destroys any shadows it finds. Beyond the transparent barrier at the front of the cell, the brig is dark. The sound of the station is muted here, dwindling to almost nothing.

Turns out there were six stompers, not three. I'm still not sure how they knew where I was going to be. I can only guess that I must have been caught on a surveillance cam somewhere: when so many have failed over the years, you forget that there are some that still work.

The moment they grabbed me, I started demanding to know what they wanted, but all I got was an order to shut up, and they marched me right back into Apogee, to the same prison that Darnell was in yesterday. There was a small crowd outside the prison. They started shouting the moment they saw me, but I was hustled straight through and pushed into the cell. When I realised where we were going, I started hoping that Royo might be there, but he was nowhere to be seen.

After I was thrown in here, and after I'd finished banging on the plastic in frustration, screaming at the backs of the retreating guards, I collapsed on the cot, lying back on the thin mattress.

The water point in the cell isn't working, and nobody's given me any food since I landed in here. My stomach is rolling with nausea. I'm back where I started, my crew has no idea where I am, and outside is a mob that wants me dead.

Brilliant.

Sometime later—hours, maybe—I hear a noise from beyond the cell. The main lights in the prison were turned out some time ago, and I can't see anything. I sit up on the bed, squinting, trying to peer into the blackness. There: footsteps. Very faint. Someone approaching from the end of the block.

In an instant, I'm up and banging on the plastic. "Hey," I say, my voice ringing inside the small space of the cell. "Need some more water in here!"

As my voice fades, I hear the footsteps again. If whoever it is heard me, they give no answer, and continue walking steadily towards the cell. I fall silent, waiting, my hand on the plastic, and Janice Okwembu walks out of the darkness.

She wears the same white jumpsuit. Her expression is grave, her lips set in a thin line. She folds her arms, and her luminous eyes lock onto mine. I'm so surprised that I just stand there, staring back at her.

"You'll have to forgive my lateness," she says. Her voice is dulled by the plastic barrier, stripped of its warmth. "I was in Apex when I heard you'd been found, and it took me some time to make my way over."

My voice comes back. "What am I doing here?"

"You're here for your own protection. Or wasn't that explained to you?" Her voice is even, her expression impossible to read.

"I can take care of myself."

"No, you can't."

I don't have an answer for her. She pauses, then continues: "People seem to believe you are responsible for the bombings today. I can't allow any more vigilante justice. Not now."

"But it's not true. I had nothing to do with it!"

She doesn't say anything.

"You can't think I did?" I stammer, my confidence leaving me. The room seems suddenly smaller, the darkness at the edge of Okwembu's feet becoming thicker.

"All you have to do..." My voice cracks. The thirst is raging worse than ever. I start again. "All you have to do is get on the comms and tell people that I'm not responsible. That way, I could move freely. My crew could protect me. And I saw the people outside—if they get in here, I'll be trapped. Out there, I can run. Please."

I'm regretting the last word the second it leaves my mouth. Okwembu seems to sense the give, the little pressure point, and steps forward, closer to the barrier.

"How much control do you imagine we have, really?" she says. "The only way we keep the peace any more is by letting people do what they want. We have to give them so much room. If the council were to crack down, to try and force people to do things in a certain way, even on the smallest thing, we'd be destroyed in hours. The only thing we can do any more is advise, and protect."

"So you're just going to leave me in here?"

"Until this crisis is over, yes."

Something occurs to me. I stare at her through the plastic. "And you came down here personally to tell me this?" I say, fear lending an edge to my words. "With Darnell about to destroy the station, you come down to Apogee to tell me that you're going to keep me in jail? I sort of knew that anyway. Why are you *really* here?" I'm slightly out of breath, but I hold her gaze.

Eventually, she says. "I'll be honest with you, even though you haven't been honest with me. When I asked you if there was anything else you wanted to tell me about Oren Darnell, you said no. You lied."

"What?"

"If you'd told me what you knew, we might have been able to stop Darnell's plan before the bombings. But that doesn't matter now. What matters is that you tell me everything, before more people die."

My heart is beating too fast. I turn away from her, my hands on my head. "This is crazy."

There's something else in her voice now, and it takes me a second to pick it up: she sounds almost excited. "Marshall Foster's assistant is missing," she continues. "A woman named Grace Garner. She worked with him for years on the council, and now she's vanished. Nobody's seen her since the bombings."

"So?" I shrug, feigning nonchalance. "What if she was killed in the blast? Or maybe Gray took her. Who knows how many people he was responsible for?"

"Don't treat me like an idiot, Ms. Hale." Her voice is soft, controlled, but her eyes are angry. "She was last seen *after* Darnell was caught. Talking with you, up on the catwalks. Oh, don't look so shocked. Do you think we'd be able to operate without informants here?"

I'm silent, and she goes on. "Foster could have been working with Gray and Darnell. If he was one of the Sons of Earth, then Grace Garner would know.

"Riley," she says, and the use of my first name nearly makes me recoil. The word is like a pointed fingernail touching bare flesh. "I have to know what she said to you, and where she was going. Where did you send her?"

"She said she wanted to tell me something. She didn't say what. I told her to meet me in the mess later. But then, there was the explosion, so..."

"You're lying to me again."

She takes a step closer to the plastic, and this time a note of anger creeps into that silken voice. "Outer Earth is my charge and I will do everything I can to protect it. If you won't help me, then I won't help you."

"I'm telling you, I don't where she is. But she's probably still in Apogee. Maybe someone saw her in the mess."

There's a long silence. Eventually, Okwembu says, "It would be so easy to torture you. But I've seen people like you before. When you've suffered loss, physical pain means nothing. But what would you do if we were to hurt your friend Amira Al-Hassan? Or cut off Kevin O'Connell's fingers in front of you?"

Anger and fear are swirling together inside me, creating something else, a new emotion, something big and bruised and awful.

"I'm going to let you think about our conversation," Okwembu says. "I'll be back soon. And do try to remember that those prison doors won't hold forever. I can only devote so many officers to guard duty in these troubled times."

She turns and walks away, vanishing into the darkness.

I lose control. I bang hard on the plastic barrier with both fists and scream myself hoarse. The sound is the same as the one I made when I slammed my hand on the outside of Darnell's cell, but in here it's louder, echoing around the space. I shout Okwembu's name over and over, yelling that I'll kill her if she so much as touches one of my friends. I scramble around the edges of the plastic, hunting for a seam or an edge, but there's nothing, and after a while I sink to my knees, my fists sliding down the plastic.

I've never wanted to kill someone before. It's an odd thought, sitting strangely and quietly in my mind like an unwelcome guest. But instead of turning it away, I feed it, nurture it. If Okwembu hurts Amira, or Prakesh or the Twins or anybody else, I will kill her.

I whisper the words to myself, and in the cell they sound closer than they have any right to be.

I sleep in snatches. I don't dream, but I'm restless, tossing and turning on the thin mattress, trying to get comfortable. There's no way to tell time in here, but I lie on that cot for what feels like hours, grinding my teeth. Eventually, when I'm right on the edge of sleep, I hear footsteps, approaching from the far end of the cell block. She's back.

I rise off the bed, my fists clenched, my nails digging into my palms. Defiance courses through me. Whatever she does, I won't tell her a damn thing. I step to the barrier, place a hand on it…

…and have to yank it away quickly when the barrier slides quietly into the wall. Stunned, I step forward, into the tiny circle of light beyond. It's bigger now that the slightly opaque barrier is gone, but the rest of the block is still dark.

An electric charge crackles up my spine; Okwembu wouldn't let me out. That can only mean one thing: the people outside have come for me. They've overpowered the guards and they've busted their way in. I shift into a fighting stance, keeping my centre of gravity low, my arms ready. I can hear the footsteps again now, getting close.

A figure steps out of the gloom, and holds out a hand.
Amira.

40

Darnell

Oren Darnell takes a deep breath, and jumps.

For a moment, his body is suspended in space. The gap is eight feet wide, and there's nothing below him but a long fall, all the way down six levels to a very messy stop at the bottom. Just as he thinks he's misjudged it, that his body is too big to get enough power into the leap, his fingers grasp the ledge on the other side.

He slams into the wall, barking his knees on the surface, nearly toppling backwards. The ledge he's holding on to is nothing, a protuberance where two sheets of metal are joined. Hot, noxious air wafts up from below.

He tries to be as still as possible. He can hear his heart beating through his shirt, and it's as if each beat is trying to push him away from the wall. His jacket flares out behind him, and the tab screen, carefully slipped into an inside pocket, comes loose. It bounces off the walls as it tumbles, and it's a full five seconds before Darnell hears the faint smash.

"Doesn't matter," he says to himself. "Won't need that any more." He barely realises he's voiced the thought aloud.

Slowly, he begins to inch his way along, aiming for an open duct a few feet to his right. Darnell can hear his own breathing, hard and heavy. His jacket has been torn to pieces by the jagged, malformed edges of the back passages and conduits. Doesn't matter. He's here.

This gap, this empty space between the sectors, is the only way into Apex. The main corridors have been sealed off, guarded by stompers with orders to let no one in or out. Hardly surprising, given the precious jewels that Apex holds: the main control room and the council chamber. But it's not as secure as its citizens might think. Darnell traded a lot for the location of this duct, this one little glitch on the station blueprints that nobody remembered to have closed off.

Hauling himself into the opening is hard, but he manages it. For a moment, he's on all fours, and then the duct opens up into a larger space, its walls hidden behind nests of wiring and open fuse boxes. An ordinary person could stand upright, but Darnell has to walk bent over. He doesn't mind. Low lighting illuminates his lower body, leaving his face in darkness.

A few yards on, he has to drop to all fours again, to push his way past a protruding power box in the upper half of the space. This close to the ground, he can see a little light filtering through the cracks between the floor panels. When he stands, his hands are caked with dust and grime.

The access point is a neat white trapdoor, set into the floor. It's fully pneumatic, and when Darnell presses the recessed button beside it, it slides silently away.

White light floods into the space from below. Darnell listens hard, but Apex is uncommonly silent. Darnell's been there before, knows how small the sector is. He should be hearing footsteps, urgent voices, the hiss and buzz and clatter of a very nervous sector. But there's nothing. Just the thin hum of the station.

Darnell drops through the gap. He's momentarily blinded by the harsh white light, blinking as his eyes adjust. He's in what looks like a small waiting area, the walls slightly curved, the lighting coming from fluorescents in the ceiling. One wall is lined with hard plastic chairs, the other with a slim flowerbed. Darnell's gaze lingers on the flowers, on their fragile orange petals. *Nasturtiums.* He wonders where the council managed to get the water to grow them.

He draws his blade, seats it in his hand, and walks down the corridor leading off the waiting area. If he's got it right, he should be on the upper level of Apex, a few minutes from the main control room. Skeins of dust fall from his shoulders and hair as he walks, dirtying the pristine white floor.

"You took your time."

Darnell whirls around, his knife slashing out.

Janice Okwembu steps smartly backwards, and the blade cuts nothing but air. Darnell stares down at her, his shoulders heaving.

"You shouldn't have let them arrest me," he says, after a moment.

"You shouldn't have got arrested," Okwembu says. "In any case, it doesn't matter. Everything else is on schedule."

41

Riley

I pull Amira into a hug, squeezing her tight. She pauses for a moment, then squeezes back.

"How'd you find me?" I ask.

"Don't worry about that," she replies. "Are you hurt?"

I shake my head. "But what about the crowd? The stompers? How did you…"

"The crowd left a while ago. As soon as they realised that they weren't getting in."

"But the stompers…"

She pauses, and it's only then that I see the thin splatters of blood across her shoulders. She shrugs, and says, "They have no idea how to fight. They think stingers make them invincible."

I tell her about my conversation with Okwembu. But before I can finish the story, there are shouts from the other end of the block. More guards, at least four of them. Amira motions me back. "In the cell. Lie down on the bed." I'm puzzled, but I do as she asks. I see her step into the shadows, flattening up against the wall on the far side.

I'm staring at the ceiling, hands folded under my head, when they arrive, stingers out. They crowd the entrance to the cell, their stingers sweeping wildly around the tight space. They look young, almost certainly some kind of trainee unit, nothing more than kids with guns. The one who arrives first seems older than the others, but still doesn't look a minute over eighteen or nineteen. His stinger, at least, stays steady.

"What did you do?" he yells.

He doesn't hear Amira slip in behind him, or see her arms reach around his neck and over his head. She grabs and twists, and I hear his neck snap, a sound that shocks the others into silence.

It's all the opening she needs.

Amira is amazing to watch in battle. She could almost be dancing. Not a single movement is wasted, and each one flows into the next, as if she had practised the entire sequence beforehand. No matter what the stompers try, Amira is three steps ahead, driving elbows into stomachs and open hands into temples.

She knocks the last one flat, striking the heel of her hand into the middle of his face. His nose explodes in a flare of blood, the crack of the bone echoing through the brig. He gives a muffled howl of pain. As he falls, she grabs his stinger, and in one quick movement dismantles it, dropping out the clip and separating the slide from the body. She tosses the pieces aside, and they strike the floor, the noise echoing in the sudden silence.

I hop off the bed. "I could have helped, you know," I say, glancing at the moaning guards. A tiny frisson of fear shoots through me at the sight of the guard who got his neck snapped, but I tamp it down.

She ignores my comment. "Why didn't you just tell Okwembu whatever Garner told you?"

"Because she didn't tell me anything. Not back at the trial, anyway. I said I'd meet her in the Air Lab."

"So why not tell Okwembu that?"

I shake my head. "Amira, there was something... I don't know. Off about her. Like she knows a lot more than she's letting on."

Amira studies me. Her eyes reveal absolutely nothing.

"Well then," she says after a moment. "We need to find Garner. The sooner we hear what she has to say, the sooner we can stop all this."

I think for a moment. "It's too dangerous for me to go all the way up to Gardens. I should lie low. I'll go find the other Dancers, you go find Garner."

"No," Amira says. "She sought you out, not me. I don't want to get all the way there to find that you're the only person she'll talk to. We go together."

"And after we talk to her, what then?"

The oddest look crosses Amira's face. It only lasts for a split second, but it seems filled with sorrow and with anger.

"What? What is it?" I ask.

She looks away. Then says, "It's all gone to hell, Riley. All of it. It's a nightmare out there."

Her words hang in the air, a reminder of what we're up against. Eventually, she says, "We have to go."

"All right," I say. "But I need water, and something to eat. They didn't feed me in here. How much time do we have?"

Another shadow crosses her face at the mention of Darnell's countdown. "I don't know. Thirty hours? Anyway, you're right. There's some food back in the Nest. We go there first, then we head to Gardens."

And then we're running again, out of the cell block and into the main station. The guards Amira took down outside the prison are still lying there. It half occurs to me that she might have killed some of them too, but I push the thought away. Besides, I tell myself, you were ready to kill someone not more than a few hours ago. Amira did what she had to.

She takes point, her scarf billowing out behind her. It's been a while since the bombings, and the station seems to have calmed down a little. But the people we do see are harried and drawn, talking quietly in worried little groups, barely glancing at us. We're not chased, and as we approach the Nest, Amira slows to a jog, dropping in beside me, her breaths coming quickly. There's a thin sheen of sweat on her face, and she runs a hand across her forehead.

She gestures for me to go first, and I tac off the wall and pull myself up through the trapdoor. The entranceway is dark, and as Amira pulls herself up behind me, I stand and reach for the keypad.

It's only then I notice that the door to the Nest is slightly ajar, a tiny slash of light creeping through the opening. As Amira gets to her feet, I raise a hand, motioning her to be quiet. I feel her tense behind me, and a growing feeling of dread wells in my chest as I push the door open.

Whatever Carver was working on has been torn apart, thrown around the room, a blast of welded metal and chemicals. His workbench is on its side. The mattresses are upside-down, with stuffing pouring out of deep slashes. Carver and the Twins are nowhere to be seen. Yao's mural—her beautiful, beautiful mural—has been sprayed over, defaced with what looks like burn marks, angry, ugly blotches that cover the entire wall. It takes me a moment to see that the blotches form a word: TRAITOR.

Amira steps from behind me, and reaches down to the floor. She straightens up, and in her hand is a small, twisted object, burned and black. She tilts it towards me. I can just make out *Treasure Isl*...on the tattered spine.

There are no words.

We slump against the wall. My stomach aches; the food and water we had have vanished. Whoever did this—almost certainly people trying to find me—would have taken them.

"What do we do now?" I ask.

Amira's silent for a few moments. Her body is still, her eyes staring into the distance. Then she rises, leaping to her feet in one movement, and says, "We stick to the plan. But we find some food and water, because we're not making it to Gardens without."

I nod, and as I do so, something catches my eye. There's another mark on the wall, different from the others. It's as if someone rubbed their finger in the burn marks, then used it to paint a design. I lean closer, my hand resting on the wall next to it. The bottom half of a circle, with three slashes above it, running downwards from left to right. The slashes are uneven, as if drawn in a hurry.

Codes and picture ciphers aren't too common among tracers. Some of the other crews, like D-Company, have dozens of members spread out across the sectors. They use the ciphers as a way to communicate, marking out their territory or their stash locations. Unless you know what to look for, the ciphers are just one graffiti symbol among many. With small, tight-knit crews, you usually don't need them. There are a few we still use though, and I'm sure I've seen this one before. I'm almost certain that it was left by Carver and the Twins.

"Amira, look at this."

She turns, her head tilted to one side, and her eyes widen as she catches sight of the cipher. "That's a Caves symbol."

I stare at it, my brow furrowed. "You sure?"

Amira says, "That's where they'll be: in the Caves. Kev must have drawn it. His family still lives there."

I shudder. "When was the last time you went down there?"

"Must be a year ago now. I don't run to New Germany too often these days."

"Will they have food?"

"They'd better."

42

Darnell

It's not long before Darnell finds out why the sector is so quiet.

The Apex amphitheatre is packed with a hundred people—techs, administrators, council members. Their mouths are open in huge, terrified Os, and their foreheads are shiny with sweat. Darnell can see them through the big transparent doors, but he can't hear them. The doors are completely soundproof, sealed shut.

"How did you do it?" he says to Janice Okwembu. "How did you get them in there?"

Okwembu shrugs. "Called an emergency briefing. Everybody to the amphitheatre. Then all I had to do was seal the doors."

She stands, arms folded, looking at the door. Someone, a tech with thin eyeglasses, is hammering on it, pulling at the handles, screaming unheard curses. Okwembu looks back at him, impassive.

"There must be others," Darnell says. "This can't be everyone in the sector."

"Oh, there'll be a few people. I'm sure you're up to taking care of them."

"What about the control rooms?"

"Everything's automated. The techs left their stations when I asked them to."

Darnell has to admit to himself that he's impressed. When Okwembu came to him, two years ago, he struggled to believe that she really wanted the same thing he did. The end she had planned for the station sounded fascinating. Brilliant even. But even then, he was never quite sure that she'd go through with it.

But when she'd told him about her frustration, her own anger at the people of Outer Earth, how they squabbled and fought and squandered everything they had, he began to see. She was proof that his idea could infect anyone: she was just as susceptible as any other sleeper. Someone sympathetic to the human extinction movement, but who felt betrayed by it, let down, frustrated with the council's inability to get anything done.

Okwembu turns away. Suspicion floods his thoughts, automatic and instant. He puts a huge hand on her shoulder, rests it there. He can feel her bones underneath her jumpsuit, fragile and angular. She stops, but doesn't turn to look at him.

"What's to stop me from killing you too?" he says.

"Because you owe me more than that."

"Oh, do I?"

"I got you out of the brig. You wouldn't be here if it wasn't for me."

He laughs. "And you think that means I owe you something?"

This time, she does turn to face him, and there's a tiny spark of anger in her eyes. "You would have stayed in there until the end. When you screwed up with Foster's eye, and got yourself arrested, you lost any chance of doing something meaningful. But I saw an *opportunity*."

"Opportunity?"

She nods. And when she speaks again, there's a thin, weary contempt running through her voice. "The people of this station need to feel fear," she says. "They need to know what it's like to be truly powerless. It's no less than they deserve. And you do have that effect on people. Being arrested made you even more infamous than you already were."

Despite himself, he smiles.

"So yes, you owe it to me," she says. "I want to be here for the end. I want to see it happen."

"And our friend is on schedule?"

She nods.

"I want to talk to him."

"Perhaps. First, you need to make a broadcast. You can say you've taken Apex, that you've got the council hostage. Make people believe that you'll kill us, one at a time."

As she turns to walk away, Darnell calls after her.

"What about Garner?"

"It was only a matter of time before Hale's friends broke her out. All we have to do is wait and watch. They'll lead us right to her."

"And we can see her?"

Okwembu nods to the camera. "Apex isn't the only place on the station where the cameras still work. I haven't found Garner yet—she's clever, staying out of sight. But if Hale really knows where Garner is, so will we, eventually."

"We should have Hale brought here. Give me five minutes with her, she'll tell us everything we need to know."

"I prefer a more subtle approach," Okwembu says. "For example, take the people in that conference room."

The people behind the doors have stopped hammering. Their eyes are flicking back and forth between Darnell and Okwembu. Darnell can see the true panic forming, the realisation that they're not just going to be held prisoner. He can see over the shoulders of the people at the front, see those at the back running their hands over the walls, looking for an escape route that isn't there.

Okwembu turns to Darnell, and tells him how they should die.

43

Riley

We leave the Nest, not bothering to latch the door behind us. There's nothing left to take. Amira gestures me to take point, breaking into a full run as soon as I hit the corridor below.

I'm trying very hard not to think about what I'll find in the Caves. When they were building what was to become New Germany, they made some of it smaller. More cramped. Someone messed up the blueprints, or perhaps they just found that they were running out of time. Or money—that was a big thing back then. Whatever it was, what they ended with was a section of the station with only one way in or out: a single, heavy door.

The place is a breeding ground for horror stories. The last one I remember was that the walls were too thin to keep the radiation out, meaning that anybody who lived there would end up riddled with cancer.

You go down to get to there, dropping onto the bottom-level corridor and entering through a stairwell at the far end of the gallery. The door is closed when we reach it, and Amira and I both have to grab it and yank it open; the metal screeches as we pull it back, the heavy door taking what seems like an age to open.

"Riley, look," says Amira.

I'm focused on the door, and don't realise she's spoken until she turns me around and I'm staring right at Oren Darnell.

The comms screen is just above us, suspended from a catwalk. Wherever the camera is, it's looking down at Darnell from above. From where we're standing, it's a disorientating effect, as if the world has twisted on its axis. He's standing in front of a door in a corridor somewhere, and there's movement behind him, fuzzy and out of focus.

His voice, when he speaks, is distant and tinny. "Apex is ours," he says. "We've taken the station council, and we're going to kill them, one by one, for your entertainment."

I find myself wishing for a glitch, hoping that the feed will cut out. No such luck.

"Of course," Darnell continues, "you might wonder what's happened to everyone else in Apex."

He steps to one side. The movement behind him is still out of focus, but impossible to mistake. There are people, dozens of them, trapped behind a door.

Darnell's gaze finds the camera. His hand strays to a control panel on the wall, and works its way across it.

"We've modified the station's life support systems," he says. "I can control them right from here. It's very useful."

Something begins to happen to the people in the room. They start screaming wordlessly, pushing up against each other, as if they can knock down the walls through sheer numbers.

"I've just vented their oxygen into space," Darnell says. "Let's see what happens."

There's nothing we can do. Not a single thing. It doesn't stop anger and an awful, furious despair from shooting through me. Without another word, Amira turns me around, and pushes me into the Caves.

Inside the door, there's a small entranceway, with multiple corridors branching off it. We take the leftmost one, Amira letting me take the lead. From the minute we enter, it's as if something is gently squeezing my shoulders. Claustrophobia begins to build.

There aren't any main lights in the corridor, and the only illumination comes from the entrances to the dorms, set into the walls at regular intervals. It's quiet, too: the Caves might be one of the most crowded areas on the station, but there's hardly any noise.

Here, nothing has a name—only numbers and letters. We're in 1-B; it's painted onto the wall, sprayed in huge, uniform characters. A few of the doors we pass have faces peering out at us. The women have wrinkles that are too deep and the men are almost all bearded, with dark eyes. Nobody tries to stop us, but as we reach the end of the corridor one of the shadows on the walls stretches and elongates, and a man rises from where he was sitting against the wall. He's wiry, not large, but the space is tight enough that he blocks the corridor, and we have to stop. His greasy, dark hair frames a pitted face; I can't place him, but he looks familiar.

"You," he barks, gesturing angrily. I don't know if he's referring to one or both of us, but before I can reply, he says: "What's your business?"

I hear the soft squeak as Amira shifts her foot backwards, lowering herself ever so subtly into a combat position. I'm about to speak, when she says, "You've got three seconds to get out of our way, starting now."

The man narrows his eyes and takes a step towards us, but I quickly raise my hands. "We're tracers," I say. "One of our crew lives here. Kevin O'Connell."

"Don't know that name."

"Sure you do. You know his family," I say, and then I realise where I've seen him before. I smile, and it disarms him for a moment, doubt crossing his face. "Come on, Syria. It's been a little while but I know you haven't forgotten about me."

He looks blank. "Riley," I add helpfully. His expression doesn't change, and for one heart-stopping moment I'm sure I've got it wrong. But then he relaxes, his shoulders dropping as he glances around the corridor. "Sure, Riley. Sure. I remember you now," he mutters. "You took that message up the ring for my cousin a while back."

I nod. He's still not exactly friendly, but behind me I feel Amira relax. "You're not getting through here without a pat-down though," he says. "Can't be too careful."

"Is that really necessary?" says Amira "We're a tracer crew. We're not looking for trouble."

"Says you who was ready to brawl a minute ago," says Syria. Amira sighs in irritation. Before she can say anything else, I hold out my arms as far as the corridor will allow, letting Syria check for weapons.

"So, about Kevin. Know where we can find him?" I ask, as he runs a thumb between my ankles and my shoes, checking for blades.

He grunts noncommittally. "Lotta Kevins down here."

"No, there's not," I say. "There's only three. One of them's a mental case, the other runs with a gang up in Chengshi, and the third is a tracer. Take a wild guess which one we're looking for."

He starts checking Amira—she's visibly irritated, staring pointedly at the ceiling. But as he runs his hands down her sides, he relents. "Yeah, yeah. Down in 3-C. Last door on the right. Come to think of it," he says as he brushes Amira's scarf back into place, "he came through with some other guys earlier. Friends of yours?"

"One of them with an arm in a sling?" Amira asks.

"Yup."

I catch Amira's eye. So she was right about the code on the wall.

"Sorry for the shakedown," says Syria. "Things have been pretty hairy ever since that bomb went off. We've already had some trouble with those idiots from the D-Company tracers, trying to get in here."

"Oh what, Syria, you were going to take them down all by yourself?"

He smiles, displaying blackened stumps where his teeth should be. "Who, me? No. Them, though…"

He gestures behind us. At every door, there are people holding weapons: homemade blades, lengths of pipe, even one or two homemade stingers. Had we tried to fight our way through, we would have been dead in seconds.

Syria stands aside, and we head to the stairs at the far end of the corridor. We're not running, but every so often we have to flatten ourselves against the wall to let someone else squeeze past. Several times, we're looked at with suspicion, but no one else stops us. We're both on edge, and I'm aware of time slipping away. My stomach is a knotted ball of hunger. Around us, Outer Earth rumbles and creaks, the sound getting increasingly louder as we continue deeper into the Caves.

44

Riley

Kev's father is as big as I remember, and seems to open his mouth even less than his son. He greets us at the entrance to the hab, a huge, heavily muscled man, with arms thick from endless shifts lifting containers in the sector kitchens. He doesn't say anything when he sees us, just nods, and gestures behind him. There, lying on a cot and looking poisonous, is Carver. Behind him are the Twins, leaning against the wall by the bed, their arms folded.

And with them: Prakesh.

Yao spots me, then so does Kev, and then everyone is talking at once. The relief at seeing everyone there must show on my face, because Kev flashes me a rare smile.

Kev's family are clustered one bunk down, huddled together: his grandfather is nothing more than a wizened face peeking out of a bundle of blankets. His mother sits on the edge of the bunk, holding Kev's baby brother in her arms. She stands when she sees me, forcing a smile onto her face.

"You're the last, right?" she asks. The swaddled baby is held before her like a shield. She rolls the edge of the blanket between her finger and thumb, worrying the fabric.

We nod, and she shouts to her husband, "Ira, that's it. You can close the door now."

I turn to Kev. "What happened at the market…" I say, and I'm surprised to find my voice catching. "Thank you."

"Tell me you found our stash," says Yao.

"Saved my life. How many of those do you have?"

"A few," Kev says. As he turns his head, his face catches the light, and I notice the bruises there, already turning an ugly purple. I reach up, gently running my hand over his cheek. He doesn't flinch, but he must see the look on my face, because he shrugs and then looks away. "No big deal."

I catch his mother staring at me. Kev told me once that they wanted him to be a ship pilot, training at the academy in Tzevya, and they're still not happy with how he spends his time. Or who he spends it with.

Yao's face is crusted with dried blood, but she looks OK. She smiles as well, and gives me a thumbs-up. Around us, the dorm is quiet, with only a few people sprawled on the beds. They're either straining to hear us or doing their best to ignore us; right now, I don't care. Kev passes around protein bars, some fruit, some water. I'm not proud about digging into his family's food supply, but we can't do anything unless we eat.

"The Air Lab?" I ask Prakesh, as I swallow a bite of protein bar.

"Wouldn't let me in," he says. "Lost my ID in the fire."

"That means Garner could be anywhere," Amira says. "And with Darnell in Apex..."

"The what now?" Carver says. Yao and Kevin stare at us, open-mouthed. Even Kev's family start listening.

"Darnell made it into Apex?" Yao whispers. "And who's Garner?"

"You don't know?" I say, confused. "You didn't see the comms?"

"This is Caves," says Carver. "Nothing works down here."

Kev looks sideways at him. "What?" Carver says. "It's the truth."

Amira and I fill them in, starting with Darnell's latest broadcast. After we're done, nobody says anything for a minute. Carver's face has gone pale.

"How is he doing this?" asks Yao, rubbing her ankle. "You don't just waltz into Apex. They've got security codes, scanners, watchdog programs, killer robots for all I know. Things that do nothing but keep people out."

Nobody answers. It's almost certainly my imagination, but it seems like the room just got a tiny bit hotter, the air a little thicker, as if someone was blowing smoke. A thin film of sweat coats my forehead.

"I think I know," I say quietly, and everybody turns to me. I take a breath. "Or at least, I think I know how to find out."

I tell them about Grace Garner and what Okwembu wanted from her. "I was hoping she'd made it to Gardens and found Prakesh," I say.

"Why does it have to be us?" says Carver.

I look at him. "What do you mean?"

"There's got to be an easier way to find her. Why should we stick our necks out by hightailing it up to Gardens?"

"Because there's no one else. No one we can trust."

"How do you even know she's in there? P-Man said he couldn't find her."

"It's our best shot. We look there first. If she's not there, we can search the rest of the sector."

"Amira, back me up here," says Carver. "You can't think this is a good idea."

Amira's silent for a moment, looking away. When she turns back to us, her face is hard. "Well, let's see, Aaron. What I think is that I have one tracer with a dislocated shoulder, and two more who look like they tried to punch out a meteorite. My fastest tracer"—her gaze falls on me—"is currently the most wanted person on Outer Earth. And I just took down eight stompers getting Riley out of the brig."

"Amira…" says Carver, but she cuts him off: "And that's not even taking into account the rioting, the looting, or the fact that every one of us is apparently going to die in a matter of hours—and we still don't know how. Do I think going up to Gardens is a good idea? I think it's a terrible idea. But we're going to do it anyway."

Her voice hasn't risen; it's softer now, as quiet as a blade slipping out of a sheath. "We are not," she says, and her voice is a husky whisper. She clears her throat. "We are not going to rely on anyone else. If Riley thinks this Garner person has information that could stop Darnell, then she and I are going to find her. We're going to do it fast, and we're going to do it now."

There's silence. "What do you mean, 'she and I'?" I ask.

"Yeah," echoes Yao. "You can't be thinking about going by yourselves?"

"That's exactly what we're doing," says Amira.

"Come on," says Carver. "My arm's busted, but my legs still work fine, promise."

"You stay here. That's an order."

"Sorry, Amira," says Yao quietly. "But Carver's right. If you want to go to Gardens, fine. But you're not leaving us here. Not on something like this."

Amira takes a long, deep breath, fighting back her anger. "All right," she says, through gritted teeth.

"I'm coming too," says Prakesh. He's been quiet for a while, and all eyes turn towards him.

"No," says Amira, exasperated. "They're tracers. They can run. You can't. We don't have time to baby-sit."

"You're going to Gardens," says Prakesh, his voice hard. "How were you planning on getting in there?"

"We'll figure something out."

"Not very smart. Riley always told me you were better than that."

Behind us, Kev's family has drawn tighter together on the bed. His dad, Ira, is there now, his arms around his wife. Kev's grandfather is still staring at the ceiling, his lips moving silently.

Prakesh steps forward, squaring up to Amira. She doesn't move, her dark eyes locked on his. "I can't get to Gardens on my own," says Prakesh. "It's getting dangerous out there. I don't know the best routes, the ones that'll be quiet. But you do. And you won't get into the labs without me. We need each other."

For a minute, Amira just stares at Prakesh. I'm expecting her to refuse, but eventually she gives a curt nod. Prakesh is about to say something, but she raises a finger to silence him. "We won't wait for you. You run at our speed, and if you get into trouble, you're on your own."

Prakesh half smiles, and turns to me. "Ready to give me a crash course, Riley?"

But Amira isn't finished. "We take the monorail tracks. Get to the top of the sector, then cut around all the way towards Gardens. They won't be running the monorail right now, not when there's no food to ship."

"The tracks?" I ask. "You think we can make it?"

"It'll be safer than running out in the open. Quicker too, if we watch our step."

I'm about to protest further, but then I realise she's right. It's dangerous, but better than risking the catwalks.

It doesn't take us long to get ready. We leave the Caves, walking single file down the tight corridors, and this time nobody stops us. As soon as we enter the ground-floor corridor, we start running. Amira takes point, leading us up the station levels to the tracks; behind her are Yao, Kev and Carver, with Prakesh and me bringing up the rear. I'm not used to being in the back, and I'm nervous that he'll fall behind or get hurt. But although he's no tracer, and has to pull himself over jumps and walls that we take in a single leap, he stays with us. Somehow. I can hear his breathing behind me as I run, heavy and hard.

The comms screens are black mirrors, reflecting us as we sprint past. I half expect them to spring to life, the face of Oren Darnell to appear, but they stay silent.

To get to the tracks, we have to cross through the gallery, and we hear the crowd before we see it. The noise is a huge, angry buzz, as if every insect burned in the Food Lab fire came back for revenge. We're still in one of the ground-floor corridors; the lights have gone, plunging it into near-darkness, with only the distant light from the galleries providing any illumination. The horrible noise fills the space. Before us is the exit to the gallery floor, and even at a distance we can see it's packed with people.

I've already heard from Yao how different groups are reacting to Darnell. The Caves are pulling in tight, letting hardly anyone in. The rest of New Germany is in chaos, with rumours of food riots, and the other sectors aren't much better. Yao says she heard that Tzevya is doing OK—there's a curfew of some kind, and an armed group preparing to find a way into Apex.

Amira raises a fist, bringing us to a halt behind her. We pause, breathing heavily, standing in a loose circle. My hips ache with the effort, and a stitch is gnawing at my side. Prakesh comes in last, his face flushed, but Amira glances at him and his expression hardens. She turns away from him, beckoning us closer.

"No running," she says, her voice rough with exertion. "Single file through the crowd, and don't talk to anyone. Go for the corridor at the far end, and wait. We'll keep going when everyone's through." With that, she plunges into the crowd.

I pull my hood up, hiding my face, and glance at Prakesh. He gestures me ahead, and I step into the galleries. The noise explodes around me. There's a full-scale protest going on; at the far end, I can see a line of stompers with riot shields, protecting what looks like one of their captains. He has that speaking device, and as I slip through the crowd, he raises it to his mouth. "If everybody could remain calm," he begins, and is drowned out by a fresh roar of protest. Something flies through the air, and he has to leap back as the projectile smashes on the platform.

It's hard to tell what the crowd want—whether they believe their leaders can just bring them Darnell, or if they want new leaders entirely. One of the stompers raises something above his head, but before I can see him bring it down I'm given a rough push to the right. Someone gets into my face, yelling, and I instinctively raise a hand in apology before hurriedly moving on. My heart seems to have climbed from its regular position to my throat, choking me. I've lost track of both the Dancers and Prakesh.

I turn sideways to slip through a narrow gap in the thick crowd, and as I turn my head I see something that causes my heart to leap from my throat right into my mouth.

Zhao Zheng, the man who controls the Lieren, is standing a few feet away.

His back is to me, but there's no mistaking the bald head, lined with thick, jagged tattoos, or the hands, covered with tarnished metal, hanging at the end of unnaturally long arms. He wears a black, sleeveless vest, and is surrounded by four—no, five—Lieren. There's a small space around them, and people seem to be giving them some room. If I'd taken a different route, I might have gone right through the middle of them.

Someone bumps into me from behind, and suddenly I'm being propelled right towards Zhao's back.

In one horrifying instant, I see the chain of events locking into place before me, the knives coming out, the split second before I'm cut to ribbons, the triumphant smile on Zhao's face.

But I pull myself up, almost touching him, regaining my balance even as the noise from the crowd is drowned out by the roaring in my ears. At the edge of the group, one of the Lieren senses movement, starts to turn his head, but I quickly step backwards, vanishing into the crowd.

It's a little while before I breathe again.

As I reach the edge of the gallery, I can see people spilling into the corridor beyond, but I quickly catch sight of the Dancers. It takes me a second to see Prakesh as well, leaning against the wall, his hands on his knees. Amira sees me as I slip through, but then the look of relief on her face is replaced with one of horror. Before I can say anything, there's a hand on my shoulder, and I feel the cold touch of those metal rings.

Zhao Zheng leans in until his face is right up close to my ear. "Going somewhere?" he whispers.

45

Riley

There are at least ten Lieren. They stand on either side of their leader, fingering blades and flexing fists. The light from the gallery makes them into silhouettes, turning their bodies into little more than dark apparitions.

Zhao gives a nasty smile, twisted by a small scar on the right corner of his mouth. The top of the scar meets the tip of one of his tattoos: a huge, slashing black mark, running up his cheek and around his head.

Amira steps in beside me, but I raise a hand, and she stops, puzzled. The people at the edge of the crowd have seen what's happening, and have started to move away.

"Zhao, this really isn't the time," I say, but he just laughs.

"Tell that to Marco," he replies. He indicates one of the Lieren, standing off to the side, glaring at me. It's the one who led the ambush that started all this, the one I kicked in the head on the run to Gardens. His nose is a bulbous black mess. His blade twitches, gripped tight in his hand.

Hello, Tattoo. Apparently you have a name.

I look back at Zhao. "They jumped me, and they tried to take my cargo. Your boy here"—I gesture at Marco, and his eyes narrow in anger—"wanted to cut my ear off. I was just repaying the favour."

"No, it doesn't work that way," Zhao replies. The smile stays etched on his face, but his eyes are cold. "You kind of—well—you insulted Marco. And that means you insulted me."

His eyes pass over the bruised twins, the crippled Carver. They're standing firm behind me, staring down the Lieren.

"I'll offer you a way out," he continues, leering. "Call it a debt of honour. We'll leave, but we're taking a body part of yours with us. I'll let you pick which one."

Amira steps forward, her teeth bared. "Not going to happen," she says.

"I thought as much," Zhao replies. And then he drives a fist deep into Amira's stomach.

She cries out and collapses backwards, the air leaving her in one huge burst. Time slows to a crawl as she falls. I leap forwards, twisting my left elbow round in the direction of Zhao's throat, and the corridor explodes.

Sometimes, the choice about whether to fight or to run gets made for you.

Every one of the Dancers attacks at once in a wave of fists and feet. My vision blurs at the edges; Zhao dodges out of range, laughing, but it dies on his lips as I bring the elbow round into the face of another Lieren. I feel his cheekbone crack under the strike, hear the howl of pain, but I'm already bringing my right hand up, balled into a fist and swinging at the man behind him. He's short, scrawny, barely out of his teens, and for a bizarre moment I wonder how someone like him ever fell in with the Lieren. Then my fist slams into his side with a noise like a wet jacket thrown into a corner, and he doubles over, retching.

Yao takes a few quick steps back, and then launches herself towards Kev. He's already dropping to one knee, cupping his hands to meet her. With a yell, she plants a foot in them, and Kev hurls her forwards. She explodes across the passage: a screaming, airborne ball of fists and feet, knocking two Lieren to the ground. As she tries to rise, another assailant appears above her—but doesn't even get to plant his feet before Kev hits him with an enormous right hook.

Behind them, Carver is facing off against two others; his arm is useless, but at the same moment that the Twins take down their opponents he launches himself towards the corridor wall, tic-tacs off and delivers a kick to the chest of one of the Lieren, knocking him backwards. Behind me, Prakesh makes a strange groaning sound—I can't tell if he's taking a hit or giving one.

Before I can find out, someone drives an elbow into the small of my back. The pain is so sudden, so startling, that I can't even cry out. It just stops dead in my throat.

I fall forwards onto my own elbows, my vision a starburst of colours. Instinctively, I lash out with a foot, and catch something—a leg—which jerks away, accompanied by a sharp cry. A hand gropes my hair, finds a purchase and yanks upwards, snapping my neck back. I have a split second to try and pull away, but then the fist smashes across my face. I taste blood instantly, salty and metallic.

Whoever owns the fist rears back for another strike, but then vanishes, ripped away. Amira, her left arm clutching her stomach, breathing heavily through her nose, disables my attacker with a jab to the throat.

For a moment, we're apart from the battle. I'm on all fours, staring up at her. A few feet away, Carver, Prakesh and the Twins duck, block, swing, strike, retaliate. Zhao is wielding a knife, a thin blade, long as my forearm. The knife rips into Carver's right shoulder, opening a jagged wound. He grunts in anger, before grabbing Zhao's knife hand and twisting. The blade flies out of his grip, bouncing and skittering down the corridor. I'm dimly aware that the noise from the gallery has got louder, though whether in reaction to the fight or because the crowd has finally broken through the line of stompers, I can't tell.

The Lieren are everywhere. Another runs towards me, his face gleaming with triumph. I'm back on my feet now, and sidestep before whipping my fist into his stomach, sending him crashing to the floor.

And then it all goes wrong.

From somewhere behind Amira, one of the Lieren appears—one I've never seen before. He's tall, thin as a corpse, wearing a jacket of some dark blue fabric. In his hand, already raised over his head, a long blade: Zhao's knife.

It's my imagination, it has to be, but the knife is as black as the deepest space, reflecting no light, and its wielder is fast, much too fast, and before I can do anything he's swinging it down towards Amira's neck.

Every part of me kicks into overdrive, snapping the corridor into sharp, clear focus. But even as my hand is reaching out to block the blade, I already know it won't be quick enough. Amira's eyes widen when she sees me, and she begins to turn, but the knife is almost there, its point finally picking up a flash of yellow light.

And then something—no, someone—appears between Amira and the blade.

There's a horrible sound, a kind of wet thud, like something plunging into a bucket of rotten food. The attacker's knife is ripped from his hand, and he staggers backwards.

Yao falls to the ground, the thin blade buried up to the hilt in the side of her neck.

For one terrible moment, her eyes meet mine, and it's as if someone has driven a blade through me instead. The corridor has fallen silent, Lieren and Dancer pausing their attack, everyone fixated on the dark blood that suddenly begins to spurt from Yao's neck, coming in thick, gushing bursts, collecting on the corridor floor. She sighs—a soft, calm sound—and then her eyes go dark.

46

Darnell

Councillor Morton holds out the longest.

He was one of the dozen people who ignored Janice Okwembu's summons to the amphitheatre. He was in the council chamber, diagramming plans for diverting more resources to the Air Lab, when he heard Oren Darnell's voice from one of the comms screens. He looked up just in time to see everybody he ever worked with asphyxiate, clawing at the walls.

Now he's barricaded the doors to the chambers. Unlike most of the sliding doors on Outer Earth, these ones swing inwards, and he's pushed every chair in the room up against them, jamming the handles shut. It's enough to hold Oren Darnell back for a good two minutes.

Morton shrinks down behind the table, mad with fear. Darnell is using a plasma cutter, burning a hole through the steel door. The air is hot with the stench of ozone. In seconds, he's cut a hole large enough to thrust his arm through—Morton sees the molten edge burn through the sleeve of his jacket, sizzle at the flesh beneath. Darnell doesn't seem to feel it. He knocks the chairs away, then withdraws his arm and kicks the door open.

Darnell crosses the room in seconds, a black hulk silhouetted by the ceiling lights. Morton is pulled from the chamber, Darnell's hands on his shoulders. He tries to fight back, hammering on the giant's arms, but he may as well try and bend a steel bar with his mind.

Darnell drags him into the passage, spins him around, hurls him to the floor.

"Whatever you want," Morton says, and that's when he sees Janice Okwembu. She's standing behind Darnell. As his eyes fall on her, Darnell can see the pitiful hope in them, as if he thinks she's arrived unnoticed, that she can knock Darnell out and save him. When she doesn't move, he says, "Janice, help me."

Okwembu steps past Darnell, and crouches down, so that she's level with Morton. He's shaking his head now, not understanding, not wanting to understand.

"Janice, please," he says. "What you're doing... this is insane."

"No, it's not," she says quietly, her eyes never leaving him. "You know what's insane, Charles? You. Sitting in that chamber for years, trying to legislate for this station, like it could make a single bit of difference."

"But Outer Earth—"

"Isn't worth keeping alive any more."

Morton's fear is starting to be replaced by anger, furious and disbelieving. "So you kill your colleagues? Torture them? It's monstrous."

"Yes," she says, standing, glancing at Darnell. "But necessary."

She walks away, not looking back. Morton tries to rise, pushing himself up to one knee. Darnell reaches down and draws the knife across his throat.

Morton takes a whole minute to die.

As Darnell turns away, he finally registers the burn on his arm, the one he got from the plasma cutter. He runs a finger along it, registering the pain but not responding to it. His stomach turns over, not from revulsion, but from hunger. When did he last eat? Or sleep? He doesn't remember, and at that moment it doesn't seem important.

He takes a step, then stops. The corridor swims in front of him, and he has to put a hand on the wall to steady himself. The memory comes, arriving to replace the pain, and he's halfway through it before he even knows it's there. The memory of his family's hab.

Darnell had given up keeping track of the number of species he'd managed to cultivate—they all blended into each other, sprouting flowers and swollen fruit and questing tendrils. He had to be careful not to step on the plants or trip over their roots. He didn't mind.

Nobody asked after his mother. At first, he'd been worried that they would, but nobody wanted to get involved. He kept collecting food packages from the mess, and would eat them standing up, alone in the hab.

On one particular day, he was just leaving for school, closing the hab door behind him. He was thinking about a new cultivar he was trying, one which wouldn't...

"Son?"

The man's eyes were bright over thin-rimmed glasses. He wore brown overalls, and carried a tab screen in one hand. He looked down at the screen, squinting. "Hab 6-21-E... Darnell family. Your parents' home?"

Darnell shook his head. "Dad's dead. And my mom's not at home."

"Ten-year maintenance inspection, son. Gotta make sure the chemical toilet doesn't need repair. Look here, see? My ID."

He held up the tab screen, showing the Outer Earth logo along with the words *Maintenance Corps*. Underneath the words, there was a pixelated photograph, and the name *Mosely, Lewis J., Inspection Officer*.

Darnell shrugged. "I'll tell my mom you came by."

Mosely smiled. "I don't think we need to trouble her, do you?"

"I gotta go to school," Darnell said, turning to lock the door behind him.

He didn't get the chance. Mosely reached over and pushed it open, and before Darnell could stop him, stepped inside. Darnell didn't move. Didn't breathe.

"Won't be a second, son," Mosely said. "Then we can—"

His words choked off as he saw the inside of the hab. Mosely turned, his hand over his mouth. Darnell remembers stepping backwards as Mosely let go, vomiting all over the door.

"Are you coming?" Okwembu says from the far end of the corridor.

Darnell looks up, the memory vanishing like smoke. He takes off after Okwembu, stepping over Morton's body. There's a distant stinging from his arm, the smell of burned fabric, but he's barely aware of them now.

"I want to talk to our friend," he says, as he catches up with

Okwembu. She's at the bottom of a flight of steps, walking down a long passage towards a door. "I want to know where he is."

"You will," she says. "Once Hale has found Garner, and we've got what we needed."

At the mention of Hale, a comfortable rage flares inside him. All the same, he's about to tell Okwembu to do what he says when she opens the door, and then every thought he has falls away.

He's looking at the main control room of Outer Earth.

The room is as long and narrow as the corridor, with screens arrayed across each wall. Darnell touches the nearest one, and it responds smoothly at his touch, menu options appearing under his fingertips. *Orientation. Lighting Circuits. Core Operations.*

"I'll leave you to it," Okwembu says. "When you're ready, come back to the main council chamber. We'll do another broadcast from there."

Darnell barely hears her. He's moving down the room, hardly knowing where to look next, a giant grin on his face. Then his eyes fall on one particular display, and his grin gets even wider.

"I'll be along in a minute," he says, taking a seat at the screen.

47

Riley

Zhao breaks the silence. He gives an inhuman yell as he flies towards a startled Carver, his hands twisted into claws. But then Amira is there, darting across the room and slamming into him, pushing him into the wall, past a startled Kev, still frozen in shock.

"Run!" she shouts.

Prakesh grabs my arm. The Lieren are stunned, but only for a moment. Then they're giving chase, filling the corridor behind us with angry shouts. There are people further down the corridor, but they shrink against the wall with expressions of terror.

I run on automatic, my feet pulling me forwards all on their own. But my mind is lingering, staring into Yao's eyes, hearing that last whisper of her breath. Alongside me, I can hear Prakesh's breathing, heavy and ragged. There's someone else alongside us—Carver, I think. I don't know where Kev and Amira are.

Slowly, the cries of the Lieren vanish behind us. For a while, I lose track of where we're going. Prakesh is leading the way; he must be taking us towards Gardens. My chest is burning with the effort, and my calves are nothing more than twin slabs of aching flesh.

The guilt comes, blossoming in my mind like a diseased flower. If I hadn't attacked Marco, if I'd stayed down after that ambush, then Yao would still be alive. The realisation nearly doubles me over. I stumble to a halt, retching helplessly, desperately wanting to throw up, to force the feeling out of me, but nothing comes. I'm too shocked to cry; all I can do is hold my stomach as a creeping numbness spreads up my limbs.

Prakesh has run ahead, but he turns back when he realises I'm no longer with him. "What are you doing?" he rasps, his voice ragged with effort. "We have to keep moving. Come on."

There's a hand on my back. Carver is crouching down, looking up at me. His arm is crusted with jagged strips of blood.

"Ry," he says quietly. The kindness in his eyes takes a second to register. "We can't worry about it now. We have to finish this. For Yao."

Slowly, I nod.

The lights go out with a soft buzz, leaving us standing in pitch darkness. "What the hell?" Prakesh says, and then gets control of himself. "I know where this goes. Hopefully we can get to the tracks."

The further we run, the more chaotic the station seems to become. Now it's not just angry crowds hurling threats—it's full-on running battles, stompers with stingers and stun-sticks raised, plunging into huge brawls in the corridors and galleries. The fate of my crew, the death of Yao, all of it digs into my mind, and every fibre of my body tells me to turn back and find them. But I push forwards, because deep down I know Carver is right. I've got a job to do, and this whole situation is getting worse by the second. Darnell and the Sons of Earth are still in control. They could do anything: more fires, more bombs, even open one of the other airlocks and shoot all our air into space, suffocating us where we stand.

Every moment of my life—every moment of almost everyone's life—has been lived on Outer Earth. This station is my home, as familiar and comforting as an embrace. But in the hands of Darnell, it feels like it's been turned against me. Like every floor plate has become a trapdoor, and every pipe has a tripwire tied tightly around it.

We hit the stairs. They're almost silent around us; there's shouting in the distance, but I can't tell if it's another crowd or the Lieren coming after us. Little by little, we adjust to the darkness, and I find I can make out the floor ahead of us.

My thoughts drift to the asteroid catcher ships. There are only two left—big, hulking vessels with skeleton crews. What if the Sons succeed, and kill everyone on the station? The ships will return to find that they're the last humans in the universe. Where would they go? Would they try to return to Earth? Would they contact each other? Or just continue into deep space, drifting until their supplies run out and their engines sputter and die?

We've been climbing in silence, and every so often Prakesh will reach a hand back—I squeeze it, hoping that it's enough. But I'm deep in thought when I realise that the stairwell is getting lighter: whatever killed the lights isn't affecting areas above us. Before long, we hit the top level of the sector, and then we're climbing the stairs to the monorail platform.

And then, a triumphant shout from behind us: "Found you!"

Lieren: two of them, both carrying knives, their features hidden in the shadows. Can we risk running in the tunnels? Should we double back? I'm frantically running through places where we could lose them.

It's then that I realise Carver isn't with us. I turn back mid-stride, and see him standing with his back to us, his shoulders squared, facing down the oncoming Lieren. I can't see his face, but I see his fists in the low light, clenched at his sides.

"Get out of here, Ry," he says. "I'll buy you guys some time."

"Carver, come on!"

But he raises a hand, waving me away—it's his left hand, and I see his face tense as he does it; it must be screaming at him, racking his body in pain. He's in no condition to fight. I start towards him, but he senses me coming, and turns, his expression angry.

"Why can't you just do what you're told, for once?" he growls, but behind the anger I hear a note of pleading that brings me up short. The Lieren are almost on him, their blades dancing, and he turns back to them, bending his knees slightly.

Prakesh is behind me: "We have to go. Now."

I wheel around, furious. "We can't leave him!"

"Yes, you can," says Carver, and swings his good arm in a huge, pistoning strike that takes one of his attackers in the side of the head and sends him sprawling back down the corridor. The other Lieren pauses, surprised, and then Carver is on him. Prakesh grabs my arm, and then my reserve breaks and we're running into the darkness, leaving Carver fighting to the death behind us.

48

Riley

It takes a long time for us to adjust to the darkness in the tunnel. Right now, the only thing we can be sure of is that we're heading in the direction of Gardens. We have to move slowly; the ground under our feet is twisted and uneven, and the tracks are nothing more than thin black lines. Our footsteps echo into the gloom.

"Do you think they'll follow us in here?" Prakesh asks quietly.

"Probably. But they won't see us right away. And we have a head start."

"Thanks to Carver."

I don't reply.

Eventually, after what seems like hours, we reach Gardens. The platform is deserted, lit by that ghostly orange light. Soon, we're on a catwalk high above the main entrance to the Food Lab, which is still spouting puffs of acrid smoke. I can't see the floor below, but I can hear people down there: it doesn't sound like a fight, but every so often angry voices are raised: people pleading for food, demanding to be let in.

Right then, there's the crackle of the comms systems. There's an enormous screen at the far end of the gallery, and as it flashes up the station logo, a cold chill settles over me. I know exactly what's coming.

Darnell appears on the screen. He's seated at the main table in the Apex council chamber, his hands folded in front of him. His frame is too large for the chair he's sitting in, and he towers over the table. He's smiling.

"It's time to make things a little more..." He pauses, as if searching for the right word, then his smile gets wider. "Uncomfortable."

Now that he's in the council chamber, there's no need for him to hack the feed, and the lack of glitches somehow makes it even worse. "We can control the thrusters from here, turn off all the oxygen, even send a little signal down the lines that'll boil every drop of water on the station into nothingness."

Prakesh has gone very still. His hand finds mine, and grips it tight. I can't take my eyes off the screen. Darnell leans back in his chair, his huge hands laced over his stomach. "But none of that seemed to be enough. Not for the people on this station. So we've told Outer Earth's convection systems to cease functioning. It's not quite as efficient as fire, but it's so much more fun to watch." The screen cuts to black.

There's perhaps half a second of silence before the crowd below us starts screaming. I turn to Prakesh, my eyes wide. I'm no scientist, but I know how this place works. And I know that we're in serious trouble.

You can heat Outer Earth without too many problems. But cooling it? Keeping the temperature down with a million people, a bunch of power sources and the regular blasts of direct sunlight when the station swings round in its orbit? That takes a lot of work. There are big fins on the station hull, convectors which let the heat just radiate off into space. They rely on coolant, circulating through pipes around the station, an enormous nerve system of liquid which keeps the temperature stable. If they shut down, if the liquid stops flowing...

"How long do we have?" I ask, my voice high and thin.

Prakesh looks away, and for a second I think he hasn't heard, but then he says, "Probably as long as Darnell's deadline. A day. Maybe less."

"Could someone get into the main systems and turn the coolers back on?"

He shakes his head. "No way. Maybe. I don't know."

We stand, listening to the chaos unfold below us. Eventually, Prakesh takes his hands off the railing. "This way," he mutters, straightening up, but instead of moving, he just stands there, hands on his thighs. His face is slick with sweat, his breath coming in huge, ragged gasps. The signs are hard to miss: the quivering calves, the slumped shoulders. Every rookie tracer goes through them. Prakesh is muscled from constant work in the Air Lab, but he's nowhere near tracer-fit. Not even close.

I crouch down, looking up at him. He tries to force a smile, and doesn't succeed.

"Will there be food and water? In this little entrance of yours?" I ask. He nods. "Good. And it had better be all natural. I don't want to be eating any genetic stuff."

He laughs, forces himself up. I rise with him. "Come on," I say. "We're almost there. Let's get into the Air Lab, and then we can rest. Promise."

Prakesh takes the lead at a slow jog; I desperately want him to move faster, but bite my tongue, letting him go at his own pace. He leads us off the catwalk and down through a maze of corridors and stairwells, taking us through a couple of keypad-protected doors. The corridors change slightly, the sparse metal plates and recessed lights giving way to banks of computers, some of which look like they haven't been used in decades. The glaring white lights from the ceiling reflect off the dark screens.

I'm uneasy. We're so close, and the thought that we might not find Garner—or worse, that the information she has might turn out to be useless—continues to gnaw at me.

"We're here," calls Prakesh. He's gone a little way ahead, to a low door set into the left side of the corridor. He leads me through, and as I come into the room I see him twisting a panel off the wall. I help out, both of us pulling hard, and it comes off in a screech of metal. The space beyond is dusty and dirty, but I can see light leaking through from further along.

Without a word, Prakesh slips inside. I follow, and soon we're in the Air Lab.

We've come out onto one of the paths between the algae pools. The huge trees lie silhouetted against the lights. I see a couple of technicians in the distance, off to the right, doing something to the base of one of them.

Whatever carnage the fire wreaked in the Food Lab, it looks as if Prakesh really did stop it reaching the Air Lab. The air, after the stale smokiness of the gallery and the corridors, is refreshingly cool. I'm expecting the lab to be packed with techs, but there are only a few, dotted here and there among the trees. There are voices and loud banging coming from one of the smaller buildings on the other side of the lab—the structures I've heard Prakesh calling mobile labs. Must be where they've set up food production.

"Let's look in the control room," says Prakesh. He points to the huge structure jutting out of the wall, visible through the trees. It's where I handed the eyeball to Darnell. "If she isn't there, we can fan out across the lab."

We head towards the control room, jogging between the algae ponds. Their surfaces are smooth, calm, with only the odd tiny shudder floating through them, as if wind had touched the water.

Tracer

After the insanity of the battle with the Lieren and the run through the station, the ponds are calming.

The control room looms above us, staircases and power lines underneath it. The upper part is level with the tree canopies, and holds a massive window. I can just see inside from where we are, and I scan the rooms for any sign of life, but there's nothing: just more computers, blinking softly through the glass.

Prakesh points, indicating a narrow staircase off to one side, which leads to the metal gantry that curves around the structure. "What are you going to do after we've talked to her?" he says.

"I don't know," I reply. "Depends on what she has to say. Maybe she knows what Darnell was trying to get out of Foster."

"It's just…" He shakes his head. "We've come a long way on faith, Riley."

"Don't," I say. My voice, drained and weary, doesn't communicate the anger I feel.

He continues, unfazed. "What happens if she can't help us? What then?"

"I don't know," I say through gritted teeth. It sounds helpless, pathetic. And he's right: if she can't help us, then Yao—and Carver, possibly—died for nothing. Not to mention Amira, who could be anywhere.

We try to minimise the noise we make, but with every step the metal clangs and booms, sounding too loud in the quiet of the Air Lab. We're just at the top of the stairs, stepping onto the bottom part of the gantry, when a voice booms out from far below, somewhere under the trees.

"My offer's still open. Better take it—unless, of course, you want your friend to contribute some flesh in your place."

Zhao.

Prakesh and I crouch quickly, ducking behind the metal barriers on the gantry. And then I see them, through a gap in the metal. Five of them, scratched and bleeding, but very much alive. Zhao standing at the back, his arms folded, death on his face. And lying at his feet, her hands bound behind her, her eyes closed: Amira.

All at once, there's too much saliva in my mouth, like the feeling you get before you vomit. There's no sign of Kev or Carver. Zhao continues, raising his voice, and this time the anger in his voice is palpable. "You think this is a joke? I know you're up there somewhere—you and your scientist friend."

I know you're up there somewhere. We're off to one side, partially hidden by the curve of the control room wall. He's seen us go up, but he doesn't know where we are. I meet Prakesh's eyes, and I can see he's realised it too.

He leans forward, bringing his mouth to my ear. "I'm going to make a dash for the control room. Wait for my signal."

"Signal?" I hiss back, but he's up, running along the catwalk to one of the doors. I hear a shout of triumph from below as Zhao spots him, and I have to force myself not to leap to my feet.

"Hiding in there won't help you," shouts Zhao. "Hey, Riley," he continues, and the laughter in his voice chills me to the bone. "Do you think your friend here will notice when we start? Marco hit her over the head pretty hard, but I'm hoping she's awake enough to know what's happening."

I'm clenching my fists so hard that my hands have gone white. Every cell in my body is screaming at me to help Amira. There's nothing Prakesh can do: what weapons is he planning on finding in the control room? Bags of fertiliser?

49

Prakesh

As it happens, fertiliser is exactly what Prakesh is thinking. More specifically, he's thinking about ammonium nitrate.

He sprints through the door to the Air Lab control room, ignoring the shouts from the Lieren below. He's expecting to find some techs there, but they're all in the mobile labs, and the room is mercifully empty. Oren Darnell's barrels of water squat at the back of the room, their surfaces rippling.

The only internal light comes from the computer screens. Prakesh is still sprinting, and doesn't see the knocked-over chair until his feet are tangled in it. He goes down, bloodying his nose on the floor, fists pounding the metal in frustration even as he gets to his feet.

Blood gushes down his chin, and he can feel his bottom lip swelling too. He ignores it, stumbling to the screens and hunting through them for the right menu.

Prakesh knows how fire works. Every single tech on the station goes through a fire prevention course, where they learn about things like backdraught, and chain reactions, and oxidisers. Even fire which spreads like liquid and bites through chemical foam has to behave, in some ways, like fire. You can starve it of air to put it out, but it'll just lie dormant, smouldering. If you add the right mix of air back into the environment, and come up with a suitable ignition source, then you can restart that fire.

Prakesh begins to pump air from the Air Lab to the Food Lab, sucking it through the vents. He's going to have to control the flow precisely, reversing it and cutting it off at just the right moments. If he screws this up, he'll bathe the Air Lab in fire.

In seconds, the oxygen levels in the Food Lab have risen. Prakesh has already picked an ignition source. The main fuse array in the Food Lab will have been destroyed by the fire, but Prakesh doesn't need it to power anything. He *needs* it to be broken, because he needs the spark. Even a single wire, its insulation burned away, will do it.

He grits his teeth, and activates the fuse array.

Nothing. The power indicators on screen remain stubbornly blank.

Blood drips onto the screen from his damaged nose. He hits the option again, then a third time, willing the fuse array to work.

50

Riley

I risk another peek over the railing, and the sight brings my heart to my mouth.

One of the Lieren, his back to me, is crouching over Amira, dragging a knife delicately over her forehead. She shifts, groans, as the point of the blade touches her skin.

"You've got about ten seconds before we start," says Zhao. "And I should warn you: I never like telling my boys to stop once they get going."

Something tickles my throat. I ignore it, but it comes back, demanding attention.

I look up, and my eyes widen: the entire top half of the hangar is wreathed in grey and white smoke. The air-conditioning vents have been activated, and smoke from the Food Lab fire is pumping in, drifting down onto the Air Lab below.

Prakesh, you genius.

"Have it your way then," says Zhao, but then I hear a puzzled shout from one of the others. The smoke is thicker now; I drop my head to the floor, where the air is still just clean.

I take a deep breath, and hold it.

Zhao's voice drifts up from below: "Where's it coming from? Marco, I thought you said the fire was only in the Food Lab."

"It was!" says Marco, his voice muffled by his smashed nose. "Zhao, I'm telling you, I don't know what this is."

The smoke has reached the floor level, shrouding the Lieren in a white fog. And at that instant, I stand up, anger burning in my veins like a hot, bright filament, and hurl myself off the gantry.

I can't see the ground below me—the smoke has got so thick that the ground has vanished. I pull my legs up, bending my knees and tucking my arms, ready for the roll, hoping that I've done it in time. When I do hit the ground, a second later, my ankles explode with a pain that shoots rapidly up my legs and into the base of my spine.

But I was ready for it, prepared for the impact, and even before I register the pain, I'm rolling forwards. The landing forces me to exhale, and as I spring upwards from the roll, already scanning for the Lieren, I have to suck in another breath. The smoke sinks in, clawing at my throat, but there's just enough clear air left to breathe.

One of the Lieren appears out of the smoke. This time, I don't bother lashing out; I go low, channelling all the energy from the roll into a shoulder-charge which takes him at the knees.

He's a lot bigger than I am, but the rage I'm feeling gives me strength and the hit sends him flying, filling the space above with flailing arms and legs. I catch an expression of total surprise on his face, and then he's gone, hitting the ground so hard that I hear his skull crack.

No time to congratulate myself. Even before I'm up, another Lieren has materialised out of the smoke, waving a knife before him. He slashes out, his eyes wide, but I dodge to the left, grabbing his wrist and yanking it upwards. He screams in pain, a sound cut off a second later when I plant my elbow in his mouth. I feel one of his teeth break through the sleeve of my jacket, but I'm already pushing him aside.

This is different to when I'm running. Then, I'm on autopilot, my body responding to muscle memory, the focus so effortless it's like a second skin. This? This feels like someone just plugged me into the station's fusion reactor and flipped the switch. My muscles are rods of iron, my teeth clenched, my vision razor-sharp, even as the smoke gets thicker. Everything Amira taught me about fighting is right in the front of my mind, like I've opened a book. In the background, somewhere unimportant, lies the dull ache in my lungs, burned raw with smoke.

Two more Lieren fly out of the gloom; I gut-punch one, throwing every atom of energy I can find into it. He goes down, but a split second later a line of fire burns on my shoulder; the other Lieren has cut me, slashing downwards through my jacket. My arm is instantly soaked in hot blood. But the pain just focuses me further, and I swing round, ducking under his next slash, before driving the heel of my hand upwards into his face.

He tries to knock the blow aside, but he's too slow, and his chin cracks under my hit. He falls, his eyes rolling back in his skull. The smoke is almost impenetrable now. What little fresh air I was getting is gone, and the slight pause in the fight causes the ache in my lungs to rocket up into my skull, clanging with pain. I'm bent double by hacking coughs, dimly aware that my right arm is wet and sticky with blood.

As I reach up to touch the wound, Zhao Zheng lunges out of the fog, whirling two more knives in front of him, murder on his face.

I have a moment to wonder where he got the knives, whether he had more on him or took them from the fallen Lieren, before I hurl myself backwards, tucking into a clumsy roll as I feel one of the knives slash so close that the air moves across my forehead. The adrenaline that focused me, that let me take down the Lieren so easily, has drained away, replaced by a leaden exhaustion. I spring out of the roll, my chest on fire and my vision blurred, as Zhao leaps forward again.

You don't survive as a gang leader on Outer Earth without some serious moves. I dodge once, twice, desperately looking for an opening, but Zhao lets nothing through. Another slash tags my forehead, singing with pain. Blood drips into my eyes as I try to circle round him. He jabs to the right, but as I dodge away I realise it was a feint—only a nanosecond of reaction saves me from being skewered in the stomach. He dives forward, leading this time with both blades, sure of his aim.

A black form explodes out of the fog, tackling him round the waist and sending him flying through the air. Zhao and Prakesh crash to the ground, a tangle of limbs. Prakesh rolls away, and then I'm on top of my enemy, my knee in his throat. Zhao's lost one of his blades, but still has the other in a tight grip. He tries to raise it, but I grab his hand and twist.

Zhao yells in fury, dropping the blade. He tries to rise, but I slam my knee back into his throat with every ounce of venom I can put behind it. He gags, fights for breath, tries again to force me off him, but the strength has gone out of him. His arms flail against me, but I barely feel them.

I start punching him. And I don't stop.

My knuckles rip and tear and shred as his face explodes with blood and bruises. I'm yelling something, words maybe, I don't know. Everything is just white; I can't tell where the smoke ends and my vision begins. My hands go numb, and it's only when his face is a jagged mash of blood and broken teeth that Prakesh pulls me off him.

"Riley, that's enough," he says. My first instinct is to rip out of his grasp, to attack Zhao again, but I don't. Horror and elation cascade through me, colliding together.

We stand, our shoulders heaving, and it comes to me that I'm breathing actual air. I look around, startled; the smoke seems to have cleared somewhat, drifting away into the Air Lab. Prakesh must have killed the vents. Zhao lies before us, breathing in wet gasps, his face a ruin.

And then, from the trees: "Is it over?"

Her hands are clutching a blue scarf, which has slipped off her head and lies bunched at her throat. Her face is creased with worry, her shoulders trembling.

Grace Garner.

51

Riley

I have to stop myself from gulping the water in the cup. I take small sips, savouring it.

Amira, Garner and I are in one of the control rooms above the Air Lab. The room is dark, with the only light coming from the screens and control panels on the walls.

The water helps, but there's nothing for my aching knuckles. Prakesh is checking on his trees, making sure the smoke didn't damage the young ones.

I'm seated on a pile of fertiliser bags, my hands throbbing with pain. I've bent them in half-fists, and my knuckles are little more than torn shreds of flesh. The cuts in my arm and forehead aren't deep, but they're still singing with pain. Amira, freed of her bonds, is leaning against one of the control panels, massaging her wrists. An ugly, black bruise is already forming on her cheek.

She's been silent ever since we brought her up here, occasionally rubbing the stumps of her missing fingers. She's lost her scarf somewhere, and the expression on her face is impossible to read.

Beside her, Grace Garner is in the room's lone chair, hunched forwards, hands clasped around another cup of water. Her face has more lines on it than I remember. I want to ask her about Darnell, Gray, Marshall Foster, the Sons of Earth, everything, but something inside tells me to wait.

Several times, Garner opens her mouth, seems about to speak, but then stops, like she too isn't sure of where to start. Eventually, she says, "I thought you'd never come."

I smile, despite myself. "The trains were running late."

She doesn't smile. "I got caught up in the crowds after…" She clears her throat. "After the bombs went off. I didn't even know there'd been one in Gardens until later. It was awful. People screaming, people pushing me."

"How did you get into the Air Lab?"

"It took me a long time to get here, and it got worse. People were trying to break in. To salvage food, I think. There were protection officers here, trying to hold them back. I knew one of them, and asked him to hide me. The look on his face when I first saw him…it was like he didn't recognise me at all." At this, her voice cracks, and silent tears begin to run down her cheeks.

She shakes her head, and seems to be steeling herself to continue. "But he helped me, eventually. Sneaked me through a back way. That man you told me to find, the one who was with you—he wasn't here. There were others, other techs. They chased me, but I got away and I hid. Then the smoke came, and then…"

"You found us," says Amira. Her voice is an impatient croak.

"Grace," I say. "You worked with Marshall Foster. Why did they have him killed?"

Something changes in her eyes—a tiny fragment of old strength that comes creeping back. It's only then that I really notice the high cheekbones, the lips, still full. She was beautiful, once.

"I was his assistant for years," she replies. "I served under him when he was on the council. He was in charge of the Outer Earth digital systems—all the computer codes and sub-routines that keep the station running were maintained by him. Marshall asked me to come with him when he retired, so we settled in Apogee. We were close, closer than you can imagine. And then..."

She stops, her head bowed.

"Gray," I say.

Garner nods. "I was reading in our room. Marshall collected books—he hoarded them while he was on the council. Silly habit of his, but I liked them.

"I wasn't really paying attention, and I didn't even hear Marshall come in until he grabbed my hands. I'd never seen him look so terrified. He didn't say anything, just grabbed me out of my chair. He wouldn't tell me what was happening. He lifted up one of the panels on the floor that we used for storage and told me to get in. It was a tiny space, and I could barely scrunch down in it."

"So you just obeyed him?" asks Amira.

"What was I supposed to do?" says Garner, her voice turning into a wail. "I'd taken orders from him *my whole life*. He was everything to me. And I knew he wanted to keep me safe. I wanted to know what was going on, but he still wouldn't tell me. I'd never seen him like that. And still, he...he wouldn't tell me why."

"What did he say?" I ask.

"He said he was sorry. He said that no matter what happened, he...he loved me, and he was sorry for everything he'd done, but I had to hide for as long as possible. I told him I didn't know what he was talking about, that he didn't have anything to be sorry for, but then he said he needed to tell me something else, that there wasn't much time."

The tears are streaming down her cheeks. Her hands are limp

in her lap. I can't even imagine what she's been through, hiding in the trees, waiting for someone who might never show up. Knowing that the entire world was collapsing around her, and that the man she trusted was dead.

After a few moments, I rise off the fertiliser sacks and walk over, crouching in front of her. Her face is red and blotchy, streaked with the shiny tracks of tears. "I know this is hard for you," I say, "but we're running out of time. There are people who want to destroy Outer Earth, and whatever Marshall Foster told you might be able to stop them."

I don't know if this is true or not. But I have to try.

"He told me to find a tracer named Riley Hale in Apogee," she says.

"Why me?"

"I don't know. He told me I had to give you a piece of information…but it didn't make any sense. I don't know what it means. I tried to get him to tell me, but he said…he said there wasn't any time. The last thing he said to me was that you'd know what to do with it when the time came."

I raise my face to hers, and she says, "He told me to give you a word. Iapetus. That's all."

She must see the look of confusion on my face, because she says, "It's one of Saturn's moons. But I never got a chance to ask what the word meant, or what it was used for." She shrugs helplessly. "He told me that, and then he was gone. I never saw him again." More tears come.

Iapetus.

I rack my brain for any mention of the word before. Nothing comes. Why would Foster say that I'd know what to do with it? I never knew him, I've never heard the word before, and even if I had, I have no clue how it helps us defeat Darnell.

But before any conclusions can form, there's a bang. The sound is enormous, replaced instantly by a ringing in my ears. The chair Garner is in pitches backwards. Her chest flares with blood, staining her blue scarf black.

She seems to fall in slow motion, her arms thrown out to the sides, like she's trying to break her fall. For one horrible moment,

I see the surprise on her face, the life already beginning to fade from her eyes. She hits the ground, and then there's just silence. Nothing but the ringing in my ears.

I turn, and see Amira. She's holding a stinger out in front of her. And as I watch, she swings the gun around until it points directly at my chest.

52

Prakesh

The other techs must have cleared out when the smoke came down. Prakesh is alone on the floor of the Air Lab, and he can't remember the last time the place was so silent. The only sound is the distant hum of the ventilation system, sucking the last of the smoke away from the labs. Most of it's gone already, and the few wisps that remain are hanging around at canopy level.

In truth, the smoke was never really going to hurt the trees, or the algae. That was just something Prakesh told Riley to give him a chance to get away. He needed time to think.

He heads for the mobile lab, making a detour around the bloodied patch where Riley beat the crap out of Zhao. He keeps glancing up at the main window of the control room, but it's reflecting some of the light at him, turning it into a shining white beacon which reveals nothing.

He has to think of a way to stay with her.

Prakesh is well aware that he's done what he said he would. He got Riley and Amira into the Air Lab. They've found Garner. Prakesh doesn't know what she'll tell them, or what they'll do next, but he knows that there'll be no good reason for him to stay with them. Riley will tell him to lie low, to stay in the Air Lab, to let her and Amira take care of…whatever the hell they need to take care of.

Riley can handle herself. Prakesh knows that. But it doesn't stop him wanting to stay with her. If he's with her, he can…

He groans in frustration, resting his hands on the edge of an algae tank. His fingertips just touch the water, sending out a ripple which distorts his reflection.

She doesn't want you, he thinks. *Not in the way you want her.*

He pushes off, striding towards the mobile lab. He'll check on the trees anyway. Get some equipment, test soil pH levels, check the temperature of the algae ponds, do something to get his mind off it.

It takes him a few minutes to make his way to the mobile lab. Most of the equipment was in the stores, destroyed in the fire, but there are still a few units scattered across the shelves here. Prakesh looks at them without seeing. Eventually, he grabs a pH monitor, more or less automatically, and turns to leave. Maybe he's overthinking this. Maybe he can…

There's a noise, right at the edge of his hearing, almost inaudible. An echoing bang.

He pauses for a moment, confused, and it takes him a second to identify the sound. Stinger fire. A single shot. He listens hard, but the sound doesn't repeat itself. At first, he thinks it's coming from somewhere in the Air Lab, but it was barely there to begin with, and the echoes smudge the sound. He can't place the source.

Prakesh turns around, meaning to investigate.

And finds another stinger barrel less than an inch from his face.

The barrel is a giant black hole, sucking in light. Prakesh becomes exquisitely aware of every movement, of every twitch in his fingers and every breath he takes. He makes himself focus, makes himself look past the barrel and see the person behind it.

It's a stomper. The underarms of his grey uniform are soaked with sweat, and his dark skin and shorn head gleam with it. Prakesh has seen him before, although it takes him a moment to remember where. He was one of the stompers who busted into Arthur Gray's room by the monorail tracks.

"Show me ID," the stomper says.

Prakesh tries to breathe. "I'm a tech. OK? I work in the Air Lab."

"Show me ID," the stomper says again.

"Seriously, don't shoot me, my name is Prakesh Kumar. I was there when Arthur—"

"*Show me ID, now.*" The stomper's grip on the stinger makes it pretty clear that he won't ask again, and he doesn't show the slightest hint of recognition when he hears Prakesh's name.

Prakesh's hand moves to where the pocket of his lab coat would be if he were still wearing one, then stops. "I lost it."

He doesn't have time to berate himself for how stupid that sounds, because he sees the stomper's trigger finger move ever so slightly. "Wrong answer," the stomper says. "I've got techs evacuating, talking about more smoke, and now I find you. Move."

Prakesh starts to walk, painfully aware of the stinger. He doesn't know what to do with his hands.

There's another bang, distant and echoing. Both Prakesh and the stomper are facing the control room when it comes, and it's impossible to miss the flash, the tiny white-yellow burst of stinger fire, from the control room windows.

"Riley," Prakesh breathes.

And before the stomper can stop him, he's running.

53

Riley

Time stops.

Amira has the stinger clasped in both hands, her finger inside the trigger guard. A tiny wisp of smoke is curling from the barrel, catching light from a nearby screen. For one weird instant, I wonder how she managed to keep the gun on her when she was captured by Zhao.

Above it, her eyes are cold. She has the same expression she had back at the brig, when she broke me out. Sorrow and anger, fighting for control.

I slowly find the words, my voice shaking. "Amira, what are you doing?"

"Don't," she says.

Her voice cracks a little. Does she have to reload? Can she fire again straightaway? Impossible to tell.

My eyes fall on Garner's body. Her legs have tilted to the side as her chair toppled over, and she lies sprawled across the floor. As I watch, her hand, splayed out above her head, twitches ever so slightly. "She's still alive." I look at Amira, trying to hide the desperation in my voice. "We have to help her."

"I said, don't."

She takes a step forward, the gun still pointed right at my chest. "Turn around."

I do as she says, trembling. I'm running over the last few hours in my mind, trying to find out why she's doing this. I see her breaking me out of the brig. Back in the Caves, trying to get us to go to find Garner without the rest of the crew. Telling the Dancers to split up when we were attacked by Zhao. And now, her and me, alone with Garner.

"It wasn't real, was it?" I mutter, and I'm surprised to hear a tiny core of steel in my own voice. "None of it. You planned it all."

The gun lightly touches the back of my head.

"I'm sorry, Riley," she says. "I wish it didn't have to happen this way, but it does."

My gaze is drawn back to Garner, and this time the hand is still. Something inside me says to keep her talking. *Buy time. Prakesh might come back.*

"Tell me why. You owe me that much," I say.

"You're the only one Garner would have spoken to. You were the one who had to find her. But once we'd got the information, that word, whatever it is, there was no reason for her to live. And no reason for you to, either."

The realisation settles over me, heavy, like a thick blanket. "You're one of Darnell's sleepers. One of the Sons of Earth."

"Yes." She says it in a whisper.

Call it instinct. Call it whatever the hell you want, but I know that she's about to squeeze the trigger. Right now. Right this second.

I whip my head to the side. She fires. The bullet is so close that I feel it whip-crack past my ear. She screams in fury, swinging the gun around. But my instinct is still in control. I'm just along for the ride.

I snap my left arm upwards, grabbing her wrist and twisting. She snarls, but doesn't let go of the gun, leaning into the move. I can feel her shifting stance, trying to pull me off balance. Her free hand swings round, and claps me on the ear, which explodes in ringing pain. I'm immediately nauseous, and she tries to throw me off, but somehow I hold on.

It can't be her. This twisting, slashing thing on top of me can't be Amira. It's someone else, something else, some*thing* that's taken over her body. This can't be the same person who saved me, all those years ago.

But a part of me—the instinct, the part that kept me alive when Amira pulled the trigger—knows different.

Amira is the best fighter I've ever seen, anywhere. The only hope in hell I have of beating her is to get to that gun.

And then I remember something else.

She was also one of the best teachers.

We fall to the floor. She gets on top of me, her nails scratching across my forehead, reopening the cut I got from the Lieren. She jerks against my grip on her wrist, trying to bring the gun round, trying to push it into my face.

I reach up and pull, swinging the gun past my face and to the side. My breath catches in my throat—Amira is so quick that she might just have pulled the trigger right then—but she doesn't, and then the gun is on my right, and she's off balance.

I swing it back the other way in one sudden movement. The stinger flicks out of her grip, skittering across the floor. She howls in frustration, torn between fighting me and going for it. I seize the opportunity, hitting her sideways across the cheek. She tumbles off me, and I scramble for the gun, hunting for it in the half-light.

My fingers close on the barrel just as Amira lunges forward and drops a knee into my back. The agony flares upwards along my spine. I smash into the ground, and it takes every ounce of control

I have not to let go of the gun. My fist is closed so tight around it that I can feel every tendon in my hand.

I buck my body upwards. Amira crashes off me, coming to rest on her knees. With a gasping cry, I swing the gun round, the metal slipping under my fingers, fumbling with the trigger guard.

I'm lying on my side, the gun in both hands, pointed right at her. The only sound is our breathing, heavy and ragged.

She slowly raises her hands. "You don't understand, Riley. What we're doing? All of this? It's for the greater good. Humanity nearly destroyed the planet. If we continue to exist, then we'll return, and we'll do it again. The only way to make sure the Earth survives is for us not to."

My thumb touches the stinger's safety catch—it's off, and I keep it that way. But there's no way of telling how many bullets are still inside. My body is humming with adrenaline and pain, and the gun shakes in my grip.

"You don't believe that. You can't."

Unbelievably, she smiles. "You forget," she whispers. "I saved Outer Earth. I saved it. I ran the Core."

My eyes flick to her hand, her missing fingers.

"I believed in it back then," she continues. "Believed it was worth fighting for. But nothing changed. We still kill and rape and steal and destroy. We don't deserve to live. We never did. And without us, the Earth can recover."

"Shut up!" I scream. Tears prick the sides of my eyes. This can't be happening. It's as if the insane Darnell is there, speaking through Amira, using her like a puppet. "What about the Dancers? What about us? Do we deserve to die?"

Regret floods her face. "I knew none of you would understand. I wanted to make you see, but I didn't know how. You would have stopped me. You would have stopped us. I always knew I'd have to choose between the Dancers and doing the right thing. I just made my choice. That's all."

The betrayal gives way to anger, bright and hot. "The bombing, the fire, the heat convectors…is that what you want? For everyone to suffer?"

There's a flicker of doubt. Just for a moment. "No. I just did what Janice Okwembu asked me to. I had to find you, bring you to Garner, and get the code."

"But Darnell has Okwembu. He said he's going to kill her."

Now she laughs, getting to her feet. "I work for her. So does Darnell—he's just the face. She came to me two years ago and asked me to join them."

"That's impossible. Back up!"

Amira has taken a few steps towards me, and stops, her hands raised. "How do you think that idiot Darnell got into Apex?"

Iapetus. "The word Garner gave me. What's it for? What does it do?"

"If you think you can get something out of me, then I'm sorry to disappoint you. I don't know what it's for. It's something Okwembu needs, that's all."

"Some kind of destruct code, is that it? She going to blow up the station?"

"Maybe."

The ringing in my ears has gone, replaced by a dull roar. I don't know whether it's the blood rushing through my veins, or something else entirely.

"I don't know what made you think this way," I say, "but they've brainwashed you. Even if we don't deserve to live on Earth, we deserve a chance. The people here aren't monsters. They didn't kill the planet. Amira, these are *innocent people.*"

"They aren't innocent. No one here is. Everyone deserves what's coming."

I cut her off. "What about me?"

She falls silent. I keep talking: "You saved me once, Amira. If you believed we all deserved to suffer, you would have left me with the men in that corridor. But you didn't, did you? And after all we've been through, all we've done together, you want to throw it away?"

Prakesh has been gone too long. He should have come back by now. But even as the thought occurs, I realise a part of me wants him to stay away. I don't want anyone to see this. Any of it.

Right then, I see that Amira has shifted ever so subtly, rocking back on her heels.

To anybody else, it would be something almost imperceptible. But I've been running with Amira for long enough, and in one horrible moment I understand what she's about to do.

"No," I whisper. With a cry of triumph, she launches herself towards me.

I pull the trigger.

54

Riley

The sound of the gunshot fills the room. The whole world.

The bullet takes Amira in the stomach. She makes the oddest sound—a kind of *phuh*. Her grace and agility vanishes, sucked out of her, her body becoming a flying rag-doll, crashing to the ground. The fabric of her tank top is soaked with blood.

As she rolls to a stop at my feet, she begins screaming. She clutches her ruined stomach, sweat beading her forehead.

I drop to my knees, pressing down on her stomach, causing her to howl in pain again. I've gut-shot her. I didn't even aim. My hands are drenched in seconds, slick and hot with her blood.

"I have to stop the bleeding," I say. "We can get you to a hospital. I think there's one near here. If we just..."

She reaches up and grips my hand. For an absurd moment, I think she's going to continue attacking me, but she doesn't. The pain is written on her face, rippling under the surface, but it's been shrouded by a kind of calm.

"You don't have to do that," she says. A tiny sliver of blood trickles from the corner of her mouth.

After a moment, she says, "I was told to kill you first, then Garner. Not to wait, not to talk, just to do it. But I couldn't. I couldn't."

"Amira..."

Her voice, husky now, coming in bubbling gasps. "You mustn't stop Okwembu. This has to happen. It needs to happen."

The anger is back, all at once, like a light turning on. Blinding, white-hot fury erupts and I slam my fist on the ground next to her head. She barely flinches.

"Why do you keep saying that?" I scream. "There are *people* on this station. People with lives, with families. Who the hell are you to say that they should die?"

She doesn't reply. I'm crying openly now, the tears dropping off my cheeks onto Amira's chest.

I should let her die. In pain.

The thought shocks me, but I can't shake it. She lied to me, to the Dancers. She betrayed us in the worst way possible. She deserves this.

"Everything you taught me," I say. "Was it all a lie too? Was everything leading up to...to this?"

Something changes in her expression. Like a barrier falling away.

"No," she whispers. "When I saved you...that wasn't a lie. And you became everything I hoped you would be."

Blood pools around her. I reach for her hand again, grip it tight. She gasps in pain, a noise which becomes an awful moan. My hatred cracks, then shatters.

Amira closes her eyes. Her face is a pale, ghostly white, and it seems like all her will leaves her at once. "You need to get to Apex."

"I can get there from here. Maybe the code will let me in somehow."

"No," she says. The air whistles out with her voice, obscuring her words. "That's not what the code does, I'm sure of it. You can't get in from the adjoining sectors. It's more secure than here. It has to be. Even if you could somehow find a way to get the doors down, you're running out of time."

She opens her eyes again, and looks at me. For a moment, I'm back in that corridor, seeing her hold out her hand to me, her eyes burning with life, as if daring me to accept. The same fire is in her eyes now, her hand gripping onto mine.

"Riley," she says. "You have to run the Core. It's the only way you'll get there. You have to."

"I can't do it."

"You have to," she says again, the pain adding an edge to her words. "Run fast. Get ready for the gravity change. Don't stop. Whatever you do, don't stop running."

"Amira…"

But what else is there to say? I feel as if I'm in zero gravity already, tumbling out of control.

"There's only one other thing I need to ask you," she says. "You need to finish it."

I shake my head, stunned. "I'm not. I can't."

"You're better with a gun than I thought you'd be. And I've seen people shot in the stomach before. The pain is bad now, but it'll get worse. A lot worse."

Her voice cracks on the last words. Amira—my beautiful, strong Amira—is begging.

I've picked up the gun without realising it. Slowly, I move it to her forehead. I touch it to her skin as delicately as she touched it to mine.

"I'm sorry," she says.

I pull the trigger for the second time.

55

Riley

I've met death in the past. My father, blown to pieces thousands of miles from home. My mother, wasting away to nothing. Gray and Darnell, and the lives they took. Yao. Grace Garner. But I've never felt anything like this. It's as if something has reached into my gut and just torn it away. It's worse than the hottest anger, worse than anything I've ever felt, and as I stare at Amira, see her eyes, glazed over, robbed of their power, I know, deep down, that the feeling will be with me forever. I'll feel it when I awake in the dark, and everyone around me sleeps. I'll feel it when I'm hurt, or when I sense someone standing behind me, ready to strike. I'll feel it in my bones and my flesh and my heart. The tears come. And this time the trickle becomes a river, then a flood.

I'm still there, bending over her body, when Prakesh arrives. He stops in the doorway, his eyes wide. Someone else is with him. A stomper. Royo.

Royo has his stinger up, sweeping from left to right. Prakesh wraps his arms around me, pulling me away. My sobs turn to screams, racked with the worst pain I've ever felt, and I bury my head in his chest. He says nothing. Just holds me close.

"So," says Royo at length. His stinger isn't quite pointed at us, but it's held ready. "I have two dead bodies, and no answers. If I don't get the second, there's going to be a few more of the first."

"What happened, Ry?" asks Prakesh.

Slowly, between sobs, I tell them. About Amira and Garner. And Okwembu.

When I'm finished, Royo looks at me. "Why should I believe you?"

"What?"

"How do I know you didn't just kill them both?"

"You think this is an act?" I scream at him. But Prakesh raises a hand. His voice is calm.

"She's telling the truth. I know she is."

It can't be enough. Surely not. But Royo is silent. He seems to be weighing his words carefully.

"My gut's kept me alive on this wreck of a station my whole life," he says. "It's telling me to trust you, so I will, but that trust can be rescinded if or when you do anything to make me doubt you. If you're telling the truth, then we need to go. I don't know how long we've got until that monster in Apex does whatever he's going to do, but it's not long."

"He's right, Ry," Prakesh whispers to me. He's still holding me tight. "We've got less than twenty hours left. The station's getting worse—the heat's starting to build up already. And there's nothing more we can do here."

I feel dizzy. My nose is clogged, my eyes wet. But I nod, silently, and he releases me. Behind us, Amira's body lies sprawled across the floor.

A thought occurs to me. "Garner. Is she..."

Royo clears his throat. "She's gone. I'm sorry."

Prakesh says, "Maybe I'm misreading things here, but if Okwembu is behind all this, maybe there's a way we can let people know. Maybe we can stop her without having to go anywhere near Apex."

"Not a chance," replies Royo. "I'm not saying I believe that woman"—he indicates Amira—"but if the head of the council is responsible, we can't get anywhere near her. I've seen the security in Apex. After those riots all those years ago, they weren't taking any chances. You can lock the entire place down. So even if we did somehow get the word out that she's doing it, there's not a lot we could do about it."

I force myself to concentrate. "If we can get to Apex, maybe we can figure out how to use the code Garner gave me. It's the only way to stop this. I'm sure of it."

Prakesh frowns. "You don't think that maybe it's a way for Okwembu and Darnell to finally destroy the station? Something they needed for their endgame? If it is, then why don't we just drop off the radar? Hide out somewhere?"

"No," I say. "She wouldn't have started all this unless she could finish it. Not Okwembu. Iapetus isn't her way to destroy Outer Earth. It's the only way to stop it from happening. This was all about making sure there's nothing to stand in their way."

"Was Amira really serious about going through the Core? There has to be another way round."

Royo laughs, a sound with no humour in it. "Even if we wanted to, there's no way. Chengshi is tearing itself apart right now. Along with Apogee, Tzevya and every other damn sector on this station. It's going to pieces out there."

My eyes stray to Amira's hand. The missing fingers, stolen by frostbite all those years ago.

A thought occurs to me. "How did you get here?" I ask Royo.

"They assigned me to guard the Air Lab entrance. We got an

alert from a smoke alarm. I came to check it out." He gestures to Prakesh. "Met your buddy when I came in."

Silence falls over us. I think of the sun. Of wanting to feel its warmth on the back of my neck. I think of what it feels like to run, to lose myself in speed and the air rushing past my face. I think of the Devil Dancers: Carver, Kev, Yao. I think of the Nest. It seems like a million years ago.

I think of my father, of how he died. Fighting. So that the human race could keep going.

And then, finally, I think of Amira. How, at the very end, she once again told me what I had to do.

I turn to Royo. "How do we get to the Core entrance?"

"The monorail. Maybe there's a train near here. We could use it to bypass the worst of the rioting and get back to Apogee."

"You can drive a train?" I ask, incredulous.

"No," replies Royo. "But I'd say now would be a great time to learn, wouldn't you?"

56

Darnell

Darnell slams Okwembu up against the control room screens, their faces inches apart.

"You call that subtle?" he screams at her, his words made metallic by the narrow room. "Now it's even worse. Now she's got a stomper escort."

"It doesn't mean anything," Okwembu says. Darnell's hands move to her throat, but she gets her fingers up just before he grips her neck.

"Oh really?" he says, tightening his hold. "You heard them. They know what's behind that retinal scanner. The whole point was that no one but us and our sleepers would ever know. Now *she* knows, *she's* still alive, and *she's on her way over here."*

He lifts Okwembu up, so her feet are off the ground, then slams her back against the screens. One of them cracks, spitting sparks. A shard of glass scratches a thin line across Okwembu's forehead. Darnell squeezes, his thumbs hunting for her windpipe. Okwembu has her hands up, two fingers the only thing between her and strangulation.

She raises her eyes to meet his, and pulls her fingers away. "So kill me," she says, her voice thin and hoarse.

Her eyes refuse to leave his, and Darnell's fingers pause, just touching the skin above the scooped hollow of her collarbone.

"Go ahead," she says, her voice brimming with venom. "You can do it all yourself. Isn't that right? Set up the comms feed, run the camera, even figure out everything the control room can do. You don't need me. I'm not useful any more, am I?"

In the silence that follows, Darnell can hear his heartbeat, feel the blood pumping in his ears.

There's a tiny ping, an alert from one of the screens. It's a long moment before Darnell glances down at it. He drops Okwembu, and she crumples to the floor, coughing, holding her throat. Darnell kills the pinging, his fingers leaving dark smudges on the surface of the screen.

"Someone's coming in through the Core," he says. "They're opening the Apex-side doors."

Okwembu looks up at him, her face expressionless. After a moment, she rises, and begins swiping through camera feeds, hunting for the Core access in the upper level of Apex.

"It's not Hale," Darnell says. "It's too soon."

"True. Although I'm surprised it's taken the protection officers this long to get here."

The camera viewpoint appears, just in time to catch the vast doors opening. There's no sound, but they can see people slipping through the gap in the ceiling, dropping to the floor. Stompers, dressed in bulky thermal suits, their movements slow and uncoordinated.

Darnell glances at Okwembu, his eyes narrowed. "You told me those doors were sealed."

"Do you think they'd just give up and go home?" Okwembu taps the screen, pointing to the doors, where a wisp of smoke is curling away. "They blew the lock."

Three stompers are already through the gap, starting to strip off their thermal suits. Three more are clambering through, hanging off the open doors and dropping down.

"Thought they'd send more," Darnell says.

"It's a classic stomper tactic. Sacrificing numbers for speed." Okwembu's voice has been torn to shreds by Darnell's grip, but there's no mistaking the worry in her voice.

Darnell reaches behind his back for his knife. He pulls it out, running a finger across the edge. A wave of dizziness overcomes him, and his gut rolls with a burst of nausea, but it's gone almost as soon as it starts.

"I'll deal with them," he says.

Okwembu doesn't look at him. "No."

He bristles. "You think I can't handle a few stompers?"

"They have stingers. You don't. I'll wait until you get close, then kill the lights. You should have some element of surprise."

She turns, looking Oren Darnell dead in the eye. "You need me. You don't want to admit it, but you do."

Oren Darnell leaves the control room, rolling his thumb across the point of the blade.

57

Darnell

It's just like before, Darnell thinks. *They're going to take everything away from me.*

He's barely aware of what he's doing. He's walking through the top level of Apex, heading for the Core entrance, but his body is moving on autopilot. His mind is somewhere else, twenty years and two sectors away, and this time the memory is so vivid, so overpowering, that he can't fight it off. He sinks into it completely.

At first, it was just him and Mosely outside the hab, but then the corridor filled with dozens of people. He kept telling them that he had to go to school, that he was going to be late, but they didn't listen. They all kept stealing horrified glances into the hab.

The thing that used to be Darnell's mother had melted into the cot. Plants covered her, their tendrils and roots and leaves colonising the spaces between her bones. A glistening, yellow ring of fat surrounded the corpse.

Darnell didn't understand the shocked faces, the horrified looks. She'd been useless before, and now she was helping his plants grow. Didn't they see what he'd made?

The protection officers huddled a short distance away, exchanging angry words, their hands over their mouths and noses. He tried to talk to them, but they ignored him. That was when he first heard the words "Controlled burn."

Darnell went crazy. He fought, pleaded, begged. But he was still a child, a long way away from the size he would attain later. When the chemicals arrived, he tried to knock them over, but the white-clad operator pushed him away. Darnell can see the look on his face, even now. The stupid, bovine hatred.

The corridor was narrow, unable to contain too many people. But in Darnell's memory, there were dozens, *hundreds* of people there. A tiny flicker of hope sparked inside Darnell. They would help him. They wouldn't let his plants burn.

But no matter how much he pleaded, they wouldn't do anything. *They just watched.*

And when the fire started, they were cheering. More than that: they were *laughing*. Cackling as his plants burned. In his mind, he can still hear some of them jeering at him.

With an effort, Darnell pulls himself out of the memory. He makes himself focus by rolling his thumb down on the point of his knife. A tiny drop of blood wells up, and the dart of pain helps focus him. He comes back just in time to hear a noise from up ahead.

The corridor he's in ends in a T-junction, and as he looks up he sees a stomper peek round the side. The stomper catches sight of him, sucks in an excited breath, and vanishes.

A second later, the corridor is filled with shouting and the sound of running feet. Six voices shout at him to drop the knife, six stingers aim right at his chest. The six become four when two of the stompers turn, covering the corridor behind them.

Darnell stops, lowering the knife. His eyes flick up to the ceiling where, just behind one of the long recessed light bars, he can make out the eye of a camera. He looks back to the stompers, memorising their positions, fixing them in his mind. It's hard—his memories want to fight him, fuzzing his thoughts—but he manages it.

The lights click off, plunging the corridor into darkness.

Darnell reaches out, grabs the nearest stomper's wrists, and twists. He hears the bone break cleanly, followed an instant later by a scream of pain and the sound of a stinger clattering to the floor.

The other stompers open fire. A bullet grazes Darnell's shoulder, digging a furrow in his flesh. He barely feels it. He's already moving, staying low, using the flashes from the stinger fire to pick his targets.

The stompers' training takes over, and they react just like Darnell hoped they would: feet planted, not moving, aiming with two hands. They're static, slow, and Darnell is a whirlwind, smashing and crushing and slicing. His body is soaked with blood, both his and the stompers.' Somewhere very distant, his shoulder is on fire, and it's joined by a screaming pain from the side of his head as a bullet rips off the top of his left ear.

The lights come back on.

Three stompers are dead, their bodies ragged with stab wounds. Two more are down: one is unconscious, the other cradling her broken arm, moaning in pain. Only the final stomper is still standing. He points his stinger at Darnell, his hands shaking, and pulls the trigger.

Click.

The stomper tries again, and again, shaking his head furiously. Darnell towers over him. He reaches down, and plucks the useless stinger out of the man's hands. In that instant, the look in the stomper's eyes is exactly the same one Mosely had, all those years ago.

Darnell smiles.

58

Riley

There's no choice but to leave Amira and Grace Garner behind. We can't carry them, not with time against us, but I promise myself that I'll come back for them. *If I come back at all.*

I follow Prakesh as we leave the control room from the back. Deeper inside the complex, the corridors are wider, designed to let heavy equipment pass through. I've never been this way, and I'm surprised to see just how clean it is, with soft lighting and spotless floors. At one point, we cross through another hangar, smaller than the Food Lab but still enormous, criss-crossed with conveyor belts and littered with processing equipment. There's nobody around, and the black conveyors lie silent.

"Monorail's this way," says Prakesh. He's sure-footed, taking the stairs two at a time. More than that: he seems upbeat, confident even. I want to scream at him. Instead, I force myself to match his pace, pushing away the anger, trying to focus on the movement. Stride, land, cushion, spring, repeat. Behind us, Royo puffs as he tries to keep up. He's fit, but heavy with muscle, and his bulky frame—made heavier with his combat armour and equipment—isn't built for speed. He keeps snagging his gear, muttering under his breath.

What Amira did is like a splinter, lodged deep in my mind. We were hers. Her crew. Her Dancers. She was the calm, controlled centre of everything we did. We would have died for her. Yao did die for her. It wasn't just that it was unquestioned loyalty; it was loyalty that never needed to be questioned.

But it meant nothing. She betrayed us. And worse, she betrayed us over something so stupid, so pointless. She must have felt like that for years, locking the thought away in some deep, dark part of her being, nurturing it. And then one day, Janice Okwembu found her, and pulled that poisonous little thought into the light.

In the end, the Devil Dancers were just in the way.

But I can't let what she did be the end. I won't. Okwembu and Darnell betrayed the station, and Amira betrayed her crew, but it doesn't matter. Because I'm not just loyal to the people who are supposed to lead me. I'm loyal to things no one can ever change or touch or hurt. Like the memory of my dad. Like the hope that one day I might run in the sunlight.

I won't let what Amira did stop me.

My stomach growls as we walk through the processing hangar, but I ignore it. I'm hungry, and thirsty, and more exhausted than I've ever been in my life, but I can't focus on that now.

The hangar leads to a loading dock, brightly lit, and two huge rolling doors which lead onto the monorail tracks. I'm worried that there won't be a train there, that we'll have to walk the tunnels, but there's one sitting by the platform, ready to receive cargo. Most of the cars are flatbeds, lined with heavy-duty locking mechanisms designed to hold large containers. Several of these are stacked along one wall of the loading dock: huge, misshapen things, tall as two men, made of bent metal. Above the main doors, two large screens display destinations and shipment details in that orange text.

The heat hits us as soon as we walk out onto the dock. The air is muggy, cloying and thick with warmth, and beads of condensation run down the walls. At this rate, it won't be long before people start dying from heatstroke. Any longer than that, and we really will be roasted alive.

"Where's the driver's seat?" I ask Prakesh. He points to a few cars up. It's little more than a raised platform, a small space with waist-high railings and a bank of controls. Beyond it, the darkness of the tunnel. Royo climbs up, and Prakesh and I follow, jumping in behind him.

He thumbs a switch on the far left of the panel. Nothing happens.

Royo stands, brow furrowed, staring at the controls. After a full minute, Prakesh leans forward. "Ah, Royo, maybe you should try some of the other buttons?"

Royo turns slowly and stares at him. Prakesh raises his hands in apology. "OK, then. Sorry," he mutters, then glances at me as if to say, *what's with this guy*?

Eventually, Royo stabs a few more buttons, and the engine below us hums to life. The rest of the control panel lights up, clicking gently. Royo exhales, turning to us to say something, but as he does so we hear the crackle of the comms system. We all spin round at once, to see a large screen above the loading doors—unnoticed until now—briefly flash up the Outer Earth logo. This time, there's no trickle of fear down my spine. Just cold intent. Whatever Darnell's doing, I know we can stop it.

He's no longer in the council chamber. Instead, he's somewhere in Apex, and the feed is almost too glitchy to make out. His words mutate, twisting themselves into new and hideous sounds, and his face is a mess of damaged pixels. Blood soaks the top half of his body.

"It's time to talk about those sleepers," he says. "Actually, it's time to talk about one in particular."

I know what he's going to say. I squeeze Prakesh's hand tight.

"She's a tracer, and she's been planting bombs all around the station. Her name is Riley Hale. Kill her and bring her body to the gallery in Apogee, where we can see it, and you get to live. Everyone else gets to die."

He leers. "In fact, you don't have to kill her right away. If you bring her to the gallery and set her on fire"—he lingers on the words, tasting each one—"then we'll make sure that some food gets left somewhere for you.

"Until then, I'd like to show you what happens to people who think they can stop us."

The camera pulls back. He's in front of an escape pod access point. Inside the pod, hammering on the doors, are three stompers. The pod isn't big enough for all of them; I can see their bodies squashed up against one another.

Without another word, Darnell launches the pod.

59

Riley

The feed ends.

I can feel Prakesh and Royo staring at me. Below us, the train idles. Darnell kills the feed.

I turn to them. "Well, it wouldn't be much fun if it wasn't a challenge, right?" I say, but their faces are grave.

Without a word, Royo pushes a large lever forwards, and the monorail begins to slide slowly out of the station. For a moment, we're swallowed by the blackness of the tunnel, but then the massive lamp on the front of the train flickers to life, bathing the track ahead in a soft, yellow light. Royo pushes the lever forwards a little more, and we begin to pick up speed, the struts on the side of the tunnel starting to pass more quickly.

Not quick enough.

"How far to Apogee?" I say. I have to raise my voice to be heard over the train.

He shrugs, his eyes on the tunnel ahead. "Twenty minutes, maybe? Half an hour?"

"Can we go any faster?"

"We're at full acceleration already," he says.

I look over my shoulder. Behind the cabin, the empty pallet cars rumble and shudder over the track, bumping together. I turn back to Royo: "What if we got rid of the other cars? Would that make a difference?"

"Good thinking," says Prakesh, and before Royo can say anything, he hops down onto the back of the car and begins to walk his way to the end. Kneeling down, he begins pulling at the coupling. After a few seconds, he looks back to us, yells something, but in the noise of the tunnel I can't make it out.

"What?" I shout, barely able to hear myself. He jabs his finger downwards.

Realisation dawns. "Is there a control for the coupling?" I yell to Royo.

"I don't know," he says, looking around the console. "But if every car unhooks at once, this entire damn train could derail. We have to make sure that we only unhook *our* car."

Visions of tumbling train cars bearing down on our little cockpit fill my head. I glance around the console, appalled by the number of buttons and levers and switches. How many controls do you need to make a train go forwards and backwards? It's not as if this thing's going out to catch asteroids.

"Got it," says Royo, and his hand flies out, turning a raised switch one click to the right. Behind us, I hear a loud clunk over the roar of the train. The car gives a huge lurch forwards as it disconnects from the others, and as I turn I hear a cry of surprise. It's Prakesh; the car disconnecting has hurled him backwards, and his feet are hanging off the edge, his fingers frantically scrambling for purchase.

I throw myself at the back of the car, reaching down to grab his arm. He grips my wrist tight, and with strength I didn't know I had, I haul him over the side.

We lie on our backs, breathing hard. And then, to my surprise, Prakesh begins to laugh.

I stare at him like he's gone mad, but soon I'm laughing too, falling into full-blown hysterics, the sound flowing out of us like water.

"What the hell are you two doing?" yells our driver. I tilt my head, expecting to find him furious, but instead his expression is one of bemusement.

"Wow," says Prakesh, sitting up. "I think I've lost count of the number of times we've saved each other."

"Maybe you should stop getting into trouble then."

"Speak for yourself."

I shake my head. "How did none of us realise that was going to happen?"

"Oh, I knew it was coming."

"So you didn't need my help at all, then? You had it all under control?"

He nods. "Of course I did. I just thought that after running through the entire station, suffocating on smoke and then fighting off every Lieren on Outer Earth, I'd cap the day off by falling under a train."

We sit against the control platform. My feet are pulled up to my chest, my arms wrapped around my knees. Prakesh has his feet stretched out, his arms by his sides. The noise of the train has lessened somewhat; we're passing through what looks like a siding, and I can see the dark shapes of other trains to either side of our track. Prakesh finds my hand, his fingers closing over mine. This time, I don't freeze. I don't pull away.

All at once, I realise just how much is riding on me running the Core. If I can't get through it, if I'm not fast enough, then everyone on this station will die. It's all on me. And I've been wrapped up in this since the beginning. If I hadn't discovered Marshall Foster's eye in my pack, then I'd just be part of a panicked crowd somewhere, fighting for food. Like it or not, I'm in the middle of this.

The train dips into a narrower tunnel, and around us the rumble grows until it shakes my insides. We can't be more than a few minutes from the main station in Apogee.

I turn to Prakesh, trying to keep my voice steady. "If I can get to the main control room in Apex, I'll try to restore the heat convectors. I don't think they've damaged them, just shut them down. It'll buy us some time at least."

He looks worried. "If Okwembu's really responsible, that's where she'll be. How do you know she won't just kill you on sight?"

"I don't. She might. I don't know. Look," I say, trying to marshal my thoughts. "The answer's in Apex. One way or another, someone's gotta get there, and I think I might stand a better chance than a bunch of stompers."

I don't know if that's true or not. But I know that the stompers won't send more people straightaway—not when the last attempt failed so badly. By the time they get going again, it'll be too late.

"You ever been?" Prakesh says. "To Apex?"

I shake my head. Compared to the other sectors, Apex is tiny: a main control room surrounded by living quarters for the council and their families. Since the sector is so self-contained, they've hardly ever needed tracers. Strange that I've lived my entire life inside an eighteen-mile ring, and there's a whole part of it I've just never seen. I have no idea what it looks like, or what kind of security there is.

"How are you planning to access the computers?" Prakesh asks. "You don't just walk into the main control room of Outer Earth and start tweaking the systems. There'll be passwords, fail-safes."

"Well, we've got one password at least," I say, thinking back to Grace Garner. The entire conversation with her seems blurred in my memory, like something out of a dream. I shake it off. "Maybe it'll get me through the system security."

"You'll need to find a way to lock the control room down. How are you…"

"I don't know, 'Kesh!" I say—louder than I intended, and above us I see Royo look round, puzzled. I lower my voice slightly. "I don't know. But if you've got another way for us to get to Apex, I'm waiting to hear it."

"We could go around—"

"One that doesn't involve running through crowds of people who've just been ordered to kill me."

He opens his mouth, closes it again.

"What can I do?" he says, his voice steady.

"You can get me into the Core. Keep me safe. And from there…" I shrug, try to inject some humour into my words. "Well, I've always wanted to go zero-G."

"We're nearly there," says Royo.

Prakesh stands, strides to the cockpit. "Do you have a first name? Seems kind of strange to be calling you Officer Royo all the time."

Royo glances at him, irritated. "Is this really important?" He turns back to the tunnel, softening a little. "Sam," he says.

Prakesh laughs. "Pleased to meet you, Sam Royo. I'm Prakesh Kumar, and in case you haven't already met the most wanted woman on Outer Earth, this here is Riley Hale."

But I'm not listening to him. I'm looking at the tunnel ahead, into the darkness just out of the spotlight's range, and my heart has started to beat a little too fast.

There's something on the track.

I can see the orange glow of the Apogee loading dock ahead of us. But something is blocking out the light. I squint, trying to make it out, telling myself that it's nothing, a shadow. But I'm not fooling anyone, least of all myself.

"Guys," I say, trying to keep my voice even. "What is that?"

Prakesh peers into the darkness, his hands on his hips and his eyes narrowed. "Yeah, what…"

The light from the train's headlamp washes over the thing on the track. It's a huge pile of cargo containers, like the ones we saw back in the loading dock in Gardens. The rusted metal crates have been piled on the track, right where the tunnel opens up, pulled on top of one another to form a makeshift barrier.

Prakesh has seen it too. He turns to me, his eyes wide. "They can't know it's you on this train. There's no way."

"They don't," says Royo. "Assholes think it's a food train coming from Gardens."

"Can we stop in time?" I ask. Royo shakes his head, even as he yanks back the power lever. A horrible squealing sound fills the tunnel as the brakes kick in, but even as I'm trying to work out if it'll be enough, my mind is racing ahead of me. We're going way too fast, and in about ten seconds we're going to hit the crates.

Royo is hanging on to the power lever, desperately trying to coax everything he can out of the brakes. "Hold on to something!" he shouts. Prakesh grabs me and pulls me down, using the raised cockpit as a shield between us and the barricade. Royo growls in fury and abandons the brake, hurling himself down onto the car's main platform, scrambling for a handhold. The struts on the side of the tunnel are passing way too fast.

A half-second later, the train hits the barricade.

The impact is enormous, a bang that shakes the tunnel and lifts the entire back end of the car clean off the track. Prakesh and I are thrown against the cockpit platform, and I hit it so hard that for a moment the world turns a dull red. Royo crashes into us, squashing us against its surface as the train bucks and screams, and then he's over us, crying out in alarm as the momentum carries him over the cockpit, his arms flailing wildly. The tunnel is filled with tumbling shapes, and I realise we've hit the barricade so hard that we've smashed *through it*.

"Watch out!" yells Prakesh, and yanks my head down just as one of the crates collides with the spot where I was a second ago, hitting with a clang that rattles my teeth.

At that instant, the back of the car, freed from its coupling to the rail, swings out. Prakesh has just enough time to yell out something before the car flips onto its side.

We're hurled forwards, our arms thrown out in front of us. Time does its big slow-down trick again, and the crates, smashed into the air by the train, hang in space around us. I see our shadows, two huge Xs on the track, cast by the light from the platform. The tunnel is quiet suddenly, the roaring and squealing dwindling to nothing.

My muscle memory kicks in, and I tuck for a roll, swinging my body to take the force of the impact. Images of broken bones and shattered shoulder blades have half a second to dance mockingly through my memory, and then I hit the ground.

I hit it shoulder first, tumbling end over end, like someone rolling a barrel down a corridor. My left shoulder has maybe a nanosecond to realise what's happened to it, and then it begins screaming in huge, horrid pain, which rapidly spreads across my back, forcing me to cry out. I lose count of how many times I tumble, but it's punctuated by me cracking my head on the track. Twice.

Eventually, I come to a stop, lying on my back. I'm staring at the roof of the tunnel, now a mess of flickering shapes and orange light. The enormous ache comes to a stop in my shoulder, pulsing like a strobe light. I gingerly move my left arm; it hurts, but it moves freely, and I breathe a tiny sigh of relief. Prakesh would kill me if…

Prakesh. Royo. Before my body even has a chance to react I'm sitting up, causing a wave of pain so fresh and immediate that I nearly throw up. I've landed closest to the platform, a few feet into the tunnel. I spot Royo immediately: a crumpled form a few yards up the tunnel from me, his head turned away, his right arm twisted at an unnatural angle. He's not moving. Prakesh has landed a little way behind me. I see the trickle of blood from the corner of his mouth, and then I realise how glassy his eyes are, and all the blood seems to leave my upper body.

But then he stirs, shakes his head, and the blood comes rushing back, leaving a pounding in my ears and an odd light-headedness. "Riley," he calls out, his voice harsh. Unable to form words, I lift my hand, and a smile cracks my face…

…which dies when someone yells the words, "It's her! It's Hale!"

Standing on the platform are a group of people, holding knives, their eyes greedy with bloodlust.

60

Riley

"Prakesh," I say, shaking his shoulder. "Prakesh, get up."

He groans and holds a hand to his forehead, gazes blearily at me. Concussion. Got to be. But if I don't get him moving in the next ten seconds, we're going to be cut to ribbons.

I shake harder. My voice has become an awkward, hissing whisper, repeating the words like a mantra. "Get up, get up, get up."

The people have started to jump off the platform and head towards us. I recognise the one at the front of the pack. A teacher. I've done jobs for his schoolroom before. But any kindness in his eyes is long gone. "She's on the tracks!" he yells.

"Thanks," says someone from behind him, and shoves him roughly out of the way: a heavily built woman with scraggly hair, holding a metal pole in both hands. I hear her mutter, "You're mine."

I can see the desperation in these people's eyes now, even as they push past the woman. They're scrabbling for a chance at life, trying to kill me in the hope that Darnell will save the one who does.

At my feet, Prakesh groans again, tries to rise, falls back. The crowd is ignoring him, focusing on me. If I can run, draw them away, he might have a chance. I can't risk a look behind me—getting a head start is the only chance I have. But I know the tunnel is clear, and I get ready to run.

And then I pause, confused. The crowd have stopped, their eyes angry. Their weapons are held out in front of them, but almost fearfully now—and the ones at the front are trying to edge away, back into the crowd. I hear a gruff voice from behind me: "I don't know how long I can hold this gun straight. Get Prakesh, and get out of here."

Royo is on his back, between us and the crowd. He's holding his stinger, pointing it right at the attackers. His left arm lies useless, twisted and bent, and the right side of his face is soaked in blood. He catches my eye and jerks his head, gesturing me back down the tunnel. "I said, move," he growls.

"You wanna die along with her, stomper?" someone yells from the crowd. "How many of us can you shoot before we tear that gun out of your hands?"

"I don't know," says Royo, his voice thick with effort. "Thought I might fire a couple of rounds at the ceiling, see if those of you in the middle can dodge the ricochets."

I help Prakesh to his feet, throwing his arm over my shoulder. "Can you walk?" I ask him, terrified that he won't answer, but then he nods and grips my shoulder tight. We start to move down the tunnel, away from the platform, but I linger next to Royo. It seems like everyone around me today has died, and I'm not sure I can lose him too.

"Hale," he says. "If you don't get your ass down that tunnel right now, I'll kill you before they do." He keeps his eyes on the crowd, who are edging closer even as he speaks.

I shoulder Prakesh, and start walking down the tunnel, into the blackness. I force myself to picture the layout of Apogee in my head: there's got to be another platform somewhere on the line.

Then I see a glimmer in the darkness, and my heart leaps. It's far, but I can see it: the light of a second platform, a little further down. I've got no idea where it comes out, but it's our only shot.

"'Kesh, we don't have much time," I say through gritted teeth. His hand is digging into my shoulder, each step causing it to flare with pain. "Do you think you can run?"

He starts to answer, but is cut off when gunshots echo down the tunnel. I turn to Prakesh, my eyes urgent, and with a supreme effort of will he seems to clear his head, forcing away the after-effects of the crash. The blood at the corner of his mouth is just visible in the gloom. He lets go of my shoulder, and starts to jog, first haltingly, then with more confidence.

We reach the station way ahead of the crowd, stumbling and shouting in the blackness of the tunnel. I hop onto the platform, then reach out and haul Prakesh up. Every cell in my body is screaming at me to keep running, but one look at Prakesh and I know that we have to rest, if only for a minute. He's breathing heavily, almost panting, and his face is contorted with pain. My shoulder is burning. When did I last have a drink? In the control room in the Air Lab, when Garner was telling us her story, right before…

I close my eyes. A moment later, I hear the crowd in the tunnel. They're closer than I thought.

I pull Prakesh towards the station's main door; the platform is smaller than the one at the main station up the track, and I'm hoping it'll bring us out near the gallery. From there, it'll just be a matter of climbing up the levels to the Core entrance. Assuming, of course, that we don't get torn to pieces by a mob on the way.

The first of the attackers arrives at the platform just as we slide through the door. He manages to get off a strangled "They're up—" before I slam the door shut, cutting him off. I have no idea if it locks, and I don't have time to check. We're in a small open area in one of the corridors—as far as I know, the Core entrance is a few minutes away.

"This way," I say, already picturing the route. We're on the same level as the Core entrance, but there's the gallery between it and us. That means we'll need to cross on one of the catwalks.

We're almost at the gallery when we see it. The entire corridor has been blocked off, this time by a bunch of burning debris. A single sprinkler is sputtering above it, dripping white flecks of chemical foam onto the fire.

I double back. Prakesh groans, but follows, and we hit the stairwell, dropping down onto Level 5. *Please let the way be open this time…*

It doesn't take us long to reach the catwalk. The gallery below us is mostly empty, but there's bad noise filtering in from somewhere, shouts and screams and banging. There are still a few people on the catwalk. One of them, a man wearing a tattered pair of overalls, is fighting with a stomper, grappling with him, as if trying to throw him off. It's hard to tell what they're fighting about.

He takes a swing at the stomper, his fist balled up and his face a horrible grimace. The move swings him around, and our eyes meet, just for a second.

The stomper goes down. The man sprints at me, screaming. "Are you watching? I'll kill her for you! Do you see?" He's got no weapon, but the expression on his face is one of such rage and desperation that it leaves me paralysed.

Prakesh steps in front of me and swings a punch so fast it's just a blur. The man drops, out cold. Prakesh swears, clenching and unclenching his hand, but even as he does so I see the other people on the catwalk look our way. I swing around, hoping for anything, a weapon, a way to run, but we're trapped. Behind us, an angry mob, and in front, even more of them. And still, my body refuses to move.

"Riley…" says Prakesh, glancing at me. He's backing up now, his eyes on the people advancing towards us.

There's a noise from above. I look up, startled, and see someone leaning over the railing of the Level 6 catwalk. Someone shouting my name.

Carver. And beside him, hanging off the railing: Kev.

It takes me a second to understand what else Carver is yelling: a single phrase, but I can barely make it out over the shouts. He raises his voice; I hear what he's yelling, and his plan is instantly clear; he and Kev are already leaning off the railing, their arms stretched towards us. On our own, it's way too high to jump and grab.

But what Carver says is: "Tic-tac!"

I grab Prakesh, say through gritted teeth: "Up above. Follow my lead." He stares at me in confusion, but there's no time to explain. I take a couple of steps back, and then take a run at the gallery wall, taccing off it and throwing my body around, reaching up as high as I can with my outstretched hands.

There's a moment when I think I've missed them—when they're passing through my field of vision too fast and I think that I'm going to crash to the floor below—but then Carver's fingers close on my wrist, and grip tight. My momentum keeps me going through the swing, but he leans into it, adding extra weight, propelling me towards Kev, who grabs my other arm. His fingers lace tight around my wrist—and slip.

I see it in horrifying slow motion, the tip of his thumb running up the back of my hand, his fingers scrabbling for a hold. But at the last second he makes a final lunge, grabbing my wrist tight. Without even waiting for me to stop swinging, they haul me upwards, their combined strength easily lifting my slender frame. Before I've even grabbed the catwalk railing, I'm yelling, "Prakesh! Get Prakesh!"

Carver yells something I can't quite make out. I grip the metal tight, and throw myself over, aware of the need to get out of the way. I land in a sprawl on the catwalk, and scramble to my feet, running to Kev's side and looking over the railing.

They've got Prakesh. Somehow, he pulled off the move, and Carver and Kev have grabbed him cleanly at the wrists. But as I watch, I see someone else take a running leap at Prakesh. He jerks his foot out of the way just in time, and the man misses, giving a frustrated yell as he crashes to the floor. But the crowd behind him is angry, eager for blood.

Someone hurls a length of metal pipe. It only just misses Prakesh, spinning away and clanging off the wall, but then Carver and Kev haul him bodily up and over, all of them falling in a tangle of limbs on the catwalk. For the first time, I realise that it's deserted, and wonder why. But then Prakesh pokes his head out the top of the pile and grins at me.

"You all right?" I say, trying to keep the worry out of my voice.

"Hanging in there," he replies.

Under him, I hear Carver say, "Maybe chat when you're *not* on top of us?"

I don't feel like laughing, but I do anyway. Carver and Kev get to their feet. "Hell of a way to treat your rescuer," mutters Carver, which is swiftly followed by a surprised, "Whoa..." when I embrace him. I reach out an arm and pull Kev in, squeezing them both tight.

"Watch the arm," says Carver. I pull back, startled, expecting to see it hanging limp by his side, but it's back in place. The shoulder, however, is purple with bruising.

"Well, that was new," says Carver, his eyebrows raised.

"Don't get used to it," I say, ignoring the angry shouts from below us. "But I don't think I've ever been this happy to see you. When we left you back there with the Lieren..."

"With the knives? I'm surprised you think so little of me, Riley."

"And Kev," I start, turning to him. But then I see him look away, clenching his fists. Yao. His Twin. It can't be more than a few hours since she died, but it feels like weeks. I reach out a hand, but he doesn't take it, just turns away slightly. It's then that I notice his ankle. It's swollen—not badly, but enough to probably hurt like hell when he moves. Where did that happen?

A bullet ricochets off the railing. We all hit the deck. I'm painfully aware of how little protection the catwalk gives us, and I hear Prakesh yell over the noise, "The corridor! Go!"

We don't need telling twice. As one, we break for the corridor. It's no more than a few yards away, but even as we start running I hear another gunshot, this one followed by screams from below.

The far corridor is deserted; Carver, Kev and Prakesh have collapsed against the wall, breathing hard. "Why's there no one here?" asks Prakesh, looking around. "Where is everyone?"

"Glad you asked me that," says Carver. "Kev here came up with the rather brilliant idea of blocking off the stairs." He gestures towards the far end of the catwalk. "Amazing what a localised slow burner can do to encourage people to find another way round."

"A slow…" I stop. Carver's eyes are bright, and it takes me a moment to get my thoughts in order. "I thought you lost all your fire bombs to the stompers after that time in Tzevya?"

"Not all of them."

Prakesh's eyes are urgent. "The other stairs," he asks Carver. "Did you do them too?"

Carver shakes his head. "I only had the one. Those things are hard to make."

We get to our feet, but then Kev says, "Where's Amira?"

The silence that follows goes on just a second too long.

"I don't get it," says Carver. "Wasn't she with you?"

Mercifully, Prakesh comes to my aid. "We'll explain later. Right now, we need to get to the Core."

Carver glances at me. "He's kidding, right?"

"Nope," I say, sounding braver than I feel. "It's the only way into Apex."

"You're going to Apex?"

Kev's shaking his head. "Bad move."

I have to bite back the frustration. "We're running out of time," I say, looking right at Carver. "Are you gonna help us or not?"

"OK, Riley," Carver says. "First off, you look terrible. I'm a little surprised you're still standing upright. Second, you do know that the Core entrance is going to be rammed with stompers, right?"

"Yeah, but—"

"What were you planning on doing, exactly? Because even if you get inside, you've got no thermo-suit. You'll freeze solid in about ten seconds. That's if you think you're going in there alone, which you're not."

I look to Prakesh, but he just shakes his head. He's shattered. It's in his trembling legs and hunched shoulders. I must look the same way.

I turn back to Carver. "If we don't get there soon, Darnell—"

Kev slams his hand into the corridor, his fist balled up. The bang is so loud that we all jump, and when he draws it away, I'm a little surprised that the metal isn't dented.

"Yao's dead," he says quietly. "I'm not letting you die, too."

In the silence that follows, Carver says, "If we go in there now, it's over. If we take a minute, figure out a plan, then maybe we have a shot."

"Where, though?" I ask. "There's nothing left in the Nest."

"D-Company?" Kev says.

I shake my head. "Nowhere near close enough. We'd spend too much time getting there."

Carver thinks for a moment, then his eyes light up. "OK, so you know the guy P-Man laid out?"

Prakesh looks at him. "Huh?"

"The guy you knocked down. Back there, before Kev and I saved the day."

"What about him?" I say.

"I know him. He's local. More importantly, I know where he lives."

"And he's not exactly using his hab right now," Prakesh says. "Clever."

"What if he's gone back there already?" I say.

Kev shrugs. "Prakesh can hit him again. I'll help."

Carver's eyes find mine. "Food, water, some sort of plan. That's all I ask." Before I can protest, he takes off down the corridor. After a moment, the rest of us follow. I'm not wild about busting into someone's home, and there's no telling who or what we'll find there, but Carver's right.

Apogee has been torn apart. The corridors are a mess of bent metal, broken lights and power boxes that have been torn open and scavenged. Frequently, we have to travel in darkness, slowing to a crawl as we negotiate the detritus. Once or twice, we come across groups of people, either cowering in shadows or spoiling for a fight. But there's not a lot of them, and they don't seem keen to take on a large group of us.

I ask Carver if it's like this everywhere. He nods. "Every sector. Ever since that psycho turned off the convectors." He looks at me. "We heard him on the comms talking about you. You must have really pissed him off."

Prakesh slips in beside me. "You OK?" he whispers. I nod, and he wraps his arm around me as we walk. I'm glad he does because, despite the heat, I feel like I'm about to start shaking.

The hab is on Level 3, past the schoolrooms. The door's locked, but Kev gives it a huge kick, and it flies open. The place is a mess, scattered with trash and scummy food containers. The floor and walls are streaked with grime, and the bedclothes on the single cot are rumpled. Kev wrinkles his nose. It looks strange on him, like something a child would do. He closes the door behind him, almost tenderly. Whether the owner is still unconscious or not, he hasn't made it back here.

It's hotter here than outside, the cramped space collecting heat, springing more sweat from my forehead. Carver takes a quick look in the attached washroom. "Nobody here. I'm guessing the guy lives alone. Let's see if he's got a secret stash."

It doesn't take us long to find the water. A single canteen under the cot, pushed right against the back wall. I force myself to take small sips when Carver passes me the bottle, not wanting to upset my stomach. There's just enough for four of us. My thirst is still there, but it's muted now, hovering in the background. Kev disappears for a few minutes; when he returns, he has his pack, and pulls out some apples and a few protein bars.

I've never been so happy to see food. I'm a little worried that the owner of the hab might come back, but even if he did, I tell myself, what is he possibly going to do against four of us?

We eat in silence, collapsed against the wall, the ceiling light above us flickering. I try to eat as fast as I can, but my stomach won't let me. After a while, Carver says, "So are you going to tell us where Amira went? Because we could really use the extra help right now."

He says it with a smile on his face, but I see his eyes, spot the worry in them. Kev, too, is looking apprehensive. I've been dreading this moment, dreading it even before I'd really taken in that Amira was dead.

But I do it. I take a deep breath, and tell them everything. When I finish, my mouth is a desert again, my body already aching for more water.

The hab is silent; even the rumbling from the station around us seems to have ceased. Neither Kev nor Carver have said a word since I told them about Amira's death. Kev is avoiding my eyes, his hands clasped together between his knees, his jaw set. But Carver—Carver is staring at me. His mouth is a tight line, and in his eyes, nothing but raw, barely contained fury. It shocks me more than it should, and it takes me a moment to realise why: I can't remember the last time I saw Carver truly angry.

I have maybe half a second to process this thought before he forces himself off the wall and dives at me, his hands twisted into claws, murder on his face.

61

Riley

The attack is so unexpected that I just don't react. Carver slams into me, forcing me back into the wall. His hands are aimed at my throat, but at the very last second he drops them, gripping my shoulders instead. He winces in pain as the force of his grip travels up his arm into his damaged shoulder.

"You killed her!" he shouts, his mouth inches from my face, his voice cracking.

I try to say something, anything. A million emotions jumble together: disbelief, then anger, then fear, flaring one after the other, like a set of lights on a circuit. Carver's words have dissolved into incoherent yells. Tears stain his cheeks.

Kev and Prakesh wrap their arms around him and yank him back. He finds his voice again, screaming, "Get off me!" He collapses back against the other wall, stumbling, like he's drunk. For a few seconds, he just leans against it, and then sinks down, his fist slamming the floor in anger.

I can't take my eyes off Carver. He senses my gaze, and raises his head to look at me. This time, all he can manage is a whispered, "Why?"

Somehow, nothing I can say seems good enough.

For a long time, none of us do anything. Prakesh keeps a wary eye on Carver, but he just sits, his head down, his body shaking with silent sobs. Eventually, he looks at me. His face is blotchy and red, but his eyes are clear. The anger in them appears to have dimmed, but when he speaks, his voice is harsh. "Why'd she do it?"

I shake my head. It's like trying to describe something on the Earth below. Some animal I've only seen in pictures.

It's Kev who answers him. "Doesn't matter now."

"Yes, it matters!"

Carver's words reverberate within the cramped hab, leaving a cold silence behind. I rest my head against the wall, trying to stop the tears I feel pricking the corners of my eyes, squeezing them shut. Out of nowhere, I see Yao's mural, from before it was destroyed by whoever wrecked the Nest. I see its colours and its swirling shapes, the image so vivid that I can pick out the parts where the ink hadn't dried yet.

"We can't bring her back, or change what she did," I say quietly, turning to face them. The words sound awkward in my mouth, as if I'm reading someone else's writing, but I say them anyway. "She thought we'd lost our right to exist as a species. I say: not without a fight. I'm going to run the Core. I'm going to find Janice Okwembu, and I'm going to end this."

I say it evenly, trying to keep the fear out of my voice. Nearly manage it, too.

"I'll go," says Carver, getting to his feet. He won't look at me. "I can do it."

I stare at him. "You're going to run through the Core with a busted shoulder? Really?"

"I'm fine," he says. I step forward, and lightly tap him on the shoulder. He tries to turn away, but I see him grimace in pain.

"I can do it," he says again, but the fire has gone out of his voice.

From the wall, Kev says, "Why can't I go?"

"With that ankle? We don't have time for this." I shake my head, frustrated. "It's not just that I'm the fastest here, which I am. I was there when she died, OK? I was there. She played me. She *used* me. This is my fight."

"Did you see what Darnell did to those stompers?" says Carver. "The ones who went through the Core? You want that to happen to you?"

I don't have an answer.

"Riley's right," says Prakesh. "I don't like it either, but this is the best shot we have."

"I'm not just going to sit here," says Carver.

"You won't have to. The Core entrance is guarded, right? If we can create a diversion or something, we can get the doors open long enough to get Riley in. What'll you need, Ry? Five seconds? Ten?"

"Three," I say, and walk right over to Carver. He avoids my eyes, but I place a hand on his good shoulder, and after a moment, he puts his on top of it. "I can do this," I whisper.

After a long moment, he nods.

I turn to Kev. "We good?"

"We good."

"Look, I hate to be the one who drops the doom-bomb here," says Carver, "but it's like I said. We're not just talking about one stomper on guard duty. You don't get into the Core with a wink and a smile. How are we going to get past them?"

"There's always stompers," Kev says. "Five. Six."

I think, trying to picture the Core entrance. I've run past it plenty of times too: a big open room, bisected by the Level 6 corridor, with huge blast doors set into the ceiling. Equipment storerooms lead off the main area. There are control panels at opposite ends of the room—old things, with dusty digital readouts and clunky switches. Presumably, that's how you open it up.

Prakesh reads my mind. "There'll be fail-safes there, too—more than likely two keycards or passcodes that'll need to be used at the same time at opposite ends of the room."

I frown. "Can we get a keycard?"

"I could probably hack it if we had enough time."

"How long?"

He looks helpless. "Ten minutes?"

"Why sure, officer," says Carver. "This little speck on the wall is the most fascinating thing you'll ever see in your life. But you'll need to stare at it for at least ten minutes to fully appreciate all the nuances..."

"Not helping," I say.

"We could lock the place down, maybe," Prakesh says thoughtfully. "Get everyone out somehow and then barricade the entrances. It might buy us enough time."

I shake my head, frustrated.

"Hello?" says Kev. We all look at him, and he spreads his hands wide. "Just break things."

Carver rubs his temple. "Much as I love your enthusiasm, Kev, stuff tends to stop working when you smash it to pieces."

"Yes—but not the stuff it's connected to," says Kev slowly, as if talking to a child. His voice is clearer than it was before. "Smash the panels. The blast doors will think there's been a power short. Open right up."

"Any chance it could work?" I ask Prakesh. Of all of us, he's the most familiar with the station tech, especially the parts which give you access to secure areas. He thinks for a minute, his fist raised to his mouth.

Eventually, he says, "It's possible. Doors on Outer Earth *are* configured to open automatically using auxiliary batteries if there's a power cut. Or at least, they're supposed to." Then he shakes his head. "But we don't know anything about the Core system. It might not work the same way as the other doors on the station. We could spend hours wrecking the access panels, and it'd stay locked tight."

"I don't like it," says Carver. "There's just too much we don't know. We don't get a second run at this."

I choose my words carefully, looking him in the eyes. "If there's even the slightest chance that it'll work, then I'm going to take it."

He returns my stare for a long minute. I'm certain that he's going to argue some more, but then he says, "Well, you're going in there, not me. Although if the doors don't open I am leaving you there and running like hell."

"Fair enough."

Prakesh puts his hands on his hips. "I'm in too."

I take a deep breath. He's not going to like this.

"I need you to stay in Apogee. If it goes wrong in the Core, you'll need to warn people. Tell them what we know."

Even before I've finished, he's opening his mouth to protest, so I talk quickly. "We could be injured, or captured, or...anyway, it doesn't matter. We need a backup plan. You're it."

"If this is about speed, I'm not going to slow you down," he says. "I've kept up with you so far, haven't I? Let me help get you in there."

I shake my head. "It's not about that. People trust you. They listen to you. Us?" I gesture to Carver and Kevin. "We're just tracers. People pay us to take their cargo and get out of their sight."

His expression has softened a little, even if he isn't completely convinced. I lower my voice. "You have to trust us, Prakesh. We can do this."

The silence that follows seems to stretch forever, but eventually he gives a curt nod, not looking at me.

"So that's it. We go," I say. But still, nobody moves.

Which is when I realise: this is when Amira would have inclined her head, the tiny gesture indicating that this is how we proceed. She'd be leaning against the wall, just there, her arms folded, staring into the distance, as if holding up every option individually and examining it for flaws.

It's Kev who breaks the silence—and before he does it, he glances at the place where Amira would have been, as if expecting her to reappear. When he speaks, he says, "If it comes to a swinging, swing all, say I."

It takes a moment for his words to make sense. Then understanding dawns: *Treasure Island*.

With a small smile on my face, I nod. "Swing all."

Carver sighs. "Since I've agreed to this insane idea," he says, "does anybody know how we're going to get enough time to destroy these damn panels?"

"Actually, I do," I say. I'm thinking back to something Carver said. Something about running through it.

It takes me less than two minutes to outline my plan. Carver is sceptical at first, but before long he's nodding, thinking hard.

"I'll need to see if I can salvage a few things from the Nest," he says. "I don't have anything to work with here. Kev—you come with me. And you two: for the love of every god there is, stay here."

"What do we do if the man who lives here comes back?" Prakesh says.

Carver winks at him. "Like Kev said. Hit him again."

He points to a big storage locker, over by the wall. "Meantime, drag that in front of the door after we're gone."

They leave, and Prakesh and I haul the locker over to the door. When it's in place, I take a minute to stretch, working my tight leg muscles and rotating my shoulders to work out the stiffness. All the injuries from the past few days seem to make themselves felt at once—the bruised collarbone, the ring around my eye, the marks on my neck and stomach from my fight with Darnell. The gashes in my hands and forehead, healing but still ugly, and the burn on my right hand where I pawed at my jacket sleeve in the fire. And I ache everywhere, my body telling me in every possible way that I'm nearly at breaking point. But I can't stop. Not now. *Please,* I silently say. *Just a few more runs. Then we'll sleep. We'll sleep for weeks.*

I sit down on the cot to stretch out my legs. Prakesh comes over and sits down next to me. He looks worried, more worried than I've ever seen him. "What are you going to do if they come after you into the Core?" he says.

I shrug, try to act like I'm beyond worry, even though there's a band of fear that feels like it's squeezing my chest to bursting point. "What I always do, Prakesh," I say. "I run."

I'm about to say something else, but then Prakesh is kissing me with so much force that it nearly knocks me over backwards. I'm so surprised that for a second his open mouth is locked on my closed one.

I pull away. "'Kesh, I... we can't."

He's shaking his head. "Why not?"

I laugh, using it to mask the tremor in my voice. "Look at this place. It's a mess. It's not even ours."

I expect him to smile back. To let the moment pass. He doesn't. He just looks me right in the eyes. His hand touches mine, clasps it, then squeezes tight and doesn't let go.

"You remember when you said you'd have to choose?" he says. "That if...that if we were together, you'd eventually have to choose between me and the Dancers?"

He doesn't give me the chance to answer. "I wouldn't care. You hear me? Because even if you chose the Dancers, even if you couldn't be with me, I'd still have a little bit of time with you. And now you're going to Apex—you're off on this *stupid run*—and you're not giving me a choice."

"If I don't—"

"No, *listen*. I know you have to go. I get that. But you don't get to do it without giving me a chance. You don't. That's not a choice you get to make."

His other hand is gripping my forearm now, and he pulls me into another kiss. This time, I kiss him back.

"We don't have enough time," I whisper.

"I don't care," he says.

Neither do I.

His hands, wrapped around my back, slip silently under my top, and begin tracing the curve of my spine. His touch is gentle, hesitant at first, but growing bolder, faster. Little prickles of heat shoot through me.

We fall back on the cot, pushing aside the blankets, my hands pushing under his shirt, lifting it over his head. His mouth moves down to my neck, then my own shirt comes off and he moves lower still, kissing my breasts, skin on skin.

He pushes me too hard, and my head bumps against the wall. I wince, but he's there immediately, kissing my forehead and laughing. I try to tell him it's OK, but I don't get to finish the sentence, because right then he slips inside me.

He holds it for a moment, looking me in the eyes. Then he slides deeper. The aches in my body vanish, melting away. Soon, there's no hesitancy, no holding back: just us thrusting together, and my nails digging deep ridges in his flesh. His mouth, my mouth, his hands, everywhere, all at once. When I come, when Prakesh finally pushes us over the edge, it's as if every scrap of energy I have has concentrated into a single burning point, deep in my own core.

I can't move, I can't breathe. I don't want to. I'd trade everything, every run I've ever been on, every good memory I've ever had, to freeze time at this instant. His hand is on the back of my neck, his skin warm. It feels good.

Like how I imagine sunlight would feel.

Afterwards, we lie together. Our breathing has slowed, quietened. He lifts his left hand and caresses my cheek.

"You come back," he says. "No matter what happens, you come back to me. You find a way."

And I whisper, "I will. I promise."

I hold him for as long as I dare. I want the memory of his touch to be as powerful as possible. If I die, if I can't save my world, then I want this to be the last thing I remember.

I don't know how long we lie together, but by the time Carver and Kev come back, we're clothed again, sitting against the wall quietly, sharing some more water. I thought there was nothing useful left in the Nest, but I guess I don't have Carver's eyes. He's got an armful of tools and spare parts. Kev has managed to find some food: more protein bars, pulled from another of his secret stashes.

We eat while Carver puts everything together. It takes him a little longer than I'd like, but eventually, he straightens up, pulling his goggles off.

Prakesh hugs me tight.

And then we're out into the passage. And we're running. Not in single file, not this time, but in a tight group, Carver and Kev close on my sides. We run at full speed, barrelling through the station, and for a little while, it's almost as if we're not running to any destination. We're just running.

62

Prakesh

Prakesh watches her go. It's the hardest thing he's ever had to do.

He sits for a few moments longer in the hab. The air is cold, but when his hand strays to the blankets that he and Riley were sitting on, he finds they're still warm.

Riley asked him to spread the word if they failed. He tries to think about how he'd do this, but it's too big a task. Outer Earth is chaos, turned feral by Oren Darnell. How do you get people to stop fighting long enough to listen to you?

He hauls himself to his feet. It's more than that. He's a lab tech. He knows about plants, and machines, and chemicals. He can transfer smoke from one room to another. He can't capture people's minds, or change them.

I changed hers.

Whatever he has to do, it won't come from staying in here. Prakesh steps out, closing the door behind him. He can hear the fighting from here. It's a jarring rumble of noise, trapped and funnelled by the corridors, twisted and bent by every corner. The air is thick and cloying, and so hot that Prakesh gasps. It's his imagination, it has to be, but he could swear there's a heat haze rising from the end of the corridor, shimmering in the lights. Somewhere, an alarm is blaring, an electronic voice spouting unheard warnings.

The noise changes. Shouting. It's closer—close enough for him to pick out individual voices.

Prakesh wipes sweat from his eyes, and jogs down the corridor. When he comes round the corner, he sees a group of people standing in the middle of the next section. Three of them wear gang colours, blue shirts and armbands with black pants. They've surrounded two others, an old man and a much younger woman. The old man is wearing dirty overalls, with one sleeve tied off at the shoulder.

The three gang members are poking him in the stomach, laughing at him as he tries to shield the woman. She's twig-thin, her head completely bald. One of the gang members reaches over, and taps her on the dome of her skull, laughing. She shrinks up against the old man, who whirls around, screaming threats.

"Come on," says one of the others. "I seen you in the market before. You gotta have some food."

The man says something back, spit arcing from his mouth. A dot of it lands on the gang member's shoulder, and he flicks it away.

"You spat on me," he says, and shoves the old man in the chest. He slams against the corridor wall, dropping to his knees. The woman screams.

"Hey!" Prakesh says.

They all turn to stare at him. Prakesh is walking towards them, a few feet away. There's no possible way he can do what he's about to do, but he keeps coming, bearing down on them.

The gang member who shoved the old man gives Prakesh a crooked smile. "Keep walking, man."

Prakesh grabs the front of his shirt, pulling him in close. As he does so, he sees that he's just a kid. So are the others—the oldest one looks like he's barely scraping sixteen.

"Hey, what—" the kid starts.

"You think what's happening gives you the right to beat up old men?" Prakesh says. His forehead almost touches the gang member's, their skin so close that he can feel the heat baking off. "I don't give the tiniest shit who you are, or what you think you can do. You'll run, and you'll keep running, and if I see you again before this is all over I'll take that rag off your arm and stick it down your throat."

He lets go. The boy stumbles backwards, only just managing to keep his feet. The other two are shocked back to life, and the older one takes a step towards Prakesh.

Don't quit now, Prakesh thinks, deliriously. He screams in the older boy's face. "*Go!*"

It breaks them. They move away, not quite running, but not quite walking either. The one Prakesh took hold of looks back over his shoulder, his face threatening payback. Prakesh holds the boy's gaze until they vanish, disappearing round the corner. His heart is hammering in his chest, and he can't quite describe what he's feeling. It's not quite surprise. It's more like awe.

"Thank you," says the old man. Prakesh turns around and holds out a hand, pulling the man up. His skin feels hypersensitive, as if some weird drug has been injected into his veins.

The woman wraps her arm around the man, her huge eyes taking in Prakesh.

"Bastards," the old man spits. "All of them. Take and kill, all they do." The woman nods, a venomous look crossing her face.

"Yeah, I know," Prakesh says. The adrenaline is draining away, replaced by the cold glare of reality. Those three were kids. The next ones might not be.

"Madala," the old man says.

Prakesh turns to him. "Huh?"

"Name's Madala," the man says, thrusting out an ancient hand. Prakesh takes it, and the man pumps twice, then jerks his head at the woman. "This Indira. She not talk much, but she says hello."

The woman blinks at him, and nods.

"Sure," Prakesh says. "Listen, you two need to get inside. It's only going to get worse out here."

"Ha," says the old man, barking the word. "Inside? No. We come with you."

Before Prakesh can protest, Indira and Madala have grabbed him by the arms, and are marching him down the corridor. He tries to say something, but Madala talks over him. "You tell us what to do, we do it."

Well, OK then, Prakesh thinks.

63

Darnell

"Where are you?" Darnell says, his eyes on the screens.

His words are barely coherent, blurring together in a husky whisper. Around him, the control room is silent. He doesn't know where Okwembu is, and he doesn't care.

He has the Apogee entrance to the Core up on the screen. The protection officers guarding it are restless and worried, pacing with their stingers out. No Hale.

He selects another camera view—the Apogee gallery, the camera under the Level 1 catwalk, pointing down. It shows a gallery strewn with burning trash, wreathed in smoke. He's lost count of how many times he's pulled up the feed, hoping to see Hale being burned alive. Not for the first time, Darnell curses the cameras that no longer work, the blind spots in his vision.

Pain lances through him, driving a pointed tip through his torn ear, his shoulder, the scabbing burn on his arm. He growls in anger. After he was shot, the pain felt like it belonged to someone else. Now it's everywhere, ferocious, biting. He can't get away from it.

He should be savouring these last few hours, using the control room to create as much fear as possible. Instead, he's obsessing over Hale. The stompers who came through the Core provided a momentary distraction, but she keeps returning to the front of his mind. He knows that she's a minor threat at best, that she can't run forever, but it doesn't help. The fact that he can't do anything about her is infuriating. It makes him feel useless.

Like before.

And in the years following the controlled burn, he *was* useless. He was placed with different families. He had counsellors. But those years are a dark, indistinct smudge—he doesn't remember a single thing anyone said to him.

Darnell didn't feel sorry about his mother—she would have died soon anyway, and at least this way she'd been useful. Why couldn't they understand that? Why couldn't they see that the plants were just doing what was needed to exist?

He tried to rationalise it, tried to understand why they'd destroyed the plants, and why nobody had stopped them. He couldn't. It was too big, a monstrous truth that he couldn't comprehend.

And it wasn't just the plants in his hab. The Earth below them was wrecked, its environment destroyed. Humans had done that too. *And they didn't learn.* Even as they clung to existence, spinning around the Earth, they committed the same mistakes.

Darnell was a minor when he was put into the system. When he was eighteen, in accordance with Outer Earth law, his record was wiped clean. He moved to a distant sector, where no one recognised him. By that time, he had his size, and he found work in the Food Lab, toting sacks of fertiliser. It was there that he had his revelation, which arrived so suddenly that it stopped him in his tracks, the sack he was carrying swaying in his grip.

He would fix it.

A species that could destroy something so pure and beautiful didn't deserve the world they were given, so Darnell would take it away from them. Without humans, nature would reclaim the Earth. It would take millennia, but that didn't matter.

There would be no place for him in that world, either. When he realised that, the relief was exquisite, like he'd been thirsty for years and had finally found cool water.

He would have to be careful. Blend in, make contacts, accumulate power and influence. It would be immensely difficult. If his plan was going to work, it would need to be total—not a single human survivor could be left alive. He would have to wipe out Outer Earth in one go. He accepted that there was little he could do about the asteroid catcher ships, but without Outer Earth to sustain them, where would they go? The humans on board would die too, even if it took a little longer.

And it had worked. His patience, his self-control, had all been worth it. In a matter of hours, Outer Earth would be utterly destroyed. Hale couldn't stop that, no matter what she did. So why is he fixating on her? What keeps him watching the screens?

"We don't have much time left."

Okwembu is behind him; her mouth is set in a thin line.

Darnell ignores her. He's still scanning the screens.

"I know there's no point treating those wounds," she says. "But I can give you something for the pain, if you like."

Darnell opens his mouth to tell her that he's fine, but his eyes are drawn to movement on the feed. He quickly maximises the camera, zooming in.

Something is happening at the core entrance in Apogee.

64

Riley

"Ten stompers," says Carver. "This isn't a break-in, Riley, it's suicide."

I bite my lip, staring at the entranceway to the Core. We're off to one side, in the shadows of the corridor. We managed to run up the levels without encountering too much resistance; there was a group of teens looking for a fight, but they weren't armed, and even undermanned we got through them easily. Now, as I stare into the room, half of me is tempted to agree with Carver. But with less than ten hours left before Darnell destroys everything, we don't have a choice.

The entrance is pretty much as I remember it: a massive open space, stacked with pallets for transporting equipment. The walls are lined with rows of lockers, each capped with an oversized keypad. There's no overhead lighting. Instead, harsh spotlights at floor level point upwards at the roof, directed at the colossal blast doors themselves. They take up nearly the whole ceiling, reaching from one wall to the other. The seal between the two halves is like a giant set of metal teeth, decayed with age until each tooth is black with rust. The doors aren't flush with the roof, but sit slightly below it. Painted across them in enormous black letters are the words *Reactor Access*.

I can see the control panels on either side of the room. I'd like to get a closer look, but even if I could understand the readouts—about as likely as being able to grow eyes in the back of my head—there's no way I'd get near them. The stompers in the room are on edge, pacing back and forth. It doesn't look as if anybody has tried to breach their defences yet, but from the way they're fingering their guns I'd guess they're expecting an attack any minute.

And now, it seems, their first one's going to come from three exhausted tracers. Lucky them. They'll probably see it as a warm-up.

Kev squats down next to me, whispers, "Still think this is a good idea?"

"Not really. But it's the only one we've got. You ready to go?"

He grunts, hefting his backpack.

"Remember," Carver says to him. "The second it kicks off, hit the ground. They'll be shooting, and you'll be the last thing they see."

Kev nods. I busy myself with pulling on the gloves Carver gave me. They're thick, made of a stiff outer material stuffed with shreds of old fabric. They're too big for my hands. I give them an experimental flex, dismayed to find that I have to exert real effort to make even a clumsy fist. Climbing with these on is going to be nearly impossible. But they'll protect my fingers from the cold. What happened to Amira won't happen to me. *In more ways than one.*

There's a dirty black scarf wrapped around my neck. I've already padded myself out under my jacket, pulling on two of Carver's shirts and a hooded top belonging to Kev. The clothing is threadbare, barely holding itself together. The under-layer is soaked in sweat from the run. I'm worried that the sweat might freeze, drawing body heat, but I can't think about that now. It'd be great if I had a full thermo-suit to wear, but it'd just slow me down. For now, I'll have to live with the discomfort.

"Last chance to back out, Riley," says Carver.

I shake my head. My heart is thudding in my chest, and there's a curious metallic taste in my mouth. But I push it away, forcing myself to focus. "We're doing this," I say.

"I always knew being a tracer would get me killed," says Kev. And with that, he stands and walks straight into the room. I have to remind myself to breathe.

Kev walks slowly, his hands up, his pack hanging loosely from his shoulders. The stomper nearest to us—a stocky woman with a ponytail—looks up at the sound of footsteps. "Stop!" she barks. In half a second, she and every other stomper in the room have their guns out and locked on Kev.

He gives a nervous smile, his hands raised above him. "Cargo delivery," he says. "Speed run from the mess. Someone sending up food for you."

The first stomper's expression doesn't change, but behind her I see a couple of the others lower their guns very slightly, their expressions hopeful. My guess was good: they've been up here for hours, maybe days, and chances to eat will have been slim. A shipment of food would be a welcome prospect.

I'm almost sorry that we'll have to disappoint. Almost.

"Since when did the mess start using tracers for food deliveries?" says the first stomper.

Kev shrugs, and I marvel at how calm he seems. "Not my problem," he replies. "But if I go back, they probably won't bother sending another one." At this, the stompers glance at each other nervously. I can almost hear their stomachs rumbling. Still the woman with the ponytail doesn't move.

"Tell you what," says Kev. "I'll take out the cargo, and put it on the floor. Nice and easy." He keeps his hands raised, not wanting to provoke.

After a long minute, the woman says, "Take off the pack."

Kev slowly reaches behind him, pulling the pack off his shoulders and holding it out in front of him at arm's length. The stomper nods. "Good. Take the cargo out," she says.

"OK," says Kev. And tears out the hidden panel at the bottom of the bag.

The chemicals inside react to the air immediately. Kev hits the deck just as the lead stomper fires, but his body has already vanished into the huge, billowing cloud of smoke gushing from the pellets.

This was what Carver had been working on when he locked me out of the Nest for kicks. Turns out he'd been trying to build this smoke system, hoping to give us an extra escape route if we ever ran into trouble. He'd been struggling with it, not able to get the formula right. But it turned out that quicksleep—the stuff Arthur Gray used to grab his victims—was the missing ingredient. Distil it down, add a few other chemicals into it, then combine it with Carver's original recipe. Expose it to air, and you've got something that could easily help a Dancer evade someone hunting them.

With the quicksleep, and the scraps he and Kevin managed to scrounge from the Nest, there was just enough left to make a single batch. It took Carver less than twenty minutes to mix the chemicals and transfer them to a pack, storing them inside a modified water container. He had to do it pretty quickly to stop smoke filling up the hab, but he managed it.

We dash from our hiding places into the noxious smoke, the room filling with confused shouts and gunfire. It's clear that for a few seconds at least, we won't be noticed. We've got scarves wrapped around our faces, but the thick smoke still worms its way in, burning my throat. I sprint towards where I think the control panel is, and a bullet ricochets off the floor in front of me; I duck, but keep running, heading towards the far end of the room.

There's a yell from behind me. Carver? No way to tell. The smoke is everywhere now, filling the room; a stomper materialises out of the gloom in front of me, his gun raised, but I'm moving too fast. I clock him across the throat, and he gives a loud, strangled cry as he flies backwards. His gun fires, the bullet dancing off the ceiling. I wince, but keep running.

A split second later, I slam into the wall, my fingers bending back painfully where they've made contact. I bite back a cry of pain, not wanting to give away my position. I force my throbbing fingers to feel along the wall to my right, hoping desperately that I've picked the right direction.

It's impossible to see now. I'm breathing too fast, inhaling too much smoke, expecting a bullet in the back at any second. But then the surface under my fingers changes, from cold metal to the smooth glass of a screen, and I know I've found the control panel. My hands feel downwards, exploring the panel. It juts out of the wall at waist height, a bank of buttons capped with the screen, which I can now see glowing dimly through the smoke.

I dig into my pocket, fighting with the thick gloves, and pull out Carver's second gadget.

It's almost too simple to work. A tiny plastic box, filled with a small blob of explosive putty. Inside the box, above the putty and pointing right at it, is a short spike. On its tip, another chemical, harmless—until you place the box on a flat surface and slam your hand onto the lid, driving the spike into the putty, combining the chemicals. Then you have about a second to dive away before the explosion takes your hand off.

When the bang comes, it's so loud that my hearing goes completely, leaving nothing but a ringing that burrows into my skull. I've thrown myself to the side, away from the explosion. It's small, but bright and hot, and enough to blow a hole the size of a man's head in the control panel. A moment later, I feel a second thud reverberate around the room. Carver must have detonated his own device.

My hearing slowly comes back. The room is louder now, filled with the terrified shouts from the stompers, telling each other to fall back. I want to yell that they're not under attack, that we don't mean to hurt them, but with the smoke and the explosions, I think I'd just earn myself a volley of stinger bullets. Lying on the ground, my ears throbbing and my lungs burning with hot smoke, a tiny thought in the back of my mind says that this is absolutely the worst idea ever.

And then I hear it. A high-pitched mechanical whine.

The blast doors are opening.

I jump to my feet, and start running, ignoring the nausea brought on by the smoke. It occurs to me that I have no idea how you actually get through the doors: does a ladder drop down? Stairs? I curse myself for not thinking about it before. I'm looking upwards through the smoke, searching for the opening. But then, no more than five seconds after the doors started opening, the sound changes: it gets lower, more throaty. As if…

My heart sinks. The doors are closing. Some fail-safe, some little electronic gatekeeper, has kicked in, and there's no way of telling how far the doors opened before they started to shut.

A figure explodes out of the fog. It's Carver, blood pouring down his face, mouthing something I can't hear. He has to say it twice before I hear him: "Jump!"

Without breaking my stride, I push off with my left leg, launching myself upwards. At the same time, Carver drops to one knee, cupping his left hand under my foot. My body acts before I can think about it, and I push into his hand even as he forces me upwards, my own arm raised. He cries out, putting every ounce of effort he can into pushing me up with his one arm. I force my eyes to stay open in the stinging smoke, hunting for an opening.

The edge of the door takes me in the forearms, almost causing me to fall backwards, but I swing my arms down, and then I'm hanging from the blast doors by my elbows. The whine is louder now, burrowing into my head. If I can't pull myself up, the doors will cut me in two.

My legs are dangling in space, and at any second I expect a bullet to slice through them. But Carver hasn't let go of my foot, and he starts pushing upwards, standing, lifting me from below. Groaning with the effort, I haul my way upwards: first my chest, then my waist, and then my legs are up and over. I catch a brief glimpse of Carver's face through the gap in the blast doors: soaked red with the blood, but with eyes burning bright. Then the doors slam shut with a huge, echoing boom.

The silence is instant and total. As I lie there, in the semi-darkness, the cold starts to seep in, tongues of ice licking at my exposed skin.

65

Darnell

"She's inside," Oren Darnell says.

His voice is even, quiet, controlled. He grips the back of one of the chairs, his eyes fixed intently on the screen. The camera is looking down on the Core doors. It shows Hale, getting to her feet, hugging herself tightly. On the screen, the clouds made from her breath are grey pixels, blocky and stuttering.

Okwembu stands in the doorway to the control room, arms folded.

Darnell throws the chair. It crashes across the control room, knocking over other chairs as it goes. Okwembu doesn't respond, not even when Darnell walks right up to her. His body is drenched in sweat and blood.

"She's tenacious, I'll give her that," Okwembu says.

"We have to shut her out."

Okwembu shrugs. "The stompers disabled the lock. We can close the doors, but we can't seal them."

"She knows the damn code. If she were to get in the control room—"

"But she won't," Okwembu says wearily. "She isn't wearing a thermo-suit. She'll freeze solid before she gets within a mile of here. And if she does somehow make it through, she'll be far too weak to fight."

Okwembu's eyes glitter, and Darnell sees something in them that he hasn't seen before. Something like excitement.

"We can kill her together. In front of everyone. And then we can tell them what's coming."

Darnell starts laughing, and once he does, he finds that he can't stop. It comes from somewhere deep inside him—an awful, hacking noise, as if a malignant tumour has come loose in his chest. He lifts the knife, points it at Okwembu. His shoulder wound has started bleeding again, and he can feel it throbbing, a deep ache that won't go away.

"You've never killed anyone in your life," he says, between gusts of laughter. "You even had me suck the oxygen out of that amphitheatre for you. You don't *deserve* to kill her."

"If you go in there, you put yourself at risk. But if we meet her here, she'll have two of us to deal with. Let her come to us."

Darnell considers it, but only for a second. Every iota of hatred he possesses has focused down into this one thing. He's not going to *let her come*. He's going to fix it. He's going to fix her.

He steps past Okwembu, and only stops when she puts a hand on his arm.

"You're hurt," she says, gesturing at his mangled shoulder. "It'll only slow you down in there. If you're going to go, then at least let me give you something for the pain."

Darnell looks down. Okwembu is slipping the cap off a syringe, filled with clear liquid. She moves to slide his sleeve up, and that's when he knocks her arm aside. The syringe explodes against the wall.

"It's butorphanol," she says, raising her hands. "Pain meds. That's all. Just—"

Darnell hits her.

Okwembu goes down, collapsing on all fours. Darnell steps over her, striding down the passage. It's only when he reaches the stairs that he wonders if he should kill her. He half turns back, then stops himself, because all he can see is Riley Hale. Okwembu isn't important. There's nothing she can do to him.

Darnell laughs again, turning away. He begins climbing the stairs.

"Oren," says Okwembu from behind him, her voice thick with pain. When he doesn't respond, she says it more sharply. "Oren!"

He barely hears her. Barely realises what he's doing. All he can think about is how every step takes him closer to the Core.

Closer to Hale.

66

Riley

Every breath is visible, as dense as the smoke in the room below me—and every one I suck in cuts deep into my lungs. This isn't like the cold I've felt in the Nest, when I've woken from a deep sleep with the blanket bunched around my feet. That you get used to. This is dry cold, ripped from the absolute zero of the vacuum, channelled and controlled to bring down the colossal heat of the fusion reactor and the superconducting cables that carry its power to the rest of the station.

I'm at the bottom of an enormous cylinder, stretching upwards to infinity, lit with huge spotlights that nevertheless fail to cut through the gloom completely. I count six cables, each as thick as three men, spaced around the cylinder. There's a catwalk, laid around the sides of the cylinder in front of the cables, curling steadily upwards like a coiled spring.

I get to my feet. Six miles from here to Apex. If I can keep the pace up, it should take me about two hours to run the Core.

Of course, I have to do it in sub-zero temperatures, and in a gravity that will get lower with every step.

I head towards the ramp that leads to the catwalk, then stop. How do the Core techs get up there? After all, if you're in a bulky thermo-suit, carrying heavy equipment, you aren't going to walk upwards for three miles every time a pipe springs a leak.

It takes me a moment to spot it, hidden in the shadows behind where I came in. An elevator. A golden ticket right to the top. I can't help cracking a smile.

My footsteps are loud in the vast space as I cross the room. The thought occurs to me that they might have found a way to shut down the elevator after I broke in, but it opens as I touch the button. The lights on the inside flicker to life, illuminating the cramped space. Under normal circumstances, it'd probably be a chore to ride in, but right now, I can't get in there fast enough.

I thumb the Up button, fighting to push it hard enough through my bulky gloves. Despite the padding, my hands are already numb, and my cheeks are throbbing gently, as if I've been slapped. I try to stay as still as possible, hoping to conserve energy. The elevator hums to life, and with an enormous clanking noise, begins to move slowly upwards. I hold my breath, expecting that at any moment it'll shudder to a halt, and start downwards, where a group of heavily armed stompers will be waiting. But the lift keeps moving, slowly making its way up the tube. My chest is still warm, and my sweat-soaked undergarments don't appear to have frozen.

It occurs to me that this is the first time I've been by myself since I was locked in the brig in Apogee. There's nobody to back me up: no Amira, no Prakesh, no Carver or Kev. And the higher the elevator gets, the further I go from everybody else.

The Dancers would get a real kick out of this place. Imagine being able to run as you approach zero gravity. Amira would...

I shut my eyes tight. I take Amira, and Yao, and Grace Garner, and put them in a very small place, deep in my mind. I force myself to do it, *will* them to stay silent. *Later,* I tell them. *Later, when this is over, we can talk.*

At that moment, the lift gives a screeching sound and judders to a halt. I drop to the floor, out of sight, before I realise that there's no way anybody could be aiming at me through the window. Slowly, I get to my feet, but I'm thrown off balance when the elevator jerks downwards. I panic, realising that they've managed to report the attack, the intrusion, and they're bringing me back down.

I hammer on the door release button. Nothing happens. There are two other buttons indicating up and down, alongside another button that looks like it activates a communicator. I'm about to press it, but stop, irritated with myself. Yes, Riley, confirm that you're in the lift.

I try to force the doors open, to push my fingers into the crack, but it's useless with the gloves on. My heart sinks: I'll have to take them off.

I grasp one in my teeth, pull it upwards, shucking it from my hand. I do the other, then tuck both under my arm. My fingers are a pale white. Is it my imagination, or are they turning ever so slightly blue at the tips?

No time. I jam my fingers into the door, hunting for a grip. The metal burns on contact, sending jabs of icy pain through my numb fingers. Ever so slowly, with a hideous creaking sound, the doors separate, and I wedge my body between them. I'm half in and half out of the lift, my hands screaming with pain, no more than a few feet above the catwalk surface.

With a yell, I throw myself out of the lift, landing feet first on the ramp with a boom that reverberates around the shaft. One of my gloves under my arm flies forwards, bouncing towards the edge. A terrified gasp escapes my lips, and I dive forwards, scrabbling for it. My fingers grab it a moment before it flies off the ramp, into space. I lie there, breathing heavily through my nose. Behind me, the lift continues its downward path.

I sit up, and shove the gloves back on. My hands are numb, way too numb. More panic begins to seep in, clouding my thoughts. I force myself to concentrate, trying to put what I need in order. I'm cold, so my body is pulling everything to its own core, diverting blood from my extremities. I need to get blood to my hands. I stand and begin swinging my arms. The tingling that returns to my hands a second later is almost worse than the numbness, but I grit my teeth, forcing myself to push through it. After a few spins, they start to feel a little warmer. Maybe I can get through this.

It takes me a moment to notice the curious sensation in my arms. It's as if, at the top of my windmill movement, I have to force my arms downwards, rather than letting momentum carry them through. And then a small wave of nausea rises in my stomach, and I realise: gravity. I'm starting to feel the onset of zero-G—or microgravity, anyway. The closer I get to the centre of the spinning ring, the less gravity there'll be. I cast my eyes up the ramp, curling up the sides of the shaft, wondering what it will feel like.

Only one way to find out. I start running.

I have no idea how far I have to go before I reach the Core, but I start to feel the effect of the lower gravity on my running instantly. As with my arms, I have to force my feet downwards—

I'm exerting less effort on the push-off with each stride, but far more to get it to stick. I try to adapt to the gravity, using it to conserve the energy at the start of each stride, and then release it at the end. But instead, I just tire a lot faster than normal. The nausea ebbs and flows; presumably, the protein bars I ate must be starting to bob around in my stomach. I want to laugh at the thought, but I'm breathing too hard, my breath forming soft clouds of condensation.

After a few minutes, I stop for a rest beside one of the superconductor cables. I run my hand down the casing: it's not metal, more like some kind of rubber, slightly springy to touch. I can feel it humming under my hand, pulsing with energy. Is this how Darnell and the Sons of Earth are planning to destroy us? Maybe they've got some kind of bomb in the reactor. Shut off the power, kill every light and air system and source of heat, turn the station into a tomb.

I tell myself that I won't let that happen.

With a groan, I push myself off the cable, and start running again. The catwalk slopes upwards, running clockwise around the cylinder, spaced a little way from the wall to make room for the cables. The surface is perforated metal grating, uneven and sharp. Every time I take a step, the sound echoes back from the other side of the cylinder. There's a railing on the outside of the catwalk; I trail my hand along it as I run, using it to steady myself against the lowering gravity. I might be running upwards in a circle, without any changes of direction, but I find that my torso keeps tilting too far forwards, threatening to tip me off balance. I have to pull it back consciously, and every time I do so, it saps even more energy.

And there's an even stranger sensation: it's like I'm constantly tilting towards the wall, as if I'm made of metal, and the wall is a giant magnet. It takes me a moment to work out what it is: the spinning motion of the ring. When I'm heading towards the centre, moving in low gravity, the spin will start to have an effect. I'll be pushed up against one of the walls of the shaft. I can only hope it doesn't slow me down too much.

I stop again, my breathing ragged. The Core's not a vacuum,

but it feels like I have to force every breath into my lungs. Is that something to do with the change in elevation? Or is it just the run itself? The sweat under my clothes has started to turn cold, and I catch myself shivering. *This isn't working.*

The whole time, I've been fighting against the lack of gravity, struggling to run in a way that I'm used to. Maybe there's a way to work with the gravity.

This time, instead of pushing each stride down, I concentrate all my energy on the upwards spring, trying to push myself higher. The first time I do it, I put so much effort into it that I nearly hurl myself over the outside railing. I grab it with both hands, steady myself and try again—and this time I control the spring, keeping my body steady in the air. The first stride takes me a good ten feet. The next, fifteen. Then, I'm leaping higher and higher, bounding forwards in huge, springy steps, covering twenty feet at a time, twenty-five. It still feels as if the wall is trying to pull me towards it, but I angle my jumps, giving myself some room to move.

The sensation is like nothing I've ever experienced. I close my eyes, and now I do laugh, because for the first time I feel what it's like to fly. For the first time in my life, in the middle of the most impossible circumstances imaginable, I'm airborne.

I've never felt a rush like it. And I know right then that if I survive this, I'm going to spend the rest of my life chasing it.

The catwalk vanishes below me, leaving me hanging in mid-air. My heart jumps, and for a long second I think I'm about to plummet to the bottom. But then I realise that I'm still moving forwards, buoyed by the lack of gravity.

It's an amazing feeling—almost peaceful.

Five seconds later, I collide painfully with the wall of the shaft.

I bounce right off, flying across the gaping centre of the tube towards the opposite wall. I flip my body around in the air, so my legs are facing the wall.

This time, instead of smashing into it, I let my legs take the impact, then push upwards, launching my body up the shaft. Not hard enough. I shoot out a few feet, and then the wall catches up with me. I bend my legs again, then push upwards even harder. This time, I propel myself into the middle of the shaft.

Looking down, I spot the catwalk, which does indeed end abruptly just before one of the cables. Of course: techs wouldn't need it any more. Not when they could just push upwards, and fly.

It's an odd sensation. The gravity is low enough that I can fly down the middle of the shaft for lengthy stretches, but every few hundred feet, I find the wall rushing up again as the spin catches up with me. Without the act of running, I start to get colder, and before long I'm shivering. I'm painfully aware that I need to get through the Core as quickly as possible. I don't know how long my body can take this cold, and I'm already going to be dangerously weak by the time I get out the other side.

An unsettling thought occurs to me. How do I actually get through the doors on the other side? Will there be a panel that controls the door? Or can it only be accessed from the outside? I didn't even stop to check at the Apogee end of the shaft, which seems like a colossal oversight.

The sound in the shaft changes, the rumbling getting deeper, more hollow. I crane my neck upwards, and there, silhouetted from behind by a dozen huge beams, like something coming out of the sun, is the Core Reactor.

It's enormous, far bigger than I'd ever expected. The shaft opens out into a massive spherical chamber; the reactor is in the centre, an angular block, running from one wall to the other, cocooned in cables and control panels. I almost expect to see jets of steam being vented into the room, but any real moisture in this cold would be lethal to the electronics. The hum coalesces, and it's unlike any other sound I've ever heard. Like this thing has a stomach, and it's rumbling.

I'm flying out of the mouth of the shaft, heading straight towards it. I look back over my shoulder, and see that the shaft entrance is moving to the side. I'm at the centre of the ring now, and everything is rotating around me. The movement is slow, more than enough for me to deal with.

I swing my body around—it's harder with so little gravity, but I just manage it—and my legs make contact with the reactor, sending a dull clang echoing around the chamber. There's a set of handgrips to my right, and I reach out for them, letting my body come to rest. I'm about to throw myself outwards again when I hear a cry of triumph from above me.

Oren Darnell flies out of the darkness, clutching an enormous blade.

67

Riley

A scream dies in my throat, choked off by the memory of those rough, damp hands. All that emerges is a terrified mewling.

I'm frozen in place, watching Darnell bear down on me. His face is like something from the other end of the universe.

At the very last moment, just before he reaches me, I finally find the strength. I piston my legs, hurling myself towards the wall of the chamber. But Darnell was ready for the move; he grabs the handgrip I was holding on to not two seconds before, then uses it to swing himself after me, his legs making contact with the reactor and pushing outwards. I'm moving away fast, but not fast enough—his push-off was more powerful, and as we race towards the wall, he starts to gain on me.

How? How did he know I would be running the Core? How long has he been waiting for me?

The part of the wall we're heading towards is fitted with several screens, all trailing power cables. When I make contact a second later, it's knees first, and I feel one of the screens crack and buckle under me, spitting glass and sparks.

Darnell is right behind me. I throw myself off the wall, aiming over his head. But instead of trying to catch me, he swings around in mid-air, bracing his left shoulder for impact as he jabs the blade upwards, slicing through my jacket and tagging my side.

It's like a red-hot piece of metal being held to my skin. I jerk away, another scream tearing itself from my lips, as a tiny bubble of blood appears and starts to spread out, floating in mid-air between us. His strike has changed my direction, knocking me back towards the reactor.

Darnell roars, and launches himself after me, but this time I have a head start, and his direction is slightly off. He's moving underneath me. He turns his face upwards, and the sight of his smile almost causes me to lose control completely.

"I saw you come in through the Apogee entrance," he calls out. "You thought I'd just let you walk into Apex?"

The cameras. That's how. It doesn't matter if not all of them work any more; the one outside the Core does. Maybe even one in the Air Lab control room. How else would he have known that Amira had failed?

He spreads his arms wide. The movement sets him spinning slowly in the other direction, but his eyes never leave me. "Now it's just you and me, Hale. And what better place for us to have a rematch than the centre of Outer Earth itself? It's almost poetic."

The mewling is back, stuck in my throat. My side is on fire; I don't think I've been cut deeply, but I leave a glistening trail of blood as I move through the air.

I hit the reactor and scrabble at it, hunting for a hold. But this section of the surface is smooth, and with nothing to hold on to, all I do is put myself into a spin. A rolling wave of nausea spurts through me, and the tumble causes my arms and legs to flail. Darnell's also trying to get a grip on the reactor. He's taken his eyes off me, hunting for a hold.

There are cables passing below me, a tangled mess of wires spewing out of their black insulation sheaths. I reach out and snag one of them, praying that I don't rip it out of its socket; the last thing I need is to cause a reactor shutdown myself. Holding on to the cable swings my body around, until my head is pointing back towards Darnell.

Tracer

I can't beat him. Not when he's armed and I'm not. And in near-zero-G—no way. I barely survived in normal gravity. I'm breathing too hard, the cold beginning to lock down my body heat. There's an odd tingling sensation in my hands.

The cables. There's a big tangle of them, positioned slightly away from the reactor, held apart at intervals by steel brackets. The gap behind the cables looks just wide enough for me to squeeze into.

I pull myself towards the opening, trying to be as quiet as possible. I wedge myself into it, the cables pushing against my bulky jacket.

If Darnell saw me enter, he'll have me trapped, able to pick me off whenever he wants. I can see the blade shooting from between the cables, skewering me in the chest, but there's nothing, just the hum of the reactor against my back. I can't even hear Darnell any more, and when I peer through the mass of cables, he's vanished. I slow my breathing, try to remain still.

There he is, drifting slowly across my field of vision. His eyes scan the room, passing across my hiding place. I hold my breath and draw back against the wall, worried that a stray puff of breath from my mouth will give me away.

He stares for what feels like an eternity.

But then he turns his head, looks away. And I notice something. He's breathing heavily: I can hear it, a tired, wet rumble. His blade hand is shaking slightly too, as if he's gripping it too hard, and his enormous shoulders are also shaking, rising up and down with each breath. He's not as fit as I am, and his body is burning too much energy too quickly. He's injured too, with blood soaking his shoulder. His jacket doesn't fit him, and the shirt underneath looks thin and insubstantial.

He came into the Core because he wanted to take me down himself, right here. It's the kind of twisted logic that would appeal to someone like him. But he didn't think. Didn't realise how much the cold would affect him.

For the first time, I may just have the edge.

Could I wait him out? Stay here until he dies of hypothermia? It sounds so ridiculous I have to force myself not to laugh. Even if I was able to somehow not die of cold myself, and even if he kept missing my hiding place in a room with very few hiding places, there's just no time. Okwembu is still out there, and the heat convectors are still inactive.

What are you going to do if they come after you in the Core?

What I always do, Prakesh. I run.

I have to wait until he's far enough away. He's getting agitated, moving towards the bottom of the reactor. I force myself to keep breathing, to flex my fingers and toes, to keep the blood flowing. The seconds stretch into minutes.

"Where are you?" he yells.

Slowly, I slip out from behind the cables. I can see him; he's below, and won't see me unless he looks straight up. Moving very quietly, I position myself on the reactor, ready to push off towards the shaft leading to Apex as soon as it comes into view. Under me, the reactor hums, the vibration gripping the soles of my shoes.

I see the shaft entrance. With one movement, I push myself off the reactor, floating towards it.

Darnell bellows as he spots me. I sneak a glance back. He's still below me, but—no—he's gaining. Maybe he pushed off harder. I will myself forwards, tucking my arms, streamlining my body. Behind me, Darnell raves. There's no joy in his voice now; just pure hatred.

The first part of the shaft is hard. The wall rises up to meet me again, and I have to push off it, adjusting to the gravity as I go, willing myself not to look back. I can see the ramp below me. Slowly, I change my aim, bring my body around—it's hard without anything to push off, but I do it. He's got closer, no more than a few yards away. The blade glints in the dim light, and I can hear his breathing, deep and hard, echoing around the shaft. I'm shivering uncontrollably now—whether from fear or the cold, I don't know.

Then I realise: the gravity. It's coming back as we get further away from the reactor, and I can use it to my advantage. Like the Apogee shaft, the ramp here curves downwards, circling the walls. I don't have to run down the whole catwalk. I can jump from side to side, letting the low gravity cushion my fall. And the lower I go, the less problematic the station's spin will be.

"You're mine, Hale," he says.

I look back over my shoulder.

"You'll have to catch me first."

I hit the ramp, and almost immediately bounce back upwards. But this time, I push myself out over the shaft aiming for a lower part of the catwalk on the far side. The low gravity means that I can drop down a few levels of the ramp each time.

The move surprises Darnell, but he recovers quickly. I can hear him in the air behind me as I drop onto the catwalk below. My heart is pounding, but I force myself to run, to jump down again, this time back to the other side of the shaft. When I look back over my shoulder, I see Darnell: he didn't quite reach the catwalk, and is scrambling over the railing on the far side, cursing with the effort. The knife is jammed in his waistband.

"What's the matter, Oren?" I shout. "Can't jump high enough?"

He doesn't say anything. He just roars. I don't waste any more time gloating, just start moving down the ramp. It's not long before I start running. The gravity is still low, so I have to control my strides, but almost immediately I start to leave him behind. He's running now, moving down the ramp behind me, but before long I'm far ahead of him. His panting gets softer and softer. When I get to the bottom, maybe I can get out and trap him in here, somehow…

I still have no idea how I can get the doors at the bottom of the shaft open. If they can only be opened from the outside, I'll be dead in minutes.

No choice. I have to keep running.

It's an age before I reach the bottom of the shaft. The last few minutes are a haze of exhaustion and pain, coursing through my body and sizzling in the cut on my side. As I reach the floor, my feet tangle up, and I crash to the ground, crying out.

I force myself to get up. I can't hear Darnell any more, but I have to move. I'm colder than I've ever been in my life. I can no longer feel my feet, or my hands.

The bottom of the shaft here is similar to the Apogee end. Same elevator, same cable points. There's got to be a way to open these doors. Whatever's on the other side—even if it's Okwembu, waiting with a stinger—I have to get out of here.

I spot a control panel, tucked away by the elevator, and my heart leaps. As I approach, I can see it's simple enough: a small digital readout, and a single switch. There aren't any labels, but I don't need them. I hit the switch, scarcely daring to breathe.

The doors clunk, sputter and begin to open. At that same instant, I hear Darnell above me.

He's coming down the last few coils of catwalk. Without thinking, without even looking, I drop through the opening doors, into Apex.

I land heavily and roll, my side flaring with pain. The temperature changes so quickly that pins and needles cascade through my body. The room is brightly lit, a huge space with white walls and glaring fluorescents. But I don't have time to take in the details. I'm looking for the door controls. There. One on either side of the room, just like back in Apogee, much newer and better maintained than their partners on the other side.

I can still hear him, panting, as he moves towards the open doors. How close is he? No way to tell. I have to lock the doors. I spring to the first control panel, jab at the touch-screen, searching for the option to close.

Seal Reactor Access? asks the panel. I hit *Confirm* so hard that a spear of pain shoots back into my finger. No time. Run. I'm pushing my body to the limit, but I still feel as if my legs won't move fast enough, like the cold has sealed my bones in place. Then I'm at the other panel, hunting through the options.

Above me the doors start to close, grinding shut. I look upwards—just in time to see him come down the last part of the ramp. The doors are closing too slowly. He'll be through them in seconds.

Move, I tell myself, but it's like I'm back in the reactor, watching him fly towards me. My legs have turned to lead.

The doors move towards each other, inch by inch. Darnell hits the floor and makes one last desperate jump towards them.

68

Darnell

Darnell is halfway through the doors when they close on his torso.

The metal teeth bring his descent to a shuddering halt, first slowing him, then holding him, then biting down as the enormous, grinding motors try to push the doors closed.

He feels his ribs break—the sound is a soft snap, like pulling a twig off a tree. He almost blacks out from the agony. He's upside-down, clawing at the air, his face twisted with pain. Something below his ribs gives way, and he screams. The darkness rushes in.

Before it closes on him completely, he sees Riley Hale. She's standing below him, her eyes wide, staring in mute horror. No more than a few feet away.

You're mine.

Darnell starts to twist his body. He can feel his legs flailing at the air above the doors, and he plants his hands on the other side of them, begins to push. He feels bone scrape bone, and he screams again, the thick cords of muscle in his neck tight enough to snap. The doors' motors are stuck in a high-pitched whine, and he can smell the sharp stench of burning electronics.

With a final wrench, Darnell rips his body free of the doors. When he hits the ground, it's as if an enormous hand has torn away his midsection. His legs have stopped working, and a dull pain emanates from the base of his spine.

Hale is slowly backing away. As Darnell screams her name, she turns and runs.

His hands still work. He can still do something. His knife has slipped out of his waistband, and lies in arm's reach. Darnell grabs it, groaning as the world turns grey and scarlet. But he can still see her. She's directly ahead, her back to him, presenting a perfect target. Darnell summons all the strength he has left, raising his arm as high as he can, crooking his elbow.

You always pull to the right, he thinks. *You have to adjust for that.*

His muscle memory is perfect, each movement sliding into place, and his arm is fully extended when he releases the knife. It's a perfect throw.

The blade spins through the air, heading right towards Riley Hale, a flickering star in an impossibly bright universe. For an instant, Darnell thinks it's going to hit its mark. Right when it counts, he's found his aim.

The knife goes wide.

It ricochets off the wall with a clang, the blade flickering as it bounces away. Hale looks back, startled, and the stupid, animal confusion in her eyes fuels Darnell's anger. He starts to pull himself across the floor, slamming his elbows into it, his ribs tenting the fabric of his shirt. If he can just get to her…

His arms give out. His face slams into the ground, all the strength draining away at once. He lies there, heaving, his hands balled into fists. He's not supposed to die here. He's supposed to die with everyone else, the only one laughing in a sea of screams. This isn't fair.

He lifts his head once more. The tracer is still staring at him.

"You cuh. You can't imagine," he says, and then stops. His throat has forgotten how to form words, and kicking it back into action nearly wipes him out.

"You can't imagine what you'll find in there," he says. A spray of blood shoots out from between his teeth as he speaks. "You can't run from it. No one can."

His eyes find hers.

"It's going to burn you alive."

The grey and scarlet turn black, like a piece of silk in a fire, and then there's nothing at all.

Tracer

69

Riley

For the longest time, I can't move.

I'm expecting him to twitch, for him to look up and come for me again. He doesn't. I should retrieve the knife, plant it in his heart, make sure, but the thought of being close to him again makes me shudder.

Crushed. His organs turned to pulp. The old Riley would have felt something.

The new one doesn't care.

After a minute, my legs give out. I go down on one knee, breathing hard. The shivering is back, stronger now, and needle-jabs of pain are ricocheting through my body. The temptation to close my eyes and drift away is so strong that I have to will my eyes to stay open. *Focus on something. Anything.*

That's when I see it. A water point. Standing in the corner, gleaming under the lights. I'm up so fast that it's a full second before the pain in my side kicks in. I ignore it, stumbling over to the water point, fumbling with the switch. The tap clicks, whirrs, and falls silent, dry as my throat.

I hang my head, more furious than I'm willing to admit, but as I do so the tap whirrs again, startling me, and begins to gush water. I let out a small cry of relief, and stick my head under the tap, greedily sucking it in, gulping in huge mouthfuls of water. I drink, and drink, and drink.

After a while, I drink too much. Coughing and spluttering, I collapse against the water point, but I'm surprised at how good I feel. Amazing how a little water can change things around.

I wipe my mouth; I'm still shivering, but the tremors are smaller now. Slowly, I strip myself of my gloves and undo my jacket. I'm no expert on frostbite, but it looks as if I managed to protect my hands for just long enough. Before long, they're flaring with powerful, reassuring pain, flushed with red.

I'm alone. No Okwembu. Or anyone else. Every surface is a gleaming white, lit by strips of lighting where the walls meet the ceilings and floors. There aren't any crates or pieces of equipment that I can see, or even any control panels on the walls. Unlike Apogee—or any other sector—it's quiet here. I can still hear the groaning of the hull, but I have to strain to do so.

And then I notice something. It's cooler here.

When I was on the other side of the station, the temperature was almost unbearable. But here, it's actually pleasant. Darnell—and Okwembu—must have kept the convection fins active for Apex. I've got to find a way to turn the rest of the station's convectors back on. How much time do I have left?

No way to tell.

I don't look at Darnell's body as I leave. I'm done with him. Trying to be as quiet as possible, I make my way to one of the corridors running off the main room. The light is dimmer here. There are doors recessed into the walls; I'm curious to know what's behind them, but there's no time.

The small, dark place where I put Yao, Amira and everyone else pulses. I fight it back. I can't be scared now, can't afford to be scared. Darnell is out of commission—I hope—but that doesn't mean his plan is. And it doesn't mean Okwembu isn't still out there.

I hit a T-junction. As I reach it, I flatten myself against the wall and close my eyes, listening hard. If Okwembu wasn't waiting for me when I came out of the Core, then there's every chance she'll be in one of the corridors, just waiting for me to show myself so she can put a bullet in my chest. I suddenly remember Darnell's knife, and curse myself for not retrieving it.

I can't hear anything: just the quiet hum of the lights, and behind them, like a ripple in a puddle of water, the sound of the station. I slip round the corner and pad quietly down the deserted passage, almost breaking into a run, deciding that it's better to be quiet.

There are stairs at the end of the corridor. Again, I hesitate before stepping onto them, wary that Okwembu could be waiting above or below me. Again, I hear nothing. Scarcely daring to breathe, I step into the stairwell, and start down it.

It's a few levels before I'm breathing again. I'm oddly reassured by just how much noise the stairs make when stepped on, giving off odd clangs every time my feet come down. Anybody listening would be able to hear me coming—but I'd be able to hear them, too. After a few levels, there cease to be any more corridors leading off. I'm getting close.

A few minutes later, I reach the bottom level. Ahead of me is a single small corridor, and at the end of it what must be the door to the control room. I don't know what I was expecting—a set of blast doors, maybe, or some complicated locking mechanism—but it's like every other door in the station.

I walk up to it, glancing nervously over my shoulder. There's a small keypad on one side of the door. Under the usual circumstances, there'd probably be several heavily armed elite officers on guard here, so other security measures in such a tight space probably wouldn't be necessary.

Still, the sight of the keypad gives me pause. There'll be no way to guess the code. Does this mean I've got to find Okwembu? Force the code out of her? My shoulders sag. I can't spend time tracking someone in an unfamiliar sector, where they know the layout and I don't, where they're armed and rested and I'm exhausted and defenceless.

It's then that a little green light blinks at the bottom of the keypad, so quickly that I nearly miss it. I freeze, hardly daring to believe I've seen it, but after thirty seconds or so it blinks again.

The door's unlocked.

This is too easy. Okwembu is waiting inside, knowing that I'll come to her. She'll shoot me the moment I'm through the door.

But there's no other choice. I have to get in there. I cast around for something to hide behind, anything to give me cover, but there's nothing in the corridor.

What if I didn't have to take cover out here? What if I could surprise her, and get behind something inside the control room before she shoots? It might buy me a few crucial seconds. And while Okwembu might fire in the direction of the corridor, she might be a little more hesitant to shoot if she could hit the controls.

Which would be a bit more relevant if she wasn't so intent on destroying the station.

I shake off the thought, and take a step back from the door, breathing hard. I rest my finger on the keypad's Enter button, tell myself to push it, but I hold back. Every cell in my body is screaming for me to turn around, to go find somewhere dark and warm and safe, and let everything disappear. I have to remind myself that there's nowhere like that any more.

I push the button.

The door whooshes open, and I throw myself through, tucking into a roll. I catch a blurred glimpse of several terminals, and then I'm in the roll, my heart in my mouth, expecting to hear the awful bang of a gunshot. I swing my head to the side, preparing to dive behind the nearest bit of cover. But as I do so, I get a look at the room, and I check my movement, coming to a stop on all fours.

The control room is deserted.

Terrified, I flick my head from side to side, hunting out hiding places, anywhere that she could be waiting. But there's no place to hide. Slowly, I stand, gazing around me.

Wherever Okwembu is, it's not here. The main control room of Outer Earth is narrow, barely wider than the corridor outside. The walls on either side of me are crowded with banks of screens, bathing the room in an orange glow. There aren't any keyboards or control pads, so I'm guessing the screens are touch-based. Several chairs are scattered around, overturned.

Slowly, I wander down the room. It's tiny. There's not even a viewing port: just bank after bank of terminals. There's no retinal scanner that I can see, nothing that Darnell would use Foster's eyeball on. It must be hidden away somewhere.

By now, I'm expecting to hear klaxons, computerised voices reading off dire warnings, but the room is quiet. I turn back to the door, hoping against hope that there's a way to lock it. There's another keypad, but it's also blinking green, and without the code, I won't be able to close it. I walk back and thumb the Enter button, and the door shuts with a hiss.

Tracer

Okwembu's absence nags at me. Where is she? I can't think of a single reason why she wouldn't be in the control room. Maybe she's watching from a distance, or listening. Waiting for me to trigger a trap.

There's nothing I can do about it now, not unless I'm willing to waste time searching the sector for her. With one eye on the entrance, I scan the screens again. I'm looking for a login box, something that requires a password, something I can input the word Iapetus into and find out what it does.

But each screen I look at appears to be logged in already; they all display various options, ranging from Dock Access to Thruster Management to Aeronautics. Most are in English, but several seem to be in Hindi and Chinese as well. One of them shows a static radio frequency, and there's a little dust on the controls, like no one has used them for a long time. Can't say I blame them; in the decades after the nuclear war, we could still pick up radio signals from Earth. One by one, they all faded. Fifty years ago, the planet went completely silent.

I stop in front of one of the screens. I debate pulling a chair upright, but decide to stand—if Okwembu comes through that door, I want to be ready.

Hesitating—but only for a second—I place my finger on one of the touch-screens and start to navigate through the system. There are lots of false starts, and I find myself staring at incomprehensible readouts and dead-ends of reactor kilowatt graphs. Cursing, I find my way back to the main menu screen, and methodically begin to trawl through the options. It's strange to think that right now I have an enormous amount of control over even the tiniest details of Outer Earth. No wonder Darnell and Okwembu wanted to take this place for themselves.

It takes me a lot longer than I want, but I find it, hidden in a sub-menu: *Convection Systems*. I tap the option, and the screen flashes with even more graphs and readouts. One catches my eye. *Average module temperature: 46C.*

Forty-six degrees Celsius. I've got to turn these things back on now.

Forcing myself to be patient, I scan through the display. I find it at the bottom of the screen. *Convection fin status: Inactive.* I tap the option, hoping that's all there is to it. My heart sinks as another menu opens up: a circular diagram of the station, showing the location of each convection fin with a small green triangle. There look to be about a dozen, scattered across the station hull.

I lean forwards, squinting to make out the detail. Each little triangle is empty. I reach out, tapping one, and it turns solid green. On the bottom of the screen, a text box flashes up: *Fin 6E1 active.*

Smiling, I start hitting all the triangles, breathing a huge sigh of relief as they turn green. But the breath catches in my throat as an error message flashes up, freezing my finger halfway to the screen.

Warning: ice crystals detected in convection system. Temperature at sub-optimal levels.

Numbers and letters pop up underneath the message. They must be convection fin locations. The error message is slightly transparent, and as I look closely I can see that all of them are on one side of the station, covering Gardens, Chengshi, half of Apogee.

Convection pump system may malfunction if exposed to extreme temperatures, reads the message. *Continue?*

I rest my head on my arms, growling in frustration, and I can feel helplessness pulling at me.

I raise my head, looking at the screen. The ice in the pipes... it has to be there because the pumps are shut down. The liquid that was on the outside when they got turned off hasn't moved. It's been exposed to the cold in space for too long.

I can't pump it back into the system yet. But what if I can melt it somehow? Raise the temperature of the liquid in the convection fins just enough so I can circulate it back in?

Circulate...

Maybe it's not the liquid in the pipes that I need to get moving.

Maybe it's Outer Earth itself.

70

Riley

It takes an age to find. I have to keep moving between touch-screens, looking for the right menu, and on the one occasion I glance at the heat readouts, I see that the internal temperature of the station has risen another half a degree.

"Come on," I say, cutting through a tangle of readouts and obscure options. "I know you're here."

I actually scream for joy when I find it. *Rotation speed.* I know that thrusters on the hull keep us spinning, slowly turning like a wheel. If I can increase the spin rate, I can move those iced-up pipes into direct sunlight.

It'll ramp up the gravity. The G-forces will increase, pushing me into the floor. But what other choice do I have?

Another model of the station has appeared, showing position relative to the Earth, moon and sun. I spot the controls for the rotation rate, and I crank them right up.

I expect to hear something—a dull boom, perhaps, as the thrusters power up. Instead, I feel a pressure between my shoulder blades. It goes from mild to excruciating in seconds, forcing me to my knees. There's no pain, but my hands are heavy—like I'm having to force them down simply to keep them sliding off the control panel. Raising my head—it feels like my neck is going to split down the sides—I see that the on-screen station has begun to rotate faster. I need to spin it a full one-eighty to get the frozen pipes in the sun.

The gravity seems to get even heavier, and this time there's real pain: a headache so intense that I cry out. I lose my grip on the controls, and my body thuds to the floor, sending an arrow of pain into my arms when they hit the deck.

It would be so easy just to lie here. My entire body feels as if huge weights are pinning it to the floor. But I push myself up, groaning with the effort. I get my right forearm on the control panel, and raise my eyes to the screen. Chengshi has moved—it's in direct sunlight. But the station is still spinning too slowly. If I don't make this happen faster, I'm going to pass out. There'll be nobody to slow the spin rate.

Gritting my teeth, I reach upwards—it feels like my wrist is connected to the floor with huge rubber bands—and push the spin control right up.

71

Prakesh

Madala is more spry than he looks, hobbling along in an odd, loping gait. Prakesh and Indira have to jog to keep up. And he has friends. As they move down the levels, he stops to rap on hab doors. Their little group swells. First it's joined by a family—husband and wife, their teenage son—and then a thick-set man with long, pale dreadlocks falls in alongside them, shouldering a steel bar like it was made of foam rubber.

Dreads passes around a canteen, and everybody takes a long swig. Sweat is running into Prakesh's eyes, stinging hot, and he has to keep blinking it away.

"So what we do?" says Madala, turning to Prakesh.

"What do you mean?"

There's a shout from behind him. They all turn to see two men fighting, slamming into the corridor walls, tangling over what looks like a single protein bar.

Madala gestures. "That. What we do about that? About everything?"

"I don't..." Prakesh says, but he can feel everyone looking at him. He drops his eyes for a second, and only raises them again when the man with the dreadlocks speaks.

"Madala says you saved him," the man says. "He trusts you. That means I trust you. Tell us where to go."

The rest of the group murmurs assent. Indira nods vigorously, pounding her fist into her palm.

The words are on Prakesh's lips, out before he can stop them. "We can't do anything about the big fights. But maybe we can break a few of the smaller ones."

"What good will it do?" The question comes from someone Prakesh didn't even know was there, a skinny young woman with a stern face and short, spiky hair. She reminds him of Riley a little, and he has to force himself to answer.

"We stop a small one, we get more people. Maybe we can stop one of the bigger ones."

"You heard Darnell. We're all gonna cook. We should be heading up to Apex and—"

"No," Prakesh says firmly. "Apex is taken care of. Our job is down here."

Dreads says, "Why don't we go down to the mess? It was crazy when I was there earlier."

Prakesh nods. "All right."

The woman with the spiky hair shrugs. "Whatever you say, boss."

The Apogee mess hall is on Level 2, a square room with lurid orange walls—a misguided attempt, early on in the station's life, to make the place cheery. There are big metal tables and benches scattered across the room. Some of the tables have been overturned, as if to act as barricades. And there are people, dozens of them, clustered around the long food service counter and spilling out of the kitchens at the back of the room. The noise is cacophonous—the sound of people gone beyond fear and rage, into a kind of helpless panic.

Once more, Prakesh feels everyone looking at him, and when he reaches inside himself to figure out what to do, he's surprised to find the answer waiting for him.

He turns to the two biggest people in the group—the man with the dreads, and the teenager. "You two. Go break up as many fights as you can. Don't hurt anyone who doesn't try to hurt you. Everyone else, find something to make noise with. Pots, chairs, utensils."

For a moment, nobody moves. Then Dreads grabs the boy and starts jogging towards the kitchen. Madala and Indira and the others begin hunting, picking up anything that looks like it can make a noise.

Prakesh rights a table, kicking it down with a bang. The sound cuts through everything, but not one of the looters so much as glances in his direction. Ignoring the sick feeling in the pit of his stomach, he climbs up on the table, cupping his hands around his mouth.

"Everybody—listen to me," he shouts. He tries to be as strident and authoritative as he can, but he might as well be trying to shout a message to Jupiter. Nobody pays him any attention.

He looks back at Madala, intending to tell everyone to start making as much noise as possible to focus the looters' attention. He feels a twinge in his shoulder blades as he turns, ignores it, and then the twinge grabs on and pulls.

Prakesh cries out, dropping to one knee on the table, his hands flying to his neck. At first, he thinks someone hit him with something, but through sweat-stung eyes he can see that everyone else is feeling it too. The looters are screaming in pain. Madala and Indira are flat on the floor, reaching for each other.

The pressure increases, pushing Prakesh down onto the metal surface of the table. His head is pounding. *It's the gravity*, he thinks. *Darnell's going to spin us out of control.*

Just when it seems like the pressure can't get worse, it does. As his vision shrinks to a tiny bright spot at the end of a dark tunnel, Prakesh hears glass cracking, and the pained sound of metal beginning to bend.

72

Riley

The weight between my shoulder blades pushes down harder, and my raised hand slams back onto the panel. What must it be like in the rest of the station? People pushed to the floor. Metal beginning to kink and grind as the gravity forces it outwards. The trees in the Air Lab, bending under the pressure, branches snapping.

One of the screens on the other side of the room is flashing red. A calm voice echoes through the control room: "Warning. Horizontal thrusters overheating. Reduce rotation rate immediately."

Come on.

For the second time, I push myself up. My muscles feel like they're going to tear apart. One arm. Two. Even raising my eyes to the screen takes an effort, like they're being held in a vice.

And as I look, I see that Apogee has slipped into the sunlight. Gardens and Chengshi are already there. With a final burst of energy, I slam my finger onto the screen, pulling back the rotation rate.

This time, there is a noise—like a giant fan powering down. I slide to the floor, gasping for air. Gradually, the weights that have been placed across my body lift off.

It's a few minutes before the gravity is back to normal. When I get to my feet, I realise that my legs are trembling. I have to steady myself using the control panels, and it takes me a little while to get back to the other side of the room. The temperature has risen another degree, to 47.5 Celsius.

I try to activate the convection fins again, tapping the tiny triangles. The same error flashes up. Extreme temperatures.

I force myself to wait. A minute passes. Two. I try again.

This time, there's no error message. The green triangles all flick to solid. After another long minute, the average temperature reading drops to 46.

I've done it. The fins on the hull will be working again, venting the heat back into space. It'll take a while, but the temperature will come back down. The enormous amount of heat generated by the million or so people here will vanish. Whatever happens now, we're not going to roast to death.

I'm too exhausted to cheer. I just smile. And all I can think is: *you might make smoke bombs, Carver, but I bet you've never spun an entire space station.*

But something nags at me. I haven't had to use Iapetus, the piece of information Grace Garner and Marshall Foster died for. I'm missing something.

I need to get the Apex doors open—if I can get some stompers in here, this will all go a lot faster. I'm more confident now, and it doesn't take me long to find the screen which controls the doors. A wireframe model of the sector appears on screen, with red markers for where each door is. I tap the option to Open All.

The screen flashes red, firing up another error message. I very nearly put a fist through the glass, but instead, I take another deep breath, and make myself read the message.

Temperature imbalance detected.

The names of the sectors are scrolling underneath it—all over 40 Celsius, except for Apex, sitting at 22.

Access to sector will remain restricted until temperature balance has been restored. Lift restriction when this occurs?

I hit *Confirm.* No telling how long that'll take, but it's a start. As soon as the convection fins have done their work, the doors to Apex will spring open. Now I just have to figure out what to do until then.

I'm about to step away from the screens when one of the other menu options catches my eye. *Comms.*

I open it up. A list of sectors appear—numbered, not named—and they're all set to Inactive. I change that, then speak as clearly as I can. There's no way of knowing if my words are going out—there's no microphone visible. But I say the words anyway.

73

Prakesh

Prakesh comes back.

He's lying on the floor of the mess, and the pain between his shoulder blades is slipping away. The inside of his mouth is dry, as if he's woken up with a killer hangover.

He raises his head, blinking against the light. Madala and Indira are unconscious, splayed out next to each other. Prakesh gets to his knees, fighting off a sudden burst of nausea, and sees Dreads slumped against an upturned table. The man is staring up at the ceiling, as if daring it to fall on him.

Prakesh uses a chair to pull himself up. His legs feel like they're made of mashed potato, and for a second he's not entirely sure where he is. Then he catches sight of the serving area and the kitchen beyond, packed with groggy people swaying to unsteady life, and it all comes rushing back.

Prakesh grabs the table he kicked upright, and pulls himself onto it. It's all he can do not to lose his balance—the world goes woozy for a second, and the black tunnel threatens to come back, feathering the edges of his vision. He pushes past it, raises his hands to his mouth.

"Everybody—listen to me."

In the stunned silence of the mess hall, his voice is impossible to ignore. Dozens of eyes turn towards him, surprise and hostility pinning him to the spot. He pushes past those, too.

"This is what he wants," he says, jabbing a finger at the ceiling. He should have pointed at the comms screen, sitting in a top corner of the room like a malevolent god, but it doesn't matter. They know who he means.

"He wants us fighting. He wants us to hurt each other. And if we keep doing it, then he wins. Simple as that. There's enough food for everybody, if we work together."

More silence meets him. The crowd is recovering from the effects of the gravity increase now, and he can see them starting to mutter to one another. One or two are even turning away, back to the kitchens and stores, as if to get a head start on the others.

"I know everyone is scared," Prakesh says, but it's no use. More and more of them are turning away. In desperation, Prakesh hunts through the faces of the crowd, eventually stopping on a young woman. She's about Riley's age, with a red shawl wrapped around her shoulders. She's got a child pulled close to her, a little boy, her hands on his shoulders. Both of them are looking back at him, and it's not anger that Prakesh sees in their eyes. It's confusion, and fear.

He tries again, speaking to the mother, to the little boy. "I know everyone is scared. You want to feed your families. You want to get back some control. You want to protect the people closest to you."

He pauses for a second. The table creaks under him, and he feels someone moving to his side. Dreads. He glances at Prakesh, and gives a short nod.

"Right now," Prakesh says, "the woman I love is in danger. She's risking her life for us—for you—to stop Oren Darnell. And that scares the hell out of me, because I don't know how to help her, and she might not make it back. But you can't just care about the people closest to you. That's what Outer Earth has been about for so long: look out for you and yours, and screw everyone else. We can't do that. Not now. The only way we make it through this is if we help each other."

For a long second, Prakesh is sure he's blown it, that the crowd is going to ignore him. But the silence stretches on, and even those who were heading back towards the kitchens are staring at him.

The comms system crackles to life.

A horrified gasp ripples through the crowd. Even Prakesh jumps, glancing up at the comms screen, expecting Darnell's face to appear. But there's no image. There's just a voice. And as Prakesh hears it, his heart almost explodes out of his chest.

Go, Riley, go.

74

Riley

"This is Riley Hale. I'm in the control room in Apex. Oren Darnell is dead, and I've turned the heat convectors back on. I…"

I swallow. My next words were about to be: Okwembu is responsible. She did it all. But before I can utter the words, I realise that they won't help. People won't believe me. I have to find her. I have to *make* her tell them herself. Somehow.

"Whoever's listening, none of this was my fault. I am not responsible. But I will find the person who is."

I can't think of anything more to say. I step away from the screen, and cast another glance around the room. All the readouts seem to be OK, and the warm orange light from the screens seems oddly reassuring.

I'm about to leave to search for Okwembu when something catches my eye. One of the screens at the end of the room, showing a view that I haven't seen in years.

The Earth.

Scorched brown land, dull blue ocean. Swirling, simmering clouds, flecked brown and white. It's almost unchanged from the last time I was shown a picture of it, years ago.

But there's something else there.

Something horribly familiar, hanging in the middle of the camera's view, stark against the curve of the planet.

Every muscle in my body is paralysed. My mouth has gone completely dry, my thoughts frozen in place. I know that silhouette. I know it because I've seen it more times than I can think of. On broadcasts, in pictures. On the Memorial wall in Apogee.

It's the *Akua Maru*. The ship from the Earth Return mission.

I tell myself to stop being ridiculous, that it can't be the *Akua*, that this is archive video, something set up by Okwembu as a cruel, cruel taunt.

My hand moves without me telling it too, touching the screen gently. An orange square blinks around the form of the *Akua*. An option appears at the bottom, displayed in the orange light. *Ship broadcast frequencies: Inactive*.

I touch the screen, and the broadcast activates. I manage to say one word.

"Hello?"

For a long moment, there's nothing. Then there's a burst of static, emanating from speakers somewhere in the room. And I hear a voice, twisted with time and distance, as familiar as my own.

"Janice?" says the voice. "Is that you?"

I don't know what to do. My hand is still on the screen, and I can't pull it away.

"Are you there?" the voice continues. An edge of anger has crept into it. "Answer me. We don't have much time, and everything must be ready for my return. Respond."

With my eyes on the ship, I manage to speak one more word.

"Dad?"

75

Riley

At first, there's just silence, broken by the crackle of the radio signal in the empty room.

I can't take my eyes off the screen. I can see the *Akua* more clearly now: the curve of her hull, the swept-down fins jutting off the sides, the cylindrical body. It doesn't seem real.

The static swells and roars. "Who is this? Who are you?" The voice fires a bright line back down the years to a man standing tall in his captain's uniform, looking down at me, with a gentle half-smile on his face.

"It's me, Dad," I say, my voice shaking. "It's Riley."

There's contempt in his voice when he replies. "I don't know that name."

"Dad…"

"And I don't know your voice either. Whoever you are."

"Dad, I promise, I'm—"

"No!" The transmission is so loud and so sudden that I nearly fall backwards in surprise. The voice is warped now, malformed, not just by distance and signal quality, but by something else. "Riley is dead. She's dead. You're a liar!"

"No," I whisper. "I'm not dead." And then, louder: "Please, Dad. Please listen to me."

"Don't call me that," he snarls, and the venom in his voice burns a horrible, ragged hole in my mind. "You're not my daughter. Do you hear me? You're not her."

The static vanishes, plunging the room into silence.

I hammer the touch-screen, desperately trying to raise him, my voice cracking and turning from a harsh whisper into a full-on scream. Every fibre in my body wants me to run; to run and run and never look back. But I can't run from this.

It's some time before I can raise him again. When the static returns, I don't hear anything for a long time, nothing but my breathing. Someone has taken the world I knew and turned it inside out. There is so much I want to say, but every time I try, the words won't come.

Eventually, he says, "Whoever you are, it doesn't matter. You'll all pay for what you've done."

I can't make sense of his words. It's like I can hear them individually, but not connect them. There's no way my father could be the one speaking them.

I force myself to stay calm. "Dad," I start, but then my voice cracks again. "Dad, how is this possible? You're still alive—how…"

"Why do you keep calling me that?" he says, but there's something else in his voice beyond anger. A tiny, desperate note of hope.

I close my eyes, and slowly say, "Your name is John Abraham Hale. You were born on December Tenth, in Apogee. You married Arianna Tahangai on Outer Earth when you were twenty-one years old."

"None of that means anything. That doesn't prove who you are."

I keep my eyes closed. "When I was five, you showed me one of your space rocks. You got it from your missions on the asteroid catchers. Mom didn't want you showing it to me—I think she thought it was radioactive or something. But when she was away you took it out and let me hold it, one night when you were putting me to bed. The rock had so many colours in it—we tried to name all of them, and then we made up names for the colours we hadn't seen before. Afterwards, we—"

"Stop," he says, and this time his voice is quiet. "This…this is impossible. You can't be her."

"No, Dad. I'm here and I'm alive and please, please talk to me."

"Riley"—and, at last, it's his own voice that cracks, seesawing between fear and disbelief—"how are you doing this? Where are you?"

"In the main control room in Apex."

"Is Janice Okwembu with you?"

Okwembu. I'd forgotten about her. I look over my shoulder at the door, but it's still shut. "No, Dad, she's not," I reply.

Something catches my eye. A tiny lens, positioned at the top of the touch-screen. "Dad," I say. "There's a camera in the control room. Do you have one too?"

"Yes," he replies. His voice has a new note of strength in it. "Yes, of course. I'll try to establish a link."

It takes a little while, and a lot of navigating through sub-menus to do it, but eventually a tiny blinking icon appears in the bottom right corner. I touch it; the *Akua*, and the stars behind it, vanish. The screen is black, and for a moment I think the link has failed—but then the blackness moves, and I realise it's his body close to the screen, blocking out the light. The feed glitches and stutters, but it works. He moves into view, and for the first time in seven years, I see my father.

The man staring back at me is a ruin, a scarred, wrinkled old man, his face ringed by a dirty, matted shock of hair. His eyes—at first, they're as dull and lifeless as the planet he travelled too. But when they meet mine, recognition dawns, flaring like a tiny star. And in the crags and furrows on the face, I recognise him too.

He's wearing a tattered tunic. I can just make out a piece of faded red piping on the shoulder. Behind him, the cabin of the *Akua* is dark, with a few flickering lights illuminating black metal and coiled cables.

"Oh, Riley," he whispers. "I—I thought you were—she told me you were dead," he finishes, and a single tear falls down his cheek.

I had defences up the moment I first heard his voice. I didn't think about it, but I did. When I see the tear, every one of them cracks and collapses. My own tears come, too late, seven years too late.

"I'm here," is all I can get out, before the sobs come, thick and fast. Now it's not the world that's ended. It's me. Every memory I've ever had of him swims to the surface, one by one: him picking me up, holding me above his head. With my mother, smiling at me from the door of our quarters. And that last goodbye, before the Earth Return mission, standing above me, the smile on his face warm and genuine. I can't connect them to what I see on the screen.

"You're alive, Dad," I say after a time, wiping away tears. "You're alive! How? How did you do it? What about the rest of the crew? Where have you—"

He holds up a hand, and for a fleeting moment I catch a glimpse of the captain he once was.

"The first thing you need to know, my darling, is that this ship is on a course for Outer Earth. It's coming, and in less than two hours it will collide with you. The whole station will be destroyed."

"What?" I say, confused. "Dad, is there a problem with the engines? We can fix it. We can come to you."

"No!" His face twists with fury. I physically recoil from the screen; I can't understand the look on his face. "This is how it has to be. This is how it's meant to be."

"Why?"

"Because," he says, speaking through gritted teeth, forcing himself under control, "you left us to die. Everyone on Outer Earth turned their backs on us."

"I don't understand. They said the *Akua* burned up in the atmosphere."

He laughs, a sound tinged with bitterness. "We didn't burn up.

The reactor malfunctioned during the entry process. We had to crash-land, bring the whole thing down manually. And everyone, every single person on Outer Earth, let it happen. You did nothing. You just went on with your lives."

My hands are gripping the edge of the control panel, the knuckles white. I release them slowly, keeping my eyes on the figure in the screen, watching him as one might watch someone wielding a knife. What he's saying can't be true. There's no possible way a ship could crash, spend seven years on a broken planet, and then somehow manage to find its way back.

"Tell me what happened," I say. "Tell me from the beginning."

My father appraises me, his eyes locked on mine. After a minute, he says, "It took years to develop all the machines needed to establish a colony back home. Earth's biosphere was a disaster, and we had to try and fix it. Outer Earth couldn't hold us forever."

He pauses. "I should have been home in two years. With you. With your mother."

"What went wrong?"

"Something happened in the reactor. An explosion of some kind. How we didn't burn up in the atmosphere, I'll never know. We managed to put down in a place called Kamchatka, in what used to be eastern Russia. It was a miracle that we were alive. Nearly all the basic functions of the ship just shut down."

"Then why did they tell us that the ship had been destroyed? Why lie to us?"

"A man named Marshall Foster was Station Command for the mission. He—"

"I know who he was."

He gives a harsh laugh. "Then imagine if a rescue mission had been mounted. There'd be a chance to investigate the cause of the explosion properly. If it turned out that Foster was in some way responsible for what happened, if it was down to something he missed or a calculation he got wrong, then his reputation would be ruined."

"Dad, that doesn't make any sense."

"It does, if you knew Foster. He was always obsessed with his own legacy. He wanted to be on the right side of history. Better that the mission failed because of an unknown mechanical issue than because of something he might have done. He wouldn't risk it. He thought we could be forgotten about. And you—all of you—believed him. You're as guilty as he is."

"Dad, that's not true. If we'd known, if everybody had known, we would have done something. We would have sent help."

"We sent endless messages. Activated our distress beacons. And we got nothing. We thought someone would come for us. But as each day went past, and each year, we realised that Foster had left us to rot, locking our signal away, and everyone on Outer Earth just stood back and let him do it."

"No. We were lied to. All of us. If anybody had known, a ship would have been sent. You have to believe me."

He turns away from the camera. I can hear him muttering something, but I can't make out the words.

A thought occurs to me. "Dad, how did you survive? How did you eat?"

"Oh," he says dismissively, still staring at something I can't see. "A lot of our terraforming machinery was destroyed during the crash, but we managed to get some of it working again. Eventually, I worked out how to turn the power back on. How to rebuild the ship."

"But food..."

There's a long pause. Eventually, his eyes meet mine, and the face that turns back to me is filled with anguish. "I've done terrible things, Riley. Things you can't imagine. We turned on each other, and I did what I had to. I survived."

I raise my hand to my mouth, all the blood freezing in my veins.

"I worked for years to repair the system," he says. "It was so hard. And there was no one for a long, long time. I forgot how to speak, for a while. All I did was work on the reactor. I was convinced the *Akua* could fly again. But even if I did get it working, I couldn't have gone anywhere. Our guidance system was damaged. Without precise data, there was nowhere we could go. I'd almost given up hope.

"And then one day, there's a signal. And it's *her*. Telling me she knows I'm here. That she wants to help, that she wants me to use the *Akua* to destroy the station."

"But why? You stayed alive for so long..."

"The only thing that kept me going," he says, "was you and your mother. As long as you were alive, I would stay alive too. I would get back to you—that's what I told myself. But Janice said…she told me you were both dead."

"You could have come home."

"For what? The only reason for keeping myself alive was gone. Outer Earth and the people inside it hadn't just left me to die. They'd taken the ones I loved the most. I wanted them to suffer."

I don't want to picture what he must have gone through, but it's impossible not to. Seven years in the cold, alone, barely hanging on. Aware that the people orbiting the Earth could save you—and believing that they chose not to. And then, right when you've lost the only thing that keeps you going, you're handed a way out. A way to make your death mean something.

"She gave me data," he says. "Schematics, flight paths, positions in space. I'd worked out how to get the *Akua* moving again, but I couldn't steer it. Not without her help. But we did it. It took two long years, but eventually I could point the ship towards Outer Earth."

"Dad, that's impossible. You couldn't…"

"Oh couldn't I?" he says. His voice has turned to ice. "I've spent my life in space. And I've spent years on this ship. All I needed was Outer Earth's projected flight path, and I could line us up exactly."

"But she'd die too."

"Don't you see? That was her goal all along. She told me that there was no place for humans in the universe any more."

"You believed her?"

"What did I care?" he says. "She was giving me everything I needed. Her beliefs were none of my concern."

All at once, everything comes together. I see the *Akua Maru*, travelling at thousands of miles an hour, colliding with Outer Earth. I see the station tear apart, cracking in two, see it consumed in fire. No one will survive.

Your world's going to end.

I pull my jacket around me. No, not my jacket: his. The one thing he left me. I push back the urge to tear it off, to hurl it on the ground and never look at it again. He must see the look on my face, sense the horror I feel, because his own expression softens a little. "Riley, if I'd known you were alive...if I was told..."

Deep in the hurt, in the fear and the confusion swirling in my mind, there's a tiny core of hope. I lean close to the camera, forcing myself to stare into those eyes. I hunt for something beyond the hatred.

"Yes, they lied," I say eventually. "They lied about everything. About you. About the ship. Foster lied to us. But, Dad, I'm telling you the truth. I'm alive. And I love you. I love you. Please don't do this."

For what seems like an age, he stares at me. Then his face falls, and something in my heart shatters. John Hale, so proud, so courageous, has reached the end.

"I can move the station," I say, desperation in my voice. "I know how to turn it—I can figure out how to move it away from the *Akua*."

"Riley, I'm sorry," he says. "The ship's reactor is still active, but the main thrusters have died. Even if I kill the reactor now, I can't slow us down. Moving the station out of its orbit will take too long. It's too big. There's nothing we can do."

76

Riley

I expect to feel something. But there's nothing there. I find myself not wanting to look at him, my eyes fixed on the control panel instead. Looking at its lights. Its clean metal surface. It can control an entire space station—turn the lights on or off, cut the oxygen supply, kill the water or make it flow freely. All that power. And it means nothing.

Again, I search for something to hold on to. But even when I focus on the faces of Prakesh, of Carver and Kev, there's no reaction.

On the screen, my father says, "Your mother. Is she..."

My voice is flat. "She died a year after you...after we were told what happened. She just gave up."

I look at him. Sadness etches his face. "Who..." He licks his cracked lips, and won't meet my eyes. "Who took care of you?"

"Nobody. Myself. But I survived." I pause, weighing up how much he deserves to know, but then decide that I don't care any more. "I became a tracer, Dad. One of the best. Someone good taught me. She showed me how to run."

I see Amira, holding her hand out to me. Again, nothing but a creeping numbness.

"I am so proud of you," he says, and the sadness in his voice bubbles over. He's crying openly now, the tears streaming down his face. "Riley, I wish..."

"No." The hardness in my voice startles me. But I grasp that tiny thread of steel, hold it close. "It's over. We're done."

My legs give out, and I collapse to the ground, leaning up against the console. Behind me, the man on the screen tries to talk, pleading with me. I shut my eyes. Maybe if I keep them closed for long enough, I won't even feel it when the ship hits.

But something tugs at the edge of my mind. It takes me a minute to find it.

Iapetus.

Slowly, I pull myself up. My father has gone silent, but he's still there, staring at me, leaning back in his chair. He opens his mouth to say something, but I cut him off.

"There's something you're not telling me," I begin, struggling to find the words. "Marshall Foster's dead. He was killed a few days ago. But there was something he wanted to keep secret, something he locked away. A word. Iapetus."

His face, which darkened at the mention of Foster's name, creases with puzzlement. "Iapetus?" he says—then surprise turns to recognition, a brief flash across his face. He tries to hide it, but I catch him too soon.

"You know what it means, don't you?" I say.

He shakes his head. "A safe-word, that's all. Something to secure communications." But he avoids my eyes.

"Dad," I say. The word feels strange in my mouth. "You have to tell me what it means."

"It's nothing."

"You're lying," I say. "Is this what Mom would have wanted? For you to lie to your daughter?"

"Don't you talk about her."

"Why, Dad? She's gone. She's been gone for a long time. It's just me, and I'm asking you. What does it mean?"

He looks as if he's about to smash his camera, cutting off communications all together. But then he takes a deep breath. "It's an override. One half of a dual fail-safe."

"Overriding what?"

He seems to weigh up the question, deciding how to answer. When he does, his voice is resigned. "On every mission, the station command and the ship's captain choose code words. You can't use one without the other. Foster chose his, I chose mine. In the event of…in the event of an accident, when a ship malfunctions or looks like it might damage the station, both code words can be entered into the system."

I wait for him to continue, but he seems to be searching for the words. "What happens then?" I ask.

He seems to take an age to form the words. "It sends a signal which causes a reactor override. Detonation."

Detonation.

Before I'm even aware I'm doing it, my fingers are navigating through the on-screen controls. I catch the look of alarm on his face as understanding dawns. "Riley," he says, his voice thick. "What are you doing?"

"Whatever I can," I mutter. My fingers seem to work of their own accord, flying through the menus, flicking through *Capacitor Control* and *Reactor Data* and *Network Variance* until it alights on *Ship Communications*, and then—*Override*.

"Riley, please," comes the voice from the speakers. His eyes are serious now, hunting mine down, until eventually I'm forced to look at them. "I have to finish the mission."

Something snaps. We both start screaming at each other at the same time, our voices cut with anger and fear. It takes me some time to understand the words coming out of my mouth. "You want to kill us all!" I yell. "You say you love me, but you're going to destroy us. Destroy me. Is this what you want? What Mom would have wanted?"

In a rage, I stab the screen, activating the Override option. The computer begins flashing up data on the *Akua*: ship reactor temperature, rate of rotation—and trajectory. On the bottom left of the screen, a little icon appears: an exclamation mark, surrounded by a small triangle, blinking on and off. Somewhere in the control room, a calm voice quietly says: "Warning: proximity alert."

Outer Earth, it seems, has finally worked out that it's in danger.

Next to the icon are the words: *Transmit override command*. With my father still yelling in the background, I activate the option. Every bit of text on the screen vanishes, replaced by an on-screen keyboard, and the words: *Confirmation Code 1*.

I don't think. I enter the word Iapetus and hit the confirm option, wanting everything to be over, wanting the world to go away. Not wanting to face the man on the screen.

The word on the screen turns green, blinks for a moment, and vanishes, replaced by a text box labelled *Confirmation Code 2*.

Foster chose his, I chose mine.

No.

"You're like your mother," he says. The words are a shard of ice, and the chill that sweeps through me is so intense that I find I can't move my fingers. I can't move anything. "She was strong. Stronger than I ever was. She would never have wanted this. Any of it. I'm sorry. Oh gods, Riley, I'm sorry."

I want to say something. Anything. But nothing will come. Every last bit of emotion is dried up, gone, as empty as space itself.

Eventually, he says, "It's asking you for a second code, isn't it?"

I whisper, "Yes."

"I waited so long," he says, as if he's speaking to himself. "And all this time, you were right there. You were alive."

It takes me more than one try to get the words out, but as I do, I'm surprised by the strength in my voice. "Whatever you left behind, it's not like that any more. There are things on this station worth saving. Things I could show you if…" The words catch in my throat. "Things that I love. People that I love. You have to tell me the second code, Dad. Please."

"Riley, no."

"I am your daughter, and I am begging you not to do this. You wanted to die? This is your chance. You were lied to for so long. You were controlled and manipulated. Both of us were. But you can choose, Dad. You can choose."

The agony pulsing in my heart is reflected on his face. "I love you," I say again, my voice tiny, almost buried in the thrum of the electronics.

Finally, his hand touches the camera, a single finger pressing against it. It has to be soon. It has to be soon, or every ounce of me will turn to dust.

"The second code is *Riley*," he says, holding back the words, as if trying to keep them from escaping. "You need to enter your own name."

What?

"Why, Dad?"

"Because I thought that if everything went wrong, the last thing I wanted to say was your name."

It takes me a few tries to punch the letters into the display, but in what seems like no time at all, my name is on the screen, glowing in orange text over his face. Below the word blinks the option: *Confirm?*

His hand is on the monitor again. "Riley…I love y—"

My finger touches the screen for the last time.

77

Riley

I don't know how long I lie there. Time passes, but I don't know how much. I feel tears streaming down my face, and I desperately want to cry out, but nothing comes.

After a while, there are strong hands lifting me up. It occurs to me that I might be dead. The thought is vague, distant, like a shape at the end of a dark corridor. I find I don't care all that much.

I'm not aware of opening my eyes, or even of focusing on my surroundings. There are shapes, and light, but it's a long time before they resolve into something I recognise. Janice Okwembu is sitting in a chair opposite me, her hands in her lap. She looks expectant, as if I'm supposed to say something.

Hate. That seems to be the appropriate response. But there's nothing there. The numbness I felt earlier is total. My wounds don't hurt. My stomach is a hollow drum. My mind is blank. It's not that I can't hold on to any feeling; it's as if there's nothing there to hold on to.

"Can you hear me, Ms. Hale?" Okwembu asks, her head tilted slightly to one side. "I want you to listen very closely to what I'm about to say."

My eyes fix on hers. Her words stir something deep in my gut, and slowly, ever so slowly, hate begins to uncoil.

If she sees it in my gaze, she ignores it. "You'll want to hurt me. That's understandable. But I can't let you do that." She raises her hand, and I see she's holding a stinger.

"Now, I could simply kill you, right here and now," she says. "But I think you deserve better than that. You've performed brilliantly. Better than I ever could have hoped. And so, I'm going to give you a choice."

I have to will my lips to form the words. "A choice?"

She nods, and throws something at my feet. A knife. Polished steel, with a black handle. It clatters on the steel floor, spinning in place. I reach down to pick it up, keeping my eyes on her the whole time.

"You're going to die, Ms. Hale. Whether you die a hero or a traitor is up to you. That's your choice. If you try to attack me, I'll put a bullet right through you. You'll die, and I'll make sure everyone knows that you were working with Darnell, that you were part of the Sons of Earth, that you brought back the *Akua* to destroy us. The name Hale will come to mean traitor. You'll be the daughter who betrayed her own father. Your friends will be too scared to speak your name. I will destroy everything you stood for."

"They won't believe you," I whisper.

"They'll believe what I tell them. They always do. But if you take your own life—I'd suggest cutting your wrists—then I'll make sure that you're remembered as a hero. You'll be the one who made the ultimate sacrifice to save Outer Earth. And while you couldn't live with yourself afterwards, your name will be written into history. When we return to Earth, they will build cities dedicated to you."

When we return?

She dips her head slightly. "I'm offering you this choice because I respect you, and I respect what you have gone through. I'm going to lead Outer Earth into a new era of peace, but for that to happen, you have to die. Your only choice is how you are remembered."

I touch the blade to the skin of my left wrist. It's sharp. The cuts will be clean.

I can't possibly do this. I can't do what she says.

But then that quiet voice whispers, *Keep her talking. Buy some time.*

I think about attacking her, or diving away. But I know that I won't be able to move fast enough. There's only one way this can end.

In two quick movements, I cut shallow slashes across my left wrist. There's pain, but it's not the stinging agony I expected. It's a distant ache, like something felt by someone else. The blood blooms instantly, a steady, pulsing flow, running into my palm and dripping downwards. The drops drip gently onto the floor.

I try to transfer the blade to my left hand to cut my other wrist, but it too falls to the floor, the clang echoing around the control room.

Okwembu nods. One wrist seems to be enough for her. "You're going to be a hero," she says. Incredibly, she smiles.

"Why?" I ask, and it's then that the pain really comes, a stinging so intense that I have to bite my lip to keep from crying out.

"Because sometimes the only way to restore order is to create chaos," she replies, speaking slowly, as if to someone very young.

The realisation dawns gradually. "This was never about saving the Earth from humans, was it?"

"The Earth is none of my concern—not yet. I wanted to save this station."

"Save it? From what?"

"From us." She's quiet for a moment. Then she says, "The council had been losing control of Outer Earth for a long time. Gangs. Crime. One riot. Two. Then war. The station would destroy itself, and I knew that if we left things as they were, it would fall away from us. When that happened, there'd be no hope."

"So you decided to rescue Outer Earth by trying to kill everyone on it? Help me out here."

She continues as if I hadn't spoken. "So I created the Sons of Earth. A terrorist group, hell bent on wiping out humanity. When I defeated them—or helped defeat them—then the entire station would unite under me. My power would be absolute. I could fix it all. Get rid of the gangs, empower the protection officers, control the tracers. I could rule, and not as a council member, not as someone held back by others, having to put every decision to a committee of fools."

"You're insane."

"It might seem that way, but only because you don't yet understand. I've learned a few things about power."

"Like?"

"Nothing unifies people like a common enemy, and fighting through hardship which can be blamed on that enemy will forge them in steel. And Darnell did have such useful ideas about human extinction. It was so easy to let him believe that I wanted the *Akua Maru* to collide with us, for the good of the Earth."

There's a lot of blood now. It forms a dark pool at my feet, draining into the seams of the plating. The blankness has been replaced by a faint dizziness.

"Foster hid your father's beacon transmission deep in the system," she says. "It didn't show up in the logs. Until one day, I saw something in the sub-routines, deep in the code. When I realised that the *Akua* wasn't only intact but potentially still functioning, I saw the opportunity."

Another stab of pain shoots up my arm, and without thinking, I clutch my wrist. I cry out, and let go of the wrist as if it's on fire.

"Did you hear me, Ms. Hale?" she says. When I look up at her, she seems to flutter in and out of existence in front of me. "I managed to keep my communications with your father private, and with the information I gave him two years ago, we were able to plot his course exactly."

"But Foster..."

Okwembu leans forward slightly, and looks right into my eyes, like she badly needs me to understand. "For every ship mission," she says, "an override code is locked away behind a retinal scanner. The only person who has access to it is the mission commander. Standard procedure, in case a ship malfunctions and endangers the station. Foster could hide the *Akua*'s beacon transmission, but to try and erase the override code would have invited suspicion, so he just left it there. I don't believe he ever thought it would need to be used."

She smooths out a crease in the leg of her jumpsuit, picking at an invisible speck of lint.

"I knew he'd never tell me the override code. I asked anyway. He claimed he didn't remember, which was a lie. He was suspicious, of course, but he would never do anything to dig up the past. Same old Foster—always hoarding information, like little stores of food he could put away for when he needed them most. He was a real politician, that one."

"And you're not?"

She just smiles, totally serene.

It's an effort to get the words out now. "Why not just hack it?"

She shakes her head. "That's the point of a retinal scanner. It's completely isolated from the rest of the network. It can't be hacked." Okwembu smiles to herself. "Not by digital means, anyway. In any event, for everything to go as planned, I had to make Darnell believe that we had to unlock the scanner, and destroy the code."

She leans back in her chair, the gun resting in her lap. "You will never know the terror I felt when I heard how Darnell had botched the retrieval of Foster's eye—by the time I found out, the protection officers had recorded it, and incinerated it." She exhales slowly. "I should have got that eye a lot sooner."

"Why didn't you?"

"Darnell. If he'd had Foster killed too soon, the stompers might have had time to investigate, and link it back to him. He'd never allow that. It had to happen when everything had been set in motion. At any rate, it didn't matter. Garner saved us all. *You* saved us all."

"You used me."

It takes a long time for her to answer. When she does, there's something in her voice—not regret, but sadness. "If I'd had my way, you'd have survived along with everyone else, and never been a part of this. But I came to suspect that you knew where Garner was. If only you'd told me, all of this would have been easier. But you would never have given in. You're stubborn. Like your father."

"Don't you dare talk about him." I'm stunned to hear a version of my father's words fall so easily from my mouth. The pain in my wrists flares again.

"Once Foster's eye was found and destroyed, so was every hope of us accessing the retinal scanner," she says. "Garner was our only hope, and it would have taken too long to search the entire station."

"Amira."

"A shame," she replies, and my coil of hate seems to tighten. "She believed that fiction of Darnell's far too easily. If she'd shown a little vision, then she would have made an excellent second-in-command. Darnell wanted me to torture the whereabouts of Grace Garner out of you, but I preferred a more subtle approach. Amira provided it."

The dark place I've put Amira, Yao and Garner into is threatening to blow open, to spill its terrible memories into my mind. I push it back.

"I should have known that she wouldn't have the strength to kill you," Okwembu says. "It seems I'm not as good a judge of character as I thought. Still, every desperate situation will have an opportunity hidden in it. And you—oh, you—when you survived Amira, you provided the greatest opportunity yet. Because what better way to preserve order than to create not just an enemy, but a martyr to destroy it?"

I catch sight of one of the screens behind Okwembu. I can just make out the message on it. *Temperature equalised. Sector access granted.*

Doesn't matter. They'll never get here in time. And even if they do, they'll never believe me.

"When we realised that you were running through the Core to get to Apex, I knew how the sequence of events would have to play out," Okwembu says. "Darnell, of course, still wanted the *Akua* to destroy us. He was convinced you needed to die, and went into the Core to kill you."

"And you let him?"

"You must believe me, Ms. Hale. I never, ever wanted you to go through that," she says. "I underestimated just how far gone he was. I tried to inject him with an overdose of pain medication, but it didn't work. I should have taken a more direct approach. For that, I'm sorry."

I have to force myself to speak now. I've lost all feeling in my arm; the pain is a memory, but there's a lightness there that leaves me afraid. So I find that little coil of hate in my heart, and hold on to it, mentally wrapping fingers around its scales.

"You let Darnell murder the council."

"They were weak," she says. "None of them would have had the strength to go through with the plan."

It's then that I realise that she's more insane than I could ever have imagined. Her eyes show nothing: not triumph, not reason, not elation. Just a horrible, green madness. The madness of someone who views people as playthings, as pieces in a game to be moved around at a whim.

"They would have backed out, eventually," she says. "When they saw what had to be done. And after all, one person can rule just as well as many."

A thought tugs at me. "The second code," I say. My voice is croaky, and my breaths are coming too fast. My heart is pumping quickly, far too quickly. I repeat the words, then say, "There was no way you would have got it out of him. My father. He'd never have given it to you." Even as I realise the implications of my words, a fierce pride burns in my chest.

She actually laughs. "Ms. Hale. Your father gave up the code willingly."

"What?"

"The ship colliding with us would be devastating, but there was a slim chance that some parts of the station would survive. Your father knew that. So I told him that I planned to detonate the *Akua* the instant that I felt it collide with Outer Earth.

Maximum destruction. He believed me, and gave me what I needed."

Those insane, empty eyes fix on mine. "You saved Outer Earth, Riley Hale. And no one will ever forget you."

Her words are drowned out by the pounding of my heart. There's a blackness at the corners of my vision, and all I want to do is close my eyes. Close my eyes and slip away, go somewhere with no pain and no memories. I can't focus on Okwembu any more; the edges of her form keep blurring, though whether it's because of tears in my eyes or not, I can't say. There's no time left.

Noise. Banging. Something outside the room. Feet on steel plating. With an effort, I lift my head.

There's a shadow in the doorway to the control room, silhouetted against lights that seem far too bright. It's a man—he's holding a stinger, pointed right at us.

No—not at us. At her.

The man speaks. "Janice Okwembu—get on the ground. Now!" Other shapes appear behind the man, blocking out the light.

Okwembu is looking around, first confused, then fearful. She turns to me, and her expression darkens with anger.

"You're right," I whisper. "You're not a very good judge of character."

Realisation dawns on her face. Maybe she sees something on the screens, or maybe the dots just connect in her mind, but she suddenly understands.

The comms system.

The one I turned on, and never turned off. The one which broadcasts to the entire station.

I guess it really was working.

I hear the men entering the room, heading right towards us. But by then, my eyes are closed, and I've fallen sideways off the chair. The coil of hate has come loose, slipping free. There's nothing to hold on to now.

My body doesn't slam into the cold steel of the floor. Instead, I just fall.

Forever.

78

Riley

First, there's nothing.

And then, after some time has passed—hours maybe, or decades—there's something.

Voices. They're muffled, and I can't make out the words. I want to speak to them, to let them know that I'm here. But then the voices fade, and I sink back into the warm darkness.

My eyes are open, and I'm looking at a body, slumped in a chair. The head is lolling on the shoulder, the mouth slightly open. I blink, still unsure of how much time there is between when I close my eyes and when I open them. But when I do, the body is still there, and I see it's Aaron Carver.

As I watch, he stirs, then stretches, yawns, and rubs his jaw, his hand scraping on stubble. I try to say his name, but my throat is as dry and smooth as old rubber.

I must make some noise, or a movement, because suddenly, he's looking in my direction, his eyes wide. "Riley," he says in astonishment, and his voice is so loud that it causes my ears to ring. I squeeze my eyes shut, and it's at that moment that the pain strikes, stabbing into my body in so many places that I feel like I'm being ripped apart.

At the edge of my vision, I see Carver step forward and adjust something next to my head. Immediately, something cool and wonderful floods through me, first halting the pain, then turning it back. As it dwindles into nothingness, I stare up at Carver, my eyes blurring. I mouth a silent thank you, and he reaches across and places a hand on my stomach.

It's an odd gesture, but then I remember Okwembu. Cutting my wrist. Pushing the grogginess away, I sit up, my back creaking with the effort.

"Hey, slow down, Ry. Easy," says Carver.

I'm in a bed, with crisp sheets bundled around my waist. I cough. "Where am I?" I ask. I barely recognise my own voice. It's not just croaky and dry, but older somehow.

"The hospital in Apogee," he replies. As he does so, the rest of the room snaps into focus. White, and brightly lit, filled with humming machines and clean lights.

"I didn't..." I falter. "I thought I was dead."

"You came pretty close," he says, flopping back down in the chair. "You must have had some extra blood stashed behind a lung or something, because apparently you were right on the edge. That's without talking about your other bumps, like that little opening in your side. Or the borderline hypothermia."

I catch sight of my left wrist: heavily bandaged, and quite numb.

"Oh, you'll have plenty of scars," says Carver, a weird smile on his face. "But hey, wear 'em with pride, right?"

He leans forward in his chair. "You did good, Riley. We heard you on the comms. Everybody did. I don't know how you managed to get through to Apex, but after you turned the convectors back on, everybody stopped fighting."

"Okwembu? Is she..."

"In the brig, under some serious armed guard," he says. "They're talking about keeping her there for a while, trying her when there's a new elected council. But we heard everything, the whole story. You're a genius."

I close my eyes. I suppose I should feel happiness. Or at least, relief. But instead, the coil of hate, which I thought had gone, suddenly unwinds itself, flexing deep in my stomach. I wanted her dead. I wanted her to suffer.

I push it away. "And Darnell?"

"They found his body at the Core entrance in Apex."

Suddenly, my eyes widen. "Prakesh. Kev. Where are they? Are they OK?"

Carver laughs. "Would you relax? They're fine. They're both fine. Prakesh has been kind of amazing, actually. He's taken over food distribution for, like, three sectors. You should see him, Ry. It's scary. He came to visit you a few times, but you were out of it."

"And Kev?"

"Please." He spreads his arms. "You think a few fat stompers are going to stop us? After you went into the Core, we outran them in about five seconds. Kev's all good. He's back to running cargo. Although if he hasn't made some decent trades, I'm going to kick his ass."

"How long have I been here?"

"Two days, just about."

Something he said earlier tugs at me. "You heard me on the comms system. Did you hear…"

He's avoiding my eyes now, and I know that he doesn't have to answer. The conversation with my father seems like something out of a dream. I can't recall all of it, only snatches, expressions, odd words.

I swallow. "The *Akua Maru*. Is it over?"

He stares at the floor. "The pieces missed us. Riley, I'm so sorry."

And that's when the small, dark place at the back of my mind bursts open. It's the place where I put my memories of Amira and Yao and Garner and, I now realise, my father. It fractures so suddenly that it's as if someone has punched me in the chest. The scream claws its way up my throat, ripping itself out of me like some kind of horrible, angry animal. When it finally tears free, it's as if the fracture in the dark place has spread everywhere, ripping my very soul in half. I scream, and scream, and scream, until there's a tiny jab in my neck and I sink into the darkness again, the scream dwindling to nothing.

When I come back, both Carver and Kev are there. Kev has some nasty bruises, but when he sees me, his face lights up, and he walks to the edge of the bed and hugs me. Behind him, Carver hangs back, a worried look on his face.

There's less pain than before. I manoeuvre myself into a sitting position and swing my legs off the edge of the bed. There's a dull ache, but nothing more. Can we ever run together again? Will the Dancers still exist without Amira, without Yao?

The scream, born from that coil of hate, has left behind its offspring, squatting in my gut. They'll always be there.

But I show none of this. I can't.

Instead, I stick a smile on my face, look Kev in the eye, and say, "Help me up."

He lifts me to my feet, his huge arms taking the weight of my slender frame easily. He grimaces, more in amusement than anything else. "What are you wearing?"

I look down. It's a smock of some sort, reaching to just above my knees. Slowly, I reach behind me, and feel the back of it. Or rather, where the back should be.

"Please tell me someone saved my clothes," I mutter, as Carver and Kev collapse in howls of laughter. Soon, I'm laughing too, even as I keep one hand scrunching up the fabric firmly behind my back.

They find me some trousers, a loose shirt, a spare pair of shoes. There's no sign of my father's jacket, and neither of them mention anything. For a moment, I want to ask them about it, but then I realise that if I had it back, I'd never wear it again. Maybe it's best that I don't know where it is.

The guys try and support me as we leave the room, but I shrug them off, walking hesitantly at first, and then with more confidence. Two doctors try to stop us, but I wave them aside, muttering that I'm fine.

We leave the hospital, walking down one of the corridors in the direction of the gallery. Apogee is a mess. There's trash everywhere: overturned crates, pieces of equipment, smashed lights, crumpled trays from the canteen. But oddly, it doesn't feel like a bad place. Nothing like it was when we had to escape the crowds who wanted to tear us apart. The thought is a strange one, another memory that feels like it happened in a different lifetime.

The people we pass make a pretence of ignoring us, but I catch them staring at me as we walk by. A few of them whisper to each other, and one or two even point. I guess I'm going to have to get used to that. But more than once, I'm smiled at, and one old woman even pushes aside Carver and Kev to pull me into an awkward, fumbling embrace. I'm so surprised I nearly burst out laughing, but I return the hug, and she squeezes me briefly before wandering off.

"What's happening in Apex?" I ask Carver.

He shrugs. "The council's finished. Okwembu was the only

survivor, and she's in lockdown. There are some people running things, I hear. Techs mostly—nobody making any big decisions or anything, just guys keeping an eye on the main systems. I was expecting some of the gangs to try and step in, but there's been nothing."

"What's going to happen now?"

"Nobody knows. I'm kind of hoping it stays like it is for a while. I can't describe it, Ry, but I've never felt the station like this. It's almost..." he searches for the right word: "Peaceful."

"Yeah," says Kev, speaking for the first time in a while. "No fighting. It's weird."

Someone behind me barks my name, and I smile when I see who it is. Royo, limping up the corridor towards us. He's as beaten up as Apogee itself, a mess of bruises and bandages. One covers his right eye, and his arm is bound up in some kind of complicated sling. He's limping too, but still manages to look as if he could throw a punch at any moment.

I'm about to throw my arms around him, but stop just in time. He seems to catch the gesture, though, and smiles. "Nice work, Hale," he says.

"Thanks. How're you holding up?"

"Flesh wounds, is all," he says, the smile still on his face.

The moment passes, and he clears his throat gruffly, all business again. "If you're going to the gallery, I hear they're short of hands for shifting soil. She's excused from duty, but you two"—he points at Carver and Kev—"you're able-bodied. Get in there."

Carver rolls his eyes. We turn to leave, but then Royo says, "On second thoughts—give us a minute?"

He's staring over my shoulder at Carver, who frowns. "She just got out the hospital, man. Leave her be."

"It's OK," I say. "I'll be right there."

Royo puts an arm around my shoulders, turning me away from Carver and Kev. It's an unexpectedly protective gesture.

"You need to be ready," Royo says.

"Oh yeah? For what?" It's hard not to laugh at his words, at his overly serious tone. After everything I've been through, it's hard to imagine something I wouldn't be ready for.

Royo glances over his shoulder at the impatient Carver. "You did the right thing. I wouldn't have you change any part of it. But—"

"Even the part where you—you know." I gesture to his wounds.

"Listen to me. That doesn't matter. I could give you some bullshit about cause and effect, but you're smart enough to figure that out on your own. It's just...I'm going to give it to you anyway. You don't just remove a council leader like Janice Okwembu, and expect things to go right back to normal."

"I don't care who takes her place."

"Forget that. What I'm worried about are the things you won't see coming. The consequences you can't plan for, no matter how hard you try."

"And those are?"

"Stupid question, Hale."

He lets me go, nodding towards Carver and Kev. "Keep 'em close. They'll have your back."

I look right into his eyes. "What about you, Royo? Do you have my back?"

He looks right back at me, and a ghost of a smile darts across his face. "Never stopped."

We leave Royo behind, and walk into the main gallery. The noise and movement is intense. People carrying huge sacks of soil, hefting the bags between them. Others yelling instructions, telling people to form lines. But even through the chaos, I see Prakesh immediately.

He's standing with a white-coated tech, looking over a clipboard, his expression serious. The moment I see him, it's as if the noise in the room drops away.

I don't know how he senses I'm there. All I know is that one moment he's looking at the clipboard, and the next he's staring straight at me. The expression on his face is a mix of relief, of sorrow, and of joy.

I'm running, my body sloughing off the pain like old clothes, my arms pumping, my feet in perfect rhythm, the rush building. Running towards him.

And then we're in each other's arms, and we kiss, and the world disappears.

ZERO-G

Prologue

Outer Earth

A huge ring, six miles in diameter, its cooling fins slicing through the vacuum. The Core at the centre of the ring, the sphere containing the station's fusion reactor, shines in the glowing sunlight. Three hundred miles below it, the Earth is dark and silent.

To generate gravity for the million people who live on board, Outer Earth spins—just fast enough to keep everything inside Earth-Normal. The spin is almost imperceptible, the rockets on the station firing at intervals to maintain it. It has been in orbit for over a hundred years.

The side of the station explodes.

A great wound opens up in the hull, like skin parting under a knife. The hole expands faster than the human eye can register, ripping apart until the gash is half a mile long. The pressure loss rips out everything inside, forming a cloud of glittering debris. Shreds of metal collide, bouncing off one other.

And there are bodies. Dozens of them. They tumble through the wreckage, crashing into the larger chunks of debris as they hurtle away from the station. Some of them are still moving, limbs clutching at nothing, fingers hooked into claws. One by one, they go still.

All of this happens in the purest silence.

1

Riley

Two days earlier
"We've got hostages."

Royo's voice echoes around the narrow entrance corridor. The big double doors to the Recycler Plant are behind him, shut tight. A rotating light spins above them, casting flickering shadows on the assembled stompers.

"Roster says twenty sewerage workers were on duty today when it happened," Royo says, jerking his thumb at the double doors. "It's our job to get 'em out."

"How many hostiles?" I say.

A few of the stompers look round at me, as if they can't quite believe I'm actually wearing one of their uniforms. I can't quite believe I am either. Six months ago, I'd be doing my best to get as far away from the stompers as I could. I've never liked cops.

Royo glances at me. His bald head reflects the spinning light perfectly. "We don't have any intel on the situation inside. That's the problem."

"What about the cameras?" says a voice from behind me.

I turn to see Aaron Carver jogging up, the top half of his black stomper jumpsuit tied around his waist, his perfectly styled blond hair swept back. He's wearing a bright red vest, exposing his toned upper arms. Behind him is Kevin O'Connell, a head taller than any other stomper here, with a closely shorn head and dark stubble across his cheeks.

All three of us used to be tracers—couriers who took packages and messages across the station. That was before Royo got us onto the stomper corps.

Royo shakes his head. "Nice of you to join us, Carver."

"Wouldn't miss it for the world, Cap."

Royo turns back to the group. "There were two working cams

on the floor, but whoever did this shot 'em to pieces the second they got in there. Locked down all the exits, too."

Carver comes to a stop alongside me, breathing hard. "Was over on the sector border when I got the call," he says to me between breaths.

"Worried about us starting without you?" I say, out of the corner of my mouth.

He puts a hand on my shoulder, uses it to pull himself upright. "Only worried you'd make us look bad. Lucky I got here when I did."

"You got something you want to say, Carver?" Royo shouts. Heads turn to look at us. My stomper jumpsuit is made of thin fabric, but right then it feels too tight around my shoulders.

Carver gives a huge smile. "Not at all, Cap. Carry on."

"What are their demands?" says one of the other stompers, a heavily muscled woman named Jordan, leaning up against the corridor wall. Her ponytail is pulled back so tightly that it looks like her hairline is going to tear her face apart.

"Before they killed the camera," Royo says, "they held up a tab screen with a name written on it."

"A name?" says Jordan, her eyes narrowing.

But I know already. We all do. I grit my teeth, without really meaning to.

"Okwembu," says Kev. His voice is quiet, but it cuts across the hubbub in the corridor.

Royo gives him a crooked smile. "Big man gets it in one."

Janice Okwembu. Our former council leader, who nearly destroyed the station in a twisted attempt to gain more control for herself. A lot of people want her dead. More than a few have tried to break into her maximum security prison to do just that.

I guess whoever took the plant got tired of waiting.

Royo raises his voice. "We don't negotiate with hostage takers. Never have, never will. But, right now, what we don't have is—*hey*! Get those people out of here!"

I look back towards the entrance. The corridor leading to the Recycler Plant backs out onto the main Apogee sector gallery, an enormous space with multi-level catwalks running all the way up the station levels. This much stomper activity has attracted a crowd, blocking up the entrance to the corridor. They're craning their necks, looking for action. I see workers in mess kitchen uniforms, tech jumpsuits, a few people with tattoos who look like they run with a tracer crew. One man on the side is covered in filthy rags, holding on tight to a pushcart full of gods know what. Three stompers break away from our group, shouting at the crowd to fall back.

"As I was saying," Royo says. "We need intel. That means we need people inside. So while Jordan here takes point on the assault, I need our new tracer unit—" he points at us, and I feel a nervous prickle shoot up my spine "—to get inside, and see what we're dealing with."

"All right," says Carver, rolling his shoulders. "About time we had some action."

"Wait, hold on," I say, raising my hand. "You said they locked down the exits, right? So how *do* we get inside?"

Royo smiles that crooked smile again. A few of the other stompers are sniggering.

"That means the only way in..." I trail off, and, as one, Carver, Kev and I look down at the floor. The metal plating is perforated, and just then I realise what's below it.

Pipes. Conveying human waste from every hab in the sector to the plant. Pipes which we're now going to have to pull ourselves through.

Carver raises his eyes to Royo. "You have *got* to be kidding me."

2

Knox

Morgan Knox stands on the edge of the crowd, watching Riley Hale.

Zero-G

Everybody gives him space. Nobody wants to go near the man with the crippled leg, the man wrapped in filthy, stinking rags. Knox barely notices the sideways glances, the muttered insults. He just stands and watches Hale, with his hands on the handle of his cart, his knuckles bloodless and white beneath the dirt.

It's not the first time he's seen her—he's been thinking about her for months now—but it's the first time he's had such a long look. He'd gone out to get supplies, and was surprised to see Hale running across the gallery in front of him, sprinting for the Recycler Plant, where the rest of the stompers were assembling.

She's got her back to him. Her dark hair falls to her shoulders in ringlets. Her black stomper uniform is a little too small for her, like it was made for someone else, and he can see the tight contours of her toned shoulders and upper arms. The bottoms of the pants show a flash of ankle above her off-white tracer shoes.

She turns to say something to one of her companions. For a moment, he sees her in profile, caught in the corridor's flashing light. Not for the first time, he catches himself thinking that she's quite beautiful.

No, he thinks, and squeezes the cart handle even harder, as if he can pulverise the thought itself. *You're not beautiful. And you never will be.*

He spits, a giant gob of saliva spattering across the ground. He feels the crowd moving further away from him, as if he's infectious. Fine by him.

He hears shouting. He looks away from Hale, to see stompers pushing the crowd back, ordering them to move along. It jerks him back to reality, and he spins his cart, using his good leg as a pivot. The cart's wheels are old and rusted, and they squeak as he pushes it across the gallery floor. He glances upwards, at the catwalks silhouetted by the vast banks of ceiling lights, and keeps moving. He can't get distracted. There's still a lot of work to do.

3

Riley

The noise in the corridor has gone from loud to deafening. Orders are being shouted, weapons checked, tab screens sought out. Royo strides towards us, ignoring the disgust on Carver's face.

"There *has* to be another way," I say, glancing down at the metal grate.

Royo shakes his head. "There isn't. It's like I said. Exits blocked off." He keeps walking, heading back down the corridor, and we fall in behind him.

"How do you know they haven't shut off the pipes, too?" I say.

"We don't. But, right now, it's the only way in we haven't tried yet. Which means you're up."

"Cap, come on," says Carver. "You are *not* thinking of sending us down there."

Royo stops at a metal plate at the side of the corridor. Black lettering across it reads WASTE PIPE ACCESS AUTHORISED PERSONNEL ONLY, with smaller writing in Hindi and Chinese below it. There's a keypad on the door, its numbers faded with age. Royo crouches down and keys in a code, the beeps drowned out by the noise from the other stompers.

"You're going to get in there, you're going to get to a vantage point, and you're going to report back," Royo says. He taps his earpiece. "I want regular contact at all times, understand?"

I'd almost forgotten about my earpiece. Every time I think I've got used to it, I realise it's still there, clogging my ear canal. The earpiece is moulded plastic, designed to fit snug in my right ear. It links me to SPOCS: the Station Protection Officer Communication System. The stompers had it before we joined up, but it was a badly maintained network, full of glitches and dead spots. Carver's big mission over the past few months has been to fix it—his first big contribution to what he calls his straight life.

"Send someone else," Carver says, folding his arms. "I didn't sign up to crawl through shit."

"I second that," I say.

Royo gets to his feet. "Tracers go where other people can't. That's the whole point of your unit. That's why we recruited you." He taps the metal trapdoor with his foot. "And by the way, try and remember that we have twenty people being held at gunpoint right now. Let's help them out. What do you say?"

Carver and I glance at each other. After a long moment, we both nod.

I look around, and something occurs to me. "Where's Anna?" I say.

"Miss Beck is currently on a staggeringly important mission further up the ring, my dear," says Carver, imitating Anna's accent perfectly, adding the twang that people get when they grow up in Tzevya sector.

Royo glances at me. "Some punk group of tracers are getting themselves into the drug trade. She's getting dirt on them for me."

My anger flares at his words. Not too long ago, we were a punk group of tracers, too. But, secretly, I'm glad she's not here. The fourth member of our little unit is the last person I want to deal with right now.

"We've already stopped the flow into one of the pipes," Royo says. "It'll back up nasty down the line, but Level 3 is just going to have to deal with it."

He reaches down and hauls open the trapdoor. The space beyond is as black as space itself. A second later, the smell nearly takes my head off.

"Gods," says Carver, his nose and mouth buried in the crook of his elbow. Kev makes a strange noise, half retch, half disgusted groan.

"Tell me you've got some full-face filters," I say to Royo.

He shakes his head. "Those are back at HQ. We're only supposed to break them out for emergencies, not bad smells."

I close my eyes, willing the contents of my stomach to stay put. Royo calls out for a tab screen, and another stomper brings one over. As he passes it to Royo, I catch him staring at me. I meet his gaze, and he looks down, disappearing back into the chaos further up the corridor.

Six months on, I'm still the woman who had to kill her own father, plus the leader of her tracer crew, to save Outer Earth. Six months on, people are still treating me like a freak, or a saviour, or both. That includes other stompers. I don't mind the stares—I've got used to them. They're part of the job, and the job is what takes my mind off what happened. It's what makes going to sleep easier.

I turn back to Royo. With a few taps on the screen, he calls up the schematics of the plant.

"There are access points for maintenance here, and here," he says, pointing at the outline on the map. "My guess is the hostage takers won't know about them, but it won't stop them from spotting you if you get careless. I want to know how many, their approximate positions, what they're armed with. Once we've got that, we'll hit the door with shaped charges and come and get you."

He snaps the tab screen off. "Carver, Hale, get going. O'Connell, you come with me."

"Wait—what?" Carver says. "Since when is Kev exempt from shit-pipe duty?"

"Since he's too big to fit in the shit-pipe," Royo says. "Besides, we don't want him getting an infection."

"Oh come *on*," says Carver. "His op was months ago."

He jabs at Kev's midsection, aiming for the spot where the scar is. Kev dodges back, smirking.

It took us a while to recover from the insanity of a few months ago. We were all injured—cuts, bruises, deep muscle strains. Carver's shoulder was dislocated, and it took quite a few physical therapy sessions before it was back to full strength.

Kev got it the worst. The ligaments in his ankle were torn, and while the surgery to fix them went OK, there were complications. Pulmonary embolism, Kev told us—a blood clot that originated in a leg artery and travelled upwards, lodging itself in his lungs. He collapsed a few days after the first op, spilling a cup of homebrew all over the floor of his family's hab. Emergency surgery, followed by months in hospital—that was his reward for helping save the station. It's only in the last few weeks that he's been back at full strength.

I was worried about him for a while—and not just because of his physical injuries. His closest friend, Yao, died last year. But he's thrown himself into his new life. Out of all of us, he's the one who's settled in the best. It's like he was born to be a cop, and being a tracer was just an interlude. I actually heard him telling some of the other stompers a joke—when we were tracers, he hardly ever spoke unless you asked him something first.

Royo looks Carver and me up and down. He steps in closer, lowers his voice. "I send any of my guys in there, they'll get caught. You've got agility, you've got speed, you've got your stingers, and you've got each other. We'll be right on the other side of the door if things go wrong."

I nod, suddenly aware of my stinger, the small pistol holstered on my left hip.

Royo claps his hands. "O'Connell. On me."

Kev fist-bumps Carver, squeezes me on the shoulder. "Stay in touch," he says, tapping his ear, and then jogs off after Royo.

"Riley," says Carver quietly, as soon as they're out of earshot. "I can take this if you want. You don't have to go down there."

I look up at him, surprised, thinking he's suggesting I can't handle it. But there's nothing but concern on his face, and my irritation drains away.

"Not a chance," I say, forcing a smile. "If I'm not there to help out, you'll make us look bad."

He returns the smile, then digs in his pocket and hands me a stomper-issue torch. Its grainy metal surface is ice-cold. I click it on and off, and he winces as the light flicks across his face.

"Want some after-market gear?" he says.

"Like what?"

He digs in his pocket, and hands me a small box. It's a good thing the bottom is covered with sticky adhesive, because I nearly drop it when I realise what it is.

"I can't carry a *bomb*," I say. Carver raises his eyebrows, motioning at me to stay quiet. I look over his shoulder, but nobody appears to have heard me.

I thrust the box back at Carver. When we were tracers, he was the one who built us gadgets, who designed our backpacks and shoes. And, occasionally, he'd make something a little more deadly.

The box is a sticky bomb. It's palm-sized, modified from a small plastic food container with a tight-fitting lid. Inside the lid is a sharp spike, tipped with chemicals. Just below it, on the other side of the box, is a wad of explosive putty. Slam your hand down on the box, and you've got four seconds to clear the hell out.

"Relax, Ry," Carver says. "This one's self-assembly."

He holds out his hand. The explosive putty is in his palm, a shiny blue glob. "Totally inert," he says. "Until you combine them."

"And what exactly do you think we're going to need these for?"

He gives me an evil grin. "Use your imagination."

I shake my head, but I know he's not going to take them back. I put the box in my left jumpsuit pocket, and the putty in my right, as far away from each other as possible. The gunk has left a little residue on my hand, and I wipe it on my leg, which does nothing more than add a thin layer of lint to my skin.

Carver nods at the pipe. "Ladies first."

I lean away from the smell, taking a last breath of cold air. Then I slip down into the darkness of the tunnel.

4

Prakesh

Prakesh Kumar takes the stairs two at a time, his arms pumping.

Suki is screaming at him to hurry. He can see the intense lights from the Air Lab ceiling through the open door at the top, and he raises a hand to his face, shielding his eyes.

He takes the last step and explodes out onto the roof of the control room complex, jogging behind Suki. Her hair—green this month—flares out behind her. Prakesh still has his heavy lab coat on, and he rips it from his shoulders as he runs, letting it fall to the ground behind him. They're running down a narrow canyon, bulky air-conditioning units on either side humming quietly.

"This way," Suki says over her shoulder. He can see the tear tracks down her face, gleaming under the lights. He nods, trying to control his breathing.

They sprint out of the mouth of the canyon. There's an open area on the roof, and Prakesh sees that there are other techs there, huddled in a small group off to one side. Prakesh doesn't know all of them, but he recognises Julian Novak from genomics, and the new guy, Iko, from maintenance. Prakesh isn't particularly fond of Julian. The man's lazy, prone to taking shortcuts in his work. He gives Prakesh a guarded nod. His dark hair hangs down over his face, and he's chewing something, his mouth moving mechanically.

Suki comes to a clumsy stop, pointing to the other side of the roof, beyond another bank of aircon units. "He's over there. We found him when we..." she trails off, doubling over and clutching her side.

"It's OK," Prakesh says. But it doesn't feel OK. Not by a long shot. He can feel his heart pounding, the sweat soaking into his shirt. "Do we have a name? Do we know who it is?"

"It's Benson," says Julian, talking around whatever he's chewing.

Prakesh's eyes widen. James Benson. Quiet, cheerful, hard worker. He's been at the Air Lab forever—Prakesh remembers working with him on some project years ago.

"Did he say why he's doing this? Did you talk to him?"

Julian shrugs.

Prakesh's anger flares. How can the man be so calm? He has a sudden desire to tell him to handle it, see if he keeps that smug look on his face then.

But he can't. He's in charge of the Air Lab now, and that means this is his show.

"How long's he been up here?" he asks Suki.

She takes a moment to answer. "Twenty minutes," she says. "I think."

Prakesh grabs her shoulder "I want you to get a Mark Six and jack it all the way up. Make sure he doesn't see you doing it."

"It'll never work!"

"Just do it, Suki. And do *not* put it in place before I tell you."

He strides off without waiting for her to reply. The aircon units run right up to the edge of the building. The control room complex is in the corner of the hangar, six storeys high, and Prakesh can see the Air Lab stretching out below him. He can see the enormous man-made forest dotted with algae pools. From up here, it seems like every square foot of extra space has been given over to growing food. Prakesh sees dark soil, brown climbing frames, the emerald green of the plants, the blinking lights of the hydroponic systems.

He looks down at the edge of the roof. There's less than a foot of space between the aircon units and thin air.

Prakesh takes a deep breath, holds it, then lets it out through his nose. He puts one foot on the edge, slipping his body around the aircon unit, his hand hunting for a hold.

Benson is a little way along. He's middle-aged, with the lean body and huge arms of someone who has spent years carrying heavy sacks of soil and fertiliser. His face is ashen-grey, his eyes closed. He's facing outwards, his hair buffeted by a stream from the aircon unit, and beyond him, a single step away, is a sixty-foot drop to the ground below.

5

Riley

The smell in the drained pipeline is like a living thing. It crawls into my nose and squats there, prickly and burning. I almost gag, manage to keep it down. The floor in the pipe is uneven, criss-crossed with ridges and bent metal, spotted with puddles of soupy water.

Zero-G

I'm on all fours, a few feet into the tunnel, when I hear Carver come down behind me. I flick on my torch as he lands, illuminating walls stained with gunk.

"Well, Royo was right," Carver says. "Kev would *never* fit down here."

I look back, playing my torch across his body. For me, the space is tight, but for Carver it looks as if he's been squeezed into the pipe, his shoulders bumping up against the roof.

We start forward. As I push myself around a corner, forcing my body into the wall for balance, my hand slips. My forearm slides into the muck, which soaks through my jumpsuit. It takes every ounce of willpower I have not to start hammering on the walls.

"Everything OK?" Carver says.

"Couldn't be better," I say through clenched teeth.

Another right turn, then we'll be in the plant itself. The next T-junction should have a grate which we can lift up.

It doesn't take us long to get there—the *patoosh-patoosh* of the machinery in the plant is coming down into the pipe, more felt than heard. The smell has grown stronger, too—something I didn't think was possible. The inside of my nose feels scoured.

There's a crackle in my ear. Royo. "Tracer unit, come back."

I look down at my wrist, at the thick flexible rubber band with the small digital display. It's the companion to my earpiece—each stomper unit gets its own dedicated channel on the system, and ours is 535.

I touch my wrist, keying the transmit button. "Copy. Loud and clear, Captain."

"Report."

I keep my voice low. "We're getting close. We should be inside the plant in two minutes."

"Good. We've got a team standing—"

There's a burst of static on the line, fading and vanishing inside a second. It's loud enough to make me wince.

"—static, Carver. When are you fixing it?" Royo says. If anything, he sounds even more annoyed.

"Gimme a break," Carver says from behind me. "I'm still trying to find out why it's even there. The frequencies on SPOCS are supposed to be discrete, so we don't pick up any radio—"

"*Carver*."

"Fine, fine," he mutters. "Hope you and Kev are having *fun* up there."

I crawl round a corner, and suddenly there's a grate above my head, sending thin strips of light down into the pipe.

"We're here," I whisper. "Gotta go."

"Copy that," says Royo.

Someone walks across the grate.

The light blinks out. I see boot soles, and footsteps boom down into the tiny crawlspace. I wait until the owner of the boots recedes into the distance, then keep crawling.

I can see the exit up ahead—it's another grate, with pinpricks of light leaking in. I look back over my shoulder as I get close; Carver catches my eye, and nods. Very slowly, I put a hand on the grate and push.

The metal grinds as it lifts up, and I freeze.

There are no shouts, no running feet. I lift it up the rest of the way and haul myself out.

I've come up behind one of the waste vats. It's an enormous metal cylinder, one of dozens dotted around the walls of the room, gleaming under the spotlights in the ceiling. The vats form a loose U-shape around an open area on the plant floor. The smell here is a little better, the stench of waste cut by the tang of disinfectant.

I pad to the side, moving on the balls of my feet, and Carver slips out of the grate behind me. He gets to his feet, hugging the wall as he moves into the shadows.

I rest a hand on the cold surface of the vat. I can feel it humming and vibrating as it churns the wastewater, separating out the good and the bad. They mix the water with bacteria to eat the waste, sending the oxygen produced back into the system. When the water's clean, it recirculates, flowing to water points across the lower sectors.

I sneak a peek around the side of the vat. I don't see the hostages. What I do see is a man with a stinger coming right towards our hiding place.

6

Prakesh

For a terrifying second, Prakesh doesn't know what to say. If he startles Benson, the man could slip right off the ledge.

Benson saves him the trouble. The eyes in that grey face slide open, and he looks over.

"What do you want?" he says. His voice is calm, as if he's asking Prakesh to deal with a routine lab matter. But Prakesh can't stop looking at Benson's feet, the toes already out over the edge.

"Hey, James," he says, going for nonchalance and failing. "I was, um...I was hoping I could talk to you."

"Oh yeah? About what?"

About what? Prakesh almost laughs. He can feel his palm sweating against the metal aircon unit. There's no manual for these kinds of situations, no step-by-step procedure you can rely on.

"Let's talk about why you're up here," Prakesh says. "How about it, huh?"

"Do you know how long I've been at the Air Lab?" Benson says, looking out at the vast hangar.

Prakesh's mind whirs away, trying to remember. "I don't—"

"Twenty years. I was here when old Xi Peng was running the place, long before you came along." He says it without malice, as if it's just a fact he's learned to live with. Prakesh supposes he has.

"Twenty years," Benson says again. "And I've hated it for nineteen and a half of them."

"We can change that," Prakesh says. He can hear noise on the ground below. He has to keep Benson's attention. If he jumps before the Mark Six is ready...

"Really?" Benson actually laughs. "How? You think changing my role or putting me at a better time on the shift roster is gonna make me *happier*?"

Prakesh starts to speak, but Benson talks over him. "I got nobody.

Never had nobody. Didn't think I needed them, neither. But it wears you down, you know?"

He jabs a finger outwards, pointing at the hangar wall.

"They," he says. "Them. They take us for granted. We give them food, all of them, and they treat us like dirt."

"James," says Prakesh. "You have to listen to me. We need you. *I* need you."

Benson ignores him. "Even you. Especially you. With that genetic breakthrough of yours, they should have put you in charge of the whole damn station. How do you stand it?"

"They made me head of the Air Lab," Prakesh says. "That's enough for me." He's feeling embarrassed somehow, like he shouldn't be talking about his success. He desperately wants to look back over his shoulder, hoping against hope that a stomper or a councillor or *someone* will appear on the rooftop, ready to step in.

"I always respected you," Benson says. "You seem like a decent guy. But I don't want to do this any more. You can't make me."

And before Prakesh can do anything, Benson closes his eyes and steps forward off the roof.

7

Riley

The man is my age, his face pockmarked with acne scars, wearing an old flannel shirt under a khaki jacket. When he comes round the side of the vat, Carver and I are pressed up against it, deep in the shadows.

The man stops, looking back over his shoulder. The stinger in his hands is homemade, cobbled together from spare parts, but perfectly capable of ruining your day.

I feel Carver tense beside me. I'm already working out the angles, the fastest and quietest way to take him down. If he gets even a single word off—

"We don't need any heroes here," someone says from across the room, out of my field of view. The man in the flannel shirt turns, striding back across the floor. I breathe out, long and slow.

The voice is faint, but I can just make out the words. "Everybody just stay on the ground, and we all walk away."

I sneak another peek round the side of the vat, taking in the floor of the plant. I can see some of the hostage takers, their backs to me, and a few people lying face down on the floor, but I can't get a clear look at the whole plant. Carver slips past me, placing a hand at the small of my back, moving silently to the next vat along.

I hear another voice—one of the hostages, I think. There's a muffled thump, followed by a groan of pain.

"Ivan," the first voice hisses.

"Sorry, Mikhail."

Carver puts up a closed fist: *Wait*. He takes a look of his own, scanning the plant, then pulls back into the shadows.

I catch his attention, pointing in the direction of the hostage takers, then hold up six fingers, three on each hand.

He shakes his head, quick-quick, then holds up a fist and two fingers. Seven.

I risk another look. There he is: he was out of my field of view, standing off to one side, over by the far wall. I can't pick out his features from here, but he has a massive beard, falling all the way to his stomach.

Carver taps his ear, looking at me questioningly. I nod, then key the transmit button on my wristband.

"Captain Royo," I say, keeping my voice to a low murmur. "This is Riley, come back."

"Copy, Hale. What do you see?"

Carver has moved further along the back of the vat, and is peering round the far end. He looks back at me, flashes seven fingers again, then a thumbs-up.

"We've got seven of them. They're carrying stingers, homemade. I don't see any other weapons."

"And the hostages?"

"They look OK for now."

Mikhail speaks again. "We don't want to hurt anyone. Not unless we have to," he says. He's just in my field of view. His accent is syrup-thick. The set of his shoulders and his posture speak of a man in his thirties or forties, but he has an ancient face, jagged with wrinkles and scars. His head is ringed with grey hair, long and greasy.

"Confirm seven hostiles," says Royo. "Can you—"

As he speaks, the earpiece gives off a burst of static, so loud I almost tear the unit from my ear.

My heart starts hammering. I slip around the back of the vat, praying the sound didn't go further than my ringing eardrum. I flick the SPOCS to a dead channel.

"You hear that?" someone says. Whoever it is starts walking towards my hiding place, his footsteps getting louder. Not good. I shrink back against the tank, willing myself to be as still as possible. Carver has dropped to one knee, so deep in the shadows that I can barely make him out.

"What is it, Anton?" says the leader from the other side of the room.

"Heard something," Anton says. "Just checking it out."

"OK. Be careful."

The man is going to be on me in seconds—and this time I can't count on him turning away. If I run, he'll hear me. If we take him out, if the others don't see him again in a minute or two, they'll come looking for him. I hear his footsteps, getting closer, see his shadow growing larger on the wall.

And then, all at once, the idea is there.

I can see Carver getting ready to move, a shifting shape in the shadows. I signal him with a raised hand, then shake my head.

The gap between the wall and the vat is maybe four feet. I push my back against the vat, facing the wall, then raise first one leg, then the other. When I'm locked into position, suspended a few feet off the ground, I start to push my upper body a little way up the side of the vat. One leg at time, I walk myself up the wall, always sliding my upper body first, always keeping my feet below waist level.

Zero-G

Being a tracer teaches you about friction. Friction maintains grip. Friction keeps you defying gravity in places you shouldn't be able to. Friction—perfectly calibrated pressure between two surfaces—can keep your hand on a wall, or your fingers on an edge for the extra half-second you need to pull yourself over. Friction keeps us alive.

I try to keep my movements smooth. When I'm on a run, sprinting through the station, I don't worry too much about making noise—matter of fact, the more I make, the longer people have to see me coming, and get out of the way. But if I make a sound now, I'm dead.

"If anybody's back here, come out now," Anton says again, the word given a metallic edge in the tight space. "We won't hurt you."

I'm ten feet up, but it's not enough—he'll see me. I force myself to keep sliding upwards. A foot. Another. The muscles in my thighs are starting to burn.

Anton comes into view. He's a tall man, heavily muscled, wearing a ragged blue jumpsuit. He's right underneath me. I can feel sweat pooling in the small of my back. If he looks up, he can't possibly miss me. He won't even have to aim. I feel a burning need to look at Carver, to see if he's still there, but I don't dare turn my head.

Just as these thoughts run through my mind, my shoe slips on the metal wall, giving off a tiny screech.

He had to have heard that. He must have. Any second now, he's going to look up and put a bullet into me.

But he doesn't. He looks everywhere, except above his head.

The burn in my thighs has become a raging fire, adding to the ache in my knees and ankles. I can't stay where I am—if I don't go up, or slide down, I'm going to fall right on top of him.

I will my legs to stay locked, keeping me in place.

He turns, and begins to walk the other way, intending to check behind the other vats. If Carver doesn't move, the man is going to trip right over him.

Carefully, I look to my left. Carver isn't there. He's moved away, slipping down the vats. I can just see him at the far corner of the room. "I'm OK," he says, his voice barely audible on my SPOCS.

My lungs feel like they're going to rip through my torso, but I exhale as quietly as I dare. I'm about to slide down when I stop.

Climbing is quiet. Getting down is always noisy. No matter how carefully you do it, there's always sound. I might bring the man back this way, even more determined.

But if I go up, I can stay quiet, and get an even better view of the plant.

Slowly, ever so slowly, I begin sliding up the vat, walking up the wall, treating each step as if there's crushed glass under my feet.

"What are you doing?" Carver says. I don't answer.

It seems like hours before I reach the top of the vat. Getting onto it isn't easy—I have to stretch out as I come over the lip, and for a minute the edge digs painfully into my lower back. But then I slide onto it, face-up, pulling my feet off the wall.

The air up here is just as dank, slick with the stink of human waste. The voices below me are muffled. Not knowing what's happening in here must be driving Royo insane. He'll be pacing, furious at us for going silent on him.

You're in a world of shit, I think, and have to force myself not to laugh.

"Carver," I whisper.

Carver speaks almost immediately, frantic with worry, abandoning SPOCS protocol. "Riley, talk to me."

"I'm up on one of the waste vats. They haven't seen me."

"You need to stay where you are. They've got two of them looking for us now. They know something's wrong."

Royo must have been listening in. "Tracers, report. We're ready to go out here. Give me hostile positions, *now*."

"Standby," I whisper. I slide across the top of the vat as I talk. The surface is convex, and as I near the edge I have to work to keep myself in place, but I finally get a good view of the plant.

The waste vats line the walls, surrounded by a ganglia of pipes and valves. The hostage takers are spread across the floor, talking in low voices. Two of them are patrolling the vats on my right, looking for Carver. Two more stand over the hostages, all lying in a small cluster on the floor. Mikhail is over by the main door.

"You find anything back there?" one of them yells.

The answer comes from below me. "Nothing, man. I don't like this."

The questioner nods, turning to the others. "Spread out. There's someone else here."

I look down. And that's when I see a woman, one of the hostage takers, staring up at me.

8

Prakesh

"Now, Suki!" Prakesh shouts. *"Do it now!"*

Everything happens at once. Benson screams—the scream of a man who realises what he's done, and desperately wants to take it back. He throws his arms out as if he's about to hug someone. At the same time, Prakesh hears metal on metal as Suki, or whoever she's with, shoves the Mark Six into place.

Benson vanishes. A half-second later, there's a strange sound, as if a giant has been punched in the stomach. It's followed by a crack so sharp that it reverberates off the walls of the Air Lab. Benson screams again, and this time it's a scream of pain.

Prakesh closes his eyes for a moment, then looks over the edge.

The Mark Six is destroyed, its surface pushed inwards. It's a transparent, inflatable greenhouse, six feet square, a lightweight alternative to the steel and plastic ones they used before. Suki did what she was told, pumping it up out of sight, then pushing it into place when she heard Prakesh call out.

Benson hit hard enough to rip the surface. If it had been pumped up even a little bit less, he would have gone straight through it. But it was enough to bounce him sideways, stopping the fall. He's broken his leg—Prakesh can see the bone poking up through the fabric of his pants. Benson is writhing in pain, surrounded by techs, who are calling for stretchers and medkits. No one is looking at him except for Suki, who looks like she wants to throw up.

Slowly, very slowly, Prakesh finds his way back onto the roof. He puts his hands on his knees, bending over. He's curiously light-headed. *Depression*, he thinks, not entirely sure what the thought is connected to until he remembers what Benson said. *That can't happen again. I need to pay more attention to the techs. I'll get Benson help, whatever he needs…*

He hears applause and raises his head. The group of techs on the roof are cheering, running towards him. Only Julian Novak hangs back, still chewing, his expression entirely neutral. Then Prakesh is surrounded by beaming faces and eager voices, and he lets Julian slip from his mind.

9

Riley

Before I can pull myself back onto the vat, the woman raises her stinger. "Up there! On the tank!" she shouts.

"Where?"

"Third from the right! By the pipes."

"Just one?"

"Watch the hostages."

"Somebody fire!"

I hear the crack of the stingers, and the bullets pinging off the metal. I'm on my back, frantically looking for an escape route. I have to move—a single ricochet off the roof or one of the pipes could end me.

Carver's in my ear again. "Riley! I'm coming!"

"No!" I say, shouting over the gunfire. "I got this."

I regret the words the second they're out of my mouth. A stinger bullet slams into the vat ahead of me, spitting up sparks. The bullets aren't designed to go through metal, but they'll make a real mess of anything softer. Another bullet whips by, scoring a hot line above my ankle, only just missing.

Royo is barking in my ear. "Hale, we're hearing gunfire! I need an update!"

I'm trying to stay as low as possible. Maybe I can slip off the back of the vat, drop down, make a run for it. I could draw my stinger, return fire. But I'm an awful shot, always have been, and finding a target under fire will just get me killed. I dig in my pockets, feeling for anything that could help. Half a protein bar. A tiny battery. I'm going by feel, and I'm about to admit defeat when my fingers grasp something else.

The box. Carver's sticky bomb. I'd forgotten all about it.

"The sticky," I say, hoping SPOCS picks my voice up over the gunfire. "How big's the blast?"

"Not big enough to take out seven people with guns!"

"Just humour me."

"You set that thing off, you're looking at a powerful, concentrated blast of three or four feet. Maybe less. But I don't see how…"

I've already flipped myself, and begun to move on all fours towards the edge. There's a seam, running down the middle of the vat, a vertical weld joining the two halves. Before I can even think about it, I'm scooting around on my stomach, ducking as another stinger bullet hits the metal above my head.

"Hale!" Royo shouts. "Get to cover. We're breaching now."

I fumble with the box, popping the lid off and squashing the putty down. I replace the lid, then slam the whole thing down on the seam.

I roll right off the side of the vat. A second later, the sticky explodes.

10

Riley

The sticky doesn't just blow a hole in the vat. It *ruptures* it, ripping the welded seam apart.

The bang hits my ears right as the shock waves ripple across my falling body, followed a second later by the sharp stench of shit and piss. I hear the terrified shouts of the hostage takers as a tidal wave of waste rolls towards them. An image flashes into my mind of the hostages, caught prone, submerged in the filth.

I twist in mid-air, tuck my arms, hit the ground, roll, come up on all fours in the torrent. There's not enough sewerage to flood the plant, but it rolls out in a great, sluggish, frothing wave. It's a dark brown, almost black, with misshapen lumps floating in the slurry. In the distance, an alarm is blaring.

I'm up on my feet, bursting into a run, when there's another enormous bang. The door to the plant explodes inwards, and stompers surge into the room. Kev is among them, sprinting to the side, trying to flank the hostage takers. His feet kick up huge waves of liquid as he runs. He hits one of the gunmen shoulder first, knocking him flying, then swings a punch at another. The floor is a confusion of brown sludge and screaming, scrambling, sliding bodies. Carver is roaring in my ear

Mikhail. It takes me a minute to pick him out in the chaos. He's raised his gun, taking aim at the nearest stomper.

He's the one. I can't take down every hostage taker, not on a floor that's this slippery, not in the chaos of a firefight, but if I get their leader…

I'm already running, the sea of muck rising up my shins, soaking through my pants. Mikhail fires. The stomper gives a strangled cry, flying over backwards as the bullet takes him in the chest.

My foot connects with something loose and slippery, and with a sick horror I feel myself flailing forward. On instinct, I tuck for a roll. The wet muck soaks through my jumpsuit and the shirt beneath it to touch my bare skin, shockingly cold.

But then I'm through the roll and on my feet, still running. For a moment, I can't see Mikhail—just stompers and hostages, diving and slipping across the floor. Then I spot him. He's almost at the doors, elbowing stompers out of the way when they try to grab him.

"Move!" I yell, dodging past a hostage. Her huge, panicked eyes are the only thing in her face not slick with filth.

Mikhail is past the doors now. Two stompers are giving chase, but they're not fast enough, and they can't risk firing—a missed shot would go right into the gallery.

I bolt through the doors, now no more than shredded chunks of metal. As I pull free of the muck, as my feet kiss solid ground, I lean forward and drop my centre of gravity, swinging my arms, pushing myself into a full sprint.

Think you're fast, Mikhail? Let's see if you can outrun me.

The shadows from the catwalks cut the floor into pieces. The area past the plant is filled with the crush—the people that pack the floor of every gallery and corridor in Outer Earth, a slow-moving morass of humanity. Mikhail is still shoving people out of the way, powering through the crowd. I do the same, trying to keep sight of him, shouting his name as I elbow people aside.

No one tries to stop him. They're all gawking at the scene in the plant. He's at the edge of the gallery, pulling away, sprinting into one of the corridors leading off the floor. I see him look back over his shoulder as he does. I'm still fighting my way through the crowd. If I don't get free in the next five seconds, I'm going to lose him.

"No!" I scream as he slips out of sight. I'm furious with the people in the crowd. They stand there like statues, not moving until I put a hand on their chests or pull their shoulders to the sides.

My SPOCS unit is filled with shouted orders from dozens of stompers, coming across the all-channels setting. "Carver?" I shout, hoping that I can be heard through the chaos.

The noise vanishes, replaced by his voice, calmer than it should be. "Copy, Ry."

My words are rendered ragged by my running. "I'm chasing Mikhail. We're on the bottom level, heading towards the furnaces. I need you to cut him off for me."

"No can do. I'm *way* behind you."

"Kev?" I can feel a stitch creeping down my left side as I run, jabbing me with every step.

"He's here. Beating someone to a pulp with his own stinger."

I don't respond, partly because I'm trying to save my breath, and partly because I know what he's going to say next and don't want him to say it.

"You'll have to call Anna."

There's a sharp turn in the corridor. I'm coming up on it too quickly, and jump towards the wall, using it to arrest my momentum and change direction in one movement. I see Mikhail, pushing past a group of people standing outside the door to the furnaces. He's sprinting past, heading for the stairwell at the far end.

"She's on a different channel today. Uh...349," says Carver.

I have to glance down at my wristband as I flick through the channels. I spin past 349, and have to pull the dial back.

"Anna, this is Riley, come back."

For a moment, there's no sound except the pounding of my feet. "Anna," I say again. "Riley here. You copy?"

"What do you want?" Anna says, her crisp accent coming through on the line perfectly. She sounds like she just woke up from a nice doze.

"Where are you?" I say.

She pauses before answering. "Level 6 in New Germany."

Mikhail hits the stairs, taking them three at a time. I'm closing, but nowhere near fast enough. "I've got a runner heading your way," I say. "He's climbing the stairwell on the Apogee border side. I need you to take him out."

Static explodes in my ear, and I nearly tear the SPOCS unit out and hurl it at the wall.

The noise dies, and Anna snickers. "What's the matter? Too fast for you?"

"Just do it," I say, as I sprint past the door to the furnace. A blast of dry heat whips by me as I pass, and then I'm at the stairs.

"If you're going to give me orders, I'll let you keep chasing him."

I can hear Mikhail above me. His thundering footfalls shake the stairwell.

"Anna, now is *not* the time," I say, the words burning a stitch in my side. Above me, Mikhail's thundering footfalls shake the stairwell. "He's coming from below you. Middle-aged, long hair, dark overalls, backpack."

Anna yawns. I hear it come over the comms, a little swelling exclamation mark, and I want to reach through the frequencies and smack her.

"I'll see what I can do," Anna says.

The bottom of the stairs is littered with garbage and scraps of twisted metal. I take the steps as fast as I can, dodging around wide-eyed onlookers, tracking the noise of Mikhail's thundering footsteps above me. He's got too much of a head start. Anna might get there in time, but she might not. I need to close the gap.

I climb as fast as I can, my legs pistoning out in front of me, my thighs screaming. The stairwell is a dark, tight space, with half the lights missing from their sockets. There's a woman working a plasma cutter just below Level 3. I smell her before I hear her, the scent of ozone sharp and pungent, and I have to shield my eyes as I dash past. I'm already looking up towards the next set of stairs, and that's when I see it.

The landing above me isn't flush with the wall. There's a gap. Five feet wide, an open space beyond the railing at the landing's edge. I didn't realise I was on this particular stairwell—the gap reaches all the way from Level 1 to Level 6, something the construction corps used to get building materials between the levels, back when the station was built.

There's a railing, waist-high and flecked with rust, separating the landing from the gap. Before I can even think about it, I jump. My right foot lands square on the rail, and I use it to launch myself at the wall, flying into space.

If I don't pull this off, if I don't swing my body a hundred and eighty degrees at just the right moment, I'll fall, screaming, all the way to the bottom.

My left foot connects with the wall, sending a shock wave up into my knee.

Time slows, then stops.

I can pick out every detail. The rough texture of the metal. My pants stretched tight against my leg as my knee bends. The feeling in my hips as I start to twist.

The word running through my mind is *friction*. My foot needs to stay in immobile contact with that wall. If it doesn't, I'm finished.

And then, as time begins to speed up again, the yell escapes my lips, forcing its way out as I push back off the wall and spin my body, injecting that tiny bit of extra energy into my movements. I throw my hands up, as high as they can go.

My palms slam into the edge of the landing above. There's a split second where I'm scrabbling at it, but my body takes over. I swing forward, then on the way back I use the momentum to thrust myself upwards. A second later, I'm up and over the railing. My arms are burning, and I can actually feel the blood powering through my veins, but I'm alive. And I can hear Mikhail, closer now. His breathing echoes off the walls, hot and ragged.

I ignore the pounding in my own chest, ignore the stitch which has turned my side to a searing flame, and charge after him into the corridor. I'm frantically scanning my mental map of New Germany—where does the corridor lead? The hab units? Or is this the sector where they've got the mess hall on the upper levels?

The lights above us flicker, then die completely, plunging the corridor into darkness. When they click back on, Anna Beck is there, in front of Mikhail, running right at him, her slingshot raised in front of her like a shield.

She fires, the slingshot strips snapping forward with a high-pitched *crack*. Whatever she's loaded it with whips through the air, too fast to see, and takes Mikhail dead in the chest.

11

Knox

Knox strips naked, then washes his hands, holding them up so the water drips down his arms. It's scalding hot, and the industrial detergent he uses makes his skin feel as if it's been scoured.

He shakes the water off into the metal basin, then turns his attention to his chest. Two strips of tape, their edges peeling, form an X above his heart. He peels the tape off, wincing, using one finger to hold the tiny transmitter underneath it in place.

Two thin wires run off the transmitter, terminating under his skin, and he touches the entry wounds gingerly. No infection. Good.

He replaces the tape, smoothing it down, then washes his hands again. The skin on them is red and raw, peeling away on the ball of his left thumb. He bites down on a stray piece, tearing it off and spitting it into the basin, then gives his thumb and forefingers another quick scrub.

The cart, and his rags, lie behind him, pushed into a corner of the storage room, below the shelves that line the walls. He hates that he has to keep them here, but he doesn't have a choice. He's lucky to have this place: these tiny, forgotten rooms on the bottom level of Apogee. And he needs his cart, the rags that keep other people away from him. It's his protection, his shield. The only way he can pass through the rest of the station unnoticed.

He pulls a set of clean scrubs from a hanger next to the basin, and slips them on. His mind is racing ahead, checking and rechecking, making sure he hasn't forgotten anything, and the cool cotton soothes him.

His hand darts through the air, plucks an object from a shelf. He cobbled it together from scratch—his electronics knowledge is passable, at best, but he worked at it until he had it right. It's a misshapen metal box, a foot square, an antenna sprouting from it. He made sure that all the messy wires and circuit boards were packed away, out of sight.

He hits a switch on the front of the box. A light flickers on, and a dial leaps into life. The storage room fills with static, words pushing through it, barely audible.

"—Go left! On your left!—"

"Confirm we have the hostiles in custody, repeat, confirm we have—"

"—Drop your weapon!"

He snaps it off, satisfied.

He exits the storeroom, leaning on his good leg. The space beyond is in darkness, but his hand finds the bank of switches on the wall to his right. The lights flicker on, one after the other, illuminating a room so clean that the floor shines. Banks of medical equipment line the walls, their surfaces spotless, and his eyes land on the wheeled tray with his tools: the forceps, the clamps, the retractors, the syringes. His lone good scalpel, its edge still razor-sharp.

In the centre of the room is the operating table, its metal surface glaring under the lights. Knox limps towards it, running his hand across its cold surface. He should clean it again. It wouldn't do for his patient to get an infection.

12

Riley

Mikhail's breath explodes out of him. He stumbles, trying to right himself, but his feet get tangled up with each other and he crashes to the ground.

His backpack splits down the side, disgorging its contents. A stinger flies out, skittering across the metal plating. A canteen, its top popping open, paints the wall dark with water.

Mikhail tries to get up, but Anna is already there. She drops a knee into the small of his back, locking him to the floor. He tries to roll over, swinging his arms behind him, striking at Anna.

"Nice try," Anna says, and drives a fist into the side of his neck. His body crumples. When I reach him, he's wheezing and clawing at the floor, his face a horrified grimace.

Anna flashes me a self-satisfied smile. She's sixteen years old, her blonde hair spilling out from under a green beanie, pulled down to just above her eyes. Her stomper jumpsuit is immaculate, with only the merest suggestion of dirt on the knees and elbows.

She waggles the slingshot in the air. It's a Y of welded metal, with a thick rubber strap hanging off the top end, bouncing off her wrist. One-Mile, she calls it.

"There," she says. "Easy."

Mikhail lashes out. Before I can yell a warning, he grabs Anna round the ankle and yanks her towards him. She topples backwards, howling in pain as her coccyx hits the deck.

Before Mikhail can rise, I'm on top of him, slamming my knee into his back. I reach for his arms, yanking them behind him. With my other hand, I reach into the pocket of my jumpsuit, then pull out a plastic zip tie and slip it around his wrists, cinching it tight. Mikhail's yelling is incoherent now, nothing more than cries of fury.

I keep my knee in the small of his back. Anna has risen onto her elbows. "I had him," she says, speaking to me but staring angrily at Mikhail.

"No, you didn't," I say.

"If I hadn't been here, you would've lost him."

"If *I* hadn't been here, he would've got away."

I grab Mikhail by the arms and pull. He groans as I yank him upwards, first to his knees, then to his feet.

"Mikhail, right?" I say. "You're under arrest. You don't have to say anything right now. You're entitled to a trial within three days. You're entitled to space in the brig until your trial. If you resist further, I'm authorised to subdue you. Have I made myself clear?" The words sound odd in my mouth. But I know I've done it right, just like Royo explained.

"Are we clear?" I say to Mikhail, when he doesn't answer. The look he gives me could turn a planet to ash, but he gives a terse nod.

I gesture to Anna. She rolls her eyes and grabs him by the other arm. As she holds him in place, I shove as much as I can back into his pack—may as well check for anything we could use as evidence. There's the canteen, plus a homemade stinger that looks like it would explode if you tried to fire it, and a broken tab screen. There's a small cloth bag, and when I shake it over my palm a tumble of seeds fall out. Bean seeds, from what I can tell.

Anna picks one up, shrugs, then drops it back into my hand. I shove everything back into the pack, zipping it shut. We march Mikhail back towards the stairwell. I call Carver, let him know where we're taking our prisoner. He says he'll meet us there.

Anna and I don't speak, but, then, we've never really had a lot to say to each other. She was Royo's final recruit to the tracer unit. To hear him tell it, she made waves up in Tzevya, where she was running with her own crew—*fresh blood*, he called her. And right from the start, she made a point of getting in my face.

The first time we met, at the stomper headquarters in Apogee, she walked up and challenged me to a race, right in front of everybody. She wouldn't leave it alone, even when I told her no. Royo had to tell her to can it before she backed off. Even then, she's always been distinctly cool towards me, always quick with a snide comment.

We're at the top of the stairs when Mikhail makes a break for it.

Anna's holding his right arm, and I've got his left. He hurls himself forward, out of our grip. Of course, he happens to be at the top of a flight of stairs with his hands bound behind him, so all he does is lose his balance, crashing down the steps. He comes to a skidding halt on the landing below, groaning in pain.

Anna has collapsed against the wall, bent over with laughter. I'm about to head down to him when she puts a hand on my shoulder. "No, wait. I want to savour this," she says between gasps for breath. "The worst escape attempt in history."

Despite myself, I can't help smiling back. We walk down and haul Mikhail to his feet. Anna leans forward and sniffs the air delicately.

"You smell," she says to me.

I reach up to rub my face without thinking. There's a streak of shit caked on my cheek, already dry and hard. I wipe it off, embarrassed, especially since Anna's skin is almost completely free of dirt. How she keeps herself clean in this place, I have no idea.

When we get to the brig, Mariana is on guard duty outside, leaning up against the wall. Carver's with her. He flashes me a thumbs-up when he sees Mikhail.

"Who's this?" Mariana asks. She's as squat as a turnip, with broad shoulders and piercing blue eyes. Unlike the other stompers, she doesn't carry a stinger, preferring an enormous iron bar strapped to her back in a homemade scabbard.

"He took a bunch of people hostage in the Recycler Plant," I say, pushing Mikhail towards her. She and Carver grab him, and Mariana taps at the keypad by the door.

"Oh yeah," she says. "A few of your friends are already inside, *hijo de puta*. Move."

Mikhail says nothing. Mariana glances over her shoulder at us. "Nice job."

"Nothing to it," says Anna, her arms folded. She sees my look, and rolls her eyes, before handing Mikhail's pack to Carver. He roots around inside it, muttering to himself. He takes the homemade stinger, the canteen and the little cloth bag, dropping them into his own backpack.

"Are you *trying* to get me fired?"

It's Royo. I turn to see him and Kev walking up towards us, and I've never known him to look more like a stomper than he does at that moment. He points a thick finger at me. "I asked you to go in and observe, not blow things up. It's going to take *months* to repair the damage. And what the hell is that smell?"

"What do you think it is?" I say, too weary to argue. Anna smirks.

"Captain Royo," a voice says from behind us.

Royo looks up, and his eyes narrow in disgust. I look round, and realise why.

13

Riley

Han Tseng is striding towards us, hands clasped behind him.

The acting council leader for Apogee wears a long brown coat, buttoned to the neck. His eyebrows are like beetles, close together, always moving. Acolytes trail in his wake.

"What's he even doing here?" Carver mutters, turning away.

"Acting councilman," Royo says, as Tseng walks up.

If Tseng notices the tone, he doesn't say so. He doesn't even look at us. "That did not go well, Captain. I want a full briefing. Immediately."

"I'll have one of my men take you through what happened," Royo says, turning back to us. "Now, Hale—"

Tseng puts a hand on Royo's shoulder. The captain slowly turns around. His face is stone.

"What did they want?" Tseng says. "Food? Better accommodation? Whatever it is, this can't happen again. With the *Shinso Maru* coming back into our orbit, we're not going to have much chance to pander to these people."

"What's the *Shinso Maru*?" Carver whispers to me.

"Asteroid catcher ship," I whisper back. "Do you even *listen* in briefings?"

"They want Janice Okwembu," Royo says to Tseng.

"Then we should have given her to them. It makes no difference in the end. If we could just..."

Royo's look pins him to the spot. "How many people are on the new station council at the moment, exactly?"

Tseng's mouth flattens into a thin line. "The representatives from Tzevya and Gardens should be chosen soon. Until then—"

"Until *then*," Royo says, "there'll be no decision on any prisoners. You might want to read the station constitution sometime, acting councilman. Everybody's entitled to a fair trial by a full elected council. That includes her."

Right then, the lights above us flicker, and die, plunging us into darkness. Everybody goes quiet for a moment.

A moment later the lights flicker back on.

"I were you, I'd stop getting involved in hostage situations, and start worrying about the lights," Royo says to Tseng. He jabs a finger at the ceiling. "They're getting worse."

Tseng seems about to interject, but Royo pointedly turns his back. The councilman's eyes fall on me, and after a moment he stalks off.

"See what I have to deal with, Hale?" Royo says, lowering his voice. "I've got Han Tseng crawling up my ass, along with a pissed-off crew of waste technicians who now have to put an entire plant back together. Care to explain?"

"I'd like to hear this, too, actually," says Anna.

"Shut up, Beck," says Royo.

"How many hostages died?" I ask him.

"Don't get smart with me, Hale."

"How many?"

Royo gives a long sigh. "It's not just about getting the minimum amount done, Hale. You don't win just because everybody's still alive at the end of it."

"I'm going home now," I say, then turn and start walking, heading back towards one of the corridors.

"I'll come with you," says Carver.

My first instinct is to tell him no. After the chase I've just been through, I could use a few moments by myself, a slow jog back to my hab to warm down my muscles and calm my mind. But he's going in the same direction I am anyway, and I don't have the energy to protest.

Carver flips Kev a salute, nods to Royo and Anna, and jogs to my side. Nobody tries to stop us.

We accelerate to a jog. Carver sticks close, saying little, letting his breathing match mine as we head back towards Chengshi. As we reach the sector border, he indicates a nearby water point, its lone light gleaming in the darkness of the corridor. The water is cold and crisp, much better than it should be.

"Sorry about earlier," I say, wiping my mouth.

"Huh?"

"When I decided to climb on top of the vat in the plant. That was a really dumb idea."

"Oh. That." He gives a lopsided grin. His tugs at the goggles around his neck. "If I'd tried to stop you, you'd have just called me names and done it anyway."

"True."

"I have to admit I'm impressed. That was a very cool use for a sticky bomb."

"Thanks."

"Kind of genius, actually."

I can feel myself blushing. "Well, I wouldn't say *that*."

"Oh, I wasn't talking about you. I was talking about the bomb. Only a true genius could have constructed it."

"Really?" I say, raising an eyebrow.

"And you should see what I'm working on now," he says. "It's big. I mean, when this thing is done, it's going to change *everything*."

"Like SPOCS?"

Carver grimaces. "Forget SPOCS," he says. "It's not right yet. Too much static, and I can't figure out where it's coming from. No, this other thing is much cooler."

I think of Carver's requisitioned workbench at Big 6, the stomper headquarters. "I haven't seen you building anything at HQ?"

His smile gets wider. "Who said I've been building it at HQ?"

"So what is it?"

He opens his mouth—and then stops. His eyes drop. "Not ready yet," he says.

We fall silent as we walk away from the water point. When we cross the border, he turns to me. "Wanna go on an old-fashioned cargo run with me?" A small package appears in his hand as if by magic.

I look at him. "You serious? Being a stomper isn't good enough for you?"

"I—" He looks away. "I miss it. I didn't think I would, but I do. There's something about taking cargo jobs that's just *easier*."

I don't have a response to that, and I don't like the way he's looking at me.

"Do you ever go back to the Nest?" he says.

I get a flash of memory just then: a room, hidden between levels in Apogee, where our crew, the Devil Dancers, lived. Carver's workbench, Yao's mural on the wall, the pile of mattresses and blankets where we slept.

I shake my head.

"Would it make you feel better?"

I squint at him. "What?"

"Ever since the thing with your dad…"

"Don't."

He stops, aware that he's gone too far. Remembering what happened to my dad is still enough to stick a sour lump in my throat.

In order to save the station from Okwembu's insane scheme, I had to kill him, detonating his ship before it could collide with us. It's a memory I try to keep locked away, deep inside me.

He clears his throat. "I guess I'll see you tomorrow."

"Yeah."

He turns and jogs away, not looking back.

That's when the fatigue really hits me. It's all I can do not to slump against the corridor wall. But I know if I do that I'll never get up again. Better to keep going, to make it all the way home, where there is Prakesh and food and soft, cool blankets.

My SPOCS unit bleeps once. "Hale, come back. Dispatch calling Riley Hale."

It's a man's voice, one that I don't recognise. I toy with not answering, but that would mean pointed questions later. Royo's already pissed at me, and this wouldn't help matters.

I close my eyes and key the transmit button. "Copy, this is Hale."

"We have a 415 with your name on it, confirm code."

"A 415?"

The dispatcher pauses, as if he can't quite believe that I don't have all our call codes memorised. "Domestic disturbance. A woman's been hurt, keeps asking for you. Location is A1-B22."

Of all the things I've had to get used to as a stomper, it's how they talk about locations on the station. As a tracer, I thought of places with pictures and memories, but stompers think of them in terms of letters and numbers. My mind whirls as I try to decode the dispatcher's words. A1—that's Apogee, Level 1. And corridor B, junction 22...that would be over by the heat exchangers, past where the silkworm merchant sets up. Not too far from here.

I really don't want to take this call. For a second, I nearly tell the dispatcher no. Then I see Royo's face in my mind again.

"Confirm code," I say. "On my way."

"Copy. Out."

I avoid the gallery floor, not wanting to run into Royo again, or any of the crew who have to clean up the Recycler Plant. It takes me a little longer than I'd like, and by the time I reach the silkworm merchant, the fatigue has settled into my legs, intertwining my muscles with cords of lead.

"Get 'em hot," the merchant intones, not looking up from the sizzling platter on his cart. "Hot silkworms, get 'em hot." I ignore him, jogging past, turning left at what I'm pretty sure is junction 22.

I thought I knew the station well enough, and that goes double for my home sector of Apogee, but I'm in a corridor I've never seen before. The walls are covered in a mess of red graffiti, tag on tag on tag. There's an odd smell, too—at first I think it's the silkworms frying, but it's sharper somehow, more unpleasant.

There's no woman here. There's no one at all.

I frown, slowing to a walk. The corridor splits again at the far end, and there's a door set into the wall. As I get closer, I see it has a faded sign bolted to it. ROOM 18.

I tap my wristband, annoyed. "Dispatch, this is Hale, come back."

Silence.

I look down at the wristband display—I'm on an open channel. I should be hearing sporadic stomper chatter, bad jokes, bursts of static.

Something's not right.

"Dispatch?" I say again. "Dispatch, I need a check on the location of that 415."

Movement. Behind me. I feel it before I see it, feel the air shift. I spin round, dropping into a fighting stance, and see a dark shape looming over me, a man, his features in shadow.

Every muscle in my body explodes with pain.

I go rigid, trying to scream. There's static everywhere now, crackling in fury, and then I'm gone.

14

Knox

Knox doesn't like the taser. It's a crude, ugly weapon, but it gets the job done.

Unlike the old models, which used electrode darts and conductor wires, this one is completely wireless—it uses field induction, with a ten-foot range. Put 2000 volts through someone, and the loss of neuromuscular control is instantaneous. He flexes the handheld taser in his fingers, ready to give Hale another blast if she shows signs of coming round. She twitches, conscious, but only just.

Knox looks round to see if he's attracted any attention, but the corridor is silent. He drops down onto one knee, an awkward movement that nearly unbalances him. The syringe goes into Hale's neck—a sedative, not suitable for long procedures but more than enough to keep her down after the taser effects wear off.

He grabs her under the arms. Hale is heavier than he expected—he nearly drops her, and, with his bad leg, it's all he can do to lift her up. He has to pause, taking a few deep breaths before rolling her into his cart.

She hits the bottom with a thud, her body contorting. She groans, and he can see the muscles in her neck standing out. How could he ever think she was beautiful? She's as ugly as the rest of them, flawed, imperfect.

Working quickly, he buries her under the stinking rags. She becomes nothing more than a shape at the bottom of his cart, a piece of trash that no one but him would ever want. In the distance, he can hear the merchant's refrain: "Hot silkworms, get 'em hot, hot silkworms."

He looks up and down the corridor again, then swings the cart around, its wheels squeaking on the metal floor as he pushes past the wall of graffiti.

"Hey, you."

He closes his eyes, astonished and furious, then looks around. Three people have appeared in the corridor behind him. Two women and a man—gang members, judging from the identical black tears tattooed on their cheeks. The man is munching silkworms, stuffing them into his face from a dirty cloth bag.

One of the women tilts her head. "What you got in there?"

She and her companions start sauntering down the passage towards him, spreading out. He tries to keep any expression off his face. His hand is already in his pocket, where he keeps his knife. *There's no way you can fight them off, not a chance.*

But he can't let them discover Hale. He's worked too long and too hard to get her here.

The woman stops, wrinkling her nose. "Gods. You shit yourself or something?"

The other two pick up the scent. "Oh, that's rough," the man says, swallowing a mashed mouthful of silkworm.

Morgan Knox puts all the confused anger he can into his face. "Leave me alone!" he shouts at them. "They're listening to me! I'm talking to them right now!"

He's babbling, saying the first things that come into his head, but it's working. They're laughing, making exaggerated expressions of disgust. One of them digs in the bag, rooting up a handful of worms, then throws it at him. They smack into his cheek, dribbling down the front of his coat.

But they're leaving, still laughing among themselves. Knox waits until they're around the corner, then lets himself relax. His mask worked. It always works. Show the world your real face, and they'll tear you to pieces, but if you can disguise yourself, if you pretend you're not a threat, they'll let you pass on by. Pathetic.

He pushes the cart, shoving it with his thigh, getting it moving again. His surgery is close, and it's prepped and ready to go. Under the rags, his patient is silent.

15

Prakesh

It's only when he shuts the door to his office that Prakesh finds he can breathe again.

He sits down on the edge of his desk, letting his chin touch his chest. *That could have gone very, very wrong.*

After a moment, he drops heavily into his chair. The room itself is tiny, with no windows. The desk is battered and ancient, covered with tab screens and old drinks containers, taking up half the room. The only luxurious item is the chair behind it, a curved combination of mesh and black straps that fits his frame perfectly. It's much too comfortable—he doesn't think he'll ever get used to it.

The Food Lab used to be run by Oren Darnell, but he was killed in his insane attempt to torture the station. After it was all over, after Darnell was dead and Okwembu arrested, Outer Earth was hit by the worst food shortages in its history.

Prakesh and the other techs had already been working on creating genetically modified plants, and they stepped up their programme, working impossibly long hours to make plants that would grow faster, stronger, with more fruiting bodies.

And Prakesh was the one who cracked it. He'd worked all night on a hunch, focusing on the telomere caps at the ends of the plant nucleotides. He planted a single runner bean seed, then passed out, exhausted, leaning against one of the algae ponds. When he woke up, the bean plant was exploding out of the soil. A few hours later, still not entirely sure it wasn't a dream, he bit down on a fresh green bean.

After that, even Prakesh was amazed at the progress they made. The Food Lab was still being rebuilt, but the floor of the Air Lab became a tangled mess of grow-ops, and every day it seemed like there was a new plant variety. For the first time in months, Outer Earth had more food than it could ever need.

The techs told Prakesh that they were putting him in charge of the Air Lab, and they told the current head, a sleepy man named Archer, that he'd better step down. They even offered him Oren Darnell's old office: a huge space above the control room, with massive glass windows that looked out onto the trees.

He turned it down. Darnell had nearly destroyed Outer Earth and Prakesh didn't feel like occupying the man's old space. The office is now the most well-appointed storeroom on the station, which suits Prakesh just fine.

He doesn't need much space to work, anyway. He glances across the three tab screens on his desk: monorail shipping manifests that need signing off, fertiliser test results, a message from a tech asking him to resolve a work dispute. He picks up the test results first. If he can power through all this, he can go home, forget this day ever—

"Anybody home?" Suki says, sticking her head around the door. A frizz of red hair tickles her cheek. "We're going for drinks. All of us. That includes you, 'Kesh."

"I don't feel much like Pilot's," Prakesh says, thinking of the grimy bar in the station dock.

"Who said anything about Pilot's?" Suki says. "My brother's got these watermelons, right? He's been soaking them in homebrew for like a week."

Prakesh smiles. "You go on ahead. I might see you down there later."

He looks down, intending to get back to the test results, half of his mind already thinking about the dispute message. He looks up when he hears Suki crossing to his desk.

She perches on the end. She's one of the only techs—scratch that, one of the only people on the whole station—that he's ever seen wearing a skirt. It peeks out from the bottom of her lab coat, over black leggings. He can smell the soil on her as she leans in.

"You did good, boss," she says.

"Benson—is he—"

"Already took care of it. He's on suicide watch, and the psych docs are on it. He won't be back until they give him a clean bill."

He smiles thanks. "Good job with the Mark Six, too."

"How did you know that was going to work?"

He shrugs. "Didn't, really."

She smacks his shoulder, then hops off the desk. "Be downstairs in ten, or I'll come and drag you out of here."

"I'm really OK."

"No way. You need a drink."

"I said *no*, Suki."

He doesn't mean for it to be harsh. But he can't control it—his tone just changes, dropping his voice low. He's instantly sorry, furious with himself.

But the last thing he wants to do is go and socialise, and Suki's closeness, the smell of her, has just made him think of Riley.

Suki looks like she's been slapped, but only for a second. She composes herself, a neutral expression sliding back into place. "Well," she says. "I guess I'll see you later, then. You should bring Riley by sometime."

Her last sentence is said without enthusiasm, more of a reflex than anything else. The door clicks shut behind her.

Prakesh turns back to his tab screens, but finds he can't concentrate. He sits back, rubbing his eyes.

He'll never get used to Riley as a cop. Every time she suits up, it's like she becomes a different person. She moves with purpose, like the last six months haven't happened, and there's a look in her eyes every time she heads off to work. Like she can't wait to get out there, can't wait to *move*.

But when the jumpsuit comes off, she changes. Everything that's happened to her—her dad, Janice Okwembu, Amira—all comes rushing back. She's quiet at home, her mind off somewhere else. Prakesh has done his best, tried to fill her world with colour and love and as much good conversation as he can, but it's never enough.

And going home at the end of the day has lost its spark.

For the hundredth time, he bites back on his frustration. He tells himself to ease up. She just needs time. He shuts off his tab screens, one after the other. They can wait. He's going home, and he's going to see Riley.

He leaves the office, snapping the door closed behind him. As he walks down the passage, he wonders idly what she's doing at this moment.

16

Riley

I'm stuck in the nightmare again.

I'm running down the middle of a long, dark corridor, moving faster than I ever have before. There's a man standing at the end, his body cloaked in shadow. I can't see him clearly, but I know it's my father. It always is.

Any moment, I tell myself, I'm going to wake up. I'll be in our bed, with the blankets knotted at my feet and the mattress drenched in my sweat, Prakesh's arm around me and his hushed voice in my ear.

But it's different this time—the darkness isn't the darkness of a dream. And the pain rippling up from my legs isn't the dull, distant pain of exertion. It's horrible, needle-sharp, bigger than life.

My father raises his head towards me. His eyes—angry, confused, terrified—lock onto my own. I see my name appear over his face, blinking bright orange. *Riley. Riley. Riley.*

I jerk awake, a strangled cry bursting out of my throat. The dream vanishes. The pain doesn't.

This is all wrong. There's too much light. The surface underneath me is hard, nothing like the soft warmth of our bed. I don't have to reach my hand out to know that Prakesh isn't with me. I'm lying face down, one arm tucked underneath me. My tongue is a dry, dead thing, and my throat screams for water. I can feel my heart pounding, pulsing in my chest and neck.

Slowly, my surroundings come into focus. I'm lying on a metal table, gleaming under a single harsh light. The light is focused, a tight circle on the table, and the rest of the room is in darkness.

The pain in my legs chooses that moment to really wake up. It's in my knees, biting and tearing. Before I can stop myself, my hand is moving down towards my right knee.

My jumpsuit is gone. I've still got my tank top and my underwear, but the flesh on my bare legs has risen in heavy goose bumps. I push my fingers down my right leg, my movements jerky and shuddering. I have to find the source of that pain. If I do that, I tell myself, I can get through this. My fingers track across my skin. The pain isn't in my kneecap, it's deeper, somehow...

Then I touch the tough, spiky thread of a stitch, and I scream.

I twist myself around, my fingers exploring in horrified bursts. The stitches are on the back of my knees: tiny, thick lines buried just under the surface of the skin, as if a parasite has wormed its way into my flesh. The stitches run horizontally, tucked between the bones. They zigzag back and forth, and the thick ends jut out at awkward angles. The flesh is horribly tender, and even touching it lightly makes the pain spike.

Get them out. Get them out now.

My fingers snag the end of the stitch on my right knee. I grit my teeth, getting ready to pull.

"I wouldn't do that."

The voice is cold and businesslike, coming from the darkness at the edge of the room. I freeze, trying to squint past the light.

"Who's there?" I say.

No answer.

How did I get here? My memory is in fragments. I was on a run—what was I doing? Was I delivering cargo? No—that's wrong. Then I remember the call, the empty corridor, the movement behind me.

Something flies out of the darkness, bouncing off my chest. I grab it just before it skitters away. It's a small bottle, off-white plastic, the blue label faded and peeling. Whatever's inside gives a dry rattle as I turn the bottle in my hands.

"You should take one," the voice says. It's a man's voice, soft and precise—the same voice as the dispatcher who called me over SPOCS.

The hell with this. I swing my legs off the table, calculating how far away the voice is, already lining up the angle of attack. I'm going to get whoever's out there and drag them into the light, make them take back whatever they—

The second I touch the floor, there's a horrid, searing explosion in my legs. I collapse, howling in pain, the pill bottle locked in my hand.

I raise myself up on one elbow, sweat pouring down my face, staring in horror at the stitches. They're already beginning to bruise, the skin fading from red to a sick, mottled purple.

My eyes are growing accustomed to the darkness beyond the pool of light. The room we're in is small, the surfaces dull metal and clean, white ceramic. There are banks of equipment lined up along the wall to my right: water basins, blank tab screens, shelves stacked with bottles and medical instruments. There's a small storage area leading off the main room, its shelves groaning with even more equipment.

The table I was lying on isn't a table, but a hospital bed, minus the mattress. There are restraints hanging off it, wrist and ankle cuffs, soft fabric hanging open. Dark brown stains run over the edge of the table. Blood.

My blood.

Movement, at the far side of the room. I finally spot the owner of the voice. He's older than me, in his forties at least. He has thick black hair and a neatly trimmed beard. His right hand grips a battered cane, the metal worn down in places and the rubber foot cracked and peeling. His scrubs are white, and, except for the dots of dried blood on the front, they're impossibly clean. He wears dark pants underneath them; they hang loose on his left leg, as if it doesn't fill them properly.

He limps over, the cane hitting the floor with a soft thud at every step. He crouches down in front of me, his bad leg folding under him. Before I can move, his hand darts out, grabbing my right knee in a pincer grip, his thumb digging into the stitches.

I snap my head back and scream. It rips around the room, turning it into a horrific echo chamber.

"Take your medicine," he says.

He lets go of my leg. I scrabble at the bottle cap, hating myself for it. The tablets are blue, chalky and bitter in my mouth, accenting my raging thirst.

The man glances at my bare leg with a grimace. Before I can do anything, he produces a pair of surgical scissors, and calmly snips the stiff ends of the stitches off. The cool metal of the blade just touches my skin.

"There," he says. "Perfect."

He lifts his other hand. He's holding a thin, black, rectangular box, with a single raised button in the centre. No—not holding. It's taped to his hand. *What*...

"At the back of the knee," he says, tracing the stitches with the tip of his finger, "is a gap in the muscles called the *popliteal fossa*."

"I don't—"

"An object of up to half an inch in diameter can be inserted in the *popliteal fossa*, without interfering with the normal movement of the leg."

His eyes find mine. "There is a device in each of your *popliteal fossae*. Each device carries a small but extremely powerful explosive charge. If the devices detonate, there will be significant damage to surrounding tissue: bone, muscle, blood vessels, nerves. Assuming you survived the resultant blood loss, you would almost certainly lose both your legs below the knee."

I can't move. I can't look away from the box taped to his hand.

"Don't worry," he says. "The trigger mechanism takes quite an effort to push. I won't hit it by accident. But if you try and attack me, or do anything other than *exactly* what I tell you, I *will* push it. And when I do, it'll make that little squeeze of mine feel like a flu shot."

He stands, then limps over to one of the machines in the corner. "And the operation went perfectly. As I said, the devices will not inhibit your normal running motion in the slightest. There'll be some pain, but it might even be manageable—if you keep taking your medicine."

The sob comes out before I can stop it. He's lying. He has to be. I'm staring at my knees, as if I can make the stitches melt away.

"And just in case you're thinking about running to the hospital to have another doctor remove the devices, don't bother," he says. "I'm the only one who could do it without setting them off."

My lips are forming words, and I have to will myself to turn them into sounds, pushing them past my shredded throat. "And what if I kill you first?"

In response, he pulls at his scrubs, undoing the knot at his side and lifting them away from his bare chest. There's a second box taped to his skin, nestling in thickets of wiry black hair. Two red wires run out of the box, burrowing into his skin, right over his heart. There are tiny, crusted rings of blood around the edges of the insertions.

"That wouldn't be a good idea," he says.

Very slowly, I get to my feet. Every movement sends a dull boom of pain echoing through me, radiating out from the stitches.

"Every second," he says, "the devices inside you send out a signal. The device on my heart answers it, and it only works as long as my heart does. If your devices don't receive that answering signal, they'll detonate. Keeps things honest, wouldn't you say?"

He turns back to the machine, bending over it.

"Look," I say. "I don't know who you are, or what you want. I don't understand why you're doing this."

"Do you remember Amira Al-Hassan?" he says, not looking round.

Amira. My crew leader, my mentor, my friend. The head of our tracer crew, the Devil Dancers—the fastest package couriers on the station. The woman who tried to murder me on Janice Okwembu's orders, who I killed in self-defence.

He looks at me, and taps his scrubs over his heart. "My name," he says, "is Morgan Knox."

I can just see the words stitched into the fabric, so faded they're all but vanished. "Amira and I were in love," he says. "And you took her away from me."

I stare at him. "Amira didn't have a..."

"You think she told you everything?" he says. His voice is nothing more than a hiss, the hatred in his eyes spreading out onto his face, twisting it into a rictus of anger. "You think she shared every part of her life with you?"

His fingers twitch, brushing the detonator button. I choose my words very carefully. "She never said anything to any of her crew. I swear."

I pause. Could Amira have had a secret lover? It's possible—she certainly kept a lot of things from us.

"She loved me," Knox says after a moment, looking away. "I know she did. She delivered cargo to the hospital I was working at."

Remorse has crept into his voice. "She was beautiful. I felt like we could talk for hours. Every time I saw her..."

I can fill in the blanks myself. This is not good. Not good at all.

"It took me months to find out what happened, but I did," he says. "You killed her."

I take a deep breath. Every word feels like a step on a tightrope, like a single wrong move could send me plummeting into the abyss. "She was trying to kill me, so I fought back," I say. "It's what she trained me to do."

"I know," he says. "It's why I'm giving you a chance to make it through the next few days."

"I don't get it. You got to put these...these *things* inside me. What more do you want?"

"You?" he says. "You're not what I want. You killed her, and you deserve everything that's coming to you, but I'm after a bigger prize."

For the first time, he smiles. "I want you to bring me the person who brainwashed my Amira. I want you to bring me Janice Okwembu."

17

Riley

His words hang in the air between us.

"No way," I say.

"You're not exactly in a position to refuse."

"No way, because it's impossible. She's in max security. There's no way to get her out."

I can already hear Royo's words in my mind: *Everybody's entitled to a fair trial by an elected council. That includes her.*

"You'll just have to figure it out," he says. He turns, his leg making the motion awkward and jerky, and limps over to the other side of the room, yanking open a drawer and rummaging through it. "After all, if you can travel all the way through the Core and take out Oren Darnell, a prison should be no problem."

I screw my eyes shut, hoping that when I open them it'll all go away. It doesn't.

"If you feel you need more motivation," he says, "I could always perform the same procedure on one of your friends. Except in their case, I'd implant the charges directly into their brains. I haven't done neurosurgery in a while, however, so I may not remember which parts are safe to cut into."

The thought of Carver, of Kevin, of *Prakesh* being subjected to this monster gets my legs trembling again, and I have to consciously force them to stop.

"I need time," I say.

"You've got forty-eight hours," he says over his shoulder.

"It's not enough."

"That's your problem," he says conversationally, as he turns and walks towards me. "You should be grateful I'm giving you even that."

He hands me a small tube of cream, the surface cold to the touch.

"Of course, as your doctor," he says, "I advise you to get plenty of rest and keep yourself hydrated. You need to be performing at full capacity."

He gestures to the cream. "Apply that three times a day, and keep taking your painkillers. I like to make sure my patients are comfortable after an operation."

It's all I can do not to lash out at him. I have to contain my anger, my frustration, locking them away behind clenched teeth. "I run, OK?" I say. "I run, and roll, and knock into things. If I hit my knee too hard—"

"And are there many situations where you take a blow to the back of your knee?"

"You think I can run with these things inside me?"

"Of course. I designed them that way. Or were you not listening when I explained about the *popliteal fossae*?"

He points. "Your clothes are under the table."

As if in a trance, I pull my jumpsuit out, then sit down again to put it on. Bending my knees all the way hurts, an electric sting shooting up through my legs.

Knox tilts his head to one side, looking at me as I slip my arms into the sleeves. "Tell me—do you miss being a tracer?" he says. "Do you miss not being able to run where you like?"

When I don't respond, he says, "You couldn't keep the Devil Dancers together, could you? After Amira died. You didn't have her spirit. You had to go begging to the stompers."

"It wasn't like that. They—"

I lower my head. I'm not giving him anything more. He has way too much already.

"Here," he says. "I've charged it for you. You shouldn't have to worry about running out of power."

I turn back to look at him. He's holding out my SPOCS unit. It's strange that in the time I've been awake I haven't noticed its absence. I guess I still haven't got used to it.

"I need the wristband," I say. Knox hands it to me, and I snap it on.

"I'll turn that back on for you after you leave," he says. "I made a few changes to the basic design. I can listen into your conversations whenever I feel like it, and I will, so please keep it in your ear at all times. I've also added a small external microphone, so I'll know what's happening around you. I like to know that our little arrangement is just between us."

I stare at him. "How did you…"

He ignores me. "Don't take it out. Not ever. And don't think you can switch channels to get rid of me. Whatever you hear, I hear."

"And if I have to talk to you?"

"Just say my name. If I hear you and respond, it'll lock out anybody else on the channel. They'll think it's a glitch, and we'll be able to talk."

He gestures to the door. "Get going."

I don't need an invitation. But as I walk towards the door, each step sending prickles of pain shooting through my legs, I get an idea.

"You're bluffing," I say, turning back to face him.

"Am I?"

"I think it'll take a lot for you to hit that button. You want Okwembu, and so you need me."

He nods, as if he expected me to say this. "I need you functional, that's true. But go ahead. See what happens."

His smile is one of the most terrifying things I've ever seen.

"You won't do it," I say.

"But what else will I do?" he says. "You think I've told you everything? Test me, and you'll suffer in ways you can't even imagine."

With that, he closes the door in my face.

The sound of the door shutting fades away. I look around me: the walls in the corridor outside Knox's surgery are caked over with rust. A beam of light cuts across the darkness ahead of me, picking out dust motes hanging in the air.

I close my eyes, listening hard. I can just make out the cries of the silkworm merchant, far in the distance.

With my heart in my mouth, I go from a walk, to a jog, to a sprint. I expect to feel the devices Knox put inside me—in my head, I picture them grinding up against the bone, making themselves felt with every step. But he was right: they don't stop me moving. Not even a little. There's stiffness, and the pain is still there, only partially dulled by the drugs, but that's all. It's only when I hit the corridor with the red graffiti that I stop, one hand on the wall, nausea doubling me over.

This isn't happening. It can't be. *Knox is lying. There's nothing inside you.*

But I only have to focus on my knees to realise that that isn't true. It's not just the stiffness: there's a *pressure*, a feeling that wasn't there before.

I stand up straight, breathing deeply, taking my hand off the wall. The dust sticks to my fingertips, and the edge of my palm.

Write it down.

How could I not have thought of that? I can't talk about what's happened to me out loud, not with him listening in over SPOCS, but I can write it down—hell, I could use the dust on the wall if I had to. I could find Carver, or Royo, and tell them. After all, Knox can't *see* what I'm doing, and if I keep talking while I do it…

Then I remember what he said. That if he found out that I told anyone he'd blow the bombs. And then go to work on whoever I told.

Can I risk that? Can I put other people in danger?

Not yet. If it comes down to it, if time starts running out, then I'll tell someone. But for now, this is on me to handle.

I make myself focus. Okwembu. Just the thought of her—of what she did—causes a little bubble of hatred to rise up through me. Sometimes I go days without thinking about her, but she keeps coming back, like a cut on the roof of my mouth that I can't stop touching with the tip of my tongue.

I clench my hand into a fist. It's still on the wall, and my fingernails scrape across the metal. I pull it away, tiny jolts of pain shooting up my fingers, and jog away down the corridor, thinking about where I have to go next, and hating myself for it.

It doesn't take me long before I reach the max security brig. I have to work hard to convince the guards outside that I need to get in—there are eight of them, wearing full body armour. Can't say I blame them. There have been plenty of pissed-off people trying to get in, to take revenge for what the occupant put Outer Earth through.

But, for once, my reputation helps. The guards know me, they know what I've done, and they know my history with the person inside. It helps that I can fabricate a plausible reason to be there: I make out like it's to do with the Recycler Plant, that we need to make absolutely sure that it had nothing to do with *her*.

The inner door opens up into a narrow corridor. There are four cells in this particular brig, two on either side, spaced at wide intervals. The lights are harsh, not even letting a shadow escape, and the frosty air bites through my clothes. It's easy to find the cell I need. It's the only one that's occupied.

I reach the cell, and see her lying on the bed, her arms under her head. I rap hard on the transparent plastic covering the front.

Janice Okwembu rises up on her elbows, staring at me.

18

Riley

"Ms. Hale," Okwembu says, moving to a sitting position on the bed.

The last time I saw her was in the control room in Apex, right after I had to kill my father. She looks, like she always does, as if she's in complete control. As if she was in a council meeting, or broadcasting a message to the station, rather than locked away in a cell. She was a computer programmer before she became a councillor, and it's easy to imagine her parsing real life like she did computer code, cool and logical and unhurried.

"I hear they're close to reforming the council," she says. "I assume that means I'll be on trial soon. I'd be lying if I said I was looking forward to it, but perhaps I can show people what I was trying to do. Tell them that I was acting in their best interests."

I barely listen to her. I'm scanning her cell, looking for any weak spots. The plastic is sealed tight into the walls and ceiling—no cutting through. The door release mechanisms are by the entrance, but there's no way I could spring them, and get her out, before the stompers outside gun me down.

She sees where I'm looking. "I assure you, I'm most secure in here. Just as well."

I don't look at her. "Shut up."

"Didn't I give you a choice? Didn't I acknowledge your sacrifice? Isn't that worth more than hatred from you?"

"It's worth nothing to me," I say, instantly furious at myself for letting her draw me in. The scar on my left wrist starts itching, and I have to force myself not to scratch it. Hell of a choice. Cut your wrists and be remembered as a hero, or take a bullet and go down in history as a traitor. Okwembu's twisted way of making things right.

Too bad I'd turned on the station's main comms and unlocked the entrance to Apex. Everybody heard what she'd done, and they came for her.

Just in time. I'd almost bled out.

She folds her arms. "I can only tell you how sorry I am so many times before it becomes pointless. If it were up to me, you would never even have been involved. All I wanted was to bring peace to Outer Earth."

"With you in complete control."

She laughs. "Do you know how the moon was formed, Ms. Hale?"

I don't respond. There's got to be a weak link, something, *anything* I can use to get her out of there.

"A long time ago," she says, "another planet collided with the Earth. It shattered our newly formed crust. It turned every part of the Earth's surface into magma. An ocean of lava. And it created an enormous body of material orbiting our planet—rock, dust, debris."

I want to tell her to stop. I can't quite manage it. Okwembu seems to sense this, and takes a step towards the plastic barrier.

"Over time, that debris came together as one object—a ball of rock known as the moon, orbiting Earth and changing the surface. The oceans, when they formed, had tides. The impact from that other planet knocked our own a little off its axis, angling it towards the sun. From chaos, Ms. Hale, comes life. From adversity, comes strength."

"That's a great story. I'll tell it to the people you nearly wiped out."

"I was only—"

"You can talk as much as you like. You're still in there, and I'm out here. All you have to look forward to is a trial, and the firing squad."

Okwembu says nothing. My shoulders are too tense, and it takes me a moment to realise that I've got closer to the plastic. I'm almost right up against it.

She raises her chin. "*That's* why you came to visit me."

"What?"

"You want me to be evil. You want me to be insane, because it would absolve you. It would mean that killing Amira and Oren Darnell and your own father wasn't your fault."

Okwembu puts a hand on the plastic. "Do you dream, Ms. Hale? I do. And I'm sure my dreams are easier than yours."

My right hand twitches. Before I can stop myself, I slam a closed fist on the plastic barrier. The bang rockets around the cell block. Okwembu takes a step back, startled, a flash of fear appearing in her eyes. It vanishes an instant later, replaced by that cold stare.

My hand is humming with pain. I shake it out, not looking away from her, only becoming aware of the guards when one of them puts a firm hand on my shoulder.

They yank me away from the cell, pulling me by the arm towards the entrance. Then they shove me outside, and close the barred door behind me.

19

Knox

The picture of Amira Al-Hassan is old, taken when she was still a teenager. She hadn't yet developed the high cheekbones, the dark eyes. But it's unquestionably her. There's a warning in her face—she's staring back at the camera as if daring it to make a move.

It's the only file photo they had, and it took Knox a long time to track it down. He has it maximised on his tab screen, and his thumb traces the delicate curve of her jawline. What he wouldn't give to have a more recent picture of her. What he wouldn't give to have seen her one last time.

He puts the tab screen down, then pushes himself up from the hard chair in the corner of his surgery. He knew this would be the worst part of the entire operation. The waiting. Hale is in play now—sufficiently motivated, he hopes—but even she will take a few hours to come up with a plan.

His hand finds the tab screen again. Amira's photo has shrunk back down, and for the hundredth time he reads her file information, lined up alongside the photo. Born in Apex. Orphaned at an early age. Recognised by the council for bravery and personal sacrifice during the lower sector riots. Declined council post. Last known affiliation: Devil Dancers tracer crew, Apogee.

There's nothing else in the file. As he always does, Knox feels a surge of anger. The file doesn't record how she died. It doesn't record how she was *murdered*.

He should have said something to her when he had the chance. He remembers when he first saw her—over time, it feels as if the memory has grown sharper, new details popping up. The way she strode through the hospital doors, the way her eyes picked him out of the crowd instantly—and never left him. He remembers the impossible curves of her body, the shrug of her shoulders as she shucked her pack, the touch of her fingers when she passed him the cargo. He couldn't say anything, could do nothing but nod a mute thanks.

And, as it always does, the anger gives way to blind fury.

Riley Hale might have been responsible for Amira's death, but she was only in that situation because of Janice Okwembu. Okwembu got to her, poisoned her mind, twisted everything good about her. Hale was just the one who pulled the trigger.

His finger brushes the button on the unit taped to his palm. For a moment, the desire is there, burning hot. He wants to press it, right now, and listen over the SPOCS channel as Hale screams and screams and screams.

He lets his hand fall to his side. Not yet. He'll give Hale a little more time, then he'll use the hacked SPOCS receiver to call her. He hopes for her sake that she has something to tell him.

20

Riley

After the situation with Okwembu and my father, the few interim council leaders made a big deal about giving me my own place. Prakesh and I now live in Chengshi, on Level 3, a few minutes from the mess.

We were there maybe two days when the tributes started arriving.

I can see them now, even as I jog down the corridor. A sea of flowers, bags of food, trinkets and tokens, pushed up against the wall and stacked around the door. People just keep bringing them, and no matter how often Prakesh and I ask them to stop, they won't. Some even hang around, wanting to speak to me, to thank me for saving the station. I try to be as polite as I can, hating myself for wanting to tell them to go away, feeling selfish and petty for wanting to be left alone.

Then I see it. Graffiti, sprayed on the wall next to our door. HONOUR HALE.

That's new.

It's not the hastily sprayed, ragged graffiti you see elsewhere on the station. The letters are carefully formed in blue ink, with minimal drips. I stare at it, a mess of feelings mixing in my stomach. My chest is heaving, though whether in exhaustion or anger I can't tell. There's a tightness in my chest, too, and an odd tickle in my throat. Like I'm getting sick. The stitches in my legs feel bigger than they are, throbbing with pain, despite the pills.

I wait until my breathing has calmed, then push open the door to our hab.

It's a tiny room, no more than a few yards across, with an even smaller washroom attached. We haven't got around to decorating the bare metal walls, but we've filled the room with plants. Every spare surface is covered with pots and sprouting greenery.

My eyes are drawn to the pot by the wall. It holds an orchid, with bright red flowers and leaves curling like old paper. A twenty-first-birthday present from Prakesh. Genetically engineered. He said it would last years before losing a single petal, but it's already shedding.

Prakesh is sitting on the double cot, propped up against the wall, flicking through a hand-held tab screen. The hab is hot, as it usually is at this time of day, and he has his shirt off. A couple of rivulets of sweat run down his dark chest, pooling in his abdominal muscles.

"Hey you," he says, swinging his legs off the bed. I bury myself in his arms, resting my head on his chest. I can hear his heart pumping against my ear, and a bead of sweat tickles my cheek. I don't mind.

"Long day?" he asks.

"You have no idea."

"Same here."

The urge to tell him everything wells up again, and it takes me quite an effort not to say anything. Knox might be listening. Right now, just being close to him is enough.

I look up at Prakesh. "Don't kiss me, by the way. I think I might be getting sick."

He wrinkles his nose. "Kiss you? When you smell like that? What happened?"

"I'll tell you while you feed me."

"And if you're getting sick, you need to get checked out. You know how fast bugs spread in here."

"...And when I get sick for real, I will."

"I'm not kidding, Ry. You might even be infectious already. How many people did you come into contact with today?"

I rub my eyes. "I don't know. A lot."

Truth is, he's right. Annoyingly so. Outer Earth is a million people packed closely together. You get so much as a cold spreading around, and whole sectors can get quarantined off.

"I promise I'll go get checked out," I say. "But I really am starving."

He rolls his eyes. "So demanding. Fine."

We eat sitting cross-legged on the bed. Crisp green beans and tofu, slathered with salty, tangy beetle paste Prakesh managed to score. The normality of it, the routine, makes me breathe a little easier. I can forget the stitches, forget the devices behind them.

I tell him about the siege—he grimaces when he hears about how close I came to being discovered, but he's known me too long to get angry or anxious. He tells me about what happened to the tech, Benson. Halfway through, I put a hand on his leg, squeezing tight. He puts his over it.

After he's finished, we're silent for a few moments. "There's new graffiti," I say.

"I saw. Maybe now they'll do an HONOUR KUMAR sign."

"They should." I'm not kidding, either. Before his breakthrough with the genetically modified plants, I barely saw him. There were times when he would come home, mutter two words to me and crash out for four hours before trudging back to the Air Lab. He and his team worked on the problem for months, struggling to get plants to grow fast enough to feed a million-plus people. For a while, the big joke was that prisoners in the brigs ate better than everyone else—they got the dud batches, the ones where the genes weren't quite right. Prakesh told me that it usually made them taste terrible.

After Prakesh cracked it, he was the centre of attention. For a while, I could slip into the background, which was just fine by me. But masterminding a new food supply isn't as flashy as saving the station from being smashed to pieces, and pretty soon the tributes started coming back.

"We sent out a new batch today," he says, swallowing a lump of tofu. "The fruiting bodies are even better this time around. Did you know that they've now got as much energy in them as two protein bars?"

"Oh yeah?" My mind is drifting, drawn back to that graffiti.

"Right. And—"

"How long do you think it'll be before they find someone else?" I ask.

He frowns. "How do you mean?"

I nod towards the hab entrance.

"It's not so bad," he says. "I get to live with a hero."

"I don't feel like a hero." I feel selfish admitting it, the words bitter in my mouth.

He sighs. "Riley, we keep going through this. *None* of what happened was your fault. You don't have a single thing to be guilty about."

Suddenly, I want nothing more than to be under a blanket, with my arms wrapped around him. I reach out and stroke his cheek. "Come to bed."

"Oh no," he says. A little bit of the spark has come back into his eyes. "First, you need to clean up."

"I hate air showers."

"And I hate going to bed with someone who smells like shit. Literally. And then you're going to go and get a throat swab at the hospital."

I know better than to argue. I slip the top of my jumpsuit off, then pull my sticky tank top up over my head. It gets stuck, and Prakesh has to help me yank it over my arms. Before I can bring them down, he reaches in, his fingers brushing my face—

—And plucks my SPOCS unit from my ear.

I freeze, my eyes wide. Then I snatch the unit back, jamming it in. I can't describe the terror I feel at this moment. All I can think of are Knox's words: *Don't take it out. Not ever.* My legs are itching—I came this close to pulling off the bottom half of my jumpsuit. If Prakesh had seen the scars…

Prakesh gives me a weird look. "You're off duty, right?"

"Don't ever touch my SPOCS. Not *ever*." It takes a moment before I realise that I'm shouting, mimicking Knox's words. I fumble in my jacket, yank open the bottle of pain pills, shove one into my mouth, not caring that Prakesh can see.

"Whoa," he says. "What's going on? What's got you angry?"

"I'm on call," I say, my mind scrambling for a reason. "I can't be out of touch. Gods, Prakesh, you should know that."

I'm too embarrassed to look at him. My reaction came from the gut, a jagged bolt of animal fear that shot through me before I could stop it. What's worse is that Morgan Knox doesn't deserve that fear, especially since I'm still not completely convinced he'll really blow the bombs.

I lie back on the bed, staring at the ceiling, willing my legs to stop hurting.

"What are you not telling me?" Prakesh says.

"Nothing. I'm fine."

"The last time you said that, I ended up getting kidnapped by Oren Darnell. Remember?"

It sounds like a joke, one of his snappy lines, but when I look over I see that there's no laughter on his face. There's another expression—one I don't like a bit.

"Don't keep secrets from me, Riley," Prakesh says. "I don't keep any from you. What's going on?"

"Just stomper work. You know I can't tell you everything we do."

"More like you can't tell me *anything* you do. And you've spent more time with Aaron Carver than anyone else. Even I know that, though of course you won't tell me."

I stare at him. "The hell is that supposed to mean?"

He lies back, his eyes closed. "Nothing. Forget it. I just didn't like you yelling at me, is all."

"Carver's a friend. We work together. You know that."

I lie down, and put a hand on his chest. He wrinkles his nose at the smell, but says nothing.

"I'm sorry," I whisper.

At that moment, the tiredness crashes down on me. I can feel Prakesh's chest rising and falling, and the rhythm calms me. It occurs to me that both of us forgot about me going to the hospital, but then I decide that I'm just too tired to care.

I try to sleep, and don't quite manage it. I get up, have an air shower, slip into clothes that aren't caked with dirt, then slide in next to him to try again.

You've got to be able to tune out to sleep on the station. It's never truly quiet here, and even now I can hear the vast metal hull groaning and clicking as Outer Earth continues its slow, spinning orbit. Let your mind drift to the edge of sleep, and it can sound like a living thing, breathing and hissing and stretching blackened metal limbs.

Just before I drift off, there's a whisper in my ear, horribly alive.

"Are you there, Hale? Answer me."

Knox.

Moving as carefully as I can, I swing my legs off the side of the bed. My head is pounding, razor blades scraping across my throat. I stumble to the door, then slip out into the corridor. It's deserted, and I sink down against the wall.

"I'm here."

Another burst of static. Then: "You need to respond faster next time. Something we're going to have to work on, aren't we?"

"I was asleep. That's all."

"Sleeping? I do hope that means you've figured out a way to bring me what I want."

I rub my eyes. "I need more time."

"You're not getting it. Tell me your plan." The eagerness in his voice makes my skin crawl.

"Working on that," I say.

"Work faster."

"Go to hell."

"Go to hell, *Sir*."

I shut my eyes.

"Say it."

My hand has strayed to my right knee, touching the unbending end of the stitch. He won't blow them. He can't. They might not even be explosive. They might be dud pieces of metal, put there to trick you.

Keep telling yourself that.

"Go to hell, Sir," I mutter.

"Better. You'll have to learn respect if we're going to work together. Go back to sleep, Riley Hale. You have a big day tomorrow."

The line cuts off, leaving me in the black silence of the corridor.

21

Riley

I don't think I'll ever get used to the noise in Big 6.

That's what we call the stomper headquarters. It used to be the operations centre for all six station sectors, but now it's just a satellite office. A mess of fizzing lights and mouldy food containers, a place that nobody bothered to rename.

The stompers stand around desks, lean back on chairs, scream out orders and jokes and questions. The sound is like a forgotten engine, one which has spun up to a furious roar. Snatches of speech whiz past me as I cross the floor.

"Hey, Sanchez, you got any info on that pusher in—"

"—teenage girls up in Tzevya. He was whoring 'em out for tofu, if you can believe that."

"We need six bodies to run a show-and-go in Gardens. Don't make me ask for volunteers."

Anna's the first tracer I see. She's drinking from a canteen with her feet up on one of the desks, her ankles crossed and her shoes unstrapped. She ignores me, but Royo doesn't. He and Kev are standing on the other side of a battered desk. The wall behind it is so smudged with marker that it doesn't even reflect the glaring fluorescents any more.

"You're late, Hale," he says.

"Sorry," I say. Kev winks at me, a gentle smile on his face, then turns back to Royo. I grab the canteen out of Anna's hands and take a long slug of water.

"Get up on the wrong side of the bed this morning, did we?" she says.

"Bad dreams," I reply, wiping my mouth and tossing back the canteen.

It's not even close to the truth. The dreams weren't bad at all. They didn't even exist. I just stared at the ceiling all night, running over the layout of Okwembu's prison again and again, looking for any possible way to break her out. Twice I had to get up to take another pain pill, and it was all I could do not to burst into tears.

When I woke up, Prakesh was gone. The other side of the bed was cold.

At least I don't feel sick any more. As I got out of bed, I noticed that the tickle in my throat was gone. The flesh on the back of my knees has swollen slightly—not enough to stop me running, but enough that I feel it every time I move.

"What's on the board today?" I ask Anna, more out of habit than anything else.

"Now she's talkative," she says to herself. "No idea. I haven't talked to the Captain yet."

"Wouldn't advise it on an empty stomach," says Carver, sauntering in through the door with his jacket tied round his waist. He tosses me a protein bar, handing one to Kev as he walks past. I smile thanks. The slab is sickly sweet, but it fills me up.

Royo waves us over. "Everybody here? OK. We've got the *Shinso* coming back into orbit tomorrow, so I need everybody on high alert. You know what this place is like when there's a fresh asteroid. Now, the regular officers're taking care of most things today, but we've had a report of a disturbance up in Gardens."

Gardens. I feel a pang of concern for Prakesh, but it passes as quickly as it came. If the last year has taught me anything, it's that he can take care of himself.

"Why can't the stompers in that sector deal with it?" says Anna. "Why do we have to clean up their mess?"

"We already had officers go in, but they haven't reported back. Probably a glitch on the feed, but we're not taking chances here."

"Any word on our Recycler Plant guys?" says Carver.

Royo shrugs. "Not that I've heard. The one in charge, the one Beck and Hale took down. He hasn't said much. Anyway, we've got more pressing things to deal with."

Royo turns back to the wall. "After you see what's going on in Gardens, I need you to..."

I'm not listening any more. An idea is slowly starting to take root in my mind—maybe the first good idea I've had since this all started.

"Captain?"

He doesn't look round. "What?"

"I was thinking. Why not let me stay on the hostage case?"

"I see I'm going to spend the day repeating myself," he says, looking over his shoulder. "It's a waste of time."

"What if they were just the start? There's a lot of hate for Janice Okwembu. Maybe this isn't the last hostage situation we'll see."

"No way, Hale. You go where you're needed. And, right now, that's Gardens. I'll assign someone else to the hostage thing."

"Just let me do a little digging. I'll head right up to Gardens afterwards, I swear. Surely three tracers'll be enough?"

I have never longed more to tear the SPOCS unit from my ear and smash it on the ground. I have to make this work. If I'm going to make it through the next twenty-four hours, I *need* to get away from regular stomper duties.

Royo sighs. "Fine. Do what you have to do. It's not like you idiots listen to me half the time anyway."

"Now that isn't fair, Cap," says Carver. "We listen to you at least three-quarters of the time. Maybe more."

Royo points at me. "But when you're done, Hale, you get up to Gardens double-time."

While Carver and Kev fill up the reservoirs in their packs from the Big 6 water point, I sit down in front of one of the tab screens. There's a bank of them on the wall—probably the largest number of working screens on the station, outside of the control room in Apex. I grab one of the battered chairs from a nearby desk. Its wheels have long since been cannibalised for other things, and its legs screech as I drag it across the floor. That's when I realise that I don't have my stinger with me—I must have left it back in the hab. I feel a guilty relief. I never liked the thing, never liked feeling it against my hip.

Carver puts a hand on my shoulder and squeezes. "See you in a few?"

I put my hand on his. "You know it."

They head out. Pulling the chair up to a screen, I call up our database.

Back when I was just a tracer, I thought I knew a lot about how the stompers worked—I'd tangled with them often enough. But I didn't know about their database. The official name for it is SCRD—Station Criminal Records Database, as the logo flashing up in front of me says—but you won't find a stomper on the station who calls it that. To us, it's just the Wall of Shame.

Aware of Royo hovering, I tap the name "Mikhail" into the system. It's not a lot to go on, but as the results pop up, blinking onto the screen one after another, it becomes clear that there are only a handful on the station. It takes me no more than a few seconds before I'm looking at the right one—that snide face framed with greasy hair is impossible to miss.

"Mikhail Yeremin," says Royo from over my shoulder, making me jump. He scans the rest of the information—what little there is. "Forty-six years old, born Tzevya sector, no known kin. Dock worker. That's the thing about the Wall, Hale. It hardly gives you anything useful. He's only in the system because he's been arrested before." He leans in closer. "Water racket."

Royo taps his knuckle twice on Mikhail's picture, accidentally making it full-screen.

"Stop that," I say, minimising the picture.

Royo clears his throat. "Sorry. I'll leave you to your detective work."

I stay on Mikhail's entry until I can see that Royo is absorbed with what he's doing—giving another stomper hell, it looks like—and then I bring up the search bar. I tap KNOX, MORGAN into it and hit *Go*.

Until now I've been focused on doing what Knox says. What if I can find something on him? A weak spot I can use? Not that I'm holding out much hope. I'm almost certain that he won't be in the system.

But, to my surprise, there's an entry—and the Wall has far more on Knox than it did on Mikhail.

I scan the words. Knox, Morgan Joseph. Forty-two years old, born in New Germany. Qualified as a medic from the sector hospital at age twenty-two, specialising in musculoskeletal surgery. Assigned to work in Medical Unit 262, wherever that is. And he has a record: stole drugs from the same hospital he qualified at. It's recent—no more than a few months ago. Spent a few days in the brig, medical licence revoked. Last known habitation is a corridor code close to where his current surgery is. No known kin. Arresting officer: Royo, Samuel.

I glance over at Royo. He's talking with another stomper, bent over one of the desks. The only person I know who's had contact with my nemesis, and he may as well be a million light years away.

The idea unrolls itself slowly. What if I could take Knox out of action from afar? Once he's in the brig, he won't have that remote any more.

Putting out an arrest warrant for Morgan Knox is the work of a few taps. So is entering the last place I saw him, and the reason for the warrant—drug trafficking, of course. I punch in the corridor and level location, and sit back, exhaling deeply. There. At some point today, a dispatcher will get over SPOCS and ask a couple of stompers to swing by that room of his.

The question is whether he'll blow the bombs as soon as they do. I don't think he will, not if I'm still out there. That's *if* his threat is actually real in the first place, and he isn't playing me.

It's a gamble. But it doesn't feel like a reckless one.

I stare at the screen, thinking hard. The arrest warrant is a start, but I still need to work on breaking Okwembu out, just in case.

My eye lands on *Medical Unit 262*. Something about it kicks my mind into gear.

Working quickly, I pull up the location. It's in the Caves—the run-down, cramped, overcrowded part of the sector that anybody who wasn't born there tries to stay away from. Kev's parents live there, but his family aren't the only people I know in that part of the station. There's someone else.

He might not know how to take down Knox.

But if it comes to it, he might be able to help me break Okwembu out of prison.

22

Prakesh

The first thing Prakesh sees when he walks into the Air Lab is Suki looking apologetic. The second thing he sees is Han Tseng.

The councilman is standing over by one of the algae pools, his arms folded, a thunderous expression on his face. Prakesh groans inwardly. His sleep was full of ugly dreams, and it's left him groggy and irritable.

And now he has to deal with Tseng. Great.

No point avoiding it. He squares his shoulders, then walks over. The councilman watches him approach—he's actually tapping his foot, as if Prakesh is an errant student. Above them, the leaves of the giant oaks move gently in the blowback from the air exchangers.

"Councilman," says Prakesh.

"No more putting this off, Kumar," Tseng says. "I want you to show me the new security measures now."

"You've picked a bad day, Sir." Prakesh keeps walking, moving between the algae pools. "We've got test results due in from a new strain of soya, and I have a dozen other things on my desk that need attention."

"Three months ago, you said you'd be implementing stricter controls," Tseng says, striding after Prakesh. "Chain-of-custody signatures, technician background checks, closer collaboration with the protection officers." He ticks each item off on his fingers.

Prakesh has to suppress the urge to roll his eyes. "If you make an appointment with Suki, I promise I'll give you a full briefing." He looks for Suki, but she's vanished.

"We can't afford another robbery," Tseng says. "The people of this station need to know that it's unacceptable behaviour."

That's one way of putting it, Prakesh thinks. Three months ago, just before Prakesh had his breakthrough with the genetically modified plants, a shipment of food was stolen. In this case, it was a dud batch, a failed experiment, destined for the brigs in each of the station sectors. A group of assailants managed to board the monorail, stop it in the tunnel and make off with several crates of food. Prakesh was amazed that it hadn't happened sooner.

They never caught the people who did it, and as far as Prakesh was concerned it hardly mattered. With more than enough food for everybody on the station, securing shipments had slipped way down the priority list. But still Tseng had been onto him, demanding that he take steps.

Tseng is still speaking, lecturing him on how to do his job. "Actually," Prakesh says, cutting the councilman off in mid-flow.

"I have a meeting with the local protection officer captain this week. We'll be addressing these issues." Thinking: *Better make an appointment as soon as this idiot leaves.*

Tseng folds his arms. "Really?"

"That's right." He places a hand on the councilman's elbow, starts guiding him back towards the entrance.

"Yes. Well," Tseng says. "I expect a full report by the end of the week."

"You got it," Prakesh says, as they reach the open area by the entrance. The sliding door is twenty feet high, hastily cut through the existing wall. Before Oren Darnell, you got to the Air Lab by going through the equally cavernous Food Lab. That changed when Darnell torched the latter.

The councilman stalks off, not bothering to say goodbye. Prakesh watches him go, then rubs his eyes, massaging away the gritty sleep. He would do anything to blow off today. The thing with Riley is still going round and round in his mind—he can't understand what got her going last night. He's never seen her lash out like that before, not at him, anyway…

Raised voices, outside the doors. Prakesh looks round, and sees two stompers talking with Tseng. They're pointing to the Air Lab, and Prakesh doesn't like the looks on their faces.

He starts walking, picking up his pace. He's thirty feet away when Tseng charges towards him, shouting, "Seal the door! Seal it now!"

23

Riley

By the time I get to the Caves, a deep itch—so ingrained it feels like a part of my body—has set into the backs of my knees. It takes every ounce of will I have not to yank the stitches out.

As I get close, I slow to a jog. My skin crawls at the thought of having to talk to Knox again, but it has to be done. He'll still be there—I've issued arrest warrants before, and they take a while to move through the system.

I turn to what I hope is a dead channel. "Knox," I say, as quietly as I can. The SPOCS unit hums and clicks in my ear. There's a burst of static, and then a stomper says, "Come back? Didn't catch—"

Then Knox's voice is in my ear, cutting the stomper out. "What?"

"I'm going to get help for the thing you asked me to do," I say. Then, taking a deep breath: "Someone I think might be able to… you know."

"No, I don't think I do," he says, and his voice is deathly quiet. "My instructions were that you were to tell no one else. You need to learn to listen."

"I'm serious," I say, dropping to one knee. There's a pool of liquid—oil, judging from the colours on its surface—puddling on the floor, and I only narrowly avoid it. "I can't do it on my own. And I won't tell him about you, I swear."

"Who?"

"You won't know him."

"Answer the question."

When I tell him, Knox barks a laugh in my ear. "Him? He's useless. He'll never help you."

"I'm going to ask him anyway."

"Tell him whatever you want. Just remember: time's running out, Riley."

Not if the arrest warrant catches up with you, I think. I rise to my feet, and walk on.

When Amira and I tried to get into the Caves a year ago, we were met with suspicion and bared weapons. They've always seen themselves as slightly apart from the rest of the station—anybody who tries to muscle in, any gang that wants to get a foothold, finds themselves going home minus a few members and a couple of important body parts.

When Oren Darnell took over the station, Caves drew in on itself, full lockdown. This time, the big metal door—the only way in or out—is wide open. The corridor beyond it is poorly lit, the walls marred with ancient, scabby graffiti.

I step through. A hand comes out of the darkness, grabbing my shoulder.

"Stomper," says the person attached to the hand. He keeps his face in the shadows.

"I'm not here on stomper business," I say.

His grip tightens. "Better not be." He releases me, pushing me backwards, and goes back to where he was sitting, on what looks like an upturned barrel. I still haven't seen his face.

"I'm looking for Syria," I say.

The man in the shadows waves a hand in the general direction of the rest of the universe.

I hold my ground. "Help me out here."

The man grunts. "You need Syria's help? You must be in bad trouble."

"The worst kind."

There's a long silence. Then he says, "1-E. Down by the water point."

As I walk away, he shouts, "Better *not* be stomper business, or I stomp you, you get me?"

"Got you," I mutter, pushing my way through a group of sullen women milling around a corner in the corridor.

The water point is the closest thing that the Caves have to a gathering place. The lights in the ceiling burned out a long time ago, never to be replaced, and the only illumination comes from small fires, scattered across the floor. The big water tank bolted onto the wall towers over a line of people topping up their canteens. Small groups hang around nearby, playing cards, talking, laughing in quiet bursts. I can feel eyes on me the second I draw close, and not all of them are friendly.

Syria has his head bent, greasy hair falling over his face, shoulders bent and angular. Down on one knee in a card game, every other player watching to see what he does. As I get closer, I see they're playing acey-deucy, and that Syria already has three twos down. One more, and he wins the game.

"Show 'em," mutters one of the players.

"He got nothing but odds," says another.

"Odds and faces."

"I got what I got," says Syria. "You just sit there while I think it over."

It's impossible to make out his face, hidden under the strands of greasy hair. I hover on the outside of the circle, willing people not to notice me. I'll talk to him when the game's finished, when he's—

Syria looks up and sees me.

"Everybody clear out," he says quietly.

The other players have seen me by now, eyeing me warily, but now they turn back to Syria, cursing and complaining. He silences them with a wave. "I *said* clear out."

In seconds, they melt away. And I become aware of something else: no one is looking at me any more. I've gone from being an object of interest to not existing. That's what happens when you go and speak to the single most powerful person in the Caves—a man who, if you believe the stories, has never set foot outside his sector.

I don't know if Syria is his first name, or his last. He's not a gang leader, or a power-hungry maniac like Oren Darnell. He just keeps the Caves safe. I did one or two deliveries for him while I was with the Devil Dancers, although he's not what I'd call a regular client.

Syria folds his feet under him, sitting cross-legged. He shuffles the cards, and I see he's wearing a thin, highly polished silver ring on his hand. It seems out of place amid the dirt and grime on the rest of his skin. I sit opposite him, my legs complaining as I do so. He says nothing.

"How are you, Syria?" I say.

It's a few moments before he replies. "You're a stomper now. Got nothin' to say to you."

"Come on, Syria," I say, feigning bravado I don't feel.

He says nothing. I exhale slowly. No point trying to convince him that the stompers aren't about to come busting in here. Better just to be out with it.

"I need your help," I say.

"And what exactly do you think I can help you with?" He looks up at me again. The spark in his eyes has faded a little, replaced by an amused curiosity.

I look behind me, at the queue of people by the water point pretending to pay no attention to us. "Can we go somewhere private?" I say.

"Don't get cute." His eyes find me again. "You got two choices. You can speak your piece here, the whole of it, no lies, or you can get out. There's a third option, but it's not one you want to pick."

I lean in as close as I can. "I want your help to break Janice Okwembu out of the brig."

Syria rockets to his feet. Before I can react, he grabs me by the arm, marching me away from the water point.

"What's the deal?" one of the men yells.

"Back later," Syria says. He rips open a door, and shoves me inside. It's a dormitory hab, with neat rows of bunk beds lined up along the walls. Drying clothes hang from lines strung wall-to-wall, and there are kids' toys underfoot. The air is thick and muggy.

Syria leads me to a bed, and pushes me down to sit on it. He stalks around the hab, and, when he's satisfied that we're alone, he sits down opposite me.

For a long time, neither of us says anything. My SPOCS unit is completely silent.

"Do you have any idea," Syria says, "of what would happen if any of my people heard you say that?"

"I—"

"They've been wanting to take a crack at her for months. It'd be like putting a torch to a line of fuel."

"I don't understand."

"Oh, don't you? A stomper, with inside knowledge of the whole system, comes into Caves talking about a prison break. They'll either think you're on a sting operation, in which case you won't make it out of here alive, or they'll go off half-cocked, and get themselves killed. Not to mention bringing every stomper on Outer Earth into the Caves, looking for payback."

He sits back on the bed, his shoulders sagging, as if he used up all his energy on the outburst. "What are you doing, Riley? I know what happened to you. Everybody does. But you aren't thinking straight."

I look down at the floor. There's a chalk drawing on it, a child's drawing, all big heads and misshapen eyes. A man and a girl, holding hands.

I stare at it, picking my next words carefully. I don't dare tell him about Knox—not yet. But I have to make him help me. It's the only idea I've got.

"And why shouldn't we go get her?" I say. "She's been in there for months. There's no council to convict her. It's time she got what's coming."

"Were you not—"

"Your guys are right. I *do* have inside knowledge. I could protect you. I could make sure the stompers never come near the Caves."

He looks at me, his eyes giving away nothing.

Eventually, he shakes his head. "Sorry. There's no way. You get safe passage out of the sector, but that's all I'm—"

Someone starts yelling for him in the passage outside.

"Busy," he shouts.

But there's more sound coming from outside. Panicked voices, the noise of running feet. Syria looks towards the door, starts to rise off the bed.

The shout comes again. "Syria, get out here!"

Syria takes off, sprinting out of the room. I'm right on his heels.

The line by the water point has scattered, people running in all directions—all except one man, on his hands and knees. He wears a dirty, tattered flight jacket, his long hair hanging down around his face.

He's coughing—huge, hacking bursts. And every time he coughs, he sprays thick, black, shiny tendrils from his mouth.

24

Prakesh

Prakesh gets to the doorway a second before Tseng does. He knows what Tseng means to do—there's a control panel on the other side of the door. You need a code to access its functions, but you can use it to seal the Air Lab. A safety precaution, built in when the door was installed.

"Whoa, hey," Prakesh says, slamming his hand around the door frame. "What's going on?"

Tseng stumbles to a halt, staring daggers at Prakesh. Stompers are closing in behind him—there are more now, Prakesh sees, at least half a dozen.

"Emergency situation," Tseng says. "Step aside. We need to seal the lab."

"Not a chance," Prakesh says. He knows he's on shaky ground—technically, a station council member can make that particular call. But there's no way he's letting them seal the techs in. Not without knowing why.

"Step *aside*, Kumar," Tseng says, looking over his shoulder at the stompers. "This isn't your concern."

"Yeah, don't care," says Prakesh. It's then that he sees the tracer unit, running towards them from the far end of the corridor. Kev is in the lead, elbowing his way past the other stompers. Carver is trailing him, along with the other girl Riley works with—*Anna, that's her name.*

All three of them are wearing face masks. The masks are thin plastic, covering their mouths and noses and chins.

"Sir," says one of the other stompers—a thin man with an even thinner mouth. "We need you to step back, and secure your employees."

"Not until—"

"Now."

Prakesh can feel the other technicians congregating behind him. He looks over his shoulder; they form a loose semicircle, dozens of them, staring in confusion at the standoff. They've seen the masks, too, and they're whispering to each other, already nervous. He has to get control of this now.

"Look," he says, spreading his hands. "You need to tell me what's going on. If you're going to shut us in here, then we should at least know what's happening."

"Virus."

Everyone turns to look at Anna Beck, jogging to a halt. She rests a hand on Kev's shoulder, bent over, holding her other hand at her side.

"Officer," Tseng says, all but hissing the words. "You're not authorised."

Anna ignores him. "It's bad," she says, looking at Prakesh. "People coughing up black gunk everywhere. It was in the mess first, but we're getting reports from all over."

Prakesh hears gasps from behind him. He lets out a shaky breath. "Just in Gardens?"

"Other sectors, too."

"Might not be a virus," says Kev. He shrugs when everybody turns to look at him. "Just saying. Might be a bacterium."

Prakesh briefly closes his eyes. It's a nightmare. Virus or not, even non-lethal diseases can spread like wildfire in Outer Earth. This one does not sound like a non-lethal disease. And if there are multiple infection sites, multiple vectors...

He flashes back to the previous night, to Riley's sore throat. He dismisses the thought immediately, refusing to entertain it. *She's OK. She has to be.*

"Listen," he says. "No one's infected here, right?" He looks around at his team, who shake their heads. "If you give us face masks, we can keep working."

"P-man," says Carver, and Prakesh rankles at the nickname. "You shouldn't have this door open. We can't afford to have any techs coughing up black slime. They're too important."

"We're fine, Aaron."

"Don't be an idiot."

"You're *not* locking us in here."

Before Prakesh can blink, Carver is in his face. He crosses the floor in seconds, fists clenched.

"Get inside. Now," Carver says. His voice has gone deathly quiet.

"Or what?" Prakesh says. Deep down, he can see Riley's face.

Tseng is almost apoplectic. "That's enough!" he says.

Anna steps between them, turning to Carver and putting a firm hand on his chest. "We do *not* have time to argue over something like this. Let them shut the doors, and we can get out of here." The other stompers are crowding in, as if they trust Carver to handle things, but only to a point.

"Stay out of this, Anna," Carver says, trying to push her aside. She plants her feet, not moving. He pushes harder, and, this time, she shoves back, her hands balled into fists.

Carver stares at her. "Are you insane? This should not be this big an issue. We need these people to keep us alive, so we have to get them locked down. It's the most important thing we can do."

"Important?" Anna hisses. "More important than what's happening in the rest of the station? In Tzevya? My *family* are up there, Carver..."

Kev steps in. "And mine are in Caves. We all have people we need to take care of."

"You heard your friends, Aaron," says Prakesh, pointing a finger at Carver over Anna's shoulder. "Go find the ones who actually need your help. Don't bother the ones who can handle themselves."

The impasse is broken by several sharp beeps. Tseng is at the door's control pad, his finger hammering on it. There's a longer beep, and then the door plummets towards Prakesh.

Carver acts fast. He plants his hand on Prakesh's chest and *shoves*. Prakesh flies backwards, his feet tangled, landing hard and skidding across the floor into the Air Lab, just as the massive door slams shut.

25

Knox

Knox is spooning beans into his mouth when he hears his name over the hacked SPOCS line. When he does, he nearly spits them across the room.

He drops the food container, grabbing his stick and limping across the floor of his surgery, turning up the volume on the transceiver.

"Suspect last spotted in A1-B22. Richards, we have you and Olawole on duty in that area, confirm?"

"Come on, dispatch," says an irritated stomper. "It's almost the end of my shift."

The dispatcher ignores him. "Repeat, your suspect is Morgan Knox, forty-two years old. Physical description is dark hair, Caucasian, six feet. Pronounced physical disability."

Knox grips the sides of the transceiver. *This can't be happening.*

"Copy that, dispatch," the stomper says, resigned. There are a few seconds of silence. Then: "Dispatch, this is Richards. I'm getting a lot of chatter on the private channels about a situation in Gardens, and another in Caves. You sure you don't want us to help?"

"Negative. We need continued stomper presence in the other sectors. Go and do your job."

"Copy," Richards mutters.

For the first time in months, Knox doesn't know what to do. Did he make a mistake somewhere? He's committed plenty of crimes in the past, but the stompers never caught on—why is he being targeted *now*? He has to leave. He has to—

Richards' voice bursts through the SPOCS transceiver. "Sarah, you read me?"

A crackle. Then: "Danny Richards. What's up?"

"You in Big 6?"

"Affirmative."

"Look up something for me on the Wall, would you?"

"Sure. What do you need?"

"We just got an arrest request on a Morgan Knox. I want to find out who issued it."

Knox stiffens, turning his head back towards the transceiver.

"OK…why?"

"Because it's keeping me from my homebrew. I'm at the end of my shift, and dispatch hits me with this. Whoever wants this son of a bitch arrested, I'm gonna—"

"Yeah, yeah, yeah. Here we go. Morgan Knox. Warrant issued by Junior Officer Hale, R."

"Damn tracers don't know how things work around here. I'll have to show her."

"Good luck."

"Hey, you got anything on what's going on up in Gardens?"

It's all Knox can do not to swipe the transceiver off its shelf. *Hale*. Did she think he'd go quietly? Did she think he wouldn't fight back? His fingers caress the remote taped to his hand. One push, that's all it would take.

He should leave. He should get far away from here. If he's arrested now, then he'll never get near Okwembu. He can deal with Hale later.

But as he looks around the room, Knox realises that he doesn't want to leave. His surgery is perfect. It has everything he needs, everything he ever *could* need, and he worked very hard to make it this way. Out there is chaos, ruin, disaster. In here, he is fully in control.

No, he's not going to run. Hale isn't going to chase him out. He'll wait, and he'll deal with the stompers she sent, and then he's going to make her realise the exact consequences of failure.

26

Riley

"Everybody get back," Syria shouts.

The man tries to stand, but his hands slip, sliding in the black gunk. He falls face down in it, shivering uncontrollably. A bubble of black slime expands in one corner of his mouth, popping gently.

Syria turns away. His eyes pass across me, but it's like I'm not even there. He points at two men standing nearby. "Bruno, Tamir," he says. "Get everyone inside. I don't want to see a single person in the corridors."

A yell comes from behind us—a man's voice, thick with fear. "We got another one!" We all whirl to see a teenage girl stumbling down the far passage, her back to us. She half turns, and I see the shimmering black threads hanging off her face. Her eyes are rheumy, unfocused.

Panic is starting to crackle through the Caves. There are shouts about something in the water. Doors are slamming shut, and running feet form a thundering undercurrent. Syria and his men take off, moving at a brisk walk, barking instructions.

My thoughts race ahead of me. I'm thinking about what Prakesh said the night before, when I thought I was getting sick. No matter what Syria does, other stompers'll be here soon. And if they close off the Caves with me still inside, then I'll never meet Knox's deadline.

I don't waste any more time thinking. I just run.

The cramped corridors pulse with bodies as the word boils up the line. People come scrambling out of the habs, heading for the exits. They begin to push tighter around me, slowing me to a jog, then a twisting, stumbling push through the packed crowds. An elbow jabs into my neck, another into my stomach. The noise is horrific: a screaming roar that the corridor magnifies and turns into a huge blast of white noise. *One exit. How could they design this place with a single exit?*

There are more people piling into us from behind, more hands raised, as if they can pull the exit towards them. The air is hot and sticky, and less and less of it is reaching my lungs every time I take a breath. Parts of the corridor are pitch-black under the burned-out lights. I have to look ahead, plan my angles, work out where each person is going to be two seconds from now. My legs move of their own accord, powering me forward as I dodge and weave through the corridor.

I'm not moving fast enough. A man goes down, his arm raised in one final plea before he vanishes under a sea of stamping feet. There's a hand in my face, pushing against my cheek and nose, a finger jamming into my mouth, arms against my back, too hard, way too hard…

And then, all at once, the bottleneck breaks. The crush surges forward. The hand whips away from my face, and then we're all running again, tripping and stumbling through the corridors.

Ahead of me, someone falls—a tall man, with no shirt and a pair of ragged shorts. What little light there is is reflected on his bald head. In half a second, I'm going to crash right into him. It'll send me sprawling across the floor, trampled underfoot.

I jump, flying over his body even before he hits the floor. I stumble on the landing, pitch too far forward, and have to throw my hands out. My palms scrape metal. As I look up, an arm swings at my face, the elbow rocketing towards my forehead. I twist to the side, and the elbow rushes past me.

There's only room in my mind for one thought: *Keep moving.*

The crowd has bunched up again, fighting for space. They've done it at a corner, where the passage narrows slightly. The door to the galleries is just ahead—I can see the light from it bathing the walls of the passage. Beyond it, two stompers are sprinting for the doors, guns up.

Amira's words whisper in my mind. Her presence is unwelcome. Her advice isn't. *Don't just run on the floor. Run on the walls and the ceilings. You can use every surface on the station to get where you're going.*

I look up at the roof. There's a fluorescent light bar, running from wall to wall, the glass thick and dusty. The bulb itself is burned out, which means the bar will be cold to the touch. I tic-tac off the wall, jumping towards it, leading with my left foot and using it to push myself off it. In the same instant, I reach up, stretching as high as I can, and grab the light with both hands. The glass cracks under my fingers, a tiny splinter needling my skin.

I exhale, and as my swing hits its apex I push my legs out so I'm parallel to the ground. Then I piston my arms, and let go.

If I miscalculate this, if I'm off by even half a foot, then I'm going to hurt a lot of people. Including myself.

The crowd is moving beneath me. The gap I'm trying to launch myself through, between the tops of their heads and the ceiling, is maybe a foot and a half. I feel their heads brush my back, raised hands across my legs.

And then I'm through. There's an *absence*, a feeling of space below me. I lean to one side, tuck my legs and hit the ground rolling.

The world goes upside down for a split second, and then I'm up and running, my muscles twanging, the cold shock of impact spreading through me.

At that instant, a transmission comes over my SPOCS, crystal clear through the static. "All points New Germany, quarantine Caves. Repeat, quarantine Caves."

No.

But the stompers ahead have heard it, too. They're already moving, guns up, and the few people still ahead of me come to a stumbling halt. I push past them, spinning around their bodies, keeping my balance as I hurl myself at the door. Not fast enough. It's already closing, one of the stompers pushing against it.

I'm ten feet away when it slams shut.

27

Riley

I'm hammering on the door even before the rest of the crowd get there. It refuses to budge. Even when other hands join me, other voices pleading to be let out, it doesn't move. Locked tight.

I find a spot against the wall and collapse against it, chest heaving, vision blurred. I feel like I've got up too quickly from a chair—like all the blood is rushing around my body, unsure of where to settle. How many hours do I have left? Eighteen? Less?

"Quiet!"

Syria. I don't know where he came from, but his presence shuts the crowd down instantly. He turns his glare on them, and they shrink away, forming another crush as the ones at the front try to back up.

"Get back to your habs," Syria bellows. "Get in there, stay in there."

They head back down the corridor in twos and threes, muttering among themselves.

Syria turns, looking down at me. "You're OK," he says, reaching down and pulling me to my feet. His skin feels calloused and worn. Once I'm up, he strides away.

"Hey." The word barely makes it past my lips. I have to clear my throat to make it come out right. "Hey!"

I jog up behind him. Syria doesn't look in my direction, but when I put a hand on his arm, he stops, his shoulders heaving.

"There has to be another way out of here," I say. "There has to be."

Syria finally looks over his shoulder at me, firmly removes my hand from his arm. "My advice? Find somewhere to hunker down until this is all over."

I try to pull my thoughts into some kind of order. Prakesh

would know what to say. He'd know how to convince someone like Syria.

Then, inspiration. "If it wasn't for me, you'd all be dead."

"Excuse me?"

"What I did…" I swallow. All at once, I'm back in the nightmare, seeing my father's face, my name splashed across it in orange letters. "With the *Akua Maru*. I saved this station. You *owe* me. So get me out of here, and we'll call it even."

It's the first time I've used what happened to me to get something. It feels weird, like I'm breaking a rule.

Seconds tick by. Shouting echoes through the Caves corridors, along with more doors slamming shut. Somewhere, very distant, the station hull is creaking and groaning.

"Follow me," says Syria. Before I can say anything, he strides away, slipping into the shadows. I bolt after him, jogging right on his heels. In my ear, SPOCS hums with traffic, almost all of it about the Caves lockdown.

He stops at one of the doors, nestled next to a giant 1-B spray-painted on the wall. He has to knock hard a few times before the door opens a crack.

A voice comes from behind it. "You get out of here now or—Syria. You OK?"

"Fine, Jamal," Syria says. The door opens wide, revealing a skinny guy with no front teeth and a shorn head. Three children cower behind him, huddled on a battered single cot, wrapped in thick blankets. The hab is cloaked in shadows, lit by a lone electric light bulb, hanging off the end of the cot. The floor is covered with patches of wet grime.

"Who's she?" Jamal says, pointing to me. Syria ignores him, picking his way across the floor to the wall at the far end. I follow, nodding at Jamal, hoping against hope that there really is another way out of here.

One of the kids slips from the bed and walks alongside me. She's a tiny girl, no more than five, wearing a dirty pair of pants and a red sweater so huge that it hangs down to her knees. She stares up at me, her brow furrowed.

Her eyes light up. "You're the lady who blew up her dad."

"Ivy!" says Jamal.

I'm too stunned to respond. Before either of us can say anything more, there's a huge screech. Syria has lifted a panel from the wall. Grunting, he sets it down. "There," he says. "It's a tight fit, but it'll pop you out by the power couplings on Level 2."

I look back once more at Jamal and Ivy, still not sure what to say. At that moment, the stitch in my left knee starts itching again, as if to hurry me along, and I step into the wall.

"Thank you," I say, as Syria lifts the panel again. Ivy has taken Jamal's hand, staring at me in wonder.

"Just go," Syria says.

Then he slots the panel back into the wall with a clunk, leaving me in darkness.

28

Knox

The two stompers—Richards and Olawole—walk up the passage towards Knox's surgery. Richards is lean, more gristle than flesh, with a gaunt face. Olawole is a foot taller than him, massive, with a trim goatee. His left eye is gone, the socket sewn shut.

"Morgan Knox," Richards says, as he slams his fist against the door a second time. "Station protection. Open the door please."

Silence. In the distance, a merchant is yelling about hot silkworms.

"This is bullshit," mutters Olawole, as Richards hammers on the door again.

"Knox!" Richards shouts. "Respond, or we're breaking in."

To Olawole he says, "Damn right. Hale is going to be one sorry piece of ass tomorrow, I'll tell you that."

Olawole smirks. "Hey, tell me something. Would you ever hit that?"

"Who? Hale?"

"Yeah."

Richards thinks for a moment. "Nah. Not my type."

He steps back, removing a tiny hand-held plasma cutter from his belt—useless for thick steel, but easily capable of melting a lock. "Knox, last chance," he shouts. "Open this door now."

There's a barked voice from behind them. "Not there."

Richards and Olawole spin around, their hands automatically going to the holsters on their belts. Olawole pauses, the fleshy part of his thumb resting on the butt of the stinger. Then he relaxes. It's just an exile—a vagrant, someone without a hab to go back to. You can recognise them a mile away, usually by the stench. The first whiffs of it reach the stompers now, thick and foul. Richards wrinkles his nose.

The exile is dressed in rags, his face lowered, as if in deference to the stompers' authority. He has a thick coat, caked with dirt, the collar pulled up around his neck.

"Move along," says Richards, his hand still on his gun.

"Not there," the exile says again. He's mumbling, like he's got a mouth full of something. "Saw him go out a few hours ago."

"You hear that?" Richards taps the back of his hand on Olawole's chest. "He's not here. Let's call it in and go home."

But Olawole is standing stock-still, his one good eye locked on the exile. The man twitches, scratches his neck, and Olawole can see the dirt caked under his nails.

"You listening to me?" says Richards. But Olawole is already moving, and in moments he's standing over the exile, towering over him. The man shrinks against the wall, cringing. He still hasn't looked up.

"Kind of interesting, you just showing up here," Olawole says. He leans in close—the smell scours the back of his throat, but he ignores it. "Knox say where he was going?"

The exile shakes his head, a furious back and forth, still staring at the corridor floor. "He didn't say anything to me, man. Anything. But I saved you the trouble right? Of knocking the door down? Right? So you can look after me?"

"What's your name?" Olawole says.

The exile mumbles something, more to himself than to the stomper. Olawole frowns, leans in a little closer. He turns his head to one side slightly. "What was that?"

He doesn't see the taser until it's too late. The exile pulls it out of his jacket pocket and activates it in one movement. Olawole rockets backwards, his arms flailing, and there's a crack as his teeth smash together. His one good eye rolls back in his head, showing nothing but white.

"Shit!" Richards says. He's already pulling his weapon from its holster, already gauging the distance, but Morgan Knox is one step ahead of him. The field-induction discharge sends him slamming into the corridor wall, barely conscious, every muscle burning with white-hot fire.

Knox checks the taser. Still at three-quarters charge. He has to move quickly—they won't stay down for long. He limps over to the big one, the stomper with one eye, then points the taser at him and holds down the trigger until the horrid smell from his rags is chased away by the smell of cooking flesh.

Richards is starting to come back as Knox walks towards him. He can move his mouth, but he can't form words yet. Drool leaks down his chin. He swivels his eyes towards Knox, but all he can see is the bulbous end of the taser, two feet from his face.

Knox drains the taser battery. When it clicks off automatically, he notices that the stomper's jacket is smouldering. He puts a foot underneath the body, then rolls it over to starve the fire of oxygen.

He looks around the corridor, but he's alone. He pockets the taser, and walks back to his surgery. There's a furnace nearby, rarely manned—he'll get his cart, dispose of the bodies, and then he'll finally get to deal with Riley Hale.

29

Riley

Syria wasn't kidding. At times, the passage through the wall is so tight that I have to shuck the top half of my jumpsuit to make myself thinner, trailing it behind me. Dust is everywhere, tickling the back of my throat, and the only light comes from cracks in the panelling.

The exit comes sooner than I anticipated. I have to crawl to reach it, flattening myself under a coil of power cables, and I nearly bang my head against the wall as the passage dead-ends. But the panel is unsecured, with no screws in place, and I lift it gently away. It's at floor level, and I can see feet in the corridor beyond. Nobody's running, which means news of the disease hasn't spread yet.

Working quickly, I slide my way out, getting to my knees and slotting the panel back in place. I'm unsteady on my feet, my body trying to process the insanity I've put it through over the past hour. The corridor thrums with activity around me, but nobody notices me slipping out of the vent. Just as well.

Royo hails me over SPOCS, and I key my wristband to transmit. "Copy, Hale here," I say.

"New orders," he says. "Rejoin the unit at the hospital in Chengshi, Level 2. Beck can brief you on the way. Confirm."

I try to ignore the prickles on the back of my neck. "Everything OK in Gardens?"

"It all went to shit," says Carver. "People spewing black gunk out of their mouths. We've got hotspots popping up all over the station."

"What?" The prickles have spread, fizzing up onto my scalp and down my spine. It couldn't have made it out of Caves. Not this soon.

Royo tries to say something, but I cut him off. "Is it in Gardens?

The Air Lab?" I try to disguise the worry in my voice, and fail miserably.

"Negative," says Royo. "Han Tseng shut it down."

"What do you mean *shut it down*?"

"Locked the techs inside," says Anna.

"Can't risk whatever this is getting into the Air Lab," Carver says. "And before you freak out: Prakesh is fine."

"Well, Carver nearly knocked him out," Anna says, "but generally speaking, everything's OK."

I take a deep breath. "Could someone please explain to me what the hell is going on?"

"*Tracers*," Royo says. "Hospital. Chengshi. *Now*."

"We'll tell you when we get there, Ry," says Carver. I don't waste time trying to argue. I take off, pushing my body into a sprint.

30

Riley

My throat is already burning, but I don't dare stop running.

The strange thing is seeing how normal the rest of the station is. Everybody's going about their business, still unaware that there's any kind of outbreak. I pass a group of men sitting on the benches in one of the galleries, talking among themselves. One of them is at the climax of a story, and they burst into laughter as I dash through the middle of them.

The motion of running calms me, like it always does. My body comes first, the muscles relaxing into a well-oiled routine, burning brightly as I run through Apogee. My mind follows as I climb the stairs towards Level 2 on the Chengshi border, dodging around the small clusters of people standing on the mezzanine.

I might be sick, too. Whatever this...*thing* is, it might be cooking in my lungs right now. Maybe my scratchy throat last night was just the start. I lick my dry, cracked lips. There's nothing I can do about it. If I so much as hint that I was in an infection zone, they'll quarantine me, lock me away, just like Prakesh. At that, I get two shots of guilt at once: one for possibly being a moving disease carrier, and another for how Prakesh and I left things. At least he's safe. At least he's with his people.

It occurs to me that Knox might be behind this. He's certainly got the skill to do it. But it doesn't make sense—he doesn't care about the rest of the station, just me and Okwembu. He's not like Oren Darnell, who was quite happy to take himself out along with the rest of us. He wants to live just as much as I do.

The area around the hospital entrance is quiet. It's in a larger corridor than most, better lit and free of graffiti. The other tracers are standing over by the closed double doors, and the metal surfaces reflect my body as I run towards them.

Carver gives me a wordless wave, and it's only then that I see that he and the others are wearing flimsy white face masks over their mouths.

Kev looks over. Above his mask, his eyes are more alive than I've seen them in months. "Got one for you, too," he says, digging in his pocket.

"Glad you could make it," Anna says, folding her arms.

I ignore her, slipping the scratchy mask over my face. "Where is everybody?" I say, gesturing to the empty corridor. The mask makes my voice sounds weird.

"On the way," Anna says. "We just got here first."

"The Air Lab. What happened?"

"Your boy was—" Carver says, then doubles over with a coughing fit, his paper mask ballooning out. He looks up to see us all staring at him. "Would you relax? Gods."

"Prakesh is fine," Kev says. He puts an enormous hand on my shoulder. "Air Lab is secure. No disease, no nothing. Not that I could see. You're good."

I smile up at him, then remember that he can't see it under the mask. Instead, I tilt my head pressing it against his hand. "OK."

Kev squeezes once, then lets go.

"We talked to the docs?" I say, gesturing to the doors.

Anna nods. "Stay indoors until the shooting stops."

"This thing's nasty, Ry," says Carver. "And it's everywhere. Air Lab might be the only place we *haven't* seen it."

My SPOCS unit crackles, and a dispatcher comes over the line. "This is a priority call," he says. "We have a medical update on the disease. The next voice you hear will be Dr. Elijah Arroway, chief medical officer in Apex."

Anna starts to speak, but Carver gestures her to be quiet. His head is tilted slightly, listening hard.

There's a pause, another painful crackle of static, then Arroway comes on.

"I'll be as brief as I can," he says, his voice tinny over the comms. "We've tested some samples, and it's not good. It's a virus—we've taken to calling it Resin. We don't know where it came from, but we do know that once it hits the human body, it works fast. Our drugs don't seem to have any effect on it, and patients aren't producing strong enough antibodies. Unconsciousness occurs at twelve hours. Extrapolating from the cases we're seeing, death occurs within eighteen."

"Holy shit," Anna says.

"Yup," says Kev.

"It attacks the lungs and the nasal mucosa," Arroway says. "We do know that it's airborne. Anybody with it is a walking cloud of infection—touching someone, or even just being in close proximity to them, will cause the virus to enter your system. The virus does not—I repeat, does *not*—survive in water. You can treat all water points as active.

"We're working on a cure now, or, at the very least, a mix of drugs to slow the spread of the virus in the body. We're also working on our processes and manufacturing equipment to produce it as fast as possible, but we don't know if we'll be able to keep pace with the infection. Until then, keep your masks on, keep—"

At that moment, the hissing static in my SPOCS unit cuts out, and Knox says, "Riley."

I turn away from the others, trying to ignore the fear in my gut.

"Not a good time," I say, keeping my voice low. Anna and Carver are deep in discussion, and Kev is staring into the distance, eyes scanning the corridor.

"Do you know what I'm looking at right now?" says Knox.

The fear in my stomach grows colder, sending tiny chips of ice through my body.

"Two stompers," he says. "Two *dead* stompers. They came to arrest me. Why do you think they did that?"

This isn't happening. This *can't* be happening.

"I don't know," I say, through gritted teeth.

"You must think I'm simple," he says. "It's the only explanation. They mentioned your name when they were told to bring me in, by the way." His voice turns mocking. "*Warrant issued by Junior Officer Hale, R.*"

And, right then, I decide I've had enough. I'm sick of his games. I'm sick of his poison voice in my ear. Time to call his bluff.

"Go ahead then," I say. "Do it. I don't think you can. I think you still need me, because without me you'll never get Okwembu."

"Who are you talking to?" says Carver. I can feel him and Anna looking at me. The corridor is deathly silent, as if the station is holding its breath.

"Tell me," says Knox. "Is Kevin O'Connell with you?"

The chips of ice expand, freezing the blood in my veins. My eyes find Kev. He sees me looking, and gives me a quizzical glance. When I don't look away, he slowly pulls his mask down.

"Everything OK?" Anna says, looking between us.

Knox's voice is as smooth as silk in my ear. "I want you to watch your friend Kevin very closely."

"Riley?" says Kev.

The words come out of me as one long, agonised howl. "*Kevin! No!*"

There's a wet, distant thud. Kev doubles over, clutching his stomach, as if his hands are trying to cover up the red stain spreading across his shirt.

31

Riley

What happens next is difficult to follow.

I'm at Kev's side, kneeling over him, my hands hovering above his body. There's blood on the floor, soaking through my jumpsuit.

At the same time, I'm seeing him running with his partner Yao, seeing him swing her into the air to catch the edge of a catwalk. She's sitting on his shoulders, legs dangling, talking non-stop while he shakes his head at her bad jokes.

I'm being shoved aside by Carver. He flips Kev over, grabbing his shoulders, shouting his name.

In my memory, Kev is sitting against the wall of the Nest, reading our copy of *Treasure Island* for the tenth time, his lips moving ever so slightly.

I see Anna, her hands over her mouth, staring down at Kev's empty face. I see Kev smiling, lopsided and goofy, feel his hand on my shoulder.

And in my ear, I can hear the very quiet hiss of Knox's line.

"Move, Riley!" Carver pushes me back a second time, so hard that I tip over backwards. He looks up at Anna. "Get a doctor."

She doesn't move. He jabs a finger at the hospital doors. "Get a fucking doctor!"

She turns and runs, slamming through the doors. The bang echoes around the empty corridor. Carver's hands track across Kev's stomach, hunting for the source of the wound. Blood soaks his forearms. He's talking to himself—no, he's talking to Kev, telling him to stop it, telling him to say something, anything.

And then there's a doctor, a white blur with wrinkled hands, and he's lifting Kev's tattered shirt, and the look on his face shocks me to my core. By now I'm standing, staring in mute horror at Kev. My face is wet from tears. I hear words like *internal*, and *organ damage*.

It all falls into place. Kev's operation—the one he had to remove the pulmonary embolism after they fixed his ankle.

He was operated on in Caves, where he could be close to his family. Was it at Medical Unit 262? Knox's old hospital? It had to be—it's the only way Knox could have sneaked the explosive into Kev's abdomen. Maybe he even performed the operation himself. He must have been planning all this for months, planning far enough ahead to know who I ran with, to figure out how to get to them. He saw an opportunity, and moved on it.

The doctor vanishes, calling for more help, for a stretcher. But it's far too late.

Then there's silence. The corridor is still.

"What happened to him, Riley?"

Carver's voice is different: brittle, fragile, like a thin pane of glass with nothing but the blackness of space beyond it. He stands slowly, one movement at a time, and turns to look at me.

"You knew what was going to happen," Carver says. "You and whoever you were talking to."

Anna's eyes are huge under the edge of her beanie. "This—I don't—"

"Tell me," Carver says. His voice hasn't changed. But there's no mistaking the raw fury in his eyes.

I say the only thing I can think of.

"I can't."

And then before either of them can react, I turn, and run.

32

Riley

By the time I reach the Chengshi border, the stitch in my side is an inferno, and Outer Earth is coming apart around me.

I expected Han Tseng to announce Resin on the comms. He doesn't. Not that it matters—by now, rumours have spread around the station, helped along by the tracer network. Even if people don't know exactly what's happening, they'll know that something bad is going on. I'm expecting panic, but the corridors are emptying. People are withdrawing into their habs, shutting themselves away. Nobody wants to come into contact with anyone else.

I can't think about the confusion and betrayal that Carver must feel. It's beyond words. He and Royo keep trying to call me over SPOCS. Their voices are eerily calm.

I make it as far as the Apogee gallery before I have to stop. I collapse against the railing on the Level 4 catwalk, sinking to the floor. Around me, the cavernous gallery is shockingly empty, and so quiet that I can hear the clanking of distant pipes. Someone has left a child's toy, a patchwork doll, in the middle of the catwalk, as if its owner decided not to go back for it.

The sobs are coming fast now, the tears streaming down my face. I keep seeing the blood, and Kev's face.

"You son of a bitch," I say, not knowing—not *caring*—whether or not Knox is listening. My voice is thick and gummy.

"Now do you see?" he says. His tone is quiet, almost regretful.

"I'm going to kill you," I say. "I'm going to rip your head off and stick one of these bombs down your throat."

"It had to be done. You had to see that your actions have consequences."

"He didn't do anything to you!"

I shouldn't be yelling. I shouldn't attract attention. But right now I don't have a choice in the matter. I think of Kev's family, in the Caves. His parents. How am I going to face them? How am I going to tell them that their son is dead because of me?

"You were at his operation, weren't you?" I say. "That's when you did it." I don't know why I'm asking him. I don't need confirmation—it's the only way that Kev could have had that *thing* inside him.

"He was harder to get to than you were," says Knox. "He had a prototype version of the device—a bulkier model. I put it next to his right lung, and sent him on his way. And that was months ago."

"Are there more?" I say. "Others?"

He actually laughs. "Maybe. Maybe not. Either way, you're running out of time."

"I don't have anything," I say. "Do you understand me? She's in a maximum security cell, and I can't get her out."

But he's gone.

I get to my feet. My legs are trembling—I don't know whether it's from exhaustion, or terror. I have to do it. I have to find a way. If I don't, then Kev will have died for nothing. Whatever happens, I have to get Morgan Knox what he wants. But it's too big a job—I can't get a handle on it, can't stop my mind from dashing itself against the problems.

Wait.

I pause, staring off into the distance. A man runs across the floor below, gesturing at someone else to hurry. His shadow tracks its way up the wall, as black as the fluid coming from the lungs of the infected.

Resin, whatever it is, is spreading. That means more quarantine zones. More quarantine zones mean more stompers will be needed to enforce them. Which means fewer stompers guarding Okwembu's cell.

That's it.

That's how I save myself.

33

Knox

It takes Knox longer than he'd like to dispose of the stompers' bodies. By the time he's finished, his bad leg is on fire.

He limps back into his surgery, teeth gritted, prickles of sweat standing out on his forehead. As he digs in one of his cabinets, hunting for a bottle of pain pills, he realises that the room is a mess. Hale's blood, dried to a thin black crust, still speckles the operating table. The wheeled surgical stands, usually lined up against the wall, are out of place, tilted at crazy angles to each other. A tray of surgical tools is on the floor, and he can't remember how it got there.

He finds the pills, and dry-swallows two of them, the bitter taste rolling around in his mouth. He should clean up—put everything back in order, scrub the table, make the room perfect again. But before he can act on this thought, a wave of exhaustion crashes over him. He's not used to physical activity—as if anybody could be used to dumping two bodies into a furnace. He limps to his chair, finds it with his right hand, then sinks into it. A minute. That's all he needs.

His mind drifts back to Amira. To the woman he loved. He had to work hard to see her again—he couldn't be sure she'd ever visit his hospital, and he might have spent months without seeing her. That was unacceptable. He began to use every excuse he had to get out of his shifts, throwing himself into finding out who she was. His supervisor, a pallid, careful man named Goran, tried to discipline him, but he barely noticed.

He saw her for the second time in the Apogee gallery. He was up on the Level 1 catwalk, and she was passing below him, sprinting across the floor. He couldn't take his eyes off her. It couldn't have been more than a few seconds before she vanished into one of the corridors, but those seconds are etched into his memory. Every movement she made, every turn of her head, every adjustment of her pack. It's all there.

He gropes for his tab screen, a sudden longing shooting through him. In a few taps, the sketch program appears. The drawings are right where he left them—his finger is a clumsy tool, but he was always skilled at anatomy, and he's drawn her perfectly. The curves of her muscles, the sharp angles of her jaw. The only thing he couldn't get right are her eyes, but he doesn't blame himself for that. No painter could. Her body was perfect, as if a goddess had decided to walk among humanity. Even her missing fingers, taken from her by the sub-zero temperatures in the Core, seemed to enhance her beauty.

He zooms in on the drawing, scrolls down. What would her thighs have tasted like, he wonders. He tries to imagine it, imagine *her*, naked, opening her legs to him, beckoning him…

No. He shuts the tab screen down, lets it drop onto his lap. Best not to. He'll never get that chance. Not after Hale and Okwembu snatched her away from him. The familiar anger returns, burning hot. Hale should have thanked him for being merciful, for sparing her life. That won't happen again.

He gets to his feet and stands, swaying. For a moment he feels dizzy, and puts out a hand to steady himself against the wall, then coughs. His chest feels a little tight.

34

Riley

"No way," says the stomper.

The stomper I'm talking to is holding two stingers, one in each hand. His jacket is off, and he wears a brown undershirt, soaked with sweat. His mask is slightly askew on his face. The outer door, made of criss-crossing metal bars, is locked shut. His partner leans against the wall, arms folded.

I was right. There are no longer eight stompers outside the maximum security brig. There are only two. Doesn't look like it's made things any easier for me.

"You think Captain Royo wants me to go back empty-handed?" I say. "It's like I said: I *have* to check the prisoner for Resin exposure."

The lie sounds ridiculous even as I say it. But it's the best I have. Two stompers is as good as my chances are going to get, and I have to get inside.

"Will you relax?" the first stomper says. Tomas, I think his name is. "We're all fine down here. No virus, inside or out."

I can feel the eyes of his silent partner on me, studying me, like I might start coughing myself.

"Orders have changed," I say, through gritted teeth.

"Until I hear it direct from Royo, orders stand. If you were coming, he would have called us."

"He's a little busy right now. In case you hadn't noticed, there's a bug going around."

Surprisingly, he seems completely unmoved by my death glare, staring down at me over the top of his mask.

"Royo's going to be pissed when I tell him you didn't listen," I say, but Tomas is ignoring me, his gaze somewhere over my shoulder. Inside, I'm screaming at myself for not coming up with something better. After all I've been through, *this* is the best I can come up with?

I trudge away. Amira's face jumps to the front of my mind—for her, it would have been easy. She took down eight guards breaking me out of a brig, like it was nothing. She'd go through these two in about five seconds.

I could probably do the same—I've fought bigger men before—but even if I did, all they'd have to do is broadcast one alert over the comms, and stompers would swarm all over us. And with no more than a dozen hours left on Knox's deadline, I need to come up with something. Fast.

Think, Riley. Think.

Slowly, I turn around, and get right in Tomas' face.

"The hell are you still—" he starts, but I cut him off.

"Listen to me carefully, *stomper*," I say, channelling the tracer I used to be. "Do you know what's going to happen if we don't uncover where Resin came from? Total anarchy. I've been ordered to eliminate this prisoner from the investigation."

I jab a finger on his chest. "Now, I could call Royo," I say, tapping my SPOCS earpiece. "Ask him to reconfirm his orders. I'm sure he'll be *thrilled* to hear from you. After all, it's not as if he has a lot going on at the moment. When this whole thing blows over, he's going to remember that you insisted on checking in. But, hey, you want to spend the rest of your career cleaning out the toilets back at Big 6, you go right ahead."

Tomas glances back at his buddy, who hasn't moved from his place against the wall. Without another word, I turn around and start walking.

It didn't work. They're not going to let me in. I have to think of something else. Maybe I can knock them out somehow...

"Hold up."

It's Tomas. "One minute, in and out. Then I don't want to see you back here."

Speechless, I just nod. We walk back to the entrance. The other stomper taps a keypad on the wall, buzzing me in. As I step through, the first door closes behind me. The control pad to open the cell doors is on the wall to my left, but I don't dare touch it.

There's a beat, and then the inner door slides back.

I jog down the cold passage towards the far end. If anything, the brig is even colder now—when I breathe, the air burns on the way in, and becomes crystal-white vapour as it comes out. The block is in darkness—I can't tell if it's another power failure, or if they're turned off deliberately.

The light's off in Okwembu's cell, too. But then there's a shifting form in the darkness, and I see her asleep on the cot, her body curled under a thin blanket.

I need to get the stompers to open the door to Okwembu's cell. I need her ready to go, not fast asleep. And, somehow, I need to surprise the stompers before they can transmit an alert call, and take them down. Preferably without killing them.

I have absolutely no idea how I'm going to get all those things done.

I rap on the plastic barrier. The shape under the covers shifts slightly, curling in on itself, as if caught in a bad dream. "Okwembu," I say.

That's when I hear shouting from outside—shouting, and gunshots.

I stop, hardly daring to breathe. There are scuffling sounds, another two gunshots, and then silence.

My body reacts before I can think about it. I have to hide. I spin in place, looking for somewhere to hunker down, but there's nothing. I'm in a short corridor surrounded by locked cells. Not good.

There's a bang, and the inner door slams open. In surprise, I lose my balance, skittering backwards, only just managing to stay upright.

I slip into the shadows at the far end, pushing back against the wall, hoping that I'm not too noticeable. My hearing comes back slowly. Okwembu's up, her hands on the plastic, staring at me.

I look back down the block. There are people stepping through, silhouetted from outside. There's no way to make out their features, but I count six at least. One of them turns to the keypad that controls the cell doors.

"Which cell?"

"Doesn't matter."

"Open 'em all."

There are several clicks, and then all the cell doors slide open, vanishing into the ceiling. I don't waste any time. I slip into the cell opposite Okwembu's, pressing up against the wall, hoping the darkness keeps me hidden.

Footsteps pound down the passage. Okwembu has shrunk back into her cell, her body nothing more than a dark form against the far wall. She has to know why they're breaking in, and what it means for her. Someone's had the same idea as me—they're using the chaos to get to Okwembu. But, unlike me, they'll be wanting her dead.

Do something.

The men find Okwembu, crowding around her cell. Their shapes are dark silhouettes, but I can see their shoulders slump in relief, and I hear a couple of exhausted cheers. I have never wanted to be holding my stinger so badly, to feel its weight in my hand and the rough edge of the trigger on my index finger.

I shrug my stomper jacket off my shoulders. I'm wearing nothing more than a tank top underneath it, and the cold air cuts right through the fabric. It dances across my bare arms, raising thousands of tiny bumps.

With no weapon, with nothing to hold them off, I have exactly one option. It's a terrible, terrible idea, but it's all I've got.

I bolt from the shadows, running right towards them.

35

Riley

In the split second before I reach the man at the back, I have just enough time to be grateful that he's the same height as I am. One arm goes around his throat, the other slams into his temple. He gives a strangled cry of surprise, and I feel his body go rigid as I pull him close to me.

The others spin around, guns up, pointing right at us. "Anton!" someone shouts.

"Don't move," I yell, trying to keep the tremor out of my voice. "Come any closer, I'll snap his neck."

But my mind is reeling. I've heard the name Anton before. He was back in the Recycler Plant—the one who I had to hide from by climbing up the vat. Are these the same people?

Can't worry about that now. I squeeze tight, and Anton cries out. Snap his neck? What was I thinking? Now I have to sell it, to make them *believe* that I can do it. I can barely make the others out—just dark forms with raised arms. My heart has climbed up into my throat. At any moment, I'm expecting to see muzzle flashes, to feel bullets tearing through us.

"Easy," says one of them.

Anton tries to pull away from me, attempting to shrug out of my grip. I pull harder around his throat, and he gives off a horrible choking noise. "Bad idea," I hiss into his ear, before raising my voice. "Okwembu! Get out here."

There's no movement. The men stand frozen, not knowing where to look. My eyes have become accustomed to the darkness, and I can see that they've got scarves over their noses and mouths.

Janice Okwembu glides through, passing between them like a knife through ribs. Her face is blank, expressionless, as if being broken out of prison is the most natural thing in the world.

She stops in front of me. "What comes next, Ms. Hale?" she says, clasping her arms in front of her.

I jerk my head behind me, and without another word she steps in that direction.

"I can take her," says someone from the edge of the group. From the sound of his voice, he's younger than the rest. I can see his gun trembling slightly in the air.

"Quiet, Ivan," barks one of them. Before they can react, I start dragging Anton backwards, following Okwembu. He takes awkward, stumbling steps as he walks, and I have to fight to keep him upright.

"Where do you think you're going to go?" says one of them, spreading his arms. "You can't drag him forever."

"Watch me."

"Outer Earth's finished. People are dying out there. Why don't you come with us? We can protect you."

"Not convinced. Sorry."

"What else are you going to do?"

I'm no more than a single step ahead of them, the plan forming in my head as I go. With their stingers raised, the men start to take hesitant steps towards us.

Okwembu speaks from behind me. "If you've got a plan, Ms. Hale, now would be the time to share it."

Ivan's stinger goes off.

The bullet ricochets off the floor in front of me, dinging off the metal. Without thinking, I shove Anton forward. Choking, he stumbles into the group, knocking another man off his feet. They all start firing, muzzle flashes lighting up the dark cell block, the bangs echoing off the walls. I grab Okwembu by the shoulder and run, head down, heart jackhammering in my mouth, my shoulders itching as I wait for a bullet to slam into my back. Some pass so close to me that I can feel the blowback.

We've got no more than a couple of seconds' head start, and I can already hear running feet behind us. I shove Okwembu through the door to the brig—out of the corner of my eye I catch sight of Tomas and his partner, laid out on the ground, dark pools of blood around their bodies. I jab the keypad by the doors, hitting every button, hoping it'll do something.

With a metallic buzz, the barred gate slams shut. A second later, a man slams into it, snarling in anger.

We take cover, flattening ourselves against the wall. I glance over at Okwembu. She's looking around her, squinting in the bright lights. Her eyes widen as she looks in my direction. "Behind you!"

I'm just in time to see someone's hand, clutching a stinger, thrust out of the bars and point in our direction. Its owner twists his arm around, hoping he might hit us when he pulls the trigger.

I dart forward, gripping his wrist. In one movement, I jerk upwards, twisting as I go. His wrist snaps cleanly, and he screams in agony. The stinger clatters to the floor.

I don't have it in me to thank Okwembu, or even to meet her eyes. "Move," I tell her, pointing back down the corridor.

We bolt, putting distance between us and the brig. I can hear her breathing as she runs beside me, low and even.

It's a few minutes before we stop. We duck into a side room, an abandoned hab of some kind. No telling if its owners are dead or have simply walked away, but the place has been stripped. Bare metal cots and overturned lockers make the place look as if the station stopped spinning, let the resulting zero gravity lift everything up, then kicked back into gear.

Okwembu sits down on one of the lockers. Her shoulders rise and fall in huge, juddering gasps. I lean against the wall, breathing hard. I did it. I got her out.

Now I just have to get her all the way across the station to Knox. Without being seen.

36

Prakesh

Prakesh is on the other side of the lab when he sees Julian Novak leading a group of people for the doors.

He ignores them at first, looking back down at the rows of soybeans planted in the giant troughs which run along the wall. He told the techs to carry on as normal, and he's trying to do the same.

He looks up again. There's something about the set of Julian's shoulders that he doesn't like.

"pH levels are good," says Yoshiro, frowning over a tab screen. "I could adjust the lights a little, get the soy to reproductive stage even faster."

"Yeah, yeah, fine," Prakesh says. He straightens up, dusting off his hands on his lab coat. "Back in a sec."

He strides across the Air Lab, cutting across the pathways between the giant oaks, keeping his eyes on Julian. The tech has at least ten people trailing in his wake. Two of them are carrying something, swinging it between them—there are too many bodies there, and Prakesh can't quite see what it is.

He knows that the shutdown code Tseng used sealed off all the Air Lab exits, including the ones at the monorail docks. There used to be plenty of other entrances—little access points dotted here and there, loose panels and ventilation shafts and forgotten corridors. Prakesh used one of them himself, during the Sons of Earth crisis. Tseng, of course, doesn't know about them.

When Prakesh was made head of the Air Lab, he thought long and hard about whether to leave them open. In the end, he gave the orders to have each and every one of them closed off. The Air Lab was the single most important part of Outer Earth. Despite what Tseng thinks, he does take its security seriously. He checked each of them himself, Air Lab and the old Food Lab, checking the welded seals over the panels and the steel bars over the ventilation ducts. *No way in. No way out.*

And as much as he hates to admit it, it has to stay that way. It doesn't stop his mind from being drawn to Riley—it's impossible not to think about her, impossible not to feel sick with worry about what she's facing out there.

And because he's thinking of Riley, he can't help but think of Carver. His anger rises, and he pushes it away. Nothing he can do about that now.

He reaches the open area near the front of the lab, and moves diagonally across it, heading right for Julian. He's picked up an entourage of his own—Suki and a few of the others are jogging towards him. Yoshiro trails behind them, still carrying the tab screen.

Julian has stopped a few feet from the doors. "Bring it closer," he says to one of his followers, and that's when Prakesh sees what they're carrying. It's an old plasma cutter—one of the models that relies on an external fuel source, a big, heavy box that needs two people to carry it. Julian himself has the cutter head, a long tube with a red handgrip on the end. Prakesh can see the metal nozzle, gleaming under the lights.

"Julian," says Prakesh, ignoring the flutter of fear in his chest.

Julian looks up and sees him, along with the rest of the techs. For an absurd moment, they freeze. The plasma cutter quivers, held a few inches off the floor. Prakesh recognises one of the men holding it—Iko, who was up on the roof the day before, when Benson took his plunge.

Julian gives him a tight nod.

"Want to explain what you're doing?" Prakesh says. He keeps moving, getting himself between Julian and the doors.

Julian tosses his hair back, then raises his chin. He's not heavily muscled, but he's tall, and looks down at Prakesh along the bridge of his nose. "Getting out. What do you think?"

"No, you're not," Prakesh says, folding his arms. Suki and Yoshiro and the others are standing off to one side, waiting to see how this plays out.

Julian half smiles. "I quit. There. I don't have to take orders from you any more." He looks behind him. "I think everybody here's had enough of being ordered around. Right?"

There are nods and murmurs from behind him. The plasma cutter fuel container drops, its clanging echoing off the door.

"Doesn't matter," Prakesh says, holding Julian's gaze. "You're not leaving. Turn around, take that thing back where it came from."

"What do you care?" Julian says. "Weren't you trying to stop them sealing it off in the first place? You just rolling over and letting it happen now?"

Prakesh opens his mouth to tell Julian about the closed ecosystem again, and the variables at play, and the probability of infection, and stops. He's remembering James Benson. His words on the roof of the control room, just before he stepped off. *They take us for granted. We give them food, all of them, and they treat us like dirt.*

Maybe Benson was right. But it doesn't matter. Being head of the Air Lab may be difficult, it may not be perfect, but Prakesh loves it. He loves being here, among the soil and the trees and the algae pools.

If he lets Julian through, if he opens up the sealed Air Lab, Tseng will see him fired. He'll never set foot in the Air Lab again. He should have thought of that before, when he and Carver nearly got into it. He wasn't thinking straight.

He can't lose this job. He won't. *If Julian wants out, he's going to have to go through me.*

Prakesh walks up to Julian. "Last chance. I don't care what you do, but you leave that cutter here, and you walk away." He raises his voice. "All of you."

He can feel Suki and Yoshiro stepping in behind him, along with a dozen other techs, and a small smile slips across his face. Julian's group are muttering among themselves, casting dirty looks in his direction.

Julian turns away, and Prakesh feels a surge of elation. "That's right," he says. "Move on."

Julian turns back. He's holding a stinger in his right hand.

Suki lets out a strange noise—a squeak and a cough, melded into one. Yoshiro spits a hushed curse.

Slowly, Julian raises the stinger and points it at Prakesh's face.

37

Riley

My right knee groans in pain. Without thinking, I scramble in my pocket for the pill bottle, twisting it open and pulling down my face mask.

Last one. The pill rattles around the bottle, and I knock it back, swallowing it quickly, getting only the barest hint of bitterness. The mask goes back on, covering my mouth and nose. I throw the bottle behind me, and it clatters off one of the lockers and out of sight. I'd do anything for a drink of water. Sell my firstborn. Trade a kidney. Anything.

"Why are you—" Okwembu takes a ragged breath. "Why are you wearing a mask? And why did those men have scarves around their faces?"

I swallow. "Disease," I say. "They're calling it Resin. It's going through the whole station."

Okwembu looks away. "Perhaps I should have stayed in prison," she says to herself.

I glance at the door. "We need to keep moving," I say. "There's a place on the sector border. We'll be safe there."

"Why did you get me out?" she says.

"Don't worry about that," I say, keeping my eyes on the door.

"How do I know you aren't planning to kill me, Ms. Hale?"

"I just saved you. Or weren't you paying attention back there?"

"Yes, but you still haven't told me why. You, a station protection officer, just broke me out of the brig. You're risking everything to do this. And if you don't want me dead, then what exactly *do* you want?"

I want to bring you to Morgan Knox. I want him to take these things out of me. I want my life to go back to normal.

I lean forward, looking her right in the eyes.

"If you try to run from me," I say, "I will chase you down and snap your neck."

"Would you? After all you've gone through to get me here?"

"Try me. Find out."

She goes silent, staring at me. Eventually, she says, "So why shouldn't I have gone with the others? The ones we're trying to run from?"

"Because they *definitely* want to kill you. With me, there's a chance you might actually survive. Logically, which one would you pick?"

"Oh? I have to say, Ms. Hale, for people who wanted me dead, they seemed very intent on marching me out of there alive."

We fall silent. Okwembu watches me. Ever since I've known her, she's been able to do that—find the weak spot in any argument, pin it down, drill right to the heart of a problem in a second. It's as if she still views the world like it's made up of code. Like humans are just strings in a program, designed to be shifted around at will. Her eyes make me think of camera lenses, capturing everything, storing it for later use.

"This isn't a negotiation," I say. "I don't owe you a damn thing. You either go where I tell you, or I'm going to chase you down, knock you unconscious, and then we'll get there anyway. Your call."

"And drag me through the station? Hardly becoming for a lightning-fast tracer."

I take a step towards her, and she raises her hands. "I can help you. We can work together."

There's a long pause. Somewhere, in a distant part of the station, there's a deep bang, turning into a rumble as the sound travels through the levels.

"Someone wants to talk to you," I say. "He asked me to get you out." A cold shiver runs up my spine, but whether in fear or anticipation I don't know.

"He must have been offering something very important to you," she says.

"You have no idea."

She walks to the door, peering out into the corridor. It's a deliberate move, but I can almost see the cogs in her mind turning, weighing the odds.

She turns back to me, gives me a tight nod. "All right. I'll come with you. Lead the way."

The old Riley couldn't do it, couldn't lead her to her death, would never have even considered it. No matter what crimes Okwembu had committed, the old Riley would have found a way around it, done everything she could to stop it happening.

The new Riley? She's thinks a little differently.

Okwembu did worse things than you ever will. Than you could ever think of doing.

But the guilt comes anyway, surging up through me, hot and acidic.

"Wait," I say. I head to the back of the room, hunting around the smashed lockers. Earlier, I spotted a pile of what looked like clothing. It's now little more than rags, ripped and shredded, but perfect for what I need. I select a long strip of rough fabric, dark blue in colour. I hand it to Okwembu.

"Wrap it around your face," I say. "Resin is airborne. This'll keep you safe." *And anonymous.*

She takes the cloth, holding it awkwardly in her hands. "Thank you," she says, after a moment.

I walk out into the corridor, my centre of gravity low, ready to bolt at the first sign of trouble. It's empty, and I relax, but only a little.

"She trained you well," Okwembu says from behind me. The sound of her voice is muffled by the fabric. "That move, back at the brig, where you broke his wrist—you could have been Amira."

Unwelcome memories fight for attention. With an effort, I force them back down.

"You run in front," I say, pointing. "One wrong move, and I'll end you."

38

Prakesh

The techs scatter.

They just bolt, heading for the algae pools. Prakesh feels an urge to go with them, to get as far away as he can.

He doesn't.

Keeping his eyes on the stinger, on the black hole of the barrel, he raises his hands. He immediately feels stupid—Julian knows he doesn't have a weapon, and really, what is he going to do, block the bullet? But it's an instinctual reaction, and when he tries to put his hands down, he finds that his arms aren't listening to him.

He sneaks a look over his shoulder. Suki and Yoshiro are still behind him, and Suki's face has gone completely white. Prakesh looks back at Julian, trying to meet his eyes.

"Put it down," he says.

Julian shakes his head. "No. I don't think I will." He's moving slowly towards the three of them, almost sauntering. Behind him, one of his followers breaks and runs. It unbalances Julian for a moment, but then he sees that the rest of the group isn't moving, and he relaxes.

Prakesh tells himself to stay calm. He tries to remember everything he knows about stingers: their range, their velocity, their stopping power. They're designed to go through soft targets, like humans, and not to penetrate metal—useful for a space station hanging in orbit, with the vacuum on all sides. Prakesh knows that the rounds are small-calibre, but can still make a real mess of whatever they hit.

On the other hand, actually getting a hit with one is a trick in itself, especially if you don't fire them regularly. Could he disarm Julian before the man takes a shot? What if he's wrong? Where did Julian even get the stinger in the first place?

He keeps very still. "Julian, listen to me—"

"Move aside," Julian says, jerking the gun.

"Think about what you're doing. They'll put you up against the wall in front of a firing squad."

Julian hangs his head. For a half-second, Prakesh thinks he's got through, but then he sees that Julian's shoulders are shaking with laughter.

"Oh man," Julian says, his fingers flexing around the stinger. "You don't understand what's happening here? The whole station's finished."

"You don't know that."

"Whatever. I'm not spending my last few days trapped in here with *you*," Julian says, ignoring Prakesh. "I got friends out there. Me and mine. So does everybody here." He jerks his head at the group behind him, then starts walking towards Prakesh. Prakesh feels Suki stiffen behind him.

"Now move," Julian says.

Prakesh shakes his head. "Not going to—"

Julian smashes the pistol into his face.

Prakesh's head snaps sideways, and it's as if someone has let off a firework right in front of him. Sparks fizzle and crackle in his vision. The pain wipes them away, huge and sudden, expanding outwards in a slow-moving wave of fire from his right cheek. There's something loose inside his mouth, one of his teeth, scratchy against his tongue.

He's lying prone, and pushes up onto his right elbow. Yoshiro is cursing every god he can think of, backed up against the wall. Prakesh blinks, unable, for a moment, to move.

"Last chance," Julian says. The barrel of the stinger seems to swell as Prakesh looks at it. He can see a slick of blood on the tiny spike of the stinger sight.

Yoshiro runs at Julian. He explodes off the wall, sprinting towards him, his arms pumping. Julian swings the stinger around.

"Don't!" Prakesh shouts. But the booming gunshot drowns out his words, and when the report fades away, all he can hear is Suki screaming.

39

Riley

Any hopes I had about not being recognised vanish with the first person we come across.

It's an old woman, a few corridors down. She's sitting against the wall, her threadbare dress pooled in her lap. She either doesn't have a place to live, or doesn't care about Resin, because she looks blissfully unconcerned as she spoons a thick soup into her mouth.

Unconcerned, that is, until she catches sight of us. Her eyes hesitate on me, but grow huge when they hit Okwembu. The spoon pauses, quivering by her mouth.

"Oh gods," she says, rocketing to her feet.

"Hope you can run," I say to Okwembu, and charge into a sprint. No time to keep her ahead of me now.

More people are looking out of their habs, spilling out of the doors. Arms reach for us, trying to grab hold of our clothing, and we duck under them or knock them away, sending their owners flying. Under my face mask, my skin is slick with sweat.

As we burst out into the gallery, onto the Level 4 catwalk, we see a large group up ahead of us. Like the men back in the brig, they've got fabric wrapped around their faces and they're all holding weapons. I even see a few children there, hefting steel bars as big as they are. They look from me to Okwembu, not sure what to do, not sure how to take seeing me running with someone like her.

"Wrong way," I say, already starting to turn. My mind is racing ahead. If we double back, we can drop down two levels by the power couplings. There's a gap we can slip through, so it should be easy to—

Okwembu puts a hand on my shoulder and shoves me towards the edge of the catwalk.

I see the railing coming towards me in slow motion. I'm already off-balance, and the railing will take me in the waist. I'll topple right over it, right off the edge.

The railing collides with my stomach, not my waist, knocking the air out of me but keeping me on the catwalk. At that second, I feel something whoosh past my back and bounce off the far wall of the gallery. It rebounds onto the catwalk, skittering to a halt.

I get a look at it as Okwembu pulls me upright. A spear. A metal pole, filed to a rough spike. If Okwembu hadn't pushed me out of the way, it would have skewered me in the small of my back.

For a moment, I marvel at how quickly the crowd decided I was a threat. They jumped straight to that conclusion, without even trying to talk to me, acting before I could stop them. The thoughts are strange, like broken puzzle pieces that can't quite fit together.

Okwembu doesn't give me a chance to really process it. Just drags me along until we're running again, away from the crowd. They give chase, but there are too many of them, and they get bunched up at the entrance to the corridor. Their angry shouts vanish behind us.

A few minutes later, we reach a gap between the power couplings, leading down to the level below. I drop first, then help Okwembu down.

"Thanks," she says. It's hardly a word—more like an exhausted exhalation.

"I owed you one," I say before I can stop myself.

I've lost track of the number of Resin hotspots, but it's everywhere now. New ones keep being reported over SPOCS. Apogee, Level 2. New Germany gallery. Outside the habs in Gardens. For now, only Apex and Tzevya remain unaffected. Hospitals and furnaces across the station are full to bursting. Whatever this thing is, it's eating Outer Earth alive. More than once, we come across a body, sprawled across a corridor, or curled into a foetal position in a corner. Black liquid is spattered on the walls and floor, shining like foul oil. And at each one, I have time to think the same thought: *why am I not sick yet?*

"How much further?" Okwembu says. Surprisingly, she's managed to keep up.

"A few minutes. Keep moving."

The words burn my throat. I focus on the image of a bottle of water, letting myself imagine the condensation dripping down the side. More than once, I hear Royo trying to hail me. He sounds worn out, like he doesn't care whether I respond or not. News of the jail break hasn't found its way onto SPOCS yet, not that I can hear. I guess with everything going on, two stompers not reporting in from maximum security has got lost in the shuffle.

As we get closer to Knox's surgery, I look back at Okwembu. She's spent. Her face has gone a strange grey colour, and she keeps coughing—quick bursts, like gunshots. My legs are hurting again, but I don't care.

I've done it. Gods help me, but I've done it. He can get these things out of me. I don't know how I'll square things with Carver and Anna, with Royo, how I'll explain my role in breaking Okwembu out. But I'll get to see Prakesh again. I picture his face, keep him uppermost in my mind.

Thinking about him leads my thoughts onto Kev. That only lasts for a second. It's too painful, too raw—I squeeze my eyes shut, shaking my head, as if to physically dislodge the memory.

The door to the surgery is shut when we arrive. It gives me a moment's pause—did he tell me a way to get in if it was locked? But I can't think of anything, and after a moment I rap hard on the door.

"Knox."

No answer. I knock again. "Knox, it's Riley. Open the door."

Nothing. Frowning, I grab the handle and pull.

The door slides open easily, taking me by surprise. Knox is nowhere to be seen.

The blood on the operating table has dried to a dark, crusty brown. Okwembu stares down at it, but for once I'm not paying attention to her. There's a canteen on one of the shelves, dark green against the grey metal, and before I can even think about it, it's in my hands. It's wonderfully heavy, full to the brim. I drink most of it in three seconds flat, gulping it down. The relief is exquisite.

I wipe my mouth, then, without thinking, offer it to Okwembu. She's still by the operating table, her finger just touching one of the streaks of dried blood.

"What is this?" she says. She's gone very quiet, her eyes locked on mine.

"Nothing. He's a doctor, that's all."

She turns and runs.

I drop the bottle. The water bursts out of it as it hits the floor, splashing across the metal. I barely notice. In two strides I'm on her, gripping her shoulders just as she reaches the threshold. She gives a howl of fury and tries to twist away, but I hold on, throwing her backwards. She stumbles across the room and slams into the far wall, sliding down it as her legs give way. Her prison jumpsuit is soaked with sweat. The cloth around her mouth and nose has come away, hanging around her neck like a noose.

I walk towards her, ignoring the guilt surging through me. She shrinks back against the wall, like she's trying to vanish into it. Reaching down, I yank up the leg of my jumpsuit, exposing the stitches, then turn to show her.

"Bombs," I say. "I deliver you, he takes them out. Sorry, *Janice*, but your life isn't worth losing my legs for."

A part of me is recoiling in horror at my own words, but on

one level it feels good to say them. It's good to have *her* scared for a change.

"So this was all about saving yourself," she says, and shakes her head. "Of course it was."

I have to hold her here. She's already taking little glances at the door, and I can see her trying to work out how to get past me. I can't turn my back on her, not for a second.

The operating table. The restraints hanging off it are padded fabric, flexible and strong. More than enough.

I grab Okwembu, pull her to her feet. She starts fighting me, clawing frantically at my skin, but she's too exhausted from the run. I jam her body into the head of the table. It knocks the air out of her, and she doubles over, moaning in pain.

I lean over her, using my own body to keep hers in place. I pull her arms across, cuffing them. Secured as she is, her hands are far enough apart that she can't use one to free the other, and the fabric cuffs are tight enough that she won't be able to pull away from them.

Okwembu goes still. She lies under me, trying to get her breath back. As I pull the final strap, she mutters something.

"What's that?" I say.

"You're not the Riley Hale I knew," she replies.

For a reason I can't quite figure out, that hurts worse than anything else.

I shake it off. Knox. Shouldn't he be here by now? This place isn't *that* big. I wasn't thinking about him while I was dealing with Okwembu, but now...

He must be in the other room. The one off to the side. I haven't even looked in it yet, and it's shrouded in darkness.

"She's here," I say, raising my voice. The darkness doesn't answer back. Behind me, I can hear Okwembu tugging at her restraints.

"It's over," I say, walking to the storeroom, stepping over the threshold. "I did it. Take them out."

Still nothing. I fumble for a light switch, my hand questing across the wall. It takes me a second to find it, but the lights are still working, and they flicker on.

Knox is in the middle of the floor, lying face up, unconscious. His cane is trapped underneath him.

And around his mouth: black slime, spattered across his lips and chin.

40

Prakesh

Yoshiro dies before Prakesh even gets to him.

The side of his neck is gone, torn away. His blank eyes stare at the ceiling as his blood pools on the floor around him and Suki screams and screams and screams.

Prakesh shuts his eyes. This doesn't seem possible. Five minutes ago, he and Yoshiro were discussing soybean plants, debating soil quality. He wonders if he's dreaming, if the blow to his head caused some kind of hallucination. But Julian is shouting at him, waving the gun in his face, and it feels far too real.

"See what you made me do?" Julian is furious, his face blood-red. His whole body is shaking. He swings the gun from Prakesh to Suki, who cringes, holding her hands up to her face. "You see what happens?"

"Take it easy," Prakesh tries to say. The words feel as if each one is wrapped in thick layers of gauze.

"Gods," says Iko. Prakesh turns his head to look at him—it seems to take a long time—and sees that he's gone white. "You killed him."

Julian is shaking his head, as if he can bring Yoshiro back to life. Suddenly, he raises the gun, jabbing it in Iko's direction. "Shut up!" he shouts.

Suki has started screaming again, dissolving into hysterics. Julian hears, and Prakesh sees him tensing, ready to swing in the other direction. Fear brings clarity, chasing away the fuzz in his head. If he doesn't get control of this, Julian is going to shoot Suki.

He could let them go. He could promise not to interfere, take Suki away and join up with the others. But something burns inside him—an anger, hot and fierce. Maybe it's Yoshiro, or maybe it's the sight of Suki, cowering and helpless against the Air Lab doors, but he doesn't want to let Julian win.

He gets to his feet, moving slowly and carefully, making sure Julian has plenty of time to see him. It's just enough to pull the man's focus off Suki, but it means that the gun is now pointed at Prakesh. He swallows hard, choosing his words carefully. "There's another way out of here," he says. "You don't have to cut through the door."

Julian's eyes narrow in suspicion. He knows that Prakesh had all the other exits sealed shut. Prakesh speaks before the thought can get a grip in Julian's mind. "I left a way open. Thought it might come in handy one day. I'll take you there, right now. Just...just don't hurt anyone."

He's lying, and he desperately hopes that Julian is too wired to see it. There's no secret exit. But his first job is to get Julian away from Suki, away from anyone he could hurt. And he knows that Julian will take the easy way out, just like he does with his lab work.

"Where?" Julian says.

Prakesh points. Julian's eyes flick to the side, following his finger. He's pointing to the wall nearby, to the sealed double doors leading to the destroyed Food Lab.

"You're lying," Julian says, training the pistol on Prakesh.

"No," Prakesh says. "I kept one open for myself. I'll tell you where it is."

Julian smiles. His teeth are bad, brown and craggy, and they look strange in his flushed, sweaty face. "Of course you did. Of course. It's just like you, isn't it? Keeping things from everyone else."

Prakesh doesn't know what to say to that, and doesn't get a chance to. Julian steps towards him, wrapping a hand around his arm above the elbow. He jabs the barrel of the stinger into the small of Prakesh's back.

"You're not going to tell us," he says, as he pushes Prakesh towards the Food Lab. "You're going to show us. Iko! Roger! Bring the cutter. We're not leaving it here."

Prakesh's head is pounding. His sense of balance is shot, and he struggles to stay upright, nearly falling, correcting himself just in time. *Don't do that,* he thinks. *You fall, and he'll put a bullet right through you.*

Julian leans in close, whispering. "You'd better be telling the truth. If you aren't? I'll come back for Suki after I do you."

41

Riley

I can't take my hand off the switch.

It's stuck there, as firmly as if it's been nailed down. Knox's chest rises, holds, trembles and then slowly falls, like a deflating balloon. I'm holding my breath, and as I force myself to exhale, I manage to pull my hand off the wall.

I drop to my knees next to Knox, my hands gripping his shoulders, shaking him, yelling at him to wake up. My voice sounds like it's coming from a long, long way away.

After a while, I sit back, cradling my head in my hands. After everything I've been through, after everything that happened in the past day, I'm going to lose. The second his heart stops beating, the return signal will stop firing and the devices will detonate.

I stand up, getting to my feet slowly, like an old woman. I walk back into the operating room, where Okwembu is still bent over the table. Her eyes are narrowed, vicious, brimming with fear and anger. Gods know what I must look like.

I reach for her cuff, intending to release her. There's no point now. I don't even want revenge any more. I just want to find somewhere warm and dark, and crawl inside and wait for it all to be over. I want someone's arms around me—Prakesh, Carver, anyone. I want to bury my face in their shoulder and have them tell me it's going to be all right, even if it isn't.

"You're letting me go?" she asks, disbelief fracturing her voice.

My hand stops, my finger just touching the cuff. I think of my father, of how he reappeared again after seven years, screaming towards Outer Earth, intent on destroying us all. I think of how I stopped him. Right at the end, when it looked like there was no way I could do it.

Knox isn't dead yet. All I have to do is find a way to keep him alive, to make sure the Resin doesn't stop his heart. I could find somewhere to hide and wait for death, or I could do what I always do. Run. Fight. Find a way.

Doctor Arroway must have made some progress by now. He said they were working on drugs to slow down Resin. It's the slimmest chance in a universe of slim chances, but so was getting Okwembu out of the brig.

There's no way I'm making it all the way to Arroway's lab, then all the way back here, by myself. Not with every stomper looking for me. I need help. And with Knox out of commission, I might just be able to get it.

Okwembu sees my hesitation. "Ms. Hale—Riley," she says. "If you leave me here, you're condemning me to death. That's not you. You'd never—"

"Shut up," I say.

Okwembu starts cursing, yanking at the cuffs, the rough fabric abrading her skin and leaving thin red weals as she pulls at them. I grab her arm, gripping it tight.

"I'm going to make a call," I say, gesturing to my ear. "Don't say a word. You may just make it out of this."

She shakes her head, looks away.

I don't want to speak to Carver right now—that's a conversation I'll have another time—but I can still find Anna.

Our channel is filled with the soft hiss of static. I take a deep breath. "Anna, this is Riley, come back."

Nothing. A drop of dread lands in my stomach, sending ripples across my body. I'm gripping the operating table with my free hand, so tight that it hurts.

"Royo? Anyone? This is Riley, come back."

The line crackles.

I stop, hardly daring to breathe. For a second, I'm sure I imagined it, but then the crackle comes again, louder this time, and I hear someone speak.

"Where are you?" Anna says. She sounds awful—not sick, just tired, her cut-glass accent shattered.

"Never mind that," I say. "I've got a problem, Anna. You're the only one who can help me."

This kind of flattery usually works with Anna. This time, however, she just sighs, a horrible, rattly sound that seems to resonate with the static. "Not this time. Not unless you tell me what happened to Kevin."

"I'll tell you when I see you. I swear. Anna, I'm running out of time. I need you to help get me to Arroway."

"*You're* running out of time?" Her voice drips with scorn. "Clock's ticking for all of us, my dear."

Okwembu speaks up from behind me. "Ms. Hale, I can help you. Let me go, and we can solve this together."

"Who's that?" Anna says.

"Nobody. It's nothing," I say, turning and walking back towards Knox's body.

Anna is silent for a long moment—so long that I think the channel's got cut off. When she speaks, her voice is brittle. "Before everything went to hell," she says, "there was a snap on SPOCS about an assault on one of the brigs. We couldn't respond to it, not with the number of people we had left, but I heard it was the max security prison."

She pauses. "Please tell me it wasn't you, Riley. Please tell me you didn't do what I think you did."

I open my mouth to reply, but what am I even supposed to say?

"Oh gods," she says. I can even see her, standing there with her eyes screwed up tight and her hand massaging her neck. "You did, didn't you?"

"...Yes."

There's a long silence on the line, broken by Anna letting her breath out in an equally long sigh. "Riley, I know you want revenge, but please trust me, this is not the time..."

"It's not about revenge," I say, cutting her off. "Look, why don't you meet me somewhere? I'll explain everything."

"I doubt it. With you gone, and Kev out of the picture—"

Her voice hitches, and she stops. There's a silence over the comms. Then: "What did you do to him, Riley? Why did you run?"

I close my eyes. When I speak, the words are pushed through gritted teeth. "It wasn't me. You have to believe me—I would *never* hurt Kev. Never."

"Then who?"

I glance over at the still unconscious Knox. Then I take a deep breath, and tell her, going as fast as I can. Knox, Okwembu, all of it.

When I'm done, Anna draws a shaky breath. "Well, this explains a lot," she mutters.

"How bad is it out there?" I say, trying to bring the subject back around to Resin.

"It's hit the whole station," Anna says.

"What about Tzevya? Apex?"

"Not yet, but soon."

I push the thought out of my mind. "What about the *Shinso*?"

"The what?"

"The asteroid catcher. The ship that was due back."

"Oh. That. I heard Royo say he'd told them to hold their position in station orbit. They must be getting pretty worried out there."

At least there's one pocket of humanity with no Resin. If it really does get as bad as I think it's going to, then at least they'll survive. At least they're used to each other's company: asteroid catcher ships run on a skeleton crew. They're built for utility rather than comfort, and most of their body is given over to the enormous engines needed to bring an asteroid to a halt, and the machinery to reel it in. They tow it behind them, anchored with enormous cables.

"Why aren't we sick?" Anna says.

"Huh?"

"Have you been coughing? Got a tight chest, anything like that?"

"No, but…" I trail off, not sure if it's worth mentioning that I *was* sick, but got better.

"Me neither. You, me and Carver. We're not sick."

This is harder to process than I thought. If it's not just me, then what the hell is going on?

"We're wearing masks, Anna," I say.

"So were a few of the stompers, and they're all down. Royo's not sick yet, but they've switched the stomper commanders to full-face respirators."

She takes a breath. "Listen—you're right about Arroway and the other doctors. They haven't cured it yet, but they've made something that can slow it down. Some kind of drug mix that's keeping people alive."

I breathe a long, slow sigh of relief. So Arroway came good. "OK. Tell me more."

"How long it lasts depends on who you give it to—some people only get a few hours, but others have lasted a lot longer." She pauses. "Can you bring this Knox person to us?"

"Not a chance. I'll have to come to Apex and bring the drugs back here."

There's silence for a moment. "I'll do you one better," Anna says. "You know the broken bridge in Gardens?"

I do. It's a Level 6 catwalk on the border of Gardens and Apex, named for its railings, torn and shredded in a long-forgotten attack.

"I'll meet you there," she says. "It'll save you going all the way."

"OK," I say. "And listen, Anna…thank you."

"Don't mention it. Just get here."

"Copy. Out."

Okwembu, silently listening to my half of the exchange, speaks up. "Will you at least tell me what's happening?"

I ignore her, stretching my legs out, doing my best to work up my tired muscles into something resembling a fit state to move. I'm going to have to run faster than I've ever run before—and I've already run so much today.

My eyes are drawn to Knox's hand, lying splayed out on the other side of his body. The remote unit is still held in it, secured to the palm with thin strips of tape. I walk over and crouch down, yanking it back and forth. After a few moments, it rips free. Knox groans, his lips twitching, sending a drop of Resin running down his chin.

One less thing to worry about. But what to do with it? I can't just leave it here. And if I have it on me, and accidentally hit the button during a roll or something, I'm done.

I cast around the shelves, looking for something to use. My eyes land on a small box, made of hard plastic. It's almost identical to the ones Carver makes his stickies out of, only slightly bigger.

I pop the lid off. It's got cream in it, white and glistening. I rinse the box out over the basin, then wipe it off, making sure the inside is completely dry.

I jam the remote into it. It barely fits, but I tell myself that that's a good thing—it means the unit won't rattle around inside while I'm running. I slip the box into my pocket. It's uncomfortable, but it'll have to do.

Okwembu clears her throat. "Can you at least pull the scarf over my mouth before you go?"

She nods at Knox. The tendrils of Resin creeping out of his mouth are shiny under the storeroom lights, shimmering wetly.

I walk over and pull the scarf up, knotting it loosely behind her head. She's still bent awkwardly over the table. Her back's going to start hurting before long. Tough.

The canteen is still in my hand. I take a long drink from it, then set it down in front of Okwembu, between her bound hands. I spotted a length of rubber tube earlier, coiled in a box on one of the shelves. I retrieve it, then slip one end into the bottle and drop the other close to her mouth, hanging off the end of the table. All she has to do is bend down to drink.

She leans back, giving me some space. "Someone you love has got sick, just like him," she says, nodding at Knox. "It's written all over you."

She's wrong, but I don't say anything, just fiddle with the rubber tubing, adjusting its position on the edge of the table.

"It's Prakesh Kumar, isn't it?" she asks. "I'm so sorry, Ms. Hale. I hope you find what you're looking for."

I don't bother to correct her. "So do I."

Suddenly, she leans forward, planting her elbows on the table, her face inches from mine.

"Your expression barely changed when I said his name," she says, her eyes glinting. "It's worse than that. Someone is dead. And since you don't have any family to speak of, that must mean someone other than dear Prakesh has become important to you. Was it Kevin O'Connell? I heard you say his name earlier. What about Aaron Carver? Maybe even Samuel Royo? Are you going to be able to save them, Ms. Hale? Or are you just going to save yourself?"

Before she can say anything else, I'm running, charging out of the door and taking off down the corridor, heading towards Gardens.

42

Riley

I run. Faster than I've ever run before, pushing my body to the limit. The few people still in the corridors have to dodge out of my way, cursing as they flatten themselves against the walls. I don't care. I can't stop. Not now.

A smell has crept into Outer Earth. The air is thick with it, cloying and sweet. It tickles the back of my nostrils, and I can't escape it no matter which route I take. My paper mask does nothing to stop the stench. The mask itself is drenched with sweat, starting to tear. I don't even know if it's worth keeping, but I don't dare take if off yet.

When I cross the Chengshi gallery, high up on one of the catwalks, I'm startled to see black smoke curling in the air. Looking over the side, I see a pile of bodies being burned, attended by stompers wearing full-face respirators.

Standard procedure on the station is to cremate dead bodies, but this...have the furnaces given out? This kind of manual cremation won't work forever. Will we start putting them out of the airlocks? Leaving them where they fall?

There's too much to think about, too many questions I'd rather not answer.

I make good time, reaching the broken bridge in just under an hour. If I get the drug mix from Anna now, I might just be in time to save Knox.

She's waiting at the far side, in the shadows of the corridor entrance. She looks up as I approach, waving me over. She's abandoned her face mask—guess she decided there was no point, since she's not getting sick. Her cheeks are stained with dirt, black rivulets running down them like tears. Strands of hair stick to her forehead under the lip of her beanie. There's no sign of Carver. Probably a good thing.

"You took your time," she says as I come to a halt. "I thought you weren't going to make it."

I lean against the wall, breathing hard. It's a moment or two before I can raise my head to look at her.

"I'm just fine," I say, throwing a weary thumbs-up.

"Any Resin symptoms?"

"Not with me. Did you bring the drugs? I need to get going."

"Riley, you can barely stand."

I don't want to admit she's right. My legs are trembling, like a baby standing for the first time.

"Doesn't matter," I say, holding out my hand. "I don't have a choice."

But instead of handing me the vial or test tube or whatever it is, she places a hand on the corridor wall, and shakes her head. A ringlet of blonde hair, stained with sweat, falls over her face, and she pulls it back. "It's not just Resin. There are other things now, too. Dysentery." She says it *die-sentree.* "The last time we had someone with it was over two hundred years ago on Earth. *On Earth*, Riley."

"Anna, give me the drugs. Please."

"Do you think it's us?" she says. She keeps looking back over her shoulder, and over mine, to the other end of the catwalk. "Do you think we've got something to do with it? Why else wouldn't we be getting sick?"

What little radar I have is starting to ping repeatedly. I reach forward, grip Anna's shoulder. "Just give me the drugs, and let me take care of this."

"Stop being so bloody selfish. Come in. Let the doctors test you. They got nothing from my blood, or from Carver's, but maybe yours will be different. And they can take the bombs out."

"Are you insane? If I don't get those drugs to Morgan Knox I'm as good as dead." I jab a finger at my shaking legs. "And there's no taking them out. If I try, then what happened to Kev..." I trail off.

She stares at me, her eyes hard. "In that case, I'm sorry Riley. I didn't want it to be this way."

They're at the other end of the corridor, just where it takes a turn. Stompers. Grey-clad, with full-face masks like the heads of beetles, all tubing and shining faceplates. Stingers out, pointed right at us.

Royo and the others must have been listening in when we spoke over SPOCS. They lured me right in.

Anna flattens herself against the corridor wall. She doesn't look at me.

I'm already moving, sprinting back the way I came, but there are stompers on the catwalk, their feet pounding the metal as they run towards me.

Something deep inside me snaps.

I want it to be over. Not just the bombs, but everything: the guilt, the nightmares, the days of trying and failing to make any sort of difference at all. Because, the truth is, Outer Earth doesn't need me. Maybe I saved it once, but I can't save it now. I can't stop Resin, any more than I could save my father.

Turning in mid-stride, I put one hand on the railing of the catwalk, then get a foot up on it. We're high up enough. It'll be quick.

I try to picture Prakesh's face in my mind, but it won't come, like the connections have been severed. Carver's, too, and Kevin's. Right then, as I feel myself going over, it's my father's face I see. The look in his eyes, right before I executed the on-screen command that killed him. My name, glaring orange over his face.

The stompers running towards me on the catwalk are in another universe. Gravity takes hold of me, caressing my stomach, getting ready to grip tight and *pull.*

43

Riley

But there are hands on my back, my shoulders, my arms. Gravity's grip loosens as they pull me back, hauling me off the railing. I'm airborne for a split second before slamming into the floor of the catwalk.

My head cracks the metal, turning my vision grey. I'm shouting: not even words, just inarticulate yells which turn into sobs as the tears run down my face, staining my face mask.

I'm hauled to my feet, hands gripping my upper arms tightly. Royo is there, staring daggers through the faceplate of his mask. Through a gap in the stompers, I see Anna. Her face is cold, set with purpose, but her eyes tell a different story.

"I thought I could trust you, Hale," Royo says, his words distorted by the mask.

I swallow. "Sam," I say, using his first name. He does nothing. I continue: "You don't understand. I had to—"

"You split from your team. You break Janice Okwembu out of the brig. You're not getting sick from Resin. You are possibly responsible for the death of Kevin O'Connell. You're damn right I don't understand."

"You know about what's inside me," I say. "You heard me talking to Anna, and you know what'll happen if I don't get back. Sam, *please.*"

He talks over me. "You're under arrest, Hale. And if you try to run, then so help me I will put a bullet in your head and walk away whistling."

I'm hustled past them, marched so fast down the corridor that my feet barely touch the ground. I try to find some energy. Maybe I can fight them, make Royo put that bullet in me. But there's nothing. My legs feel like pieces of lead, dead and useless. They take my wristband, pull my earpiece out.

"Where are we going?" I say eventually.

"Apex," says the stomper on my right. "We need to get a blood sample."

I don't remember half the journey to the hospital. We have to pass through multiple checkpoints, each one guarded by stompers with full masks. They've locked down the entire sector, surrounding it with stompers—the last stand against an encroaching tide of Resin.

The walls of Apex are a dazzling white, glaring under the ceiling lights. The harsh light brings back bad memories—the last time I was here, I'd just run through the Core, almost hypothermic with cold.

What little order there was in the sector's hospital is gone. Beds have spilled out of the doors, makeshift mattresses littering the floors of the wards and the surrounding corridors. There are huddled shapes on them, wrapped in blankets, shivering. Several are still, with the fabric pulled over their faces. Doctors move between the mattresses, bending down to their patients, occasionally rising to glance at each other and shake their heads.

They take me to a small ward by the main offices. It's strikingly similar to Knox's operating room; there are the same units and basins lining the walls, the same hospital bed in the middle. The bed is a little more comfortable than the one Okwembu is currently chained to, with a padded mattress and a raised headrest, but there are the same wrist and ankle cuffs hanging off the side. Before I can argue, the stompers lift me up onto the bed, strapping me down, pulling the velcro tight. I can move my hands and feet a little, but not enough to make any difference. The mattress feels rough and clammy on my skin.

One of them brings over a canteen with a straw attached. The water soothes my parched throat, and I can feel my body relaxing into the bed.

At least I don't have to run any more.

Han Tseng walks in, along with a doctor. It's Arroway—he doesn't identify himself, but he's still wearing his name tag. He looks familiar, and I remember running a hospital job for him before, back when I was still with the Devil Dancers. I remember him looking tired back then—right now, he looks like he's about to fall over.

"Don't look so terrified," he says, washing his hands in the basin. "It's not as if we're going to operate without anaesthetic. I just need a blood sample."

"Do you think there's any chance it'll work?" I ask. But he doesn't meet my eyes, just raises a syringe to his face, tapping the needle to knock the air out. My arm is swabbed with alcohol, icy-cold, followed by the bite of the needle as it goes in. I hiss, failing to clamp the noise down in time.

"Of course it won't work," says Han Tseng. "You'll have the same things in your blood as your friends Beck and Carver. Just a lot of highly complex antibodies that we can't replicate. But we have to at least try."

Arroway draws the needle out. The blood in the syringe—my blood—is a red so dark it's almost black.

"I heard there was a way of stabilising people with Resin," I say.

Arroway shrugs. "It's a mix of furosemide and nitrates we cooked up. Stops the lungs filling completely with fluid. But it only slows Resin down. Eventually, everyone dies."

"Did they tell you about the bombs?" I ask.

Tseng shakes his head. He's not saying no—he's shaking it in disbelief. When he looks back up, there's contempt on his face. "You use Resin as an excuse to settle a score with Janice Okwembu? And then you cook up this story? What do you want me to say here?"

Anger surges through me. "It's not a story. Pull up my pants leg. Look for yourself."

His eyes linger on my legs for a moment, but he makes no move towards them. "You can't put remote-control bombs in someone. It's insane."

I try to keep the fury out of my voice. "Just look. You'll see the stitches. Or better yet—there's a control unit in my left pocket. It's right there."

Han Tseng loses it. He walks over, slams his hands down on the bed, stares right into my face. "We've lost *everything*. The only thing I can do now is try to save what's left. See him?" He points to Arroway. "He and his colleagues are working overtime, trying to figure out how we beat this thing. Do you imagine for a moment that I'm going to pull him away from that so he can perform exploratory surgery on your say-so?"

"*My friend* is dead. His name was Kevin, and he was killed the same way."

Tseng turns, and strides to the door, not looking back.

"Just put me under then," I say. "Knock me out. I don't want to feel it. *Knock me out!*"

But he and Arroway are gone. The stomper standing outside the door looks in, his gaze lingering on my prone body. Then the door shuts, sliding closed, and I hear it lock with a click that echoes off the walls. I yank at the restraints, but they stay strapped tight.

It doesn't take long for me to wear myself out. There's nothing I can do now.

Distantly, I wonder how long I have before Knox's heart stops beating and the signal is transmitted. An hour? Two? I still can't quite believe that the drugs to keep him alive, to keep *me* alive, are right here in this hospital. They may as well be on the other side of the moon.

I can't even work up any anger against Anna. She may have betrayed me, but it feels like something that happened a long, long time ago.

Will Carver come and see me? What will he say? And when it's all over...will they stick me on one of those funeral pyres? Will they tell Prakesh?

The room is quiet—even the hum of the station is muted here, reduced to a low hiss. Time passes—I don't know how much. There's a security camera in the top corner of the wall by the door, flashing a tiny red light every few seconds, its black lens staring down at me. I can see the hospital bed reflected in its gaze. I expect Royo to come and question me, but it doesn't happen.

I close my eyes. The light in the room turns orange under my lids. I try to picture myself on Earth, running through that field of grass that I've dreamt about so often, under a warm sun, and a sky so blue that it hurts to look at it.

There's a loud click.

Just as I open my eyes in surprise, the lights in the room flicker and die, plunging me into darkness.

44

Prakesh

They cross the hangar in silence, heading for the Food Lab. Prakesh is acutely aware of the stinger jammed in his back, but even more aware of the man holding it.

Julian is hanging on the end of a very thin thread, and Prakesh doesn't want to think about what will happen if it snaps. He isn't crazy—at least, Prakesh doesn't think so. But he's very scared, and that means he'll be quick to do something stupid.

"That's it," Julian says, as they pass under the oak trees running along the side of the lab. "Keep walking."

The men carrying the plasma cutter—Iko and Roger—walk behind them. Prakesh can hear them struggling with it, swearing under their breath as they lug it across the floor. The other people in the group walk ahead of Julian, as if scouting the way. Prakesh can tell that they're on edge as well, can tell from the set of their shoulders that they don't like this. Then again, they aren't the ones with a stinger in their backs.

This isn't the first time Prakesh has been in danger. He was abducted by Oren Darnell, nearly lost his life. And he and Riley have been in plenty of other scrapes. But something about this is different. Maybe because it's his own techs holding him hostage—

people he worked with, people he trusted. Whatever it is, it's enough to make cold sweat break out across his back.

"So this exit," says Julian. "Tell me about it."

Prakesh has to hunt for the words. Then he has to work his swollen mouth hard to try and form the words. "Wall of the Food Lab."

"I know that." He sounds bored. "Where does it lead?"

"Out into the ventilation system."

"OK." Julian digs the stinger barrel into Prakesh's back. "And where does the ventilation system get us? Where's the nearest exit point?"

"The water point on Level 2. Near the hospital."

Instantly, he realises his mistake. Julian stops dead, then grabs Prakesh's shoulder, spinning him around and jamming the gun into his cheek. "You're sending us to a *hospital*? Where do you think the disease is? I don't feel like dying today."

That's when Prakesh sees them.

There are five—six—Air Lab techs, crouching behind one of the algae pools that run alongside the trees. They're armed: Prakesh can see fire extinguishers, metal rods. He doesn't know how long they've been following Julian's group for, but it's clear what they plan to do. They're going to attack. And even if they succeed, not all of them will make it. Julian won't hesitate before shooting them, just like he shot Yoshiro.

Julian's stinger is still in his face. He speaks as fast as he can. "You won't get infected," he says. "I said it's *near* the hospital. You can just go the other way. Besides, for all we know they could be containing it right now."

Julian looks around, as if hunting for support among the others. Prakesh looks over his shoulder, over to the algae pools. He can just see Suki's terrified eyes looking over the top. Prakesh gives a very gentle shake of his head, desperately hoping that Suki understands.

He doesn't get a chance to find out. "I say we use the cutter on the main door," says Iko. "I don't like this one bit, Jules."

Prakesh can see Julian thinking. He closes his eyes. If Suki and her group attack, if Julian doesn't lead them into the Food Lab, then this could go very badly. He looks at the gun, held tight in Julian's hand, now pointing slightly away from him. *I could take it*, he thinks. He feels a sudden urge to reach out, pulls it back just in time.

Julian shakes his head, then spins Prakesh around again, putting the pistol in its accustomed position in the small of his back. "Let's go," he says.

They resume their march towards the Food Lab, the doors looming large. Prakesh knows what's beyond them: a dark, soot-stained hangar, filled with scaffolding and building equipment. Construction stopped a few months ago—they need building materials from the asteroid, the one the *Shinso Maru* is bringing into orbit. The ship might be ancient, barely functional, but it's still got enough juice to bring an asteroid back. Once they've got that, they can start rebuilding.

Assuming we're still alive, Prakesh thinks.

Julian pushes him over to the doors. There's a keypad set into the wall. Prakesh set the code himself, months ago—another part of his plan to keep the Air Lab secure. He punches it in now: 0421. Riley's birth date. Easy to remember.

Prakesh pauses for a moment before hitting the final number. He would do anything right now to be back in his hab with Riley. He doesn't care about their fight any more. He just wants to hold her.

"What are you waiting for?" Julian says.

Prakesh shakes his head, and hits ENTER. With a hiss, the doors to the Food Lab slide back into the wall. There's nothing but darkness beyond them.

"We're going to need some light," Prakesh says. He glances at Julian. "They turned off the power couplings. Overheads won't work."

"Oh, we got light," says Julian. He looks at Iko, who lifts the hooked nozzle of the cutting torch. He flicks a switch, and the end of the nozzle sparks to life, a point so bright that Prakesh has to shield his eyes.

Julian shoves Prakesh with the small of his hand. "You're in front," he says.

45

Riley

The blackness is total. There isn't even any light coming from under the door to the outside. The whole hospital must be down—I can hear confused shouts from somewhere in the corridor.

I expect the emergency lighting to come on. It doesn't. I yank at the restraints again, as if the velcro was somehow only strapped shut because of the power. It doesn't give, and I slam my head back on the pillow in frustration. There's hammering on the door, and I yell at them to let me out, but then I hear running footsteps, getting fainter. Doesn't matter—not to me anyway. I'm still stuck here. Still dead.

I hope Han Tseng feels really shitty afterwards, I think, and surprise myself by giggling. It's a weird sound, tiny in the darkness. I shut my eyes; apart from a few muffled voices, somewhere in the distance, the hospital is almost completely silent. I could be lost in space, drifting further than any human has ever gone.

There's a noise above me. A grinding sound.

My eyes fly open, but I see absolutely nothing. Just pitch darkness. My breath has caught in my throat—I imagined the sound, I had to have. But then it comes again, directly above me. A sound like metal on metal, as if someone was—

Pushing back the plates in the ceiling.

Whoever it is chooses that moment to drop. One of their feet takes me in the breastbone with the force of a meteorite impact, sending a huge shock wave of pain slamming through me. I yell out, half in surprise, half in total agony. My attacker's other foot has landed on the mattress; they're off balance, and their arms windmill as they fight to retain it.

The foot digs into me, jabbing hard. "Who the hell is—" I manage to say, but my next word is swamped as a hand clamps over my mouth.

I whip my head from side to side, trying to shake it off, grunting frantically, even trying to open my mouth so I can bite down on one of the fingers. Right then, there's a voice, next to my ear.

"If you don't stop thrashing around," says Carver, "I'm going to suffocate you with a pillow."

I'm breathing hard through my nose. Only when I'm completely still does he take his hand away. He does it slowly, as if I might start yelling again. No chance of that—I'm still working out what I'm actually going to say to him.

I finally settle for "What are you doing?"

"Practising my landings."

I feel his hands moving along my right arm, until he finds the cuff. He rips the velcro away. I start on the other, while Carver works his way round to my feet. Halfway there, he knocks his shin on something and swears loudly.

"Carver, why are you doing this?"

"Has anyone ever told you that you ask far too many questions?" he says. I feel tugging on my right ankle, hear the rip of velcro. "I'm getting you out of here."

"But what happened earlier. With Kev..."

"So what, you don't want me to get you out?"

"I didn't—"

"I still don't understand what happened to Kev. But I'm not letting it happen to you, too."

He keeps working on my cuffs. "We all agreed that if you tried to contact anybody, we'd get you to come in. It was just luck that you got through to Anna first, really. I don't think Royo would have managed it—he was never very good at asking nicely."

"Luck? Anna betrayed me."

"Don't start with that, Riley. She did what she had to do. And I still can't believe you wouldn't tell me what was happening to you."

I try to make my reply strident, strong, but it doesn't feel that way. "I didn't want you to get hurt. I had to handle this myself."

"How'd that work out for you?"

The last cuff falls loose. I stand carefully, putting my feet on the floor as if the bombs will trigger from the slightest impact.

"They tested your blood," Carver says. "You and Anna are both immune to Resin."

"What about you?"

"Same thing," he says. "They're not sure why. We've got the right antibodies, but they don't know why, or how to replicate them. Anyway, doesn't matter. Tseng's not letting anyone leave."

"He thinks if we can hold Apex, we can save the station. That about right?"

"Uh-huh. But, right now, we're the only ones who could get anywhere—any stomper with a respirator wouldn't make it ten steps before being killed for it."

I hear another sound from where he's standing—like liquid in a small container being shaken.

"Furosemide-nitrate compound," he says. "Single dose. Got it from one of the labs. If this Knox person is real, and if you really die when he dies, then it'll buy you some time."

I feel myself smiling. It's a tiny chink of light in a very dark world, but it's there.

"We'll have to force the door," I say, stepping my way around the debris.

"Actually, if I have my timing right, we can use the handle."

There's another loud click from above. The room is flooded with dim red light—the emergency power, finally kicking on.

Carver's face, hair and stomper jacket are streaked with sticky, oily dirt from the ducts. "Deactivate the emergency backup, smash the main power coupling, slip into the ventilation system before they arrive," he says. "Easy."

He slips past me to the door and tries the handle. It doesn't move. His brow furrowed, he tries again, rattling it harder.

"Problem?" I ask.

"This should be connected to the emergency power, right?"

"It's a manual door, you moron. They all are."

"Yeah, I see that now, thanks. What do we do?"

I think for a moment, casting my eyes around the room. In the corridor outside, I can hear running feet and urgent voices. How long will it be before they check on us? No way to tell.

My gaze falls on one of the units lined up against the wall. It's about chest-high, the metal shelves stocked with pill bottles and plastic containers filled with viscous liquid. I step towards it, pulling it away from the wall on its casters, struggling to keep it straight. "Help me with this," I say to Carver.

He's shaking his head. "If you're trying to reach the ceiling vent, it's no good. It's too high up."

But for the first time in what seems like a year, I'm smiling. "Better idea. There's a guard outside the door, right?"

He nods, confused. "There should be. Why?"

I point to the unit. "Just help me. Then get on one side of the door."

Puzzled, he complies, pulling the unit over to the door, then pressing his back to the wall on the right. I take the left. "Ready?" I say.

"Ready for what?"

"This."

I put one foot on the unit, and shove. It topples over with a colossal crash, sending bottles flying across the floor. Almost immediately there's a startled cry from outside. The door flies open, and a stomper runs into the room. He's got his stinger out, but before he can turn around I hit him in the back of the neck, right in the pressure point.

He goes limp on his feet, and I shove him to the floor. He turns his face up to the light, his eyes clouded, and just before Carver pulls me out of the door I recognise him. Sanchez—one of the guys from Big 6.

There's no time to feel bad. He'll live, and that's good enough for now.

The corridor is bathed in the red emergency lighting, turning it into something from the depths of hell. There's a strange buzzing sound, like the power cables are frying in their rubber insulation, cooking the entire hospital.

"How did you know there was only one stomper outside?" Carver says over his shoulder.

"I didn't."

"You could have told me."

"You had a better idea?"

"Not really," he says.

As the words leave his mouth, two stompers materialise in front of him, stingers out. I see their eyes widen above their masks, see them raise the stingers. Carver drops to his knees, skidding along the corridor.

I know what he's doing. It's a move Amira taught us, years ago, and I wasn't even aware that I'd remembered it until now. I take off with one foot, planting the other firmly on Carver's back and launching myself upwards, going so high that my forehead taps the roof of the corridor. I fling my legs out in front of me, as if I'm sitting in mid-air.

My feet hit the stompers at the same time. My left foot takes one of them in the throat; his gun goes off, the bullet slamming into the floor somewhere behind us. My right foot hits the other stomper square in the face, the heel smashing into the faceplate of his respirator. I hear it give under my foot with a *crack.*

They're both down before I land. I barely manage to get my feet under me before I do, but as I make contact I see the one I smashed in the face try to rise. Carver jams a fist into his neck, sending him sprawling. Then we're both up and running, charging down the corridor.

The buzz in the walls is louder now, like the hospital is angry at us for overcoming its guards. We don't see any more stompers—wherever the rest are, we seem to have slipped past them. We sprint out into the hospital atrium, heading for the exit. The atrium has high ceilings, going up at least two levels, with balconies clustering around it—another one of those vastly impractical designs that our ancestors seemed to specialise in. There's an admissions desk in our way, between us and the door, a chest-high slab with overturned chairs scattered before it. We vault over it in unison, landing with a bang on the other side, no more than a few strides from the doors.

We're almost there when we hear a shout from behind us.

"Hale!"

It's Royo. He's standing by the desk. His respirator has been ripped off, hanging on his chest, a tangle of black tubes and straps. His bald head is shiny with sweat under the lights.

And the stinger in his hand is pointed right at us.

It's only when he fires that we stop. We're nearly at the doors, and we skid to a halt. Carver nearly tumbles, his feet catching under him. Royo fired upwards—a warning shot, buried in the ceiling.

"Next one finds its target," he says.

His gun hand stays steady, but there's something in his eyes. Like he doesn't quite know where he is. We're too far away to jump him—and too close to run.

I shake my head. "We're on the same side, Cap."

"And what side would that be?" he says.

"Yours," I say. "Outer Earth's."

"No. No, no, no, no. You and Janice Okwembu. You're all in this together. You made the virus. It was you."

Carver steps in front of me, his hands held out in front of him. "Put the gun down, Captain."

Royo takes a step forward, the stinger aimed right at Carver's chest. Above and around us, the darkened balconies stare down. "You're helping her, Carver? Can't say I'm surprised."

A tiny flash of anger crosses Carver's face, but he doesn't move. Instead, he says, "Whatever's stopping Riley and me from getting sick, they can't build it in a lab. There's nothing more we can do here."

"You're wrong. We have to hold the sector."

"With who?" Carver says. He raises his arms, pointing to the empty balconies. "Where's your backup? How many stompers have we lost today?"

"I don't care."

"Cap, listen to me," I say. I can feel the stitches in my legs burning, like lit fuses. "Everything you heard me and Anna talking about was true. If I don't do this, I'm dead."

"It's the *Shinso Maru*, isn't it?" he says. "That's your plan. Kill as many people as possible, then capture the ship."

"Captain…Sam…"

"You're trying to go back to Earth. Finish what your old man started, all those years ago. Okwembu got in your head, just like she did with your crew leader. You shouldn't have listened to her, Hale."

His words aren't true, aren't even close to being true, but they cut deeper than they should. I'm about to say something very stupid when I freeze. What I see stops the words in their tracks, cutting them off as effectively as someone grabbing me round the throat.

A line of thin black liquid has started to run from Royo's nostril. It reaches his lip, moving almost imperceptibly. He coughs, reaching up to wipe it away almost absent-mindedly. It leaves a black streak on his face.

"We're going now, Cap," Carver says quietly.

Slowly, he turns, and starts walking towards the doors. After a moment, I turn and follow. Behind us, I hear Royo take a step forward. "Don't make me do this," he says.

Carver jabs at a button by the doors, and they slide soundlessly into the wall.

"Is this how you want it to end? With a bullet in the back? Hale, I am your commanding officer, and I am ordering you to stop. *Now.*"

And then another voice speaks, from the shadows. "Put it down, Captain."

Anna Beck steps out, One-Mile raised high, her fingers clenched around the steel bearing in the cup. She walks towards us, never taking her eyes off Royo, tracking him with the slingshot.

He lowers the gun, just slightly. "So it's like that, huh?"

Anna nods. "It's like that." She's at our side now. I can't look at her. I want to tell her to stay away, that I'll only get her killed. Instead, as one, we turn and start to make our way out. Our walk turns into a jog, then a run.

"Dammit, *stop.*"

Even without looking round, I can tell that Royo has raised his stinger again. Anna isn't aiming at him any more—she's moving with us, away from Royo. Then we're into the corridor, the lights in the ceiling whipping past above us, the passing struts in the walls punctuating the beating of my heart.

Royo howls—it's a cry of agony, like he's being tortured, like he's going through the worst pain imaginable—and pulls the trigger.

46

Prakesh

The harsh light from the cutting torch throws the structures in the Food Lab into sharp relief. Scaffolding rises above them, ladders and pipes etching rigid shadows onto the walls. The floor is smeared with soot, with tools scattered across it, hammers and welding masks and angle grinders. The greenhouses, destroyed in the fire, are nothing more than shells, their thick bases almost melted away.

The door to the Food Lab whines shut behind them, clicking into place.

Prakesh coughs. Even now, months after the fire, the air is still thick with a sour chemical tang. Julian gives him a shove and he stumbles forward, almost tripping over a welding mask. He whirls, on the verge of anger now, but Julian has the stinger pointed right at him. Iko sweeps the cutting torch from side to side, the shadows moving with it.

Prakesh starts walking, keeping his hands visible at his sides. The group falls silent as they move through the hangar, stepping single file between the melted greenhouses. Prakesh's mind is on fire, anxiety poking holes in his plan. He should make his move now. *No.* He's still an easy target. But the longer he waits, the further he gets from the Food Lab entrance...

"I don't like this place," Roger says.

"Same here," Iko replies. "Hey, Prakesh," he says, raising his voice. "Weren't you here when the fire started?"

Prakesh says nothing.

"Sure he was," Julian says. "He watched old Deacon go up in smoke. Didn't you?"

Prakesh keeps his eyes fixed on the floor ahead of him. He'd rather not think about that particular day—the day when Deacon, one of Oren Darnell's co-conspirators, strapped on a vest containing packs of flammable ammonium nitrate and then set himself on fire.

Prakesh nearly died in the inferno. So did Riley; she ran in there to save him.

If I get out of this, he thinks, I am going to hug her so hard she won't be able to breathe.

His shin smacks into something hard. A piece of sheet metal, laid between the remains of two of the greenhouses to form a low, makeshift table. He lands on it hands first, soot scratching at his palms, scattering the tools lying across it.

There's shouting from behind him. Julian is there instantly, jamming the gun into his neck, a sweaty hand against his hair.

"Watch where you're going," he says, hissing the words into Prakesh's ear, then hauling him upright. Prakesh can feel blood soaking into his pants, oozing from where the metal edge sliced through them.

Julian kicks the table aside, the crash echoing off the walls. They keep marching. This time, Julian makes Iko and Roger take the lead, keeping the stinger wedged firmly in Prakesh's back.

He directs them to the end of the hangar, to the massive structure that rises almost to the ceiling. The walls still stand—the support struts are made of thick steel, and they managed to withstand the fire. But the inside is a tangle of melted metal and plastic, and there's another smell in the air now, earthy and sour.

"The Buzz Box?" says Julian. "Your exit's in the *Buzz Box*?"

Prakesh meets his eyes, and nods.

"And you had to lead us here? You didn't think to mention that this was where we were going?"

"You didn't ask," Prakesh says.

Julian falls silent, staring up at the structure. The Buzz Box. Ten million beetles and twenty million silkworms—the station's single best source of protein, before they were all burned to cinders. It deserved its name. Prakesh remembers the noise, a hum so intense that it vibrated your stomach. It's darker inside than it is on the hangar floor, as if the light from the cutting torch can't quite penetrate.

"At the back," he says. "There's a loose panel on the wall."

Julian pushes him inside. "Show us."

The top sections of the structure have burned out, collapsing inwards, and the floor crunches underfoot. At first, Prakesh thinks it's just debris, but the fragments are too small. It's only when Iko plays the light over it that he realises what they're walking on: dead insects. Millions of them, frozen in puddles of melted plastic.

I'm in a nightmare, he thinks, and almost laughs. He expects someone to make a joke, Iko maybe, but nobody says a word.

He's running out of time. But Julian has the gun at his back, and Iko's cutting torch is just a little too close. Sweat beads on his forehead, dripping into his eyes.

After what seems like an age, they reach the back of the Buzz Box. Julian lets him go, and Prakesh makes a pretence of moving along the wall, running his hands across the panels. *Please, please let this work.*

"Here," he says, nearly swallowing the word. He raps on one of the panels—a panel he knows has nothing wired behind it. "This one."

Nobody moves.

Julian gestures with the stinger. "OK. So open it up."

Prakesh crouches down, pretending to work on the bottom of the panel. He looks over his shoulder, finding Iko's eyes. "I need some more light."

Iko glances at Julian, who shrugs. He steps forward, raising the tip of the cutting torch so it's above Prakesh's head.

Now.

Prakesh reaches up, grabs the cutting torch cylinder, and wrenches it out of Iko's grip. Before the man can do anything, Prakesh pulls it downwards, his fingers hunting for the ON switch.

He finds it just as the nozzle touches Iko's thigh. The plasma slices through fabric and skin and flesh. Iko howls, more in surprise than pain.

Prakesh hears the stinger go off, drowning out Julian's shout of surprise. But he's already gone, sprinting back the way they came in.

47

Riley

The bullet buries itself in the wall somewhere behind us. There's no second shot. We turn a corner in the corridor, and Royo is gone.

None of us says anything as we run. There's too much to deal with: Anna's betrayal, what happened to Kev. My body feels like a canteen, drained of its last sip of water.

The time I spent in the hospital, off my feet, has restored some of my energy. Carver drops behind the more we run, first alongside me, then behind me. Initially, I think it's because he's letting me lead the way, but then I realise it's more than that; he's not as fit as me, and not as fast over long distances. I can hear him breathing, ragged and quick.

Anna is hurting, too. I can see it in her stance, in the set expression on her face. But she keeps pace with me, refusing to drop back.

When we slip through the door into the surgery, Okwembu is still strapped to the table, bent over. The bottle I put in front of her has been knocked onto the floor, and, judging by the red marks on her wrists, she's been trying to pull loose. She gives us a cold look, tight-lipped.

Carver stares at her for a moment, fascinated, as if he's never seen her close up. I guess he hasn't. Anna leans up against the door, trembling, pushing against the stitch that's trying to bend her in two.

Carver points to Okwembu. "You actually managed to get her all the way here without killing her?" he says. "Not sure I'd've managed it. Not after what she did."

"I was trying to save Outer Earth, young man," Okwembu says.

Carver leans forward over the table, so close to Okwembu's face that their noses are almost touching. "My crew leader died after you and Darnell got in her head. Didn't save her, did you?"

"Carver," I say. I can't even look at the other room, where Knox is. Not until I have the drug compound.

He shakes his head, then reaches inside his jacket and pulls out a small bottle and tosses it to me. It's about the size of my palm, filled with something that looks like thick urine. Spotting a syringe on one of the shelves, I grab it and yank the cap off before jamming it into the mesh stopper on the top of the bottle. My hands are shaking so hard that I almost drop the syringe. I sprint into the other room, skidding to my knees in front of Knox.

For a long, horrible moment, I'm sure he's stopped breathing. Then he gives a tiny exhalation, almost like a cough, his chest fluttering. There are more Resin strands on his face, fresh ones over the dried tracks. I don't waste another second. I grab his arm, pull back his sleeve and jam the needle into a vein. I push the plunger, and dark blood wells up alongside the wound.

Knox's arm jerks, sending the needle flying. He coughs, then groans in pain, twisting his legs, his back arching so far that it pushes him off the floor. His breath is coming in short gasps.

"Did it work?"

Carver is standing in the doorway, his arms folded, Anna peeking over his shoulder. I can see Okwembu behind her, straining for a better look.

Knox's breathing has settled back to a regular tempo—shallow, but consistent. His eyes flutter open, fix on mine. A capillary in his left eye has ruptured, staining the white matter bright red.

"I was..." he starts—but another coughing fit overtakes him, grabbing his body in a giant fist and shaking.

Carver speaks from behind me. "You awake yet, asshole?"

"Carver," I say. "How long?"

"What?"

"The drugs. How much more time do we have?"

He shrugs. "Half a day, maybe? I don't know. Resin's tough to figure out."

"Resin?" says Knox, rising up onto his elbows. He nearly makes it, but his body starts trembling and he collapses. "Is that what it's called?" He rolls onto his side, pulls his legs up to his chest. "Throat hurts."

"Get used to it," I say.

He glances towards Carver and Anna. "You brought someone else in here?"

"They're friends. And they helped save your life, in case you're wondering."

"Not that you deserve it," Anna says.

He doesn't respond. He's bathed in sweat, and every cough sets his body trembling like a leaf in airflow.

"I did what you asked, all right?" I say. "I broke her out. Time to hold up your end."

He stares at me, uncomprehending.

A tiny seed of panic begins to flower, deep inside me. "I brought her to you, just like you wanted," I say, as if repeating it enough will get it through his skull. His pupils are unfocused, his mouth slightly open. When he licks his cracked lips, I see his tongue is almost completely black.

"Who?" he says. "Amira? You brought me my Amira?"

Carver rockets off the door frame, fists clenched, mouth set in a thin line. Anna grabs him, pulling him back.

"No," I say, forcing myself to stay calm. "Okwembu. Janice Okwembu."

I jerk my head towards the operating table. He glances behind me, sees the former council leader strapped down. She stares back at him, refusing to let fear show on her face.

"Very good," he says. He closes his eyes and lets his head fall back on the floor.

I grip his shoulder. "Take these things out. Now."

"Ah yes," he says. "I should keep my promise."

He raises his hands, and with a kind of dull horror I see that they're shaking. He can't keep his fingers still. I grip his right hand—it's ice-cold under my fingers, the skin damp with sweat, and, no matter how I squeeze, it won't keep still.

"I could take the devices out," says Knox, "but doing it without setting them off? Or leaving the surrounding tissue intact? That I'm not sure about."

I throw his hand down. It bounces off his chest, coming to a rest by his side. His eyes are closed. I want to scream at him.

But he's right—there's no way he can carry out any sort of surgery.

Carver leans over him. "Then tell us how to deactivate them. There's gotta be a way."

But Knox is gone—fallen back into unconsciousness, his chest rising and falling. No telling how long he has left. How long *I* have. I'm back to the beginning. I walk past Carver and pick up the pills, then lean on the edge of one of the basins lining the wall. I hang my head, trying to focus on my breathing.

"Riley," Anna says. "What exactly was he going to do to Okwembu? Please tell me this isn't what I think it is."

I backhand her across the face, my body moving before my mind registers what's happening. It knocks Anna backwards, the sound cracking around the room. I grab her by the front of her shirt and slam her into the wall. Her beanie falls over one eye, and the other one looks back at me in fear and incomprehension.

"*None of this* is what you think it is," I say. "Being a tracer, being a stomper, all of it. You treat it like a game, but in the real world people die. People we care about."

She struggles in my grip. "All I'm saying is that we should—"

"You wanna trade places?" I say. "Fine. *You* can be the one who gets turned into a walking bomb. You can make the decisions."

Carver pushes between us. When I resist he shoves me away, and when I try to rush back he puts a hand square on my chest. "Everybody just calm down."

"Why did we even let her come?" I say through teeth clenched so hard that my jaw clicks.

"Riley, I—"

Carver pulls me away. I try to wrench free, but he wraps me in his arms, burying my head in his shoulder. That's when I realise I'm crying. The tears are ice-cold against my skin.

"Easy now," Carver whispers. "Easy."

"Kev was my fault," I say, amazed that I can still find words. "I killed him."

"*No.* You didn't. You understand me? That was all Knox. And when this is all over, we'll go and talk to Kev's parents together. Promise."

The oddest feeling comes over me then. It's the same feeling I have when I'm close to Prakesh, when we're lying in bed and I have my head buried in the side of his neck. At first, I think it's just me missing him, but it's more than that. Being this close to someone, being *held*, feels good. Good enough that I don't want to let go.

When I look up, after what seems like entire minutes, Okwembu is watching me intently.

"Riley," Anna says, her voice very small. "I'm so, so sorry. Captain Royo told me that we had to bring you in, so I...I mean, if I'd known, I would have..."

"It's OK," says Carver. "Everybody screwed everybody. We've balanced the karma."

I take a deep breath. "Yeah."

I glance at Anna. Carver's got no family to speak of, but she's different. "If you want to get back up to Tzevya, look after your folks, that's fine."

She opens her mouth to speak, pauses, shakes her head. "If my father knew I left you, he wouldn't let me back in anyway."

"What's the word on SPOCS?" I say.

Anna tilts her head. "Oh, right. You don't have yours. Resin's all anybody's talking about. We've dropped right down the priority list."

"Good to know."

She narrows her eyes. "Okwembu—she hasn't got sick either?"

Anna's right. I look back at the former council leader—bound, but healthy.

Carver thinks, then shakes his head. "There's a connection, but not one that I can see. Anyway, it's not important right now—we've *definitely* been exposed to Resin, we *definitely* aren't sick and we can *definitely* move faster than anyone else. So what do we all have in common?"

Anna sucks in a breath. "*Of course.*"

Carver and I stare at her. She looks back at us, her eyes wide.

"Mikhail," she says. "He's what we all have in common. He's why we aren't sick."

Neither of us responds. She looks between us, back and forth. "Think about it. Riley and I arrested him, and Carver, you were there when we brought him in."

I shake my head. "So was Royo. And he's got Resin."

"And Mariana," Carver says. When he sees Anna looking confused, he goes on. "The guard at the brig. She died earlier."

"Right," says Anna, grimacing. "But name *one other thing* that connects us. It's him, I'm telling you."

An idea flickers at the edge of my mind. Something I saw. Before I can get a fix on it, it's gone.

At that moment, there's a noise from the corridor outside. The sound of people trying to be quiet and failing. A single glance between Carver and me is enough.

We start moving. But we're barely halfway to the door when it flies open, and people with guns charge into the room.

48

Riley

I let muscle memory take over.

The closest attacker is a woman, her long brown hair pulled back into a ponytail, her lower face hidden by a green scarf. I knock her gun aside, and follow it up with a jab to her throat. She crumples, retching. I'm dimly aware of Carver moving alongside me, grunting as he takes another one of them down.

I drop and spin, lashing out with my left leg, catching another one of them in the shin. I get a glimpse of Anna. She's grabbed a scalpel, and has thrown it, flicking her hand out. It fails to connect, bouncing off a jacket-clad chest. Okwembu is shouting, pulling at her restraints.

I use my momentum to spin myself upright, ready to take out the rest of them. I don't know who they are, or what they want, but they're not getting it.

Too many of them. They're pouring through the door, stingers out, eyes flashing in triumph. Carver and I are slammed up against the wall, and one of them has his arms around Anna, lifting her off the ground. She's screaming and kicking, but her hands are held tight against her waist.

I look around, and a stinger barrel is inches from my nose.

"Stop moving," says the owner. It's the woman I attacked first, the one with the ponytail, and her voice is hoarse from the blow across her throat. Above the green scarf, her eyes are murderous. I subside, breathing hard. Carver does, too—he's got three guns on him. The surgery is packed with people.

That's when I recognise them. Even with their faces covered, I pick them out. There's Anton, holding a gun on Carver. And Ivan, his arms wrapped around Anna. These are the men who took hostages in the Recycler Plant, who later interrupted my attempt to rescue Okwembu, back in the maximum security brig.

Who the hell are these people?

Anton glances at me, and under the rag he smiles. "You left a trail a mile wide," he says. "Would have been here sooner, if you hadn't locked us up."

"There's someone back here," a man says. He's over by the storeroom, standing above Knox.

Anton glances over. "Resin?"

"Yup. Dead." The man nudges Knox with the heel of his boot.

The room falls silent. And, finally, all eyes turn to Okwembu. Their prize, the person they've been hunting across the whole station. She stares back at them. She's still cuffed, still bent over the table, but there's defiance in her eyes.

Anton walks up to Okwembu, his hands clasped behind him. "I've waited a long time for this," I hear him say.

She's finally going to get what's coming to her. Anton's going to kill her in front of all these people, and I'm going to have to watch. It's strange—now that I know it's actually going to happen, I'm not sure I want it to.

Anton leans over her. He undoes her cuffs, ripping the velcro off.

"You have something we need," he says. "You're going to give it to us, whether you want to or not."

"And what is that?" Okwembu says, massaging her wrists.

Anton grins. "The Earth."

49

Riley

Dead silence.

Okwembu looks from Anton to Ivan, and back again. "And how exactly do I give that to you?" she says, her tone apparently one of honest curiosity.

"Not here," Anton says, shaking his head. "I'll explain later. You come with us, and you do what we say. Understand?"

Okwembu rolls her wrists, stretching them out. "And if I do… you'll guarantee my safety?"

"That's right."

There's a long moment of silence. My mind is reeling. What can Okwembu possibly have that will give these people… *the Earth*? What does that even mean?

Okwembu nods. "Fine. Let's go."

"Good." Anton barely looks in our direction. "Put the rest up against the wall and shoot them."

Anna starts howling, twisting in the arms of the man holding her. Carver and I are marched at gunpoint towards the storage room. Knox hasn't moved a muscle. A thin line of Resin has trickled down from his nose, pooling on the floor. My heart feels like it's about to stop.

"Why don't we take them with us?"

It comes from one of the others, a woman, leaning up against the wall. She's wrapped a scarf around her entire head, so that only her eyes are showing.

Nobody says anything for a second. Then Anton says, "We don't need them, Hisako. Anyway, I told you back at base. We're stretched thin enough as it is."

"Right, right, I know," says the woman. "But think about it—if we could bring them over to our side, we'd have people with inner knowledge of Apex." She shrugs. "After all, they're stompers. They've been there. We haven't."

Carver and I exchange a glance. Just what are these people planning to do?

Anton walks over, conversing in whispers with Hisako and two of the others. They pull Okwembu in, too, and she talks quickly and quietly. More than once, I hear the words *kill* and *important*. Anna's eyes are huge.

After a minute, the huddle breaks and Anton walks over to us. "Hisako's right," he says. "Much as I hate to admit it. You're coming with us."

I let out a thin breath. Anton smiles, revealing crooked and broken teeth. "I do owe you one for the Recycler Plant, though."

He leans back, and throws a punch across my face.

There's enough force in the blow to snap my head back. My teeth clack together, and I feel one of them break, almost delicately. There's blood in my mouth, and my cheek is already starting to hum with pain.

Carver shouts in anger. Our arms are pulled behind us, twisted sharply backwards. My hands are snapped together, and I feel something hard and sharp-edged being slipped over them—a zip tie of some kind. It's yanked tight, cutting into my wrists, and I grunt in pain.

Hisako tears a strip of cloth from her scarf. She blindfolds me with it, knotting it tightly behind my head, plunging me into darkness.

50

Knox

Morgan Knox isn't sure if he's awake or not.

At first he thinks he's dreaming. Or hallucinating. Hale and her friends are restrained, blindfolded, and his room is filled with strangers. One of them leads Okwembu to the door. She looks back at him in the instant before she crosses the threshold. Her eyes meet his. Triumph sparkles in them, and she's actually smiling.

It's that smile that jolts him fully awake. It's not a dream, not a hallucination. They're taking Okwembu and Hale both, and it's happening right in front of him.

He tries to move, to cry out. But the only sound he can make is a gurgling wheeze, and it costs him dearly. Pain radiates through his body, boiling up in his throat.

Resin. That's what Hale called it. He must have got it from those stompers, the ones who came to arrest him. Or perhaps he got it from Hale herself. Knox claws at the floor, breaking his nails on it, leaving thin smears of blood behind. He coughs, and it's such an awful sensation that it nearly knocks him out. He can't get enough air into his lungs—they feel stretched, like a rubber bladder, filled to the brim. He's dimly aware that his nasal passages are blocked, jammed solid with muck.

He opens his eyes again. His surgery is empty. Okwembu and Hale are gone.

Anger explodes through him, blocking out the pain. He won't let that happen. Hale is going to learn what it means to fail.

The remote. It's in the pocket of his scrubs. It takes him a minute to work up the strength to roll over, another to lift his hand to his body. His fingers fumble at the hem of the pocket, but when he finally pushes them inside, he feels nothing.

No.

Perhaps he got the wrong pocket. He shuts his eyes tight, willing his arm to move, but there's nothing in the other pocket either. *She's taken it.*

He coughs again, and something rolls inside him: a long, slow movement that tears his chest wall apart. This time, he screams. The world goes dark.

When he comes back, his thoughts are a little clearer. Hale gave him something, he remembers that. Some kind of intravenous fluid. Whatever it was, it's had some effect—he's still having trouble breathing, but he *is* getting air into his lungs. That means he has a chance.

But for how long? He may need another dose, and it doesn't seem as if he'll be getting one any time soon.

His medical training takes over. It's as if he's standing above his own body, looking down on it, another doctor assessing a patient. *He has fluid on the lungs, and in the pleural space behind them. We need to drain them.*

Standard procedure is to do a tube thoracostomy, inserting a static drain in the chest to release the fluid. No chance of that. He can barely move, let alone carry out a surgical incision. He'll have to use a syringe. He can insert the needle into the cavity, draw out some of the fluid. It'll hurt like hell, but he doesn't have any other choice.

He could let himself die. It would be easy. All he has to do is lie here. The transponder is still attached to his heart—he can feel the wires itching beneath his skin. That means Hale's devices would detonate. The thought gives him bitter pleasure.

But then he looks up, and sees Amira.

He knows it isn't real. It can't be. Amira is dead. And yet there she is, sitting on the edge of the operating table, her legs swinging back and forth. Her dark eyes are locked on his. Her tank top is soaked with blood. She runs a finger along it, and it comes up dark and shining.

"Help me," he says. His voice is nothing more than a whisper.

He blinks, and she's gone.

They killed her. Hale and Okwembu. They took away the only perfect thing in his world. He can't let them get away with that. He won't.

Zero-G

The syringes are in his surgery, on one of the wheeled stands next to the operating table. Every movement is agony. When he rolls himself onto his stomach, it's as if he's falling from a great height, slamming into the ground with the force of a meteor.

He lies there, breathing hard. After a moment, he tries to rise. He barely makes it to one knee before his muscles fail, sending him crashing back down. He tries to slow his breathing, tries to ignore the horrid sucking feeling in his chest.

There's no way he's going to be able to walk. He'll have to crawl. He gets one arm out in front of him, then the other and pulls.

He makes it three feet before another cough explodes out of him, spraying the floor in front of him with sticky black fluid. He stares at it, bewildered. Blood? Pus? Whatever it is, he has to drain it, and soon.

He pulls himself through gunk. It's sticky, like snot. He has to stop to rest more than once. On the third time, a coughing fit nearly tears him in two. But somehow he keeps moving, putting one arm in front of the other.

The stand is in front of him. He's going to have to get to his knees again.

He moves as carefully as he can. A single cough, a single tremor in his fragile lungs, could unbalance him, and he doesn't know if he can get up a third time. Slowly, oh so slowly, he gets his right leg underneath him, then raises himself up on his knee like a sprinter at the block. He can see the tray of instruments on the stand, see the scalpels and forceps. The syringes, he knows, will be in a small plastic case, just out of sight.

He touches the tray, and that's when the cough explodes out of him.

His hand comes down on the tray's edge, sending the instruments flying through the air. He tumbles onto his side, retching, as they roll and skid across the floor away from him.

51

Prakesh

Every step Prakesh makes is as loud as an explosion. He stumbles into one of the Buzz Box supports, bounces off it, nearly loses his balance on a pile of loose metal pipes. Behind him, Julian's stinger fires a second time, a third, the bullets ricocheting off the floor behind him. Iko is still screaming.

Julian stops firing. Without the muzzle flash, Prakesh is instantly cloaked in darkness. But his retinas haven't adjusted yet—he's running through a bright, black void, hands out in front of him, hot breath tearing his chest apart.

"Find him!" Julian says.

Not if I can help it, Prakesh thinks. The thought is interrupted as something collides with his shin.

It could be anything: a piece of scaffolding, a stack of metal sheeting, a machine battery. It hits him in the same spot as before, when he was walking through the Food Lab. The first time, he was moving at walking pace—now the sensation is so sharp that he's convinced his legs have been sliced right off. He tumbles end over end, landing on the floor beyond the obstacle, cracking his skull so hard on it that the black void blossoms with colour.

He pushes against the pain, telling himself to get up. He rises to his knees, fingers bent on the slimy floor, and stops.

The Food Lab has gone silent. No explosions of sound. No crashing of metal. As long as he stays down, he can control his movements. Adrenaline made him run, but he can see past it now, and it's a much better idea to stay hidden.

There's a flicker of light from the Buzz Box—Julian, sparking the plasma cutter back to life. Prakesh sees the obstacle he tripped over. It's a corrugated metal sheet, propped horizontally between two supports. He ran right into its leading edge. His fingers find his right shin, and he feels a slick wetness. The wound is skin-deep, nothing more, but he still has to bite back a hiss of pain.

Iko is moaning now, and Prakesh hears Julian telling him to shut up. "Roger. You, Owen and Jared spread out. Sweep the floor. *Find* him." To Prakesh's ears, he sounds insane: someone at the very end of a very long tether.

Roger says something Prakesh can't quite hear. "Neither does he," Julian replies. "You find him, and you beat the shit out of him."

They only have one stinger, he thinks. Should he make a run for it? All he has to do is get to the entrance to the Air Lab, and he can seal them inside. No. From where he is, it's too risky. He can't track them all, and he doesn't know how fast they can move.

He can hear them now, their footsteps crunching on the melted plastic. He closes his eyes, trying to pinpoint them on the floor, but there are too many echoes. The sounds fold in on themselves, multiply, coming from a dozen directions at once.

Prakesh opens his eyes. The metal sheet he's crouched behind is long—fifty feet, at least. He can move along it, and then...yes, there, a stack of yellow plastic barrels he can hide behind. He doesn't know what he'll do when he gets there, but it's the best chance he's got.

Keeping his head down, Prakesh moves on his hands and knees, listening hard, trying to time his movements to coincide with the hunters.' He feels like the only thing louder than his hands on the grimy floor is his heartbeat, thundering loud enough to blow a vein in his neck.

"Come on out," Roger says. His voice is distant, coming from the other end of the floor. The light has grown dimmer, as if the search has moved away. With any luck, they haven't spread out too far.

Ten feet away from the end of the metal sheet. Five. Still nothing. Prakesh stops a foot from the end, dropping down onto his elbows. The barrels are a few feet away. To reach them, he's going to have to cross a gap on the floor—a gap dimly illuminated by the flickering light of the plasma torch.

Prakesh listens hard. He can hear them: footsteps, a bang followed by a muffled curse, Iko's helpless whimpering. He *thinks* they're at his four o'clock—no way for him to tell if they're looking in his direction or not. Nothing for it. He can't stay here.

He looks up at the barrels, takes a deep breath. He'll move on the balls of his feet, like he's seen Riley do, staying low and quiet. He tenses his thighs, preparing to move.

He sees the shadow a second before he leaves his position. He freezes, and that's when the voice comes, shockingly close, no more than three feet above his head. "He's not here!"

The speaker is standing on the other side of the metal sheet, his filmy shadow stretched out across the gap in front of Prakesh. Slowly, very slowly, Prakesh turns his head and looks up. It's Roger—Prakesh can just recognise the shape of his head and shoulders. He's looking back towards the Buzz Box, and as Prakesh watches, he idly rests a hand on the metal sheet. It shakes slightly, just touching the edge of Prakesh's shoe.

"Keep looking, then." Julian sounds hoarse and anxious.

Roger drums his fingers on the metal. Prakesh can't look away. If Roger turns his head, even a little, and looks down, there's no way he'll remain undetected.

Roger grunts in frustration, shoving off from the metal sheet. Prakesh breathes a long, low sigh—then chokes it back when he sees where Roger is going. The man is coming round the end of the metal sheet, between Prakesh and the barrels. There's nothing Prakesh can do.

52

Riley

The blindfold is hot around my face, and my fingers are already starting to go numb from the biting pain of the cuffs. I can't stop running my tongue over my jagged tooth, and my cheek is still burning from Anton's blow.

My entire sense of balance is gone, destroyed by the blindfold. My feet are constantly tangled up, and my captors have to hold me upright to stop it happening. A few times, I really do start to fall—my stomach lurching as my centre of gravity topples—and they have to pull me back.

I don't know how long we walk for, or where we go. For a while, Anna and Carver are alongside me—I hear them spit the occasional curse as they, too, struggle for balance—but after a while they go silent. My imagination runs away from me: maybe we've been split up, our captors taking us to different places so they can break us individually.

Whoever they are.

My legs are burning. It's been a long time since I took any pills, and the stitches have become hot lines, flipping back and forth between bright sting and maddening itch. There's nothing I can do. I try to ignore the burning, pushing other thoughts to the front of my mind. *Prakesh*. He's never felt further away than he is now. At least he's safe—I don't like that he's sealed away, but the Air Lab is a lot less chaotic than it is out here.

After a while, the sound around me changes—it feels muted somehow, like we've moved away from the main body of the station. I start to hear other noises—people shouting orders, the clanking of machinery. A few minutes later, we come to a stop. The noises have got louder now—it's as if I'm in an enormous factory. Every muscle in my body feels ready to collapse.

"What do we do with her?"

"Take the blindfold off. I don't think it matters now."

I feel the material being unwrapped, light slipping in as the layers come off, and when the last one falls away I have to squint against blinding overhead lights. My eyes fill with tears, and, as I blink them back, I see Carver standing alongside me. His blindfold is being pulled off, too. Anna is being brought up behind us. Okwembu is there as well, her hands clasped behind her.

I look around, and my mouth falls open.

We're in one of the old mineral-processing facilities, where they bring asteroid slag and turn it into something useable. There are dozens of these places across the lower sectors, so it's impossible to figure out the exact location. Smelting kilns line the walls, bracketing enormous centrifuges. They'll spring to life when the *Shinso Maru* comes in, delivering its asteroid cargo. The space construction corps will break it down, and the tugboats will bring the pieces in to be turned into slag, which will be processed to get the minerals out. The asteroids are our building material, our fertiliser, our chemicals.

A metal frame for holding heavy equipment runs around the walls of the rectangular room, reaching to a ceiling that must be sixty feet up. Right above us, I can see a smaller gantry, a set of tracks with what looks like a miniature train car on it, just as high up but with a tangle of cables hanging down from the body. The cables end in a shredded mess of torn wires.

The place makes me think of Big 6. Same energy, same movement. There must be more than fifty people—men, women, children, entire families. Everybody is moving, everybody is doing something: shifting crates, wheeling pallets of equipment. Even the kids.

A few people glance in our direction, but nobody pays much attention to us. Off to one side, a group of them stand around a table, checking weapons. There are homemade stingers, more than I've ever seen before. Other weapons, too: long metal tubes, lined up alongside a strange type of ammo, black and squat. As I watch, one of them hefts the tube onto his shoulder, as if to aim it.

Resin has sucked Outer Earth dry of life, but it's like this one little room has managed to fight it off—to stay alive in all the chaos. I don't see anybody sick. It's like they're preparing for something, a journey maybe.

Or an invasion.

I glance over to the man holding my left arm. He's pulled down the cloth over his face, and I can see that he's not as old as I thought he was. Stubble coats his face, but the eyes above it are young—a bright, anxious blue.

I wriggle my arms. "Any chance you could take the cuffs off? I can't feel my hands."

He shakes his head. "Sorry."

"How about some water, then? We could really use a drink."

He seems about to respond, but then he suddenly snaps to attention. I feel the other man holding me do the same, jerking me more upright.

Mikhail is walking towards us.

They must have sprung him from the brig. He looks less gaunt, his prison jumpsuit exchanged for a dark blue jacket and pants over a patched, untucked cotton shirt. His hair has been swept back, pulled into a neat ponytail, and he's wiped the grime off his face. He stands erect, too, with the bearing of a ship's captain. Something about it bothers me, and it takes me a second to realise why: it's the same posture my father had, before he left on the Earth Return mission. Straight-backed, chin up, daring the world to test him.

A ghost of a smile flickers across his face. "We meet again," he says, his eyes finding mine.

The words sound odd in his mouth, as if he read them somewhere and is trying them on for size. I want to ask him about Resin—about why nobody here is sick, and what they're preparing for.

The man with the blue eyes jogs my shoulder. "They're just stompers. We should—"

Mikhail silences him with a look.

"If you're thinking we're going to help you break into Apex," Carver says, "then you need to think a lot harder."

Mikhail glances at Carver. He takes a step closer, and I feel the grip on my shoulders tighten. "I'm going to give you a few minutes to think about what you wish to contribute to our cause. I would think hard, if I were you. Hisako can be very persuasive."

He holds Carver's gaze a moment longer, then turns away, looking towards Okwembu. "You," he says. "My colleagues tell me you were a computer programmer. Before you joined the council."

It's an odd thing to say, out of place in the current circumstances. Okwembu barely blinks. "I was," she says.

"What operating systems did you train in?"

"Operating systems?"

"When you were at the academy."

Okwembu frowns. "Ellipsis. Deep-OS. But those are outdated systems. I don't see what—"

Her eyes go wide. She stares at Mikhail, understanding dawning.

Not that it helps the rest of us. The names mean nothing to me. I look round at Carver, but he's just shaking his head, as confused as I am.

"You're going *back* to Earth," Okwembu says, her voice filled with wonder.

Mikhail smiles. "And we need the *Shinso Maru* to do it. You're going to deliver that ship to us, whether you want to or not."

He's talking about the asteroid catcher, the one currently in orbit around the station. And with Resin out there, they'll never have a better opportunity to take it. The pieces are starting to slot into place. The *Shinso Maru* is one of the oldest ships we have. It's a dinosaur, a relic, something that should have been replaced decades ago.

Those operating systems—they must be what the ship runs on. Somehow, these people are going to use Okwembu to gain access to the ship.

"Why me?" Okwembu says. "There must be dozens of people who can use Ellipsis."

"There aren't. We've looked. If there's anyone around who still knows how to use it, we can't find them. Dead or missing, we don't know." He shrugs.

"This is…" Carver says, trailing off.

"But I don't understand," Okwembu says. "We've run data on Earth before. There's nothing down there any more."

Mikhail doesn't answer her, and she bows her head, as if thinking hard. Then she composes herself, locking eyes with Mikhail.

"I'm done with this station," she says, and it's impossible not to hear the bitterness in her voice. "It doesn't want to be saved."

"So you'll help us?" says Mikhail. He sounds wary, like he's expecting a trick. Like it shouldn't be this easy.

"Gladly," Okwembu says. She cocks her head. "Tell me about Earth. Tell me what you've found."

Mikhail turns to the men holding us. "Get them out of here."

"Hey!" says Anna. But we're hustled away, marched off as

Okwembu and Mikhail huddle together. Someone is working with a plasma cutter above us, and, as we pass underneath, sparks prickle my face.

None of this makes any sense. They can't use the *Shinso* for re-entry. It's got no heat shielding, nothing that'll stop it from burning up in the atmosphere. And even if they make it down, how are they going to survive? We *know* Earth is a dead shell: a world of dust storms and frozen wastelands. That's why my father went down there in the first place—to see if he and his crew could make a part of the planet habitable again.

But he didn't succeed. The mission was a failure. So why does Mikhail think humans will be able to survive down there? What have he and his people found?

I want to talk to Carver, see if he can help me figure this out, but he's too far ahead of me.

My eyes are drawn to something at the back of the room—two people, hunched over a machine of some kind. At first, I think it must be a bomb—my mind kicking into overdrive—but then I see it's something else. There are old-fashioned screens on it, displaying odd shapes, like spiky blots of ink. And there's a keyboard, jutting out from the main body. There are two antennae on top, swaying gently. Before I get a better look, the machine is out of sight.

Another piece of the puzzle, and I have no idea where it fits.

Our captors march us to a corner of the room. Carver, Anna and I are shoved up against the wall, our faces are pressed into it. The men spin us around, then push us down. My bound hands are cramping behind me, sending little darts of pain up my arms. Anton is watching us, sitting on a nearby crate, his stinger resting on his knee.

Carver's brow furrows. "I don't get it," he says, more to himself than to us. "There's no heat shielding on that thing."

"I know," I say. "They'll never make it."

"What's happening?" Anna says. "Why are they talking about old computer systems?"

Carver shrugs. "It's for the *Shinso*. But they'll burn up before they get halfway down. Why do you think nobody's..."

He stops. There's the strangest look on his face.

"What is it?" I say.

"The asteroid. That's genius."

Anna glances at me. "Do you understand a single thing he's saying?"

"They're going to use the asteroid as a heat shield," Carver says, his voice filled with wonder. "They're going to ride it all the way down."

53

Riley

"Is that even possible?" Anna says.

"In theory," Carver replies. "Something's gotta burn up. If they can go down asteroid first, then that's what'll catch fire."

"That's insane," I say.

"Hey," says Anton. Our voices must have risen, and he's looking over sharply at us. Carver subsides, shifting his shoulders to stop his bound hands hurting.

"What makes them think they can go back?" I say, barely speaking above a whisper. "What do they know that we don't?"

Carver shrugs. "Beats me."

Anna leans in. "But if they've figured out a way to survive on Earth, why haven't they taken it to the council? Why do they need to *hijack* the asteroid catcher?"

Carver grimaces. "Because we can't fit the entire station into the *Shinso*'s escape pods."

We stare at him.

"Think about it," he says. "They can use the asteroid as a heat shield, but they'll still be travelling a billion miles an hour. They'll never be able to land the ship. Their only shot is to bail out."

Of course. Asteroid catchers have escape pods, but there aren't that many of them. They're designed to carry the small crew of the asteroid catcher, maybe a few more. You could get everybody left on Outer Earth onto an asteroid catcher, but only a few of them would make it to the ground. These people—Mikhail and Anton and the rest of them, along with Okwembu now—are just putting themselves at the front of the queue.

"Earthers," Carver whispers.

"What?"

"That's what we should call them. They want to get back to Earth, right? So they're Earthers."

Anton's become bored. He's still sitting on his crate, but he's fiddling with his stinger, slipping the clip in and out with a rhythmic clicking. Our legs aren't bound, but there's no way we're going to slip past him.

Anna sees me looking. "If we're going to get out of here, we need to get these cuffs off," she says, keeping her voice low. She shakes her shoulders, frustrated with the bonds. "See anything?"

I look around, hunting for something we can use. Might as well try and teleport away—there are no tools within reach, no scissors or knives we could use. Not that Anton would let us try anyway.

I lean over a little too far to my right, and overbalance. I almost fall on my side, only just managing to pull myself back. As I do, I catch sight of the wall.

It's made up of interlocking metal panels. The panels are old, dented, and the edge of the nearest one is bent outwards a little. It's not sharp, but it's rough and rusted.

I scoot across, lifting my backside up to move myself along. Anton is still tinkering with his stinger.

"Riley," Carver says from behind me. "What are you doing?"

I push my back up against the edge, my bound wrists against it. "Using friction," I mutter.

I brace myself, and begin moving my arms up and down, sawing the zip tie against the edge as fast as I can.

"*Really?*" says Carver.

Anton looks up.

I freeze. My wrists are still tightly bound. I can feel his eyes on me. *He's going to see you've moved. It's over.*

Anton grimaces, as if our presence offends him. He goes back to his stinger.

I keep sawing, trying to go as fast as I can without making too much noise. I grit my teeth as the spot between my wrists heats up. As I do so, the zip tie snaps. Blood rushes back into my hands, pins and needles dancing under the skin.

"You're crazy," Carver says. It comes out as a hissed whisper.

"It's our only shot."

Anna is shaking her head. "Shot is what we'll be, if we go through with this."

Anton is picking something out of his teeth now. There's no point doing this slowly. If I'm going to take him down, I have to cross the gap before he can call for help. A pressure-point strike should do it. Right on the back of the neck.

The pins and needles swell, shooting up my forearms. I grit my teeth, flexing my fingers, waiting until the pain subsides. I don't know what's worse: the pain, or making myself wait.

Thirty seconds goes by. I get my legs under me, get up on one knee. Anton still hasn't noticed.

"Riley," Carver hisses again.

I spring forward, rocketing to my feet. I'm trying to stay quiet, but Anton looks up almost immediately. His eyes widen, and I see him raising the stinger, lifting it towards me, his mouth opening to cry out.

But I'm way, way too fast for him. I cross the gap in seconds, whipping my right fist around in a long arc, driving it into the back of his neck, aiming for the pressure point.

It doesn't work.

Anton squawks in surprise, clapping his free hand to his neck, toppling off the crate, upending it and spilling its contents. Soil explodes across the ground with a muted hiss. Anton is already getting to his feet, already trying to bring the gun around. I don't give him the chance. I dart forward, driving a knee into his chest. He coughs, hot air blasting into my face. Then I roll off him, and swing my hand a second time into the back of his neck, following it up with a jab to his throat. Nerves and oxygen—shut down.

It disables Anton completely. His eyes roll back, his body twitching.

I lie next to him, breathing hard, waiting for him to move again. He doesn't.

A hand shoots into view, so suddenly that I almost lash out at it. It's Carver—he pulls me to my feet. The world tilts sideways for a second, the blood rushing back to my head. Anna is working on her bonds, sweat beading her forehead as she burns through them on the metal.

Her wrists snap apart. She doesn't waste time, jumping to her feet, and gesturing at us to hurry. Carver pulls me along—I have to blink a few times to get the world to stay put. I glance down at Anton, still on the ground. He's breathing—shallow and irregular, but it's there. A thin line of drool has leaked out of his mouth, staining the floor.

I glance at the overturned crate. It wasn't just filled with soil—there are tiny plants dotted in the debris, half grown, each one sprouting immature bean pods.

My stomach rumbles. We should get out of here while we're still alone, but none of us has eaten for hours, and, if we do make it out, we're going to need food. Working quickly, I strip the beans from the plants, stuffing them into my pockets.

"No time," Carver says.

"Just a second," I say, grabbing another handful of beans.

"We gotta *go*."

We run. We're in the shadow of the kilns now, slipping from one to the other in short bursts. My heart is firmly lodged in my throat. When we reach the end of the line of kilns, I have to stop, just for a second. There are crates stacked here, lined up on wheeled pallets. How are they planning to get this—all of this—onto the *Shinso*?

"Where's the exit?" I say to Carver.

But he's not looking at me. Instead, he's looking back down the line of kilns. Where a child is standing, staring at us. A young girl, frozen in mid-step.

Everything stops. Even the noise from the crowd fades away.

The girl opens her mouth. I can see her getting ready to scream, can feel Carver tense alongside me. But then she tilts her head, her eyes narrowed, looking right at me. "You're the lady who blew up her dad."

My eyes go wide. It's Ivy. The girl from the Caves.

"That's right," Anna says, giving Ivy a radiant smile. "She's the lady who blew up her dad. I'm her friend Anna, and he's Aaron. It's nice to meet you."

The girl nods, as if all of this was the most normal thing in the world. "I got bored with the grown-ups," she says, rocking back and forth on her heels. She stops, looks from me to Anna, then back again.

There's a yell, over from where we were sitting against the metal sheeting. Anton. His voice is hoarse, but unmistakeable. *Shit*. I should have squeezed harder, knocked him out properly.

I turn back to Ivy, on the verge of telling her to run as fast as she can, when the first of them comes around the crates. He starts to yell, a noise which is cut off as Carver jabs him hard in the throat. He goes down, heaving, banging his head on the side of the opened crate as he does so. It overbalances, then topples off the pallet, spraying more soil across the floor.

Ivy is pushing up against the wall. I'm not sure what's open wider: her mouth or her eyes. More running feet, charging towards us. They'll be on us in seconds. And they're coming from *both* directions—from where we were up against the metal sheeting, and from over by the entrance. Hemmed in by the crates and the kilns, we're in a bad place to run from.

Anna is in a half-crouch, one hand hovering over the floor, outstretched fingers just touching it. "We split up," she says. "Go in three different directions."

"Won't work," Carver says. "Too many of them."

Anton comes round the corner.

His face is pale, the skin on his throat a blotchy red. But he's awake, and angry. He's at the head of a pack, all of them armed with lengths of lead pipe or small blades. In a few seconds, they're going to be on top of us.

So I do the only thing I can think of doing.

I drop to one knee in front of Ivy, and put a hand on her cheek. Her skin is smooth under my touch, as warm as a kiss.

"Honey," I say. "We're going to play a game. OK? No matter what happens, remember it's just a game."

Before she can react, I scoop her up, hoisting her to shoulder height. I wrap my left arm around her neck, pushing her throat into the crook of my arm, just like I did with Anton.

Then I pull tight.

54

Prakesh

Roger stands in the dim light, looking around him. Prakesh tries very hard not to move a single muscle.

Seconds tick by. Prakesh becomes exquisitely aware of every part of his body, down to his fingertips, which are just touching the grimy floor. He stopped breathing some time ago, and his chest has begun to ache.

Roger scratches his nose. Then he actually yawns. Prakesh has to suppress the urge to bolt from his hiding place and throttle him. He has to push it back, telling himself to stay put.

Roger turns and walks away. "Nothing here, either," he shouts, as if he'd spent the past few moments looking in a completely new area.

He walks out of sight. Prakesh waits ten seconds, counting them off. It's agony, and his mind can't help racing ahead of him, constructing a scenario where Roger and Julian and the rest of them are watching the gap in silence, waiting for him to make a move.

But he can't stay here. Sooner or later, one of them is going to think about looking on the other side of the metal sheet, and then it's all over. He has to get to the exit.

He allows himself two quick breaths. Then, with his blood hammering through his veins, he takes the gap. He runs bent over, doing everything he can to keep his footsteps silent, not daring to look round. He keeps his eyes locked on the barrel.

He's almost there when Julian spots him.

Prakesh hears him yell out from the other side of the hangar, quickly followed by the sound of running feet. His body doesn't react fast enough, and slams shoulder first into the barrel. It's empty, *bonging* as it bounces away from him. A shot from Julian's stinger rings out, the bullet ricocheting off the ceiling above him. How many bullets does the man have left? No time to find out, no time to do anything except sprint for the exit.

Prakesh can hear them behind him, all of them running, all of them coming straight towards him. They've got the advantage—with the plasma cutter, they'll have all the light they need. He can see his shadow spread out, its arms blurring as he runs, but most of the way ahead of him is cloaked in darkness. If he hits another metal sheet, or runs into one of the pieces of scaffolding…

"Get back here!" Julian sounds like he's lost his mind. He tries to fire again, but this time there's nothing but an audible click. He's out of bullets. Not that it matters: he couldn't hit anything anyway. And if Prakesh doesn't get out of here soon, these people are going to catch him and beat him to death. He's as sure of this as he is of his own heartbeat.

A shadow, darker than the rest, looms in front of him. He doesn't have time to see what it is. He hurdles it, the toe of his right shoe just brushing its surface. If he were Riley, he'd probably tuck into a roll on the landing, preserving his momentum. But he's not Riley, and he lands awkwardly, very nearly falling flat on his face. His throat is a parched desert, cracking under the searing wind of his breath. *Come on, come on, come on.*

A figure lunges at him from a set of scaffolding on his right. Prakesh only just manages to duck under the man's arms, lashing out blindly. He feels his fist hit an arm, hears a soft grunt of anger.

There. The exit. Prakesh can just make it out, can just see the tiny green light on the keypad next to it. He sucks in another acid breath, and runs even faster. There's a giant crash behind him, as if one of Julian's men has run right into one of the stacks of metal pipes.

And as Prakesh reaches the door, as his hand finds the keypad. *Riley's birthday.* He punches in the numbers, *2104*, fingers fumbling on the keys.

The keypad gives a dull beep. Incorrect code.

He wants to laugh. It's absurd. He made the code so it would be easy to remember.

The footsteps behind him fill the world, thundering closer. At the very last second, Prakesh realises what he's done. He switches the code, punching in *0421*, slamming his hand on the ENTER button.

With a whining hiss, the door begins to slide back, letting in an intensely bright ray of light from the Air Lab.

Prakesh doesn't wait for it to open fully. He squeezes through the gap, blinking against the harsh light. He's vaguely aware of people on the Air Lab side, but doesn't have time to look. He reaches for the keypad on this side of the door, punches in the numbers, hits ENTER.

Nothing happens.

Prakesh's already overstretched mind nearly snaps in two. The door continues to slide away, and it's only after a second or two that he realises it has to go all the way before he can close it again.

He looks up, without wanting to. Julian and Roger are sprinting for the door. Fifty feet away, closing fast.

Prakesh can do nothing but watch them. As the door clicks into its fully open position, his hand is already on the keypad, his fingers jumping to the numbers. He hits ENTER, and the door begins to shut, closing agonisingly slowly. There's no way it's going to shut in time. Prakesh tells himself to move, but his feet have stopped listening to him. All he can do is watch.

55

Riley

"Riley, what are you doing?" Carver says.

I don't know. I'm making it up as I go along. Anna is looking at me like I've gone insane, her eyes darting between me and the approaching Earthers.

I can feel Ivy's throat pulsing in the crook of my arm. She's dead still.

Anton comes to a juddering halt, the men and women behind him nearly knocking into him.

"Stay back," he says over his shoulder. His eyes are locked on me and the girl, shot through with fear and fury.

"Gods, she's got—"

"Let her go."

I raise my chin, staring them down. "Listen up," I say, raising my voice so that it fills the room. "Everybody back off. We're walking out of here, and I don't want to see anybody in our way."

Ivy is still frozen. I can't tell if she's scared solid, or just playing along.

Mikhail arrives, pushing his way through the crowd, thunder on his face. He ignores the girl, focusing on me. "Put her down," he says slowly.

"You think I'm joking?" I say, hefting her higher, using the surface of my arm to lift her chin. "I'll do it." Somehow, I manage to keep the trembling out of my voice.

A man falls out of the crowd. It's Jamal. There's anger on his face—anger, and a terror so raw it takes my breath away.

"Please," he says. It's the kind of whisper that stops everyone speaking. "Please don't hurt her."

"She won't."

Okwembu steps out behind Jamal—the latest arrival to our little game, calm and composed. Mikhail tries to speak, but she places a hand on his arm. Carver and Anna have drawn closer to me, almost touching on either side, their bodies tense.

"Neither of them will," Okwembu says. "They don't have it in them."

She turns Jamal's face towards her, and smiles gently. "Your little one is going to be fine."

Her words snap Carver out of his trance. He steps in front of me. "Only if everybody locks their feet to the floor," he says. "We're going to walk out of here. If anybody gets in our way, we'll kill her."

A small part of me burns with revulsion at his words, but I ignore it. There's no other way out of this.

Okwembu's smile gets even wider. "Two of the young people in front of you have never killed before," she says to the crowd. "The other one, the one holding the girl, is Riley Hale. You probably know her. She *has* killed before—she murdered her tracer crew leader, and then own father. But she did it to save Outer Earth, and she feels so guilty that she'd rather die before taking another life."

She turns to face me. Her expression is completely neutral. "Did I miss anything, Ms. Hale?"

Right then, Ivy decides she's had enough.

Maybe she realises that it isn't a game, or that it's not fun to play-act any more. She screams. And it's the kind of high-pitched scream that makes you want to put your hands over your ears and scream back, just to shut out the noise.

I let her go. I don't put her down—I *drop* her, not meaning to, but watching it happen anyway, horror rising inside me. The girl's face goes from surprise to terror in about a third of a second, and then she slams knees first into the ground. Jamal goes from standing to sprinting in the same amount of time, running for his daughter.

Mikhail steps in front of Okwembu and points at us. The anger on his face is like steam trapped in a broken vent.

"Take them."

56

Riley

We run. Back down the line of kilns, ahead of the mob. A hunk of metal bounces off the ground in front of me, and another smacks me in the small of the back. I don't dare look around.

Carver is alongside me, his breathing hot and hard. Anna is just behind. We're nearing the back of the hangar, which either means we're going to have to double back or go all the way around, outpacing the mob.

We come to the back wall, and hang a hard left. There's an old slag container pushed up against the wall—big and clunky, open at the top, as tall as I am.

"Over there," I shout, pointing. Carver follows my gaze, then looks at me like I've gone mad.

"We can't hide in there!" he shouts back.

"She means above it," says Anna.

He looks up. Hanging over the container is a claw-scoop, the kind that looks like a giant, stubby fingered hand. The arm attached to it extends upwards, a mess of thick cables and pneumatic sections. The arm reaches its apex about twenty feet up, before curving down and terminating in a control cab, bristling with levers and dials. But a few feet above the top of the arm is the metal frame of the gantry.

Before Carver can argue, I scrabble up the side of the container. I take a split second to get my feet on the rim—the crowd is closer now, shouts coming from everywhere, Mikhail's voice roaring above them—and then I jump.

My fingers snag one of the cables on the crane's arm. For a horrible moment I can't get a good grip. Then I lock in, and the rounded part of the scoop slams into my torso. My legs swing in space, but I use the momentum as they come back to push myself higher, my shoes scrabbling for purchase on the metal. The joints above me groan in protest, like an ancient monster, woken from its sleep. I'm moving as fast as I can, trying to climb, trying to make space for Carver. He jumps, and there's an enormous bang as he grabs the scoop. It lurches, swinging like a pendulum, the metal under my hands vibrating.

Anna cries out in alarm. I look back and down over my shoulder—they've got her. Two of them, Hisako and a man. He's holding her around the chest, pinning her arms to her sides, and Hisako is trying to capture her thrashing legs.

I don't know what to do. If I drop down now, the mob will be on me before I can get back on the crane arm. But I can't just leave her there.

Anna solves the problem for me. She twists her body to the side, slipping out of the man's grip, lashing out with her foot. She connects with Hisako's stomach, and I hear the woman's breath leave her body in a pained *whoop*.

Anna stumbles away, dropping into a fighting stance. Hisako and the man are between her and the crane arm. They're trying to flank her, sidestepping, Hisako rolling her shoulders like she's been waiting for a fight. And there are others coming up behind her.

Anna looks around, then up at us. "Keep going!" she shouts. "I'll find you."

With that, she launches herself at one of the nearby stacks of crates, scrambling onto the top of it. Then she's jumping along them, the pallets rocking under her weight. Angry shouts follow her, trailing in her wake. She takes one last look back. Then she's gone.

I was never the best climber. That was always Amira. She could get up a sheer wall, given a little time and a good pair of shoes. But she did teach me a few things. Even as I start to climb, I'm spotting handholds, seeing parts of the arm I can slip my fingers over or jam a foot into. The route unfolds like a puzzle. Someone fires a stinger, and I hear the bullet *ping* off the wall. I'm less worried about being shot than I am of falling, but it still makes me jump.

I hear someone yelling to go round the other side, to get the ladders.

"There's a *ladder*?" Carver says.

"Shut up and climb!"

My fingers nearly slip off one of the ledges on the metal tube, the rust scraping across my skin. I hiss with pain, and my left leg swings out into space, threatening to take my body with it. I put everything I can into stopping the swing, pulling it back onto the arm. I'm breathing too fast, and I have to force myself to find the next hold, to keep going.

The arm starts to curve as I climb, bending inward on its arc. It makes things easier. The gantry is almost within reach now, although I don't dare to look further down it. If I see people running along it towards us...

Carver is right behind me, climbing so close that he has to wait a half-second for me to lift my feet so he can use their positions as handholds. I'm at the apex of the arm, steadying myself, when I feel him slip.

Time slows, then all but stops. He's clear of the arm, holding onto nothing. He has the most indignant expression on his face, like he can't *believe* the handhold betrayed him.

Usually, when you're climbing something, it's just you and the wall. Nothing else matters. Every so often, when you're high above the ground and balancing on a knife edge, it's just you and the hold you're reaching for. Everything else is blackness, and silence.

Right now, right this second, there's just my hand, and Carver's.

I reach for him. I put every ounce of power into it, but my hand is too far away and it's stuck in its own gravity well, drained of momentum.

His fingers touch mine. Move inch by inch up my hand. Every muscle in my arm is its own entity, hanging in space, burning with power.

And then his hand is gripped in mine, and he's swinging, transcribing an arc under the crane. The noise rushes back and his enormous weight pulls my stomach into the metal, knocking the air out of me. He's screaming, a yell that is half adrenaline, half terror, so heavy he nearly pulls me right off the crane. Somehow, I manage to hold on, using my thighs and the tops of my feet to anchor myself to it.

I swing him back, aiming for the downward part of the arm, and he snags a cable. His chest is rising and falling with jagged, jerky motions. When he lets go of my hand, my arm starts shaking uncontrollably. But he starts climbing straight away, and in moments we're balanced on the gantry, our feet planted on the metal railing.

I look up, and my heart sinks. The ladders weren't tall enough to reach the gantry, but they're tall enough to get to the top of a stack of slag containers, piled high in a corner of the hangar. There are already people on the top, and they're pulling up one of the ladders—intending, no doubt, to use it to reach the gantry. The crane we climbed is at the back of the room, towards the centre, and the ladders are being positioned ahead of us. I spin round, nearly losing my balance, and put a hand on the metal to steady myself.

"You OK?" I say to Carver, who looks more unsteady than I do.

He nods. We start heading down the gantry, away from the ladders, moving in a weird half-jumping gait that keeps us on the struts. There's no sign of Anna on the floor below us. Under our feet, I can feel the gantry vibrating as our pursuers finally climb onto it. We keep moving, and before long we've reached the wall closest to the entrance. But it's a dead end—the gantry runs up against the wall, and there's no way down, no handy claw-arm or ladder in sight.

Real panic starts to build inside me. I think of Mikhail's face again, of steam trapped in a vent, growing hotter and hotter.

The miniature train car. The one on the gantry tracks that was hanging over us when we were brought in. It's at ninety degrees to us. That part of the gantry is separate from ours, too far away to jump to, and the car itself is all the way down the other end.

But that's not what gets my attention. It's the car's power line: a single cable, thick as my wrist, sheathed in black rubber and connected to a power box, a foot or so above our heads.

Carver sees where I'm looking. "If we climb along it, it'll snap in two."

"Better idea."

I squeeze past him, nearly overbalancing, and put my hands on the power box. The cable goes right into it, into a slot bracketed by thick plastic. I grab the cable and pull, as hard as I can; he joins in, his muscles bulging.

The gantry under our feet has started to sway slightly, bending as too many people converge on one spot. I hear Mikhail shout something, and realise that not only is he up there with them, but that they're closer than I thought.

"Riley, please tell me we're not doing what I think we're going to do," Carver says. We're both wiggling the cable, teasing it out of its socket.

"I'll hold onto you, OK?" I say. "You're heavier."

"Oh, *thanks*."

Another shot rings out. This one is closer, ricocheting off the power box itself. Slowly, ever so slowly, the cable gets looser, like a rotten tooth coming out of a gum. I can see the black edge of the rubber peeking over the white plastic.

There's a scream from behind us, and a second later there's a sickening thud from below. Someone took a plunge.

"Careful," Mikhail shouts. He sounds like he's right on top of us. This time, I do steal a glance over my shoulder. He's a few feet away, his arms out, trying not to overbalance. There are three men behind him, all armed with stingers, all pointed at us.

"You've got nowhere to go," he says. The words are a growl.

The cable snaps out of its plastic socket. Carver yanks on it twice, making sure his grip is steady. I wrap my arms around his waist. Mikhail's eyes go wide, and he takes a wobbling step forward.

I close my eyes. Carver jumps.

57

Riley

It feels like we free-fall forever. Like the cable in Carver's hands is attached to nothing.

That doesn't last long. The cable goes taut, snapping so tight I nearly lose my grip on Carver, and then we're swinging, just like Carver did under the claw-arm, only much faster. The train car on the gantry squeals in protest. I force my eyes open, and see the ground rushing towards us. The cable is too long, and if we don't let go at exactly the right second, we're going to slam into it at full speed.

"Now!" I shout. A split second later, five feet above the ground, Carver lets go of the cable.

I twist my body sideways, letting my right shoulder take the impact. As I roll, I do everything I can to keep my legs out of the way, tucking them up. It hurts like hell. I tumble, pummelled by the ground, and then I'm on my feet, adrenaline fizzing in my veins, sharpening everything in my vision.

We've come down a few steps away from the entrance. Carver is getting up, unsteady on his feet. He's actually laughing, although his eyes are still back on that gantry. Mikhail is ordering his men to the ladders, his face in a rictus of fury.

There are others on the floor, running towards us, but they're some distance away. "Time to go," I say to Carver. I focus the adrenaline rush, my eyes on the big door set into the wall. It's on a roller, way too big for us to push—and right now it's shut tight.

"Where's the door release?" I say.

"Hold them—" Carver says, then stops and tries again, steadying his voice. "Hold them off."

He sprints away, leaving me pushed up against the door, facing down the approaching Earthers. Six of them—two men and four women. No stingers that I can see, just lengths of pipe, and they're approaching cautiously. One of them has a limp, favouring his right ankle, and one of the women looks barely out of her teens.

Janice Okwembu is nowhere to be seen. Not surprising—she always vanishes whenever the action starts.

I step forward, squaring my shoulders. "The first person to try it gets one of those pipes wedged in their throat. Any takers?"

The group stops, hovering a few steps away. The young woman takes a step forward, her face set. Above and behind her, I can see Mikhail's group racing across the gantry, heading back towards the ladders.

"You think we'd just let you go?" says the woman. She's got one of the pipes, and, as she takes another step forward, she grips it in two hands to steady herself. "After what you did to Jamal's girl?"

I step forward to meet her. She refuses to step back. The others, emboldened by her example, line up on either side of her.

Better hurry, Carver.

The door gives a huge rumble, and begins to move on its rollers behind me. The woman sucks in a breath—like she really, really didn't want to have to do this—then hefts the pipe and swings it at me, in a horizontal sweep. I was looking back towards the door, and only just catch the swing out of the corner of my eye. I dodge back, and the pipe whooshes by me, grazing my chest. The woman curses, tries to bring the pipe back, but I'm already running, with Carver on my heels, out of the door and away.

The Earthers chase us, shouting at us to stop, but we're in the open now—and there's no way they're outpacing a pair of tracers in the open. Their cries grow fainter and fainter behind us. It's impossible to work out where we are—the corridors around us could mark anywhere on the station. It's only when we emerge onto one of the stairwells that I realise we're in New Germany. The Caves are below us, and the Tzevya border is off to our left.

The power's off in the stairwell, and there's that stench again, wafting up from the bottom. We stop on a landing, breathing hard. The light is out, but as we arrive it flickers back on. An old woman is leaning up against the wall, dead eyes locked on the ceiling. Resin has sprouted out of her mouth like an obscene afterbirth, almost gluing her head to the wall.

We look away, and I catch Carver staring at me.

"What?" I say.

He shakes his head, as if banishing unpleasant thoughts. "Where did Anna go? She's not still in there?"

"I don't know. She'll be OK." I can't say whether this is true or not.

"Right," he says. "And we need to get back to your psycho doctor anyway."

I can feel the incisions in my knees throbbing. Part of me is amazed that I'm still whole, that Knox hasn't died yet. "What do we do then?"

"We get him to Apex. We warn them about the Earthers."

"Do you think Anna was right? That they're behind Resin?"

He shakes his head again. "No idea, Ry."

Without another word, we start running again, pushing our exhausted bodies further, heading back down the ring.

58

Knox

Morgan Knox doesn't know how he gets hold of the syringe. But it's in his hand, his thumb resting on the depressed plunger. It takes all his effort just to remember what he's supposed to do with it.

Tube thoracostomy. That was it. He's got to drain some of the fluid on his lungs.

Every breath sends a constricting black corona into his vision, and, with each one, the corona gets bigger, narrowing his sight down to a small, bright circle.

He's lying on his back on the surgery floor, holding the syringe up to the light. It's a black shape, the needle appearing to grow before his eyes. He flips the cap off with trembling fingers, then lowers the syringe to his side. He's going to have to punch right through his tunic.

His right index finger feels out a space. There—between the second and third ribs on his right-hand side. He'll be able to get the needle into the pleural space, the area between the lungs, draining off some of the fluid. It'll buy him some time to address the underlying pathology, assuming he can stay awake to do it.

He doesn't know if it'll be enough. But if it doesn't do something, he'll fade away, and he can't allow that. Not while Janice Okwembu is still walking around.

The needle rests against the fabric of his tunic. Knox can't take enough of a breath to prepare for it, so he doesn't bother. He just pushes the needle in, right through the skin.

It's the worst pain he's ever felt in his life, slicing right through his chest cavity and out the other side. He can't scream. He can't do anything. It takes him a moment to get up the strength needed to pull the plunger back, and when he does so, the agony is almost unbearable.

He pulls until the plunger stops, then rips the needle out. There's another feeling now, beyond the pain: a searing stab of cold, right into the centre of his being. It's air, travelling in and out of the tiny hole he made. He holds the syringe up, pushing back against the darkness in his vision. The space in the syringe is filled with greyish-black ooze.

He lets it go, his hand dropping to the floor. He should do it again, withdraw more fluid, but he can't face going through that pain again. He concentrates on getting as much oxygen as he can from the tiny breaths he's able to suck into his lungs.

The corona leaps forward, driving his sight to a hot pinpoint of white light. Then even that vanishes, and Knox is gone.

59

Prakesh

Julian only just makes it through the doors.

He has to turn sideways, jamming his body into the crack. His one hand—the one not holding the stinger—lashes out at Prakesh. His face is contorted with rage.

Roger's hands enter the crack, wrapping around the frame, trying to push the door back. The motor starts complaining, grinding as it pushes against the obstacle. Julian growls in fury, swinging his arm again, his fingers hooked into claws.

It's impossible not to think of what happened to Oren Darnell. He was crushed by the massive doors leading to the Core, caught between them while trying to chase down Riley. This isn't the same thing: the door and the motor behind it aren't strong enough to do permanent damage to Julian. And, Prakesh can see, it's not enough to hold him either. Julian is pushing through, inch by inch, the growl turning to a groan as he fights through the gap.

Prakesh starts to back away. It's only after he's taken a few steps that he remembers that Julian is out of bullets.

The realisation floods through him, an electrical storm crackling through his muscles. Julian wants him? Fine. Prakesh strides towards him, grabs his upper arm and *pulls.*

With a squeal, Julian pops out of the door. Prakesh collapses backwards, and Julian lands on top of him, his skin hot and greasy, stinking of adrenaline. Prakesh sees, with unsettling clarity, the door close on Roger's fingers. He hears a cry of pain, and then the fingers are gone and the door clicks shut.

He tries to push Julian off of him. He's rewarded by Julian's fist driving into the side of his face, cracking against his cheekbone. The world flashes grey. Prakesh is dimly aware of another pain at the back of his skull, where he must have impacted with the floor after Julian hit him. He has just enough time to process this when Julian hits him again.

This time, the man's fist lands right on Prakesh's upper lip, splitting it open. Blood, hot and bitter, coats his tongue.

Julian's hands wrap around Prakesh's neck, thumbs digging into his throat. Julian is shouting—a sound filled with insane fear. Prakesh realises this distantly, almost academically, as if Julian is a plant specimen that has developed an interesting characteristic. Another thought follows it: he can't breathe. Can't get enough oxygen into his lungs. It's important, Prakesh knows it is, but he doesn't know what to do about it. Julian's face is inches from his, spittle flying from his mouth.

Prakesh can't feel the pressure on his throat any more. He's at the bottom of a deep, dark hole, looking up at a dwindling circle of light.

Something appears in the light, above Julian. No, not something. *Someone.*

With the same distant recognition, Prakesh sees that it's Suki. She has a fire extinguisher in her hands, a squat, red cylinder, heavy and rusted. She holds it horizontally, one hand gripping its nozzle assembly, the other holding the base. Prakesh notes all this, and wonders what she plans to do with it. There's no fire, and that's what you use fire extinguishers for...

With a desperate cry, Suki slams the extinguisher down onto Julian's head.

He stops shouting, and the most curious expression crosses his face. Part surprise, part anger. He doesn't look around, not even when Suki hits him again. The second blow turns him into a ragdoll, and he collapses on top of Prakesh, spasming.

The fingers around Prakesh's throat loosen and fall away. Oxygen comes rushing back, and, with it, reality. He shoves Julian off him, and the tech thumps onto the floor.

Suki raises the extinguisher again, tears falling down her face. She's shouting, too, as if Julian's fear fled his body and found a home in hers. Just before she brings the extinguisher down, Prakesh grabs her wrists. He doesn't remember getting off the floor, and the extinguisher bounces off his chest. It hurts.

She tries to shove him aside, tries to bully past him with the extinguisher. He still has hold of her wrists, and he grips them even tighter.

She drops the extinguisher. It lands nozzle first, and shoots out a spurt of white foam as the handle makes contact with the ground. Prakesh lets go of Suki's wrists, more in surprise than anything else. She yelps, then covers her mouth with her hands. Above them, her eyes are enormous.

"It's OK," Prakesh says. They barely count as words: his throat is a piece of rust-caked metal. His skin feels as if a steel band is locked around his neck, hot and constricting. He tries again. "It's OK, Suki. You're all right."

She wavers for a moment, then hugs him, burying her face in his shoulder. A part of Prakesh doesn't believe any of this is real. The lights are too bright, every sensation magnified.

"What about the others?" Suki says, her voice muffled in the folds of his lab coat. "Roger? Iko?"

"Trapped. They're not getting out of the Food Lab." He looks over towards the door, half expecting to see Roger forcing it open with his fingertips. But it's shut tight, the light on the keypad blinking a reassuring red.

Suki pulls apart from him. She opens her mouth to speak, but she's interrupted by the sound of cheering. She and Prakesh turn, and see the other techs charging across the floor towards them.

Prakesh tries to speak, tries to raise his voice. He wants to tell them that it isn't necessary, that any of them would have done the same thing. He wants to point them towards Suki, tell them how she saved him. But as they surround him, as they pound him on the back and reach for his hand, laughing with relief, shouting his name, he wonders if that's true. For the first time in forever, Prakesh Kumar feels like a hero.

60

Riley

Knox has got worse.

I can hear him breathing the moment we enter his surgery. There's a guttural quality to it, like his larynx is falling apart. The dark skin of his face is pallid as a block of tofu, stained with dark drips of Resin. He's managed to crawl halfway into the surgery.

Carver fills up a canteen with water while I examine Knox. I fold my jacket underneath his head—it helps still his ragged breathing a little.

"Here," Carver says, passing me the sloshing canteen. As I drink deep, he nods to Knox. "We should go. The people I've seen like that...they don't last too long."

I take a slug of water. "How long?" I say, trying to keep the tremor out of my voice. Almost manage it, too.

He shrugs. "An hour. If that."

"I can't get him another shot of the drugs in an hour. I wouldn't even know where to start."

"There's plenty in Apex."

"That's a two-hour run. At least. And that's without having to carry someone. What about the monorail?"

For a moment, Carver's eyes flicker. Then he sighs in frustration. "Not running, last I heard. We could find a train car at the top of the sector, but it could take us most of an hour if there isn't one nearby. And if we don't luck out, we won't have time to do anything else. Is there any way we could get those bombs out of you?"

I shake my head. "He said that if anybody but him tried to take them out, they'd blow." I suddenly have a picture of a bomb—a big one, a real monster—with all its tangled wires.

"How sure are you?"

"I'm sure, all right?" I say, anger flaring, thinking of Kev. I force myself to walk away, leaning my hands on the operating table. "Get out of here, Carver. If you stick to the top level, you should get to Apex before—"

"I'm not leaving. Not when you're like this. Not when you're making stupid decisions."

I stare at him.

"I'm not just talking about this death wish of yours," he says. When I don't respond, he shakes his head. "The kid, Riley."

"I am *not* going to have you be angry with me for what happened back there," I say. "We've got other things to worry about."

He kicks the leg of the operating table, hard. The bang echoes around the room. His voice follows it, raised in an angry shout. "You almost strangled her!"

I can see the fury building in his face. I'm reminded of how much he keeps hidden away—when I told him about Amira's death last year, he nearly throttled me.

"How could you do something like that?" he says. "She was a *kid*." He turns away, rubbing the back of his head, his other arm on his hip. It's such an exaggerated posture of frustration that I almost laugh, but then he turns back to me and the look on his face kills the laughter.

"I was *bluffing*," I say.

"We should have come up with something else. If I'd had two more seconds..."

"We didn't have two seconds."

"You're out of control. You're not thinking straight, and you're not letting us help you. This whole time, you've been trying to handle everything yourself. Remember what Amira taught us? Crew first, Riley. Dancers over everything."

"Amira *betrayed us.*"

"And that makes everything she did null and void, does it?" He shakes his head. "You don't get it. Amira was the greatest teacher anybody could ever have, but she went bad, and she went bad because she didn't trust us. She bottled all her feelings up inside, just like you're doing now."

"I'm not her." The words are hissed through gritted teeth.

He talks over me. "She took it all on herself. All that responsibility. You're doing the same thing."

I turn away from him, trying to shut him out. It doesn't work.

"But—no, *listen to me,* Riley—you're not responsible for what happened to Kev. Amira was self-defence. And your father?"

"Shut up, Carver."

"Nobody should be in that position."

"*Stop.*"

There are a million things I want to say, and a million more I don't even want to think about. Around us, the station is horribly silent.

"You don't get to send me off and die by yourself," he says. "Not happening. Not ever."

And then I'm kissing him. Hard.

My lips land on his with such force that it nearly knocks him over. I wrap my arms around his neck and pull tight. My tongue finds his, slipping past his open lips. It's only when he starts to return the kiss, a shocked second later, that the full knowledge of what I'm doing comes rushing in.

And yet, I can't stop. I don't want to. I know it's wrong, but the need for human contact, the need for something *normal,* is impossibly powerful. It's all I want. I want to bury myself in his arms and forget about everything. I soak up the kiss like water, like I've been wandering thirsty for months.

It's Carver who pulls away. He does it gently, leaving just a hint of warmth on my lips. It takes him a moment to speak. "Riley..." he says.

My cheeks are burning with guilt. All I can think of is Prakesh, lying next to me in our bed in Chengshi, his eyes closed, his mouth slightly parted as he sleeps. I can see the image clearly, as if I'm right there next to him.

I hear Carver suck in a quick intake of breath. My first reaction is to glance at Knox, but he's still out, his chest trembling. When I look back to Carver, I see a strange glint in his eyes.

"Carver, listen, I didn't mean—"

"All right, what if I had this thing?" he says, then stops. "But it's not ready yet," he mutters, more to himself than to me.

"What?" I ask, more confused than I'm willing to admit. I have to repeat myself before he looks up.

"The station's pretty empty now, right?" he asks.

I think of the thousands killed by Resin, and shudder. "It'll still take us too long to get to Apex."

"No, no, listen: anybody left alive—they aren't going to be hanging around in the corridors, are they?"

"Probably not, but what difference does it make?"

"It's perfect," he says. "I should have thought of this ages ago. Sorry about that."

He jerks a thumb at Knox. "Can you pick him up and bring him to the main corridor? I need to go and check on something."

I try to make sense of everything he just said, and come up with nothing. Carver doesn't wait for my response; he's already heading for the doors.

"Carver, wait up," I say. I only just manage to catch him before he runs into the passage. "*Carver*."

"We need to get him to Apex in under an hour, right?"

"Yeah…"

"So I might have a way to do that." He starts to move again, stops. "Only: we might die."

"*Might?*"

"It's no more than a ten per cent chance. Twenty, tops."

"Excuse me?"

"But I think it'll work. Almost positive."

"Carver, now would be a great time to tell me what's going on."

Every second we stand still seems to make him more anxious. "OK, you remember I told you I was working on something big?"

A dim memory surfaces, of our conversation following Mikhail's arrest. "Sort of. Why?"

"Well, this is it. The thing that's big."

Without another word, he bolts.

"Get him to the main corridor," he shouts over his shoulder. "I won't be long."

"Carver!"

But he's gone.

With nothing else to do, I head back into the operating theatre. When I first woke up here, it was clean and ordered—Knox's perfect little world. But it's a mess now, with bottles and medical supplies scattered across the floor.

My mind keeps coming back to the kiss. Every time it does, I push it away. I can deal with it later. I have to. If I give it any attention right now, I'll collapse completely.

It takes me a few minutes to work out how to move Knox. I find myself wondering if it's even safe to move him, if that'll just add to what Resin is doing to his lungs, but it's not like I have an option.

He's my height, but he's heavy. It's impossible not to think of the expression *dead weight*. I have to psych myself up into hoisting him, getting my arms under his and linking my hands across his chest. He moans as I lift him up, and a thin streak of black drool trickles down his chin. I almost let him go, desperate for the slime not to touch my hands, but I force myself to hold on. My legs protest as I drag him out of the room, and his rubber-soled shoes screech as I drag them across the floor, his legs bouncing whenever he hits the edge of a metal plate.

If I wasn't so exhausted, if my neck wasn't starting to hurt from looking back over my shoulder to see where I was going all the time, this would almost be funny.

Somehow, I manage to get through the corridors surrounding the operating theatre. By the time I reach one of the larger corridors, my entire body has become a conductor for pain, a magnet for it. Aches and stinging and a needling itch in the back of my knees.

I drop Knox, and he groans again as his head thumps off the metal. The corridor is deserted. No Carver.

I sit up against the corridor wall, relishing the chance to let my body do nothing for a few minutes, keeping an ear out for any sounds. If the Earthers come, I want to be ready. But outside of the rumble of the station, the only sound is that of a flickering light further down the corridor, the filament buzzing and clicking. After a few moments, it sputters out, leaving that section in darkness.

Knox isn't the only reason to get to Apex quickly. If the Earthers get to the ship dock, if we can't get the people in Apex to mount a defence, they'll overwhelm the remaining stompers, and take the *Shinso*. I still don't know how Okwembu, and her knowledge of old operating systems, is going to help them. If we can't defend the dock, it won't matter.

There's a sound. One I can't place. I open my eyes.

It's a rumbling—distant and dull, like a mythical creature at the bottom of a cave. Is it the Earthers? I bend down to grab Knox and drag him to a hiding place, but then I stop. The rumbling isn't human. It sounds almost like a monorail car. But that's not possible—there's no monorail down here.

The rumble gets louder, revealing details of itself, unfolding into a high-pitched, whining growl. It's not static—it ebbs and flows, revving like...

Like an engine.

Carver.

The blackness further down the corridor is obliterated by a blinding white light as *something* comes round a corner.

The rumble becomes deafening, and it changes to a squeal as the light rushes towards us. Gaping, I flatten myself against the corridor wall. If this isn't Carver, then my life is about to get even more complicated than it is already.

Just as the light seems like it'll swallow us, it swings round, revealing what's behind it. The roar cuts off, grinding back to a low rumble as whatever it is skids to a halt, turning sideways in the corridor. It's Carver, and he's on top of a machine so strange that I have to focus to take it all in.

It has to be seven feet from front to back, with four black wheels. They're huge, each of them a foot and a half across, bracketing a crazy collection of piping and wires and cables, jumbled together like a child's puzzle. At the centre of it all, a massive, grooved steel block. A pipe shooting out of the back spits black blurts of smoke.

Carver straddles the body, his legs splayed out alongside him. His hands are gripping a control stick. He's grinning like a madman.

He shouts over the rumble of the engine: "Like I said. I was working on something big."

61

Riley

I don't get a chance to say anything. The thing's engine gives a massive, grumbling belch and cuts out, spitting a final blast of smoke out of the tailpipe. The corridor stinks of oil, and the silence is almost as loud as the engine was.

Carver thumps the engine block with his foot. "No, no, *start*, you stupid thing."

He reaches down and yanks on a cord, pulling it once, twice. The motor gives a tiny puttering cough, but fails to catch.

"What. The hell. Is this?" I say.

"When it works, I call it the Boneshaker." He's off the vehicle now, crouching down, doing something clanky to its innards.

"*When* it works?"

"Yeah, well, I sort of only turned it on for the first time ten minutes ago."

"Carver…"

"I know what you're thinking," he says, without looking up. He's gone back to his tinkering, his hands jammed deep in the machinery. "How did he manage to build a working four-wheeler in six months? Ow!"

He pulls his hand back with a start. There's a small gash in his thumb, already bleeding. He sucks on it briefly, and plunges it back in.

"Actually, I was thinking that you've finally gone insane," I say.

He continues as if I hadn't said anything. "I just wanted to see if it could be done. I got tired of building little gadgets. I knew I had to work on something bigger."

"So you built *this*? Where did you get the parts?"

"Here and there," he says. "Trade for this, bribe someone for that, steal the other."

I open my mouth to speak, then decide that there's nothing I could say that would sum it all up.

I settle instead for hauling Knox upright. Unbelievably, it feels like he's got even heavier. When I lift him up, he starts coughing, his unconscious body shuddering as his throat tries to get rid of the gunk in his lungs.

I have to shout at Carver more than once to get him to help. We manage to get Knox sitting on the machine. His body is barely upright, his head lolling on his chest. I step back, my skin caked with sweat.

With a muttered prayer, Carver gives the cord another abrupt tug. This time, the motor jumps into life. Carver yanks his hand away, and then the thing is running—coughing and spluttering, but running. Carver pumps his fist and vaults onto the machine, landing in front of the comatose Knox. He tweaks the throttle and backs the machine up, lining it up straight, and then jerks the throttle, revving the engine.

"Climb on," he says. He has to raise his voice to be heard above the roar.

I jab a finger at Knox. "You sure he can ride this thing? It might make him worse."

"It's the only shot we've got. This is the fastest way up the ring."

"You'll never get through the crush!"

"There *is* no crush!"

I stare at him. Because he's right. There isn't. Not any more. The crowds of people that normally clog every public space in the station are gone. They've barricaded themselves inside their habs, shutting themselves away. For the first time in forever, the corridors and galleries are empty.

Before I can stop myself, I'm on top of the machine. *Boneshaker* is right—the vibrations from the motor travel up through my body, rattling my skull. With Knox and Carver on the thing, there's barely enough room for me—my backside is hanging right off the body.

Tracer routes unfold in my mind, corridors and passages that I've run a million times. Jumps I've done, walls I've climbed, stairs I've leapt down. My favourite spots. The ones I always try to avoid. All spread out in my mind, like a map on a desk, one I can run my finger over and plot the best route.

I reach forward and wrap my arms around Carver's midsection, sandwiching Knox between us. He trembles, and I feel a dot of Resin speckle the skin of my arm.

"We'll need to go up through Tzevya," I say. "We don't have time to go the long way round. Go to the end of the corridor, then hang a left."

"What about if we go down by the air exchangers?"

"My way's faster."

Carver guns the throttle and the world goes blurry.

62

Riley

I've never moved this fast. Not on a monorail car, not when I ran the Core, not on my fastest, most effortless sprint, when it feels like a fusion reactor is powering my legs. The speed is intoxicating, a thing of raw power, exploding through my body as the Boneshaker bucks and shudders underneath us.

I have to use my feet to stay on, hooking them into the guts of the machine, desperately trying to keep my balance. For a few seconds, I forget everything: Knox, Resin, Royo, Okwembu, the Earthers. Prakesh. I'm laughing, a furious, joyous howl that I couldn't stop even if I wanted to. I don't know if Carver can hear me, and I don't care.

We shoot out onto one of the catwalks, high above the New Germany gallery. There's nobody in sight. My mind is racing ahead of us, and my laughter cuts off abruptly as I realise where we're heading.

"Whoa, whoa, Carver, stop!" I shout.

He looks over his shoulder. The movement travels down into his hands, and the Boneshaker jerks a little. "What?"

"I forgot! This'll take us down the stairs."

"It's the only way. Trust me!" He twists the throttle harder. The machine surges ahead, and it's all I can do to keep my grip while holding Knox up.

The entrance to the far corridor looms, and then we're through it, in blackness for a few seconds before we emerge into a lit part of the corridor. Carver jerks the stick to the side, and it's only when the right wheels jerk upwards and rumble over something that I realise why. We just ran over someone. A body. I flick a glance back over my shoulder, but the corpse is nothing more than a shadow, fading fast.

Carver shouts over his shoulder. "Hold on tight!"

I lift my ass off the seat to get a better look. The stairs are short, no more than ten steps, but steep, and coming up fast. Carver twists the brake—until now I hadn't realised that there *was* a brake—but then changes his mind and guns the throttle again. I barely have time to process what Carver is doing before we're airborne.

We're going so fast that, for a moment, we don't actually fall. We just keep flying forward, and it's only when we're about to collide with the ceiling that the Boneshaker drops. The thought comes to me—much too late—that we should have slowed and then driven down the stairs. I feel the ceiling just touch the top strands of hair on my head. In a weird way, I'm too fascinated to be scared—everything is moving at light speed and in slow motion, all at once.

Carver leans back, pulling the nose up. We slam into the ground with a bang that shakes the corridor. The wheels squeal as they try to keep contact. Carver is screaming, fighting with the control stick. I see him tweaking the throttle, desperately trying to speak to the skid—and then we're out of it, running straight, zooming down the corridor and laughing so hard with relief that I think we're going to fall right off. I'm astounded that Knox hasn't snapped out of his unconscious state; then, I wish I hadn't thought about it.

"Next time," I shout, "go *down* the stairs!"

"How about next time you take us somewhere where there *are* no stairs?"

"I'll try. You know where to go from here?"

He nods. "You're not the only tracer on Outer Earth."

As the words leave his mouth, the Boneshaker's engine gives an almighty cough, bucking so hard that it lifts me off the seat. It sputters and dies, and we coast to a halt at a T-junction, bumping up against the wall.

"Shit, shit, shit," Carver says. He slams his foot down on a lever on the side, then does it again, but each time the motor refuses to catch, giving a sullen clicking sound before fading. The Boneshaker has left enormous, curling black lines on the floor, like question marks.

"Told you we should have gone down slowly," I say, dismounting. My legs are trembling.

"And where's the fun in that?" He follows me, bending down to ram his hands into the motor. The metal is steaming slightly.

It takes me a few moments to realise that Knox has lifted his head. He's staring at me, his eyes rheumy, almost clouded. Little black bubbles pockmark his cheek and lips, dotting his pale skin.

He opens his mouth, the words dropping out of it like hanging spit. "Wuh. Wuh. Where. Where are wuh?"

"He speaks," Carver says, not looking up.

I try not to meet Knox's eyes. "Getting you to safety."

"Wuh-why?"

"You die, I die, remember?"

He doesn't have long left. I close my eyes, trying not to pay attention to the hot, itching stitches. "Carver, we're running out of time," I say.

"I know, I know. It's the batteries."

"Just fix it."

"I'm trying."

That's when I hear the voices. They're distant, and it's impossible to make out the words, but it sounds like they're coming from behind us.

"Carver?" I say.

"I hear 'em."

The Boneshaker gives another roar, briefly catches, then dies. That nasty clicking sound ratchets out of the engine, followed by more curses from Carver as he gets ready to try again. I drop down into a combat stance, my hands at my sides, ready to take whoever comes first. *Buy some time. That's all you can do.*

It's a gang. I see it the second they come round the corner, colours out, vibrant purple, splashed across bandanas and tattoos. I don't know them, but it's easy to see what they've been doing. They're carrying boxes of stuff—food, parts, batteries. I guess it's easy to go looting when the station's locked down.

The leader is a short, stocky guy, with a shaven head and an ugly, badly healed facial tat in the shape of a scythe. He comes up short, staring in confusion at the Boneshaker. Then he grins and turns to his buddies, barking something at them in a language I don't understand. The ones carrying boxes put them down, and start to saunter towards us. They don't have any weapons that I can see, but I can tell they're ready to fight, and that they know how to do it.

Right then, the Boneshaker catches and holds. Hot smoke swirls around my legs, and I leap back on before I can think about it, wrapping my arms around Carver a split second before he guns the motor.

I'm sitting a little forward this time, squashed against Knox, but I feel hands brushing my back, scrabbling for a hold.

The front of the Boneshaker rises upwards, like an ancient beast rearing to attack. For one insane second I think I'm going to fall right off it. Then I see that the gang leader has grabbed onto the back edge of the Boneshaker and is being dragged along. His boots judder as they fly along the floor, bouncing off the metal.

I reach back to push him off, but Carver jerks our ride to one side. The man swings around, smashing into the corridor wall with a sound like a melon splitting open. He tumbles away, lifeless.

We're heading back the way we came—the Boneshaker came to a halt facing the wrong direction, and Carver didn't get a chance to turn around. "We're going the wrong way," I say.

"Better hang on, then."

Leaning to one side, he tweaks the brake, twisting the control stick and spinning the Boneshaker so fast that it nearly pushes us right off. Somehow, I manage to keep both Knox and myself on.

The gang is back on its feet ahead of us. There aren't that many, but they crowd the corridor. Carver shouts something, his words lost in the roar of the engine, then twists the power so hard that the grip almost comes off in his hand. The Boneshaker surges forward, its vibrations threatening to shake me apart, and we head right for the middle of them.

At the very last second, the gang scatters, diving out of the way.

One of them doesn't move fast enough, and the Boneshaker rumbles over her ankle. Her scream drills into my ears, but it's gone almost as soon as it starts. I expect to hear stinger fire, but we've knocked them down, and soon we've left them behind.

"Whatever you did to the batteries, it worked!" I shout.

Carver nods. "How's our patient doing?" he says.

I lean forward, studying Knox. He's unconscious again. The drool on his face has dried to a thick crust.

63

Riley

The power failures have grown worse—there are large parts of the station in darkness now, whole corridors blacked out. I think of the cities back on Earth. Or, at least, how I imagine them to have been. Huge buildings, towering to the sky. Thin streets winding between them like pieces of string, pulled tight. Easy to imagine them teeming with millions of people. What's hard is to imagine them empty, after the nuclear war. It must have been like Outer Earth is now.

The closer we get, the more scared I feel. It's impossible to know how Knox is doing, or how long he has. There's no telling whether more of the drug will even help him. Maybe it's something you can only take once.

Don't think about that.

There are more bodies, and the sickly sweet smell of decay is thicker, ebbing and flowing through the corridors. But there are no more gangs, and nobody stops us. It's not long before we cross the border into Tzevya.

Ahead of us, the corridor becomes a T-junction. Someone has scrawled a message on the wall in black ink, and, as Carver slows to take the corner, I see it clearly. *Resin? Turn back we shoot on sight.*

They might *shoot on sight*, but so far Tzevya looks deserted. I'd expected to find the corridors blocked by debris or something, but they're wide open, although the doors alongside remain closed.

We trundle down a short flight of stairs onto the bottom level. There's another corridor ahead of us, long and empty. Most of it is in darkness, but here and there a few lights flicker, still holding out.

I feel Carver hesitate for a moment, as if reluctant to go back up to full speed. But then he guns the Boneshaker. The wheels squeal, spitting up smoke, and we speed down the centre of the corridor.

We're about halfway down when I see it.

It's so fleeting that I'm almost ready to believe I imagined it, but then it catches the light again.

"Stop!" I scream at Carver.

He turns to look at me, his eyes narrowed in confusion. We're still going way too fast. I hurl myself forward, pressing up against Knox, scrabbling for the brake. Carver yells in surprise.

The Boneshaker starts to skid. Its wheel clips the wall, and we nearly unbalance as the vehicle lurches the other way.

My hand is on the brake, pulling it hard, my feet gripping the body of the Boneshaker in a desperate attempt to hold on. Carver is screaming, trying to control the machine, his hand fighting with mine for the stick.

I feel the machine tilt...

We come back, slamming into the ground and ending in a screeching, grumbling halt in the middle of the corridor. The engine cuts, leaving nothing but the sound of our breathing.

Carver starts to turn around, on the verge of asking me what I was doing—

And stops dead as the wire strung up across the corridor just touches the side of his neck.

I still can't believe I saw it. I can barely see it now—it's only really noticeable through the impression it's leaving in the skin of Carver's neck, a thin channel just to the right of his Adam's apple. Somewhere, very distant, an alarm is blaring.

Very slowly, Carver leans backwards. His finger searches for the wire, finds it, twangs it gently. The light dances off it, zipping up and down its length.

"Like I said," I say. "Stop."

When he looks back to me, his eyes have gone huge.

Right then, what feels like every door in the corridor bursts open. There are people everywhere, ripping us off the Boneshaker and throwing us to the ground.

I try to stand, but I'm forced down by a foot in my back. I see Knox fall to the ground on my right, see a strand of dried Resin gunk fall across the floor.

Shoot on sight.

Before I can even articulate the thought, they've spotted the strand. Their angry shouts coalesce, turning into cries of "He's sick!" and "Do it!" I try to scream, but there's a gun barrel jabbed deep into the back of my neck. I see one being put to Knox's head, forcing it down.

My heart flash-freezes. It just cuts off mid-beat. I can't take my eyes off the stinger against his head, against the finger round the trigger. I can see every groove, every wrinkle. The joint is scarred, filigreed with white lines, and a thin silver band shines at its base. The finger begins to squeeze.

All at once, I remember where I've seen that ring.

"Syria!" I shout.

The finger pauses, just for a second. The hand holding the gun is shaking ever so slightly.

And then there's a voice, cutting above all the others. "Riley?"

The gun is lifted off my neck, and I'm pulled to my feet. My heart kicks back into gear, and it feels like the Boneshaker starting up: all noise and vibration. Part of me is still waiting for the gunshot that will end Knox's life, but it doesn't come.

Syria turns me to face him, both of his hands on my shoulders. He's wearing a medical face mask—gods know where he got it from. Greasy hair sticks to the mask in sticky strands, and the eyes above it are grim.

Anna is standing behind him.

Her expression dances between joy and confusion, shouting at the others to stand down. They stare at her, not sure whether to put the guns away, and it's only when she gets between them and me that they start to lower them. Syria is staring at me, recognition dawning.

I have a million questions—how Anna escaped the Earthers, how Syria ended up in Tzevya, what happened to the Caves. I don't have the energy to ask any of them. Behind me, I hear Carver hauled to his feet, shouting at the others to get off him.

From somewhere on the floor, Knox gives a hitching cough.

"He's sick," someone behind me says. "No exceptions, remember?"

The words kick the crowd back into gear. Syria steps forward, raising the stinger.

"*No,*" Anna says, inserting herself between us and the crowd. "This one comes in."

"You giving *me* orders now?" Syria says, elbowing her aside.

"And who put you in charge, Caver?" one of the others says.

"Shut up. All of you," Anna says. She points to me and Carver. "I'm immune, so I'll take him—me and them, too. We'll put him in the hospital, in one of the iso wards."

"Out of the way, Anna," says a woman at one side of the corridor. She has a face mask, too, and short black hair that sticks up in untidy spikes.

"No, listen." Anna looks right at the woman. "Walker—you know me, and you know I'd never ask you this if I didn't have a good reason."

Walker raises an eyebrow. Anna looks over at me, then back at her.

She points a finger at my chest. "If he dies, so does she."

Silence in the corridor. Anna senses the hesitation, and presses home her advantage. "Donovan. Rama. Shanti," she says, looking at each of them. "Please. You have to trust me."

I badly want to say something—to tell them just why Knox's death means mine as well. But if I mention that I'm a walking bomb, it could disrupt the precarious position we're in. And even if Anna succeeds, what then? I need to get Knox to Apex. It's the only way he survives.

"Isolation ward," says the woman Anna called Walker. "We'll clear a path. But if one more person dies, it's on you."

Anna nods, then squats down next to Knox. I follow, lowering my head to hers.

"Anna, you don't understand," I say, but then I stop talking. Because Anna has reached in her pocket and drawn something out.

It's a tiny vial, no longer than her palm. It's just like the one Carver and I took from Apex—the furosemide-nitrate. The drug compound.

"We've still got a little left," she says.

64

Riley

The Boneshaker won't start. Anna, Carver and I have to carry Knox through the sector—Carver and I on each arm, and Anna on the feet. A squad of Tzevyans clears the way for us, ordering people back into their habs.

We'd never have got through Tzevya on the Boneshaker anyway. Most of the corridors are blocked off, guarded by people in makeshift face masks. They've done a good job; the wire that nearly cut Carver's head off was an early-warning system, attached to a home-rigged alarm somewhere else in the sector. It was never meant to be a weapon, even if it came horribly close.

Tzevya has drawn into itself, shutting off contact with the outside, hoping Resin will burn itself out. I don't know what world they thought they'd emerge into after it did, but it's a relief to be somewhere where the smell of decay isn't syrupy-thick.

The hospital is deeper into the sector, a few minutes from the border with Apex. Our honour guard peels off as we get there, as if they don't want to be near the place. It's small, with a narrow central corridor bordered by a few wards and offices. I expect it to be full, heaving with Resin patients, but the beds are empty. The wards are a mess, too, with upturned furniture and equipment scattered across the floor. As if they were the sight of a brawl.

Shoot on sight, I think, and shiver.

We put Knox into one of the isolation wards at the back of the hospital, a brightly lit room with a single bed and a keypad-locked door. By now, he's dosed up on furosemide-nitrate, and he doesn't wake up when we heave him onto the bed. There's no telling how effective this second dose will be. No way of telling how long I have left before Knox's body loses the fight.

There's no point taking him to Apex now, but we still need to warn the council about the Earthers. We can't let them take the *Shinso*. It's not just the fact that they'll be leaving us behind—we *need* that asteroid. It's the source of our minerals, our building materials, the things we need to keep this place going. The things we'll need to rebuild.

Walker, the only one of the Tzevyans to have seen us all the way here, volunteers to guard Knox's ward. Anna smiles thanks, and she and Carver and I make our way back through the hospital.

"We should go," I say. My voice sounds like it's coming from someone thirty years older. "Get to Apex."

Carver gives me a sideways look. "Shouldn't you…I don't know. Stay here with him?"

"Would it make a difference?"

He looks helpless. "I guess not."

Anna clears her throat. "It'll be tough to get inside. I'll get us some reinforcements."

I grind my teeth together. "They'll slow us down."

"You go up to Apex by yourself, or even if it's just us three, and they'll arrest you like they did the last time. You think they'll pay attention to anything you have to say? It'll be safer if we have an escort."

"Right," says Carver. "I'll get the Boneshaker fixed."

"Is that what you call that contraption?" Anna says. "Can you not just leave it here?"

"Leave it alone with a bunch of Tzevyans? Do you have any idea what the gangs up here would do to get their hands on that thing?"

Anna rolls her eyes, then turns to me. "What do you want to do?"

There are a few scattered chairs in the main lobby, and I sit down heavily in one of them. I don't have much choice—it feels like my legs are going to give out. "Think I'll just sit here for a minute," I say. "Come and get me when it's time to go."

"Right," Anna says, dragging out the word. She's about to say something more, but Carver shakes his head. They jog away, and the hospital doors close behind them with a hiss.

I lean back, rolling my shoulders, trying to sort through my thoughts. On the one hand, we need to get to Apex as soon as possible, before the Earthers do. On the other, they've got heavy equipment, supplies, and it'll take them a little while to get up there, even if they hurry.

There's got to be a way I can keep Knox alive. Maybe they've got something new in Apex—a more advanced drug compound, perhaps. But, really, what good will it do? Even if one exists, it's just delaying the inevitable.

At that moment, I feel the same way I did when I almost threw myself off the broken bridge. It would be so easy to go and find a high place, with no stompers around to stop me. One last run, and then it would all be over.

The thought is calming. I hold on to it, pull it close. If it comes to it, that's what I'll do.

I don't know when I fall asleep. The first I know about it is when I jerk awake, my head snapping forward. I was dreaming about my father again—I don't remember the dream, but I can feel it, like it's left some kind of psychic residue. My mouth is covered in sticky saliva. How long have I been out?

I stand up, surprised to find that my body doesn't just give up and fall apart at the seams.

With my legs aching in protest and my body pleading with me to go back to sleep, to sink into oblivion, I force myself to get up. I need to find Anna and Carver.

Although I've been to Tzevya before, I'm not as familiar with it as I am with the other sectors, and pretty soon I realise I'm lost. I'm on the top level, in a darkened corridor bordered by hab units. There's a hissing nearby, like steam escaping a trapped pipe.

I see a man at the end of the corridor. He's hunched over, adjusting something on the enormous stack of old crates that make up the blockage. Maybe he'll know where the sector hospital is.

I take a step towards him, and my leg gives out.

I don't realise it's happened at first. The next few seconds are a series of quick jerks, like I'm jumping forward in time between each awful moment. Then I'm down, crumpling to the ground, damn near bouncing off it as I skid to a halt, screaming.

The bombs. Knox is dead. Knox is...

But when I look down, I see that my legs are still in one piece. No bloodstains on the fabric of my pants, no splinters of shattered bone poking through. And it's only my right knee that's in pain, bright and sharp. The muscles are acting up, complaining about what I've put them through.

I feel pressure under my arms, and then I'm lifted right off the ground. The man is there, pulling me up with a strength that his wiry frame shouldn't possess.

"Easy now," he says. I have a moment to register that his accent is the same as Anna's, crisp and sharp, and then he's pushing open the door to one of the habs running alongside the corridor. He uses his foot, nudging the door open and turning sideways to pass through. My own foot bounces off the frame, and I bite my lip as the shock travels up my leg, like a finger twanging a taut wire.

The light in the hab is low—nothing more than a dim bulb on the ceiling. I have time to make out two cots, a double and single, before I'm lowered onto the bigger one. I put my head back, waiting for the numb feeling in my knee to pass.

"Any permanent damage?" he asks.

My face is prickly with sweat, but the pain has come down a little. For a long moment, I'm too relieved to speak. I really thought the bombs had gone off. I was so sure.

"Fine," I manage to get out. I try to sit up, but he puts a hand on my stomach.

"Easy," he says again. "Your body's just telling you to take a few minutes out. From what I've been hearing, you've had quite a journey."

He stands. "There's some water in Jomo's hab, I think," he says. "I'll be back in a minute."

Before I can reply, he's gone, the door clicking closed behind him.

I can hear my heartbeat in my ears, loud and insistent. I lay my head back on the pillow. As I do so, I catch something out of the corner of my eye, on the wall by the single cot.

I raise myself up on my elbows, getting a better look at the hab as I do so. There are stacks of clothes on the thin shelves running along the wall, lined up neatly next to a small pile of wrinkly apples. The single cot has been neatly made up, its threadbare blanket positioned carefully on the mattress, its pillow just so.

The thing I saw is a drawing. The light's too dim to make it out from where I'm sitting. Slowly, I swing my legs off the bed, waiting to see if they can take the pressure.

They can. I walk over to the single cot, squinting in the low light.

Whoever did the drawing is pretty good. It's executed in black ink: a single figure, running down a cylindrical passage, its walls delicately shaded. There's someone, the outline of a person, standing at the far end, and the central figure is running towards them. Looking closer, I see that the figure is female. Her hair streams out behind her, and she's wearing a jacket that looks like...

The picture snaps into focus. The passage is the Core, and the figure at the end is Oren Darnell. And the one at the centre... there's no mistaking it. Whoever did the drawing got my dad's old flight jacket perfect.

Very slowly, I reach out. My finger is about to touch the ink when I hear a voice behind me.

"Best not. It's murder to get off your hands."

The man has come back. He's holding out a canteen to me, and, as he moves into the light a little, I realise that he's Anna's father.

There's no mistaking it. The skin on his face is shot through with a filigree of lines and wrinkles and tiny scars, but his eyes are the same as his daughter's. He sees me staring, and raises his eyebrows quizzically.

"I brought you that water," he says.

I want to say something, but the words won't quite come yet. The water is delicious—cold and clear. I nod thanks, wiping my mouth and passing the canteen back.

"Frank Beck," he says, thrusting out a meaty hand. His grip is dry and firm.

"Riley Hale," I say, amazed that I can get the words out.

Frank steps past me, pointing to the picture. "I'd almost forgotten that was there. Used to it, I guess."

"Anna did that?"

"She's quite good, isn't she?" he says. "She drew that after the whole Sons of Earth thing calmed down. She wouldn't stop talking about how you ran the Core. Went on about it so much that Gemma—that's her mother—she told her to use some of the old matt-black we had lying around and..."

My voice feels like it's made of old glass. "Matt-black?"

"Oh—chemical residue stuff left over from water processing. I work down at the plant, you know. Anyway, she drew, er...well, this."

He raises his hand, sweeping along the length of the drawing.

I'm transfixed by it. I expect it to stir old memories, bad ones, but it doesn't. Instead, I find myself picking up the smaller details: the pattern on the bottom of my shoes, the way the figure at the end of the Core has the same hulking profile as Oren Darnell. She's even drawn the gloves I had on, which I used to fight off the freezing temperatures in the Core.

"I don't understand," I say to Frank Beck. "Anna and I—we don't exactly get along most of the time."

"Really?" he says, his brow furrowed. "I'd never know it from the way she talks about you. There was a new story every day when she was growing up, even before that bastard Darnell. Riley Hale ran New Germany Level 3 faster than anyone ever. Riley Hale jumped all the way off a gallery catwalk and survived. Riley this, Riley that. Said one day she was going to be faster than you."

"You're kidding."

"Not a bit of it."

I shake my head, still staring at the drawing, then sit down on the single cot. "But *we don't get along*. At all. We never have." I think back to the first time Anna and I met—how she got in my face, challenging me to a race then and there.

Frank shrugs. "She's always refused to be second best at anything. She was running with a crew of lads up here, but she jumped at the chance to go and work for the stompers—mostly because she'd finally get to run with you."

"Was it you who taught her to use the slingshot?"

He gives a small smile. "Anna's always wanted to be the fastest person on Outer Earth, but it doesn't take much to see that her real talent is shooting. Drawing, too, but mainly shooting. I made that damn slingshot for her when she was a girl, and I don't think there's another sharpshooter in the six sectors who can aim like she can. I remember once when we..."

"Dad, you in there?"

Anna appears in the doorway. Frank Beck smiles. "Hey, sweetie," he says. "I was just helping your friend Riley here."

Anna steps inside. She briefly hugs her father, then turns to me, not looking at the drawing (*her* drawing) on the wall behind us.

"Carver's machine won't start," she says. "He's got one of the guys helping him on it, but it'll be a while."

Frank Beck holds his hand out. I take it, and he pulls me up off the bed.

"I've got some people together," Anna says. "Safety in numbers, right?"

I take a deep breath. "OK," I say. "Let's go."

65

Riley

We're halfway across the Tzevya gallery when the lights go out. This time they don't come back on.

We all stop, just for a second, waiting. The Tzevyans have been pretty good at keeping their sector clear of Resin victims, but I can still smell the dead here, the sickly-sweet scent of decay sticking in my nostrils.

"Any time now," says one of the others—Walker. But the lights stay off.

Syria clears his throat. "Let's go," he says, pointing to one of the corridors leading off the gallery floor. The lights are still on there, flickering gently.

There are ten of us, walking slowly up towards Apex. Syria leads the way. He's barely said a word to me. Every so often, I'll catch him looking in my direction, but when my eyes find his, he looks away. I don't mind. I'm not sure I know what to say to him. No one's said a word about the Caves, but I only have to look at Syria's drawn face, at the bags under his eyes, to know that the news isn't good.

It feels strange to be moving through Outer Earth in a big group. More than that, it feels strange to be moving so *slowly*. I'm used to taking the corridors and catwalks at a run, not at an infuriating trudge. I bite back the urge to shout at them, to tell them to hurry. It'll just piss them off, and, right now, I need them on my side.

"Hey, tell me something, Hale," says Walker. "These people want to take the *Shinso* back to Earth, right?"

"Yeah?"

"How're they even planning to get on board? I mean, they take a tug, OK, but then what? The crew isn't just gonna open up and say, come on in, right?"

"They're using Okwembu to do it," I say. I'm thinking hard, trying to get my thoughts in order. "She knows something about the ship's operating system. I think they're going to use her to gain access."

Walker points to the floor. "What makes them think there's anything down there? Whole planet is a wreck."

I shrug, thinking back to Okwembu and Mikhail, back to the facility that served as the Earthers' base. "I don't know. They didn't exactly tell us their plans."

Walker is silent for a moment. Then she says, "Why don't we let them?"

"Why don't we let them what?"

"Take the ship."

"You're full of shit, Walker," says a man at the back. He's Donovan, I think.

"I'm serious," she says over her shoulder. "There's still the *Tenshi Maru*. Isn't there?"

"Way too far out," Syria mutters.

"And hang on," Donovan says. "You're proposing we let these people take one of our two remaining asteroid catchers, and just leave? What about the rest of us?"

"I just—"

"No. Not happening. Besides, we *need* that asteroid if we're going to have any hope of surviving."

"I'm just saying. These people want to try dropping this thing into Earth's atmosphere without heat shielding? Good luck and good riddance."

Donovan scoffs.

"They're going to use the asteroid as heat shielding," Anna says.

"Bullshit."

I shrug. "Actually, it makes sense. They'll have to be damn careful, though."

Walker ponders that. "But you said they didn't tell you anything about their plans."

"They didn't," I say. "Carver worked it out. He..."

I trail off. Something is jogging my memory, something I saw when we were captured by the Earthers.

It slips away, back into a mess of thoughts. There are still far too many loose ends, too many things we don't know.

"They've got weapons," I say. "They're ready to fight their way into the dock. The people in Apex need to know they're coming."

Walker shrugs. "People in Apex need to find out what this Resin thing is. That's what they need to do."

"Got that right," says Donovan. Syria huffs, flicking an irritated glance in his direction.

Anna falls into step alongside me. For once, her beanie is off, tucked in her jacket pocket. Her blonde hair is stuck to her forehead in untidy strands. Was she right about Mikhail? Is he the connection between us, the reason we aren't sick?

And if he is, does that mean that he and the Earthers cooked up Resin?

That thought again, flickering at the back of my mind, vanishing before I get a fix on it.

When we do reach Apex, it's a relief to see that most of the lights are still on. Of course, the doors are shut—huge slabs of steel, blocking off the wide entrance corridor.

Anna stops, resting her hand on the door.

"Now what?" says Syria.

"Why don't you knock?" Walker says.

"Wow. You're a genius, Walker," says Donovan.

"And you're an asshole."

"Yeah, well," says Donovan, walking over to one side of the door and dropping to his haunches. "I'm an asshole who's going to get us inside."

He's pulling at a panel on the wall—trying, I realise, to get to the wires behind it. He thinks he can short-circuit the doors somehow. I want to tell him not to bother—this is Apex, where if they want you outside, you stay outside.

At that moment, the doors give a massive mechanical whine and begin to slide open.

Behind them is a stomper, stinger up, aimed right at us. Syria swears, dropping the stretcher and scrabbling for his own. Walker, Donovan and the others already have theirs out.

The stomper is huge—a heavily muscled woman, not tall but built like a human version of the Boneshaker. Her name comes to me out of nowhere: Jordan. She was there when Royo sent Carver and me into the pipes outside the Recycler Plant.

The eyes buried in the black beetle-mask of her respirator are cold. "Don't move," she says. "Not a damn step, you hear me?"

"We're not sick," Anna says, raising his hands.

There's a second stomper now, coming up behind the first. I see his eyes widen. "It's Hale," he says to Jordan. He notices Donovan, still crouched by the side of the door, and trains his stinger on him.

"Get her into a brig somewhere," Jordan says. "Rest of them can go on their way." She looks at Anna and the others. "Thanks for the delivery."

"Step aside, stomper," says Syria.

Jordan raises her stinger and fires. The bang is enormous, the bullet burying itself in the ceiling. We duck on instinct, and two of the people in our party take off, bolting away from Apex.

"Next one won't be a warning shot," Jordan says. "Hale—come with us."

"Just *listen* to me," I say. "Do you think I'd come back here if there wasn't a damn good reason?"

She doesn't lower her stinger. *I was wrong*. I thought I could negotiate with them, get them to give us passage. But none of this is working out like I planned.

"You've got one minute," she says.

I let out a shaky breath. "Is Royo—" I begin, but Jordan cuts me off.

"Still alive, for now," she says. "I'm in command. Now talk."

It takes less than that to tell them all about the Earthers. But when I'm finished, the stompers don't put their guns away. "Crap," Jordan says.

"But…"

"No. It's crap. I don't believe a word of it. Now you—"

There's an enormous roar, and then the Boneshaker bursts into view behind us. Carver is leaning back, as if trying to control a rampaging beast. Both the stompers are staring at the Boneshaker.

In the next instant, two things happen.

Donovan explodes off his haunches, moving faster than he has any right to. He shoulder-charges the nearest stomper, sending him sprawling.

The move distracts Jordan for a split second. I use it. I dart forward, jabbing at her gun arm. The heel of my left hand smacks her on the back of her wrist. The heel of my right hits the stinger itself.

It's a move that could get me killed if I miscalculate it, but it works. Jordan's stinger goes flying, ripped out of her hand before she can squeeze the trigger.

The Boneshaker comes to a screeching halt, rocking from side to side. Carver cuts the engine. He looks at me, then at the stompers, then at Anna, then back at me.

"What'd I miss?" he says.

66

Riley

After the tangled mess of Tzevya, Apex feels sparkling clean. The brightly lit corridors and white surfaces are free of the smell of decay.

Jordan and the other stomper are in the middle of our little group, their stingers confiscated, their arms held tight. Jordan's colleague got hit by Donovan in the scuffle, and blood is caked on his upper lip. Both of them are silent. We all are—we wouldn't really be able to hear each other anyway. Carver drives the Boneshaker behind us. He has the motor at just above idle, but in the tight corridors the noise is amplified. Every so often, Jordan looks back at it, a confused look on her face.

Apex is smaller than the other sectors, but it'll still take us a few minutes to reach the council chamber. I'm on the lookout for more stompers, and I can see Anna doing the same thing. Last thing we need is to run into an ambush. But there's no one around. Even Apex, it seems, has drawn into itself, like a freezing body diverting all its blood back to the core organs.

We're starting to get into a part of the sector that I recognise. It takes me a moment to work out where we are. A couple of levels below us is the main control room, where everything happened with my dad. Thinking of it is like touching an open wound.

Anna signals me to head down a corridor to our right, and that's when the Boneshaker cuts out again. The engine gives a giant, choking splutter, replaced by a resigned hissing noise, spraying clouds of noxious steam. Carver groans in frustration, his voice rising to a high whine. "Come *on*, you bastard, *come on*."

"Just *leave* it," says Syria.

Carver looks up at him. "Screw you."

Suddenly, everybody is shouting at everybody else, long-held tensions spilling out. Even I'm raising my voice, yelling for calm. At this rate, we're not going to get into an ambush—the stompers are going to come right down on top of us.

Somehow, Jordan's eyes find mine. I've walked into the fray, and I've ended up next to her. I can hear her voice clearly through the chaos "What are you doing, Hale?" she says.

I ignore her, but she keeps talking. "*Even if* these Earthers did exist," she says, building up steam. "*Even if* they actually managed to hijack the *Shinso*, they're not making it back to Earth. That thing's got no way to make it through the atmosphere without burning up."

I don't bother to tell her about the asteroid heat shield, and she doesn't give me a chance to. "Not to mention the fact that there are zero provisions left on that ship. They've been out there for nearly two years. I have to keep telling them that we can't send a tug, which is pissing them off because they're cooling their heels in Outer Earth orbit. So unless your *Earthers* have food of their own stashed away, they're not going anywhere."

I turn my head to tell her to shut up, and stop.

She stares at me. "What's wrong, Hale? Run out of lies to tell?"

But her voice sounds very far away. My mind is racing, connecting the dots faster than I keep track of it.

Jordan's words.

What I saw in the Earthers' camp.

The idea, dancing on the edge of my mind, steps into the light. I see everything, like when Anna's drawing suddenly snapped into focus.

And I really, really don't like what I see.

"Hey!" Anna says, all but bellowing the word. Finally, everyone stops talking. I barely notice. I'm rolling the idea around in my mind, desperately trying to find a weak spot in it, something I missed that will puncture it and sink it.

"Carver: leave it. We have to keep moving. Riley...Riley, what's wrong?"

Getting my tongue to form words is almost impossible. "You go on ahead," I say.

Anna narrows her eyes in confusion. "What?"

"I just..." I'm moving away, turning, breaking into a run. "There's something I have to do," I say over my shoulder.

"Riley!" Carver says. But I've already left them behind.

67

Riley

Doctor Arroway is slumped across the table in his office, his head resting on his forearms, slightly turned to one side. He's discarded his face mask—it's on the table in front of him, crumpled up. I can see the nail marks in its papery surface, as if he held it tight and scrunched it up before throwing it onto the table.

His office is at the back of the hospital, a messy room that looks as if someone has been living in it for the past few days. He probably has. I can still hear the sounds of the hospital—the moans of the patients and the barked commands of the few nurses and doctors that still remain—but they're muted here, and they're cut off completely when I shut the door.

Arroway jerks awake. He looks around him, and when he turns his face towards me I see that his eyes have sunk into his face, swallowed by huge black circles. He wavers for a moment, then realises who I am, and explodes out of his chair.

"No, no, no. Get away," he says, staggering backwards. His foot catches the chair leg as he does so, sending it crashing over. I can see him looking around for a weapon, something he can use against me.

He must think I want revenge, for not examining me when I told him about the bombs, back when I was captured at the broken bridge.

"Relax, Doc," I say, raising my palms. "I just want to talk."

"Talk?" Sweat beads on his forehead, and his eyes won't stop moving, still hunting for a weapon.

I force a smile. "Calm down. I'm not here to hurt you, or anyone else. I promise."

It feels like I do a pretty good job of keeping the nervousness out of my voice, considering. It feels like I'm hanging over a giant pit, dangling from a frayed rope, with a new strand snapping every minute. My earlier realisation is like a monster waiting in the pit, skulking in the shadows. I don't dare look at it, or even think too hard about it, or I'll fall from the rope.

I push on, using the words to strengthen my grip. "When you tested me—when you tested my blood. You didn't find anything useful, right?"

He's still looking at me like I'm going to lunge forward and bite him. After a few seconds, he gives a tight nod.

"I've got something for you," I say. "I think—"

My throat suddenly goes very dry, as if it doesn't want to say the words. I force them out. "I think it might help you figure out where Resin came from."

Arroway's eyes narrow. "How did you even get in here? They told me they sealed the sector."

"Never mind that. Here."

I dip my hand in my pocket. In the second before I pull it out, I pause. *You could leave it alone*, I think. *Just turn and run. Pretend you don't know anything.*

Then I take my hand out my pocket, and place what I'm carrying on the table.

The beans are a drab green colour, thin and curled. They're the ones that I took from the Earthers, thinking that I might need them as food further down the line.

"I don't understand," Arroway says. "What is—"

"Just test them." I've already got one hand on the door, pulling it open. The noise from the hospital floods back in. "Then come and find me. I'll probably be in the main council chamber."

Arroway stares at me, as if he still isn't sure whether I'm a dream or not.

"Come and find me," I say again. Then I'm gone, pushing my way through the hospital, not looking back.

I try to quieten my mind as I run through Apex. It's just as well I don't run into any other stompers—I'm so wired I'd probably try and take them head on. I try to sink into the movement, let the rhythm take me away, but dark thoughts tug at the edges of my mind.

It's not hard to find the council chamber. I can hear Syria bellowing from three corridors away, his voice ringing out, turned metallic by the corridor walls. "You're cowards! All of you!"

I step up my pace, breaking into a jog. Someone tries to answer Syria, but he cuts them off. "I don't care. You're just gonna let them take it? I swear to my gods, you walk out that door, and I'll use it to take your head off."

I've never been in the council chamber before, but I've seen it plenty of times on the station comms screens—the council leader would occasionally broadcast messages to the station from here. Okwembu did it all the time. It's smaller than I thought it would be, and, right now, it looks awful. The big centre table is strewn with detritus: discarded food containers, wrinkled jackets, tab screens. A glass of water has been knocked over, spreading a puddle across the middle of the table that nobody has bothered to mop up.

Syria is still shouting, threatening violence if anybody leaves.

He, Anna, Carver, Donovan and Han Tseng are on one side of the conference table. Walker is on the other side, along with the rest of the Tzevyans. Jordan and her colleague are seated in one corner, sullen and silent.

Syria pauses for breath, and Walker cuts in, jabbing a finger at him. "We've been through plenty worse before. You think we can't survive a couple more years without asteroid resources?"

"I think you're a coward, that's what I think," Syria says.

Tseng looks as tired as Arroway was. There's no sign of his functionaries. "I absolutely forbid you to leave," he says to Walker. "If these people are really coming, then we can't let them leave. They are *not* taking that asteroid catcher."

Anna tries to cut in. "Everybody just—"

Tseng talks over her. "I order you to go down to the dock, and start fortifying it. You hear me?"

That causes laughter from everyone on the other side of the table. Walker tilts her head, looking Tseng right in the eyes. "Not a chance."

I hover in the doorway, not sure whether to intervene or not. I guess Walker had more supporters than she thought. But as I stand there, I think how easy it would be to agree with her.

It would be incredibly difficult to survive without the resources from the asteroid. That's our building material, our soil nutrients, everything. With the *Shinso* and its cargo gone, we'd have to rely on the one last ship out there: the *Tenshi Maru*. It might be months, even years, before it finds a suitable asteroid to capture and bring home. But we could hold out—especially now that there are far fewer of us left.

It's an uncomfortable thought, and it brings another. If the Earthers really want to take the *Shinso*, why should we risk our lives trying to stop them? Let them take the damn ship. If they think they can survive on Earth, then Walker is right: good riddance.

Anna sees me, and gestures me inside. Syria has started shouting again, and this time Walker has had enough. She and the others start picking their way across the room, heading for the door. One of them catches my eye, and half smiles, like we're both in a private joke.

Tseng has his hands flat on the table. For a tiny instant, I can see him as a council leader. It's a strange sensation, and I'm brought back to reality when he shakes his head furiously, making his greasy hair flick from side to side.

"They can't take the *Shinso*," he says. "We can't let them. We need to fortify the dock *right now*."

Walker ignores him, pushing past me with a muttered apology. Syria is shaking his head, as if he can't believe what he's seeing.

That's when Tseng really loses it. He hammers the table, once, twice, three times. "Don't you idiots understand? This isn't just about *holding out*. If we don't get that asteroid, this entire station is finished. It's over."

Something in his voice stops all movement in the room. Walker and her companions turn to look at him. Tseng falls silent, a deep expression of worry crossing his face. Like he's said too much.

At that moment, the lights in the room flicker, plunging us into darkness. Another power failure, identical to the dozens I've seen over the past few weeks. After a moment, the lights kick back on again in sequence, *click click click*. All of us look up at them when they do.

"What," says Syria quietly, "is so important about that asteroid?"

Han Tseng's indignant exterior has cracked. What's underneath is pink and tender, and he swallows, his Adam's apple bouncing.

"If we lose the *Shinso*'s asteroid," he says, "we lose the fusion reactor. If we lose the reactor, everything stops working. No heat. No air. Nothing. Outer Earth dies."

68

Riley

The silence feels like it has weight, like it's an actual presence in the room.

It's Anna who breaks it. "The tungsten," she says, her eyes wide.

Carver stares at her. "Holy shit. Of course."

His hands grip the top of a chair, and a deep growl of frustration rises in his throat.

"I don't get it," I say.

"I second that," says Walker.

Han Tseng sighs. "It's not the reactor per se. It's the shielding. It's made of tungsten alloy, which is ideal for absorbing the heat from the plasma core."

"This is just...*perfect*," Carver says.

"The tungsten shields have degraded over time," says Han Tseng. "We've been throttling the power grid to reduce the strain on the reactor, but it's not enough. If we don't get the tungsten out of the *Shinso Maru*'s asteroid and repair the shields, then the reactor fails."

"Fails how?" Anna says.

"The second there's a shielding breach, it'll shut down. Just stop cold. Everything on the station that uses power is finished."

"What about backup systems?" Anna says. She's taken her beanie out of her jacket pocket and is knotting it in her hands.

Tseng gives a bitter laugh. "For an entire station? *Maybe* some of them are still working. Enough to power a sector or two, for a few days."

"Why didn't you tell people?" I say. "Why keep it a secret?"

Tseng notices me for the first time. "It would have caused a panic," he says. "And up until a few minutes ago, none of us was aware that the *Shinso* shipment was in danger. If everything had gone to plan, we would have had those shields fixed before anybody even noticed the power failures were a problem."

The question comes to the front of my mind, as if it was just waiting to be asked. "These people—the ones coming to take the *Shinso*. They think they can survive back on Earth."

Tseng shrugs, looking helpless.

"We *do* monitor the Earth, right?" says Carver.

Silence. Tseng won't meet anyone's eyes. After a long moment, he shakes his head.

The groan is involuntary, uttered by everyone in the room, brimming with disgust. Tseng swallows. "There's no point. Why spend time listening when we were never going to hear anything?"

Carver stares at him. "But you must have had software listening out. A sub-routine that would ping us if…tell me you had *something*."

Tseng gives a helpless shrug. "You don't understand. We listened for years. *Decades*. When we sent Earth Return down, we were monitoring non-stop." A note of defiance creeps into his voice. "But we heard nothing. It's dead down there, and we had to focus on surviving up here. There was no point hunting for transmission from a planet we were never going to go back to."

"So go and find out what changed," Walker says.

Donovan nods. "Yeah. Let's go and take a look. See what has these people thinking they can run out on us."

"*No*," says Syria. He looks thunderous. "Forget all that. It doesn't matter what these people know, or what they think they can do. We've *still* got a reactor, we've *still* got people, and we've *still* got our home."

Syria glares at us. "They could have come forward. They could have told him—" he jabs a finger at Tseng "—what they found. But they didn't. They wanted it for themselves. No way we're letting that happen. If we can really survive down there, then everyone deserves a shot at it. We need time to figure all that out, and time is one thing we don't have."

Tseng looks at me. "Is there any hope they'd listen to reason?"

I think of Mikhail and the Earthers. Of Okwembu, and how quickly she fell in with their cause. I think of the atmosphere in the old facility: that nervous tension, electric in the air. The stacked supplies, the shouted orders.

Slowly, I shake my head.

Tseng takes a long breath, lets it out. "I'll go and talk to the stompers. Maybe we can take these people down."

Syria shakes his head. "Not gonna work."

Tseng raises an eyebrow. "Excuse me?"

"We go on a hunting mission, we're going into unfamiliar territory."

"It's not unfamiliar," I say, nodding to Carver and Anna. "We were there."

"Right. But the rest of us weren't. And we know they're going to the dock—they'll need the tugs to get out to the *Shinso*. They'll have to come all the way across the station, and when they get here we'll be ready. Why exhaust ourselves chasing them down when there's no guarantee we'll even find them?"

The room is silent again. Tseng is shaking his head.

Before anybody can say anything, there's the sound of running footsteps from the corridor outside. A moment later, Arroway comes round the door, moving so fast that Tseng has to make a surprised leap to the side.

At the sight of him, the fear that I pushed to the back of my mind scrambles into the light. I lick my suddenly dry lips, knowing what he's going to say. In that moment, I wish I could take it all back. I wish I had never given him the beans.

Arroway is out of breath, his shoulders trembling. He puts his hands on the conference table, tries to speak, doubles over with a cough.

"Doctor Arroway," says Tseng, his tone shocked, as if he can't believe that Arroway would just barge in like this.

"Resin," Arroway says. It's impossible not to hear the excitement in his voice—no, not excitement, more like joy. He coughs again, then straightens up. "We have the source. We know where it came from."

He points a shaking finger at me, a tired smile creeping across his face. "You were right. You are absolutely right. Those beans… how could we not see it?"

Tseng looks as if he's about to explode. "Doctor Arroway, *explain yourself.*"

Anna laughs, like she doesn't quite dare to believe it. "We can cure it, can't we?"

Arroway nods. "We've already isolated the components we need. It won't take long to start producing a cure—maybe not even an hour. We've already got all our production machines running full speed, for the furosemide-nitrate. Hell, with enough time, we could produce a vaccine for it. And it's all thanks to her." He nods in my direction, still smiling.

Everyone turns to look at me. I don't let myself pay attention to them. I march over to Han Tseng, and grab him by the front of his tunic.

"The Air Lab," I say.

"Let go of me."

"How do I unseal it?"

When he doesn't respond, I shake him so hard that his teeth clack together. *"Tell me."*

"18623," he says. "The code is 18623. But I don't—"

I let go of him, already turning away, moving towards the door. I can feel a room full of shocked eyes on my back.

At the last second, I turn and point a finger at Arroway. "I want the first cure that comes off the line. You find me, and you give it to me."

"Ry, hold up," Carver says. "Ry!"

I launch myself out the room and take off down the corridor. Fear and guilt match every step I take.

69

Prakesh

The headache is cranked all the way up, and his throat still feels like it's being squeezed by a thick steel ring. But the soil under Prakesh's backside is cool. He digs his fingers into it, letting the grains collect in the fissures on the underside of his knuckles.

Ordinarily, he'd never do anything to compress his good soil. But, right now, all he wants to do is be close to it. He has his back to a tree trunk—the rough bark is uncomfortable and knobbly, but in a way he needs that, too. He's on one of the tree beds, a little way down from where he fought Julian Novak. The giant oaks tower over him, shade dappling his face.

At some point, he'll have to get up. Yoshiro's body will need to be taken care of. He's not relishing the task at all—every time he thinks of it, he feels a hot spike of anger towards Julian—but at least, he thinks, it's a task he knows he can do.

He feels a presence close to him, and opens his eyes. Suki is standing there, hands clasped in front of her. From this angle, she looks younger than she is. Her expression is slightly embarrassed, like she's interrupted a private ritual.

Prakesh smiles up at her, nods. "How are you doing?" he croaks.

She lets out a shaky breath. "Fine. Forget that—what about you?"

He waves the question away, nodding instead towards the part of the Air Lab where Julian almost choked the life out of him. "He under control?"

Suki flashes a pained smile. "Some of the guys took him back to the control room. Locked him in one of the storage units."

Prakesh feels an unwelcome flash of guilt. "He doesn't need to be looked at by a doctor, or..."

"Nah. He'll be OK. I don't hit *that* hard, you know."

She sits down next to him, as if she's had enough of waiting for an invitation. She crosses her legs underneath her, smoothing down her skirt.

"So what do we do now?" she says.

Prakesh shrugs. He starts to speak, but is interrupted by more cheering. A group of techs are crossing parallel to them, along one of the passages between the algae pools, and they're shouting his name. He raises a weary hand, flashes a smile. It satisfies them, and they move on.

"Carry on as normal," he says to Suki. "Although we need to set up testing protocols for whatever this disease is. Can't risk it spreading in here." He's already thinking ahead, thinking what needs to be done, of how best to isolate anybody who might be infected.

Suki puts a hand on his knee. "I'll take care of it."

"You sure?"

"Well, as we've already established from the extinguisher incident, you can't do everything."

"The *extinguisher incident*? Is that what we're calling it?"

"You can call it whatever you want. I still saved you."

"Yes, you did." He reaches over, squeezes her shoulder. His eyes find hers. "Thanks. I owe you one."

Before she can reply, he hears the sound from the other end of the hangar. The hissing of the door to the outside world.

Prakesh is on his feet before he can stop himself, stumbling towards it. The door is opening, and on the other side of it is—

Riley.

He breaks into a run. In moments, he's on her, pulling her into his arms. A part of his mind registers that she looks awful—run ragged, stinking of sweat, her stomper jumpsuit torn in a dozen spots. She's pale, her mouth a tight line. But he doesn't care. She returns his embrace, holding him tight, and that's all that matters.

"Is it over?" he asks, when they pull apart.

Riley looks up at him. And that's when he sees the fear behind the exhaustion. Sees that she's holding something in. Something bad.

"Riley, what is it?" he asks. "Tell me what's happening."

He grips her shoulders, pulls her close so they're face-to-face. "Gods, Riley, *talk to me*."

"Resin," she says. "It's you, Prakesh. Resin came from you."

70

Riley

Prakesh's eyes narrow in confusion. His head is tilted slightly to one side.

"I don't understand," he says. His tone is light, like I'm fooling with him.

I have to be the one to tell him. It's the only way I can handle this—if I know the news is broken by someone he cares about. But when I try to speak again, I can't find the words.

"Riley, what is this?" he says.

I force my voice to work. "You're behind Resin. You created it. Not on purpose," I say, when I see him about to interrupt, "but through what you were doing. It…it was an accident."

"Riley," he says, his voice even, calm, reassuring. "You're not making any sense. There is no way—*no way*—that I engineered Resin. Not even by accident."

The other techs have come up behind him, clustering in a loose semicircle. Above us, the Air Lab's trees stretch to the ceiling, the lights filtering through their canopies. We could be in an old story—one that takes place back on Earth, with mythical monsters hiding out in the dappled half-light. I wish we were. It would be easier to fight those monsters.

Slowly, I reach into my pocket, and pull out one of the beans. It's one I took from the crates in the processing facility, where the Earthers were camped out. I gave ones just like it to Arroway, so he could test them. Beans that come from seeds identical to the ones Mikhail had when Anna and I took him down—the ones in the cloth bag that spilled out of his pack.

I drop it into Prakesh's hand. He stares at it, using the fingers of his other hand to turn it over. There's a faded, pale stripe down the side of the bean, masked with thin hairs.

"This is from a previous batch," he says, then shakes his head. "Where did you get this?"

He turns the bean over and over in his hands, his calloused fingers running up and down it, as if trying to make sure it's real.

I try to keep things ordered in my mind. "Some of us weren't getting sick. Me, Carver, Anna. We hadn't contracted Resin. Okwembu hadn't either."

"OK…" he says.

"Remember how you told me that the defective batches couldn't be wasted? That it was being fed to prisoners?"

"They tasted terrible," Prakesh says. There's no humour in his words, just an undercurrent of fear, and it nearly rips my heart in two.

I keep going, telling him about the Earthers. How they weren't sick either. "I still don't know how they got hold of the beans, but my guess is that they stole them. They need provisions for the trip back to Earth."

"Trip back to—*what*?" Prakesh looks back at the techs. Some of them are shaking their heads in disbelief, but I can see the wheels turning, see them making the connections.

"Nobody in the Air Lab got Resin," I say. "Right?"

He's shaking his head, more in disbelief than refusal. "Riley, this is crazy."

"Because you were exposed, too. After all, you created them."

"It doesn't prove anything. There must be others on Outer Earth who aren't sick. Maybe some people just have a... a *natural immunity*."

"Maybe," I say, trying to hold back the tears and failing. "But, Prakesh, so far everyone we've seen who isn't sick has been exposed to those beans in some way. We've all come into contact with one of your previous batches. We either ate them, or touched them."

Prakesh slams the heel of his hand into his forehead, screwing it in, his eyes closed. "No, no, this is all wrong," he says. He's gone deathly pale, his walnut skin turning sallow.

I try to keep things ordered in my mind. It's hard, but I manage.

"When we were exposed to that batch, we got a low-grade version of the virus. It was like those flu shots we get sometimes—we build up antibodies, and then we don't get sick. Because we'd been exposed, we had antibodies that everybody else *didn't* have.

"The beans that came afterwards had a much stronger version of the virus. The rest of us—you, me, the techs, the prisoners—the antibodies we had kept us safe. We could fight the newer, stronger one off. Nobody else could, because they never had a chance to develop those antibodies."

I close my eyes. "The genetic engineering you did to the plants created Resin. You made the latest batch, thought it worked, put it on the monorail and shipped it out to every mess hall and kitchen in the station. People ate it, and they got sick. The only ones who didn't were those who had been exposed to a previous batch."

He actually takes a step back, like I'm going to lunge out and bite him. It takes everything I have not to reach out for him. But I can't do that—not yet. If I do, I'll just collapse.

Prakesh looks back at me. "A virus can't jump from plants to humans," he says, speaking to me as if I'm a child. "It doesn't happen. That's not how it works."

"Do you have any proof?" says one of the other techs. She's come up alongside Prakesh, her arms folded, fury on her face. "If you're going to come in here and accuse us of…"

"Suki, back off," says Prakesh.

"Boss…"

"I was in charge of production. This is for me to deal with. All right?"

Suki looks at him like he's gone mad, but nods. There are footsteps behind us, and I turn to see Jordan, along with Carver and a couple of other stompers. From the looks on their faces, I can tell that they've worked out what's going on. I gesture at them to wait.

"This can't be true," Prakesh says. "Tell me this wild theory has been tested, Riley. Tell me this isn't just a hunch."

And I do.

I tell him what Arroway found. How the link between Resin and the beans became apparent as soon as he began testing the samples I gave him. "They're developing the cure right now," I say.

A cure. Unbidden, the ghoulish face of Morgan Knox swims up from the depths of my mind. *I'm going to be OK.*

It takes me a second to realise that Prakesh is walking away.

He isn't running. He's just walking away from the group, his hands laced behind his head, his shoulders trembling.

"We need to take him in, Hale," says Jordan.

I didn't hear them come up behind me. I turn to face her. "What?"

"He's behind one of the most awful genocides in human history. Hundreds of thousands of people…"

"It was an *accident*."

"He's still responsible."

"So what are you gonna do?" I'm shouting now, but I don't care. "Lock him in the brig? In the dark? Make him invent, I don't know, time travel so he can reverse what happened?"

"Hale, listen to me."

"No, you listen. We're going to need everybody we have to defend the dock. You touch him, and you answer to me."

Prakesh is sitting up against one of the algae pools, staring into the distance. The techs are standing around, talking in hushed voices, looking as if they're not quite sure what to do.

"Go talk to him," Carver whispers. I look up at him, and he nods gently.

I walk to Prakesh. Every footstep echoes off the walls of the hangar.

He doesn't look at me, even when I slide down next to him. After a moment, I rest my head on his shoulder.

"It's too big," he says. "I try to look at all this, and I can't figure it out. It's like looking at the Earth. You can't see all of it at once. I keep looking at it from different angles, and—"

A single tear falls from his left eye, leaving a dark track on his cheek.

"I was just trying to stop people from being hungry all the time," he says.

"You weren't doing this alone," I say. "All the other techs..."

"Did what I told them to. I was the one who rewrote the genes of the plants. I mapped them, I coded them to make them grow faster. Maybe I didn't test them enough. But I thought I'd cracked it—all the others did was help the plants grow. Not one of them could have seen this happening. None of them should have had to. It was my responsibility."

"I know what you're going through," I say, thinking of Amira and my father.

"Do you?" he says, finally turning to look at me.

I open my mouth to reply, and find I have nothing to say. The guilt I experienced after killing Amira and then my father was awful. Sometimes it felt like it was going to burn me up, turning my insides black and dry. But this? This is monstrous. I don't know what he's going through. What I know is only the barest fraction of it.

My mouth has gone as dry as frost on the station hull. "I don't care," I say. "You didn't do any of it on purpose. You were trying to help." I reach out and take his hand. "And none of this changes anything," I continue. "Not between us. I love you, and I'll always be here for you. No matter what you're going through."

But as I say the words I can't help but taste Carver on my lips. Feel his arms around me. That truth—if it is a truth—feels as enormous as the Earth itself. And like Prakesh said, I can't see all of it at the same time.

He gives my hand a squeeze. Very gentle, but it's there.

I hear the soft clinking of body armour, and look up.

"Time to go," Jordan says.

71

Riley

I want to bring the techs with us, thinking that we'll need all the manpower we can get. Jordan doesn't let me. "There aren't enough weapons," she says. "Besides, these geeks wouldn't know which end of the gun to hold."

Prakesh gives her a vicious look. I put my hand on his shoulder and his anger fades as quickly as it came. The sadness that replaces it is even worse.

In the end, we compromise: a few techs come with us, and the rest head up to the Apex hospital, where they'll help Arroway produce the cure for Resin.

"What do you want to do?" I ask Prakesh. More than anything, I want him by my side. I want him close to me, where I can keep him safe. But I know better than to voice these thoughts.

He takes a long time to answer. "I'll be along a little later. I need to think."

Without another word, he walks off across the Air Lab.

There's nothing left to do but head for the dock.

I've been here before, on a cargo run years ago. It's in Gardens, right on the border of Apex. The entrance is on the top level by the monorail tracks, with a massive corridor leading off it. One wide enough to allow big shipments of asteroid slag to pass through.

The doors at the front of the dock stopped working a century ago. Nobody ever fixed them. So as we're walking up, I can see right inside the huge, cavernous hangar, just as big as the Air Lab. I'd forgotten how enormous it is—and how hard it's going to be to defend.

On the far side are the giant airlock doors, bisected by a magrail similar to the one that powers the monorail cars. From the little bit of knowledge I have of how the dock works, the magrail extends outside, running along the hull. Tugs match the speed of the spinning station, then latch onto it so they can come inside the dock without having to worry about crashing.

The tugs are lined up along each wall, squat and menacing. There are only a few left—over the years, plenty of people have managed to steal one, desperately hoping it'll have enough range to get them back to Earth.

Tseng is nowhere to be seen. Can't say I'm surprised. The remaining stompers are gathered by the rusted hangar doors. Usually, there's a hardened group guarding the dock from intruders, so it's jarring to see such a small crowd there, dwarfed by the entrance. Anna, Walker and the rest of the Tzevyans are with them.

Syria is there, too. One of the stompers is looking down at him. He barely reaches the height of her shoulders. This time, she's the one doing the shouting, while Syria stands mute, with his back to us.

"Maybe you aren't understanding the maths here," she says. Her finger jabs his chest. Once. Twice. "*Six* crowd barriers left in this sector, and the entrance is about three times their length."

"I heard you," says Syria, slapping her hand away. Carver glances at me, his eyebrows raised. Prakesh shakes his head. He hasn't said a word since we left the Air Lab, lost in his own thoughts.

The other stompers watch silently, their faces grim. Whatever they were doing before, it's like they've been drawn to this. Like they want to watch things coming apart.

The woman doesn't relent. "Unless you personally want to go

dragging back the ones we've deployed already, we aren't going to be able to defend the dock. It's not going to happen. We're better off getting in one of the tugs and heading out to the *Shinso* ourselves."

"So you're just going to give up?"

"Stompers!" I shout. "Eyes on me."

Everyone looks at me, eyes huge with surprise. It unbalances me for a moment—the words just burst out of me, and I'm still not quite sure what to say next.

Somehow, I find my voice again. "We are going to find a way to defend this dock, crowd barriers or not. Give me a headcount."

There's the oddest feeling coursing through my body. Like the feeling I get after a sprint, or a well-landed jump, when every muscle is humming with adrenaline. Carver has his chin to his chest, his eyebrows raised, looking at me with comical shock.

I glance at the woman who was complaining about the barriers. Her name pops into my mind from nowhere. "Officer Iyengar. Headcount."

She clears her throat. "Outside of the people you brought with you? Fifteen. That's all that's left."

I expect her to tack a snide remark on the end, but she just holds my gaze. My mind is whirling, thinking that we might have to pull some Air Lab techs from the hospital. But it won't help—much as I hate to admit it, Jordan was right about not giving them weapons. Even if they know how to use stingers, and even if we have enough, we can't guarantee they'll stay cool-headed enough to make a difference. It'll be better if the majority of the people in the dock are stompers, or Tzevyans.

Right then, at that very second, I almost turn and run. As far and as fast as I can, away from everything and everyone. I keep my feet planted.

"All right," I say. I start pointing, jabbing my finger at each of them in turn. "You and you. We need every weapon we can get our hands on. Every stinger we can find. You: go to the hospital, see if anyone's responded to the cure yet, and get them down here. We need manpower. You three: start moving those crowd barriers. See if we can bottleneck these people."

Anna says, "Can we get word to the Earthers, somehow? Maybe if we tell them about the reactor, they'll..."

"Not a chance," Carver says. "They'll think it's a trick."

"It's worth a shot," I say. "We have to let them know what'll happen if they take the *Shinso*."

"No," Iyengar says. "We don't know where they are. We could miss them entirely, and they might not listen to us if we find them."

I think hard, picturing the Earthers in my mind. "They've got weapons, and they've got heavy equipment with them, plus supplies. My guess is they'll be sending an advance force to clear us out, so they can take the tugs. There won't be as many of them, but they'll be heavily armed."

Behind us, Jordan shakes her head. "They'd be walking right into the line of fire. They'd have to know that."

"Maybe," I say, choosing my words carefully, aware of the need to have Iyengar onside. "But I don't think it'll stop them. They want to get off this station bad."

Without another word, I walk past her into the hangar, looking around for something we can use to create longer barricades.

An idea forms. "The tugs," I say, pointing at one of the ships. "Can we get them going? Position them in front of the entrance?"

Jordan interjects. "Flying a tug in an enclosed space? That's a bad, bad, bad idea. Not even seasoned pilots try that one."

"This is insanity," says Syria. "Why don't we just blow up the tugs? Hell, I've got demo experience—I could do it." He takes a step towards the nearest tug, but Carver stops him.

"If we survive this, we're going to need to get the broken-up asteroid inside for processing," he says. "We can't do that with disabled tugs."

Taking a deep breath, I turn to Jordan. "Find us a pilot. Somebody with tug experience. I don't care how dangerous it is—it's all we've got."

"I don't even know if there are any pilots left."

"Just look."

As she turns to leave, something else occurs to me. I call her back. "Find Tseng. Get him down here. And get on the line to the *Shinso*. Tell them to get as far away as they can."

Shaking her head, Jordan walks off. Syria and Anna follow her, leaving Carver and me standing by the tug.

"They won't have time, you know," says Carver.

"Who?"

"The *Shinso*. They're in orbit around us, and they won't be running their engines. They won't have time to get out of range of the tugs before this is all over."

"Doesn't matter. We need to warn them."

"Right." He lets out a long, slow breath, staring around the dock. "What about us?"

"What do you mean?"

"Well, Captain Riley's dished out orders to everyone," he says. "And hasn't left any for herself. Or her trusty sidekick."

Before I can answer, he says, "Listen, about earlier..."

I cut him off before he can remind me of our kiss, hating myself for having to do it, hating myself for not knowing what to think. "We'll deal with that later, OK?" I say. "After all this is over."

"Right," he says, a small smile crossing his face. "When we've saved the world. Again."

"From what I remember, *I* was the one who saved it last time."

The words are out before I can stop them. But when the memories come—Amira, my father, Okwembu—I'm surprised to find that they don't feel quite as sharp as before. Carver stares at me, and then bursts out laughing. "Of course," he says. "Sorry. Then this will be my first time. You can show me how it's done."

I hear my name shouted from across the dock. I turn and see a white-coated figure jogging across the floor towards us. It's a young woman, not much older than me, with golden-brown skin and a bob of dark hair.

At first, I think it's one of Prakesh's techs. I'm on the verge of telling her to get lost, but then I see that she's wearing the insignia of the station medical corps: two curved snakes around a vertical staff, the faded patch stitched onto the top pocket of the coat.

"You're Riley Hale?" she says, as she comes to a stop.

"What is it?"

She digs in her pocket. "Doctor Arroway told me to give you this."

My hand is moving even before she pulls out the vial of liquid.

It's transparent, viscous and slimy, clinging to the walls of its tiny cylindrical container. "This is it?" I say.

"First off the line. Why did he want me to give it to you? He didn't say."

I tuck the cylinder into my pocket. "Never mind that. How do I give it to a patient?"

"You just inject it into any vein. But that should be done at a hospital, so I can't see what—"

I don't let her finish. I start moving, walking towards the dock entrance. After a few moments, I turn around and shout a thank-you in her direction.

I'm going to have to move very, very fast.

Carver jogs up alongside me. "Want to me to stay here? Or come with you?"

He's right. He should be helping prepare the dock. But I can't find it in me to tell him to go. I need someone next to me. What I have to do next is going to take every ounce of will I have.

"Come with me," I say.

He smiles. "Sure."

72

Knox

Beep.

Morgan Knox hangs on to reality by the thinnest of threads. He's awake, his eyes open, staring up at the ceiling of the isolation ward. Somewhere in the space below his neck, there is appalling, awful pain, as black and dry as space itself. He knows that if he pays attention to it, even for a second, it will overwhelm him, and he won't be able to hang on. Instead, he focuses on the sound of the EKG machine. As long as he can hear it, he's still alive.

Beep.

For the first time in what feels like decades, but must surely have been just a few hours, he's fully lucid. He knows where he is, and what has happened to him. And he knows that he doesn't have long left. Like the pain, he has to approach this thought at an angle, look at it from just the corner of his eye.

Beep.

If he had any strength left in his lungs at all, he would laugh. He set up his revenge so perfectly, executed it with the utmost precision...and then he was laid low by *this*. A disease. Something he couldn't possibly have anticipated. If he'd put his plan into action only a few days earlier, he would have carried it off.

Beep.

It maddens him that he can do nothing about Janice Okwembu. But there is one bright point in the darkness: the little transmitter attached to his heart. The moment he dies, it will send out a signal to detonate the devices implanted in Hale. They will both die. But she's the one who will die screaming.

No.

It takes Knox a few seconds to register that the sound has changed. His eyes track down from the ceiling to the wall, and it's only when he gets halfway down that he recognises the sound he heard as human. Is someone with him?

No. You're not going to die.

Amira Al-Hassan is leaning up against the wall. She wears the same faded red scarf, and blood has soaked the front of her top, wet and black. She shouldn't be standing with a wound like that. She shouldn't be alive. But it's as if she barely notices it. She twists the end of her scarf in a clenched fist, and her eyes bore into Knox's.

He tries to speak, but barely has enough strength to move his lips apart.

No. Don't speak. Just listen.

She propels herself off the wall, moving with an uncommon grace. She walks to the bed and stands over it, looking down at him.

You think Riley Hale will suffer when you die? Sure, the explosives will hurt, but she'll bleed out fast. You know that, even if she doesn't.

Amira leans in closer. Her lips don't move when she speaks. *We could have been together, Morgan. We could have spent our lives together. She took that away from us. You think she should die quickly? It's not even close to what she deserves. Her death should take days.*

He reaches out to her, lifting his hand off the flimsy mattress. Trying to touch her.

Stay alive, Morgan. For me.

Beep.

He blinks. The movement seems to last an aeon. When he opens his eyes again, Amira is gone and in her place is Riley Hale.

73

Riley

It's a very good thing that Carver and I used to be tracers.

It means that we get back to the Tzevya hospital fast. We sprint across the sector, not talking, just running. I can feel the cure pressing against my hip, and some part of me thinks that every step is going to be my last, that we're not going to get there in time.

The hospital is still quiet, its beds empty. That won't last. Now that we've got a cure—or what might be a cure—they'll start distributing it quickly. Hospitals like this will become staging points, pulsing with energy, as Arroway and his colleagues start handing it out.

Uncertainty nags at me—we don't know how long we have before the Earthers reach the dock. We don't even know where they are, or how many there'll be in the first wave. But I can't defend the dock until I've dealt with Morgan Knox.

We find the isolation ward quickly. Knox's face is caked with strings of Resin, and he's still unconscious. But I can see him breathing, his chest shuddering as it expands and contracts. I don't waste any time. I grab a syringe from a nearby tray, then jam it into the steel mesh cap of the container holding the cure. Carver grabs Knox's arm, angling it towards me. With shaking hands, I inject every drop of the cure into his body.

Nothing happens.

"Is that it?" I say, watching Knox. There should be movement—when I injected him with the furosemide-nitrate, his entire body bucked and writhed as the medicine worked its way through him. Now, he's still. Comatose. My nerves feel like frayed cables, their strands pulled impossibly tight.

In that moment, I can feel the shape of the remote control, the one that would trigger the bombs. It's still in my jacket, wedged in its container. But I have it, and Knox doesn't.

I snap my fingers in front of Knox.

Nothing.

"Let me try," Carver says. Then he slaps Knox across the face.

He pulls the slap at the last moment. Knox cries out, a gurgling sound coming out of his throat. His eyes fly open, track across us, not seeing. Carver grabs Knox's chin, holds tight. "Wakey wakey," he says.

"Chest…sore."

"They've got a cure for Resin," Carver says. I stop him with a hand on his arm.

I take a deep breath. I'm thinking back to that little girl, Ivy. The one I grabbed when the Earthers were almost on us. Carver was right. I shouldn't have done that. But I can draw on that same desperation, channel it into what I'm about to do.

And Carver's right. It's easier when you're not alone.

"You haven't seen people die from Resin, have you?" I say to Knox.

Carver picks up what I'm doing immediately. "We have," he says.

"You're awake for most of it," I say. "The last half-hour or so. People cough up their own lungs. They go blind. They die screaming."

None of this is true. But Knox doesn't know that. His breath is coming quicker now, rattling in his chest.

"They've got a cure," I say. "For Resin. You haven't been given it yet."

"So," he says, and coughs. It's as if he has to use every muscle in his body just to form words. He tries again. "So cure me. I die, you die."

"Yeah. But now you die in agony, too."

I catch the spark of fear in his eyes. It flares for less than half a second, but it's there. I lean forward, getting in his face. "And you don't want to die, do you? You never did. You want to *live.*"

"Help me."

"No."

"Help me."

"You want that cure?" says Carver. "Let's trade. Her bombs come out, your lungs stay in. How's that sound?"

"Can't…operate. Too sick."

I keep my voice as steady as I can. "You're never going to touch me again. You're going to tell me how to remove them, and I'll find another doctor to do it."

Anger and fear and loathing combine on his face. It's one of the most terrifying expressions I've ever seen. I make myself keep looking into those eyes.

"You killed my Amira," he says.

"She wasn't yours, man," Carver says. "She never was. She belonged to us. She was a Devil Dancer."

He doesn't speak for a long moment. Then he says: "Left…wire."

I lean in. "What?"

"Cut…the left wire. My left."

"So that's it?" I say. "They open me up, pull out the bombs and cut the wire on the left? And what happens if they cut the wire on the right?"

He doesn't respond.

"Bullshit," Carver says. I look at him.

He returns my gaze. "He could be lying. The second those wires are cut, the bombs will go off."

"Telling…truth. *Please.*"

But there's no way of knowing. He could tell us anything, and we wouldn't know until it was too late.

I lick my lips. "You help me, I help you. You prove you aren't lying, and I'll inject the cure myself."

A little strength comes back to him then. He bats at Carver's hand, trying to push it away. "I'm not lying," he says, each word punctuated by a breath. "Cut the left wire on each bomb when you remove it. That's all. Now cure me, because if I die, the transmitter on my heart dies, and it won't send the answering signal back."

His words dissolve into a coughing fit. Carver sits back on his heels, his brow furrowed. "I don't know, Riley. I'm not sure how we can—"

I reach forward and grab Knox by the shoulder. "What did you just say?"

He raises his eyes to mine. "What?"

"No, no. You said—" I pause, trying to get the words right. "You said that if the transmitter dies, it won't send a signal back. And that means the bombs explode. Right?"

He stares at me in confusion, then nods.

My heart is beating faster. "What kind of signal is it?"

He points to his ear.

All this time, it was right in front of me.

Carver sucks in a shocked, delighted breath. He's already way ahead of me. "I can do it," he says breathlessly. "Won't take long."

"You can duplicate the signal?"

"Oh yeah. Just have to find the frequency he's using, which I can do because—"

"You're a genius. Got it."

He flashes a huge smile, his eyes shining. "It'll take him out of the equation. Even if he goes under, the gizmos inside you will still get that answering signal."

He punches me on the shoulder. It hurts, but I don't care. I close my eyes, feeling relief too exquisite to describe.

"Come on," says Carver, pulling me up. "Let's get back to the dock."

We're halfway across the ward when Knox shouts after us, putting all the energy he can into his voice. "We had a deal," he says, and coughs again. "You have to cure me."

I look over my shoulder, at the broken man on the bed.

"I already gave it to you," I say. "You're cured."

Knox's scream of fury follows us all the way out of the hospital.

74

Prakesh

Prakesh sits on the edge of the roof, his feet dangling in mid-air.

Two techs are crossing the floor below him, six storeys down. He's amazed that they can't hear him breathing—to his ears, each inhale is as loud as an engine turning over, each exhale an explosion of exhaust. But neither of them look up, and, in moments, they're out of sight.

Vertigo takes hold, the floor rushing up to meet him. He blinks hard, then squeezes his eyes shut, tilting his head back.

"I have to think," he says.

The words come out as a confused mumble. But he's been thinking from the moment he left Riley, from when he dodged the other techs and found his way up here, from the moment he swung his legs out over the edge. The result is no different. It's as if something blocks the thoughts from forming, as if his mind is trying to protect itself.

What keeps coming up, what keeps pushing past the mental barricades he's hiding behind, are numbers.

Population figures. The number of canteens in each station sector. Batch numbers, stencilled onto crates of produce in big black lettering. Monorail shipment times, printed in dull spreadsheets on his tab screen. There are strings of letters mixed in with the numbers, too. Cytogenetic locations: reference points for particular genes on particular chromosomes. Genes that he altered. Genes that he intuited would make the plants they belong to grow faster, bear more fruit.

The numbers don't matter. He can express the result in any equation he likes. He can rationalise it, tell himself that what he did made complete scientific sense. But at the other end of the equation is a single, stark figure. It measures in the hundreds of thousands, and it's growing by the second.

Zero-G

How could he have let this happen? How could he have been so short-sighted?

Nausea takes him. He clutches his stomach, appalled at the sick pain. He is desperate to throw up, but the tiny, clear section of his brain tells him not to. It would spatter on the ground below, attract people's attention, and he can't face that. Using every ounce of will he possesses, he holds the tide back, clamping his mouth shut, gritting his teeth.

Slowly, the feeling subsides. What's left behind is even worse.

Who is he kidding? He's not up here to think. He's up here because he saw what James Benson was planning to do—what James Benson *did*. He's up here because it's six storeys to the ground, a hundred feet up.

A bitter smile sneaks onto Prakesh's face. How could he have had that much hubris? Who was he to stop James Benson from taking his own life? He barely knew the man. That he could judge him, that he could try to control whether or not he lived or died... it's *obscene*. If Benson felt there was nothing left, that the rest of his life was beyond saving, then who's to say he wasn't taking the honourable way out?

And Prakesh's situation is far, far worse than Benson's. He can feel it pressing down on his shoulders, an almost physical weight.

That number again. The one on the other side of the equation. Six figures, growing by the second. Because of him.

Riley would miss him, for a time. But he saw how she looked at him, when she delivered the news, and he knows that taking himself out of her life would be a mercy. And his parents...it will be hard for them, yes, but it's better this way.

Prakesh is suddenly aware of his fingertips, clamped onto the edge of the roof. He can feel the grainy surface, scratchy under his nails. It would take the slightest push. A tiny amount of force. And there'll be no Mark Six to catch him.

His fingers start to move, his hands pushing downwards.

Halfway through the motion, he opens his eyes. The floor rushes towards him, as if he's already falling, and vertigo locks his head in a vice.

It doesn't matter. He's almost off the roof, almost in the grip of gravity. In the next instant, it'll take him.

Prakesh lets out of thin cry of horror. His body is off the surface of the roof, on the edge of tilting into oblivion. He tries to pull it back, but he can feel gravity taking hold of his stomach. His fingers scrabble at the roof, his palms digging into it.

No good. He's falling.

With a panicked howl, he tries to dig his feet into the side of the building. His arms are the only things supporting him now, the elbows bent at a strange angle, wrists screaming with pressure, his feet kicking in mid-air.

Mastering every last ounce of energy he has, Prakesh swings his right leg up, hooking the heel on the lip of the roof. The motion is enough to shift his centre of gravity backwards. The edge of his ass touches solid metal. He teeters, every muscle straining, and then falls back onto the roof, slamming into it thighs first.

"Oh," he says. "Oh no. No."

He's barely aware of what he's doing: crawling away from the edge on his hands and knees. He goes ten feet before he collapses, hyperventilating. The nausea is back. This time, he does throw up, retching thin streams of gruel onto the roof.

The seconds tick by. With each one, he tells himself that he's still alive.

Killing himself would be the easy way out. That he could have thought otherwise amazes him. He would have regretted it immediately, cursing himself, horribly aware that there was nothing he could do to fix what he'd just done.

And, really, what would his death mean? It would just be another number in the equation, another victim of Resin.

Riley told him they were developing a cure. Resin won't last much longer. Prakesh can do nothing about what's already happened, but he might be able to change what happens next. He's responsible for hundreds of thousands of deaths; surely the only thing he can do now is to help save as many lives as possible?

He can go to the dock, make himself available, do whatever they need him to do. Maybe he can convince the people trying to take the *Shinso* that there's another way. And when it's all over, he can help distribute the cure. Not make it—he'll never set foot in a lab again—but he can get it where it needs to be.

He lies there for a few more minutes. Then he gets to his feet, his legs shaking with effort, and walks back to the stairwell.

75

Riley

The floor of the dock is humming with activity.

The stompers have returned, lugging crates, filling the room with the sound of clanking metal. They drop the crates with an enormous bang, and start pulling out weapons—not just stingers, but other guns, too. I see Syria rubbing his hands with glee.

Carver didn't come back with me. As soon as we left the hospital, he was off, saying he needed to find a working SPOCS unit and a soldering iron. Now I'm jogging down the middle of the floor, wondering how I'm going to fit into the chaos. I do a quick headcount of my own as I go. Fifteen stompers, excluding Carver, Anna and me. Plus nine Tzevyans. Just under thirty souls. It'll have to be enough.

"Hale."

Iyengar is waving me over. Han Tseng is with her. He looks even more exhausted than before.

"This man claims he can fly," she says.

I try to keep the surprise off my face. *"You?"*

Tseng shrugs. "You think I've been a councilman my whole life? I can fly a tug."

"Not for twenty years," says Iyengar, sniffing in annoyance.

He glares at her. "The technology's the same. You asked if I could fly? Well, I can fly."

"Yeah, but can you fly in here?" I say.

Tseng's eyebrows look ready to fly off his head. "In the dock?"

"We need those tugs—" I point to the ships along the wall "—over there." My finger jabs towards the door.

"You're crazy."

I smile and shrug, my eyes locked on Tseng's. For the first time in days, I feel alive. "Well, if you can't do it..." I say.

He folds his arms. "Young lady, I once flew one of these tugs through a field of asteroid slag debris, *and* it had a damaged thruster. I'm probably the only person who *can* do it."

Without another word, he spins on his heel and walks to the closest tug. "Just make sure nobody is standing underneath it when I turn the engines on," he says over his shoulder.

He walks to the back and reaches up, standing on tiptoe. There's a hiss, then a clunk as a ramp drops down from the back of the tug. Tseng pulls it down the last few feet, then clambers on board. The tug itself looks like an enormously fat man, with a bulbous nose and tiny fins jutting out of the sides. Even though it's in the smallest class of ships, it still dwarfs us.

Iyengar is shaking her head. I don't give her the chance to comment. "Make sure everybody has a weapon," I say, as Tseng appears in the tug's cockpit. "And make sure they've got something to hide behind."

"I can't do both," she says, sounding sullen and resigned.

"Then pick one, and find somebody to do the other."

With a guttural roar, the tug's engine springs to life.

Tseng might be right about the tech being the same, but the moment the tug lifts off the magrail, I find myself wondering about that little trip of his through the debris field.

All activity in the hangar comes to a screeching halt. Watching the tug jerk itself upwards, seeing it nearly clip the wall and spin out of control prompts a burst of horrified gasps from across the floor.

It doesn't help that the tug looks about as manoeuvrable as a chunk of rock itself. I can just see Tseng at the controls, his head visible in the cockpit, high above. I see him look down, then the tug slowly begins to drift forward, moving towards the middle of the dock. The roar of its engine is huge.

It takes me a second to notice that it's still rising. It's only a few feet from the ceiling, on the verge of clipping it.

"Look out!" someone yells. It's impossible to know whether Tseng hears them, but the tug drops, plummeting to the floor. Just as it's about to crash, Tseng gets it under control. It rocks from side to side, hovering over the magrail track, its engine thrumming with a sound like water being sucked through a distant pipe.

After a moment, Tseng starts to move forward, scattering the crowd which had gathered to watch. He brings the tug to a grinding stop near the doors—I can hear the metal keening as the tug judders to a halt.

I don't stop to watch him climb out. Moving is good. Moving means that I have to pay attention to my body, working out how to minimise the impact of each step to lessen the pain in my knees.

I'm at the entrance of the hangar, helping Iyengar move a crowd barrier into place, when I almost back right into Prakesh.

He's aged ten years. It makes my breath catch in my throat. His face is haggard, his eyes red and raw. When I hug him, it's as if he barely has enough energy to squeeze back.

"How you holding up?" I say, as we pull apart.

He looks away, shrugs. At that moment, I want nothing more than to go back to our hab in Chengshi, curl up with him on the bed, and go to sleep. I want to pretend my kiss with Carver didn't even happen.

There are a million things I want to say to him. I want to tell him it'll be OK, even if it won't. I want to hug him again, and not let go.

Instead, I say, "We could use some extra hands. Can you help me with—"

"We can't do this, Riley."

"What?"

He waves at the rest of the hangar. "This. We can't let more people die. If I can go and talk to whoever is coming, try and convince them, then maybe…"

He trails off. I open my mouth, then close it again, not sure what words to use. We don't have time for this.

My eyes find his. "I know what you're saying, but we've met these people. They want off the station, and they're prepared to go through us to do it."

"They'll listen to reason. They have to."

"'Kesh—"

"You don't understand," he says, pushing me away and holding my shoulders at arm's length. "This is the only way I can make it right. I *have* to help. Please tell everyone to stand down."

I take a deep breath. "No."

It's one word. Two letters. A single syllable. But in that instant, it's heavier than any word ever uttered. Prakesh's body sags, as if I'd just punched him in the gut.

"They won't listen," I say. I've never been more sure of anything in my life. It's all too easy to see the weapons they were stockpiling, the determined look in Mikhail's eyes. "Either we stop them here, or they'll kill us all."

His shoulders sag. After a few seconds, he says, "What do you want me to do?"

76

Riley

The next twenty minutes are one big multi-stage cargo run.

Anna and I zip back and forth across the hangar, ducking and diving and dancing past anybody who steps into our way. We ferry stinger parts and help lift barriers and deliver messages from one end of the dock to the other. I break off every so often to direct operations.

The tension builds so slowly that it takes me a little while to realise that the friendly chatter has ceased. I can feel people becoming more harried, dropping things more often and cursing when they do.

After a while, there's not a lot left for us to carry. We rest for a moment, over by one of the remaining tugs.

"What are you idiots standing around for?" says a voice.

Royo. He's pale, haggard, and moving with increased care. But he's upright, being supported by Carver.

"Captain," says Anna solemnly, "you have an ability to take a beating that is nothing short of outstanding."

"Why, thank you, Beck," Royo says. "You have an ability to never shut up that I find similarly awe-inspiring."

His gaze finds mine. I can't describe what passes between us at that moment, but it's not something I have words for.

"Resin," I say. "Is it..."

"Getting there fast. Not everyone is responding to the injection Arroway cooked up—I think some are too far gone. But for what it's worth, yes, we beat Resin. Not that it helped ninety per cent of this station."

There's an uncomfortable silence.

"We'll deal with that later, Cap," says Carver. He reaches over, and passes me something. A SPOCS unit. It's been torn apart, and put back together again—when I jam it into my ear, it makes an uncomfortable fit.

"Is it working?" I say.

He nods. "Yeah. I think I got the frequency. But..."

"What is it?"

"Ry, there's no way of testing it. Not unless your friend Knox puts a stinger to his head. And it's a stop-gap at best—you'll have to keep it charged up."

"*Shinso*'s started moving," Royo says. "But they're not going to have nearly enough time to get clear, Hale. These tugs look small, but they've got plenty of range."

"It'll help," I say. "It has to."

Another wave of exhaustion slips through my barricades, and I have to bite my lip hard to get enough pain to fight it off.

Royo is eyeing us. "Where are your weapons?"

"We'll get there, Cap," Carver says. "Besides, who needs weapons when you have the Boneshaker?"

Royo raises his eyebrows. "You mean that thing?"

He jerks his head at the dock entrance, where the Boneshaker, black and hulking, is parked up against the wall.

"Run it right at 'em, and they scatter like bugs," Carver says, a huge smile eating up his face. "Riley's got her speed and Anna has One-Mile."

"Nope," Anna says. "Earthers took it." She casts a dirty look at the entrance to the dock.

As I look at her, an idea comes to mind. "Anna?"

"Huh?"

"Come with me."

Before she can say anything, I'm striding out across the dock floor, hopping over the magrail. I hear Anna following, calling my name, but it's drowned out as Tseng swings another tug overhead. I don't have to look up to know that I could probably reach out and touch the bottom of it.

I don't stop until we reach the weapons crates. The stompers are there, cleaning the stingers, and the bright smell of oil gets stronger as I approach. One of them looks up, then reaches down to get me a gun.

"Not one of those," I say, and he looks up, puzzled. I point to one of the other weapons in the crate. One I saw earlier, when they were first brought in.

"The long gun?" he says, his brow furrowed. "I was leaving that until last. I don't even know if it'll fire—last time this thing saw action was the Lower Sector Riots."

"Pass it here."

"Think you can handle it? It's heavy."

"It's not for me."

He shrugs, then lifts out the gun. Anna's eyes go wide.

It's long—as tall as I am, easily. A thin barrel, an extended stock, and, screwed onto the top, a scope. It stains my hands black, turning them gritty with oil.

She hesitates before grabbing it, like she isn't quite sure it's real. When she does, the expression of wonder in her face is just amazing. Anna hefts the rifle to shoulder height, jamming the stock into her shoulder and welding her cheek to it, squinting down the scope. When she lifts her head off, there's a black mark on her cheek. It's at odds with the white gleam of her smile.

"Do you even know how to use that thing?" asks the stomper cleaning the weapons.

Anna racks the breech, clicking it back, then glares at the stomper. When she speaks, her voice is a low growl. "Just give me the ammo."

77

Knox

The sheet on Knox's bed is stiff with dried Resin. He's been coughing for the past hour, and the fluid coming out of his lungs has gone from thin streams of liquid to sticky chunks. With each cough, he is able to breathe a little more easily.

And with each cough, his hatred for Riley Hale grows.

He curls on his side, tucking into the foetal position. Pain racks his body, and another round of coughing lodges a gluey hunk of Resin behind his back teeth. He sticks a finger in his mouth, fishes it out, and flicks it away. His head is clear—clearer than it's been in what feels like years. He knows what he has to do, and the sheer force of that knowledge, the clarity of purpose, is enough to make him swing his legs out from the bed.

He almost falls. He has to grip the mattress to steady himself, nearly pulling it off the bed. His nose is blocked, and, in the silence of the isolation ward, his breathing sounds harsh and hot.

He needs a weapon. Taking Hale on bare-handed is a non-starter. After all, her crew leader taught her to fight, didn't she?

From the door of the ward, Amira says, *That's right. She'll break you in half if you let her, just like she broke me.*

"I don't know where she is," he says. "I'll never find her."

You do know. Think back.

He pauses, his hand still gripping the mattress. That was it.

Hale's friend, the blond one, said something important. *Let's get back to the dock.*

Knox runs a hand across his sticky lips, looking around him. His eyes fall on the wheeled instrument tray beside the bed. There's a syringe on it—the same one that Hale used on him, he's sure of it. Its plunger is depressed, and he can see a drop of liquid beading on the end of the needle.

He scoops it up, holding it in a two-fingered grip with his thumb on the plunger. Amira smiles, then turns and walks through the closed door. This bothers Knox for a moment, but then he pushes the thought aside.

He still feels horrible. Every muscle aches, every movement bringing agony. He makes himself walk, pushing open the door of the ward and shambling through the hospital corridors. Some of the lights are out, and he has to grope his way through. Several times, he bangs his shin or his hip into something in his path. Each impact feels like it vibrates his very bones.

He starts to hear voices, which grow clearer as he makes his way towards the entrance. He tightens his grip on the syringe. As he approaches the lobby, the voices grow even more clear. There are two of them: two men, silhouetted in the main doorway, facing each other. They both wear the off-white uniforms of medical orderlies, and they look bone-tired.

From somewhere out of sight, Amira says, *Wait*.

The man on the left scratches his head. He has an untidy ponytail, and he keeps tugging at it. "How many we got coming?"

"Gods know," the other replies.

The first man yanks his ponytail again, his arm cocked over his right shoulder. "It's going to be a nightmare. How can Arroway expect two people to run this place?"

"Gods know," his partner says again. "You start setting up. I'll see if I can scrounge up some more volunteers."

"Seriously? You think you're actually going to find any?"

But the second man has already gone, his footsteps fading into the distance.

Ponytail shakes his head, then strides into the lobby. He's muttering to himself, and Knox can hear the words clearly. "Sure,

sure, I'll just do all the hard work, why not?" he says. He starts clearing the main desk, shifting tab screens and food containers out of the way.

Now. Go, Amira says.

Knox crosses behind the man, trying to be as quiet as possible. He's almost at the door when he hears the man turn. "Hey. Whoa, hey!"

Knox doesn't look round. Ponytail pads up behind him, moving quickly across the floor. "Hey, you all right?" he says, putting a hand on Knox's shoulder. "You were inside? We've got a cure, so you can just hang out here and—"

In a single movement, Knox turns around and brings the syringe up, burying it in the man's eye.

He almost doesn't get there. The muscles in his arm feel like they're made of glass. And Ponytail sees the needle coming, tries to deflect it. But he's not fast enough.

He starts to scream, and Knox puts a hand over his mouth, shoving him backwards. They fall to the floor, the man bucking and writhing underneath him. Knox leans on the syringe, pushing it further in, and he feels the needle scrape bone. It isn't nearly long enough to penetrate beyond the eye socket, but it gives Knox the opening he needs.

He yanks the needle back, pulling it out of the deflating eye. Ponytail is still trying to push him off, but his hands have strayed to his face, exposing the rest of him. Knox takes a split second to locate the carotid artery in the man's twisting neck, and then he stabs the needle downwards, again and again.

Soon, the man's struggles begin to get weaker. When they stop completely, Knox is drenched in blood.

He gives the syringe one final twist, then gets to his feet. He's shaking, and he knows that it was stupid to burn so much energy so fast. But his head is clearer than it's ever been, his purpose a bright shining light.

He looks down at the man one last time. "I'm discharging myself," he says, and keeps walking towards the doors, moving in long, loping steps.

78

Riley

It's while he's piloting the third tug that Tseng spins out of control.

He's put two of them across the entrance. The one he's piloting would block off the entrance completely, but when he tries to position the ship, it all goes wrong.

I'm running with Carver when there's an enormous grinding screech, and we look up to see the tug tilting forward. Its cockpit glass has smashed, and the ceiling of the dock has a huge black gouge ripped into it. Before I can process this, the tug lists to one side, and the stompers scatter as it smashes into the ground.

The ship bounces once before slamming into one of the tugs he's positioned across the entrance. The engine of Tseng's tug cuts, replaced by the crunching bang of the impact.

There's a stunned silence. I'm holding my breath, and Carver has grabbed my hand so tight that it's gone numb.

The hatch on the top of the tug snaps open, and Tseng crawls out. He tries to stand, and then topples off the top of the tug, his body falling out of sight. Two Tzevyans rush to his aid, and Royo immediately starts directing the other stompers to different positions across the dock.

"We are so screwed," says Carver, looking at the enormous gap in the hangar entrance between the wall and the parked tugs.

"Maybe not," I say, resuming our walk to the Boneshaker. Carver shakes his head, and follows. Glancing over my shoulder, I see Anna setting up behind some crates, with a clear line of sight down the entrance corridor. The long gun is balanced on the top of the crate, and she's got her eye glued to the scope.

When we reach the Boneshaker, Carver vaults onto it.

"How are you planning to use this thing?" I say.

"I'm gonna take them from the side. They won't know what hit 'em."

"Don't drive into the line of fire, then. OK?"

Carver flashes me a smile, then reaches out and pulls me into an unexpected hug.

"What are you going to do?" he says.

I point to the gun station, to one of the crates loaded with ammo.

"I'm a tracer," I say. "I'm going to run."

And without another word, I take off down the hangar.

I can feel the tension rising, crackling through the air. Stompers and civilians hunker down behind hastily placed cover. Stingers are checked, sighted, checked again. Everyone's eyes are on the corridor leading up to the dock. Royo's at the weapons table when I get there, talking to the stompers behind it. He's still pale, but seems more upright, somehow. By now, the combined noises in the hangar have become so loud that he's having to shout to be heard, but he stops when he sees me.

"Can't be more than a few minutes before they get here," Royo says. "You ready?" He hands me a stinger of my own, greasy with oil.

I don't get a chance to respond. At that moment, a rocket—a whirring, spinning projectile, propelled on a roaring cone of fire—comes howling through the entrance of the dock.

79

Riley

The rocket corkscrews through the air, detonating right above the middle of the hangar, sending out a cone of flaming, spitting shrapnel. One piece lands near me, charred black, crunching off the deck. Somewhere distant, there's a roar as Carver kicks the Boneshaker into life.

I dive behind a line of crates, my stinger out and trained on the doors. Two more rockets explode through the gap. One of them takes out a crane near the side of the dock, knocking two stompers sprawling. I see one of them skidding across the floor, a dark, smoking stump where his left leg should be. His face is a mask of pain and shock.

We're returning fire—I can hear the boom of the long gun, the spitting bang of stingers—but it isn't stopping the Earthers' advance guard from charging through. There are more of them than I thought, using plate metal as makeshift shields, dropping them to form cover.

I've never been a good shot—and that's under firing-range conditions. But I start shooting anyway, targeting the gap. One of them is running right at me—I fire once, twice, but hit nothing. As I get ready to fire again, I hear a thundering shot from my right. Anna: down on one knee, the long gun resting on a crate. She took down the Earther on the run, tracking his movement across the floor before shooting.

I don't have time to thank her. I keep firing. This time, I find my mark, my bullets taking one of the Earthers in the shoulder. She spins out, knocked backwards. The air is thick with acrid smoke.

More of them. Now they're using their own supplies as cover—crates on wheeled pallets, absorbing the gunfire, their surfaces denting as the bullets ricochet. Still more are breaking through the gap, running left, right, dodging out of the way. I hear Iyengar curse as a man she was aiming at vanishes behind cover.

There's no sign of Mikhail, or Okwembu.

I'm useless here. It's a damn miracle I hit even one person. I should be transporting ammo, keeping everyone else topped up. Frantic, I look around for the supply, spotting it a few yards away behind another barricade. I sprint for it, pumping my arms to push myself forward—and have to duck and roll as a length of metal pipe swings forward, nearly taking me in the face.

The Earther wielding it has come right through the lines, his eyes wild. The pipe is huge, so big that it looks like a roof strut, and he has to lean back to get enough force to swing it again. I feel rather than hear the pipe, like a sick vibration in the air. Just in time, I roll to the side, coming up as it bangs off the floor.

The Earther roars in anger, but I'm too fast for him, up in half a second and chopping him across the throat, right above his Adam's apple. It knocks him back—amazingly, he's still upright. Before he can regain his balance, I drive a knee into his stomach. That does the job.

Before he even hits the ground, there's a whooshing thud to my left. I look around to see that Iyengar is on fire.

One of the makeshift rockets hit her. She's screaming, tearing at herself in agony as flames bloom around her. With a horrible clarity, I see the skin on her face start to blister. Her fingers are stuck together. She falls face down, twitching.

Prakesh jumps to the front of my mind, and the feeling that comes with it is an impossible terror. I can't see him anywhere. I don't know whether that's good or bad. There's too much noise, too much drifting smoke. Royo is shouting, trying to regain control.

I feel the rumble of the Boneshaker before I see it. Then Carver is pulling alongside me, sweeping me onto it. He hands me a clip over his shoulder, the metal slick with oil.

"I'll drive, you shoot," I hear him say.

I don't have time to tell him that I'm a terrible shot. He guns the engine, and I nearly topple off the back as we scream off down one side of the dock.

80

Prakesh

"Get down!"

A hand on the back of his neck shoves Prakesh to the floor. Bullets whine overhead, the air rippling as it's pushed aside. The front of the makeshift barricades, where his head was a moment before, cracks and splinters as a volley of gunfire tears into it.

The man who shoved him down is peering over the top of the barricade, his hand still on Prakesh's neck. Prakesh can feel some sort of ring on one of the fingers, the metal cold against his skin. He looks up, the coppery taste of fear coating the inside of his mouth. The man has lank hair and an angular face. *Syria,* he thinks. *Riley called him Syria.*

There are two stompers alongside them, and, as they return fire, Prakesh gets to his knees. They're in a good position in the shadow of one of the tugs, but even as he raises his head, another bullet whistles past his ear and he ducks.

Syria moves with him, grabbing the front of his shirt. He pulls Prakesh close, all but snarling his words. "You gonna start firing any time soon?"

Prakesh is holding a stinger with both hands. He doesn't remember how he got it, who gave it to him, but he knows he hasn't fired a single shot. Every time his finger finds the trigger, he freezes.

Syria throws him aside, blind-firing over the top of the barricade. Another rocket detonates, filling the air with the hot stench of smoke.

What am I doing here? Prakesh thinks. A few hours earlier, he was in the Air Lab, outrunning and out-thinking Julian Novak, protecting his colleagues. Now he's in the middle of a firefight, asked to take even more lives than he has already.

"If you're not gonna fire, give me your ammo," Syria says, fumbling at the stinger in Prakesh's hands.

In response, Prakesh raises himself up, swinging his arms over the top of the barricades. He pulls the trigger once, twice, three times, not even aiming. He knows there is almost no chance of hitting anyone, and he doesn't care. He just wants it to be over, and the quickest way to do that is to drain his ammo. At any other time, the logical part of his mind would have protested this. But now, with the smoke invading his nostrils, it's all he can think to do.

His stinger clicks empty. In the instant before he ducks under the barricades again, Prakesh sees Riley. She's on the back of Carver's contraption, tearing across the floor, drawing fire from the Earthers.

81

Knox

Knox sees Okwembu first.

She's around the near side of the dock entrance, squatting on her haunches, utterly untroubled by the chaos going on around her. She wears the same prison jumpsuit she had on when Hale brought her to his surgery. She wears a thick jacket over it, the faux-fur collar bunched around her neck. There are other people around her, their heads bent close together. Knox can see their mouths moving, but he can't hear their words over the gunfire. One of them—a craggy, scarred man with long grey hair—is gesturing wildly, jabbing a finger at the dock.

There's a bang, and he ducks instinctively. He is on the other side of the dock entrance from Okwembu, leaning up against the wall. Whatever's going on here, whoever these people are, none of them has noticed him yet. They're focused on the battle, on pushing deeper into the dock.

He still has the syringe, its needle caked with dried blood and aqueous humour. He grips it tight. He'll walk across, come up on Okwembu, and jam it into the side of her neck.

No, says Amira, crouched next to him. *You won't get within ten feet before they cut you down.*

She's right. Of course she is. He shakes his head, angry with himself. He has to keep it together. He's still not strong enough—the walk over here has exhausted him, draining what little energy he has. His lungs are clear, but feel brittle, as if a breath that's too strong will crack a hole in them.

"You!"

Knox feels a hand on his shoulder. He tenses—his reactions might not be what they should, but he's still got the syringe, and he can still fight off whoever this is.

No, Amira says again.

Knox looks around. The man is tall, easily over six feet, with broad shoulders and a carefully trimmed moustache. He's clutching a tattered backpack in his hand, and he looks Knox up and down, his eyes narrowed. "The hell happened to you?" he says, raising his voice as a fresh volley of gunfire crackles through the air.

Knox tenses his fingers on the syringe. Whatever Amira says, he can't afford this delay. Hale is in there, he knows it, he just has to get to her. And he is acutely aware of how he looks, his face and clothing crusted with the evidence of Resin.

But the man's eyes are jumping, unable to focus, brimming with adrenaline. "Doesn't matter," he says, almost to himself, digging inside the backpack. "Take this. Stick to the left flank, and we should be able to take out a few more of them."

The stinger is black, home-made, the metal edges badly machined. Knox takes it with his free hand, palming the syringe with the other, leaving the needle sticking out between his middle and index finger. "Thanks," he says.

And looks up to see the man's shoulder explode with blood and bone.

Knox throws himself to the floor, out of the line of fire, pushing the screaming man aside. He doesn't know where the shooter is, and he doesn't care. He crawls into the dock, staying as low as possible, heading for one of the wheeled pallets stacked high with crates. His hand is sticky with sweat, and he keeps a tight grip on the stinger.

Somehow, he makes it to the cover. There's a body behind it, curled in on itself, like it's trying to protect its stomach. Knox shunts it aside, tries to think, tries to form thoughts under the noise. He's lost his syringe somewhere—it must have fallen from his hand as he crawled. Doesn't matter. Amira is there, down on one knee beside him. A thin stream of blood issues from her mouth, trickling down her chin.

He takes two quick breaths, then raises himself up, sneaking a look around the side of the crates.

The dock is coming to pieces around him. The parts he can see through the drifting smoke are a tangle of muzzle flashes and sprinting bodies. He tries to stay calm, knowing that it's what Amira would do. *Hale. Where are you?*

He spots her at almost the moment the thought forms. She's on the back of the vehicle, the one they had him on earlier, tearing across the dock with her friend at the controls.

And as soon as he spots her, he hears Amira speaking in his ear, the anger in her voice as clear as a pane of glass. He turns to look at her, and sees that the blood coming from her mouth has covered her entire face. Her eyes are black holes in a sea of dark red.

There she is. There's the bitch. Kill her.

82

Riley

There are three Earthers crouched down behind one of the barricades. They've killed the stompers who were behind it, taking it for themselves. We're heading right towards them—a thought has just enough time to form in my head, a crazy jumble of words like *Can't* and *Aim* and *Impossible.* Then I'm firing.

I rise up off the seat to do it, aiming over the top of Carver's head. I don't even see where most of my shots land. But then one of the Earthers goes down, blood exploding out of a gaping wound in his temple. The other two turn, their eyes wide with shock, and then the Boneshaker is on them. The one on the left manages to get out of the way, diving right over the front of the line of the crates. The other isn't as lucky. I feel his body crunch under our wheels as we ride right over him, the vehicle bucking so hard that it nearly kicks us off.

Carver hangs a hard right, the Boneshaker screaming alongside the tugs barricading the entrance. As he does so, I get a good look at the dock. My stomach drops, and it has nothing to do with the speed we're moving at.

We're losing. It only takes me a second to see that. The few stompers and Tzevyans left are pinned down, hunkered behind the barricades with only the tops of their heads visible. I can't see Anna—just the tip of the long gun, standing upright. She's either reloading, or she's dead.

More Earthers come tumbling out of the gap. In seconds, my clip is dry, the slide slamming open. I raise myself up, putting one leg on the seat.

"The hell are you doing?" Carver shouts. He's pulled the Boneshaker to the right, shooting diagonally across the dock, crossing the gap while there's no gunfire from the others.

"Just keep going!" I shout. And at the moment where we zip by a tightly clustered group of Earthers, I hurl myself off the seat.

There are three of them, crouched low as they run, heading for cover. They turn at the sound of the Boneshaker, and I see the shock in their faces as I fly through the air towards them. My legs are tucked, with my knees pulled up to my chest and my arms out, elbows cocked back. In the split second before impact, I see that the one closest to me is Anton—the Earther who captured us back in Knox's surgery. His eyes are huge, his mouth open in horror.

I have just enough time to think the words: *I came back for you.* And then my shin takes him in the face.

I'm moving so fast that his mouth is still open when I hit it. There's a crunching sensation as his jaw shatters. It happens so quickly that he doesn't have time to cry out; he just drops.

I'm already tucking for the roll, the ground rising up to meet me, and when it does it's like sliding on oil, my body tucked in the perfect position. I rise up from the floor as the roll brings me up, striking out as I do so. Fist to stomach, elbow to chest. The last two Earthers go down.

Another *boom* followed by a crumpling sound behind me. Another Earther—one I hadn't seen, a younger man with a trim beard—came up behind me. Now he's nothing more than a trembling body, his chest a dark, open wound.

I turn my head to see Anna flick me a salute. The barrel of her gun is still smoking. More rockets, shooting out from somewhere unseen in the entrance passage, exploding above us in a crash of noise and smoke. I start to run to the side of the hangar, away from the line of fire, when one detonates right next to me.

It's like someone took the world and yanked it away, leaving nothing but darkness and silence behind. Slowly, very slowly, flickers of light start to fade in, accompanied by a dull roar. My body has stopped responding: everything below my neck has checked out.

Amazingly, I don't feel fear. I don't feel anything.

I close my eyes.

I don't know how much time passes before I open them again. Some sounds have come back: the booming of gunfire, people shouting. But I barely notice them.

Because Morgan Knox is standing over me.

Somehow, he made it into the dock. He crawled out of the hospital, found his way here, wound his way through the battle. He's turned into something awful, barely a human being. His face is black with dried Resin. His mouth is open, and I see it's coated his teeth, filling out the thin gaps between them.

He's got a stinger. He's holding it in both hands, aiming carefully. It's less than four feet away. Impossible to miss.

Move, I tell myself. But the thought comes from far away.

Knox's open mouth forms a twisted smile. He sights down the body of the gun.

I try to form words, but I can't. I can only watch as he squeezes the trigger.

83

Riley

In the instant before Knox shoots me, I move.

It's more in desperation than anything else. I roll to the side, using my shoulders to wrench my body.

Knox fires. The bang slams my eardrums shut, and the bullet hits the floor right where my neck was. I can feel the vibrations travelling through the metal.

I let the energy in my shoulders travel. First to my torso, then my knees, then my ankles. I'm lying on my side now, my back towards Knox, and I kick out with my right leg.

My shin collides with his. He goes down, howling in fury. But as I roll back the other way, I see that he still has the stinger. He's up on one elbow, trying to get a bead on me.

I get to my knees, my head pounding, white heat burning in my throat. *Not fast enough.* He's going to aim and fire, and this time I'm not going to be able to stop him.

"Hey you."

Knox pauses, looks to his right.

Carver's boot takes him across the side of his head. He crumples instantly, folding in on himself. His head thuds off the floor, and the stinger spins away.

"That was for Kev," says Carver.

He stares down at Knox a moment longer, then looks over at me. "You OK?"

I'm too stunned to speak. Knox is still breathing, but he's unconscious, sprawled awkwardly across the floor.

"I'm fine," I say. We're off to one side of the dock, behind one of the tugs and out of sight of the entrance. The Boneshaker sits nearby.

"Can that thing still run?" I ask Carver, pointing to the Boneshaker.

He shakes his head. "Lucky shot hit the engine."

I point to Anna's shooting nest. Carver nods, and we sprint towards it, keeping as many barriers as possible between us and the entrance to the dock. Even so, we have to hit the ground a few times as bullets slam into them. There are bodies back here; too many of them.

Anna is crouched down when we get there. Her beanie is pulled down low on her head, and the eyes visible underneath it are glowing white-hot. There's no sign of Royo, or Syria, or anyone else we know. No Prakesh, either.

I lean up against the crates, breathing hard, feeling fury coursing through my veins.

"Are they *still coming*?" Carver shouts to Anna.

She nods, slamming the breech of the long gun shut.

"How many?" I ask.

"Hard to tell," she says through gritted teeth. "A lot."

"Can we hold out?"

But even as I ask the question I know what the answer is. The dock is filling with smoke from the detonated rockets. Every breath burns, turning the back of my throat to acid. And everywhere I look, I see bodies. Stomper, Tzevyan and Earther, piled together. Even if we've taken down one of them for each of us, it's still not enough.

Carver grabs two nearby stingers, checks them, then tosses them aside with a snarl. "Empty," he says.

"Got anything else?"

Before he can answer, there's the rough whistle of another rocket. It detonates above us, and I go deaf again, the afterimage of the explosion imprinted on my retinas. Anna fires, her eyes just visible over the long gun's stock.

Right then, I get a glimpse of the back of the hangar, and my stomach goes into free fall.

Royo is sprawled out on the dock. The floor around him is slick with blood, gushing from a wound high on his right leg. His face is twisted with pain and fury.

Okwembu is walking towards Royo, a stinger of her own clutched in her hands.

But she's not firing. Because between her and Royo is Walker, swinging an enormous chain, daring Okwembu to take another step. She swings so hard and so fast that Okwembu has to dodge back, the thick chain striking the metal floor.

But none of that is what causes my blood to freeze.

It's Mikhail.

Royo hasn't seen him. Neither has Walker. But he's moving fast, coming up from behind them, his footfalls masked by the noise of battle. There's something in his hand. Something that catches the light from a rocket detonation nearby and reflects it back, turning the burning orange glow into something sharp and bright.

I boost out of my crouch into a sprint. I can feel from my screaming muscles that I'm moving faster than I ever have before, but it's like I'm running on the spot. The distance between me and the back of the hangar seems to grow, even as Mikhail closes it.

I try to shout a warning, but it comes out as little more than a husk of itself, thin and empty. My legs are still moving, and the sparks of pain shooting from them tell me how fast I'm going, but I'm not going to make it. I'm not even halfway there when Mikhail reaches Royo.

Walker is regrouping after her last swing, setting her shoulders to move the chain again, and Royo is almost catatonic, his hands dark with blood as they grip his leg.

At the very last instant, Royo sees Mikhail. He tries to raise himself up, an expression of astonished anger on his face. Okwembu is smiling, serene.

Walker whirls around, but it's too late.

Moving casually, almost gently, Mikhail puts a knee on Royo's chest. He hesitates, just for a second, and then he slides the blade into Royo's throat.

84

Riley

Royo goes still.

Walker screams in anger, lifting the chain high over her head. Before she can bring it down, Okwembu steps forward, and puts the stinger against her neck. I see her lips moving, but her words are lost in the wash of battle. Walker's shoulders slump, and she hurls the chain down, the links crashing to the ground.

Mikhail removes the blade, wiping it on the sleeve of his jacket.

The strength goes out of my legs, and I'm brought to a stop completely when Okwembu glances in my direction and pushes the barrel of her stinger harder into Walker's neck.

Mikhail raises the blade over his head. It must have been some sort of signal, because the gunfire coming from the entrance lowers, then stops completely. There are a few isolated pops from the remaining stompers, and a boom from Anna's gun, but then even those die away. Smoke drifts across the hangar floor. I can see Anna reloading. She hasn't seen what's happened to Royo.

"It's over!" Okwembu shouts, her sharp voice cutting through the fading echoes of gunfire.

Carver and Anna spin around, aiming their guns at her.

Okwembu flicks me a glance. "Careful, Ms. Hale," she says, more quietly.

I realise I'm still moving towards her, and stop. I can't take my eyes off the gun at Walker's neck.

"No one else has to die," Mikhail shouts. "Not if you surrender yourselves."

There's silence in the dock. I look back across the floor, and I see with dismay that there are only a few of us left. Me, Carver, Anna, two Tzevyans, two Stompers. No: there are two more. Prakesh is over by the right-hand wall, leaning up against one of the tugs, his expression grim. Syria is with him.

But there are still at least a dozen Earthers, walking through the entrance to the dock. Mikhail brings the blade down, pointing it right at us. His eyes flash above it, green and clear.

And at that moment, one of the tugs at the entrance springs to life.

The Earthers around it scatter, and surprised shouts reach us across the dock.

Tseng. I can just see him behind the controls. What is he doing?

The tug starts to rise. I look back at Okwembu, but she and Mikhail are frozen in place. It's only when Tseng tilts the tug towards them, its shadow growing on the ground as it rises, that they start to move, taking halting, panicked steps backwards, Okwembu pulling Walker with her.

One of the Earthers emerges from the entrance. It's Hisako—I remember her from when Carver, Anna and I were captured. I can barely make her out through the smoke. There's a tube on her shoulder. She points it at Tseng's tug, which is gathering speed, flying right across the dock towards us.

Okwembu sees it, too. "No!" she shouts.

Hisako fires.

The rocket hisses through the air, and hits the back of Tseng's tug with a bang that shakes my teeth. The tug lurches forward, propelled on a cone of fire. It starts spinning, whirling on its horizontal axis. Carver screams my name.

The roar of the tug becomes a tortured, metallic scream. I feel it pass overhead, and hurl myself to the ground. Its shadow passes on top of me. Mikhail and Okwembu bolt, sprinting towards the wall of the hangar, heading for the other tugs.

Walker runs, too. But not fast enough.

The tug hits the ground.

It's bouncing, breaking up, shedding pieces of itself like torn clothing. The cockpit vanishes, engulfed in a wave of fire which explodes from the tug's belly. Walker looks up, then the tug is on her. She vanishes in a whirlwind of torn, screaming metal.

Carver's grip on my arm is iron-tight. The destroyed tug is still going. The wrecked body is tumbling across the floor, heading right for the…

For the airlock doors.

They loom at the far end of the hangar. Big enough to let a whole tug through. Surely they'll withstand a hit—they're too big, too solid.

But the destroyed tug is coming in too fast.

It hits hard enough to shake the ground. Above us, the roof struts keen and screech, knocking loose dust and metal shavings. The boom is subsonic, catching in my bones.

The only thing louder is the silence that follows it.

When I look up, I see that the tug has smashed *through* the first set of doors, ripping right through the metal, knocking one door right off its tracks, coming to rest up against the outer doors.

Slowly, Carver and I get to our feet.

At that moment, the outer doors give off a low, metallic grinding sound. It's the sound of metal splitting. They're not holding—and beyond them is nothing but the vacuum.

"Oh gods," says Carver.

Zero-G

85

Prakesh

They used to tell stories about hull breaches when Prakesh was a kid.

They were scary stories—tales the grown-ups would weave while they gathered around, wrapped up in blankets while their parents sipped homebrew in the dim light. They would talk about the monsters lurking on the other side; how they would reach through the hole, open their giant mouths and inhale, sucking everything out in an instant.

Prakesh knows better now, and he wishes he didn't. Every fact about rapid decompression is flashing to the front of his mind. When those doors split, anything not nailed down will be dragged right out into space—including people. If by some miracle they manage to hold on, they'll have about ten seconds before the loss in air pressure rips consciousness away from them. Two minutes later, they'll be dead. That's if the whirlwind of flying debris doesn't kill them first.

In a hundred years, it's never happened, not once. The solid steel skin of Outer Earth has never been cut.

They have to get away. They have to move now. But Prakesh is already running the equations in his head, doing it involuntarily, size of the hole versus air speed versus tension on the station hull.

They'll never make it.

And, all at once, the idea is there, burning bright. Prakesh stands and runs, pushing past Syria, scanning the bottom of the tugs. *Come on, come on, where are you…*

There. The ramp access button, a bulbous red mushroom on the tug's underside. He hammers on it, and the ramp begins to drop, lowering down from the back of the tug. It's their only hope: get inside a sealed environment, away from the deadly effects of the decompression.

The ramp moves slowly, issuing a thin mechanical whine, and Prakesh has to suppress an urge to scream at it. Instead, he turns and cups his hands to his mouth. "Everybody! Get inside, now!"

Syria reacts first, his big feet hammering across the floor, his arms pumping. He gets there just as the ramp fully extends. He grabs Prakesh's shoulder, trying to pull him up the ramp. Prakesh twists away. "You go," he says. "I'll get the others on board."

Syria wavers, then bolts up the ramp, using the handholds on the inner walls to pull himself along. Prakesh turns, and sees Janice Okwembu sprinting towards him. There are Earthers with her, some of them still clutching their weapons.

He almost stops her, then shakes it off. He has to preserve life now, no matter whose life it is, no matter what they've done. He gestures them onwards, urging them to hurry, and they sprint past him, pounding up the ramp. It bends and creaks under their weight. There's no time to open any of the other tugs' ramps—he'll have to get as many people into this one as he can.

Prakesh's heart is pounding, every muscle tense, waiting for the airlock doors to give way. He tells himself not to hold his breath if it happens—his lungs will rupture if he does. Every instinct he has is to get into the body of the tug himself, but he stays at the bottom, looking for more people he can save.

Riley. Where's Riley? Prakesh shouts her name, but he can't see her.

86

Riley

The airlock doors give another grinding screech. An alarm blares in the distance. The smoke in the hangar clears for a moment, as if it wants to give us a full view of what's coming.

The doors give off another keening groan. The hangar is a grey nightmare, glowing orange in places from dozens of tiny fires.

Anna is with us, appearing as if from nowhere, her eyes wide and panicked. And I can't see Prakesh. I don't know where he is any more. I'm pulled in a thousand different directions.

"Can we seal the hangar?" I say to Carver.

"It won't work," he says. "The doors, remember?"

I can't even see the entrance to the hangar—it's vanished behind a curtain of smoke. But then Carver's words sink in: we can't seal the place off. The doors don't work—and the tugs won't block the entrance completely.

I hear my name being shouted, and see Prakesh. There he is, through a gap in the smoke. He's over on the other side, underneath one of the tugs. Somehow, he's managed to get its ramp open, and he's waving people on board. Okwembu and Mikhail move past him. They're all getting onto one tug. The thought of him on board with *her*…

"Come on," I say. Carver and I start running, and it's only a moment later that I realise Anna isn't following. I look back to see her still standing there, the long gun by her side. I don't like the way her mouth is hanging open, or the distant look in her eyes.

Ignoring Carver's protests, I run back to her, grabbing her by the arm. "Anna, we have to go."

She pulls away from my grip. "I can't leave."

"What?"

"My family. They're still here. They're still in Tzevya."

"You'll never make it."

She gives her arm a vicious shake and knocks my hand away, her eyes blazing, every moment of her sixteen years radiating out. "I *said* I'm not going."

"Anna, please," I say, and I'm startled to feel tears staining my cheeks. There's another groan from the outer airlock doors.

Anna puts her hands on my shoulders, letting the long gun fall to the floor. She stops being sixteen, just for a second. The distant look in her eyes has vanished, replaced by an eerie calm.

"You never gave me that race," she says, and then pulls me into an embrace, her small arms tight around my shoulders.

"You'd never have beaten me anyway," I say, my words muffled as I hug her back.

I want more than anything to pull her along with us. Instead, I whisper words into her ear. Words Amira might have said to me, in another time and place.

"Run. Faster than you ever have before. Watch your take-off spots on the jumps, tuck your arms for the rolls. Make sure you're always looking ahead."

Anna nods, tears of her own touching my skin. She breaks away, gives Carver a brief hug, and is gone, sprinting towards the dock entrance. She moves fast, vanishing down the corridor.

"Time to go," Carver says.

And at that moment, the airlock doors give way.

87

Riley

The rush of air knocks me off my feet.

I'm tumbling, my body slamming into the ground, skidding across it. The smoke turns into huge curls as it's sucked towards the breach. The roar is enormous.

Carver grabs my hand. He's got hold of one of the tugs, his feet planted on the floor and the fingers of his other hand gripping a handle on its underside. I swing my other hand up, gripping his wrist. He starts to pull, his eyes squeezed almost shut. The muscles in his arm stand out like power cables. He jabs at the tug's body with his elbow, and then the ramp is coming down, the whining of its motor cutting through the roar.

With a horrifying clarity, I see the drops of sweat on Carver's face wicking away, sucked off his skin by the force of the breach. One touches my own cheek, a tiny spot of wetness, gone almost instantly.

I don't feel fear. I hardly feel anything—just a thin, burning need to survive. I can't get any air into my lungs, and blackness starts to creep in at the edges of my vision. I catch a split-second glimpse of the airlock doors—or where they used to be. The space beyond them is endless.

Movement. Coming right at me. I duck just in time for a spinning crate to shoot past. If I hadn't, it would have taken my head off.

The pull of the air is like an arm around my chest, refusing to let go. Someone—Earther, stomper, no way to tell—shoots by us, tumbling out of control, their scream fading as they're sucked towards the breach. I want to look to the side, to find Prakesh, but I know that if I take my eyes off Carver I'm done for.

Then one of my feet is on the ramp. I finally risk a glance over to the other side of the hangar. I can't find Prakesh's tug—they all look identical, lined up along the far wall, entrance ramps shut. With a sickening lurch in my stomach, I see that they're rocking on their magrails.

I'm barely conscious now, with no oxygen in my body, moving by sheer force of will. I propel myself forward, dragging myself into the tug. There are handholds just above the ramp, and I wrap my fingers around them, the tendons in my arms screaming in protest. There's a push from behind, Carver's hands flat on my back, and then I'm sprawling across the floor. I hear Carver come in behind me, grunting with the effort. The ramp starts to close, its electronic whine louder inside.

The ramp shuts with a loud clack. I take a breath, but there's no oxygen. Nothing at all. It was all sucked out the moment the ramp began to open.

The blackness closes in completely.

I don't know how long I'm out. I know it can't be more than two minutes, because if it were I'd be dead. An alarm is blaring, the speaker painfully close to my ear, and a calm, mechanical voice is saying, over and over again, "Danger. Pressure Loss. Emergency O2 activated."

I roll over, trying to inhale as much air as I can. My lungs feel like they're being burned away, and each breath stokes the fire. I concentrate on the motion of taking each breath, pushing back against the pain. The world has shrunk to the space around my lungs, blacking out everything else.

Slowly, the fire recedes, the oxygen trickling into my system, my lungs finally settling back into a rhythm. We're in a small rectangular loading area in the middle of the tug. Readouts and storage lockers, some the size of a grown man, line the walls, and everything is bathed in a low red light. I get to my feet, struggling to hold myself upright. I'm trembling, but quickly realise it isn't just me: the whole tug is shaking, straining at its coupling.

Carver is already on his feet, stumbling past me. "Move, move, move, move!"

I get to my feet, unsteady but spurred on by adrenaline, nearly falling as the tug lurches to one side. There's a grinding noise from below, and as I duck through the low doorway into the cockpit, I can feel it shuddering through the tug.

There are two chairs made of bucket plastic, low to the floor, surrounded on all sides by switches and glowing readouts. Carver is already sliding into the left-hand seat, throwing switches and tapping readouts. Two control yokes jut out above the seats at chest height—for a second I can't help thinking of the Boneshaker.

I follow Carver, slipping into the seat next to him. I'm not sure what's louder: the hammering of my heart, or the terrifying grinding sound from the tug's coupling. Carver gives an experimental pull on his yoke, and mine matches its movement, nearly taking me in the chest. Someone has tied a slip of paper to the handle; I get a glimpse of the message written on it as the yoke is pushed back. *Alison—fly safe, fly straight. I love you. Kamal.*

It takes a few seconds for me to tear my eyes away.

There's a glass screen in front of us, curving around the tug's body. My breath catches as I look through it. The dock is a nightmare world of flying debris and whirling smoke. Bodies spin through the air, grab hold of something, are wrenched away.

On the other side, a tug has lifted off its railings and is moving towards the breach. There's no way to tell if its engines are on, or if it's being dragged by the force of the vacuum. My heart feels as if it's being physically pulled out into the dock, as if it can find Prakesh's tug all on its own.

Carver punches the air as our tug rumbles to life. Needles jump and skitter behind their transparent housing, and the yokes shudder with the force of the engine. "Strap in," he says, reaching behind him and fumbling for a belt. I scrabble for mine, finding it above and behind me; it goes down over my shoulders and between my breasts, clicking into a buckle between my legs. As soon as I slide it home, the straps pull tight, forcing me into the seat and knocking a little breath from me. Another tug is moving, tumbling clumsily across the floor, spitting sparks as it scrapes across it.

Carver has his hands on the yoke, staring intently at the read-outs.

"You *can* fly this thing, right?" I say.

"Sure," he says. But he doesn't move, his fingers still wrapped around the yoke. Below us, there's another metallic growl as the tug strains at its magrail.

I close my eyes. "You can't fly it, can you?"

When I open them again, Carver is staring at me. There's a small, apologetic smile on his face.

With a final, fatal wrench, our tug tears loose of its coupling, and we're spinning and crashing towards the void.

88

Knox

Morgan Knox comes to just as the airlock doors breach.

For a few confused seconds, he doesn't know what's happening. He's pulled across the dock, and his lungs feel like they're being crushed in a vice.

Stop, he thinks.

But he can't. His hand snags something, one of the wheeled pallets the Earthers were using for cover, but he's pulled away almost immediately. His head collides with the floor, and brilliant sparks explode across his field of view. A second later, a whirling dagger of metal buries itself in his thigh. He has no air to scream with, can only watch in horror as the shard is ripped out by the pressure, trailing a fan of blood.

He can do nothing. He is a small child in the grip of a giant. The world around him is a roaring nightmare, a maelstrom of debris and bodies.

And then it...*changes.*

The sound dwindles, then vanishes. Knox is out of the storm, and he's looking at Outer Earth. It's huge, bigger than he could have ever imaged. He can see it curving away from him, see the glittering convection fins on its hull. Beyond it, the blackness of space is split by a billion tiny pinpricks of light.

Time slows to a crawl.

He can't breathe. He can't do anything. But as he looks at Outer Earth, Morgan Knox is gifted a moment of clarity. He realises what's happened, realises that Outer Earth has suffered a breach. And that's when the real fear grips him, pushing past the confusion.

Because he knows what's going to happen next.

He feels it on his tongue first. A prickly sensation, like a mouthful of iron. It's the moisture boiling off. His face is swelling, the skin stretching and warping. His eyes...oh gods, his eyes. The pressure is unbelievable.

And yet, he can still see. His vision has shrunk to two small circles, but it's enough to see Amira Al-Hassan, floating in front of him.

Morgan, Amira says.

And then she screams.

The sound tears Knox apart. What's happening to him is happening to her as well. He can see her skin starting to stretch, the tissues in her face swelling up. Her limbs contort, bending into impossible positions. She's dying, she's dying again, and there's nothing he can do about it.

Morgan, help me!

He tries to move. But his body has stopped listening to him. He needs air, needs oxygen, but there's nothing he can do.

Amira's eyes are horribly distorted, swollen red bulbs with a misshapen iris at the centre. She stops screaming, and suddenly her voice is full of scorn. *You can't do it, can you?*

He tries to speak.

You failed me.

Then she vanishes. Like she was never there. Like she never existed in the first place.

Knox's vision shrinks to a pinprick, then vanishes completely.

89

Riley

If we weren't strapped in, we'd be smashed to pieces in the tug's insides. The entire body shakes as we roll end over end, slamming again and again into the walls and floor of the dock. Another tug looms in the cockpit glass, but I barely register it's there before we hit it. The bang throws me back into my seat again as we spin off.

I get a split-second glimpse of the airlock doors, of torn and shredded metal. And then, all at once, we're out.

The only sounds are the tug's humming engine, and my own shaky breathing. We're still tumbling, with debris flying past us, but it's now against a backdrop of inky blackness. Every few seconds, the side of the station swings past, huge and dark.

"Yeah. OK. All right," Carver says, more to himself than to me. He's got hold of the yoke again, and is hesitantly reaching out to the instruments, flicking switches and running his finger along labels. I look away from the spinning hell outside the window, trying to ignore the lurching in my stomach.

Something hits us, bouncing off the roof with a dull boom. When I open my mouth, my voice is louder than I intended. "Get us under control."

"I'm trying."

"Try harder!"

"Why don't you stop giving me shit and look for the thruster controls?"

I start scanning the dials and digital readouts, but it's like I'm looking at another language—one made of numbers and arrows and strange symbols. My finger hovers over the controls, and I have to exert real effort to move it. *Zero-G. We're in zero-G now.* It's impossible not to think back to when I ran the Core, a year ago. When I fought Oren Darnell in the microgravity.

"Got it!" Carver says, and twists a knob on the control panel. There's a low groan as the tug jerks itself into life. The spinning world outside the window is slowing, coming to a rest. For some reason, I expected everything to be darkness—for the blackness of space to be total. But it's as if we're floating in a chamber bathed in brilliant light. Objects slowly rotate, catching the light and holding it: a crate, a discarded stinger, the arm of a crane. A little way away, another tug spins gently, the cockpit dark and empty.

And then Outer Earth comes into view, and my mouth falls open.

We're about a mile away from it. Part of the station is cloaked in shadow. But the rest of it is awash with sunlight, gleaming like a jewel. The convection fins on the hull are huge, glittering slabs. The core at the centre is a mess of protruding cylinders, all radiating out from the central reactor. I can make out the tiny puffs of fire as the hull lasers open up on approaching objects, vaporising them, preventing them from damaging the station.

"No," Carver says, sucking in a horrified breath. I follow his gaze, and a breath catches in my throat.

The dock. It's as if a deity, angry and vengeful, made a giant fist and punched out the side of the station. The breach has torn a hole right through, a jagged wound that must reach into Apex itself. There's a cloud of glittering debris above the breach.

"Anna," I say, and it's a full second before I realise I've actually said her name. I turn to Carver, tearing my eyes away from the station. "Do you think she..."

"Don't worry," he says. "She'll have got clear."

But his eyes say something different.

He rotates the tug—I can hear the thrusters shooting off, like compressed air. The station swings away. The glow of the Earth, far below us, is just out of sight.

"There!" Carver shouts, pointing out of his side of the cockpit. I raise myself up as high as the straps will allow, my body assisted by the low gravity.

The asteroid is so big it takes my breath away. I know it's smaller than a single sector on Outer Earth, but at that moment it looks impossibly large. It's steady against the blackness, pitted and pock-marked, with shadowy craters and a trailing veil of ice reaching out behind it.

And on one side, dwarfed by its cargo and only just visible: the *Shinso Maru*. A tiny speck, connected to the asteroid with dozens of thin, silver threads. Each one of them will be a flexible carbon-fibre cable, twenty feet across.

It's hard to believe that the Earthers' plan will work. I try to picture them entering Earth's atmosphere, coming in behind the asteroid, using it as a shield against the intense heat.

"How far away are they?" I say.

"Close enough," Carver replies, pushing the yoke forward. I can feel the thrusters kicking in. The rumble comes up through my seat.

I push myself up out of my seat again. "I don't see the other tug."

"They got a head start."

"Or they didn't make it at all."

"Calm down, Ry. They'll have got there. Prakesh'll be OK."

He tries to make the words sound comforting, but doesn't quite get there. What comes out sounds almost mocking, and I can see that he knows it, refusing to meet my eyes. The memory of the kiss surfaces, and won't go away.

"Did you see any kids?" Carver says.

"Kids?"

"The Earthers—they had children with them, back in that mining facility."

We fall silent as the implication sinks in. The children have been left behind—every one of them, including Jamal's little girl, Ivy.

"Hey, look on the bright side," says Carver. "Your bombs haven't exploded. Guess my solution worked after all."

I touch my ear, without meaning to. There's no way Knox survived a dock breach. I guess Carver's right.

Against all odds, I feel relief. Sweet, beautiful relief. I hold onto it, just for a moment.

Carver corrects the tug, pulling down on the yoke, but it just slides the other way, nearly vanishing below us. "I wish I knew how to read this thing's instruments," he says. His forehead is shiny with sweat, his mouth set in a thin line.

We fall silent. My gaze drifts to the ship, larger now. It's in the full glare of the sun, and what I see takes my breath away. It's like something from a distant galaxy; from a civilisation much older than ours, one that has been around so long that they've evolved in a completely different direction. The ship is a huge, slowly rotating cylinder, half a mile long at least. It looks awkward and ungainly, with enormous thruster cones jutting off its body. The surface isn't a uniform grey like I thought at first. It's mottled blue and brown, too, with an almost plant-like texture. It's a little below us, off to the left. I point to it. "Can you bring us around?"

Carver pulls the yoke down, but nothing happens. His brow furrows, and he does it again, harder this time.

"Carver?" I say, trying and failing to keep the nervousness out of my voice.

"The thrusters." He breaks off, pulling the yoke towards him again. "They're not responding. They must have been damaged when the airlock blew."

I grab my own yoke and pull. A strange image comes to mind: a picture I saw years ago, in a school lesson I thought I'd long forgotten. A boat of some kind, the couple in it rowing hard against an unforgiving ocean current. When I pull the yoke down, the tug remains locked on its course, the hum of its engine steady. If we stay on our current course, we're going to shoot right past the *Shinso* and its asteroid, with no way to make it back.

"Can we fix them?" I say.

"Sure," Carver says. "If we had a few hours and I actually knew something about tug engines."

He's pulling at the yoke now, hurling it in different directions, the asteroid looming large in our field of view. "Come on, you piece of shit, work," he says. "Come on. Come on!"

90

Prakesh

It's all Prakesh can do to hold on.

They're flying away from Outer Earth, stars whirling past the cockpit viewport. Movement inside the tug is practically impossible. They might be floating in zero gravity, but there are at least twenty people inside, and there's hardly an inch of free space. Earthers and Tzevyans mingle together, huddled in the dim red light.

One of them floats past Prakesh, a knee half an inch from his nose, and he pulls back reflexively. He bangs his head on the wall, and gasps, tightening his fingers on the handhold. The lack of gravity is tearing his stomach apart—some of the others couldn't take the pressure, and there are already chunks of vomit floating in the stale air, glistening, catching the light.

He keeps seeing the airlock doors give way, keeps hearing the terrible roar as the air was sucked out. He doesn't know if the station can survive a breach that big. Riley will be OK, he knows it, refuses to think otherwise, but what about his parents? They're still on board.

He makes himself focus. He's near the front of the tug, near the two pilot seats. They're taken up by Okwembu on the right, and Mikhail on the left. They've managed to strap themselves in, and Mikhail is fighting with the control stick.

"Everybody hold on," Okwembu says. "It's all under control."

"*Under control?*" Syria's voice comes from the back of the craft. "You just blew a hole in the side of the station."

"It's the only chance we have," Okwembu says. Prakesh stares at her in silent wonder—she sounds calm, almost bored, like the breach was part of her plan.

He makes himself speak. "We have to go back. We have to help them."

"Help who, Mr. Kumar?" She doesn't turn to look at him. He wants to reach out and grab her by the hair, shake some sense into her, but he can't seem to remove his hand from the wall. His fingers have stopped listening to him.

"Everybody on Outer Earth," he says. "They're still there. We can't just *leave them*."

Now she does turn to look at him. In the red light, her eyes look like black holes.

"We can, and we have to," she says.

He feels anger, real anger, at the thought of following Janice Okwembu into anything. But, then, what choice does he have? What choice do any of them have?

Preserve life, he thinks, and grips his handhold even tighter.

Sweat is pouring down Mikhail's face. "All right," he says to Okwembu, almost mumbling the words. "We should be in range."

"Where is it?" she replies.

"Jacket pocket. You'll have to reach over."

Prakesh sees Okwembu shut her eyes, just for a second, then lean over to Mikhail. She's exhausted—he can see that now. Despite her calm demeanour, there are dark shadows under her eyes. She sticks a hand in Mikhail's jacket, and it emerges holding a small tab screen, a bulky antenna jutting out of it.

"You know what to do?" says Mikhail.

Okwembu mutters something unintelligible, tapping her way through the opening menus.

"*Hey*," Mikhail says. "You make it work. That's the only reason you're still alive."

He doesn't see the look Okwembu flashes him, and the pure poison on her face is enough to make Prakesh's eyes go wide. In that instant, she doesn't look human.

But she says nothing, turning back to the tab screen.

"What's happening up there?" Syria shouts.

"Yeah," comes another voice. "We can't see anything."

Okwembu is using a program Prakesh hasn't encountered before: all green backgrounds and sparse text. "It's going to take a few minutes," she says. "I haven't used Ellipsis since I was at the Academy."

"I thought you said you could do it," Mikhail says.

She rounds on him. "I can. I'm the *only* one who can. You should remember that. You just need to give me time."

And Prakesh understands.

The crew of the *Shinso* would never let them on board. They'd know what was happening on the station, and they'd have been told to get as far away as possible. So the Earthers are using Okwembu to override the ship, using her experience of the *Shinso*'s dated operating system. It wouldn't take much—all she'd have to do is force the ship's airlocks to activate, to let them dock.

And, on cue, the *Shinso Maru* slides into view, a tiny speck in the void, shadowed by the giant asteroid behind it.

91

Riley

Before I realise I'm doing it, I'm unbuckling my straps. They whiz back into the seat, and I float upwards, my stomach rolling uncomfortably. Carver stares at me in disbelief. "Where are you going?"

I don't have time to respond. I'm trying to bring to mind everything I know about moving in zero grav, remembering my journey through the Core. There are hand grips on the wall, awash in the red light from its interior. I use them to pull myself up, wincing as I bump into the ceiling.

Each move you make sends you in a new direction. Go slow.

It takes an enormous effort not to rush. Carver has unstrapped, too, floating behind me, his feet tapping against the cockpit glass. When I look back, I see that he's left a smeared boot print behind.

It's hard to pick out details in the hellish red light. I don't even know what I'm looking for—I half hope that there'll be an escape pod of some kind, but I know even before I get to the back that there's no way there'll be one on a ship of this size. My eyes rove over the back of the tug, looking for anything that might help us.

"Riley?" Carver says. It comes out as a nervous shout, the cramped space amplifying the word, hurting my ears. But I don't reply, because right then I see the lockers.

The man-sized ones. The ones I passed on my way in.

My breath is coming in quick gasps as I tug on the handle. The locker opens with a creak of metal hinges, and inside...

"Are those what I think they are?" says Carver.

I grab onto a hand grip to steady myself, a stupid grin plastered across my face. There are three space suits inside the locker, each with the block letters SCC stitched on the chest. *Space Construction Corps.*

Carefully reaching into the locker, I pull the first of the three space suits out, and push it towards Carver.

"Riley, it won't work," Carver says, even as he spins the suit, looking for the seals. "There's a procedure for putting these on—you're supposed to check each other for breaks, spend an hour depressurising."

"Carver, now is *not* the time."

My own suit is made from what feels like grainy rubber, inflexible and tough. There are arches of plastic on the shoulders, one on either side, bracketing the space where my head will go. Here and there, dotted across the body, are tiny vents edged in hard plastic. It's dusty, too, the grains hanging in the air before me. How long have these suits been here? Will they still work?

My fingers find the seal running down the torso, and even as I yank it open I'm trying to recall what I know about the construction corps suits. The one-piece units are supposed to be easy to use—or easier, at least, than the ones our ancestors wore. The backpack unit has air, and power thrusters that let you move around—those must be the vents. I can't think of anything else, so I just concentrate on getting inside it.

Legs first, then arms. The inside is made of the same rubbery material, and it rucks my jacket sleeves up as I jam my arms in. Working as fast as I dare, I close myself inside the suit. My hands feel as if they're made of lead, the fingers numb and clumsy in the thick gloves. The suit hisses slightly as the single long seal closes. It's tight around my neck, and like four small vices across my wrists and ankles. In the gloves, my fingers feel as if they're welded in place.

"Helmets," I say to Carver. "Where are the helmets?"

For a horrible moment, I'm sure that they're back on Outer Earth somewhere—that the suits will be completely useless. Carver looks like some kind of freakish doll that has come to life, moving his hands up and down his suit, patting the rubbery surface. There's a hiss, and then out of nowhere, his helmet appears: flexible plastic, sliding through grooves in the arches on his shoulders, shooting up from behind his head and over it before locking into place at the front.

He grabs my arm and jabs at something on my wrist. A small control panel, set into the suit—I hadn't seen it before. There's a loud whoosh, right by my ears, and my own helmet shoots over my head. As it seals into place, the ambient noise vanishes, and I hear nothing but the tiny hiss of the oxygen supply. That, and my own breath, coming in terrified hitches.

"—crazy." Carver's voice is tinny and faint, but there.

I try not to think about what he's saying. "How am I hearing you?"

"I don't know. Must be a frequency the suits are locked into."

"Get the ramp open," I say to Carver.

"If we go out there without pressurising properly—"

"You have a better idea?"

"There's got to be an airlock in here. We can—"

"There's not enough time!"

His fingers find the button, caressing it slowly, buoyed by the lack of gravity.

"Ry..." he says, and the fear in his voice is unmistakeable.

"Do it!"

Carver hits the button.

Nothing happens. The ramp stays obstinately shut. Carver jams the button a second time, a third. I don't dare take a look out of the cockpit window. I just close my eyes.

There's a deep click, and then the whine of a motor as the ramp starts to open. I have just enough time to catch Carver's eyes—wide with fear, just like mine—and then we're tumbling, crashing into each other, sucked sideways by the loss of air pressure.

We both hit the ramp at once, almost becoming stuck as our bodies tangle in the gap. It's like the dock breach all over again—the same rushing sensation, the same sense of panic. But this time there's no seat to strap into. No metal cocoon.

I have time to shout Carver's name, just once. And then we're pulled free of the ramp, rolling end over end, into space.

92

Prakesh

They're coming up on the *Shinso Maru* way too fast.

Its hull looms in the viewport. There's a muted bleeping sound, and a calm voice warns them of a proximity alert. Mikhail grips the stick, pushing it gently. The hull slides away as the tug tilts downwards.

Everybody inside the tug watches the movement play out. Prakesh's mouth has gone completely dry. His world has shrunk down to that cockpit viewport. It's like they're trying to sneak up on a gigantic beast, get close to it without touching it.

Could he take over the tug somehow? He and Syria could rush the cockpit, overpower Okwembu and Mikhail, turn this ship around and…

And what?

He grits his teeth, furious with himself. Without wanting to, he thinks of Riley—she would know what to do. She always has a plan, always has something she could try.

She's not here, a voice in his mind says. *It's just you.*

"Steady," says Okwembu.

"I was a tug pilot for ten years," Mikhail says, speaking a little louder than he should. "I know how to fly."

He flicks a quick glance at Okwembu. "How much longer?"

The tug's comms system crackles. "Unidentified tug ship," says a man's voice, crisp and efficient. "This is Captain Jonas Barton of the *Shinso Maru*. You are not authorised to—"

Mikhail fumbles at the control panel, snapping off the transmission. It's immediately replaced by another soft beeping. "Warning," says the tug's electronic voice. "Fuel at five per cent."

"Gods," says someone behind Prakesh. He can't tear his eyes away from the viewport.

"Are you in?" Mikhail is almost shouting now.

"Nearly there," says Okwembu. She's navigating across the screen at a blazing speed, her fingers opening and closing windows faster than Prakesh can track.

"Nearly isn't good enough," Mikhail says. He's sweating so hard that it has started to drip off his face, forming opaque globules in the air in front of them. "We dock now, or we don't dock at all."

"Almost got it."

Mikhail pulls back on the stick. Prakesh's stomach lurches as the view swings upwards, the hull rushing towards them. Mikhail hits a few more controls, and the tug stabilises. They're really close to the hull now—so close that Prakesh can make out the details on its surface. The ancient warning labels, the handholds, the vents. He can see man-sized crusts of ice adhering to the hull, jagged and grey.

The thrusters on the side of the *Shinso* fire, all at once. At first, Prakesh thinks that they're trying to get away, to increase their velocity. But the angle is wrong. The thrusters are at ninety degrees to the body.

Mikhail peers out. "What are they doing?"

"Don't worry—that's me," Okwembu says. "We have to stop the *Shinso*'s rotation if we're going to attach to the airlock."

"That'll disrupt the on-ship gravity."

Okwembu ignores him. And—*there*—the airlock. A huge, round port in the side of the ship, with three scalloped hinges around the edges. Easily the size of their tug.

Without warning, Mikhail swings the tug around. This time, Prakesh almost does throw up—he feels bile climb into his throat, feels his mouth flood with saliva. The *Shinso* disappears, replaced by a backdrop of stars. What the hell is Mikhail doing?

He looks over. Mikhail's eyes are fixed on a screen set into the main console. It's a camera on the back of the tug. The feed is glitchy, but Prakesh can see the airlock. Mikhail is going to back them in, docking so that the ramp can lower and they can enter the ship.

"I'm going in," Mikhail says. He starts to reach for the thruster control.

"No," Okwembu says, and a note of fear has crept into her voice. "I don't have access yet."

"If we don't dock now, we'll run out of fuel."

"It won't accept us. You have to give me time."

Prakesh closes his eyes. He tries to picture Riley, and his parents, and Suki. He tries to think of the Air Lab, of the light filtering through the tree canopy, of the quiet, cool algae ponds.

"Warning," the electronic voice says. "Proximity alert."

One of the Earthers starts to scream.

"Proximity alert."

Without wanting to, Prakesh opens his eyes. The *Shinso*'s airlock fills the screen on the console.

"Got it!" Okwembu says.

There's a *thud*, reverberating through the tug, shaking its occupants. The lights flicker. Whoever was screaming stops abruptly.

A second later, the tug's ramp hisses open.

93

Riley

My suit has gone completely stiff, like I'm encased in ice. All I can hear is my breathing, thick and rapid, causing condensation to form on the inside of the helmet. There's no other sound.

I'm upside down, looking at the tug as we fly away from it. It's so small—a little metal bubble, nothing more, vanishing into the distance.

"—ley, get—" Carver says, his voice crackling in and out.

"What?" I shout. My eyes are locked on the tug.

"We need to—away. The thrusters—"

I collide with Carver.

I didn't even see him. He just slams right into me. We're knocked away from each other, tumbling out of control. My breathing has never been so loud. I can hear the details of every inhale and exhale, and each one tastes sour in my mouth.

There's another fizz of static, and then Carver's voice comes again. "—losing you. We—"

"Carver, can you hear me?"

"—sters!"

"Carver! Where are you?" I can barely get the words out. Outside my helmet, the world is a spinning nightmare. I see him, just for a second, and then he's gone, spinning out of view.

I breathe deep, sucking in the damp-smelling oxygen, refusing to let myself throw up. I have to get control of my movement. Carver mentioned thrusters…

Slowly, I force my arm to lift, bringing it into view. The control panel is the size of a man's hand, nestled into the suit on the back of my wrist. No readout, but at least a dozen big buttons—ones you can hit with the thick-fingered gloves. They have writing on them—but it's like reading another language. *Trans. Mix. Gauge.*

But one of the buttons is labelled *Thrust*. With fingers that feel huge and fat, I jab at it.

It's like getting kicked all over my body, all at once. Shoulders, shins, the centre of my chest, the small of my back—all of them feel a sudden, silent pressure. An image appears on the inside of my helmet: a small diagram of a space suit, with the six points highlighted by small circles.

I can't see the *Shinso*, or even Outer Earth. I don't even know which direction I'm facing. The blackness stretches around me—I've shrunk to a tiny speck, dwarfed by it, swallowed by it.

A piece of debris shoots past me, propelled by the dock breach. I barely get a fix on it before it's impossibly distant, tumbling away from me at light speed. It's as if I'm hanging over a bottomless pit, with nothing between me and an endless fall.

My stomach is a rolling ball of nausea, vertigo twisting it back and forth. I shut my eyes, focus on my breathing, wait for the thruster to stabilise the spinning stars.

"Riley?" Carver says, his transmission suddenly crystal-clear.

"I'm OK," I say, only just managing to get the words out. My mouth feels foul. The rapid breathing has crusted on my tongue.

"I can't see you. I'm heading over to the *Shinso*. Can you make your way to me?"

I look at the display on my helmet. It's just above my right eye, and as I look closely I can see the small circles indicating the thrusters are different sizes—some big, some small.

"How?" I say.

"Move your hands to your stomach. You'll find a little stick there."

I move my hands down, fumbling with my clumsy, unfeeling fingers. The inside of the gloves is soft and padded, but the outside might as well be moulded metal, and my skin burns from the effort. Somehow I do it, and my hands close around something thick and solid; my helmet's position won't let me see what it is, but it must have popped out when I activated the thrusters. And all at once I understand what Carver means.

Incredibly, Carver laughs. "I see you!" he says. He starts to say something else, but then his voice vanishes in a painful burst of static.

Zero-G

94

Prakesh

The crew of the *Shinso Maru* don't stand a chance.

Okwembu's hack stopped the ship spinning, removed its artificial gravity. They're nauseous, disoriented, not prepared for the sudden rush of bodies out of the airlock. If they'd been smarter, they would have set a trap, but they simply weren't expecting this many people.

Prakesh is one of the last out of the tug, in front of only Mikhail and Okwembu. The noise in the narrow corridor leading from the airlock is atrocious. The *Shinso*'s crew are trying to hold out, blocking the passage, fighting off the Earthers with fists and feet. But every movement sends them flying in the opposite direction, and they're not used to controlling themselves in the low gravity. Neither are the Earthers, but at least they have a few more minutes' practice.

Prakesh comes to a halt, one hand on the roof, the other on the wall, staring in horror at the assault. One of the Earthers fires a stinger, once, twice, her body slamming back into the floor. Blood spreads out across the corridor.

If he tries to wade into the melee, he'll just get himself killed. He hates being a spectator, hates feeling so helpless—especially when people are dying in front of him. Another stinger shot rings out—it's in the hands of one of the crew, but the bullet goes wide, and it's ripped from his grasp.

There's a hand on Prakesh's shoulder. It's Syria, and he's gripping hard enough to dimple the flesh under Prakesh's shirt. His face is pale.

"Wait!" The voice comes from the other end of the corridor. "We surrender. Please."

Slowly, the movement in the corridor begins to subside. As it does, Prakesh starts counting, without really wanting to, working out how many people still live. There are six bodies, Earther and crew, dead from gunshot or stab wounds. One crew member has a broken neck, his head tilted at an impossible angle.

Four crew dead. Two Earthers. The remaining two crew members are cowering, floating in an almost foetal position, their palms out. A man and a woman, gaunt from years spent in space.

Okwembu pushes past Prakesh and Syria, her face expressionless. She doesn't seem bothered by the lack of gravity, her arms akimbo, fingers just brushing the walls. "Put the bodies somewhere out of the way," she says, propelling herself down the corridor. She stops when she reaches the two frightened crew members.

"I'm sorry that had to happen," she says. She's speaking quietly, sincerely, so much so that one of the crew members actually nods. "You need to take us to the bridge now."

The other crew member isn't swayed so easily. "Why are you doing this?" he says. "You're a councillor. You're supposed to be on the station."

"I *was* a councillor." A note of impatience has crept into Okwembu's voice. "Not any more. The bridge. Now."

95

Riley

"Carver!"

There's nothing. The panic starts to creep in again, tightening my chest and forcing the air out of my lungs. I'm not cold inside the suit—this is nothing like Outer Earth's core—but a chill creeps in nonetheless.

I tell myself to focus, to concentrate on getting the suit under control. I push the stick up, towards my stomach. Nothing happens.

For an awful moment, I think my thrusters aren't working. Then my fingers feel buttons on the stick—one on the front, one on the back, perfectly cupped by my thumb and forefinger.

I hit the one on the back. My chest thruster puffs out a cloud of gas, and I feel myself moving backwards. Experimental pushes to the left and right make the circles on the corresponding legs and shoulders grow bigger as the others diminish. *Stick for direction. Buttons for thrust.*

Scanning the blackness for the ship, I push the stick down again, spinning in a slow vertical loop.

My hands are completely numb inside the space suit gloves, and they're *hot*, as if all my blood has drained into them. But after fumbling for a few moments, I spot the *Shinso*, shining in the void as it reflects back the light from the sun. My breath catches—the distance is impossible to judge, but the gap between me and the ship feels like it stretches for miles.

I jam the thruster controls on the stick. My thumb is aching now, throbbing with pain, but I feel the kick at the base of my spine.

My eyes are drawn to a green bar, positioned alongside the thruster display in my helmet. It's filled to about two-thirds, and, as I look at it, it ticks down another measure.

As if my fuel is being used up. Or my oxygen.

Will I have enough to make it to the *Shinso*? No way to tell. It doesn't even feel like I'm getting any closer. I breathe as slowly as I can, taking small sips of air, trying with every ounce of will I have to control the frustration. If I was on Outer Earth, I could run this distance in minutes, just sprint across the gap.

I grit my teeth, keeping my thumb pressed down on the controls, ignoring the pain.

Slowly, ever so slowly, the ship creeps closer. Details start to resolve, shadows becoming clear on the surface.

There's a crackle over the radio. "—ley, come in! Do you hear me?"

"I'm here."

My words come out in a rough whisper. I clear my throat, and try again.

"Gods, I thought you were…Listen, don't come in too fast. You won't be able to stop in time."

I'm almost on top of the ship now, its hull swelling beneath me.

I see him. He's got his back to the ship, as if he's lying prone below me. Incredibly, he manages to wave: a single movement, long and languorous.

"We don't have much time left," he says. "I don't know how much juice you've got in your thrusters, but I've burned half of mine."

We glide above the surface of the ship. I can only see the edge of it, peeking over the bottom of my helmet.

"Shit," Carver says.

"What?"

"How are we going to get inside?"

"We go in the airlock," I say, confused.

"And how do we get them to open it for us?"

I open my mouth to reply—then stop. How could we be so stupid? The sensation in my mouth has got worse. When I lick my lips, my tongue is utterly dry.

"How are you doing for fuel?" I ask, stealing a glance at mine. One-third left, assuming it *is* fuel, and not my air supply.

"Almost out," he says, his voice steady. "Can you see their tug?"

"Where?"

"Down there, near the front of the ship."

I tweak the stick, just a little, and spot the tug even before he's finishing speaking. It's docked with the ship, clinging onto it like a bug. Its front end points outward; the ramp at the back must be connected to an airlock.

Relief floods through me—Prakesh made it. He's alive.

I push down harder on the button on my stick. We move towards the *Shinso* in slow motion, and I want to curse with frustration.

I don't. It would just waste air.

"It's stopped rotating," Carver says, puzzled.

"Let's go for the tug," I hear myself say. "Maybe we can get inside it."

We keep moving, pointing ourselves towards the front of the craft. We're almost there, the tug looming large in front of us, when the white cone in Carver's thruster sputters and dies.

"No juice. I've got no juice," he says. I can hear him trying to keep the panic out of his voice. He's a little ahead of me, to the left.

"Hang on," I say, angling myself towards him. I have to slow myself down. If I overshoot and have to come back for him, I'll run out of fuel myself.

Almost there.

Almost...

I slam into Carver, taking him around the waist, pulling him along with me. My meter has started to blink red, a flashing beacon at the edge of my vision.

I can only just see past Carver's torso. His hand floats in front of my face, and just beyond it I can see the surface of the tug.

"Steady," says Carver.

"You need to guide me. I can't—"

"Riley, reverse! Reverse thruster!"

We're skidding above the tug's surface—too far above it. If I don't stop now, we're going to overshoot. I lift my finger—slowly, so slowly—and force it down on the second stick button. I feel a juddering in my chest, and Carver's body, pressed close to it, is pushed upwards. He grabs my hand, stretched out above me, and I can hear his breathing in my helmet. It sounds like water rushing through a pipe.

We come to a halt.

When I look down, I see that my foot has caught on a cable that stretches along the outside of the tug's body. If it hadn't been there...

Slowly, my muscles aching with the effort, I pull Carver down, onto the surface of the tug. Soon we're both kneeling on it, hooked onto the cable. There's almost no fuel left in my tank.

"Shit," Carver says again. This time, it comes out in a long, slow exhalation.

"Too close."

"Yeah."

"Can we disconnect the tug? Go in through that airlock?"

"No good. It'd take too long. Let's see if we can go round to the other side."

I was hoping he wouldn't say that. I steel myself, getting ready to pull Carver close to me and inch along the tug's body.

There's a sudden pressure in the small of my back. "I've got one of your thrusters," Carver says. "I'll hold, you pull."

"Letting me do the heavy lifting, huh?"

"Yeah, well, you can handle it."

There's another handhold a little further along: another cable, lifted slightly off the surface. I reach for it, using tiny taps of my shoulder thrusters to keep me steady. When I manage to get a grip on the cable, the sweat on my face is so thick that it's started to float off, coating my helmet. I can barely see out of the smeared surface.

"Keep going," Carver says.

But when I look up, I see there are no more cables. Nothing to hold onto. The back of the tug sweeps away from me, and I know that if I try to climb down it with Carver in tow I'll drift away. Beyond the tug's body, there's nothing but space.

"It's no good," I say. "We're out of holds."

"We can't be out. Keep looking."

"Carver, I'm telling you, we need to find another—"

I stop. As I speak, my free hand—the left one, the one not gripping the cable—drifts into view, and with it the wrist control. There's one button I hadn't noticed before. The writing on it reads: PLSM.

"These are construction suits, right?"

"Yeah, why?"

"I've got an idea. Is there something you can grab onto?"

"Hold on."

The pressure in the back of my suit takes an age to fall away. I force myself to stay still.

"OK, I'm holding onto the tug's body."

My right hand sweeps towards my wrist control, and thumbs the PLSM button. Another display pops up in my helmet: another bar crossing horizontally across the bottom. Words flash beneath it: *Plasma cutter arming*.

At almost the same instant, there's a flash of blue on the back of my left wrist. A nozzle has appeared; it flicked up from the suit with a tiny rumble of motors that I can feel in my chest. The light sparks, vanishes, then appears again: a thin streak of blue-white flame, reaching out beyond my hand. There's no sound at all.

Plasma cutter ready.

Carver whoops with joy. "Easy," I say, wincing at the burst of noise.

"Sorry," he says, at a more manageable volume. "Good thinking."

I bring the flame down towards the surface of the tug. My wrist has locked in position—a safety measure, presumably, to stop me from bending it and cutting through my own suit. When the flame makes contact with the metal, there's a silent spray of sparks, drifting upwards and winking out instantly.

"I just tried my own cutter," Carver says. "Not getting anything. Keep going."

The metal has started to glow—first red, then white. I've been holding my breath, and let it out in a thin whistle.

"You holding on to something?" says Carver. "There's going to be a pressure blowback when we cut through, so we'd better—"

A section of the metal suddenly pops outwards like it's been hit by stinger fire. I'm still caught on the cable, but for a moment the whoosh of pressure knocks me off balance. The flame lifts off the metal, traces an arc through the vacuum—

—And cuts across Carver's chest.

Neither of us speak. I can see his eyes, wide with confusion, then horror. I've stopped breathing again. There's a burn mark on his suit, slicing across the middle of the letters SCC.

I hear him breathe over the radio. "I'm OK," he says. It's more question than statement. "Just…I'm OK. There wasn't much contact."

Slowly, I bring the flame back around. I start cutting again, trying not to look at the readouts in my helmet, stopping every so often to adjust my hold on the cable. My hands are impossibly numb. I cut in a rough rectangle, big enough for us to slip through in our bulky suits. The initial rush of air has stopped; the inner airlock door must have sealed. The inside of the tug is starting to become visible, awash with red light.

My gauge is only a quarter full now. I'm about to start cutting the final side of the rectangle, already thinking about how I'll push the cut panel away from us, when Carver says, "Riley, there's something wrong."

I force myself to keep the torch in contact with the metal. "What is it?"

"I'm getting a warning. On my suit display," he says. The words come out in chunks, like he can't put them all together. Or like he's finding it difficult to breathe. "Some kind of…oh gods, Riley, it's a pressure warning."

The plasma cutter. The burn mark on his chest.

"Don't worry," I say, not daring to look at him, moving the cutter as fast as I can. "We'll be inside soon, OK? Just hold on for me."

"Lot of warnings popping up here, Riley."

"I know, I know."

Eight inches to go. Seven. I try not to think of what we were taught about the physics of space. And what happens to the human body in a vacuum.

"My tongue. I can feel it on my tongue."

Five inches. "Carver, we're nearly there." Four.

Suddenly he's screaming in my ears. "It hurts, Riley, make it stop, *make it stop*!"

96

Riley

The next few moments are a confused blur.

I cut through the final edge and grab hold of Carver's suit, only just remembering to shut off my plasma cutter before I do. Carver has stopped screaming.

The chunk of metal that I cut out of the tug's body drifts away. Somehow, I manage to haul Carver through the opening. I'm fighting against the lack of gravity now, forgetting that I have to control my movements. But then we're inside the tug, drifting in the red-washed interior. I'm yelling Carver's name, and getting nothing, nothing but the crackle of the radio back.

I manage to get us over to the ramp, which leads down to the airlock. The thought occurs to me that there might be a welcoming party on the other side, but there's no way I'm staying in this vacuum a second longer than I have to. Not with Carver passed out, the pressure being sucked from his suit. I might be too late.

Don't you think that.

I hammer on the release, and pull Carver through into the airlock space—he feels light, like there's nothing inside the suit. The outer door closes. I hear the hiss of the airlock pressurising, and then the second one opens and we're moving through.

I grab at Carver's wrist panel, fumbling with it, and when his helmet shoots back into the suit I see that his face is almost drained of blood. His lips are a horrific shade of purple.

I shout his name, loud enough that it hurts my ears inside my own helmet.

I stab at my wrist, retracting the helmet, not caring about the change in pressure. It's like someone is jabbing hot needles into my ears. The familiar nausea is back. I groan with pain, but somehow I manage to keep my eyes locked on Carver.

I reach out, pushing past the pain, my suited hand finding Carver's face.

He doesn't move. Doesn't speak, or open his eyes.

I'm trying to form words, but they don't quite make it out of my throat. I try to slap him, but in the low gravity I can't get enough force. My hand just taps his cheek. I bite my lower lip hard enough to bring a trickle of blood, tasting the coppery tang of it, the sting taking attention from the horrible feeling in my ears and stomach.

"Carver," I say through gritted teeth. "Wake up. Please, Carver, wake up."

I take in a huge breath—the air tastes stale here, and dry—and scream into his face. "Carver, *don't leave me*!"

At first, I think I've imagined it. But then his lips move again, very slightly. I hold the movement in my mind as I would a very fragile piece of glass in my hand.

Carver coughs, then sucks in a huge *whoop* of air. He does it again and again.

"Riley…" he says, his voice barely a whisper. And then I'm burying my face in his chest, pushing us right into the wall.

"I think you can start calling me Aaron now," he says.

I can feel my tears falling away from my face, drifting past us. His arms go around my body, and although they don't pull me close, I can feel them there.

Good enough.

After a few moments, he whispers, "You need to let go."

"Not ever."

"No, you really do." He pushes me away, turns to the side and throws up.

I try not to look at the vomit; the slick globules hang in the air, splitting and turning, as if they're floating in a glass of water. The pain in my ears and stomach has dropped a little. Now that I have a chance to actually look at the surroundings, I can see we're at the end of a long passage. It's smaller and more cramped than the corridors on Outer Earth. There are banks of bright white lights in long lines across the ceiling. Somewhere, very faint, there's a buzzing sound, like a machine starting up.

"How you holding up?" I ask Carver, as I pull him along.

"Feels like someone hit me in the stomach with a steel pole," he says. "Eyes, too."

"Try swallowing. It helps a little."

"I can barely talk, you want me to swallow?"

"Make an effort."

He smiles a little, then groans in pain. I'm worried he's going to throw up again, but he gets it under control.

"Come on," I say. "We've got an Earth trip to cancel."

"You need to—" he stops, steeling himself. "You need to go on ahead."

I stare at him, confused. "I'm not leaving you."

"I can barely move two feet without wanting to spill my guts. I'll just slow you down."

"Aaron…"

But I see his hand gripped tight to the wall hold, and I know he's serious. I swim back towards him and hug him again, resting my head on his shoulder. "Promise me you'll try to get somewhere safe?" I say.

"Not a chance. I'll be right behind you, soon as my stomach stops trying to crawl out of my mouth."

I kiss his cheek—his skin is like ice. Then I'm gone, moving away before I have a chance to think about it.

97

Prakesh

Prakesh has never been on the bridge of an asteroid catcher.

It's enormous, far bigger than he would have expected for a crew of six. It's arranged like an amphitheatre, with three tiered levels. The captain's chair is right in the middle of the bridge, tilted slightly back. Workstations surround it, and there are dozens of other screens positioned around the walls, Prakesh can only guess at some of their readouts. He's floating near the back wall, doing what he can to keep the contents of his stomach in place.

What captures his attention is the front of the bridge. It's taken up by a huge viewport: a curving, rectangular sheet of toughened glass. Through it, Prakesh can just see the edge of the Earth.

What's down there? What have the Earthers found that makes them think they can survive?

The bridge is packed. The two remaining crew members have been pushed down into their seats, each of them surrounded by a group of Earthers. Okwembu is bent over one of them, her body twisting as she floats in mid-air, clutching her tab screen. Prakesh catches snippets of conversation, and realises they're trying to restart the ship's thrusters, get it spinning so that they can get the gravity back. He hears them talking about their course—they're going to put the ship into orbit around the Earth, plan their next move.

He feels someone slide in behind him, and then Mikhail is whispering in his ear. "Don't even think about it," he says, his breath hot and dank on Prakesh's skin.

Anger floods through him, but it's a weary anger. He turns himself around to face Mikhail, putting his hand on the wall to steady his body. "Think about what?"

"Doing anything stupid." Mikhail's eyes bore into his. "You think I don't know who you are?"

For a horrible moment, Prakesh is sure that Mikhail knows about Resin—that he'll tell everyone. But instead, the Earther leader says, "You fought against us, back in the dock. You try and get in the way here, and I'll break both your arms."

Prakesh almost laughs. What is he possibly going to do? Take out a bridge full of armed Earthers by himself? Even if he enlists Syria—currently against the back wall, fighting against the nauseating effects of the lack of gravity—he'd end up dead.

"Get the hell away from me," he says.

"You just—"

"*I said*, get away from me." He shoves Mikhail in the chest. They fly apart, Prakesh bumping into the ceiling. A couple of the Earthers cry out in alarm. Before they can jump in, Prakesh raises his hands, meeting Mikhail's thunderous gaze. "I'm not going to do anything. Just leave me be."

Mikhail looks as if he wants to break Prakesh's arms right there and then. Instead, he pushes himself off the wall and floats back onto the bridge. "One move," he says, as he passes Prakesh.

But Prakesh doesn't respond. Because he's looking at something over Mikhail's shoulder.

It's on one of the screens at the back of the bridge. It's filled with fast-scrolling text, the background the same sickly green as Okwembu's tab screen. The text is too far away to read, but Prakesh can just make out the enlarged writing in the giant, blinking text box superimposed over it.

PRESSURE LOSS IN AIRLOCK 3A. OUTER DOOR COMPROMISED. DO NOT USE.

Prakesh stares at the screen, thinking hard.

It takes a hell of a lot for airlock doors to fail. Short of a speeding tug smashing through them, it's extremely rare to get something like an unplanned pressure loss. When they came in the airlock, it was a clean entry. The seal was good.

Could the tug have dislodged? Could there be a problem with the seals? It's always a possibility, but Prakesh doesn't think so. Someone else is trying to get through that airlock.

Riley.

It's impossible. His mind is playing tricks on him, letting him believe something is true when there's no possible way it could be. He's only setting himself up for a disappointment, and he's had about as much of that as he can handle.

And yet…

Prakesh looks around, taking in the bridge. No one is paying attention to him—not even Mikhail, who is talking with Okwembu.

There's no way he can take back the *Shinso*'s bridge.

But that doesn't mean he can't go find out what's causing the pressure loss in airlock 3A.

Moving as quietly as he can, he swims over to the bridge doors, scraping his fingers against the floor. Halfway there, he looks up to see Syria's eyes on him, narrowed in confusion.

Prakesh shakes his head, very gently, side to side. Then with one last look back over his shoulder, he pushes his way out through the doors.

98

Riley

Moving down the corridor is easy. I shoot from one handhold to the next, ignoring the nausea still bubbling deep in my stomach.

There are no doors along the walls to break the monotony of the steel panelling. There aren't even any signs or power boxes—and certainly no graffiti, like you'd see on Outer Earth.

The corridor takes an abrupt left turn, heading deeper into the ship itself, and I push my way around it. The buzzing sound is still there, but now it's joined by others: the slow, creaking groan of the hull, louder and more insistent than Outer Earth's. The low rumble of the engines, felt more than heard. And somewhere deep in the *Shinso*'s guts, there are voices. Almost impossibly distant, but there.

Guts. The word feels right; the corridor seems to go on for miles, like the intestines of some enormous creature. One that's spent its entire life in the deepest reaches of space.

Somewhere, deep in the bowels of this thing, is Okwembu. And with her: Prakesh.

I screw my eyes shut. *No.* He's not with her. He might have helped her and the other Earthers inside a tug, but that's just how he is. He wouldn't have let them die. There is no way that he'd have helped them beyond that. He would have tried to stop them. They could be holding him prisoner right now. They could be torturing him. They could—

I make myself stop.

I can't just run in without a plan. If I take off, if I try to save Prakesh, I could get myself captured. I have to be careful. I don't know what condition Outer Earth is in after the breach, but I *do* know that if anybody is still alive there, they need that asteroid.

More than anything else, I have to stop the ship. That might mean going in the opposite direction to Prakesh.

I have to trust him. Trust that he'll be OK.

After an age, the corridor opens up into a spherical chamber, with other passages leading off ahead of me, and to the left and right. The voices are louder now—ahead of me, I think—but I still can't hear the words.

There's a sign set into the wall at the entrance to each passage. I move around to the one on my left. The words are grimed over, their cleaning neglected by astronauts who know their way around the ship blindfolded.

I rub the dirt off to read them, and the granules hang suspended as I knock them off. Some of the fine particles drift up my nose, and I sneeze—the motion pushes me back, sending me into a fast tumble, and I have to grab a handhold on the floor to steady myself. I'm hyperventilating, the air coming and going so fast that I'm suddenly light-headed. The sign I was cleaning swims in front of me, upside down now. I'm angry at myself, furious that I'm not better in zero gravity.

It takes me a few minutes to get my head right. The sign indicates a corridor heading to *Mining, Astronautics, Engines.* Moving around as carefully as I can, I get my bearings. I can go straight ahead to *Ship Bridge,* or drop down the passage to the right, to *Crew Quarters, Mess, Gym, Reactor Access.*

Bridge is out. Sure, I could stop the ship from there, but not without fighting through Okwembu and her Earthers.

So what, then?

My eyes drift back to the other signs—and settle on *Reactor Access.*

At the very edges of my mind, a plan begins to form. Before I can poke holes in it, I'm pulling myself down the right-hand corridor.

If anything, the passage is even narrower here. I find myself drifting towards the ceiling, and more than once I get caught up against it, the impact jarring my stomach and sending little shocks of nausea up my throat.

It's not long before the passage opens up again—this time, into a dimly lit hallway lined with six closed doors, three on each side. In the middle of the hallway, there's an abandoned plastic food carton, slowly rotating as it hangs in the air. There's a tiny slick of something brown in one of its corners.

I move past it, glancing at the doors as I do so. Each one has a name stencilled onto the wall next to it, in block capitals: DOMINGUEZ, LEE, BARTON, OLAFSON, SHALHOUB. Right at the end, perched on top of KHALIL, someone has drawn a surprisingly detailed grinning cartoon devil, looking over its shoulder at me, pulling down black pants to flash a bare ass. Next to it, in black ink, someone has written: *Rashid, the demon of the Asteroid Belt.*

The passage gets narrower again, and this time the lights fade entirely, either dead or turned off. I can just see by the light of the crew quarters behind me, and, at the far end, there's another glimmer of white light. By the time I reach it, pulling myself out into another spherical chamber, a spiky fear has joined the nausea, jostling for space in my stomach.

There's a passage in the floor this time, dropping down into darkness. There's a big sign next to it, laid out in more stencilled letters:

REACTOR ACCESS

WARNING AUTHORISED PERSONNEL ONLY.

I grapple towards it, steeling myself for the darkness, when I happen to look up and see something strange.

There's another passage, heading off to the right. According to its sign, it leads to the *Mess*. At first, I think that there's just a lot of grime covering the wall, but I stop myself, my body half in the lower passage, and take a closer look.

It's not grime. It's too thin, too wet looking.

Almost without realising it, I'm pulling myself out of the passage, heading towards the mess hall, wanting to know and desperate to get as far away as possible. The splatter I saw is blood. There's not a lot of it—it wasn't shed by anyone living.

And when I get through the passage—when I pull myself out the other side—I find them.

Four bodies. All *Shinso* crew. Suspended in mid-air, loose-limbed, with eyes that are glazed and dead.

99

Riley

I turn away, pushing myself tight into one of the walls, my cheek against the cool metal. It's at least a minute before I have the strength to look at the bodies again.

My gaze drifts along the wall. There are seats built into it, with heavy straps that would go across the chest. I guess if you're eating in zero gravity you need your hands free. There are lockers running along the wall opposite me, and there's debris floating around the room, too: half-empty, opaque pouches of liquid.

The bodies are clustered together in the centre of the room, their loose limbs bumping up against each other. Two men, two women. One of them is facing me, and I can see the gaping stinger wound in her chest.

There's nothing I can do for the crew now, but perhaps there's something in the lockers that would come in useful. I pull myself along to them, swimming across the bottom of the room to avoid the bodies. When I get upright again and spring the lockers, the items inside tumble out, joining the cloud of debris scattered across the room. More food pouches, bars, pressurised water canisters. An entire sealed plastic container of straws tumbles out of one and drifts away, its contents bouncing around inside it.

There's a knife inside the locker, velcroed to the back. For a moment, I'm confused—you don't use knives and forks to eat in zero gravity—but then I see that it's more like an old hunting knife. I've seen a few like it on Outer Earth—heirlooms, objects from the planet below us. This one has a wooden handle, worn smooth, but the blade has been kept good and sharp. It must have belonged to one of the crew. I reach out and grab it.

Now I have a weapon.

I tuck it into my belt, telling myself to make sure it doesn't drift loose. Then I take two deep breaths, and pull my way out of the mess hall.

I've nearly reached the spherical chamber leading to the reactor when there's a voice not ten feet away.

"You think they got aboard?"

I choke back a breath, not letting a single sound escape, and push myself against the wall. My hand just touches a slick of blood, and I have to force myself not to yank it away again.

In the chamber, the owner of the voice floats past, his back to me. He's with another woman, moving slightly above him. Both of them are Earthers—I recognise them from the battle in the dock. How many made it on board? Those tugs aren't big enough to fit more than a dozen people—maybe twenty, at a push. Strange to think that of all the Earthers I saw, only a tiny fraction made it here.

"Of course they got on board," says the woman. "You saw the airlock alert."

"I'll push 'em back out if they're still there."

"She wants them alive. You know that."

They've headed back into the passage, moving towards the crew quarters. I can't risk following them. Even with the knife in my belt. I wait for a beat, two, three, until the voices are gone completely. Then I slip out into the chamber, and pull myself into the passage leading to the reactor. I go feet first, and the darkness swallows me.

There's a ladder running down the one side of the shaft. I fumble more than once, cursing under my breath as I lose my grip on the rungs. But there's a light at the bottom—a tiny, bright, yellow glare—and it keeps me centred. Before long, I'm pulling myself out of the shaft into the passage at the bottom.

It's at right angles to the drop, the ceiling low and cramped. The metal here is rusted in spots, coated with a kind of yellowish rime. The floor below me is a grate, laid on top of a tangled mess of pipes and wires. The sounds I heard earlier are muted—all except one. The buzzing noise. I'm closer to the machine now, and the sound has become a growl, so low it rattles my insides.

I have no idea what I'm going to do when I get to the reactor. I know it's a fusion core, like the one on Outer Earth, only much smaller. It'll have shielding, but there's got to be a way inside.

I have to disable it somehow—it'll stop the *Shinso* in its tracks, cut all power to the engines. Of course, I might blow it, and myself, into the next world. And it might cut power to everything else, too, including the life-support systems. But there should still be enough air to breathe for a while, and if I can get Carver and Prakesh, if we can then make it back to the tug…

I stop counting the ifs and the mights. Instead, I look around the cramped passage for a handhold, and pull myself along it, heading in the direction of the buzzing noise.

I'm expecting another airlock at the end of the passage. There is one—but it's been left open, the doors recessed into the wall. Good. That means there won't be any alarm triggered when I go through. I can see part of the reactor chamber on the other side, bathed in a clinical white light.

The room is laid out in a circle, like a rotunda, and the floor slopes away from me, with strips of light leading to the machine in the middle. It rises in a giant cone to the ceiling, twenty feet above me. Like its bigger brother at the centre of Outer Earth, its body is cocooned in cables.

I push myself off towards it, looking around the room for a control panel. I'm half hoping that it'll be as simple as telling a computer to shut the reactor down, but there are no controls anywhere. The only thing that disturbs the shape of the walls are several metal storage boxes, each one five feet long, held to the walls by more velcro.

As I get closer, I can see the body of the reactor underneath the tangle of cables. Thick steel plates, the joins between them sealed with thick, grey rubber. The same substance runs around the cables where they meet the body.

I circle it, running my hands along the plates and the seals, looking for a weak spot. Nothing. No panels, no screens, not a single thing that will let me get inside. I make my way over to the boxes, hauling them open. They're all empty. No tools, save for a small screwdriver, strapped down inside one of them. Useless.

And it doesn't help that I know almost nothing about fusion reactors. Assuming I do get inside, what would I see? I picture a glowing ball, hanging suspended in its own nest of cables, and curse myself for not knowing, for not asking Carver if he knew what to expect.

I pull the knife out of my belt, and jam it into one of the seals as hard as the low gravity will let me. It only just pierces the rubber-like material. I wiggle it back and forth, feeling the sweat pop out on my forehead, but I only manage to get a little bit deeper into the seal. It'll take hours to get through.

Could I cut into one of the cables, maybe? I throw the idea out almost as soon as it occurs. Which one? And how would I do it without frying myself?

I've left the knife caught in the seal. As I watch, it comes loose, spinning slowly in the space in front of the reactor. After a few moments, the blade is pointing right at me.

I freeze, unable to look away from it. Because, right then, I get another idea. But this one is like a poison of its own, seeping right through me, corroding everything it touches.

I can't cut through the steel plating, or the rubber seals.

But what if I could blow up the reactor?

100

Riley

I turn away from the knife, determined not to look at it again.

But I can't stop my mind from weighing up the possibilities. They stretch outwards in my mind, three steel cables stretching away from me in different directions, pulled taut, like the cables tethering the asteroid to the *Shinso*.

Along one, I fight my way through to the bridge. I manage to avoid being captured, or killed, somehow, and I take control of the ship. I turn it around, bring it home. The station gets the tungsten it needs to shore up the reactor. Outer Earth survives.

But that cable snaps in an instant. Getting past the Earthers by myself? Taking every single one of them out of commission with no backup, no gadgets from Carver, and no idea of the bridge layout? It's a possibility so remote as to be almost non-existent.

Cable two. I try to get to the bridge. I'm captured or killed, and the *Shinso* continues its journey. There's no asteroid slag, no tungsten for the station's reactor. Outer Earth dies. Anna, and everyone else, dies.

Along the final cable, I...

I cut into myself. Knox told me how to get the bombs out—*cut the left wire*. I somehow do it without dying from blood loss, or passing out from the pain, or blowing myself up. I get the bomb out—it'll have to be one; the thought of cutting more than once causes my gorge to jump—and use it to blow up the shielding around the ship's reactor. Knox said the bombs were sensitive to impact—I can use the storage boxes to detonate one of them.

The blast probably won't be enough to disable the reactor entirely, but it might let me get inside, assuming I'm still conscious or coherent enough to do something about it.

Let's say I do it. It'll be just like back in the Recycler Plant—I simply have to put the bomb in the right place. The *Shinso*'s power dies. Those aboard it have no option but to make for the tug, and head back to Outer Earth. The chances that we can stop the *Shinso* from drifting too far and bring it and its cargo back into station orbit are slim, but still there.

No. I won't. I can't.

I'm already thinking about all I've been through. Everything I've survived. I'm thinking about Kev, and Royo, and everyone else who has died to stop this ship from leaving. I think about what I had to do to my own father to save my home. I'm thinking about Anna and her family. About Jamal, and his daughter Ivy. About everyone I know on Outer Earth.

A voice drifts up from a very dark place in my mind: a place I'd almost forgotten about. A little black box where I put the things I never want to think about again.

There's nothing you can do to save it, Amira says. *It's finished. We were never supposed to live this long.*

And somewhere else, a tiny thought crystallises. It glows like a star, full of immense power, but so far away that it's nothing more than a pinprick of light in a black void.

I'm not you, Amira. And I never will be.

I turn around, gripping one of the cables to spin my body. The knife is bumping off the body of the reactor. Slowly, I reach out for it, gripping its wooden handle.

101

Riley

I'm up near the ceiling, next to the cables that run from the reactor. I've got a cable around my right arm, hooked into the armpit. I've jammed my left ankle into a cable further along, tilting the back of my knee towards me.

It's an awkward position, and a tight fit—the cables push at the back of my neck and head. I've torn a strip off the bottom of my shirt, pulling it tight around my left leg, midway up my thigh. I have no idea if that's the best place for a tourniquet, but I know it has to go on somewhere. I've already taken one of the storage boxes from where it was velcroed to the wall. If this works, I'm going to need to hit the bomb with something to detonate it. The box floats next to me, gently rotating.

I've pulled up the leg of my jumpsuit. The air in the reactor is chilly, and I can feel it prickling my skin. I take a look at the stitches again, running a finger along them and fighting back the dry taste in my mouth. The stitches form a puckered line, running across the flesh at the back of the knee. Most of the stitch, save for the spiky ends, runs under the skin. I think back to the words Knox used: *popliteal fossa*. A gap in the muscles.

I run my finger across the part above the stitch. The thought of cutting into it is enough to bring more cold sweat out across my body. It's all too easy to imagine never being able to run again, miscalculating the cut, damaging the muscles themselves...

I can't do this. I can't.

Several deep breaths later, the blade is a few inches above the skin. If I can cut along the line of the stitch, it should open up a little. I should be able to see the bomb.

And remove it without blowing myself up.

Around me, the buzzing of the reactor feels softer, as if the machine is waiting to see what happens. I can hear my own heartbeat, and my breathing, exquisitely precise.

The knife hovers, trembling.

And before I can do anything, my hand acts on its own, jamming the knife into my flesh.

I let out a shocked gasp, staring at the blade sticking out of my flesh, coming out at an angle. *There's no pain. There's no—*

Blood wells up around the knife, floating in huge bubbles. And it's then that the pain comes. A giant, searing bolt. I throw my head back and scream.

Surely the bombs can't be worse than this. It feels like someone is holding a red-hot brand to my leg: holding it and twisting it.

Tears double and triple what I see, but I can still make out what I have to do. The knife has cut through the part of the stitch closest to the bone on the left. If I keep going, I can go right through the stitches, and open it all up.

My right hand, gripping the handle of the knife, is trembling so hard that I have to use my left to steady it. I grit my teeth, and begin pushing it outwards, sawing gently up and down, cutting through the stitches.

My back aches from having to twist my body, but I barely notice—compared to the pain from my knee it's almost nothing. Every single movement brings a stab so intense that it greys out my vision. Every cut stitch brings such a wave of relief that I nearly cry out, and every one seems to be more painful than the last. By the time I sever the final stitch, my legs and the space around them are a red hell, and the grey at the edge of my vision has turned black.

But I can see the bomb. I can see it.

The wound is open now—a gaping purple-red mouth, with ragged edges. I can see the muscles and the gap between them, just visible under clouds of blood. And *there*: a metal casing. A flat, dark-green square, half an inch across, with a raised circular segment in the middle. It looks impossibly small—there's no way something that tiny could do any damage.

I think back to Kev, think back to the bloodstain spreading across his shirt.

I need to see more. And I need both hands to do it. Somehow, I get the knife away from the wound, and put the handle between my teeth. The blood that stains it is still warm, coppery on my tongue, and that alone is almost enough to make me pass out. I bite down on the handle, and use my shaking fingers to gently pull the gaping mouth open some more.

This time, I do pass out.

When I come to, the knife has dropped out of my teeth and is floating in front of my face. I don't remember what the pain was like; I just remember it being *there,* so enormous that I couldn't even comprehend it.

I snatch the knife out of the air and look back down at my destroyed knee. My head feels clearer now, as if it's been wiped clean by the pain.

I grip the bomb between thumb and forefinger, and begin to slide it out from the gap.

Knox was wrong. Anyone could have removed it. It would have been better if it—

Something pulls at my muscle, something between it and the bomb. I freeze.

Working as gently as I can, trying not to touch the edges of the wound, I slip my finger underneath the bomb. Wires. Two of them, sheathed in rubber and slick with blood, running from the body of the bomb to the muscle itself. *Attached* to the muscle, wired into it. Had I kept pulling, I would have ripped them right out. In the haze of pain, I'd almost forgotten Knox's words. *Cut the left wire. My left.*

The knife is already back in my hand, and, working as slowly as I can, I slip it back under the metal casing. I feel it touch the wires, and the thought of cutting the wrong one is enough to make me gasp.

I make sure the blade is right between the two wires, resting against the bomb casing. My hand is trembling so hard that I can hear the tapping of metal on metal. His left would be my right. So I have to cut the right-hand wire. I rest the blade against it, ready to cut. I need to do it in a single movement, yanking the blade across and cutting right through.

What if Knox was lying?

Out of nowhere, a memory surfaces. The memory of being ambushed by the Lieren, back when I was just a tracer. They had me pinned against the corridor wall, and one of them had a blade at my face. He was going to cut off one of my ears. He was flicking the blade left, right, left, right, trying to decide which one.

Each breath is shaking now, barely making it out of my lungs. I have to decide.

I flip the knife, angling it towards the other wire.

Then I flip it back, and cut the first one.

102

Riley

I scream.

It lasts for perhaps half a second, cut off as my throat slams shut. The knife is through. It skidded off the edge of the cut, but I barely felt it, the adrenaline knocking away the pain.

I did it.

I slice through the remaining wire, and then I'm holding the bomb in my hands.

The entire casing fits into my palm. I'm laughing now. It's a horrible sound, lumpy and angry. My entire body is drenched with sweat, and my knee...I can't even look at my knee. When I lift my arms from around the cables, pulling myself out, the muscles in my upper body scream in protest.

I swim towards the reactor as if in a dream. With every beat of my heart, darkness pulses at the edge of my vision.

You will not pass out. Not now.

Time skips forward again. I'm in front of the reactor. The bomb is suspended there, nudging one of the rubber seals. The storage box is positioned on my shoulder like a rocket launcher. I'm aiming it right at the bomb. One hit. That's all it'll take. I have enough presence of mind to throw the canister, rather than swing it—no telling how big the explosion will actually be.

There's a voice. The words hang in the air as if caught in the low gravity themselves, and it takes me a few moments to understand them.

"Riley, what have you done?"

Very slowly, I turn my head.

Prakesh is floating in the open door of the airlock, his eyes wide with confusion and horror.

I try to say something, but the words won't come. He puts a hand on either side of the door, and launches himself into the room, heading right for me.

No—not for me. For the box I'm holding on my shoulder. I grip it tight, ready to launch it at the bomb.

"Stay back, Prakesh," I hear myself say.

He's grabbed hold of a cable, pulling himself to the stop. "Ry, you're hurt—we need to get you some—"

"I said, *stay back*."

"OK," he says, raising a hand. "I'll just talk then. All right? I'll just talk."

He can't keep his eyes off my knee, a thin stream of blood still trailing from it. When it touches the metal on the reactor, it spreads out, so dark it's almost black.

"We're too far away now," he says. "If you blow the reactor, we'll never make it back."

I say nothing.

"They know you're here—I only just managed to get ahead of them. Come back with me. Please."

I don't hear the rest. I'm looking past him. All the way to the reactor airlock.

Okwembu is there, along with Mikhail.

They've got Aaron. Mikhail has an arm around his throat, and a stinger pressed to the side of his head.

103

Riley

I can't move.

I have to blow the bomb. But if I do that, Aaron dies.

All I can see is the stinger, jammed up against his head. He's barely conscious, and there are dark rings under his eyes, standing out against his pale skin.

"Better put it down," says Mikhail, pulling his arm tighter around Aaron's throat.

"I didn't want it to come to this," Okwembu says. She's moved into the chamber, a few feet away from Prakesh. "But, Ms. Hale, you need to do what he says."

"I can't."

I'm crying now, the tears spurred on by the waves of pain coming from my knee. They fall out of my eyes, drifting in front of me.

Okwembu speaks slowly, as if carefully examining every word. "Outer Earth is lost. It's finished. Even if we somehow repair the Core, we've lost too many people to Resin."

I think of Anna, her father, all the others left behind. "You're wrong."

But it's as if she doesn't hear me. "The only thing that matters now is that humans survive. And the best chance of that is this ship."

"Don't listen to them, Riley." Aaron's voice is almost inaudible under the noise of the reactor, but there's still some strength in it. "Just…" His words are choked off as the arm pulls tighter around his neck.

"Riley, please," says Prakesh. "Just do what she says. Do it for me."

I stare at him, not understanding his words. When comprehension comes, it's as if a bullet has gone through my own head. "You're with them?"

"You know I'd never want this. Any of it. But I can't let anyone else die. Not you, not Aaron, not anyone else in this room or this ship. And if you blow that bomb, that's what'll happen."

"And Outer Earth?" I say. "What about them?"

The regret on Prakesh's face is infinite. "We can't help them, Ry. *I* can't help them. I never could. The only thing I can do is protect what we have now. I can help keep this ship safe."

"Prakesh—"

"You have to let me do this," he says.

Is he telling the truth? Would Prakesh lie to me? It's impossible to think. It feels as if there are more people in the room than the five of us. Kevin is there, and Yao, floating just out of sight. Royo, his dark eyes locked on mine. Amira, right behind me, whispering in my ear.

My father is here, too, with my name in orange letters over his face. I can't quite see his eyes.

"I'll give you three seconds," says Mikhail.

Okwembu glances at him. "No, Mikhail. I have this under control."

"Three!"

"Riley, I love you, but you have to stop," says Prakesh.

"Two!"

"Mikhail, *stand down*," says Okwembu.

"One!"

"Do it, Ry," Aaron shouts. "Do it now!"

I throw the box.

104

Riley

But not at the bomb.

Instead, I throw the box away from me, so hard that it bounces off the floor with a dull boom. The bomb floats in front of the reactor, its wires just touching the surface.

Silence.

Relief is written on Prakesh's face. "Good. That's good, Riley."

I look down at my hand. Somehow, the knife is back in it. I don't know how—I can't even remember seeing it since I used it on myself. And, right then, it's as if all the voices, all the people crowding the reactor chamber, the buzzing of the reactor itself, just vanish. My mind is wiped clean. There's just me, and the knife.

And Janice Okwembu.

She's floating in front of me. Her eyes sparkle with triumph. Everything that's happened, all of it, from my father to the Devil Dancers to Resin to the dock to Morgan Knox...all of it is because of her. The chain of events she set off, by bringing my father back, put us here: on a hijacked vessel, with the station in ruins behind us, and hundreds of thousands of people dead.

She's the origin point. She's responsible. She wanted power, and control, and it tore Outer Earth apart.

I'm barely aware of what I'm doing. I feel my hands grab hold of something, and use it to spin me around. I move my right leg, the undamaged one, swinging it around so that my foot is in contact with the surface of the reactor. The knife is pointed upwards, gripped tight in my hand. Its blade is crusted with dried blood.

I push off the reactor in what feels like slow motion, but somehow I know that I'm moving faster than I ever have before. Everything I've gone through coalesces, simmers down into those two things. The triumph fades from her eyes, replaced by fear.

And the sight of it, that naked terror in her eyes, is wonderful.

Someone grabs me around the middle. The world comes rushing back—Aaron, Mikhail, the reactor, all of it. The knife is gone, flying away from me. Okwembu, too, pulled back by Mikhail. He throws Aaron aside as he does so, sending him flying.

I'm shouting, hammering on the arms that grip me tight. It's Prakesh. We slam into the wall of the chamber, and my knee flares with impossible pain. He just pulls his way up my body until he towers over me, pulls me into an embrace, locks me in it. My words turn to nothing, to incoherent screams.

I fight to get away from Prakesh, but there's no strength left in my arms. Eventually, all I can do is stare at him. Betrayal, hatred, love, pity—I feel every single one of them.

"No more deaths, Riley," he says. "No more. Not even her. It's over."

105

Riley

There's food, water and a room with very bright lights. The *Shinso Maru*'s medical bay—I don't really remember how I got here, but Aaron is with me, strapped into one of the other beds.

I can't feel anything below my left knee—the man working on it puts a huge needle into my leg, and the pain simply melts away. I'm strapped down, held in place by wide velcro straps, but my arms float freely. I can barely move them.

The man is muttering to himself as he works on the cut. "You did this to yourself?"

"There was a bomb in me," I say. "I took it out."

I hear him pause for a moment, as if waiting for more. When it doesn't come, he goes back to work.

"There's another one," I say. I barely recognise my own voice. "Other knee."

His eyes go wide. Then he shakes his head sadly. "I don't..." he says, and trails off.

"Please. You have to take it out."

"Dominguez was our medical officer," he says. "I'm doing what I can, but I'm out of my depth here. I'm sorry."

He's right. Better to leave it where it is, for now. As long as that transmitter in my ear stays charged, I'll be OK.

It's then that I notice the patch on his chest, faded and frayed, but still legible. KHALIL, ASTRONAUTICS OFFICER.

"The demon of the Asteroid Belt," I say. I don't know if he hears me. I'm drifting down a long, dark tunnel, shot through with flecks of fire. I expect to see my dad, with my name obscuring his eyes, but I'm way too deep for that.

When I wake up, Khalil is gone. In his place there's one of the Earthers, floating by the door. I vaguely remember him from the attack on the dock—a giant man, with a face that looks as if he hasn't smiled in years. "Are you here to make sure I don't kill anybody?" I ask. My throat feels as if it's filled with razor blades.

He doesn't say anything. Lifting my head, I get a look at my knee for the first time. It's wrapped in bandages; a swollen ball of white fabric, dotted with blood.

I rip off my velcro straps. Using the wall for control, I move over to Aaron's bed. He's flat on his back, his eyes closed. The glaring lights show up the purple circles underneath his eyes. There's a drip stuck into his arm, hooked up to a bag of yellowish liquid.

"They said not to wake him yet," says the man by the door.

I put a hand on Aaron's shoulder, and squeeze. Instantly, the man is by my side, moving between me and the bed. I didn't realise how big he was—my head barely reaches his shoulders.

"Best do what you're told," he says, staring down at me.

I return his gaze. "What are you, then? My bodyguard?"

"Mikhail says to keep you in here. He'll figure out what to do with you later. You and your friend."

I'm already working out how to take him down, working out the best way to disable him in low gravity. Then I realise I've only got the use of one leg, and that my other limbs feel like thin glass. I've as much chance of taking him down as I have of surviving in space without a suit. I turn and push myself back to my own bed, pulling myself down onto the edge of it, strapping myself back in.

Sometime later, I look up to see Prakesh.

His eyes are drawn, but he tries to smile as he moves towards the bed. The bodyguard floats between him and me, his hand raised.

"Let me see her," Prakesh says.

The man doesn't move. Prakesh's eyes flare with anger. "If I was going to try something, I would have done it by now. *Let me see her.*"

After a long moment, the giant lets him past. Prakesh pushes himself around him towards the bed.

I can't look at him.

I keep seeing Okwembu. I was so close. And *he* stopped me, pulled me away just before I could have my revenge. For Outer Earth, for my dad, for everything.

I should hate him. I want to.

But as he reaches the bed, as I see the pain in his eyes and feel his hand on my shoulder, that hatred cracks and crumbles.

I can't blame him for not wanting anyone else to die while he stands aside and does nothing. How can I turn him away, when he's in so much pain? It would be the worst thing possible.

I reach out for him, and we embrace. I bury my head in his shoulder.

Neither of us speak. We don't need to. We just hold each other tight. Both of us have made mistakes. Both of us are broken, in our own way.

I don't mention what happened with Aaron. I don't know how.

"What's it like?" I say. "Up on the bridge?"

He rests his forehead on my shoulder. "They're working out how to shape the asteroid. It has to be structurally sound for re-entry. They're going to need to go outside to do it."

"That's enough," says the guard, appearing behind Prakesh.

I squeeze him tight. "Go," I say. "I'll be all right."

"You sure?"

In answer, I squeeze even harder. I don't tell him the real reason I want him to go. It's because Aaron is awake, and watching us, and the confusion in his eyes is too much to bear.

"I'll come back, OK?" Prakesh says. "I'll come and get you."

He looks back at me one last time.

"I love you," he says.

"I love you, too."

He leaves, and the door slips shut behind him. The guard doesn't say anything as I unstrap and float over to Aaron's bed. He's sitting up, drinking from a pouch of water through a straw.

"Guess we're going to Earth then," he says, pulling the straw from his mouth.

"I guess."

He shrugs. "Gonna be interesting to see how they do it. Even after they get through the atmosphere, they'll still be going a billion miles an hour. I'm thinking they'll use the escape pods, bail out..."

He trails off as I wrap my arms around him. It's all I can do not to start crying again. He hugs me back, then lifts my head to his, his lips brushing mine.

I pull away.

Gods help me, I pull away.

His eyes meet mine. "I just thought—after all we've been through, we could..."

"Please don't ask me this, Aaron. Not now."

I reach up to touch his cheek, but he pushes me away, anger blazing on his face. "I was there for you. This whole time, I've been right alongside you. Back at the hospital in Apex, the Boneshaker, the fight in the dock, the tug—all of it. Doesn't that mean anything?"

His words echo my thoughts about Prakesh. My heart feels like it's about to shatter, like a single tap on my chest would kill me. I have to fight back the tears.

"You really still love him?" Aaron says. "After all that he's done?"

It comes out as a whisper. "I don't know."

"Then why did we kiss? You tell me that. Why?"

When I speak, each word is like a weight being hung around my neck. "I wanted to be close to someone. I wanted something normal."

"Excuse me?"

"I shouldn't have done it, Aaron. It was wrong. You're my *friend*."

He's crying too now. "You don't understand," he says. "You two have each other. Who do I have, Riley? Who do I have?"

I can't answer him. I wouldn't know where to begin. I don't know what I'm becoming, or what to think any more.

The door opens behind us. I hear Prakesh's voice. "You're OK to come through to the bridge, if you want."

"Don't go with him," Aaron says in a whisper. "Stay with me. Please."

But I don't.

We leave the medical bay, Prakesh and I, the bodyguard floating along behind us. He hasn't said a word. I take one last look back at Aaron—only for a second, because any longer and I'll crack in two. He's turned away from us, facing the wall.

On the bridge, banks of glowing screens are lined up like soldiers. A giant screen hangs from the ceiling; it's displaying what looks like a projected course, the *Shinso* a tiny dot in the top right corner. The Earthers are here—at least twenty of them, floating in small groups. Syria is there, too, huddled by the wall. He doesn't look at me.

The far wall is transparent. I can see the Earth. The sun is just peeking over the far horizon. A band of colour spreads out from it, dark blue becoming crimson and orange and white.

That's when I see Okwembu.

She and Mikhail are floating just below the window, deep in discussion. Mikhail's body has been caught by the sun, but the top half of Okwembu's body is cloaked in shadow. She turns to look at me, and her face is a black hole, silhouetted against the light. It's impossible to see her expression, and she doesn't move—just stares at me, her chin slightly lowered. I get a ghost of the anger I felt in the reactor, when it was just me, her and the knife. Prakesh seems to sense it, and holds me tighter.

We're not done yet, I think, looking at Okwembu. *You and me. Not even close.*

It's Mikhail who comes forward, using the railings that buttress each level to pull himself towards us. I expect him to be angry, but as he comes towards us he actually smiles. "I'm glad to see you up," he says.

I flinch from him, doing it before I can tell myself not to. He stops, and raises his hands. "You have nothing to be afraid of. Not from us. You understand that we have to keep a watch on you—" he gestures to my guard, still floating behind me "—but I hope you will help us when we reach our destination."

I'm shaking my head, and when I speak I struggle to keep the rage out of my voice. "Destination?" I say, jabbing a finger at the window, at the black mass under the sun's band. "There's nothing there. Nothing and nobody. We destroyed it, remember?"

"You haven't told her?" Mikhail asks Prakesh. He shakes his head.

"Told me what?"

Mikhail gestures to the big man. My bodyguard. "Alexei. Bring the recording."

"What is this?" I ask Prakesh.

"You need to hear it," he says.

As Alexei moves to the other side of the bridge, Mikhail turns back to us. "It's true that most of the Earth is a wasteland. The nuclear bombs saw to that."

"Then what—"

"Don't interrupt. The climate on maybe ninety-eight per cent of the planet's surface is completely destroyed. But we've discovered a part of the Earth where it's starting to clear."

I'm shaking my head, not quite believing it. "OK, so what? Starting to clear isn't the same as completely clear. You still don't know what's down there. If it's even habitable."

Alexei comes back. He has an ancient recording unit, no bigger than my hand. Mikhail takes it, and presses play. Static hisses out of the tinny speaker. Around us, the room has gone silent.

"I don't see—" I start, and then a man's voice is coming out of the speaker, so crackly I can barely make it out. I have to listen hard, but soon I hear the tonal vowels, the clipped words.

"It's Chinese," I say.

Mikhail nods. "The English message will come in a moment. We think they're broadcasting in different languages to reach as many people as possible."

"We haven't had any communication from Earth in fifty years. Not one."

"That is correct," Mikhail says. "And so we stopped listening. That device in your ear—" he points to my SPOCS unit, still there despite everything I've been through "—it runs off cell frequencies, as you know, which means it can't pick up old radio transmissions."

And all at once, it clicks into place.

The static. The bursts across the SPOCS line. The interference that Aaron could never fix, that hurt my ear whenever they came through.

I remember the thing I saw in the old mining facility that the Earthers had taken over. The device with the old-fashioned screens, displaying the strange shapes.

We weren't listening. The Earthers were. They found something—something that convinced them that they could survive on Earth. They didn't tell the council because they knew that only a few people would ever be able to return to the planet. They wanted it to be them.

There's a pause in the recording, and then it switches into English.

"If anyone can hear us, we are broadcasting from a secure location in what used to be Anchorage, Alaska. There are at least a hundred of us here, and we have managed to establish a colony. We have food, water and shelter. The climate is cold, but survivable. If you can hear us, then know that you're not the only ones out there. Our coordinates are—"

Mikhail turns off the recorder.

"Do you see now?" he says quietly.

I can barely find the words. "It's an old message. It has to be."

Alexei shakes his head. "At the end of it, he gives a date. One which was only two months ago."

"They live," Mikhail says. "The broadcast was meant for survivors on Earth, but we heard it, too. And we're going to find them."

It feels like everyone in the room is watching me. Okwembu hasn't moved—her face is still cloaked in shadow. Slowly, I raise my head towards the window.

The world looks back at me, dark and silent, with the sun coming up over the horizon.

IMPACT

Prologue

The meteor tears a hole in the sky.

The low-hanging clouds glow gold, as if the sun itself has dropped into the atmosphere. Then the white-hot rock rips them in two.

There's a shape behind the flames, just visible past the corona. A long cylinder, black against the clouds, attached to the meteor by a shimmering cord. The cord breaks, and the crack is loud enough to knock frost off the trees below.

The man on the ground throws himself to the dirt, hands over his ears, as if the pieces were passing right above the tree line. Icy mud soaks his skin, but he barely notices.

His cheek is pressed to the ground, the world turned sideways, but he can still see the pieces. Their white heat has faded to a dark red. Most of them are vanishing over the eastern horizon, but at least one seems to be plummeting right towards him, screaming down through the air.

He scrambles to his feet, trying to run. But the piece is nowhere near him—how could he have thought it was? It's going down in the east, the red metal fading to scorched black. His heart is pounding, and in the split second before it vanishes over the horizon, its shape leaps out at him.

That's not just a meteor.

It's a ship.

Slowly, ever so slowly, the roar begins to fade. There's a final crackle, like fading thunder, and then it's gone.

His legs are shaking, but none of his companions notice. They're as stunned as he is, staring up at the sky.

One of them is moving, pushing through the brush, yelling at them to follow him.

"Think there'll be survivors?" someone shouts.

"No one survives a crash like that," comes the reply.

But the man isn't so sure. A long time ago, he was in one just like it.

1

Riley

The alarm starts blaring a split second before the shaking starts.

Aaron Carver is floating in the centre of the ship's medical bay, and Prakesh Kumar and I get thrown right into him. Everything else in the room is strapped down, but I can see the instruments and the bottles shaking, threatening to tear loose.

"What the hell?" Carver rolls away from us, putting his arms out to stop himself from crashing into the wall. The ship is rattling hard now, the metal bending and creaking, caught in the fist of an angry giant.

"It's re-entry," Prakesh says. He's holding onto the ceiling, and his body is swinging back and forth as the pull of gravity increases.

"Can't be," I say, my words almost swallowed by the noise. "It's too soon!"

But it isn't. We've been in Earth orbit for a week. Normally the ship would be spinning to generate gravity, but we've spent the past day in zero-G as we prepare to plunge through the atmosphere. There was supposed to be plenty of warning before we actually started re-entry—enough time for everyone to get into the escape pods. It shouldn't be happening this fast. The G-forces were supposed to come back gradually.

My stomach is doing sickening barrel rolls, and my hands feel *heavy*, like my fingers are weighed down with rings. "I thought this was supposed to be a smooth ride," I say, trying to keep my voice calm. "The asteroid—"

"No good," Carver says. He grabs hold of a strut on the ceiling, the muscles standing out on his powerful upper arms. His hair is almost as long as mine now, although he doesn't bother to tie it back, letting the blond strands float freely.

"I *told* them," he says. "You can shape the damn asteroid as much as you want but if you're using it as a heat shield, things are going to get—*shit!*"

He spins sideways as the ship jerks and kicks, flinging him against one of the cots bolted to the floor.

"It's OK," says Prakesh, sweat pouring down his dark skin. Neither he nor Carver have shaved, and bristly stubble covers their faces. "We just sit tight. They'll come get us."

We all stare at the door. The alarm is still blaring, and the hull of the ship is screeching now, like it's being torn in two.

"They're not coming, are they?" says Carver.

"Just hang on," says Prakesh. "Let's not—"

"They would have been here by now," says Carver, horror and anger flashing across his face. "They're not coming, man."

I close my eyes, trying not to let frustration overtake me. He's right. The Earthers—the group who took control of this ship to get back to our planet—don't trust us. Not surprising, given that I tried to destroy the ship's reactor in an attempt to prevent them from leaving.

There's no way of stopping the ship. It'll be travelling at 18,000 miles an hour, even after it's passed through the upper atmosphere and burned off the asteroid it's tethered to, acting as its makeshift heat shield. Getting off the ship means being in one of the two escape pods, and it's easy to picture the chaos as the Earthers rush to get inside them. They've either forgotten us, or decided that we aren't worth saving.

I scan the walls and the ceiling, looking for an escape route that we missed the previous dozen times we tried to find one. Not that we tried that hard—after all, if we got out of the medical bay where else would we go?

Carver half swims, half crawls his way over to the door, pushing Prakesh aside and twisting the release catch up and down. When that doesn't work, he kicks at it, but only succeeds in pushing himself away.

Prakesh stares at him. "What are you doing?"

"What do you think?" Carver makes his way back to the door, kicks it a second time. It shudders but stays firmly shut.

"It's locked, Aaron."

Carver swings round, staring daggers at Prakesh. "You think I don't know that?"

"Then why are you still doing it?"

"Because it's better than doing nothing, like *some of us*!"

"I'm trying to—"

"Both of you! Shut up!" I shout. I can't afford to have them bickering now. They've been sniping at each other ever since we were locked in here—Carver has feelings for me, and he's still furious that I turned down his advances to stay with Prakesh. It's something I've tried not to think about, a problem I've pushed to the back of my mind again and again, not wanting to make a choice, not even knowing how to start.

"We kick together," I say. "All at once."

I don't have to explain. I see Carver's eyes light up. He moves next to me, bracing himself against the wall.

"Aim for just above the lock," I say, as Prakesh gets into position on my left. "Hit it on zero. Three! Two! One! *Zero!*"

The door bangs as our feet slam into the space above the handle, but remains stubbornly shut. The force pushes us backwards, nearly knocking us over. Somehow we manage to stay upright.

"Again," I say. There's a hold on the wall, and I grab onto it with an outstretched arm, bracing us.

"Three! Two! One! *Zero!*"

The door explodes outwards, the lock ripping off the wall, and we tumble into the corridor. The alarm is piercing now, ear-splitting. Carver pumps the air in triumph.

The ship jerks sideways. For a second, the wall is the floor, and everything is a nightmare jumble of limbs and noise. Prakesh falls badly, his head slamming into the metal surface with a clang that I feel in my bones. In the moment before the ship flips back, I see his face. His blank, uncomprehending eyes. A trickle of blood runs down his forehead.

2

Okwembu

The ship's movement knocks Janice Okwembu onto all fours.

She staggers to her feet, leaning against the wall, trying to control the nausea. There's a blur of movement on her right, and one of the Earthers shoves past her, pushing her out of the way.

Okwembu tries to stay calm, but she can't stop her hands from shaking. She barely makes it to the corridor hub before she stumbles again. Her green flight jacket is bulky, but she can feel the frigid floor plates through the thin fabric of her pants.

The asteroid was supposed to have held up, dissipating the massive heat and shock wave of re-entry. Every calculation they did showed that the vibrations wouldn't start until they were deep into the atmosphere. But they got it wrong—a missing variable, something they didn't take into account. The asteroid is fracturing, leaving everyone on board the ship to scramble for the escape pods.

She looks up. Mikhail Yeremin, the leader of the Earthers, is at the other end of the corridor. His greasy hair frames a face locked into deep panic. In that moment, it's as if he doesn't even recognise her.

He vanishes, ducking out of sight. Okwembu curses, tries to get to her feet, but the ship lurches again. The back of her head smacks into the wall, and bright stars glimmer in her vision.

There's a hand reaching for her. It's another Earther, a young woman—one of those who went outside the ship, using plasma cutters to shape the asteroid. She's wearing a ship jumpsuit two sizes too big for her, and her eyes are bright with fear. Okwembu grabs her hand, lets the woman haul her up.

The movement of the ship stops, just for moment, then becomes more violent than ever. Okwembu goes over backwards. The Earther reaches out for her, misses, her fingers brushing the front of the fleece she wears under her jacket.

They snag on the lanyard around her neck.

It pulls tight, the cord pinching against Okwembu's spine. The hold keeps her upright—just—but it's stretched to breaking point. The woman's hand is wrapped around the green plastic data stick at the end of the lanyard, her knuckles white. Any second now, it's going to snap right off.

With an effort of will, Okwembu balances herself, planting her back foot on the floor. The pressure on her neck drops, and the woman lets go of the data stick. It bounces against Okwembu's chest.

"You OK?" the woman says, trying to hustle her along, holding her by the shoulder. She shakes loose. She's got her balance back now, and she's feeling calmer, more focused. "I'll be fine. Just go."

The woman wavers, then bolts. Okwembu's hands find the data stick, holding it tight.

For the past week, while they prepared for re-entry, all Okwembu has done is scrape data, putting every scrap of information she could onto this one little stick. None of them know what's down there, what it's really like on the planet's surface—all they have is a garbled radio message, talking about how part of the planet has somehow become habitable again. So Okwembu spent her time downloading everything off the ship's antiquated operating system—water filtration methods, studies on the best soil for growing food in, atmospheric data, reactor blueprints. Maps and charts and graphs, petabytes of information. She doesn't know if any of it will be useful, or if she'll even be able to access it on the ground, but she's not going down without it. The *Shinso Maru* is worth nothing now, but its data is a price beyond jewels.

The lights in the ceiling are flickering, and the few Earthers she does see are panicked, moving like mindless insects. Contempt boils inside her, but she tells herself to stay focused. Contempt can become anger, which can mutate into panic. She can't afford that. Especially not now.

The escape pods are a short distance away, and Okwembu moves as fast as she can.

3

Riley

No matter how hard I shake Prakesh, I can't make him open his eyes.

Carver crouches down, shoving his head under Prakesh's left arm, hoisting him upwards. I do the same on the other side, heart pounding in my chest. Prakesh is amazingly heavy even in low gravity, his feet dragging on the ground between us as we try to keep our balance in the shaking passage.

There are shelves along the walls, with small plastic crates strapped onto them. One of them comes loose as we walk past it, slipping out of its fabric straps, and we have to pull to the side as it bounces off the walls and floor. The ship's jagged motion turns it into a pinball.

I pull Carver's head down as it flies towards us. Not fast enough. The crate just scrapes across his forehead, and he hisses in surprise, staggering into the wall. His hiss turns into a growl as his shoulder takes the hit.

Somehow, we manage to get moving again. I'm getting better at it now, bending my legs, anticipating the ship's movements. Carver is doing it, too. The screeching of the *Shinso*'s hull has been replaced by a crunching, grinding noise, as if bits of the ship are being ripped off by the friction of re-entry. I don't even want to think how fast we're going. I don't want to think at all. If those escape pods leave without us...

Just keep going.

We pass a window in the corridor, looking into what appears to be a gym. The treadmills and weight machines are straining against their brackets, slowly working loose. I catch our reflection in the window. We're a mess. All of us are wearing badly fitting flight gear—grey jackets and T-shirts that are too big for us. Stray strands of hair stick to my face in greasy lines. Prakesh's face is ash-grey, blood still dripping from his head wound. Carver's arms are straining, his face contorted as we pull Prakesh along.

I tear my gaze away, focusing on the passage ahead. "How long do we have?" I ask.

"Not nearly long enough," says Carver. I flash back to when we first came aboard the *Shinso,* when he asked me to use his first name: Aaron. I still haven't been able to shake the habit of using his last name.

We reach the junction. There's a sign on the wall, grubby with age: *Mining, Astronautics, Engines.* I jab a finger at the corridor on the left. "Astronautics. Let's go."

Prakesh groans again. It's like he's trying to fight his way back. I put a hand on his chest to steady him—

—And trip.

I try to catch myself, but my legs get tangled underneath me. I go down on one knee, struggling with Prakesh, Carver grunting in surprise.

Fire rolls out from the back of my knee, travelling up my leg and down into my ankle. I wait for it to pass, gritting my teeth.

Back on the station, a psychotic doctor named Morgan Knox implanted explosive charges in the muscles behind my kneecaps, blackmailing me so I would break Janice Okwembu out of prison. I cut one of the explosives out of me when I tried to destroy the *Shinso*'s fusion reactor, tried to stop the Earthers abandoning Outer Earth. It didn't work. And after we were captured, I had to beg the Earthers to take the second explosive out of me. It took a few days, but they finally did it, numbing my leg with anaesthetic and slicing me open. I'm slowly healing, but there are bandages on the backs of my knees. Both the wounds hurt like hell.

Everything that happened on Outer Earth feels like a distant dream. We still don't know if anybody on the station survived. Even if they did, we're much too far away for them to reach us.

I push upwards, straining against Prakesh's weight. The corridor is even narrower here, and at one point Carver and I have to turn sideways to get him through a door.

The escape pods are right ahead, three sets of airlock doors built into the corridor, with big letters stencilled on either side in black. EMERGENCY USE ONLY.

While some Earthers worked on the asteroid, others worked on the escape pods. They turned them from space-going vessels into something that might actually be able to land on Earth, creating makeshift parachutes from material found on board the *Shinso*.

The pods themselves are too small to have their own fusion reactors, so they run off conventional liquid fuel. They're housed inside specially designed airlocks. There are Earthers everywhere, helping each other inside the first pod's open door, stumbling, panicked. An orange light above each airlock door blinks on-off, on-off. The floor of the airlock is slightly lower than the floor in the corridor, and I feel my knees jarring as we step through.

Carver and I pull Prakesh into the pod. There's a cockpit at the front with rows of seats along each side. Each one is a mess of thick straps, with a neck guard protruding from the seat back. Oxygen masks hang from the ceiling, swinging wildly as the *Shinso* bucks and writhes. I badly want to see outside, but the only thing visible through the cockpit glass is the outer airlock door.

The pods can take twelve people each, plus a pilot. All but three of the chairs are full. Mikhail Yeremin is there—he's checking his straps, his long hair hanging down over his face. There's lettering above his head: ESCAPE VESSEL 1. Underneath it, in smaller black letters, is a vessel name: *Furor*.

Carver perches on the edge of an empty seat, pulling Prakesh onto the one next to him. I lean in to help, yanking the straps down and buckling them tight. Carver does the same with his own straps, snapping himself in. We made it.

I stand up, intending to take the one remaining chair in the escape pod, opposite Prakesh. Any second now, they'll shut the door and we can—

Carver's eyes go wide.

Two hands grasp my shoulders, pulling me backwards. I cry out, my feet tangling up in each other, catching the edge of the pod's entrance. I land on my coccyx, cracking it against the floor plates in the airlock.

Janice Okwembu is looking down at me.

I haven't seen her since the day we came aboard. She's a former Outer Earth council leader who went rogue, joining up with the Earthers. The expression on her face is completely blank.

"No!" Carver shouts, fighting with the straps holding him to the chair. "Leave her alone!"

I scramble to my feet, moving as fast as I can. Not fast enough.

Okwembu looks down at me, reaching over to one side of the frame for the control panel. "Goodbye, Ms. Hale," she says.

And the door closes in front of me.

4

Okwembu

Aaron Carver finally gets loose.

He shoves Okwembu out of the way. She collides with one of the seats, almost falling on top of its occupant, a man with tangled black hair and an acne-speckled face. Okwembu ignores him. She lifts herself into a seat, grabbing the straps, concentrating on buckling herself in.

Carver hammers at the control pad, but the door doesn't open. Of course it doesn't. Okwembu made sure to twist the rotary to the *Eject* position. It shuts the pod down in preparation for launch, to ensure that the door has a good pressure seal. It can't be opened again. Behind it, the inner airlock doors will be closing.

She hopes that Riley Hale has the good sense to get out while she still can.

Mikhail Yeremin is staring at her, and she doesn't like the expression on his face. She turns away, ignoring him, busying herself with her straps. She's still looking down at her buckle, and so isn't prepared when Aaron Carver slams her back against the seat. His face is inches from hers.

"Open it up," he says. When she doesn't respond, he barks the words in her face. "Do you hear me? Open it up."

"You should sit down, Mr. Carver," Okwembu says.

He rips her straps away, lifts her up, throws her out of her seat. She hits the floor, wincing in pain as her right hand takes the impact, bending at the wrist.

Carver grabs the back of her jacket, dragging her to the door. Mikhail is almost out of his seat, huge fingers fighting with the catch on his chest. The other Earthers watch without saying a word.

Okwembu attempts to spin away, trying to get her arms out of her jacket. Carver sees the move, stops her, pulling her up so her face is level with the lock. "*Open the door,*" he yells, right in her ear.

When she doesn't move, he wrenches at the rotary switch alongside it, trying to get it back to *Doors Manual*. Okwembu wants to tell him not to bother. The most he'll be able to do is tear the switch itself off the control panel.

"We need to launch *now*," shouts the pilot from the front of the craft. "Everybody better strap in."

"We're not leaving," Carver says. "Not until—"

Mikhail grabs him around the shoulders, shoving him backwards into his seat. Carver tries to get back up, but Mikhail won't let him, holding him in place as he clicks the catch shut.

"You don't strap in, you die," he says.

Okwembu takes the gap. She staggers back to her seat, heart pounding, strapping herself in. She looks up to see that Carver has stopped fighting. He's gripping his straps tight, his fingers bloodless. Mikhail is making his way back to his own seat, grabbing at the straps.

"She'd better make it," Carver says, looking Okwembu right in the eyes. "Or I'm going to *end* you."

In the moment before the pilot launches the pod, she wonders about Carver. She shouldn't be surprised at his actions. He doesn't have any sort of vision or understanding of the wider consequences of what's happening here. What he has are mechanical skills, and Prakesh Kumar, sitting next to him, has agricultural ones. The moment she saw the make-up of this pod, she knew it was the one she needed to be in.

The people inside it—Carver, Kumar, the other Earthers—all have skills that can be used on the planet below. Hale doesn't. She can run, and she can fight, and as far as Okwembu is concerned neither one is particularly useful.

It's more than that, she thinks. *You wanted to do it. You wanted to put her in her place.*

Okwembu closes her eyes, and the pod explodes away from the ship.

5

Riley

I lose control.

If the pod's door wasn't made of metal, if it wasn't completely beyond human strength to do anything to it, then my fingers would be digging long channels in the surface. I kick and hit and hammer and try to wedge my fingers into the whisper-thin gap. I scream Okwembu's name, but the only thing that comes back at me are the waves of vibrations tearing through the *Shinso*.

"What are you doing?"

It comes from beyond the inner airlock door. Syria is standing there, staring at me like I've gone crazy.

He was a community leader from Outer Earth, from a place known as the Caves. He fought hard to stop the Earthers from taking the ship, but ended up here with them. Like Okwembu, I haven't seen him since the day we boarded the *Shinso*. He must have been locked up somewhere else—there's no way he would have helped Okwembu and Mikhail. He's tough and wiry, wearing a bright red flight jacket, and his dirty hair is thick with knots.

He works his way into the airlock and grabs me, then has to do it again when I tear my way out of his grip.

"Hey!" he says, grabbing my arm. "Are you crazy? There's a second pod."

"My *friends* are in there," I shout back. At that moment, the word doesn't seem adequate enough. Carver and Prakesh aren't just friends. They're everything. They're all I've got left.

Syria pulls me through the outer airlock door. It's starting to shut, the mechanisms sliding the door closed. "And we'll be right behind them," he says. "Guaranteed."

The second pod is twenty yards down the corridor. Before I can blink, Syria hustles us inside, shoving me into a seat and buckling me in. I don't have the energy left to fight back. The seat straps are tight around my chest and stomach. The shaking is getting very bad now.

"Release in ten seconds," shouts the pilot from the front of our pod.

"We have to go now!" another voice says.

"Negative. We need to give the other pod time to get clear, or we'll smash into it," the pilot says. I can't see his face, just the back of his head. A woman opposite me is muttering something that sounds like a prayer, her eyes shut tight. The name of the pod is above her on the wall: *Lyssa*.

I think back to Prakesh and Carver, tight on either side of me, our legs raised to kick down the locked door. All of us together, acting as one. I try to hold onto it, but it sends an unexpected spasm of anger through me—and this time I'm angry at myself.

I spent a week with them in that damn medical bay, a week where I could have talked to them, a week where we could have straightened out where we stood with each other. I wanted to be with Prakesh, told Carver as much, but it didn't stop the choice gnawing at me, making me wonder if I'd made the right decision. It didn't stop me thinking about how I kissed Carver while we were dealing with the last few hours of insanity on Outer Earth. I had all the time in the world to say something, and I didn't, and now I might never see them again.

And on the tail of that thought comes another. Janice Okwembu took them away from me. When I see her again, I'm going to make her pay.

I'll find you, I say, willing the thought to reach Prakesh and Carver, knowing it won't and not caring. *I don't care what happens. I'll find you.*

"Release!" says the pilot.

But there's no bang. No shuddering explosion. Nothing happens.

The pilot hammers on the control panel, each hit more and more frantic. But no matter what he does, our pod refuses to launch.

6

Prakesh

Prakesh is back in the Air Lab on Outer Earth.

He can see the ceiling lights through the canopies of the enormous oak trees towering above him. He can smell the damp scent of the algae pools, the thick musk of soil.

His parents are there, his father's arm around his mother. He can see every detail—his father's prosthetic leg, his mother's scarf, the earrings she wears. He tries to say their names, but when he moves his lips, no sound comes out. And they're not smiling—they're just looking at him, sadness lining their faces.

Then they're gone, and Riley Hale is there, standing before him. The woman he loves. He doesn't want her to speak. He knows what she's going to say.

Impact

Resin, Prakesh. The words come in her voice, even though she hasn't opened her mouth. *Resin. It came from you.*

He doesn't want it to be true. The virus that tore through Outer Earth can't have come from him. It's a dream, that's all. A bad dream. Any moment now, he's going to wake up in bed with Riley, in their hab in Chengshi.

The Air Lab is shaking. The tree branches are swinging back and forth, groaning, as if caught in a hurricane. Riley is gone.

There's a *bang*. It explodes through Prakesh's body, filling every cell, blotting out the world. His eyes snap open. For a moment, he doesn't know where he is. Then he sees Aaron Carver next to him, his eyes squeezed shut, G-forces rippling his cheeks.

Prakesh remembers everything. His gaze darts around the packed escape pod. Janice Okwembu is near the front, her eyes closed, her head tilted back. Mikhail is a few seats down from her.

They're in-flight. They have to be. That means the escape pod jettisoned from the *Shinso*. Prakesh tries to turn his head, pushing against the Gs, and gets a brief look out of the cockpit glass. It's a mess of black and red, matted with a dull grey. *Clouds*, he thinks.

The headache comes suddenly, flaring at the base of his skull. It's like a red-hot needle, jamming upwards into his brain. There's blood on his face—where did it come from? The last thing he remembers is kicking the door down, holding tight onto…

Riley. Where's Riley?

At that moment, the shaking stops. The escape pod stabilises, and the roaring from outside vanishes, replaced by the gentle hum of the engines. The G-forces holding Prakesh against his seat disappear, although the headache remains. An audible sigh of relief rises from the cabin and someone gives a weak cheer.

Carver still has his eyes closed, his head tilted back.

"Everybody sit tight," says the pilot. "Parachute's out."

"What's our location?" It comes from Janice Okwembu, her voice calm and controlled.

Prakesh doesn't hear the pilot's answer. "Where's Riley?" he says to Carver.

No answer. Prakesh licks his lips. "*Carver*. Why isn't Riley here?"

"Ask her," Carver says, jerking his head at Okwembu, thunder on his face.

Prakesh's eyes find hers, surprised fury igniting inside him. "What did you do?"

Okwembu doesn't hear him, or, if she does, she doesn't say anything. Prakesh twists his head, looking back at Carver.

"But they got off OK, right?" he says. "They're behind us?"

Carver doesn't get a chance to respond. There's a distant boom, almost too soft to hear, like thunder from an unseen storm.

"There goes the *Shinso*," says the pilot.

7

Riley

The control panel of the *Lyssa* is a chaos of flashing lights. The pilot is panicking, shaking the stick back and forth.

This is what my father must have felt.

The thought is clear in my head. My father was on a mission to return to Earth, to establish humans on the planet again. His ship, the *Akua Maru*, suffered a catastrophic explosion during re-entry. He must have felt this, too. The same shaking. The same terror. My knuckles have gone white, my fingers gripping the seat.

"Gunther," someone shouts. "Check the couplings."

"Couplings are fine!" Gunther says over his shoulder.

"Then cycle the software. There must be—"

The bang feels like it shatters my eardrums. The G-forces rocket up, slamming me back into the seat and holding me there as the pod spins away from the main body of the *Shinso*. My eyes feel like they're going to drill out of the back of my skull.

A moment later, there's a second bang—the *Shinso* finally tearing itself apart. The sound reaches into the *Lyssa*, ripping through it, knocking us into a crazy spin. My head snaps to the side, then the other, at the mercy of the G-forces.

The other pod got off OK. I know it did. I heard it launch. I repeat the words in my mind, one after the other.

A hand grips mine. Syria. I want to look at him, but I can barely move. Everyone in the pod is screaming, held fast to their seats.

The G-force changes direction suddenly, knocking my head back the other way. I'm still squashed against the scratchy fabric of the seat, but I'm looking towards the cockpit now. I can see right out of the glass.

There are flecks of grey vapour spinning around us. The sky behind them is a dark blue, and at its bottom edge I can just see it turning to scarlet.

In a split second, the view changes. The grey vapour blocks out the sky—we must have fallen into a cloud bank. And there's burning debris, screaming past us—huge chunks of it, trailing fire. It's impossible to tell which chunks are asteroid and which were part of the *Shinso*.

There's a *thunk* as a piece hits us. I'm almost certain that the *Lyssa* is about to tear in two, but then our spin begins to slow.

"Drogue's out!" says Gunther from the cockpit. "Looking good. Everyone hold tight."

The parachute deploys. Our wild movement doesn't just slow—it comes to a sudden halt, snapping us upwards against our straps. I'm holding onto one at my shoulder, and two of my fingers get caught underneath it, burning as the fabric bites into them.

The noise vanishes, draining away. The view outside the window is swinging, left to right. It's not just sky now—there's something in the distance, a jagged shape, brown, capped with white.

"Gods," says Syria. It takes me a moment to see where he's looking.

Gunther's head is lolling onto his right shoulder. His eyes are dull and glassy, and I can see his right hand, drooping off the armrest of his seat. I've seen snapped necks before—it must have happened when the main parachute deployed. Maybe his straps came loose, or he hadn't secured them tight enough.

The air rushing around us is louder now. We must be getting closer to the ground. The pod gives a sickening lurch, and the side

I'm on drops, sending my stomach into my throat. I'm looking up at the people strapped in opposite me, all of them tilted forwards.

The parachute. Whatever construction the Earthers cobbled together from the *Shinso*'s supplies isn't holding. It's all too easy to imagine a hole in it, the air rushing through, our drag decreasing as we plummet towards the ground, the hole getting wider with every second. And there's nothing I can do. Nothing *any* of us can do.

Through the cockpit window I see the ground. We're close enough to pick out every rock, every crack in the terrain. It's rushing towards us, way too fast.

"Everybody hang on!" Syria says. We're skimming over the ground now—it's moving too fast, the texture of the dirt blurring as I look at it. I try to picture Carver and Prakesh, holding them uppermost in my mind.

There's a grinding, wrenching crash. The pod flips over, and then everything goes away.

8

Prakesh

They should be drifting down slowly, held up by the billowing parachute. Instead, they're moving sideways, as if the wind has caught them, tossing them like a leaf.

"Too fast, too fast, too fast," Carver says, as if that alone will be enough to slow them down. He speaks more to himself than to anyone else, but Prakesh can still hear him over the rushing air. The man opposite him is praying audibly now, invoking Shiva's name, Vishnu's, Buddha's.

It occurs to him that they might not make it. It's all too easy to see the pod slamming into the Earth at hundreds of miles an hour, vaporising on impact, turning everyone inside to burning dust.

Impact

"Listen up!" It's the pilot, shouting back over his shoulder. "We're coming in over the water, and we're coming in hot. There's going to be one hell of a bang, so everybody—"

Prakesh doesn't hear the rest, because that's when he sees the water. Whatever they're above—a lake, a river, the *ocean* for all he knows—fills the cockpit window, glittering in the distantly setting sun. It's rushing past at an impossible speed.

Okwembu turns her head away, tensing in her straps. Prakesh does the same, holding on tight, thinking of Riley, picturing her in his mind, but all he can hear is Carver screaming, "*Fuuuuuuuuuuuuu*—"

The impact lifts Prakesh out of his seat, ripping his head back. The whiplash takes him, snapping his head forward. A bright stab of pain lances through his neck.

They're airborne again, moving above the water. He can hear the rushing air above the screams from the pod's passengers. How are they still in the air? He remembers video footage he saw once, archival stuff: a stone skipping across a pond. Get the angle and the velocity right, and that stone could skip for a hundred yards.

But the pod is no stone. Prakesh has half a second to realise that they've flipped upside down, that he's hanging awkwardly in his straps, and then they hit the water again.

The impact this time sounds muted. It's a whooshing thud, vibrating up through the pod. Prakesh fights to stay conscious, to not let the pain in his neck and head overwhelm him. He opens his eyes—it feels like it takes him days, but he does it.

The pod is still moving, but much more slowly now. It comes to a rocking halt, still upside down. Prakesh can hear rushing water. He raises his eyes to where the ceiling of the pod should be, down below him, and sees why.

The water is coming in. As Prakesh watches, one of the panels shears off and a fist of water hits the man opposite him. The man chokes and splutters, his eyes wide with shock.

We have to get out of here.

The thought comes to Prakesh from a great distance. He wants to shout it to everyone, but his vocal cords have stopped working. His fingers move on their own, finding the strap release buckle on his chest.

He has the presence of mind to take a single, deep breath. Then he clicks the catch open, and drops.

9

Okwembu

The water knocks the breath from Okwembu's lungs.

For one terrible moment it shuts her body down completely. She is entirely submerged, hanging upside down in her seat. Her arms and legs won't move.

The need for air overpowers everything, short-circuiting every rational part of her mind. Okwembu throws her head forward, desperate to break the surface of the water, aware that she might not be able to. Her brain sends out a desperate signal to breathe, and she opens her mouth wide.

Air. Beautiful, wonderful, air. She can't get enough of it, and she can't keep it inside her. Her lungs can't hold onto it, shocked into uselessness by the water. But she's above the surface, and awake, and *alive*. Electrical connections short out in bursts of sparks, lighting up the pod's interior.

A moment later, the water rises over her face. In a panic, Okwembu thrusts herself upwards, but she's strapped in tight and can't keep her head above the surface. The air vanishes, ripped away.

The other passengers are just like her, upside down, the water over their chests. They're thrashing in place, fingers fumbling at the straps, desperate to get loose. Okwembu keeps her eyes open, forcing her body to cooperate. Through the dark water, she can see a huge hole in the back of the pod, edged with jagged, torn metal. *That's* her way out.

She is going to survive this. It's insanity to think otherwise. She is going to find the source of that radio transmission, make contact with whoever is sending it and continue her life. That's all that matters.

Okwembu works quickly, unstrapping herself, pushing past the panic, working the buckles on the safety straps. They come loose, but she's tangled up in them, her left arm pinned in an awkward position. She wrenches to the side, popping it free.

She doesn't know how to swim. None of them do. Nobody in this pod has ever encountered this much water in one place. She has to work it out as she goes. The water makes fine motions impossible, the cold robbing her of control. But she can still move her arms and legs, and she propels herself towards the hole. She forces her eyes to stay open, even though it feels like they're going to freeze in their sockets.

A hand claws at Okwembu. The face behind it is upside down, eyes wide with terror, like something out of a nightmare. The fingers are in her hair. For a horrifying second, she's caught, stuck fast. Then she twists away, pushing through the jagged hole.

Her next stroke gets her clear. It takes every burning atom of energy she has to keep going, but she does it, breaking the surface.

And all she can see is fire.

It takes her a confused second to work out what's happening. The surface of the water is burning, the flames licking against a darkening sky. *The fuel.* It's draining from the pod, ignited somehow, burning hard. Smoke stings her eyes. Heat bakes the water off her face, but below her neck she's almost completely numb with cold. Her clothes are heavy with water, holding her in place.

Movement, off to her right. Coughing and spluttering. A shadow, pulling itself out of the water, heaving its way up onto—

The shore. It's visible through the smoke, close enough to get to. She can make it.

Okwembu starts swimming, winding a path through the burning fuel. But her movements are slower now. Underwater she could swim, but here it's almost impossible. Every stroke feels huge, but seems as if it propels her no more than a single inch. Her vision shrinks down to a small, burning circle.

It can't end like this. She won't let it. But the circle threatens to wink out, and she tastes the water in her mouth, cold and sour.

Then she's being lifted up. Hands under her arms, pulling her bodily out the water. She slams into the ground on the shoreline, mud spattering her face, tongue touching dirt. Her limbs twitch spasmodically. She rolls over, without really meaning to. Her clothing clings to her like a second skin, and her legs are still submerged in the water.

Mikhail Yeremin stands over her, breathing hard, his shoulders trembling.

10

Riley

What happens next comes in flashes.

The seat straps are digging into my shoulders, biting down through my jacket. They're digging in because I'm tilted forwards, all the way, on the edge of my seat. My left thigh hurts, but it's a distant pain, and it doesn't seem important right now.

The bottom of the *Lyssa* is gone. The space where it should be is filled with rocks and dirt, jagged and uneven, the shadows falling in strange shapes. The rocks are speckled with ice, painted in a dozen drab shades of white and grey and brown. Here and there is a flash of colour: dark purple, like a plant clinging to the surface.

When I open my eyes again, there's movement. Hands. Feet. Someone falls, their body plummeting past me.

I don't see them hit the ground. My eyes are already closed. All I hear is the hard thud, and the piercing scream that follows it, trailing off as I sink into darkness.

I come back when something grips my shoulder. A hand. Syria's hand. His face is taut with concentration. He's hanging off the side of the *Lyssa*—the pod has been torn to pieces, the metal shredded and pierced. Torn wires spit showers of sparks.

"Come on, Hale," Syria says. His voice sounds like it's coming from another dimension. "You're the last one. Don't make me wait here any longer than I have to."

I close my eyes again.

Just before I go away, I feel Syria fumbling at my chest. His fingers are caught on something.

The buckle, I think. *It's connected to the straps, and the straps are—*

My eyes fly open just as Syria pops the catch.

I drop, tumbling head first out of the seat. Syria grabs me around the wrist, holding tight. I can see the muscles in his arm straining, the drops of sweat pouring off his brow. I swing in place, clutching at him with my free hand, holding on with everything I've got.

The *Lyssa* is tilted at a sharp angle. What I thought was the floor was actually the wall opposite my seat, and there's a fifteen-foot drop from where we are to the ground below. The dark purple things on the rocks are the shredded fragments of our parachute.

There's a body on the ground. A woman, writhing in agony, clutching her leg, her blue jacket spread out around her like angel's wings. She's half lying in a pool of water. It stains the rocks, creeping up their sides.

"Just drop me," I say to Syria.

"What?"

I don't wait for him to get the idea. I shake loose of his arm and drop, tucking my legs.

For an instant, I get a clear view past the edge of the *Lyssa*. More rocks, some the size of the pod itself, resting in a sea of dirt. The ground is steeply sloped. A giant gash has been ripped out of it, the *Lyssa* tearing up the hillside. We must have come in at an angle, crashing across it. I catch a glimpse of grey sky, the clouds low and dark.

I hit the ground. Hard.

My muscles aren't primed for it. It's uneven, nothing like the hard, flat surfaces on Outer Earth. I land at the edge of the pool of water, try to roll, channelling my vertical energy at an angle, twisting so the impact travels across my spine, but my feet sink into the dirt. It absorbs the energy, trapping it, and the precise roll I was planning turns into a clumsy tumble.

I somersault, landing face first, a dagger of rock jabbing into my cheek. My thigh is screaming at me, as if someone stuck a hot knife in there and is slowly twisting it back and forth.

I ignore it, forcing myself to get up, shouting for Syria before I'm on my feet. He's halfway down, clambering past the bottom edge of the *Lyssa*. The pod itself is almost torn in two, resting up against a boulder. There's a smell in the air I can't place, thick and pungent.

"Come on!" I shout at Syria. My words form puffs of white as I speak, and I suddenly realise how cold it is. The dry air scythes deep into my lungs. I'm aware of my fingers straying to my thigh, aware of them brushing something hard that sends little sparks of pain shooting through me. I look down, but my vision is blurry, unfocused. I can't see anything.

Whatever it is, it isn't slowing me down. It can wait.

The woman in the blue jacket is still on the ground. She's passed out, and two more Earthers are dragging her to safety. Their faces are smeared with dirt and blood.

I run in, intending to help, then stumble to a halt.

The ground on the side where the woman lies is churned up, with dozens of depressions formed by everybody dropping down. Depressions filled with liquid that I thought was water.

It isn't water.

It's fuel.

Highly volatile, flammable fuel. So unstable that it's not even supposed to be exposed to air.

There's a steady stream of it trickling down the large boulder. That's what the horrible smell is. And, above us, shredded wires are raining sparks.

"Get out of here!" I scream at the two Earthers dragging the unconscious woman. All I can think about are her clothes, soaked in fuel. There are two more Earthers beyond them, sprinting across the slope.

Syria is hanging, getting ready to drop. A thin stream of sparks rains down around him, and for the first time I see that he's wounded, blood running from a huge gash in his shoulder.

He lands awkwardly, stumbling. I sprint towards him, pulling him away from the crashed pod, my feet catching on the uneven ground. I can't seem to focus on any one object—the world is a mass of grey and brown, the freezing air slicing into my lungs. I almost fall, sliding down the slope a few feet, and have to use my hands to steady myself.

There's no telling how long we have, or how big the explosion is going to be. I don't even know if there'll *be* an explosion, but I've seen fuel before and I don't want to be around if it goes up.

"What about the others?" Syria shouts, looking over his shoulder.

"We don't—*watch out*!"

I grab Syria's shoulder, stopping him cold. What I thought was a pile of rocks concealed a short drop, the mucky ground sloping away at a steep angle. There are more rocks piled at the bottom of the slope, some as large as I am.

I hoist myself over, dropping down, telling myself to be careful. There's a crack behind us, a big one, like the boulder holding up the *Lyssa* is giving way.

Whoomp.

For a split second the world is completely silent. There's no air in my lungs—it's been sucked away, pulled towards the *Lyssa*.

There's no bang. No explosion. Just a sound that goes from a murmur to a *roar* in less than a second.

Syria screams. I'm looking up at him, and in that instant there's a halo of white fire around his body. His jacket is burning. With a kind of horrified fascination, I see his hair start to smoulder.

Then the shock wave knocks him off the ledge. He collides with me and sends both of us tumbling down the slope.

Sky and dirt whirl around me. I roll end over end, screaming, fingers scrabbling at the ground, legs kicking out as I try to stabilise myself, my thigh sending up frantic signals of pain.

The tips of the fingers on my right hand snag something—a plant, growing out between the rocks. I don't get a chance to make out the details—it snaps almost immediately, but it's enough to slow me down a fraction. I'm on my back, my legs facing downhill. I spread them wide, my heels bouncing off the uneven ground. It's crusted with ice, rock-hard, and I can't break through.

Syria is just below me, still tumbling. For an instant, I see his back, a terrifying mess of red and black. Parts of his jacket are still smoking. Before I can do anything, he smashes into the rocks below, howling in pain.

I'm coming in way too fast. I lift my legs, using every muscle I have to get them off the slope. It looks like I'm doing a complicated stretch. I slam them back down, and this time my heels catch, smashing through the crust just enough to slow my descent.

I come to a stop, bumping up against Syria. Even that light tap is enough to jerk a horrified moan from him. He's on his back, his face twisted in agony, breathing far too hard.

The fire has turned the top of the slope into hell. I don't know how hot rocket fuel burns, but the rocks are blistered and blackened.

I get to my feet. I'm unsteady, off balance, but I pull Syria to his feet with a strength I didn't know I had. He screams again, tries to push me away, but he's too weak.

I don't know if we can outrun the fire, but we have to try.

I wrap an arm around him. As I try to get a grip under his armpit, my hand brushes his shoulder. It's baking hot, and the surface feels wrong: crumbly and soft, all at once.

No time to check. Moving as fast as I can, I pull Syria across the slope, away from the burning pod.

11

Riley

Gradually, the slope gives way to more level ground.

We're on the edge of a vast, uneven plateau. Behind us, a peak rises to the sky, its tip buried in the clouds. The air is hazy, but I can make out smaller hills around us, their surfaces barren.

I have to keep my eyes on the ground. There's plenty to trip over down there: slippery rock, patches of crusty ice, those weird scrubby plants with their brittle tendrils. Syria is almost a dead weight, barely conscious. I'm shivering—the adrenaline is draining out of my body, and it's beginning to wake up to how cold it really is out here.

Should we go after the Earthers? Try join up with any that survived the explosion? But even the thought of trying to get Syria back up that slope is too hard to take in. As it is, each step is a small miracle. I try to push myself into a rhythm, the same rhythm I used when I was a tracer: *stride, land, cushion, spring, repeat.*

"Stay with me, OK?" I say to Syria. He doesn't respond.

The fire might be burning hot, but it's not spreading. After a few minutes, it's a distant rumble, and the insane heat fades. I concentrate on putting one foot in front of the other.

We're on Earth.

The thought forms slowly. It's hard to take in. A few days ago, I was on the station, the only home I'd ever known. Every second of my life had been spent inside a metal ring, and I never once thought that I'd step outside it. It wasn't even something I took for granted. It just *was*, a fact of my existence that was never going to change.

I can't even begin to understand how this place exists. The whole planet was meant to be a poisoned, radioactive wasteland. Humans were supposed to have been wiped out. And yet we're here, out in the open. There's sky and clouds and ground and a horizon, stretching out in front of me.

Fear starts to gnaw at me. Just because we're walking around on Earth doesn't mean it isn't killing us right now. I could be breathing poisoned air, bathing in radiation, and not know until it was too late.

Of course, there's not a single thing I can do about it. If it's true, we're all dead anyway.

The light is changing. I raise my eyes skywards, and the strangest thing happens.

I see low-hanging grey clouds, growing dimmer as the sun sets beyond them. They run from one end of the horizon to the other, flat and unbroken, featureless, capping a world of distant, snowy peaks and barren rock. But everything is much too bright. I can't focus on things, and trying to do so plants the seed of a headache behind my eyes. I screw them shut, try a second time. Same result.

It's like I've put on someone's glasses—someone with much worse eyesight than mine.

I decide not to look at the sky again.

We enter a shallow depression in the hill, bordered by more rocks, and that's when Syria's legs finally give out. For a moment we're locked in a crazy dance, as if he's my partner and I'm bending him over in a complicated move. But he's heavy, way too heavy, and he goes down, thumping face first into the dirt. That's when I get a really good look at his back.

It's as if an amateur artist tried to mix red and black paint to create a new colour, and didn't quite manage. Most of his jacket is gone. Parts of it are fused with skin, melted onto it, along with his shirt. There's a large, undamaged section of it near his waist, flapping loose, but even that is only hanging on by a few burned threads. The skin itself is crusted black; the burned area runs all the way from his lower back up to his neck and across his shoulders. If I hadn't climbed down onto the slope first…

Don't think like that. You can't. Not now.

I don't know a lot about burns, but even I'm aware just how easy it is to get them infected. And we're out in the middle of nowhere, with no supplies, and the sky growing darker by the minute.

I need help. But any Earthers who were in the *Lyssa* are long gone, and Prakesh is—

Prakesh. Carver. The longing I feel for both of them at that moment is almost indescribable. I don't even know how to start looking for them—they could be on the other side of a hill, or on the other side of the world.

My thigh spasms. I bite back a scream, my fingers straying to it, finding the hard thing again. With the adrenaline draining away, I'm starting to feel more pain, and even touching my thigh sends a thin whine hissing through my teeth.

At first, I can't figure out what's wrong. I'm feeling a hard edge, but I can't see anything, just—

Then I see. There's a piece of metal embedded in my thigh. Shrapnel from the crash. Has to be. It's two inches long, almost flush with my skin, hiding under a thin slit in my pants fabric.

The wound is on the inner curve of my thigh, a few inches below my pelvis.

I can't leave it in there. If it starts festering, it might stop me walking, and if that happens I'm as good as dead. I won't be able to help myself, let alone Syria. My mind takes this thought and amplifies it. *Take it out, take it out now.*

I slip my pants down, the cold raising goose bumps on my flesh. The fragment is deep, but there's enough above my skin for me to grip onto. It doesn't look too big—I should be able to yank if out in one movement.

But isn't there an artery in the leg? Doesn't it curve around the area the shrapnel's in? I think back, trying to recall everything I know about how the human body works. *Prakesh, where are you when I need you?*

I take three quick breaths, grasping the ragged edge of the metal. I'm on the verge of stalling when my fingers act on their own, ripping out the fragment.

12

Riley

I don't hear myself scream. But I do see all the colour in the world drain away. Everything goes grey, the pain so sharp that I almost pass out.

Somehow I stay awake, looking down at the piece of metal. It's long and thin, no more than half an inch wide. It was embedded lengthwise in my thigh, the wound a shallow cut. My fingers stray to my skin—there's blood, but nothing like the amount an artery would pump out. I hang my head, sucking in deep breaths through my nose.

The wound still hurts like hell, but it's a manageable pain. I rip a length out of the bottom of my shirt, binding the wound tight. That makes everything go grey again, but only for an instant. *You can deal with this. You have to.*

That's when I hear it.

At first, I mistake it for the noise of the fire. But that faded long ago. This is different: a distant rushing sound, so quiet that I think I've imagined it at first. But then I get a fix on it.

That's water. There's water near here.

Syria is awake again, groaning. I crouch down, resisting the temptation to put a hand on his shoulder.

"Hey," I say. "Can you hear me?"

His voice, when it comes, sounds as blistered as the skin on his back. "Where are we?"

"I don't know. But I'm going to get you some water, OK? I think there's some of it close by."

"Hurts," he says. "Hurts bad."

"I know. Just…hang in there. I'll be back as fast as I can."

I walk a few steps, picking my way up the edge of the depression, and stop.

How am I going to find my way back here? It's all very well heading for the water, but I don't know how far away it is. I could get lost on the return journey—there are no landmarks here, nothing but rocks and dirt. Syria would…

Syria. That's it.

I turn back, kneeling next to him. Then I snag the undamaged part of his jacket, working it loose as carefully as I can. It would be better to use my own clothing, but the bright red cloth will be easier to see in the fading light—and since I used a strip of my shirt to bind my thigh wound, I might not have enough.

I'm a little worried about hurting him, but the piece comes away easily. I start tearing it into strips. They don't need to be that big, and soon I have a dozen or so in my hands.

"Just hang in there," I say again. It's all I can think of.

I climb over the top of the depression, clambering over the rocks. One of the plants is there, its branches trembling in the frigid wind. I take a strip of fabric, and tie it on. It's caught by the wind, a bright red flag, easy to pick out even in the gathering dusk.

There are other plants dotted here and there. I make my way down the slope, skidding every so often as I lose my footing on the rocks. Just when I'm about to lose sight of the first strip I take another and tie it onto a second plant.

I don't know what'll happen if I run out of strips before I reach the water.

But the sound is louder now, somewhere ahead and to the left. My legs are shaky and uneven, and I'm conscious of how hungry I am. Cold, too, with every breath showing itself in a puff of white vapour at my lips.

My dad's ship crashed in eastern Russia. I don't know how close that is to where we are right now. He spent seven years trying to stay alive, desperately trying to get back to us. I had to destroy his ship to save the station, and, in the few minutes I had to talk to him, he told me about where they landed. Kamchatka, it was called. Cold, barren, hostile to life, the air a toxic soup, the environment battered by deadly dust storms. The craziness of this entire situation crowds in on me again—how am I able to walk around out here, without freezing solid or suffocating? How am I even here?

I take a deep breath, pushing back the panicky thoughts. I don't know where I am, or what I'm dealing with. I can only focus on what's in front of me.

The slope steepens slightly. I have to place my steps carefully, stopping every so often to tie a strip of fabric to a branch.

Soon I'm down to three pieces of the fabric. A few more steps. The slope is getting even steeper now. Two strips.

I stop, listening hard. I've been heading towards the water for the longest time, but now I can't place the source of the sound. It's coming from everywhere, as if the boulders themselves are picking up on it, twisting its direction.

I look back. The third-to-last strip of fabric is just visible, flickering in the dusk.

I head to my right, where I think the water is. But the sound doesn't change. If anything, it gets even harder to figure out its location.

With a shaky breath, I tie the last strip of fabric onto a plant. I can go a short distance from here, but not too far. If I get lost, I'm finished.

A few more steps. A few more. The sound is really loud now. I have to be close. But where is it?

Come on.

And then I step through a gap in two boulders, and see the stream.

It's barely worth the name. It's a trickle of water, a foot wide, narrowing to inches in places. The noise is coming from a waterfall, maybe five feet high, spattering onto the rocks from a hollow in the slope. The rocky surroundings amplified it, made the noise sound as if it was a gushing torrent.

I stare at it, feeling absurdly cheated. And yet, as I do so, the oddest thought occurs. It's still more water than I've ever seen in one place.

Thirst claws its way up my throat. I scramble across the rocks, dropping to my knees at the edge of the water, ignoring the pain in my thigh. The water is so cold it stings my lips. It isn't like the water on Outer Earth—it's sweeter, somehow. More full. I almost laugh when I realise that, for the first time, I'm drinking water without a single chemical in it.

None that you can taste, anyway.

The thought makes me lift my mouth from the water, but only for a second. I have to use the water—and not just for my thirst. I need to clean the wound in my thigh. I debate leaving it, but decide that it's more important to flush out the dirt from the wound than worry about chemicals that might not even exist.

I unbind my wound, wincing as I splash ice-cold water on it. The cut itself looks deep, despite the tiny size of the fragment that hit me. I have no idea if the water will help keep infection away, but it's all I've got.

I pat it dry and bind it up again, then sit back. Syria's still out there. I have to get this water back before it gets too dark to see.

But how? I don't have a canteen, like I would on Outer Earth. I'd give anything for my tracer pack right now, with its water compartment.

Inspiration hits. Working quickly, I strip off my jacket and the shirt beneath it. The cold is harsh enough to make me gasp. I put the jacket back on, zipping it up all the way. It's not nearly as warm as it was before, but it'll have to do.

I make my way back to one of the plants. Their leaves are small and waxy, sickly green in colour, but it looks like there are enough of them. I strip them off the bush, grazing my hands in the process. My fingers, I notice, are getting slightly numb at the tips. *Not good.*

I head back to the stream, carrying my bundle of leaves. The shirt itself is long-sleeved, made of stretchy nylon. I turn it upside down, and tie the sleeves tightly around the front below the neck, as if the shirt is wrapping its arms around itself. I stuff the inside of the shirt with the waxy leaves, pushing them down, trying to cover as much space as I can. There. A vessel, with the shirt's hem as the lip.

But will it hold water?

Only one way to find out. I crouch by the pool again, and drag the shirt through the water, open end first. A bunch of leaves float out, and when I lift the shirt up water cascades through.

I force myself to stay calm, retrieving the leaves, packing the shirt again. When I lift the container out of the pool, my hands all but frozen, there's nothing but a few steady drips leaking out of the bottom.

I breathe a shaky sigh of relief. OK. Now I just have to get it back to Syria. It's grown even darker while I've been working, and for a second I forget my rule about not looking up. The sky is turning black, with a thin band of grey on the horizon as the day fades away. Then my vision goes wonky, like it did before, and I have to look down.

It's hard to carry the water. The vessel is heavy, and I have to hold the fabric on the shirt hem tight in both hands. The fabric of my jacket is waterproof, near enough, but the shirt is still soaked through, and before long the top of my pants is dripping wet.

I can barely see the ground. The slope is steeper than I remember, and my legs are already aching. I have to concentrate hard to spot my tags. The water swings back and forth in my hands, pattering on the dirt. Apart from the slowly fading sound of the waterfall, it's the only sound.

My thoughts turn back to Prakesh, to Carver. Are they safe? Did they land close to us? I have a sudden image of them being drawn to the stream, looking for water, just like I did. I half turn, but the thought of abandoning Syria is horrifying. I stride forward again, furious with myself. I can't leave him. I won't.

That's when I realise I can't see the next tag.

I swing round, looking for the last one I passed. There. Just visible in the fading light, wrapped around one of the thin plants. *That means the next one should be visible from here.*

But it isn't.

I backtrack. Panic is sparking in my chest, tightening around my lungs, but I push it away. I look left, then right, then turn a slow circle.

Nothing. I can't see it. Did it come loose? Did the wind take it? I look downhill, but I may as well be staring into a black hole. There are nothing but shadows down there.

All I have to do is head uphill.

I keep walking, still looking for the tag, checking back over my shoulder for the previous one. And just at the point where I can't spot it any more, the slope changes. It's as if I've walked over the crest of a small hill, because the ground drops downwards again. I didn't see that on my way to the stream.

I keep going—and walk right into a wall of soil. Part of the slope is exposed, with roots poking through it, scratching my face.

"Syria!" I shout. My voice echoes into the distance.

13

Prakesh

There's a fire.

It's not big, and it won't last the night, but it's burning well enough for now. There are trees surrounding the lake; most of them are stunted and dead, their dry branches and leaves simple to collect. It was easy for Prakesh to pull in some of the burning fuel on the water's surface, lighting a dry branch while the others build a small pile behind him.

The *Furor* escape pod has long since vanished below the surface of the lake—and it *is* a lake, long and thin, stretching further than the eye can see. The forest around them is dense and dark, the wind rattling through the dry wood. The sun has slipped below the horizon, and the sky is fading to a dark blue above their heads.

The survivors huddle around the fire. Like everyone else, Prakesh is soaked to the skin, and he can't stop shivering. Every part of him, from his ears to the toes in his squelching, sodden shoes, is numb.

And yet, despite everything that's happened, he feels excitement. These trees didn't grow in a lab: they're entirely natural, sprouting from soil that might not have been touched by humans in a hundred years. He can't wait for dawn, can't wait to see what the forest actually looks like in the daylight.

Of course, that assumes they *make* it to daylight. Prakesh is painfully aware of how poor a fire is at transferring heat. They should find something to put behind them, something to reflect the warmth back. But he can barely move, doesn't even want to try it. They're lucky they've got a fire going in the first place—without it, they wouldn't last long.

"Rub your chests," says Janice Okwembu. She's kneeling close to the flames, and her eyes land on each survivor in turn. There are six of them: Prakesh, Carver, Mikhail, Okwembu, the pilot, plus the man who was sitting opposite him on the *Furor*, the one praying to every god he could think of. Prakesh struggles to remember his name. *Clay*. That was it. He's young, slightly plump, with long brown hair tied back in a ponytail. He's rubbing the chest of the sixth survivor: the pilot, one of the *Shinso*'s original crew. The man is barely conscious, a thick trail of drool snaking down his chin. *Khalil*, Prakesh thinks. *His name's Khalil.*

No one else in the escape pod made it to shore.

Carver gets up. He has to do it in stages, going first to both knees, then to just one, then to his feet, tottering like an infant taking his first steps. He's breathing hard—his jacket is gone, lost in the lake, and his shirt is a sodden, steaming mass.

"So now what?" he says.

Mikhail seems to be less affected by the cold than the others. He clears his throat, but Okwembu gets there first. "Well," she says. "We—"

Carver lurches forward, moving on legs that look as stiff as the dead branches on the trees. He's heading right for Okwembu, his fists balled up.

Prakesh forces himself to his feet, his own limbs aching with the effort, and gets in front of Carver. "Not a good idea," he says.

Carver bumps up against him, tries to push past, but Prakesh moves with him. Mikhail is up, too, reaching past Prakesh, his hands on Carver's chest.

"Aaron, not now," Prakesh says, somehow managing to push the words past his frozen lips. Okwembu's payback can come later. If they're going to survive this, they're going to need every pair of hands they can get.

Carver roars in anger. He tries to push past again, but Mikhail grabs his shoulders, not letting him. Okwembu watches, her face impassive.

After a moment, Carver turns to Prakesh, his face incredulous. "Are you kidding me?" he says. "After what she did to Riley? We should drown her in the fucking lake."

"That's enough," Mikhail says. He tries to make the words forceful, but they come out slurred together.

Carver sags, then points a trembling finger at Mikhail. "Your plan sucked," he says. "How many people did you lose? How many of your Earthers actually made it down? If you can call this making it." He gestures to the lake, where isolated puddles of fuel are still burning.

"They knew what their chances were," Mikhail says. "But don't you see? We *did* make it. We're back home. We can make a new life here." His tone is pleading, as if he's trying to convince himself along with them.

"We *were* home," Carver says.

"Outer Earth is gone," Okwembu says calmly. She glances at Prakesh. "Resin saw to that."

Carver stands stock still, then tries to make a rush for Okwembu again. It takes all the strength Prakesh has to stop him, but somehow he and Mikhail manage it. Carver rocks on his heels, breathing hard through his nose.

"Actually, you know what?" he says. "I'm done."

He stalks off, muttering, heading down the shore. He's shivering, clutching himself, nearly falling twice in the space of ten yards, but he keeps going.

Before Prakesh knows what's he's doing, he's following. By the time he reaches Carver, he's feeling a little better.

"Wait," he says. Carver ignores him, only stopping when Prakesh slips around him and puts both hands on his shoulders. Aaron's face is shrouded in shadow, but his shoulders are trembling, hitching up and down, vibrating under Prakesh's hands.

"Think about this for a sec," Prakesh starts, and then Carver punches him.

He's completely unprepared for it. Carver's strength has been sapped by the cold, but he still knows how to throw a punch. His fist takes Prakesh in the side of the head, and for a moment that side of his vision is gone, nothing but black. When it comes back, he's lying on the ground, and explosions are going off in his head.

Carver is yelling at him. "Where were you? She pulled Riley out of the pod, and *you were asleep*! You just passed out!"

Prakesh tries to speak, can't. It's not just that he can't find the words—it's as if the thoughts going through his head are too big to comprehend. One of his teeth is loose, jiggling in its socket.

"I'm going to find her," says Carver, staring out across the lake. "You can come with me, or not. I don't care."

Prakesh knows Carver has feelings for Riley. It was hard to miss, locked in that medical bay. He wanted to bring it up, wanted to confront him, but he could never quite figure out how. Carver danced around the subject, too, radiating undirected anger. His usual upbeat, sarcastic personality had drained away. They settled for oblique remarks, snapping at each other, circling but never attacking.

And Riley's absence is like a physical pain, deep in his gut. But it's not just her. It's everyone on Outer Earth. His team in the Air Lab. His parents. And every single person who died after being infected with Resin, the virus which sprung from a genetically modified superfood that *he* created. They're all lined up behind Riley, and all of them are staring at him.

Carver might hate Okwembu and Mikhail. Prakesh does, too. But he has far more blood on his hands than they do. Not just ten more, or twenty, but hundreds and hundreds of thousands, dead because of him. He thinks back to his parents—he doesn't even know if they're alive or not, if they survived Resin. Even if they did, he knows there's a good chance that the decompression in the station dock will have wiped out everybody in Gardens. Probably everybody on the station. That thought, too, is an almost physical pain.

The tiny group clustered around the fire is all he has left. He *has* to keep them alive. It's the only way he can make it right—or start making it right. He can't do that if he's hunting for Riley.

He closes his eyes, and says, "We can't go."

"What did you say?"

Prakesh gets to his feet. He's steadier this time, despite the pounding in his head. "If we split the group up, we die."

"Yeah? Well, that's fine by me, as long as I don't have to be near *them*." Carver jerks his finger back at the fire, and the figures around it, bathed in shadows.

"OK," says Prakesh. "Go. Charge off into an environment we know nothing about, with no map and no supplies, at night, in the cold."

"I'll stick to the shore," Carver says, but he sounds resigned now. The punch drained the last of the energy he had stored up. "Riley had to have come down close to here. If we—"

"We don't know *where* she came down. We don't even know if her pod launched."

"Don't—"

"You could hunt forever, and never find her."

"So you're just giving up? Is that it?"

"I won't if you won't. But if you head off by yourself, you'll never make it."

Prakesh twists the bottom of his shirt in his hands, wringing water out of the fabric, giving him time to articulate his thoughts. "We don't know what's out there, and we don't know what the war did to the ecosystem. Most of the planet is a wasteland, and that has a knock-on effect."

"I thought this part of the planet was supposed to be OK for humans now."

"Maybe. But there could still be extreme weather patterns, localised microclimates." Carver is about to interrupt, but Prakesh talks over him. "We could be caught in a flash flood, a snowstorm. Anything. That's without talking about any wildlife we run into, or how we actually find food."

Carver frowns. "Wildlife? You actually think anything survived long enough to get here?"

"Hard to say without data. The global population of certain species might have been decimated, but it's possible that tiny clusters could survive, assuming they adapt. If they could migrate, hunt out food sources, they might be able to—"

"I get it, P-Man."

"Right. Sorry." Prakesh is secretly relieved at hearing Carver use that damn nickname. It means he's calming down, thinking more like his old self.

He gestures to the lake. "But if we stay in a group, we can cover a wider area. We can find food, shelter, fuel for a fire. We can keep each other warm. And then I promise: we'll look for Riley. We'll find her together."

Carver hugs himself, shivering. The thunderous look hasn't left his face, but he gives Prakesh a tight nod.

"All right," he says. "But if Okwembu so much as says one word to me, I'm going to do to her what I did to you." He grimaces. "Sorry about that, by the way."

Prakesh is about to answer when he hears a panicked shout from the fireside. He and Carver swing round. Okwembu and Mikhail are on all fours, leaning in close to the guttering flames. The smoke has grown thicker, swirling in huge curls around them.

"Oh shit," Prakesh says.

He starts jogging back towards the group, Carver on his heels. He's desperately hoping that he's wrong, but even before he gets halfway back, he can see that the fire—their one source of heat—is going out.

Rob Boffard

14

Anna

The noise drags Anna Beck out of her sleep.

For a moment, she can't separate reality from the nightmare. She was lost in space, drifting, alone, unable to move no matter how hard she tried. Slowly, she convinces herself that she's awake.

The hab is dark. Her father is sitting up on the other cot, blinking in confusion. Her mother is curled up tight, still deeply asleep. There's no alarm—they cut them off to save power days ago—but she can hear running feet, raised voices.

Then the voices resolve, and Anna hears the word "Fire."

She stares into the darkness. A fire isn't a reason to panic. The sector's chemical suppression system should deal with it, stop it spreading. So why are people freaking out? Why the running feet and confused shouts?

Something's wrong.

She kicks the covers off and runs, throwing open the hab door and rocketing into the corridor, sleep falling away like shed clothing. There's a man in her way—she tries to dodge past, but she's still not fully awake. It slows her reaction times: she smashes into him, and she goes flying, skidding on her ass down the corridor.

"Where's the fire?" she shouts up at him.

The man is middle-aged, stubbled, naked from the waist up. He's holding a blanket around his shoulders, open at the front. Anna can see his ribs, gaunt and bony.

She scrambles to her feet. "Did you hear what I said?"

He blinks at her, and she wants to scream at him. Then he says, "Down in the gallery." He has the voice of a man who is not entirely sure that this isn't a vivid dream. He probably thinks he's going to wake up, and that Outer Earth will be good and whole again.

No point waiting to find out. She's already running, going as fast as she can.

Impact

At least it isn't far. She's in Apex sector: home to the station's main control room, the council chambers, the technicians who kept the place running. Outer Earth suffered an explosive decompression, a breach in the dock that rendered most of it uninhabitable. Everyone still alive—a thousand people or so—is crammed into this one sector, the smallest on the station. She can be at the gallery in five minutes.

Anna has no idea what she's going to do. All she knows is that she has to be there. So she runs, barrelling through the white corridors of Apex.

The last time she ran this fast was when the dock's airlock doors gave way, after the Earthers' attack. She almost didn't make it. The rush of air when the doors gave out almost took her off her feet. But she was in one of the side corridors then, a little further away from the dock. Someone—she still doesn't know who—grabbed her, pulled her along, got her across the border. It sealed shut behind her, leaving her sprawled across the floor, gasping for air.

Just before she reaches the gallery, up in the Level 3 corridor, she runs into a group of people packing the passage. Two stompers are just beyond them, pushing the crowd back. Only one of the lights in the ceiling is working properly, but underneath it Anna can see lazy wisps of smoke curling through the air. She can smell it, too, hot and sharp.

She pushes herself onto her toes, craning her neck, trying to see what's going on. She can just see into the gallery. There are no visible flames, but the catwalk is flickering with orange light. But why haven't the suppression systems kicked in? Where's the chemical foam?

A little way past the stompers holding the crowd back, a technician is down on his haunches, doing something to the wall. One of the panels has been removed, and the stomper is messing with the wiring, cursing and swearing. He grabs a hand-held plasma cutter, sparks it to life. That's when Anna realises what's happening: the suppression systems really have failed. If they can't fix them, the fire will rage out of control.

"What's happening?" she says to a man in the crowd.

"Electrical fire," he answers, not looking at her. "Circuit in the gallery floor just blew up."

And this is when Anna realises that there's nothing she can do to help.

She can run, and she can shoot. In the past few days, after Outer Earth shrank down to this single, tiny sector, she's discovered that she's good with kids, looking after several of those who found their way into Apex, who lost their moms and dads. Right now? None of those things are worth spit. What was she thinking?

At that moment, Anna feels every single one of her sixteen years. Sure, she could fight through the crowd, use her tracer training to get all the way to the front, but what good would it do? At least it looks like the stompers got everybody out—there should be nothing in the gallery but the escape pods, which won't do anyone much good anyway. No point escaping if you don't have enough fuel to de-orbit. Even if you somehow managed it, your pod would incinerate the second it hit the atmosphere.

She leans against the corridor wall, her eyes closed, fists knotted in frustration.

Two stompers, clad in black and grey, are trying to push through the crowd. They're a few feet away from Anna when she sees that one of them has a squat, orange gas canister in her hand. Supplies for the plasma cutters being used to weld the metal across the edge of the door.

But the crowd isn't parting. They aren't letting the stompers through.

Anna moves without thinking. She snatches the canister away. It's ice-cold, the pressurised gas inside filming the metal surface with condensation.

The stomper who was holding it lashes out at her in surprised fury. Anna ignores her. She takes two steps towards the opposite corridor wall, and jumps. She leads with her right foot, planting it squarely halfway up the wall, then uses it to kick her body upwards and outwards. She twists in mid-air, and now she's high enough to look over the heads of the crowd, all the way to the door.

Anna used to have a slingshot. She called it One-Mile. It was nothing more than crudely welded metal with frayed rubber strips, but in her hand it became something else entirely. She could plant a shiny ball-bearing in a target from fifty yards away, knock grown men off their feet, shatter jaws and break fingers. She was that good.

Impact

One-Mile is gone, lost when she and Riley and Aaron Carver were captured by the Earthers. But Anna can still shoot. She can still aim.

She throws the canister backhanded, sending it flying over the heads of the crowd. One of the technicians is quicker on the uptake than the others: he catches it, taking it in the stomach as he wraps his hands around it. Anna has just enough time to see him turn, handing it off to someone else, and then she crashes to the ground.

The stompers pick her up, slam her against the corridor wall. She even recognises one of them: Alana Jordan, a heavy-set woman with long black hair and a sour face.

That's when she hears the *click-hiss* of the suppression chemicals. The smell of smoke vanishes, replaced by the iodine tang of the foam.

The crowd is cheering, high-fiving each other, hugging. One of the technicians—maybe even the one who caught the canister—is shouting over the noise. "We got it. It's contained."

Everyone visibly relaxes, shaking their heads and laughing, like all their problems have just been solved. Jordan lets Anna go. She dusts herself off, a small smile creeping across her face.

A man detaches himself from the crowd. He's handsome, mid-twenties, with angular cheekbones. He's dressed in the white jumpsuit of a council member, and he looks exhausted, his eyes bloodshot. Anna's smile vanishes. Dax Schmidt is the last person she wants to talk to.

"Are you out of your mind?" he shouts at her.

No, Anna thinks. *I've only got one foot out the door.* She's on the verge of spitting the comeback right in his face, but he looks as if he wants to reach over and strangle her. His anger is unbelievable, and it stops the words in her throat.

"That canister could have exploded," he says. "You could have killed a lot of people."

"Well, it *didn't,*" Anna says, furious and embarrassed at the same time. People in the crowd are looking over at her, not even bothering to disguise their interest. "Besides," Anna says, pointing to Jordan. "They weren't going to get there in time."

"What? The gas? They were doing fine. They didn't need extra." Dax looks back over to the technician—they can see him clearly now that the crowd is dispersing. He's slotting the panel back on the wall, the plasma cutter by his side.

"But the stompers were—"

"I don't know how much you know about plasma cutters," Dax says. "They use them in space. They last for a really long time. You think the tech couldn't use a single canister to cut through a couple of fused power boxes?"

"But they—" Anna stops. Every word feels like it takes a year off her age. She wants to tell Dax that she's killed people. That she had a long gun, during the siege in the dock. But she can't figure out how to say it without sounding stupid.

"It's called a *back-up*, Anna. I sent word to the protection officers to bring it over in case the first one failed."

"Leave her be, Dax," says Jordan, turning away. "She's just a kid."

Dax starts to follow, then looks back over his shoulder. "You shouldn't be here. Go home."

Anna watches him leave. The exhaustion hits her like a punch to the gut, and she slides down the wall, breathing hard. She reaches up, grabs the edge of her beanie, and pulls it down over her eyes. Her blonde hair splays across her cheeks.

She would do anything to have Riley here right now. Riley, and Carver, and Kev. She has to tell herself, not for the first time, that they're gone.

It's just her.

15

Riley

I'm breathing too fast. I try to slow it down, but it doesn't help. Each breath sucks icy air into my lungs, slicing through me like a knife.

I don't bother calling Syria's name any more. I don't even know if he's able to respond. Chances are, he's probably passed out from the pain.

The wonder I felt at being on Earth has left with the daylight. The sky above me is pitch-black now. I just walk, heading uphill, trying to ignore the fact that nothing around me looks familiar. I laugh, the sound bitter against the wind—it doesn't matter. This landscape is the same for who knows how many miles in each direction. What were the Earthers thinking, coming down here?

My thoughts wander too far, and I lose control of my water container.

I'm already gripping the fabric so hard that my hands are aching and numb. I catch my right foot in a pile of rocks, or a plant root, or *something*, and the fingers on my right hand lose their grip.

There's a panicky moment where I'm scrabbling in the dark, half hoping that I can catch the edges again. Then a deluge of icy water drenches my pants. The leaf-filled shirt flops against me, dripping the last of its load onto the frozen soil.

For a long moment I just stand there, staring out into the darkness. Then I grab the shirt and ball it up, furiously scrunching the fabric. I hurl it away, and it gives a wet thud as it slaps off a nearby rock.

I howl. That's what it is: an uncontrolled, animal howl. It's a hot anger, burning bright, as if trying to force back the cold air.

And as my voice trails off, as the howl dies in my throat, there's an answering sound.

It comes from a long way away—a coughing bark, almost inaudible. I freeze, listening hard. The bark comes again. It's deeper this time, more drawn out, but then it's gone.

Seconds tick by. I let out a breath, the cloud dissipating into the night air. There's not just anger now—there's fear, too, flooding my mouth with a familiar metallic taste.

Whatever's out there isn't a picture in a tab screen or part of a story told by a teacher in some Outer Earth schoolroom. It's alive.

And it knows I'm here.

I start walking again, reducing everything to the physical motion of putting one foot in front of the other. I don't know if I'm going in the right direction, but if I don't keep moving I know that I'll just lie down and never get up again. I keep the slope ahead of me, keep climbing. *Climb high enough, and you can get all the way to the top of the mountain.*

I'm so deep in myself, so intent on movement, that I don't realise I've found Syria until I almost trip over him.

He's lying where I left him, prone in the depression. I get my footing, then drop to my knees next to him.

"Syria," I say. He doesn't respond.

My mind is already moving ahead of my words. I lost the water, but I can still hear the stream. I'll have to take him there, over my shoulders if I have to, no matter how much pain he's in.

He hasn't moved. "Syria," I say again, shaking his shoulder. The flesh beneath my fingers is a gummy crust. Even the lightest touch must cause him excruciating pain, so why isn't he—

Then I'm shaking him, trying to roll him over, screaming his name.

The screams dissolve into sobs. I sit back, shoulders shaking, breath coming in hitching gasps. It's almost completely dark now—I can't see further than a few feet in any direction.

He shouldn't have died here. He should have died on Outer Earth, in the Caves, the place he protected and watched over. He should have died years from now, surrounded by his friends. Instead, he died alone, in agony. Thousands of miles from home.

Okwembu.

Her name arrives in my mind from nowhere. It's a strange thought, as if someone else is speaking the word. I react, hammering on the ground, once, twice, a third time, tiny rocks leaving impressions in my skin. I barely notice. All I can see is her face.

She made me kill my dad, she helped destroy our home, she took my friends away from me when she shoved me out of the first escape pod. She didn't kill Syria, not directly, but she's why he's here. Without her, the Earthers' plan would never have worked. And now she's taken away the last link I had to Outer Earth.

It all comes back to her. All of it.

I've never felt such anger. The thought is so potent that, for a time, it's all I can hold in my head. When I come back, I realise I'm shivering, shaking so hard that my teeth chatter. Everything below my waist feels like it's made of ice.

I'll never find the stream again in the dark. I barely found it in the light. I decide to stay where I am—I can survive a night without water. But I *have* to get warm. The last time I was this cold was in the Core, back when Oren Darnell had Outer Earth held hostage, and that was a cold that nearly gave me hypothermia. If I don't find a way to get warm, I'm as good as dead.

I can't make a fire—or at least I have no idea how to. It's not the kind of thing they teach you on Outer Earth, where the general idea is to avoid fire of any kind. Besides, there's nothing to burn.

Inspiration strikes, and I jump up, running on the spot. But it only makes my aching muscles hurt more, and doesn't generate anywhere near the amount of heat I'd need.

I sit back down again, hard. If he was here, Prakesh would come up with a plan. And Carver...he'd have some gadget stashed away, a portable flamethrower or a miniature electric stove.

I close my eyes. *They're not here. You need to think.*

The Core. I was prepared for it then, dressed appropriately, with my dad's old flight jacket and several sweaters, plus thick gloves. Here, I've got nothing on but thin pants and a jacket—a single layer against the cold.

I need insulation. But how?

I could snuggle up to Syria's body—make use of his remaining heat. I could even take his clothes, or what's left of them. The thought makes me recoil. I won't do that. If there's nothing else, if I truly can't stay warm, then I'll revisit it. But there's got to be another way.

What about the leaves? asks a quiet voice in my mind.

I don't give myself time to poke holes in the idea. I scramble in the dark, using my hands to feel for the plants. I know there's one close by, and seconds later I find it, yanking it towards me. There aren't many leaves, and those that it has are crumbly and dry, falling apart in my fingers. I let it go, and keep searching.

I find another plant, then another, stripping them bare, and soon I've gathered enough to start stuffing them into my jacket. They're scratchy and uncomfortable, but I keep going, pushing them down into the jacket sleeves.

My hands are utterly numb, and the only thing I can see is my breath condensing in the freezing air. I shove more leaves into my pants, which feels even worse. Not that I have a choice in the matter—I do this, or I die.

Something moves against my skin.

I squeal, ripping my hand away. The thing comes with it—I can feel it latched onto my finger. I shake my hand furiously, and then it's gone. A bug. Had to have been. Asleep in the leaves, until I disturbed it. The idea that there might be others, crawling close to my body…

The cold is making it hard to think—my thoughts are coming in quick bursts, barely coherent. My stomach sends a radiating, hungry ache up through my body, and, right then, I realise just how tired I am. It's as if all the strength has run out of my legs.

I find my way back to Syria, the leaves rustling against my skin. My thigh is throbbing. I do my best to ignore it, curling into a ball, pulling my hands into my jacket sleeves and jamming them between my legs as I try to get comfortable on the hard ground. At least I'm out of the wind, hunkered down in the depression.

I hunch my shoulders, trying to get my ears into my jacket collar, but the jacket isn't big enough.

I don't know how long I sleep, but it's dark and dreamless. I only wake up when a sound steals into my mind. The sound is a low growl, and it pulls me out of the blackness.

I open my eyes. They adjust to the darkness instantly, as if I've had them open this whole time.

The animal is right in front of me, no more than three feet away, its jaws wrapped around Syria's leg.

16

Prakesh

They can't restart the fire.

The fuel on the lake has burned away, save for a few flickers of flame in the centre that provide a little light. No matter what they do, they can't get any other wood to catch.

And the fire isn't the only thing that's gone. Khalil is dead. He slipped away without anyone noticing, his sightless eyes staring at the sky.

Mikhail is on his hands and knees, blowing with all his might. It would look ridiculous, Prakesh thinks, if the situation wasn't so serious. He's already told Mikhail that it's not going to work—starting a fire from scratch requires fine motor skills. It requires time and energy to gather materials. The cold and damp is taking all of it away, but Mikhail won't quit. He keeps blowing, refusing to give up hope.

"Shit," Carver says, kicking a clod of dirt into the lake. The last cinder goes out with a puff, and Prakesh coughs as a loose wisp of smoke catches him in the throat.

Clay is praying loudly, invoking Buddha this time, praising his holy name. Carver rounds on him. "Will you shut up?"

Clay subsides, muttering. Carver looks at Prakesh, shivering as the wind scythes through him. "OK, P-Man. Your action. What do we do now?"

But before Prakesh can answer, Janice Okwembu speaks up. "We need to keep moving," she says, getting to her feet and dusting herself off. "Walking will keep us warm, and we can look for food."

"No." Mikhail has finally abandoned the fire and is sitting back on his heels. Prakesh doesn't like the look in his eyes, doesn't like the naked fear he sees there. "We stay here. You heard the radio message. There's *sanctuary* out there." He leans on the word, as if it'll keep the cold away. "They'll come for us. We swim out, we get more fuel. We restart the fire."

"And end up like him?" Carver jerks his head at Khalil's body. Mikhail glares at him.

"It won't work," Okwembu says, folding her arms. "If the people who broadcast that message are out there, we need to get to *them*. We can't wait for them to come to us."

Suddenly they're all talking at once. Mikhail and Carver are shouting at each other, Okwembu trying to intervene. Clay's prayers get louder.

"Enough," Prakesh says. When nobody listens, he bellows, "*Hey!*"

Everyone falls silent. Mikhail's shoulders are rising and falling with exertion. Above his beard, his eyes are gleaming with panic.

"She's half right," says Prakesh, pointing to Okwembu. "We keep moving."

Okwembu nods, but Mikhail growls in frustration. "We'll never make it."

Prakesh talks over him. "We're too exposed here. Feel that wind coming off the lake?"

The others nod. Of course they do.

"Moving will keep us warm. And we're not going far—just until we find somewhere out of the wind. Once we're there, we group together for warmth, wait until morning. It's the best chance we've got."

"We don't even know where we are," Mikhail says. Prakesh can hear the fear in his voice.

Clay stops praying, then clears his throat. "Actually, I think I do."

They all turn to stare at him, and he swallows before continuing. "I looked at some old maps on the ship's computer before we came down here," he says, pointing to the water. "I think this is Eklutna Lake. South shore."

He swallows again, knotting his hands. "We're north-east of Anchorage. It's far, but all we have to do is head that way." He points into the forest.

Prakesh doesn't wait for an answer. He walks away from the group, moving into the trees, rubbing his arms furiously. For a long moment the only sounds are his feet crunching on the frosty ground. *They're not coming,* he thinks. *They're actually going to sit there and freeze to death.*

But a moment later he hears them coming after him. He slows down, waiting for them to catch up. No one mentions Khalil.

The ground slopes slightly, and before long Prakesh's knees are aching from the descent. His eyes have adjusted to the dark, but it's a relative term. The forest is as dark as space itself. He can just make out the stunted trees against the black sky. Once again, he feels that excitement—a feeling that refuses to go away, despite their situation.

How can there possibly still be trees down here? Why has this part of the planet survived, when everything they know about Earth says it should be a frozen, radioactive dustball? Is the planet starting to fix itself? How long has it been like this? Surely not long—they would have seen it when they sent the Earth Return mission down, when they were scanning the planet for landing sites. That means it's only been like this for seven years, at the most. How is it even possible?

A hundred years before, the people still on Earth were using every technological trick they had to turn the tide of climate change. Cloud seeding, messing with the ionosphere, carbon capturing. None of it really worked, and then the nukes came raining down and it didn't matter any more. But here, something has changed. Something made this part of the world different.

His thoughts return to his parents, back on Outer Earth. The regret comes rushing back, rough and familiar as an old blanket.

But what is he supposed to do? How can he possibly help anybody who might be alive on Outer Earth? There's only one thing he can do now, and that's survive. If he's going to live through the night, then he's got to shut out everything else.

The wind has got worse—it's constant now, whistling through the tree branches and every gust freezes him to the bone. He keeps hoping that the slope will deviate, that there'll be a depression or gully where they can get out of the wind. But there's nothing—no matter where they go, the ground is evenly sloped.

Carver is to his right, and he can hear Mikhail behind him, swearing as he pushes through the foliage. He can't hear Clay, or Okwembu, and he doesn't want to lose them. "Everybody still here?" he calls.

"Still here," mutters Carver. The others echo him, one by one, their voices betraying their exhaustion.

Abruptly, the trees open up. They're in a small clearing, no more than fifty yards wide. There's a sliver of moonlight, peeking down through a tiny gap in the clouds—enough for Prakesh to see some strange structures ahead of them. He identifies an old wooden table, half of it rotted away. Plants have grown into it, winding tendrils through the wood. Next to it is what appears to be a large steel drum, now rusted, most of its top half gone. The bottom is still held in place by two metal brackets.

Prakesh runs his hand across the edge of the drum. It would have been installed over a hundred years ago, and probably hasn't been visited in about as long.

One thought leads to another. If humans really have survived, then they'll have managed to keep some tech going—they wouldn't have been able to broadcast a radio signal otherwise. The excitement rises again at the thought of what else might be out there.

He pulls his hand back from the drum. Wouldn't do to get an infected cut out here.

The others stumble into the clearing behind him. Mikhail collapses on the table, which groans in protest.

"Keep moving," Prakesh says.

But Mikhail is shaking his head. "No. No. This isn't right. We stay here. We can light another fire."

"Mikhail." It's Okwembu. She's shivering, too, holding herself tightly, but her voice is as calm and controlled as ever. "Get up."

If Mikhail hears her, he gives no sign. He's still shaking his head, muttering to himself.

Okwembu walks up to him, grabs him by the shoulders. "Get up," she says, and this time there's real fury in her voice. He ignores her, rocking back and forth on the rotten wood.

Carver strides off, heading for the other side of the clearing.

"Aaron!" Prakesh catches up to him just before he disappears into the trees.

The wind has got even worse, and Prakesh struggles to hear Carver's voice. "Forget that. He wants to stay where he is? Fine! Let him!"

"We need to stick together," Prakesh says, but he doesn't even know if Carver can hear him. He plunges into the trees, almost tripping over a rock, and has to put his hand against one of the tree trunks to stop himself from falling. The bark is damp and frigid against his skin, speckled with frost.

"Wait!" Clay screams the word, stumbling after them. Prakesh can feel a panic of his own rising, as if the presence of the others was the only thing keeping it down. He is colder than he has ever been in his life, and every breath feels like it has to physically claw its way out of his lungs. The wind has increased now, strong enough that he has to lean into it. He can hear the trees beginning to bend, the old wood creaking.

17

Riley

I stay as still as I can.

The animal lets go of Syria, its growl extending and twisting into a snarl. There's a gap in the clouds, enough to let in a little light from a hidden moon. I can't stop looking at the creature's mouth. Its teeth are a dull white, and saliva drips from its bottom lip.

A small part of my mind, walled off from the terror coursing through me, is fascinated. Outside of those in pictures, this is the first animal I've ever seen.

As my eyes adjust further, I pick out more details. Its two ears lie flat against its head, and its eyes have a lethal, primal shine. It's low to the ground, waist height, no more, with spiky, ragged hair—or is it fur?

The growl comes again, and that's when the fascinated part of me disappears. It might be the first animal I've ever seen, but it definitely isn't friendly.

Very, very slowly, I get to my feet. The beast takes a quick breath, interrupting the growl, but then it comes back at an even higher pitch. A tongue darts out from between the teeth, liquid and agile.

Terror has a way of sharpening my senses. How many times have I felt it on Outer Earth, and how many times has it made me a better tracer? It works now, because that's when I see the other two.

One of them is on the edge of the depression, almost invisible in the darkness. It's standing stock still, its head tilted to one side. The third is on my right: smaller, its fur darker than the others, opening and closing its mouth.

I raise my hands. The white vapour of my breath is coming in quick, trembling bursts. I'm speaking quietly, nonsense words, trying to keep the fear out of my voice.

I take a single step back, and that's when the first animal attacks.

It's shockingly fast. One moment it's motionless, and the next it's crossed the space between us and buried its teeth in my leg.

There's a frozen moment where I feel its teeth crushing through the leaves in my pants. Then they pierce my skin.

I lash out with my other foot. I'm already falling backwards, my arms whirling, but my shoe takes the animal in the head. It squeals—an oddly human sound—and lets go of my leg, its head twisted sideways.

Wolf.

The memory comes from nowhere. I was once ambushed by the Lieren, an Outer Earth gang intent on jacking my cargo. One of them had a tattoo on its neck. A red wolf.

I scramble to my feet. I don't know how fast a wolf can run, but right now speed is the only weapon I have. Ice crunches under my feet as I scramble into a sprint, hyperventilating, pumping my arms.

Behind me, the wolves give chase, their barks echoing across the plateau.

There might be a little moonlight, but it's like running through a black hole. Picking out details on the ground is impossible. I barely make it twenty yards before the wolves are on top of me.

And I'm not even close to fast enough. The wolves' speed is unbelievable. One of them lands on my back: a huge, hot, horrible weight knocking me to the ground. I feel its breath, burning against my skin. I twist and roll, shaking it off before it can get its teeth into me.

I spring onto my feet, legs apart, in a fighting stance. I'm surrounded—the three wolves have me in a loose circle, with a boulder at my back. The smaller wolf was the one I threw off; it's getting to its feet, its eyes never leaving mine. The bite on my leg is itching and burning. I'm trying to remember if wolves have poisonous bites, if that was something we were taught in school, but I can't marshal my thoughts.

All at once, the terror is gone. So is the hunger, and exhaustion. All of them burn away to nothingness, replaced by that seething anger.

I glance down. There's a loose rock, nudging up against my foot. I reach for it, eyes locked with the lead wolf.

It snaps at me, darting forward, but the anger strips away all hesitation. I bellow as hard as I can, swinging the rock in a massive sideways arc. The wolf drops before I smack it in the head again, twisting its shoulders as it skips backwards. Its legs are bent, quivering with energy.

Movement, on my left. This time, the rock connects, and the second wolf gives a pained howl as I smash it to the ground. My hand is buzzing from the impact, but I bring it back, driving it down into the animal's skull.

There's a *crunch*. Hot blood soaks the back of my hand, and the wolf's body jerks, its legs beating the air. It gives one final, piteous whine, then falls still.

I look up at the other two. They're backing away slowly, their teeth bared. Their growls fill the air.

I put my arms above my head, still clutching the rock, and scream at them. I don't even know what I'm doing. It's as if the anger has tapped into a part of me that I didn't know existed—something fundamental, a survival instinct buried deep in my DNA.

The wolves take off. The big one gives me a last look, and then they're gone, slipping into the darkness.

I'm still standing there, frozen to the spot, when there's a voice from behind me. "Guess you ain't such easy prey after all."

18

Okwembu

Mikhail is panicking.

He's rocking back and forth, trembling like a leaf. Okwembu stares at him. How did she ever think he would be useful?

If he wants to stay here, fine. She may not like Prakesh Kumar and Aaron Carver, but she's a lot safer with them than she is with him. But which direction did they go? They've long since vanished into the trees. Okwembu tries to remember. Her thoughts come slowly, the cold sapping her energy.

I have to get out of the wind.

She strides back to the table. "Move," she says to Mikhail. When he doesn't respond, she climbs on top of it, barking her knees against the wood, then puts a hand on his back and shoves. He falls forward, crying out in surprise, the sound whipped away by the wind.

Okwembu doesn't wait for him to get up. She clambers off the table, dropping back to the ground. She's not used to this amount of physical activity, and her arms are already aching. The wood is soft and rotten beneath her palms, but she pushes hard, using every ounce of strength she still has. If she can lift the table upright, she can make a windbreak. It's far from ideal, but it's the best she can do.

The table lifts an inch, then thumps back down. Okwembu tries again, leaning into it.

No good. She's going to need Mikhail's help. But when she turns to find him, he's walking away, hugging himself, head down.

"What are you doing?" she yells after him. No reaction. She abandons the table, shielding her eyes against the biting wind.

By some miracle, she manages to get in front of him. He doesn't look at her. His eyes are fixed on a point in the distance. He keeps walking, as if determined to get as far away as possible.

"Mikhail, no," she says, putting a hand on his chest.

He shrugs her off. "We have to go back," he says.

"What?" She can barely hear him over the wind.

When he doesn't answer, she plants herself in front of him. He finally looks at her, and that's when she sees what's really happening. The panic she heard in his voice, back at the lake, has taken over completely. It's the panic of someone who finally realises that all their plans are utterly useless.

"Listen to me," she says. "We—"

Mikhail puts a hand on her neck, and shoves her to one side. She goes down hard, twisting her ankle, bruising splayed fingers on the hard dirt.

"It was a mistake," Mikhail says, raising his voice so that it cuts above the wind. Tears are streaming down his face. "All of this. We should never have come."

He starts walking again, and that's when Janice Okwembu decides she's had enough.

No matter what she tries to do, no matter how well-meaning her intentions, she is met with stupidity and cowardice. She is confronted by people who hate her, who want her dead, who would take everything she's worked for and smash it to pieces. None of them realise how much she's sacrificed, how much she's put on the line for humanity. They're weak. All of them.

And she is tired of weakness.

She doesn't know how she finds the rock, but suddenly it's in her fingers, almost too big for her hand. She gets to one knee, then to her feet. Mikhail is almost at the trees.

Okwembu sprints after him. He doesn't look round as she approaches, and he doesn't see her raise the rock.

She swings it into the side of his head. He goes down, his legs crumpling, sprawling on his stomach in the dirt. Okwembu doesn't wait for him to roll over. She plants a knee in his back, and brings the rock down on the base of his skull. Then she does it again. And again.

Blood spatters her upper arms, dots her face. She barely feels the wind now.

After a while, Mikhail stops moving.

Okwembu takes a long look at what's left of his head. *I should feel something*, she thinks. Guilt, triumph, sorrow. He saved her life, pulled her out of the freezing lake. He should mean something to her.

But for all that she's done, for all the lengths she's had to go to ensure her survival, Okwembu has never killed anyone. Not directly. Not before now. And as she stares down at Mikhail's body, she feels nothing but quiet satisfaction.

She met weakness with strength. Cowardice with courage.

She tries to rise, but the wind is so strong now that it almost knocks her over. She saves herself by grabbing hold of a tree trunk. Her back is to the wind, and it cuts through her thin, damp clothing, turning her skin to ice. Strength and courage got her this far, but if she doesn't get shelter soon, she's not going to live long enough to reap the benefits.

She drops to her knees alongside Mikhail, wedging her hands under his torso. Gritting her teeth, she rolls him onto his side. Then she lies prone, curling her knees to her chest, pushing herself into the gap. The thought of being this close to his body is revolting, but Okwembu finds herself regarding the feeling at a distance, like it's someone else's problem.

She's not completely out of the wind, and she's still bitterly cold, but it's a vast improvement. They're low down on the ground, and she doesn't think a falling tree or snapped branch will hit them. She can feel the last residual heat from Mikhail's body leaching into her. Nothing to do now but wait for it to stop.

Janice Okwembu closes her eyes.

She's still lying there when bright lights illuminate the clearing.

19

Prakesh

"What the hell is happening?" Carver shouts.

Prakesh can barely hear him. It's not just the roaring wind: it's the trees. The trunks are creaking, the branches grinding together. The cacophony is unbelievable. The air is a swirling maelstrom of twigs and dead leaves, scratching at his face.

Microclimates, Prakesh thinks. *Extreme weather. We should have expected this. We should have prepared for it.* He wants to shout all of this to Carver, but there's no point. They have to find shelter, and they have to find it soon.

All three of them—Prakesh, Clay and Carver—are bent over, leaning hard into the wind. Prakesh glances back at Clay. The man's eyes are screwed shut, his mouth set in a thin line, like he's trying to pretend this isn't happening. Prakesh takes a step, then another, willing his frozen muscles to work. How strong is this wind? Sixty miles an hour? Seventy?

Carver is the first to lose his footing. He skids backwards, his feet sliding along the ground as if it's turned to ice. Then he tumbles over backwards, somersaulting, face frozen in surprise. Prakesh throws himself to the ground just before Carver smashes into him—he feels Carver's feet thump across his back, a hand scrabbling at his jacket.

He looks up to see Carver slam headlong into Clay. Somehow, Carver manages to hold on, grabbing him by the ankle. It stops him moving. He motions Clay to stay put, so they expose as little as possible to the wind. *Smart*, Prakesh thinks. If they don't freeze to death, then they might just make it through this storm. He makes himself stay down, too, tries to control his shivering.

There's a *crunch*. Prakesh raises his head a fraction, squinting against the icy rush of air.

A huge branch is tumbling towards them. It's coming end over end, ripping up the ground, and it's heading right for Carver and Clay.

They haven't seen it. They've both got their heads down. Prakesh shouts a warning, but it's lost under the wind. The branch is bouncing off the other trees, gaining momentum, smashing its way towards them.

For a second, he's amazed that they can't hear it, that they haven't noticed the presence of something that big and that destructive. Then he's moving, staying low, leading with his shoulder. A second later, he connects with Clay, his numb body barely registering the impact. Then he and Clay collide with Carver, and all three of them tangle up, a chaotic mix of limbs and dirt and wind. The crunching and cracking is deafening now.

The last thing Prakesh sees is the branch, rushing towards them. He closes his eyes, waiting for it to hit.

A bough rips across Prakesh's cheek, scratching his skin, drawing blood. Then the air rushes back into the space above them. The branch crashes further into the forest, finally wedging itself against another tree, ten feet off the ground.

The wind drops a fraction, just enough so that Prakesh can raise his head without feeling like the muscles in his neck are going to snap.

"Come on!" he shouts. He doesn't know if the other two can hear him, and he doesn't wait to find out. The ground is still a gentle slope, and Prakesh propels himself down it, the wind at his back. It's all he can do to keep his balance. There has to be a dip in the landscape, a large rock, *anything* that will get them out of the wind. Carver and Clay have caught up, running alongside him.

Abruptly, the ground levels out. Prakesh looks around, and for a moment he doesn't understand where they are. The uneven forest terrain has given way to hard-packed ground. It's a strip, around ten feet wide, stretching away into the darkness on their left and right.

Prakesh's body is firing on all cylinders, his heart hammering in his chest. He knows the strip is man-made, but he can't seem to think beyond that. Doesn't matter. They won't find shelter, not here, not out in the open. He yells for Carver to keep going.

Lights explode out of the darkness.

Two huge yellow circles, four feet off the ground, heading right for him. It's such a strange sight, so *alien*, that all three of them freeze. It's only in the last instant that Prakesh moves. He throws himself to the side, his hands out in front of him, but he's much too late. It's going to crush them.

There's a grinding screech. The lights swing to the side, and whatever is behind them turns sideways. Prakesh sees wheels spinning, kicking up huge clouds of dust which are instantly whipped away by the wind.

The thing comes to a skidding halt, rocking gently from side to side. It's solid enough to resist the wind—Prakesh can almost see the air skating over the top of it. It's like the vehicle that Carver put together on Outer Earth, only bigger. This one has a fully enclosed body, squat and boxy, with a slightly angled back. The wheels are enormous, resting in the tracks the thing made when it skidded sideways.

One of the doors on the side of the vehicle flies open. The figure in it is silhouetted by the interior lights.

"Get in!" the figure shouts.

Impact

20

Okwembu

Okwembu doesn't have a chance to process the sudden arrival of the others. They tumble into the vehicle, sprawling across the floor in a tangle of limbs.

The man who pulled them in screams over his shoulder to the driver. "Get us out of here!"

The woman next to him slams the door shut. The driver floors it, and the vehicle bucks and writhes as it fights against the wind.

The inside of the vehicle is cramped and low, with two rows of seats facing each other. The seats are covered in torn brown fabric, worn enough that Okwembu can feel the metal frame beneath digging into her back. The others throw themselves into the seats next to hers. She can feel Carver staring at her, taking in the streaks of blood on her face.

The noise makes speaking impossible. The wind has picked up again, and it's as if what came before was only a warm-up. She can feel the constant pressure on the vehicle's right-hand side, an angry god trying to shove them off the road. Okwembu can just see through the glass at the front of the vehicle. The headlights illuminate a world of flying debris, most of it moving too fast to identify.

A rock appears in the windshield, tumbling slowly, nearly as tall as the vehicle's front end. Okwembu flinches, but the driver is already spinning the wheel. The tyres screech as they dig into the dirt.

None of them have seat belts. Aaron Carver slams into her right side, squashing her up against the side of the vehicle. For a moment, her ear is pressed against the metal, and she can hear the true ferocity of the wind. She actually *feels* the rock scrape the car.

The skid has made them tilt, lifting the wheels on the right side an inch or so off the ground. The driver spins the wheel the other way, but the wind has them in its teeth. They're slowly tilting, inch by inch.

And Okwembu sees why. The skid has shifted everyone in the vehicle to one side. If they don't shift their weight to the other in the next few seconds, they're going to roll.

Nobody else has figured it out. They're all scrambling to stay in their seats, all panicking. She has to act, and she has to act now.

She manages to get a hand between her and the wall. But she's not strong enough. She gets her foot flat against it, half twisting her ankle, gritting her teeth against the pain.

She pushes hard, shoving them off her. Carver was a tracer, wasn't he? Someone used to movement and centres of gravity? Surely he'll see what she's doing. But when she looks into his eyes, she sees only anger and confusion. He's not going to do anything. It's up to her, like it always is.

Janice Okwembu scrambles off her seat, and hurls herself to the other side of the vehicle. The tilt pauses, just for a fraction of a second, but it's enough. And it's Clay who reacts, scuttling on all fours across the vehicle, pushing his back up against the right-hand door. The woman does the same, and *finally* the others figure it out.

The vehicle slams back to the road with a bang that rattles Okwembu's skull. The driver wasn't expecting it, and for a moment it feels as if the vehicle will spin out of control.

Okwembu closes her eyes.

When she opens them again, they're back on course. She can still hear debris scraping across the vehicle's body, but they're on a steady path, the headlights slicing through the darkness ahead of them.

Trembling, she pulls herself back onto her seat. The others do the same. She glances at Carver, but he's not looking at her. He's staring at the floor, hugging himself, shivering with cold.

"Almost out of it," the man says, raising his voice above the wind. His accent is unbelievably thick, like he's chewing a mouthful of food. "Everybody just hang on."

Okwembu can feel that they're descending, winding down the slope, away from the lake. Exhaustion and adrenaline catch up with her. She bites the inside of her cheek—she has to stay awake. Her hand moves to the data stick around her neck, grasping it through her shirt.

After a while, the road straightens out. They're still deep in the forest, but now the wind is nothing more than a low murmur.

The man in front reaches over the seats, resting a hand on the driver's shoulder. "We OK there, Iluk?" he says.

Iluk nods, and the man turns back to them. He puffs out his cheeks, shaking his head.

"You're damn lucky," he says to them. He's a big man, with short black hair and a neatly trimmed goatee under a pockmarked face. "You hadn't come out onto the old forest road when you did, we'd've gone right past you, praise the Engine."

Okwembu doesn't have time to question the strange phrase. The man keeps talking. "These storms can last for days," he says, looking up at the roof as if he expects what's left of the wind to lift it right off. "We get the real big ones once or twice a year. Real big ones. Nothing like the dust storms they get further south, though. Those things last for months."

"Who are you?" Prakesh says. His voice is a croak, and he's shivering badly.

"Hell—hang on," the man says. There's a storage locker bolted to the vehicle frame above him, and he clicks it open. Okwembu can see food containers, water canteens, equipment the purpose of which she can only guess at. And blankets.

It's these that the man goes for, passing them out. Okwembu gives him a grateful smile, wrapping one around her. It's scratchy, and smells of alcohol and sweat, but it's warm. Their rescuers pass out canteens of water, and they drink deeply.

"I'm Ray," the man says. "Iluk's doing the driving, and this here is Nessa." He gestures to the woman. She has a face that looks as if it's chiselled out of stone, framed by long, dirty-blonde hair. Like Ray and Iluk, she wears camouflage-patterned overalls, open at the neck, with a thick hooded sweater below them.

One by one they introduce themselves. Ray nods to each of them in turn. "Any more of you out there?" he says.

The others look at Okwembu. She shrugs. "No. There was just the one—the man you found me with."

Carver opens his mouth to speak, but she cuts him off. "He wanted to go back to the lake, and I tried to stop him. He attacked me."

"Gods," Clay says. His face is pale, his shoulders shaking.

"You're lying," says Carver.

Okwembu shrugs. "You heard him, back at the lake. He panicked, and I had to defend myself. I didn't have a choice."

Okwembu can feel suspicion radiating off Prakesh and Carver. Before they can say anything, Ray clears his throat. "What about the ship you came down in?" he says. "Where'd you land?"

Prakesh lifts his head. "We hit the lake. It's gone. Anyway, it was just an escape pod, not the ship itself. That burned up in the atmosphere."

"So no supplies? Any fuel, or anything?"

"Gone."

"Ah, shit." Ray shakes his head. "Prophet's not going to like that."

He glances at Nessa, and something passes between them, something that Okwembu can't quite figure out.

"Who's Prophet?" says Clay.

"We saw your ship come down," Ray says, ignoring him. "And I said to myself, Ray, the Engine has provided for us. It has sent survivors to join our cause. Prophet sent Nessa and Iluk and me up here, see if we could find where you landed."

He pauses. "Are you really from..." He raises his eyes, lifts his chin towards the roof.

It takes them a moment to realise what he's referring to. Prakesh speaks first. "Outer Earth?"

"I knew it!" Ray slaps his knee, a huge grin spreading across his face. His teeth have been worn down to tiny stubs.

"Outer Earth's a myth," says Nessa. But she's glancing at Ray, like she wants him to confirm it.

"Ain't no myth," Ray says, grinning. "Told you, didn't I? Where else could they have come from?"

"Why'd you leave?" Nessa says.

"Ask her," Carver says, jerking his head at Okwembu.

Okwembu's calm has returned. Carver seems to speak at a distance—he can't hurt her, not any more. She glances at him, then turns to Ray and Nessa, lifting her chin slightly as she speaks. "Outer Earth was hit by a virus," she says. "It killed almost everyone it touched. A few of us escaped."

Carver gives a bitter laugh. "She left out the part where she and her buddies blew a hole in the side of the station dock."

Stupid, she thinks, looking over at him. *Stupid and petty and small-minded. Just like Mikhail.* She exhales through her nose. "I've already explained why I—"

"You don't get to explain shit."

Ray clears his throat. "I see you folks have a lot to work out. But you're going to be fine. We're going to get you to the *Ramona*, and we're going to look after you."

Nobody speaks. The rumble of the engine is undercut by the howling wind, not as strong as it was but still forceful enough to rattle the sides of the vehicle.

Eventually, Prakesh says, "What's the *Ramona*?"

Ray smiles again. "You'll see."

21

Anna

The smell in the amphitheatre has gotten worse.

In the past, the station council used it to hold meetings, addressing the techs and functionaries that kept Apex and the wider station beyond it running. It's a huge room, two hundred feet wide, with a dozen rows of tiered seats sweeping down to a stage below.

The rows are packed with people. They lie on the floor, slouch against each other in the hard plastic seats, huddle in small groups along the walls. It's baking hot, and the thick scent of sweat hits Anna like a fist across the face.

She's still not sure why everyone congregates here. People have occupied habs and laboratories, the gallery, the mess hall. But the amphitheatre is in the centre of the sector, furthest from the borders.

It's as if Outer Earth has decided to draw itself in, as if the people inside it find comfort in spending time together here.

She looks around, finally spotting her parents on the bottom row. Her mother, Gemma, is asleep, her head resting on her knees. Her father, Frank, is deep in conversation with someone, off to one side. As Anna gets close, she sees it's Achala Kumar.

Anna only really met her a few days ago, after everyone had packed into the amphitheatre. She feels the same morbid curiosity as the first time she saw her. It was her son Prakesh who created Resin.

Achala looks as if she hasn't changed her clothes in a week. The lines on her face are like deep cuts. "Don't tell me that," she's saying to Anna's father. "Don't *say* that. I deserve a place on that ship more than anyone."

"Achala." Frank Beck puts a hand on her shoulder. "Think about what you're saying. I know you want to see Prakesh again, but—"

"I have a *right*," Achala says, raising her voice. "They can't tell me I don't."

"We don't even know if he survived." He ignores the shock and anger on Achala's face. "I'm sorry, but it's the truth."

She slaps his hand away, then turns on her heel and stalks off.

Frank Beck's shoulders slump. For a moment, he looks so defeated that Anna wants to run after Achala Kumar, scream at her, tell her to leave them alone. She settles for wrapping her arms around her dad from behind, resting her head on his shoulder. She has to stand on tiptoe to do it.

He nuzzles his head against hers. "Hey you. What are you up to?"

"Just wanted to see how you were doing."

"Fine, sweetheart. Just fine."

"What was that about?" she says, pointing at the retreating Achala.

Frank sighs. "What do you think? She wants a guaranteed spot on the *Tenshi*."

"She wants to skip the lottery?"

"Mm-hmm." He perches on the edge of a plastic chair. "Can't say I blame her. If you were down there, I'd probably be doing the same."

Anna moves in next to him. "You don't control who gets to go. Why's she bothering you?"

"That's what friends do. They listen to each other, even when one of them isn't thinking straight." He sighs, rubbing his left eye with the heel of his hand. "You'd think her husband would talk to her. He's a good man—used to work on the space construction corps, you know..."

Anna tunes him out. She's thinking about the lottery.

What's left of Outer Earth is dying. The fusion reactor keeps them spinning, maintaining the artificial gravity, and it keeps the water and the lights on. But its shielding is failing. No one knows when it'll go, but once it does, it's all over. Outer Earth will become a frozen tomb.

The asteroid from the *Shinso Maru* should have fixed it. It had all the tungsten they needed to shore up the reactor. But now it's gone, taken by the Earthers.

Their only hope is the one remaining asteroid catcher in existence: the *Tenshi Maru*. And it's still three months away. When it finally arrives, it's going to attempt the same re-entry manoeuvre that the *Shinso* did before it, using the asteroid it brought back. They'll ride it down, all the way through the atmosphere, taking their chances on Earth.

There are only a few spaces available on the ship. To get there, they'll need to leave via Apex's twelve escape pods—each of which can only take three people.

Everyone else gets left behind.

Even then, the trip will be crazy dangerous. The escape pods will get them most of the way to the *Tenshi*, but they can't dock with it directly—something about airlock compatibility. Every person in the pods will need to strap on a space suit, and transfer over to it.

Anna flashes back to the nightmare, when she was drifting in space, alone and terrified. Even the thought of going zero-G is enough to make a cold sweat prickle the back of her neck.

She needs to do something normal. Something beyond just worrying and surviving. She could go back to the Apex control room—it's not good for much these days, but in the first days of the crisis Anna spent a few hours there, trying to reach the *Shinso* on every wavelength she could think of. She got nothing but static.

She dismisses the idea—there's nothing for her in the control room any more. "I'm going to go find some matt-black," she says. "Finish the painting."

Frank gives her a tired smile, a final hug. Anna heads back up the stairs. Only a few lights in the ceiling are still illuminated, and she has to watch her step in the gloom. She picks up her pace as she hits the corridor, using the movement to chase the thoughts away.

The painting she's working on is in a corridor two levels above her: a mural of Outer Earth itself, hanging above the planet. Anna's never been outside, so she has to work from her imagination. She can't say why she's doing it—a few months from now, there'll be nobody alive to appreciate it.

She uses matt-black, a gluey residue left over from water processing. It's difficult to work with, but it's perfect for painting: a deep, velvety black that no other chemical mix can replicate. Anna loves it, even if it sticks her fingers together.

Her father used to work in the water-processing facilities, and she never wanted for matt-black. That's all changed. Still, she has at least one good source for it.

The hab is on the other side of the sector, on the top level. She comes to a halt outside the door, getting her breath back, resting her head against the cool metal wall. Not for the first time, she marvels at how white the corridors are here. How impossibly clean they are.

She raps on the door. There are muffled sounds from within, as if the occupant is getting out of bed. "Just a minute," he says.

"It's Anna," she says.

"Yeah, OK. Hang on."

The sounds continue. She's still standing there twenty seconds later, about to knock again, when the door clunks open.

All the doctors Anna has ever known look like they haven't slept in years. Elijah Arroway is no exception. It's impossible to picture him without the deep bags under his eyes, without the weary slump of his shoulders. Arroway was put in charge of fighting the Resin outbreak, and he still looks as if he hasn't quite recovered.

He's been handling water processing for Apex. It was what he did before he became a doctor, and they needed that more than they needed his medical training. All of which made him Anna's number one matt-black source.

He attempts a smile when he sees her, doesn't quite manage it. "Anna. Not a good time, I'm afraid."

"Oh. OK," Anna says, frowning. It's not like Arroway to be so abrupt. She shakes it off—they're all on edge. "Just came for the matt."

"The... right. Of course."

He turns and walks back into the hab. It's tiny, no more than a few yards across, with a single cot tucked against the wall on the left. The door to the bathroom at the back is slightly open, and Anna can smell the tang of the chemical toilet.

There's a low table in the corner. A rectangular plastic container sits on top of it, filled to the brim with the glistening black substance. Anna leans against the doorframe, and, as she does so, she notices something odd. There's a duffel bag on the unmade bed, jammed full of clothes. The bottom half of a sleeve hangs out of it, draped across the covers.

"Here," Arroway says.

Anna pulls her gaze away from the bag. She has to take the container with both hands, and the matt-black sloshes gently as she does so. She gets her forearms under it, smiling thanks.

"Moving hab?" she says, nodding at the bag.

Arroway grimaces again. "Toilet's broken. They've got a spot downstairs I can use."

"Right," she says, and then can't think of anything else to say.

"Well," Arroway says, nodding to her. He closes the door gently, clicking it shut in her face.

She stands there for a moment. Then she shakes her head, and walks back down the corridor.

The matt-black in her arms is heavier than she expected, and she has to stop to rest several times, carefully placing it next to her on the floor. The second time she stops, she idly dips the tip of her index finger in the substance, tracing a delicate curlicue on the corridor floor. She rubs that fingertip against her thumb, enjoying the slightly rubbery give of the matt-black.

She's still there twenty minutes later. Still rubbing the matt-black between her fingers.

The fire in the gallery. Arroway's bag. The lottery.

They go round and round in her mind.

She's being paranoid. She's bored, and she's scared, and she's looking for something to distract her. The things she's seen are utterly unrelated.

Anna gets to her feet, leaving the matt-black on the corridor floor. After all, it's not like anyone is going to steal it. She rubs her index finger and her thumb together once more, then jogs off down the corridor.

22

Riley

I don't know how deep the cave goes.

There's a lantern propped by the entrance, but its light only reaches a few feet in. The space I *can* see reminds me a little of the Nest, back on Outer Earth: a total mess, with blankets and tools spread out over the uneven floor. A battered metal stove is puffing away, smoke curling out of the top and collecting near the ceiling. The narrow entrance is covered by planks of rotting wood, nailed together to form a makeshift door.

The stranger is crouched by the stove. He hardly said anything on the way over, only that his name was Harlan, and that he had a place where I'd be safe. He has dark brown skin, offset by a scraggly beard. Both the beard and his hair are streaked with grey. Guessing his age is impossible—he could be forty, he could be four hundred.

He wanted to leave Syria's body behind. I wouldn't let him. He carried it on his back, bringing it into the cave. It's somewhere behind me in the darkness. I keep wanting to look, have to force myself not to.

It crossed my mind that it might not be safe, that all this could be a trap. I found I didn't care much. There's nothing Harlan can throw at me that I haven't survived a dozen times already.

He shuts the stove door with a clank, then gets unsteadily to his feet, pulling something from a pocket in his cavernous coat.

"Eat this," he says. He has the strangest accent, mushing together certain sounds, as if he never quite learned how to form individual words. "You were damn lucky with the wolves. They got a big pack round these parts, gettin' more aggressive every year. No idea why those three were off alone, but those leaves you used must have changed your scent some. You want to be careful, though. You pick the wrong kind of leaves, you get this rash all over your body. Itch'll drive you crazy."

I stare at him, my mouth hanging open.

He grimaces. "Sorry. I ain't talked to other people in a while. Guess I ain't used to it. Here."

I reach for the food, then hesitate. Alarm bells are going off already. But my hunger wins out, and after a moment I take it. It's like a strip of tree bark, brown and hard, with a grainy surface. I have to work to tear a chunk out.

The taste nearly knocks my head off. It's salty, like the fried beetles we used to get in the market, only a thousand times more intense. My stomach growls, and I take another bite, filling my mouth with the chewy substance.

"Good, isn't it?" Harlan says, grinning. "Cure it myself."

Cure. I suddenly realise what I'm eating. "This is...meat?" I say, speaking around it.

Harlan has gone back to work on the stove. There are logs piled up next to it, and he's busy jamming one of them inside. Light dances on the rock walls. "Mule deer. Caught it last spring, down near Whitehorse. First I'd seen in *years*. Didn't even think they were alive any more. Can't believe I got it before the Nomads did, I tell you that. Set a trap, over by the falls. Sucker walked right into it."

I make myself chew slowly, savouring the taste. It's not just delicious—it's incredible. For a moment I forget about where I am, forget about everything except this, the first piece of meat I've ever eaten. I tell myself to take it slowly, not wanting to upset my stomach.

"Where are we?" I say, after I finally swallow.

Harlan glances up at me. His eyes are rimmed with wrinkles, an endless field of them, reaching all the way round to his temples. "You don't know?" he says. "Seems strange, since you crashed down here. Figured you might have had *some* idea where you were going. That space station you came from—hey, is that really true, by the way? You ain't just trying to fool me? Because if you are..."

I shake my head. "No, it's the truth."

He gives a long, low whistle. "Boy. Is it still there? Or did they come crashing down, too? I think everyone else you came down with is dead, or they will be soon. Can't survive long in these mountains 'less you know what you're doing." He's having trouble controlling his volume—some sentences are almost shouted, while others drop to a whisper.

I focus on the first question he asked. "I got separated from the others," I say, doing my best not to think of Okwembu.

Harlan jams a piece of the meat in his mouth, swinging round and pulling a battered backpack from its spot near the wall. He rummages in it, then withdraws something long and thin. It's paper—a whole roll of it, torn at the edges but otherwise intact.

"Scooch over," Harlan says around the dried meat, and unrolls the paper across the dirty floor.

It's a map. I've seen plenty of them before, but always on tab screens, crisp and sharp. This one is faded, the tiny place-name letters all but gone. The land on the map, marked out with thick black lines, forms an uneven, top-heavy blob. At the top, near the map's edge, the land breaks up into dozens of tiny islands.

"Hold this side down," Harlan says, tapping the edge closest to me. The paper feels fibrous under my hands, almost alive, as if it too came from an animal.

"All right," says Harlan. He rests a finger on the map, where the left-hand part of the blob begins to curve and mushroom out. "This is where we are. The Yukon. Canada. Ring any bells?"

I shake my head, but he's no longer looking at me. "Not that it matters," he says. "Canada, the States, whole damn planet far as I know. Most of it's all dust now. Everything below this line is dry as anything." His finger traces a curve across the blob, east to west, a little below the place he called Yukon.

"So why is it OK where we are?"

"Can't say. A few years ago, we were living in one of the bunkers here." He taps a point about ten inches below Yukon, his finger nudging the faded word *Utah*. "Those were bad years. Ever since I was a kid. Dust storm three-quarters of the year and frozen solid for the rest of the time. Air was nasty. You couldn't stay above ground long, not that people didn't try. We didn't get a whole hell of a lot further than Red Rocks. I remember this one time, Garrison told us about this electrical spike he was reading down by..." He looks at me. "Doing it again. Sorry. Just, I don't know, click your tongue or something if I talk too much."

"It's OK," I say. "But...what about up here?"

He shrugs. "We got word that things were changing. That you could live outside. Trees, air, whole deal. Paradise, compared to where we were. You hear that kind of thing, you go for it. Beats living in a tunnel underground, believe you me."

Trees. I glance at the door, thinking of the barren landscape beyond. The only trees I've ever seen were the ones in the Air Lab—the big oaks. I try to picture a forest of them, stretching to the horizon. I can't even begin to imagine it.

Harlan sees where I'm looking. "They're down at the lower elevation, round Whitehorse. Not much of a forest, but it's there. Air's good, too. Go outside anywhere south of the 49th parallel, and you gotta be wearing a full-face gas mask."

"What about the wolves? How are there...I mean, we thought all the animals were dead."

He grunts. "Oh, they ain't dead. Not completely. Most parts, sure, you never see 'em, but animals are funny. They find ways to survive. Probably don't need no more than a handful of 'em to do it, neither. You ask me, I think they just kept moving. Couldn't go underground, like we did, so they found places they could get food. 'Course there's been a lot more in the last few years, now the air's cleared up."

"And there are more people here? In Yukon?"

"*The* Yukon. You gonna live here, you gotta get the name right."

He turns away, letting go of his side of the map. It curls over, covering my hand. I spread it out again as he jams a poker into the stove, muttering to himself.

"Why are you up here, and not in the forest?" I say, still staring at the map. "Is it because of the . . . the Nomads?"

He grunts. "Something like that."

"Who are they?"

Harlan doesn't answer, poking at the fire.

I don't bother repeating the question. It doesn't matter. What's important is getting back out there. Prakesh and Carver must have come down close by, and if Harlan knows this place as well as I think he does, then we might be able to find them. I actually smile—the thought of seeing them both again, of coming across them, seeing their faces, feels amazing. I could bring them back here.

And then you'll have to choose between them a second time, says the small voice in my mind.

I ignore it. That can come later. I try to picture the forest again, imagining running in the sunlight, in a place where there's air and water and food. Where I can see the sky.

"So, my friends were on another escape pod," I say, trying to keep the excitement out of my voice. "I need to find them."

"Yeah?" says Harlan. "Where were you folks headed?"

The name jumps up out of nowhere. "Alaska."

His brow furrows. "Alaska?" He comes back, bends over the map, so close that his nose almost touches the paper. "The border's over a hundred miles away. Well, what used to be the border. Plus, state itself goes all the way across to the Bering Sea. Nothing but ice out there."

A sick feeling starts to swell in my stomach, as if the meat is turning toxic. I didn't have time to think about the physics of our re-entry before, but I'm doing it now and it's chasing away the good feeling I had before. At the speed we were travelling, two pods launched thirty seconds apart could come down hundreds of miles from each other.

Not good. Not good at all.

Harlan clears his throat. "Where were you supposed to end up? In Alaska?"

My mind goes blank. My finger hovers above the map, as if a name will leap out at me, but all the letters run into each other. *There's got to be a way. I have to find them.*

Then I remember. "Anchorage," I say. "We were going to some settlement in Anchorage." I scan the map for it, and let out a cry when I find it, nestled into a small bay. "If they launched when they were supposed to—"

"Kid," Harlan says quietly.

"—then they would have landed nearby. And there are other people there, so—"

"Kid."

I look up at Harlan, and the sick feeling in my stomach expands, spreading through my body.

"What?" I say.

"I'm sorry," he says. "Your friends are already dead."

23

Prakesh

"We're here," says Ray.

Prakesh jerks awake. He hadn't even realised he'd dropped off. His neck immediately starts complaining—the vehicle's seats weren't designed for sleeping, and he'd passed out with his head at an awkward angle. His mind feels like it's floating three feet above him.

Iluk kills the engine, then bangs the door open and slides out. For the first time Prakesh realises that they can barely see out of the windows—they're grimed over, caked with dirt. Only a thin strip at the top of each one is still clear, and Prakesh can see the early light of dawn peeking through the windows on his left.

Ray opens the door. Prakesh has to shield his eyes against the glare.

"Come out when you're ready," says Ray. He and Nessa clamber through the door, with Okwembu following them. Nessa half closes it and Prakesh can feel the chill air licking at his exposed skin.

Carver rolls his head from side to side, massaging his shoulders. He looks exhausted, like he's aged ten years in a single night. Clay, too, is slowly blinking awake.

"Glad *you* got some sleep," Carver says, as Prakesh rubs his neck.

"You didn't?" He runs his tongue along the inside of his cheeks, trying to scare up some saliva. It doesn't work.

"Five minutes, maybe. We've been driving for hours."

"Right," Prakesh says. He's trying to get his thoughts in order, but it's like tying shoelaces with thick gloves on. There's something about these people—Ray and Nessa and the silent Iluk—that he doesn't like.

Carver gestures to the door. "You getting out, P-Man? Or we just going to sit here all day?"

Prakesh pauses for a moment, then pushes open the door and steps outside.

The first thing he notices is that the ground is soft—much softer than the tough, packed dirt of the forest. The second thing is the air. It *smells* different—a mix of a thousand scents, of salt and chemicals and decay and something else, something metallic and alien.

He looks up, and his mouth falls open.

Prakesh has seen pictures of the ocean before. They always showed blue sky, sandy beaches, white-capped waves. He didn't expect oceans like that to exist on Earth any more, but this…

It's a black, seething mass of water, hissing at the shore like an angry monster. There are waves, but they're stubborn little things, barely managing a fringe of froth before sinking into the edge of the water.

And there's a city in the ocean.

Or at least, what used to be a city. The buildings are half submerged, poking out of the water, tall towers reaching to the sky. In the pale dawn light, Prakesh can see that most of the towers are half destroyed, their walls and floors broken away, exposing their dark interiors to the low-hanging clouds. There are dozens of them, spread out along the shore, which curves away on either side of them.

The closest tower is barely fifty feet away—Prakesh can still see the main revolving door, water lapping at its frame, the glass long gone. The interior is dark, with gaps in the far wall that let in a little daylight. Most of the upper half of the tower is gone, the steel beams exposed like old bones.

Carver lets out a low whistle from behind him.

"Something, right?" says Ray. He has the vehicle's hood open, and is rooting around inside. With a yank, he pulls an object from deep in the engine.

"Spark plug," he says, when he sees them looking. "Make sure this old girl doesn't go anywhere." He raps a headlight with one hand. Prakesh sees that they're parked a little way off a paved road, pockmarked with potholes, vegetation pushing up through the cracks.

"What happened here?" says Prakesh. Clay is climbing out of the Humvee now, and is looking around, his eyes huge. Okwembu is standing a little way off, looking out over the water, motionless. Her blanket is loose around her shoulders, the wind playing with its hem.

Ray slams the hood closed, pocketing the spark plug. "Anchorage?" he says. "Sea claimed her, just like every other city on the west coast. East, too, for all we know. Happened long before the Engine brought us here."

There's a noise from further down the beach. Iluk and Nessa appear, dragging another vehicle behind them—a boat, the same size as the first vehicle but flat-bottomed, with a bulging motor on the back.

They drop it near the edge of the water with a thud. That's when Prakesh sees that Nessa has a gun: a lethal-looking rifle with a cylindrical scope mounted on top. Its lenses pick up the thin dawn light.

Ray reaches inside the wheeled vehicle, pulling out an empty canister and an opaque, flexible tube. He flips open a small flap on the side and winds the tube down into it. He puts his mouth around the tube and sucks in his cheeks. A second later, he turns and spits a thick stream of fuel onto the dirt, then wipes his mouth. The rest of the fuel is coming up the tube, draining into the canister.

"Where'd you get this, anyway?" Carver says, gesturing to the vehicle. For the first time, there's a glimmer of excitement in his eyes.

"The Hummer?" says Ray. "Had her for years, long before we even knew about the Engine. It was Prophet's originally. While back, some other Nomads tried to jump him, but he took 'em down and took what they had. She's still in pretty good shape, right?"

"Nomads?" says Clay.

Carver ignores him. "What's it—*she*—run on?"

"Diesel," Ray says. "Gotta look after it. Not too much around these days." He looks at Prakesh. "We were kind of hoping that you'd have some with you. Some sort of fuel anyway."

Prakesh feels a tiny drumbeat of fear in his chest, fear of something he can't quite place. Once they're in the boat, out on the water, there's nowhere to run to. He can't get over the thought, and he doesn't know why it scares him so much.

Carver hasn't noticed. "I built one, you know. Well, not one as big as this, and it didn't have the roof or anything—" he points to the top of the Hummer "—but it was *fast*."

Ray smiles and reaches inside the Humvee, emerging with a rifle of his own.

"We get animals down here sometimes," Ray says, seeing that Prakesh has noted the gun. "Wolves, mainly. Nessa swears she saw a bear one time, not that I believe her. And then there are the Nomads, of course."

He gestures to the boat. Clay is already perched on the side, and Okwembu is clambering on board. "Hop in. Iluk'll push her into the water."

"Yeah, sure," Prakesh says. He turns to Carver, who is still admiring the Humvee. "Talk to you for a sec?"

Carver looks up, but before he can say anything Ray steps between them. "Something on your mind?" he says. It's Prakesh's imagination—it has to be—but his accent has grown thicker.

"Just want to talk, that's all," he says. "The second escape pod might have come down near here. We should look for that one, too." He tries to sound natural, but struggles to keep the nervousness out of his voice.

"We just saw the one," says Ray. "Besides, we should get you fed. Cleaned up. Right?"

Prakesh tries a smile, flashes Carver a meaningful glance. "Can't leave our friend out there."

Carver stares back at him, confused and wary. Ray spits. The saliva arcs through the air, burying itself in the sand, and Prakesh smells a hint of fuel in the air. The drum in his chest is beating harder now.

Ray gestures to the ocean with the rifle. "We'll talk on the way."

So much for subtlety, Prakesh thinks. "What's the *Engine*?" he says. "Who's Prophet?"

"Get in the boat."

"Where are you taking us? What's out there?"

All the good humour has left Ray's face, and what remains is hard and cold. "Food. Shelter. A society. Just like the radio message said."

"I've been thinking," Prakesh says, deciding to plunge ahead. "That message? So you're just broadcasting your location to anyone who can listen? I don't buy it. I'm not going anywhere until you tell us—"

Ray raises his rifle, and points it at Prakesh's face. Nessa and Iluk do the same, tracking Carver and Clay. Okwembu watches, not reacting.

Ray's smile is thin and humourless. "Get in the damn boat."

24

Riley

The silence in the cave stretches on forever. The edge of the map has curled over my hand again, but I barely notice it.

Your friends are already dead.

"You don't know that," I say.

Harlan's face is grave. He doesn't say anything. And, right then, the anger comes back. How dare he? He doesn't know Prakesh. He doesn't know Carver. Wherever they are, whatever they're dealing with, they'll be OK. They have to be.

My fist is clenched, scrunching up part of the map. Slowly, I let go, pulling my hand back. Then I take a deep breath, the anger subsiding. For now.

"What's in Anchorage?" I say. The heat in the cave has built up, drying out my tongue and blocking my sinuses.

Harlan bends down to his backpack, the cave echoing with clunks and thumps as he rummages through it. He pulls out an ancient radio, one with an antenna and a big chunky knob.

There's a crank on the side, and Harlan gives it a few quick turns. A light on the radio flickers on, growing orange, and we hear the thin sound of static. Harlan mutters to himself, adjusting the knob on the front of the radio, and then there's the voice, the message, the one I heard for the first time on the bridge of the *Shinso Maru*.

This time, the message chills me to the bone.

"—can hear us, we are broadcasting from a secure location in what used to be Anchorage, Alaska. There are at least a hundred of us here, and we have managed to establish a colony. We have food, water and shelter. The climate is cold, but survivable. If you can hear us, then know that you're not the only ones—"

"They do a new one every couple of months," Harlan says, shutting the radio off. "But it's been ever since we got up here. I don't know how they get the power to do it, but it doesn't matter."

"Who's *they*?"

"We don't know." Harlan adjusts his position. "Back when I was in Whitehorse, we had a survivor come through. Russian guy. Least, I think he was Russian. Had an accent you had to really listen hard to understand. Massive beard, too, like fur on a—"

"Harlan."

"Sorry. Don't ask me how he managed to get to here from Alaska, but he did it."

I don't know where Whitehorse is, and I have only the vaguest idea of where to find Russia. "What happened to him?" I say.

"Told us he was in a big party out of Siberia," Harlan says.

"Winters had got too heavy there, so they were coming east, hoping for something better. They heard the message as they were crossing through Alaska, and decided to check it out.

"They got ambushed, even before they got to the source of the signal. Guy couldn't stop shaking when he told us. Said it was like the night just folded in on 'em. Men, women, children, didn't matter. Anchorage swallowed 'em whole. He managed to get away, along with his wife. She died on the way here."

"And you believed him?"

Harlan shrugs. "Not like we were gonna go there ourselves to find out."

"There has to be an explanation," I say, staring at the map. "Maybe something else took them. Maybe the settlement was—"

"You don't get it, do you?" says Harlan. "Don't you think it's a little strange that they're just broadcasting their location?" He waves his hands in the air, waggling his fingers. "Hey! Everybody! We got food and supplies! All you can eat! Form an orderly line!"

I stare down at the map, not wanting to think about his words.

"If they were really accepting survivors," Harlan says, "then the Nomads would have cleared 'em out long ago. Them, and anybody else who feels like livin' off what other people got. You want to know what I think? I think whoever sent this message is doing the same thing. Why go out hunting for supplies when you can just have them come straight to you?"

He puts a hand on my shoulder—then jumps when I slap it away. The anger I feel is immediately replaced by embarrassment, and I turn away, hugging myself tight. This isn't his fault.

But, right now, I feel like I did when I looked up at the sky—like the world has gone fuzzy at the edges.

"You ain't gettin' to Anchorage anyhow," he says, not unkindly. "You're four hundred miles crow flight, and you won't make it even halfway before the snows set in."

I'm barely listening. I'm back on my feet, pacing, thinking hard. Four hundred miles. It's a long way, but if I leave now I can get there in a month or two. It's nowhere near fast enough, but it'll have to do.

"The person I loved was on that ship," I say, each word carried on a hot, angry breath. "I have to find him." In that moment, I don't know if I'm talking about Carver or Prakesh.

Harlan doesn't touch me again. He just steps around until he's in front of me, leaning slightly away, as if he's afraid I'm going to lunge forward and bite him.

"I don't think you understand what you're about to do. How're you planning to feed yourself? Or navigate? That's without talking about the weather."

"I can deal with the cold."

"Can you deal with a snap that drops the temperature twenty degrees in ten minutes? I've seen that stream you were at frozen solid. And we got wind storms that come out of nowhere. They'll knock you right off your feet. 'Sides, you've already met the wolves."

He stops to take a breath. When he speaks again, his voice is quieter. "What's the biggest space you ever been in?" Harlan says quietly.

"What do you mean?"

"When we were on the way over here, I caught you looking up at the sky. Like a goddamn deer in a spotlight."

"I've been outside the station before," I say, crossing my arms. "I've been *in* space."

"Right. Right. But for how long? And I'm guessing you had a space suit."

In the silence that follows, I realise that I don't have a single thing to say.

"Your mind ain't right," Harlan says, locking his eyes onto mine. "You're snapping at every little thing, and you just ain't ready for what's out there."

I look away, refusing to give up, desperately trying to think about how I could do this. *Four hundred miles.* I'll need gear, food, a map. Maybe Harlan can help me. Maybe I can—

When I look back, I see that he's staring at my thigh.

"What's that?" he says, stepping in close.

"Nothing," I say, my mind still on Anchorage. "Just a cut."

"Lemme see." He goes down on one knee, reaching in. I shy away, startled, but stop when I see the look on his face. The worry on it.

"I told you, I'm fine," I say, baring my teeth as his fingers gently explore the cut, peeling back the fabric of my pants. "It's a flesh wound. I got hit by a piece of shrapnel, but I took it out."

He stops for a moment, grabbing a nearby lantern and bringing it closer. The heat from the glass bakes onto my skin.

"Deeper'n that," he says. "And there's still some metal in there."

"What?"

"Yeah, there, and there, and... yeah, hi, I see you. You didn't get it all out. This from the..." He lowers his hand to the floor fast, making an explosion sound with his mouth when it hits, looking up at me questioningly.

I nod, furious at myself for having missed this. The smaller shards must have broken off the bigger one when it embedded itself in my flesh.

"So we take the rest out," I say. My gut churns—more pain. I tell myself I can handle it, that it'll be worth it if it gets me moving again. It can't possibly be worse than the pain I felt when I cut that bomb out of me.

But Harlan is shaking his head, sitting back on his haunches. "Can't do it," he says. "Nope. Nuh-uh. Can't. They're too deep. Do you have any idea how much it's gonna hurt when those things come out? Do you?"

"Pretty good idea," I say, getting down to his level, stretching out. In the flickering light, the wound looks even more jagged and raw. "Just bring me something I can use. Tweezers, or pliers. A knife'll probably be fine."

"You don't understand," he says, his voice shaking. "Even *if* we get them out, I don't got the medicine to stop the cut going bad."

"You must have something," I say. I can feel my nails digging into my palm.

He shrugs, helplessly. "Had. It's all gone. Tripped and fell a few months ago when I was checking traps. Got a massive gash all the way up my arm." He points to his bicep. "Used the last of it on that. Even then, I don't know if it woulda been enough to handle what you've got."

I run through the options in my head. I could clean the cut, get the slivers of metal out, but I only have to miss one for sepsis to set in. I could burn it—pour lamp oil in the cut and set it on fire—but even the thought of that makes me want to throw up. Besides, I don't even know if that would work. It might just be inviting further infection.

"Wait a second," Harlan says. He jumps up, surprisingly spry. "This is *perfect*."

I stare up at him, not entirely sure I heard him right. "I'm going to die of infection, and that's perfect?"

"No no no," he says, waving his hands. "It's just...listen, I think I know where we can get the stuff you need."

"OK," I say slowly, feeling a tiny spark of hope flare up in my chest.

"We go to Whitehorse," he says.

It's a name he's mentioned before. "What's Whitehorse?"

"Town about twenty-five miles south from here, give or take. Except...shit, I don't know, Eric was already making noises about heading for Calgary, so there's no guarantee they'd even—"

"But they'll have supplies? If they're still there?"

"*If* they're still there, yeah. Only..." He stops, a strange expression of longing settling on his face. In the lantern light it makes him look a hundred years old. More.

"Only...what?" I say.

"You gotta do something for me," he says. "If they're still down there, you gotta tell 'em I helped you. You gotta tell 'em I looked after you, all right? Made sure you were OK."

It's such a strange request that at first I don't know how to respond. "Why?" I say, after a moment.

His expression hardens. "Does it even matter? Just do that for me. I get you down the valley, you tell Eric that I did good. That's the deal."

He's going to trick you, says the voice at the back of my mind. *He can't just want something that small. He wants something else. Something he isn't telling you about.*

I'm about to listen to the voice, but then I remember something Carver told me. It happened right after we escaped from the Earthers, back on the station. He told me that I had to let other people help me—that I couldn't do everything on my own.

I could try get to Whitehorse myself, but it's all too easy to imagine getting lost out there. If that happens, I won't survive. Whatever Harlan's doing, whatever weird game he's playing, I have to go along with it. It's the only shot I have.

"All right," I say. "Sure. I'll tell them."

He smiles, showing yellowed teeth. He digs in his pack again, tossing me another stick of dried meat. "Eat up, and get some sleep," he says. "We got a long way to go tomorrow."

25

Anna

Anna has to knock several times before Achala Kumar opens the door.

She's wearing a blue sweater with a black shawl wrapped around her shoulders. The skin on her face is puffy, her eyes bloodshot. She frowns when she sees Anna. "You're Frank's daughter."

Anna nods. "Can I come in?"

Achala considers for a moment, then shrugs, holding the door open for her.

The Kumars have taken over a hab on Level 2. It's even smaller than Doctor Arroway's, and even more spartan. Cold, too—as Anna walks in, she can just see her breath curling in the air before her.

Ravi Kumar is on the small single cot, his back up against the wall. A thin blanket covers the lower half of his body. There's a depression where his left leg should be, and Anna finds it hard to look away. Right then, it strikes her just how much his son looks like him.

Ravi smiles at her, but she can see the puzzlement in his eyes.

Achala closes the door behind her. "I'm sorry I can't offer you anything to drink," she says. "About earlier: I shouldn't be arguing with your father. It's not his fault."

"Achala, what did you say to Frank now?" Ravi Kumar says, his voice weary.

"Don't you start with me," Achala spits back. "Our boy is *alive*, and I'm not going to sit here while—"

"I need to ask you something," Anna says, speaking over both of them. She sits down on the edge of the bed, telling herself to stop looking at the space below Ravi Kumar's left knee.

She doesn't quite manage it. Ravi reaches over, taps the blanket. "Loader claw closed over it," he says. "Crushed the shin. I was lucky it didn't puncture my suit." His eyes bore into hers. "But you didn't come here to talk about old injuries."

Anna takes a deep breath, irritated with herself. This shouldn't have been difficult. "They keep space suits in the escape pods, right?"

"Space suits?" says Achala.

Ravi nods slowly, his eyes narrowed.

"OK," Anna says. "But do they keep them anywhere else in the sector? Extra suits, or something?"

"No," Ravi says. "There's no point—there are only a few places you can do an EVA from, and there's nothing like that in Apex." He sees Anna's confusion. "EVA—Extra-Vehicular Activity. Spacewalks."

"And you were in the construction corps, right?" Anna says, more to herself than to him. "So you'd know."

"Of course," Ravi says, even more puzzled. He glances up at his wife. "Unless Achala knows something I don't."

Achala thinks hard, shakes her head. "No. There's a workshop in Tzevya where they did suit repairs, but nothing here."

She looks at Anna in horror. "But you can't be thinking of going outside?"

Anna thinks back to the nightmare: drifting, weightless, in a black void. She shivers, without meaning to. "Nothing like that."

"Then why the interest in space suits?" Ravi Kumar pulls himself off the bed, hands fumbling along the wall for the cane propped against it. "What's going on?"

Anna is about to tell them, then stops. She has to be sure. She has to be absolutely positive about this before she tells a soul.

"I'll tell you afterwards," she says. She sees Achala about to speak, and ploughs on. "I'm not going outside, and I'm not doing anything bad. Promise."

She smiles, turns to go.

"Anna," Achala Kumar says, and when Anna turns back she sees that Achala is crying. Her hands are knotted at her waist, fingers clenched tight. Ravi looks down, embarrassed.

"You have to help us," Achala whispers.

Anna doesn't know what to say. She doesn't know how to tell the Kumars that she has even less pull than they do. More importantly, she can't tell them that she agrees with her father—that the lottery is the only way. The Kumars aren't the only people with missing sons, daughters, husbands, wives.

"I'll try," she says. It's not a lie, not exactly, but she feels uneasy as she says it. What she has isn't even a theory. It's a hunch, a feeling, based on a collection of things that might not even be remotely related. But what if she's right? What if this all means something? What will it mean for the Kumars?

She walks out of the hab, closing the door behind her. Then she takes off down the corridor, heading for the escape pods.

26

Riley

It's mid-morning before we reach the tree line.

We see it from far up the mountain, stretching into the distance, but it's only when we're close that I get a good look at the trees. They're nothing like the ones in Outer Earth's Air Lab. Those were enormous, with canopies that blocked out the light from the ceiling lamps. But these trees are no more than twenty feet high, and they're stunted, with stubby branches and wind-bent trunks.

Even so, I make myself stop for a moment, taking it in. These trees weren't supposed to exist. They were supposed to be gone. And yet here they are, fighting to survive, pushing back against the cold.

Harlan doesn't notice I've stopped until he's a few feet into the trees. He looks over his shoulder, nodding at me to follow. He's wearing a tattered canvas pack, his rifle strapped to the side. There are no bullets in the gun—Harlan says he ran out months ago—but it's reassuring to see it there anyway.

The ground is a mess of frost and brown leaves. It's eerily silent, and it takes me a moment to work out why that bothers me. On Outer Earth, whenever we were shown videos of forests, they were always noisy—bird calls, insects, wind. Here, the only sounds are our footsteps and the laboured sound of our breathing.

I pick one of the nearby leaves from a tree, rub it between my fingers. It doesn't feel like any leaf I've touched in the Air Lab. It feels crinkly, desiccated, and before long it comes apart in my hand.

Harlan sees me looking. "Most of this was frozen over five years ago," he says. "Kind of amazing how the forest just comes back, given half a chance. Topsoil's pretty thin, but that's changing. Twenty years, this'll be green all the time."

"How do you know it'll stay this way?" I say, dipping a hand under my jacket. Harlan gave me one of his shirts to wear under it, and the material feels scratchy against my skin.

He looks helpless suddenly, as if I've brought up something he doesn't want to think about it. "No way to tell. Better hope it does, though, or we're all done."

He strides ahead, plunging deeper into the forest, his canvas pack bouncing.

I'm trying to ignore my fatigue. My eyes are gritty with it, my muscles leaden. Harlan wouldn't let us leave until dawn—he refused to travel in the dark, told me we needed sleep if we were going to hike down to Whitehorse. I didn't want to push the issue, but even curled up in one of his blankets I only managed a couple of hours of sleep.

It didn't take long for infection to start showing in my thigh. The wound felt hot, like some of the heat from Harlan's lantern had cooked into the flesh. I couldn't tell in the low light, but it looked a little red, too. Harlan bandaged my thigh, wrapping it in a wide strip of cloth, and sometime in the night it began to itch, sending up waves of discomfort. That would have been enough, but my mind was like an engine that wouldn't shut off. It kept going round and round, throwing up every uncomfortable scenario it could think of. Most of them involved Carver and Prakesh.

I think about them now, as we head into the forest, replaying my thoughts without really wanting to. My relationship with Prakesh was supposed to be simple. After everything we'd been through, it should have been enough. We had our little hab in Chengshi, and we had each other. I didn't need anything else.

But then I kissed Carver. And no matter how many times I tell myself that it was something I did in the heat of the moment, I know it isn't true. Even then, when we were trapped on the *Shinso* and I told Carver I was staying with Prakesh, I thought I was making the right choice. But it hurt him, badly, and it was only later that I realised that it hurt me, too. More than I care to admit.

What does that mean?

I know when I find them, I'll have to make that choice again. But what if the choice gets made for me? What if I get to Anchorage, somehow, and find that one is dead, and not the other? What am I going to do if they're both dead? I know I'll have to carry on, keep surviving, but it's like looking up at the sky, like trying to take in something bigger than I can imagine.

I bring myself back. The wound on my thigh isn't slowing me down—not yet, anyway—but I can't quite hold my balance on the uneven ground, and I keep having to use the trees to steady myself. Harlan slips between them, moving with an easy grace.

It's not long before I slip, my foot skidding on a patch of ice. I have to grab a branch to stop myself falling, the bark scraping my skin.

"Whoa," Harlan says, turning. He skips back up the slope, and puts his hands under my arms. "There we go," he says, pulling me upright.

"Thanks," I say. I feel strangely embarrassed, the blood rushing to my face. I want to tell him that I'm not used to the ground, that if we were on Outer Earth, with its flat metal surfaces, I'd be the fastest person he's ever met. No point. And I don't want to think about Outer Earth right now.

"Is it always this cold?" I say instead, shaking my hands. My fingers are still numb at the tips.

"Cold?" Harlan says over his shoulder. "This ain't cold. You wait until winter."

"Does it ever get warm?" I ask.

"It's not too bad in summer. We actually get a little green, if you can believe it. That's hunting season, though, so it means harder work. Hey, am I getting better at the conversation thing?"

I smile. "You're doing fine."

"Good to know, good to know. Good, good, good."

A few minutes later, we come across a pool of water, fed by a trickling stream running down from the mountain. I fill my water bottle, shivering as my hand touches the surface, then take a long drink.

"Don't fall in, whatever you do," Harlan says. "Water that cold, it'll shut your body down in minutes. Then we'll never get you to Whitehorse. The thing you did with that man's jacket was smart, by the way."

I blink at him, trying to follow the conversational path he's laid down. When I do it, I realise he's talking about how I tore Syria's jacket into strips, used it to mark my path while I tried to find water.

"Didn't work," I say. "I still got lost."

He taps his head. "Doesn't matter. You might not know how the outside works, but you think like someone who does. The tags, getting to the water, stuffing your clothes with leaves. All smart."

"It was cold."

"Exactly. And out here, cold'll kill you faster than almost anything. You gotta stay warm. Good clothing, good fire, good shelter. You remember that, and you'll be OK. Here, let me show you something."

Without waiting for me to answer, he strides off into the trees. He's heading back the way we came, but before I can tell him that he's going the wrong direction he comes out again, carrying something in his hand. It looks like a clump of hair, only it's a pale green, with much thicker strands. When he passes it to me, the underside is slightly sticky.

"Old man's beard, we call it," he says, wetting his hand in the water. "And the gunk underneath it is spruce sap. Best fire starters nature has, these two, even when they're not together. You get a spark, these'll kindle like anything."

"How do I start a fire?" I say, stuffing the sticky bundle of fibres into my jacket pocket.

But he's off again, skipping across the boulders that ring the pool. "Come on," he shouts. "Town ain't far. I know an old forest road we can use."

The road, when we get there, is wider than two of Outer Earth's corridors laid side by side. The surface is overgrown, covered in a skin of wet leaves, but it's easier going than the forest itself. The stunted trees hug the road from both sides. Here and there, some of them have fallen, their tilted trunks slick with moss. Despite their lack of a canopy, their shapes cut the sky down to a thin sliver above us, which is just as well. I still can't look at it without getting a little nauseous.

Harlan keeps stopping to point things out, and soon my pockets are full of strange plants with even stranger names: burdock, cattail, lady fern, and a tart berry Harlan calls lowbush cranberry. It's bright red, and so sour that I almost spit it out.

I want to tell Harlan to hurry—I don't know how long I have left. But if I'm going to survive down here—if *we*, as in Prakesh and Carver and I, are going to survive down here—then I'll need to know about plants like this. I can't depend on Harlan forever.

"Who exactly are these people?" I ask. I'm still turning over our conversation of last night, when he asked me to tell the people in Whitehorse that he kept me safe. I still don't know what that's all about, but maybe coming at it at an angle might get me some answers.

Harlan glances at me, as if weighing up how much I need to know. Eventually, he says, "I used to be with this group. We'd try and stay one step ahead of the Nomads, but every year we lost more people to 'em. It got harder and harder to convince ourselves to keep moving."

"Why were the Nomads chasing you?"

He shrugs. "Nomads don't have anything against us, specifically. They just take down anybody who isn't them, grab as much supplies as they can, and keep moving. Lot of different tribes around here, all with the same MO. And believe me, you don't want to run into them."

He goes silent for a minute. I'm about to prompt him, but then he says, "We found this old hospital in Whitehorse. Place had been abandoned for decades, but it had a basement you could seal off. Plenty of space, and plenty of visibility around it."

"And if the Nomads came?"

"If the Nomads were in the area, we could hunker down, wait them out. They never found us. Not once." He gives me a toothy grin. "We had food, we had power, we even cooked up a water—"

I'm walking with my head down, moving carefully over a boggy patch, when I nearly bump into Harlan. He's stopped dead in the middle of the road.

"Hey—" I say, but then my voice cuts off when I see what he's looking at.

There's a wolf in front of us, mouth closed, eyes bright. Its fur is dark, matted with dirt and leaves, and its ears are pricked straight up, as if it's scanning the forest around us. My eyes go wide as I realise that it's the wolf from the night before—the first one that attacked me.

"Don't move," Harlan says.

My first instinct is to run at the wolf, scare it off. I've come too far, been through too much, to get scared away by a single animal now. In the daylight, it looks scrawny and malnourished. I can see the bones of its ribcage through its dirt-caked fur.

I step forward, a shout forming on my lips, but Harlan whacks me in the chest with his arm.

"I said don't move," he says, enunciating each word.

I'm about to tell him to let me past, but then I see the others.

They're on both sides of the road, silent among the trees. Dozens of them, low to the ground. Some are no more than pups, but others are huge adults, with ears the size of my palms. All of them are thin, hungry-looking.

The smaller wolf opens its mouth, letting its tongue roll out. Saliva drips from huge, gently curved teeth, and it gives a long, low growl.

27

Okwembu

The boat scythes across the bay, winding its way around the submerged buildings. Every time they hit a wave, or when Iluk turns the rudder a little too sharply, Okwembu feels a lurch in the pit of her stomach. The top half of her body is freezing, drenched in sea spray.

The only place to sit is on the side of the boat, on the stiff rubber pontoons. Ray and Nessa sit on one side, their feet braced against the centre stanchion. Okwembu and the rest of them sit on the other. Prakesh Kumar is staring up at the buildings, and the low clouds beyond them. Clay looks shell-shocked, his eyes flicking between their captors. His fingers grip the short lengths of rope on the side of the boat that serve as handholds, holding them tight.

Aaron Carver is different. He looks as if he wants to reach across the boat, grab Ray by the neck and launch him into the surf. He doesn't dare. Nessa still has the rifle, and she's pointing it squarely at his chest.

Nobody's said a word since they took off from the beach. But as they come around one of the buildings, Iluk eases off the throttle a little, compensating for a sudden swell, and Carver speaks.

"I don't get it," he says, talking to Ray but keeping his eyes on Nessa's rifle.

"Get what?" Ray is jovial again, like they're out for a pleasure trip.

"The whole act. Like we were safe, like you were going to welcome us into your *society*." He spits out the last word, like it has a bad taste.

"You *are* welcome," Ray says. "So long as you can earn your keep." He knots his hands between his knees, leaning back slightly as the boat crests a rolling wave. "There are only two kinds of people. Those who can serve the Engine, and those who can't. Some people find it hard to accept their place. They need a little encouragement. But it's a lot easier if they come of their own free will."

Iluk accelerates, powering over a wave. A second later the throttle drops and Ray says, "Nessa jumped the gun a little, so to speak. You know, when your friend started getting antsy?"

Prakesh raises his head, the expression on his face just as murderous as Carver's.

There's a haze over the water, soft and damp. Their visibility drops to a few yards. Iluk slows the boat, the motor puttering. The last of the buildings passes by on their right: a black shape in the fog, torn and twisted. Okwembu looks over her shoulder, taking it in. At some point in the past, moss began to grow up the walls. It's blossomed over the years, turning the first three levels a dark, almost luminescent green.

Aaron's thigh is just touching Okwembu's, and she can feel it twitching. All his energy and anger is bottled up, kept in one place by Nessa's rifle. At some point—maybe in a few moments, maybe in a few minutes—he'll make a play, go for the gun. It's inevitable. And if he doesn't, Prakesh Kumar will. Neither of them can see past the current situation, see the need to do nothing until they know what they're dealing with. If Ray and Nessa had any intelligence, they'd shoot them and be done with it.

Should she say something? Try to calm him down? No. He wouldn't listen anyway.

But Prophet might.

Society. That's the word Ray used. And judging by what she's seen so far, from the vehicles and weapons and the radio message, this isn't a disorganised group. It's what she's been looking for: a community, a collective of people away from the insanity of Outer Earth. It's this, more than anything else, that keeps Janice Okwembu calm, that keeps her compliant. For now.

She felt a spark of worry when the woman, Nessa, attacked Prakesh. When these people, whoever they are, showed their real faces. But it hardly matters. *They* hardly matter. They're foot soldiers, advance scouts. Prophet, whoever he is, is where the real power lies. What can she offer him? Everybody has something they want, and if she can understand his she can survive this.

First, she will make herself indispensable. Then, she will make herself powerful.

Clay's shocked intake of breath rips her out of her thoughts, and she looks up.

It's as if there's a hole in the fog: a huge, looming, black void. Not a building. It's something much bigger, rising a hundred feet above the water's surface, curving inwards like a giant wave.

"Holy shit," Carver says. He actually scoots back a little, bumping into Okwembu. For a second, she has the crazy idea that they've hit the horizon—that this *thing* stretches hundreds, maybe thousands of miles. She tells herself not to be so stupid. She can see the metal surface now, see the openings in it. But this isn't a building. It's not part of Anchorage. They're out into the bay, which means—

A ship.

A distant memory jogs her. A history lesson from far in the past, their teacher talking about the war, about different armies ranged against one another. Their ancestors used these ships to transport fighter planes across oceans, between theatres of conflict. They were nuclear-powered mobile command centres, symbols of military might.

Ray is beaming. "Welcome to the USS *Ramona*," he says.

They turn, tracking alongside the aircraft carrier's hull. Awe overrides her fear. She never thought she'd see one, not in a million years. And yet, somehow, one of them is here, parked in the waters off Alaska. Okwembu sees the same moss that was on the buildings climbing up the curved metal, its tendrils burrowing into the seams between the plates. How long has this ship been here?

And right then Okwembu notices two things simultaneously.

Ray and Nessa are both looking up at the *Ramona*, their heads tilted back.

And Aaron Carver is looking at the rifle.

He moves before Okwembu can, exploding off the side of the boat. He wraps his hands around the rifle—one on the barrel, another halfway down the stock. Nessa comes alive instantly and the gun goes off.

But Carver's move knocks the barrel upwards, and the bullet passes over their heads. Clay screams, and Prakesh rockets to his feet. Only Okwembu stays seated, her heart hammering, as Carver wrestles Nessa for the gun. The boat rocks back and forth, threatening to upend them into the icy water.

Ray and Iluk react, trying to shove Carver away. But he's ferociously strong, and in the next instant he's got the gun away from Nessa. He smashes Nessa right in the chest with the butt of the gun. She grunts, tumbles over the side, splashing into the water.

Iluk reaches for Carver, but the tracer dodges back, out of range. He's up on the front of the little boat, his foot on the edge, and he brings the gun around, seating it against his stomach.

Okwembu doesn't dare move—he'll shoot her just as easily as he'd shoot the others, without a second thought. Nessa is splashing somewhere out of sight, trying to pull her way back into the boat.

"Aaron," Prakesh says. "Just—"

"OK," says Carver, almost shouting. "I have had it up to *here* with this *bullshit*. You and you—" he swivels the gun between Ray and Iluk. "In the water. Now."

But Ray is laughing. He's sniggering to himself, shaking his head, as if Carver has played a prank on him.

"Something funny?" Carver says, stepping off the prow, lifting the gun towards Ray's face.

Ray grins. "Look up, son."

Carver gives a laugh of his own. He jerks the gun at Nessa, who has somehow managed to get both arms over the edge of the boat. "Go for a swim. Take her with you."

Okwembu looks up, and smiles.

"Aaron," says Prakesh.

"You got three seconds," Carver says.

"*Aaron.*"

Finally, Carver looks up. Okwembu gets the sense that he intends it to be a quick glance, a little upward flick of the eyes, but when he sees what's above them he can't look away.

There's an opening in the side of the ship—huge and rectangular, lit from within by a yellow glow. There are faces in the opening. A dozen of them, men and women, as ragged as Ray is. Okwembu can just make out their military camouflage. Each of them is holding a rifle, just like Nessa's, and each rifle is pointed right at the boat.

Ray sniggers as Carver lowers his gun. "That's not even the best part."

He points at the edge of the deck, far above them. There's something else there—a large metal cylinder, tilted off the end of the deck. There's a long, black tube at right angles to the cylinder—a gun barrel, Okwembu realises. It's pointing right at them.

"See, even if they missed," Ray says, pointing at the faces in the opening, "Curtis wouldn't."

"Curtis?" Prakesh Kumar's voice sounds flat and featureless.

"Took us a hell of a long time to get the Phalanx gun up and running," Ray says conversationally, folding his arms. "But Curtis kept at it. That's his baby. Hardly ever leaves. He did a test-fire the other day, and he got off a thousand rounds in one pull of the trigger. He shoots now, and you'll be in heaven before you can spit."

"So will you," Carver says. Clay is quaking behind him.

"That may be. But I doubt Curtis'd hesitate. He's always been a little bit too...*enthusiastic*, if you get my meaning."

It's everything Okwembu can do not to yell at Carver. She doesn't dare. One wrong move and they'll be shot to pieces.

That's when the idea comes to her. It arrives fully formed, blazing hot. Her bargaining chip. The thing she can offer Prophet. It's right there, but if Aaron Carver doesn't see reason she'll never get a chance to act on it.

Ray puts out his hand, looking Carver in the eye. "Now give me the gun."

Iluk pulls Nessa out of the surf. She collapses in the boat, the centre of a pool of icy water, staring daggers at Carver. For a moment, he does nothing. Then his shoulders slump and he hands over the rifle.

"Good boy," Ray says.

28

Riley

"Harlan?" I say, keeping my voice low.

The wolf barks—a high-pitched, almost whining sound, then gives another long snarl. I can feel my heart beating hard enough to punch through my chest wall.

Harlan ignores me. His eyes are locked on the lead wolf. Slowly, he reaches into his jacket, hunting for something, never taking his eyes away from the wolf. The others are moving now, coming in from both directions, low to the ground. They're just as thin and undernourished as the lead wolf, but their teeth are knife-point sharp.

This must be the pack Harlan mentioned. I hear his words in my head: *Getting more aggressive every year.* I flick a glance at the rifle. With no bullets, it'll be next to useless—and even if it was loaded, there's no way we can shoot them all.

We have to get out of here. We have to run. I have no idea if we'll be able to outpace the wolves in a flat sprint, not if they're as fast as I remember, but we don't have a choice. There's no way we're taking out this many.

I look round. There's a gap in the closing circle of wolves, at my two o'clock. If Harlan and I run at the same time, we should be through it before they take us.

"All right," I say, my voice now barely above a whisper. "See the gap? We're going to go through it. Run as fast as—"

"Stay put," Harlan says. He's found whatever he was looking for, and is drawing it slowly out of his jacket. "Gotta face 'em head-on."

Adrenaline is starting to shoot through me, a thousand tiny blades dancing on my tongue. "Too many," I say, hissing it out the side of my mouth.

"Just *wait*," Harlan says.

The thing in Harlan's hand is a metal cylinder, bright orange, about three inches tall. There's writing on it, too scratched and faded to make out. A large black nozzle sits on the top of the can, made of dented plastic. As I watch, Harlan moves his thumb, flicking open a safety catch. The lead wolf growls.

Harlan slams his thumb down on the nozzle. A jet of fine mist shoots out of the can, dull orange in colour, curling and drifting across the ground. The moment it touches the wolves, they squeal in pain, pawing their faces, snorting, shaking their heads. I catch the scent of the spray and it makes me want to put my own arm over my face. It's like food that's been heavily spiced, then left out for days to rot.

Harlan sprays in quick bursts, targeting different groups of wolves. They all react to the spray, and one or two of them take off, hurrying back into the woods.

But not enough of them. Not nearly enough. And the spray is dissipating, vanishing in the cool air. Harlan's bursts are getting weaker—whatever propellant is in the can is being drained off with each hit.

"Come on now," says Harlan, as if pleading with the can to work. He gives it a vigorous shake. Something inside the can clacks as it swings back and forth.

"Harlan, if we don't run—"

"*Never* run," he says, as the remaining wolves circle around. "They'll chase you down like a damn dog. You can't outrun wolves."

"Yeah, but that stuff's not working."

The circle is getting tighter. A couple of the wolves are darting forwards and backwards, snapping their jaws. Everywhere I look, more of them are emerging from—

The trees.

There's a fallen one close to the side of the road, its trunk tilted at forty-five degrees. I follow the trunk—when it fell, it landed on one of the thick tree branches, which is still supporting its weight. That branch is about ten feet off the ground.

At that moment, the lead wolf attacks.

It moves with a languid grace, appallingly fast. I can see the muscles rippling under its fur, see its ears flatten against its head. But I'm moving, too, pulling Harlan with me. He's off balance, and the wolf flies past him on the left, jaws snapping at the air. It slams into the ground, spraying up clods of dirt, legs scrabbling for purchase.

I can feel the other wolves pounding the earth as we sprint towards the tree. One of them appears in front of me. Its head is turned sideways, jaws open wide. Its mouth is a gaping black hole, flecked with a stardust of saliva.

I swing my fist in an arc, smashing into the side of the wolf's head. It's like punching a wall, but it's just enough to knock the wolf away. Its jaws snap shut on open air.

I can still smell the spray from Harlan's canister. It's as if a red-hot poker is being jammed into the back of my throat. My eyes are streaming, itching like crazy. I have to fight to keep them open.

I jump, my feet landing squarely on the trunk. There's no time to look back, no time to check if Harlan's all right. I move up the trunk as fast as I can. It's too steep to rely on just my feet, so I use my hands, moving on all fours in an awkward crouch. My heart is hammering, urging me to hurry.

Harlan screams.

I look back. One of the wolves has him around the ankle, its jaw locked on his foot. It's twisting its head back and forth, as if trying to rip the leg clean off. Blood wells up around its teeth. Harlan is on his backside, pulling his way up the trunk, trying to kick at the side of the wolf's head with his other leg. The wolf barely notices his blows.

I lunge backwards, lifting my leg so it travels over Harlan's right shoulder. My foot slams squarely into the wolf's muzzle. It lets go of Harlan, yelping, and topples sideways off the trunk. Its claws scrape along the bark.

The move has left me off balance again. I manage to right myself just in time, breathing hard, focusing on the top of the trunk, which is resting cleanly on one of the thick tree branches.

I reach the top, climbing onto the branch and steadying myself against the trunk. I look down without meaning to, and it almost makes my heart stop. The ground is a snarling, biting, furious mass of teeth and fur.

"We have to keep going," Harlan says. His voice is ragged with effort.

But where? There are no other fallen trees around us, no convenient branches to clamber along. We're trapped.

Think, Riley, says the voice inside. *Find a way.*

My gaze snaps to one of the other trees. It's upright, but only just—its roots are sticking out of the soil, the trunk hanging on by threads. Its branches are thin and insubstantial, but there's a tree a short distance away that has thicker ones. I track the trees, mentally jumping from one to the other. There's no telling where this is going to take us. But it's the only choice we have.

It's an easy jump to the almost-uprooted tree—a few feet, no more. I've jumped wider gaps on Outer Earth. But I have to shut my eyes for a second, *will* myself to do it. I turn my head sideways as I hit, just in time to avoid breaking my nose. The impact knocks the tree out of alignment, and I can feel it tilting.

I'm slipping, so I tense my legs, locking myself to the trunk. Below me, the wolves are throwing themselves into a frenzy.

With a crunching, crackling sound, the tree topples over. I hang on tight as it slams into the one alongside it, crashing down onto the branch. The impact nearly knocks me off, but I manage to hang on, my legs still wrapped around the trunk. I scramble up it, heart hammering in my ears.

It's just as well I made the jump first. There's no way Harlan would have managed it if I hadn't knocked the tree over. Even then, it takes him twenty seconds to make the jump, psyching himself up for it. He almost doesn't make the landing, but then he gathers himself, scrambling up the trunk. The wolves try to follow, hauling themselves over the destroyed roots, but there are too many of them, and they're too frenzied with hunger—every time one of them gets close, another one tries to push past. Harlan's eyes are glazed with fear, and his boot is soaked in blood—I can't smell it, but it's a sure bet the wolves can.

There's another branch above me, to my left. I swing up onto it, making room for Harlan. The wolves aren't giving up. As I look down, I see that they've made it onto the fallen trunk. One of them is a few feet up, trying to dig its claws in, but it topples backwards, landing on two of its friends.

Stopping, even for a few seconds, drives the situation home.

We're moving away from the road, and we can't stay in the trees forever. But I feel elation, too. It worked. Wolves can't climb. As long as we stay up here, they can't get us. They can't—

I slip. I don't know whether it's a wet patch, or just bad balance. One second I'm crouched on top of the branch, and the next I'm falling. My fingers claw at the bark, hunting for a grip, and get nothing. The familiar, sickening feeling of gravity takes hold of me, and then I'm tumbling down towards the snapping wolves.

29

Riley

It's only at the very last second, right when my legs are about to leave the branch entirely, that I realise what I have to do.

My left leg is still in contact with the branch. I swing my right leg upwards, fighting against gravity, forcing my burning muscles to react.

My ankles slam together, locking me to the branch. I start swinging, upside down now, swinging back and forth. I look down, and a pair of jaws slams shut inches from my face. The wolf falls back to earth, vanishing in a sea of barking, growling fur.

Harlan is reaching down for me, his face contorted in pain. He grabs for my hand, misses, tries again. I'm swinging too wildly. I have to tighten my ankles on the branch, slow myself down. As I do so, I feel them slipping, inching away from each other.

I bend from the waist, my torso screaming at me. It's just enough. Harlan snags my fingers, then his other hand grabs my wrist. I can see the sweat standing out on his face.

But he's got me. He's pulling me up, around the side of the branch. Away from the pack.

He wrenches me upright, and I sit, my legs dangling on either side of the branch, breathing hard, trying not to let the panic take over. The branch itself is bending and creaking, threatening to break under our weight.

The wolves are milling around below us, growling and snapping at one another, as if arguing about what to do. I risk a look down, and several pairs of eyes meet my own, bright with hunger.

Harlan is talking, more to himself than me, his words coming fast. "That was much too close. Too close. Not like that time in Dawson when we had warning. Goddamn spray. It should have worked, it should have. Eric'd know what to do. He'd get us out of here."

My nose is running, and the stinging in my eyes has changed to a horrible, maddening itch. "We have to go," I say, forcing the words out.

Harlan is still muttering to himself. I swing round and look at him. "Hey. We can do this. All right?"

He looks up. He's trembling, although I don't know if it's exhaustion, or fear, or both, but I see him nod. Moving as slowly and as carefully as I can, I make my way across to the next branch. The wolves see the movement, snarling, grinding up against the trunk of the next tree. Some howl: a noise which feels like it's going to pierce my eardrums. They're frenzied at the thought of prey, nostrils flaring, teeth bared.

Harlan is slower than I am, but he's staying with me. We move higher into the trees, testing branches, contorting our bodies as we stretch between them. It's hard going: several of the branches are covered in slippery moss, and there are others that won't take our weight. Once or twice I place a foot on one, only to have it snap and fall, crashing down onto the pack. It feels like there are more of them, like they're calling their friends from all over to join them. There's no way to tell. Everything down there is teeth and fur and horrible, burning eyes.

Even as we make progress, I know we can't keep going like this. My arms are already burning with exhaustion, and Harlan looks like he's about to fall over.

I can see sky through the trees ahead of us, the grey clouds level with my eyeline. There must be a hill, with the forest sloping down it, away from us. We can deal with that. We just have to be careful.

Then I reach the edge of the forest, and a horrified moan escapes from my lips.

It's not a hill at all.

It's a cliff.

The trees run right up to the edge of it. I could take a few more steps out onto the branch I'm on, and have nothing below me but air. The cliff itself must be fifty feet high, formed of weather-beaten rock, grey and white. It extends a long way to our left and right, curving away from us, as if we're at the apex of an enormous circle. Here and there, plants cling to the surface, small branches thrusting outwards, like they're trying to escape.

The wolves reach the cliff. We've managed to get a little way ahead of them, and at first there are only three or four, growling, running in mad circles. But then the rest arrive, bunching up against the edge.

I don't see it happen, but, suddenly, one of the wolves is falling, legs kicking at nothing. It gives a puzzled bark, and then it smashes into a jutting part of the cliff. Its head detonates, gore exploding across the rock, and the pack's howling gets even louder.

Harlan is whimpering. "We have to go back," he says.

"What?"

"We can't go down there. We can't."

"We don't have a choice." I say it knowing full well that I have no idea how we're even going to get to the cliff, let alone down it.

I look at the wolves. The small one, the leader, is staring up at me. Every other wolf is in a mad rage, pacing and turning, but the leader is still. He's waiting. Calmly, patiently. He knows that sooner or later we'll need to come down.

I lean out over the edge and scan the cliff, looking for something, *anything*, that will help us.

I see it.

Then immediately wish I hadn't.

"Harlan, listen to me," I say. "We're going to have to jump."

"What?"

I have to force the words past my lips, because what I'm proposing is completely insane. "We grab hold of that," I say, pointing. There's a tree growing out of the cliff face, fifteen feet down, slightly to the right of us. It's got two branches, shooting out at right angles to the rock face, sprouting tufts of leaves. They're not nearly as thick as the branch we're standing on, and there's every chance that they'll snap the second we hit them. But it's our only shot.

Harlan has stopped talking. Now, he's just shaking his head rapidly, back and forth, hugging the tree even tighter.

I'm not going to convince him. I could stay up here forever, and never talk him down. I've seen panic before. If you try to take a panicked person somewhere, they won't just refuse to go—they'll fight you, desperate to stay where they are.

I have to show him.

The howls get louder, rippling up from below. I look down at the plant on the cliff. It seems impossibly far away. If I miscalculate this, if I'm off by even a foot...

No. Don't get scared. Stay angry. Stay focused.

I inhale once. Exhale. And jump.

30

Riley

Most times, when I'm airborne, things slow down. It's my body's own safety mechanism, the adrenaline working to make sure I survive whatever I'm trying to do.

Not this time. This time, things *speed up*.

Almost immediately, I can tell I'm moving way too fast. I've overcompensated, overshot the jump, and the only thing on the other side is open air.

The branch knocks the wind out of me. I hit it so hard that I keep moving, somersaulting over the top. I have just enough presence of mind to bring my hands down, wrap my fingers around the wood, and then everything goes upside down. I get a momentary look at Harlan, his mouth open, and then I'm hanging, swinging in the wind.

My swing goes too far, and one hand comes loose.

This time, everything *does* slow down.

One hand. Four fingers and a thumb. That's all I've got between me and a fifty-foot drop. I can feel the grip on my thumb sliding away as the swing pulls it around the branch.

But swings go both ways, and this one doesn't travel quite far enough to pull me off. As I come back, I throw my free hand up, grabbing hold of the branch again. Slowly, I come to a stop. When I look up, I see a dozen animal faces staring down at me, saliva dripping from open jaws. The wolves are barking, harrying each other, not sure what to do.

"Are you OK?" Harlan is shouting, over and over again, the words blending into one another. I don't answer—not yet. Instead, I move along the branch towards the cliff. It creaks and bends, but it feels like it will hold. Twigs jab at my cheek, spiky and intrusive. Now that I'm down here, the adrenaline has started to ebb, and an awful worry has replaced it. What if the rock is smooth? What if I can't find handholds?

But the rock is cracked and fissured, and there are more shrubs dotted here and there—none with long branches, but they should be enough. I move carefully, placing my feet first, positioning them on a convex piece of rock. Then I jam my fingers into one of the fissures, bending my body so that my legs can take the weight. At the back of my mind, fear is trying to grab hold, but I won't let it. Not this time. If I can climb a surface on Outer Earth, I can climb one down here.

"Riley! Help me!"

I look up. The wolves have forgotten about me. They've turned their attention to Harlan, crowding around the tree below him. He has to jump. It's the only way.

"It's OK!" I shout. It still hurts to speak, my throat stinging from whatever Harlan sprayed at the wolves. "It'll take your weight."

"I can't do it."

He's still in a panic. Not good. If I don't get him down here soon...

Impact

Leave him.

The voice speaks from nowhere, and this time it's so forceful that I can't ignore it. *Leave him. You can find Whitehorse on your own. He'll only slow you down.*

I actually feel my hand start to move, as if I'm about to make my way down the cliff. I clench it deep into the fissure, horrified.

I'm not leaving him. I won't do that. He's only here because of me—he might have offered to take me to Whitehorse, but I was the one who ran for the trees, the one who led us here. More than that: he's not physically equipped for this. I'm asking him to do something that even I found nearly impossible, and I've been a tracer for years. Wherever that horrible thought came from, I can't give in to it. I have to help him.

Going first wasn't enough—I'll have to talk him through it.

"It's closer than you think," I say. "I know you can make it."

Harlan moans.

"I'm going to move further out of the way." I slide along the cliff, hunting for a hold. "We're going to go on zero."

"Can't do it. Can't."

"Yes, you can. We're going to get down there, and then we're going to go to Whitehorse. You're going to get me there safe, and I'm going to tell them you were with me every step of the way."

I don't give him the chance to back out. I just start counting. "Three... two..."

Harlan jumps.

I'm looking at the branch, so I don't even see him do it. Suddenly there's this *scream*, and then a thud as he slams into the branches. He hits them exactly as I did, toppling head over heels. But he doesn't have my instincts, and he doesn't grab hold of the branch as he goes over.

I rip one hand out of the crack in the rock, lunging for him. My fingers grip the collar of his coat.

Then gravity takes over, and he nearly wrenches me off the cliff face.

He slams back into the rock, roaring with pain and fear. I grit my teeth, plant my feet, do everything I can to keep my other hand buried in the cliff. I can feel the skin tearing off my fingers.

Somehow, Harlan doesn't fall. He finds one hold, then two, then he's being supported by the cliff. My hand is clenched so tightly around his coat that it's an effort to actually let go.

"Still with me?" I say, trying to inject a little humour into my voice. I'd almost forgotten about the wolves, but they're howling and barking, furious at the loss of the kill.

Harlan grunts. It's good enough.

"I think we'll be OK," I say. "You need to go first, all right? Just take it slow. I'll be right behind you, I promise."

He stays frozen for a long moment, long enough to make me think I'm going to have to talk him into it again, but then he starts making his way down the cliff, inch by inch. I wait one breath, two, then I follow.

More than once, I get stuck, dead-ended in an area without any holds. I have to backtrack, climbing up the cliff, and somehow those are the worst parts, the times when I come closest to letting gravity take me. But soon we're thirty feet above the ground, then we're twenty. There are more shrubs now: scrubby, insubstantial things clinging to the rock. We grab them as close to the roots as we can, clenching them in our fists. At ten feet above the ground, I take my deepest breath yet, and drop.

I'm used to landing on hard surfaces, and the soft ground catches me off balance. I tuck into a roll, feeling dead leaves and frozen, clammy dirt under my hands. I come up onto my feet, gasping.

Harlan is just below where I was on the cliff. I consider telling him to jump, but he might not know how to land properly—he could crack an ankle, or worse. I direct him, pointing out the holds, talking him down until he's a foot above the forest floor.

We're in a large clearing, on the edge of another part of the forest. Huge boulders lie scattered across the ground, as if they fell from the cliff long ago. When I look up, the wolves have gone.

"Harlan," I say. "I am so, so sorry. It was the only thing I could think of, I…"

Harlan is making an odd sound. He's standing, hands on hips, gazing up at the cliff edge, and he's laughing. Actually laughing.

"You like that?" he shouts. "Try to mess with old Harlan, eh? That's what you get! Hope your stomachs are rumbling good and proper, you bastards. Can't catch old Harlan, not in a million years. That cliff goes for *miles* in each direction. You'll never find us."

He collapses in howls of laughter again. I take a few deep breaths, feeling my heartbeat get slower and slower.

"What was in that thing?" I say, when Harlan subsides. My tongue is dry and heavy in my mouth, and it's hard to speak.

"What thing?"

"The spray can. The stuff you used on the wolves."

"Oh, that?" A dark look crosses Harlan's face. He digs the canister out of his jacket, staring at it like it personally betrayed him. "Bear spray," he says. "Guess it doesn't work if there's more than one wolf, right?"

"*Bear* spray?"

"Should never have traded for it in the first place," Harlan says. "Goddamn useless piece of shit. Now, if I was younger, I'd go back and find the guy who traded it to me and bust his head in two." He raises his voice again, shouting at the clifftop. "Just like I'll do to the next mangy rat-eared *fleabag* that comes anywhere near me! You hear?"

He grins. "Come on," he says, the volume of his voice returning to normal. "Whitehorse ain't far."

He limps off, heading for the trees. I follow, the wound in my thigh throbbing like a broken tooth.

31

Okwembu

Okwembu is the last one up the ladder.

It's made of rope, frayed and salt-stained, and it's all she can do to persuade her exhausted muscles to hang on. A bitter wind slices through her clothing as she climbs.

There are plenty of faces above her when she reaches the top, but no hands help pull her over. She has to do it herself, crawling over the lip of the opening. It's only when she's on all fours, shivering, that rough hands find their way under her elbows. She is yanked upright, and the first thing she sees is a rifle barrel, pointed right into her face.

They're in a wide cavity in the side of the ship, with ridged metal walls. There are fluorescent bulbs in the low ceiling, just like Outer Earth, and only half of them appear to be working. The space goes deep into the ship—Okwembu can see passages branching off it, sealed with thick doors.

Her captors say nothing. There are around twenty of them, men and women. Most of them appear to be around her age, and they're all dressed in overalls with the same pattern of grey and blue splotches. Both their clothes and their faces speak of hard use, of long years spent fighting against the wind. Edges are frayed, knees torn, and their shoes are as mismatched as their weapons—rusted rifles that have seen endless repair jobs.

Carver, Prakesh and Clay are all being held at gunpoint, just like she is. Behind them, she can hear Ray grunting as he pulls himself over the top of the ladder.

That's when she sees the man at the back of the group.

He's around fifty, she guesses, and completely bald, his head gleaming under the lights. His right eye is gone, the lid sewn shut. The stitch job is clumsy, with dark lines criss-crossing his skin; it reminds Okwembu of a bad tattoo she once saw on Outer Earth. In this case, she's almost certain that nobody has ever told this man how ridiculous it makes him look. There's something about the way he carries himself—he's not tall, or muscular, but there's a set in his shoulders that speaks of power.

Okwembu waits until he looks at her, and smiles. "Hello, Prophet," she says.

A murmuring rumbles through the crowd at her words. She can feel Aaron Carver staring at her, his eyes drilling into the side of her head. Not that it matters—*he* no longer matters. None of them do.

Ray gets to his feet behind them. "We got 'em, Prophet. These're the only ones who survived the crash. Only ones we could find anyway. If we—"

Prophet starts laughing.

The sound is musical, the laugh genuine and throaty. It transforms his face completely, his mouth opening wide, the skin around his one good eye crinkling.

He strides towards them, still chuckling. "Welcome," he says. His voice is deep and resonant. He claps a hand on Carver's shoulder, gripping tight, then looks at each of them in turn. "You're safe now. Praise the Engine!"

He booms the last sentence to the roof, and every other fatigue-clad figure on the deck echoes him. Most of them pump their fists in the air, but Okwembu sees that a few of them look down at the floor, their words almost inaudible.

Ray clears his throat. "They came down in an escape pod. Right into Eklutna. Reckon we could go back up there, get a diver down to attach a tow rope, but—"

"Ray," Prophet says, drawing out the syllable. "We will take whatever the Engine sends us, and be grateful."

He glances at Okwembu when he says it. She stays silent, telling herself to wait.

Carver gives an exasperated sigh. "You know what?"

"Just—" says Prakesh.

"No." Carver raises his chin, looking right at Prophet. "I don't give the tiniest shit about your Engine, whatever the hell it is. Your guys brought us here *at gunpoint*, so don't give us this line about being safe."

"But you *are*." Prophet hasn't taken his hand off Carver's shoulder. "All the Engine asks is that you give of yourself before you can rise into its grace, and all of us here—" he looks around at his group "—have given everything we could."

Clay makes a break for it.

Okwembu doesn't see him do it. One moment he's being held firmly, and the next he's running, bolting towards the edge of the deck.

Prophet doesn't blink. He holds out his hand, and Nessa thrusts her rifle into it. In one fluid movement, Prophet seats it in his shoulder, aims down the scope with his good eye, and fires.

The gunshot is a thunderclap in the enclosed space. The bullet takes Clay in the middle of the back. He spins a full three-sixty, arms wheeling, then vanishes off the edge of the platform. A moment later, there's a heavy splash.

Carver goes crazy. He fights against the men holding him, managing to get his arm around a neck. One of the others steps forward, driving a fist into Carver's stomach, dropping him to his knees.

Ray brings his rifle around, aiming right for the centre of Carver's forehead. Okwembu tells herself to stay calm.

"No no no!" Prakesh says. "We'll do it. We'll do what you want."

Okwembu glances at him, surprised that he'd submit so easily. Then again, she doubts that Prakesh would let anyone else be killed—not after he himself was responsible for so much death.

Carver subsides, staring daggers at Prophet.

Prakesh is still talking. "We can help. I can grow you food, and Aaron here can fix anything. Just *don't shoot*."

The smile is back on Prophet's face—just as radiant, just as genuine. He passes Nessa her rifle, then clasps his hands behind his back.

"A wise decision, brother," he says.

He gives no signal, no nod or raised eyebrow, but their captors move instantly. They march Prakesh and Carver away, into the ship. One of them hauls open a door further down, spinning the huge valve set into the front. Their captives are hustled inside, and the door slams behind them, almost as loud as the gunshot that killed Clay.

"And what about you?" says Prophet, his calm grey eyes finding Okwembu. "Will you serve the Engine?"

"No," she says. "I won't."

Nessa grunts in annoyance, raising her gun. A sadness comes into Prophet's eyes.

"Your Engine is broken," Okwembu says. "And I'm going to help you fix it."

32

Anna

Anna comes to a halt just before the gallery, jogging to a stop in the corridor. She stands for a moment, hands on her knees, shoulders rising and falling as she waits out the stitch gnawing at her side.

The gallery is a giant, cavernous, echoing space, reaching all the way up the levels, criss-crossed by catwalks. Most sectors have two or three galleries, but Apex has just the one. It's in better repair than the others—or it was, before the fire. At least the lights in the ceiling above her actually work.

She hears a voice, and looks up. Alana Jordan strides across the gallery, moving away from her. Amazingly, her stomper jumpsuit is still immaculate, stretched tight across her shoulders. Her dark hair is pulled back in a ponytail, which flicks from side to side as she walks. There's a huge, black burn on the gallery floor, several feet wide. Surrounding it are puddles of dissipating foam. The air stinks of chemicals. Anna watches as Jordan skirts them, then she looks beyond her, to the escape pods.

There are twelve of them, behind large circular doors, each with a small window. Anna's too far away to see any details through them, but she can just make out the interior wall of the airlocks housing the pods.

Every sector has some—or had, anyway. They were next to useless. A design screw-up in the station's distant past meant that each sector didn't have even close to enough pods for the people inside it. You could get three people in them, four at a push, and they barely had enough fuel to make it out of the station's orbit. They were token, and everyone knew it.

Not that it stopped people from taking them—people who wanted out, who wouldn't listen to warnings about lack of fuel and maximum range. There are still stories about them: ghost pods, floating in the void, carrying nothing but skeletons and evil spirits. Apex is the only sector which still has all its pods. For most of the station's history, it's been guarded well enough that no one's actually managed to take them.

There are stompers around the pod doors. Of course there are. They lean against the wall, pacing the floor, looking bored and irritable. Their grey jumpsuits stand out against the gleaming white surfaces.

Anna knows why they're there—to keep people away from the pods, to deter anybody who wants to make a break for it. She counts seven of them, but it may as well be seven thousand. There have already been a few souls who have tried to get the hell out, coast away into the void. The stompers have shut them down.

She has to get a look in those pods.

Anna pulls her beanie off her head, rolling it in her hands. After the breach in the dock, the other stompers closed ranks, shutting Anna out. Alana Jordan was the worst: she'd been a stomper for her entire adult life, and didn't exactly like the idea of someone as young as Anna sticking around. Is there any way Jordan would still listen to her? But even as the thought occurs, Anna realises it's useless. The remaining stompers are a tight-knit group, determined to hold the station even if it's going down. She tries to get past them and they'll just laugh at her.

There's a burst of childish laughter. Three kids dart into view on the gallery floor, skipping around the puddles, giving the burn mark a wide berth. They can't be older than seven or eight, and it sounds like there are more of them, just out of sight.

She sees Jordan turn, hears her shout something at the kids. But it's a distracted shout, and she immediately turns back to her colleagues. One of them reaches the punchline of a joke, and the group collapses in laughter. Jordan laughs as well, but gestures at them to keep it down, casting a worried glance towards the playing children. *Must have been a nasty joke*, Anna thinks.

And then: *they don't mind the kids being there.*

Anna's eyes widen. Any adult who came near the pods would find themselves looking down a stinger barrel. But the kids aren't a threat.

There are at least ten of them, kicking a ball back and forth—a tatty thing made of rags that looks like it'll fall apart at any moment. Three of the kids are involved in another game of their own devising, one that involves a lot of running and shouting. Anna's looked after a few children before, keeping an eye on them while their parents get some sleep, but she doesn't recognise any of these kids.

And there's one standing apart from the others: a girl, younger than the rest, with dark hair that looks like it's been drawn in matt-black. She wears a faded red sweater, hanging down over her knees, and she's walking in a slow circle, lost in thought.

Anger almost overwhelms Anna. When the Earthers headed out for the *Shinso*, these kids were some of the ones left behind. They didn't deserve that. No one did.

"Hey," Anna says, trying to keep her voice quiet. Too quiet, as it turns out: the word is lost in the shouting from the ball game. Anna tries again, and this time the girl looks up.

Anna waves her over, glancing at the stompers, who are still clustered in a loose circle around Jordan.

The girl scrunches up her face, reluctant. Anna fights back frustration—she can't go out onto the gallery floor, not unless she wants the stompers to spot her.

After what seems like an age, the girl wanders over. "I'm not supposed to talk to people I don't know," she says, folding her arms.

Anna smiles. "Then why are you talking to me? Aren't you gonna get in trouble?" She sits down on the corridor floor, crossing her legs. Now she's looking up at the girl, instead of the other way round.

"You're weird," the girl says, scrunching her face up again. It's like she's seen an adult doing the expression, and is trying to copy it.

"Maybe I am," Anna says. "But you're kind of funny-looking yourself."

She regrets the words the instant that they're out of her mouth. But the girl just giggles, her eyes bright.

"What's your name?" Anna says.

"Ivy."

Anna tries to keep her face neutral. Because, right then, she recognises Ivy. When she, Riley and Carver got taken captive by the Earthers, Riley used Ivy as a hostage so they could escape. She held a knife to the little girl's throat. Anna can only hope that Ivy doesn't remember that she was there.

"I'm Anna," she says, leaning forward and resting her elbows on her knees. "Can I tell you a secret?"

Another face-scrunch. "You don't have to treat me like a little kid, you know. I'm almost six."

Anna exhales. "Right. Sorry."

Someone from the ball game shouts Ivy's name. "I have to go," she says, turning back, about to skip away to join them.

"Wait," Anna says, a little too loudly. She drops her voice. "Can you do something for me?"

Ivy looks over her shoulder. "I'm not supposed to talk to—"

"—people you don't know. Right. But it's nothing big. You don't even have to leave the gallery."

"What do you want me to do?"

"See those doors? Over on the other wall?"

Ivy looks. "Mm-hmm."

"Do you think you can look in the windows for me? I want to know how many space suits are inside each one." She thinks back to what she knows about escape pods. "They should be strapped into lockers on the wall. Each locker has a little window in it, so you should be able to see inside them."

"Why?" Ivy says.

"Why what?"

"Why do you wanna know about the space suits?"

"I just do, OK?"

Ivy folds her arms. "If you don't tell me, I'm going to go and tell Mrs. Alana that you're here, and she'll come and throw you in jail."

"All right, all right," Anna says. She gets up from her sitting position, squatting on her haunches, beckoning Ivy closer. "I think there's something bad going on."

Ivy's eyes light up. "Bad?"

"Real bad. And I think the space suits have something to do

with it. I can't count them, because Mrs. Alana will chase me away." She looks Ivy in the eyes. "Can you do that for me?"

"No," says Ivy, shaking her head. Anna's heart sinks.

But then Ivy points to the ball game, to a particularly tall boy of about eleven or twelve, wearing a dirty blue pair of overalls. "I can't see in the windows. Marcus can."

She waves him over. Three or four children trail behind him, like a council member's entourage. Up close, Marcus is even taller than he first appeared—certainly taller than Anna, with scraggly black hair and a wide nose. The first bumps of acne are beginning to spread across his cheeks. He reminds Anna of Kev, one of Riley's tracer friends who became a stomper, too. Kev, who died when a bomb that had been planted in him—

She makes herself stop, shuts that line of thought down quick.

Anna expects him to be suspicious, but as she tells him what she wants them to do a grin spreads across his face. He starts nodding even before she's finished, rocking on the balls of his feet. His excitement is infectious, spreading to the other kids. Anna has to shush them, glancing towards the stompers at the other end of the gallery. "But you have to be careful," she says. "They can't know I'm here, or that I asked you to take a look."

"I don't like it," says one of the other boys. He has the hood of his sweatshirt up, and a froth of red hair dances under the edge of it. "We could get in trouble."

"Not if we're careful," Marcus says, echoing Anna's words.

He lifts the rag ball away from one of the other kids, tosses it back and forth in his enormous hands. Then he turns on his heel, draws back his foot and kicks the ball. It lofts across the gallery, its shadow moving along the floor, and lands squarely in the middle of the group of stompers.

Anna squashes back against the wall of the corridor as the kids barrel back into the gallery, shouting and laughing. A couple of the stompers look irritated, but the others are smiling. One of them taps the ball with his foot, sending it back towards the approaching Marcus.

In less than a minute, the kids have almost all the stompers involved in the game. Even Alana Jordan is taking part, nudging the ball with her enormous feet. Ivy takes it on the run, knocking it ahead of her, darting around another stomper as if he wasn't even there.

Anna can't help smiling. Somewhere along the way, she'd convinced herself that it wasn't going to work. That the kids would ignore her, or, worse, that they'd tell the stompers about her. But it's like Ivy said: they aren't little kids any more. Not really. They all know what's happening to Outer Earth, they're all scared, all looking for something to take their minds off the situation.

Marcus has moved away from the game. He walks casually over to the first bay door, looking over his shoulder. When he sees that the stompers are still kicking the ball around, he stands on his tiptoes and looks into the window.

Anna sinks back against the wall, looking up at the ceiling. *He's going to see three space suits in each one*, she thinks. *They're all there. You got it wrong.*

An angry shout from the gallery brings her back. She tilts her head, angling it around the corner of the passage.

What she sees nearly stops her heart.

One of the stompers has seen Marcus looking in the bay door windows. He has the kid by the front of his overalls, yelling in his face. The game stops abruptly, Ivy skidding to a halt with the ball balanced under one foot.

Anna tells herself to run. Marcus will give her up in a second, and she doesn't want to be anywhere near here when that happens. But she won't leave him. If that stomper hurts the boy, Anna tells herself, she'll tear him in half. She stays rooted to the spot, hand frozen on the wall.

The other stompers have surrounded Marcus, arms folded, all their good humour gone. Jordan is talking now, jabbing a finger in the boy's face. The stomper holding him gives him a shake. Ivy runs right at them, but the other kids hold her back, grabbing her by the hem of her enormous red sweater.

But Marcus is talking, gesturing wildly. She can't hear what he's saying, but Jordan and the stompers are listening close. The other kids are all trying to talk at once.

After a minute, the stomper lets him go.

Anna's shoulders are shaking. Before, she could hardly move, but now it takes everything she has to stay put. She wants to rush out there, drive an elbow or a knee into someone's throat, show them what happens when they threaten kids.

The game resumes—slower than before, but still enthusiastic. And Anna can't believe her eyes: Marcus is continuing to look into the bay door windows. The stomper who accosted him stays close, and he doesn't look happy at all, but he lets Marcus do his thing.

After he looks in the last one, Marcus gives the stomper a friendly wave, then returns to the game. Ivy still has the ball, kicking it up into the air now, again and again, daring someone to come and take it from her.

Ten minutes later, the game finally ends. The stompers call time—they're out of breath, standing with their hands on their knees, shoulders rising and falling. The kids take off, laughing, knocking the ball in front of them.

When Marcus and Ivy and the rest of them enter the passage, Anna is waiting, sitting against the wall. *This is it,* she thinks. If everything is still where it should be, she'll forget this insanity. She'll get her matt-black, and finish her drawing.

Marcus comes to a stop in front of her. "You OK?" Anna says. "What happened?"

He says something, but it's in a hoarse stage whisper, as if there are listening devices embedded in the walls.

"What?" Anna says, leaning in close.

"Told 'em I had a bet with a big kid," he says, grinning. "That I could touch all the pod windows without getting caught. They let me."

Anna returns the smile, more relieved than she cares to admit. "OK. What did you see?"

"There's a suit missing," Marcus says, still in that ridiculous whisper. "In one of the pods on the end. There's only two suits in the locker."

Anna sits back against the wall.

"What does it mean?" says Ivy. Her eyes are huge.

"It means," Anna says, "that we're in big trouble."

33

Prakesh

The passages are narrow—so narrow that they have to walk in single file, the struts on the walls brushing their shoulders. The stairs are the worst, steep enough almost to be ladders. The sound of their footsteps is dulled, buried by other noises.

He tries to keep track of where they're going. But exhaustion and cold prick at his mind, dulling his thoughts as they descend deeper into the ship.

He's furious at himself. He should have seen this coming. If it hadn't been for the storm and the need to get to safety, he would have. He's even more furious at the Earthers. How could they have thought things were OK down here? How could they have been so unprepared?

Without wanting to, he thinks of Outer Earth, of Riley and his parents, of his hab and his office in the Air Lab. *We should have stayed there,* he thinks. *We should have tried harder to stop the Earthers from leaving.*

Carver is still reeling from the blow to his stomach, and has to stop more than once. The second time, it's to throw up. He hunches over, hands on his knees, vomiting a thin, watery gruel.

The corridor explodes with cruel laughter. "First time anybody's ever thrown up *before* they start serving the Engine," one of the men says. He's younger than the rest, with a chin almost clear of stubble.

Another, a giant with a hooked nose, says something in a language Prakesh can't understand.

The first one laughs again. "Keep walking."

Carver puts a hand on Prakesh's shoulder, uses it to pull himself upright. He wipes his mouth, tracking thin strands of slime across his skin. It reminds Prakesh of Resin, and *that* reminds him of his part in creating it. He closes his eyes, tells himself to breathe. If they can just stay alive…

"Hey! I said, keep walking."

A few minutes later, the corridor opens up. The room they duck into is as big as the entrance platform, with a low ceiling that gives it an oddly squashed look. It's a mess hall—there's the kitchen off to the right, separated from the room by a large window. The sinks and countertops are rusted, pitted with disuse.

There are no tables or chairs in the main area. Just a group of people, around thirty of them, sitting cross-legged on the floor. Carver sucks in a breath behind him, and Prakesh can understand why. The men and women on the floor are skeletons, thin skin stretched over collarbones and hollow cheeks. They're all sitting in silence, spooning gruel into their mouths from battered bowls. Their overalls—rags, really—hang off their bodies in shreds of brown and black.

They aren't alone. Four people in camo, two men and two women, lean against the walls. One of them looks over at Prakesh, appraising him, and the expression on her face turns his stomach to lead. She has a rifle, as do the others, and wears a thick brown jacket over her overalls, its furry hood pulled up.

Prakesh and Carver are shoved forward, hands on their shoulders pushing them to the floor. No one looks at them. The captives just keep eating, moving like robots, spoon to mouth to bowl to mouth.

The woman smiles, icy and sharp. "New recruits," she says, sarcasm edging her voice. "Engine be praised."

She stalks off to the kitchen, returning with two battered tin bowls. Spoons stick out of them, held in place by the thick contents. She shoves the bowls into their hands. "Eat," she says. "You've got five minutes."

Prakesh wants to throw it back in her face. The meal is nothing more than disgusting slop: warm and slimy, with a thick skin on its surface. But he hasn't eaten in a day, maybe more, and his hunger overwhelms him.

He takes a mouthful and wishes he hadn't. The liquid coats his tongue, tasting and smelling of nothing at all. He chokes it down, aware that he needs to keep his strength up. Carver is doing the same next to him, breaking off occasionally to breathe in hard through his nose, trying to keep it down.

As they eat, Prakesh looks around surreptitiously at the others. None of them are speaking—they're just slurping back the soup, even tilting their bowls to catch the last drops. Heads stay down, eyes locked to the floor.

They're workers.

Whatever this ship is, whatever the Engine is, these people (*and us*, he realises with a shudder) are the ones who work to keep it going. Prophet and his followers take whatever supplies are brought in, then put their previous owners to work.

He screws up his eyes, driving the heel of a hand into his face. Then he takes a deep breath, and swallows another mouthful. What else is there to do?

The guards who brought them in have left, and the ones that remain in the room look bored, their rifles held at ease. Prakesh is looking around, chewing as fast as he can to get the sludge down his throat, when one of the other workers catches his eye. He's young, barely out of his teens. His face is freckled, and he's just beginning to get some fuzzy stubble on his upper lip.

He holds Prakesh's eye for a second, then looks away. It's the first time any of the prisoners has even acknowledged their presence.

"All right!" the woman with the hood shouts, snapping Prakesh out of his thoughts. "Chow time's over."

Prakesh and Carver don't react fast enough. The prisoners spring to their feet. As one, they march to the window leading to the kitchen and deposit their bowls on the surface. One of them stays behind, stacking the bowls, while the others line up along the wall. None of them raise their eyes from the floor.

"You!"

It comes from the guard, the one who'd joked about Carver throwing up. He's pointing a stubby finger at Carver. It's only then that Prakesh realises they're standing alone in the middle of the room, still holding their bowls. The boy with the freckles glances up at him from his place by the wall, then looks back down.

"We're going," Carver says, and starts to walk towards the kitchen.

He's stopped by a shout from the guard. "Did I say you could move?" The man's voice is contemptuous, almost teasing.

We shouldn't be here, Prakesh thinks, and at that moment real panic crashes over him. He should be with Riley right now. The thought of living here, of *dying* here, without ever knowing what happened to her, is almost too much to take.

Carver doesn't turn around, doesn't look at the guard until the man puts a hand on his shoulder. Then, in one movement, he spins around and throws the bowl into the man's face.

The slime splatters the wall, blobs of it sliding down the paint. The other guards react instantly. Prakesh is shoved out of the way and Carver is pushed to the floor, held there, a boot on the back of his head.

It's as if Prakesh is watching something unfold on a tab screen. No—it's worse. You can shut off a tab screen, put it away. This is like he's in a bad dream, hurtling along at full speed, powerless to stop it. He tries to form words, but his throat is locked up tight.

Carver disappears in a storm of bodies, roaring in pain. Some of the guards are using fists and feet, while others are swinging their rifles like clubs.

Prakesh makes himself move. He grabs the guard's shoulders, tries to pull him off, but it's like trying to shift a mountain. The guard shoves him backwards, and Prakesh crashes to the ground.

He gets one last look at Carver, curled up on the ground as kicks and punches rain down on him. *They're going to kill him*, he thinks. The thought is clear as a bell, perfectly formed.

Then someone is pulling him upright. He tries to shove them off, but it's the boy, the one with the freckles, and he holds on tight.

"D-d-don't," the boy says, so softly it's almost inaudible.

He pulls Prakesh out of the room, Carver's cries growing fainter behind him.

34

Riley

Harlan's torch barely makes a dent in the darkness. It's nothing more than a rag on a stick, soaked in oil and set alight. The chill wind threatens to snuff it out at any moment.

We've been out of the forest for an hour now, walking on what Harlan calls the Old Alaskan Highway. The surface is black and hard, unusually smooth. Some sections of it are split, plants pushing up through the cracks. It reminds me of the cliff we just climbed down.

My thigh has got worse. Not just a little worse. A lot. The pain is constant now, radiating upwards in long, sluggish waves. It's hard to pinpoint its exact location. I don't know how fast infection spreads, but the shards of metal still buried inside me are almost certainly speeding things along. My fingers keep straying to the cut. Even under a layer of bandage, touching it raises the pain another notch. The flesh is swollen, tight under the fabric of my pants, and the burning itch is almost unbearable.

And it's not just my leg. My head has started to ache, pain pulsing slowly but insistently at the base of my skull. Despite the cold, I can feel myself starting to sweat. *Fever.* Even I know it's the sign of a growing infection. If these people aren't where Harlan says they are, or if they're not willing to help...

Several times I catch myself breaking into a jog, and have to tell myself to drop back. I don't know the way, and Harlan won't be able to keep up with me. He's limping, his ankle swollen from the wolf bite. My own, from the night before, seems to be OK—a couple of tiny cuts, nothing more. Compared to my thigh, it's barely worth noticing.

But it does occur to me that Harlan needs to get his own wound treated. We haven't spoken much since we left the forest, and I still can't shake the guilt of having put him in danger. But he volunteered to take me, and we can't be too far now.

A building looms up out of the gloom: a squat, single-storey box, lurking on the edge of the highway.

"Edge of town," says Harlan. They're the first words he's spoken in an hour.

"How far?" I say, doing the best I can to keep the fear out of my voice.

Harlan shrugs. "Judging by the house we passed? Maybe one or two miles. Could be wrong, though—this damn fog confuses me, you know? There was this one time, I was up by the Black Rapids, tracking that deer, and got lost for—"

I interrupt him. "Tell me about these people. The ones we're going to see."

"They're just people, like me."

I take a deep breath. No point in snapping at him. "How do you know them?"

"Ran with 'em for a time. Folks tend to stick together. Gives you a better chance out here. We came up from—"

He stops.

"From?" I say.

He shakes his head, a black figure cut out of the darkness by the torchlight. "Doesn't matter. Just remember what you gotta tell 'em. Then we'll be even, you and me."

I'm about to press it, ask him why he left these people, why he wants me to tell them that he kept me safe. But then I hear the voice in my head, the one that whispered to me to leave Harlan to die. It's been silent since the wolves attacked, but now it's strident, *angry,* as if there's an actual person behind the words. *He's not telling you because he's going to hurt you. There's something he doesn't want you to know about. What is it, Riley? What's in the dark?*

"No," I say to myself, shaking my head, like I'm trying to dislodge something.

"You say something?" Harlan says.

In answer, I stride past him, moving on ahead, aware that I don't know the way but needing the movement, needing the rhythm to calm my mind. Whatever he's done, whatever his relationship is with these people, it doesn't matter. I don't have a choice. I find these people, or I die. I try to ignore my headache, which feels like it's getting worse with every step.

More buildings appear, most of them set back from the road. Like the first, they're only one storey. Some of them have dishes and antennas on their roofs. They look like alien artefacts.

At one point, we cross under a structure, built over the road's surface, fifteen feet off the ground. It's only when Harlan plays his light over it that I see it's an old sign. There are three slabs of dark green metal, each with writing on them. HAMILTON BLVD. ALASKA HWY. WHITEHORSE CITY CENTRE. There's a gap between ALASKA HWY and WHITEHORSE CITY CENTRE, like a missing tooth.

Underneath the sign, there's the oddest thing. It's a big machine of some kind, right in the middle of the road. It's only when I get closer and spot the wheels that I realise it's a vehicle.

It's like Carver's Boneshaker, only much bigger, with a closed-in cockpit and a box-shaped back end. The metal surface is rusted, the tyres long since rotted away. Harlan pays it no attention, but as he passes its front end he runs a hand along the metal, tracing the curve, a small smile on his face. It's a strange gesture, but before I can ask him about it he's walking off into the darkness.

The road begins to slope downwards, off to the left. The buildings get bigger, with larger windows and double doors. The glass in the windows is mostly gone, smashed to pieces, and some of the buildings are in ruins—missing a wall, missing a roof, sometimes no more than a few broken pillars. There are more vehicles on the road, hulking and silent.

As we walk, I hear a very soft sound, a tiny *clunk*. Off to our right, behind one of the buildings. I stop, listening hard. The sound doesn't come again.

"Harlan," I say. "You hear that?"

"What?"

The town is completely still. I shake my head. "Nothing."

Whatever it was, we don't have time to investigate. We keep walking, heading further into town, but with each step I feel like someone is watching me. Several times I look round, thinking I'll catch a shadow moving between the buildings. But there's nothing.

I feel like it's just my imagination, but then I realise that I'm getting used to the darkness—either that or the buildings are reflecting a little light, amplifying it. I can see further down the road, and I can even make out another sign alongside it. The sign reads TWO MILE ROAD.

"Not long now," Harlan says. "Almost at the river."

A few minutes later, we hit the river itself. I'm expecting a massive body of water, but what I'm not expecting is that it's choked with objects. Barrels, pieces of wood, floating structures that looked like waterborne versions of the buildings we've been passing. And there are things in the river that look a little like the vehicles on the road, only without wheels.

Boats. That's what they are. For the first time in what feels like forever, I actually smile. Back when I ran with the Devil Dancers on Outer Earth, we had one book: *Treasure Island*. We'd all read it a dozen times, burying ourselves in stories about giant ships crossing the Spanish Main, on the hunt for—

The smile drops off my face. That book is long gone. So are the Devil Dancers. There's just me, and if I don't focus, I'll be gone, too.

We cross a bridge over the river. Parts of it are gone, gaping holes in the surface, and we have to be careful as we walk around them. I manage better than Harlan, moving on the balls of my feet.

As I make my way across, I see a particularly strange boat, one I didn't notice before. It's a white, enclosed cylinder, with a cockpit up front. The cylinder is supported by two smaller ones, bobbing on the surface of the water. Along the sides of the cylinder, near the top, the metal is torn, as if something was ripped off it.

There's a light reflected in the cylinder's surface.

It's there and then it's gone—one second, no more. At first, I think it's Harlan's torch, but it was too steady, nothing like the flickering flames. What I saw is the reflection of an electric light.

Harlan saw it, too. When he turns to me, his eyes are bright. "They're still there. They didn't leave!"

I don't get a chance to answer. Harlan starts jogging, heading up the road towards the light. "Come on," he shouts over his shoulder.

The road curves sharply, and there's more forest on my right—we must be at the other edge of town. And then I see the building, bigger than any we've come across before, fat and boxy. There's a sign on the side of the road: WHITEHORSE CITY HOSPITAL.

Our path opens up onto a wider apron in front of the building, strewn with abandoned cars. My eyes have adjusted to the dark now, and I can see the double doors set into the front of the building.

Harlan slows down as we reach the doors. He's bent over, wheezing, but as I come to a stop alongside him he flashes me a huge smile.

"They're really here," he says. His accent has grown thicker, spurred on by his excitement. He pushes open the door. "We'll get inside, we'll sit down with 'em, and then they can take those things out of your leg. Then you tell 'em—tell 'em how Harlan saw you right. Tell 'em how—"

His words are cut off as a bullet blows a chunk of concrete out of the floor.

35

Okwembu

"Leave us," says Prophet.

The two guards glance at each other, then obey, quietly slipping out of the door and closing it behind them.

Okwembu doesn't know where they are in the ship. Every corridor looks the same, every stairway identical. She thinks they're somewhere high up, possibly near the deck, but there's no way to tell for sure.

The room they're in is a hab—or what passes for one here, anyway. There's a single cot, the creases in its bedding razor-sharp. A folding chair. A table, clear of everything except a battered plastic bottle of water. There are no windows, no decoration of any kind. The only light comes from a bulb in the ceiling, hidden behind a wire grill.

Prophet perches on the edge of the table, arms folded, looking at her expectantly. Okwembu says nothing. She knows that one wrong word will get her sent to wherever Prakesh Kumar and Aaron Carver have gone, so she waits for him to make the first move.

Eventually, Prophet does. "So who are you?" he says.

"My name is Janice Okwembu. I was, until quite recently, head of the council on Outer Earth."

If he's surprised, he gives no sign. "And how, exactly, did you come into the service of the Engine?"

"That's not what you're really interested in."

Okwembu looks around her. "This ship," she says, "was probably built at the same time as my station. They both run off the same type of power source: a fusion reactor, yes? Devices like that were saved for the biggest structures and military units."

She stops, raises her eyes to find Prophet's remaining one. "But yours isn't working."

Prophet smirks. "Oh?"

Okwembu starts walking, slowly making her way around the room, trailing a hand along the wall. "You're broadcasting a radio message in an attempt to gather supplies from travellers seeking sanctuary. Your colleague, Ray—one of the first things he asked about was whether any fuel had survived the crash."

"We have vehicles. Boats. The humvee. They need fuel."

Okwembu raises her finger, turning it this way and that. There's a little dust on the tip, and she rubs it away with her thumb.

"Boats can be propelled without using the motor. And your Humvee is a luxury, not a necessity. You have everything you need right here." She pauses. "Including, I assume, a steady stream of workers and supplies, thanks to that radio message."

Prophet gives a good-natured shrug. "The Engine provides for its people. We just try to save as many as we can."

"You need the fuel to run your ship. You need it to power your lights and your water purification systems. But why? After all, you have a perfectly good fusion reactor sitting right here, don't you?"

She pulls the chair out from behind the table and sits down on it, crossing her legs. Without asking for permission, she picks up the bottle of water and twists off the cap. It's tangy with purification chemicals, but it quenches her thirst.

"Your Engine is broken," she says. "Or, at least, it isn't functioning as it should do. It doesn't matter what you believe, or what you worship. Belief doesn't fix a broken machine. I think your men know that."

Prophet stiffens. Okwembu stops, wondering if she's gone too far. Belief can be a dangerous thing—people will question what's right in front of them, but swear that something invisible exists. What if she—

But then Prophet smiles. And for the first time, Okwembu sees past the mask he wears. What's underneath it is as cold as the forest wind.

"And you have a spare fusion reactor, do you?" he says. "Hidden somewhere?"

"No," Okwembu says, putting the bottle back on the table. "But I know how to fix yours."

With that, she reaches into the neck of her shirt and pulls out the data stick.

She holds it up, letting Prophet get a good look at it. Then she bends forward, removing the lanyard from around her neck, and places it on the table between them.

Prophet says nothing.

Okwembu nods to the stick. "The ship we used to enter Earth's atmosphere was an asteroid catcher. Back on Outer Earth, the asteroid would have provided us with resources, but in this case we used it as a heat shield. We spent a week in orbit, while some of the crew shaped the rock for re-entry."

Prophet picks up the data stick, resting it in his palm.

"I spent that week on that ship's bridge," Okwembu says, "downloading everything I could from the ship's computer. The operating system was ancient, but I managed to get it all into a useable form."

"Data," says Prophet, not asking a question. It's as if he's trying the word out, rolling it around in his mouth. "What kind of data?"

Okwembu shrugs. "Water filtration specs, data on plant growth, maps. Things I thought might conceivably be useful on a planet we knew nothing about." She takes another sip of water. "As I said, I took as much I could. I didn't have time to sort through what I had, and since the stick had more than enough space, I decided I didn't have to. So there's information on the ship's fusion reactor. Specifications, repair protocols, parts listings, emergency procedures. This stick contains everything you need to put a broken reactor back together."

"And yet," says Prophet, deadly quiet, "you offer it in place of yourself. Like you're above serving the Engine. People have died here for much less than what you've just done."

Okwembu has gambled a good deal in these last few minutes. She hates having to do it, hates the uncertainty, but knows that it's the only choice she has. There is a society here, a stable one, with structure and order and control. There are hierarchies, chains of command. There are workers—she saw one of them, back bent, mopping the floor as they passed what looked like a mess. There is water, and there is power. Everything she needs. She could integrate herself into the *Ramona*'s society, gather allies, make it her own.

And all she needs to do that is a little time.

"You can't afford to kill me," she says.

"No?"

"No." She folds her arms. "The computers on this ship are over a century old. I'm the only person here—maybe the only person *alive*—who can get the data off that stick in a useable form. You let me stay, you let me join your…*faith*, I suppose is the word. I download the data for you, and you get your reactor back. No more depending on fuel."

"We could torture you," he says, the grey eye never wavering.

"But you won't. You've done it before, and we both know that it never quite works. Isn't it simpler just to make the trade I'm proposing?"

She gets to her feet, steps closer to him. "You need me, Prophet. The data is there, and I'll get it for you. You just have to trust me."

He looks at her, as if sizing her up. She smiles back at him, serene. He'll do as she asks, because he's like her. He knows how to get on top, and stay there. He's created a society out of nothing—stable, controlled, self-sustaining.

There are only a few people with the will to do that. And they're very good at recognising each other.

Without another word, Prophet turns and strides to the door, flinging it open. He looks over his shoulder at her, and as she looks back into that lone grey eye, she has another unwelcome flicker of doubt.

"Come with me," Prophet says. "I want to show you something."

36

Riley

Harlan leaps backwards, yelping. His torch goes flying, extinguishing itself as it bounces across the floor.

My eyes aren't used to the darkness, and I can't see a thing. I think about running—either sprinting forwards, shoulders down, making myself harder to hit, or back through the door, putting a wall between myself and the shooter.

Before I can decide, Harlan cries out. "Wait! Don't shoot! Eric, don't shoot. It's me."

Silence.

I hear Harlan take another step forward. My eyes have adjusted now, and I can see him, a shape in the darkness. "Listen to me, there's—"

A second gunshot rings out. Harlan falls to his knees.

I'm almost certain he's been hit, the thought striking me like an iron bar. But he just lost his balance. I can hear him breathing, ragged and heavy.

There's a snap, then a hiss. A burning white light appears at the back of the room, spewing thick smoke. A flare of some kind. Tears prickle at my eyes as they adjust a second time, and I hold a hand up to my eyes. I can see people, silhouetted by the light, but it takes me a minute to see their faces.

Amira is standing in front of me.

I blink, startled, on the verge of saying her name. But it isn't Amira. It can't be. Amira's dead.

Then I get a better look at the figure. It's a man, not a woman. He's tall—six five, six six, easy. His dark hair is tied back in a ponytail, and his face could be carved from rock. It's lined and weathered, the mouth set in a thin, jagged line. He wears grey pants and a dark shirt under a knee-length coat, and he's carrying a gun—a black rifle, chunky and angular. The coat as battered as his skin; on the breast, I can just make out a logo: a bird in a golden circle, with the words ROYAL CANADIAN AIRFORCE stitched beneath it.

He has the oddest thing around his neck—a necklace, a piece of cord with something white and curved hanging off it. A tooth, as long as my little finger.

Eric doesn't move. He's looking at Harlan, and there's no mistaking the expression on his face.

"You," he says. "You'd better have a good reason for coming back here."

Harlan is smiling, getting up off the floor, glancing at me as he does so. "Oh, I do, believe me. It's good to see you again, Eric, it really is. Can we talk? I—"

"Who's she?" Eric says, jerking his head at me.

I'm about to speak, to tell them about the wound in my thigh, but Harlan cuts me off. "She's the reason I'm here. I wanted to bring her to you. She crashed outta the sky, and I looked after her. She'll tell you." He looks at me again, and it's impossible to miss the pleading note in his voice. "Go on. Tell him. Like you said you would."

Eric turns on his heel and walks away, not glancing over his shoulder. "If they aren't gone in one minute," he says to someone in the darkness, "shoot them."

I don't know if these people can help me, but I'm not letting them leave without finding out. Whatever is between Harlan and Eric, however they know each other, I have to get past it.

"Wait!" I say.

Eric keeps walking.

My mouth is dry, my head pounding, but I make myself form the words. "There's shrapnel in my leg, and I can't take it out myself."

He doesn't stop. Doesn't even register that he's heard me. I swallow, trying to keep my voice calm. "Please. You're all I've got."

Eric turns back to look at me. It's impossible to decode the expression on his face, so I don't try. I just start talking, being as clear as I can. I tell them where I come from, what's happened to me. I tell them about how I got injured, about how it's infected. And I tell them that Harlan brought me down the mountain, that he kept me safe.

I look at Eric as I say this, but his expression doesn't change. Around us, the room is silent, with nothing but the very slight shifting of bodies. Harlan, Eric and I could be the last people on the planet, locked in this circle of light.

"Why should we help you?" Eric says.

"Because I'll die if you don't."

Eric doesn't even blink. "So?"

"*So?*" Harlan's eyes are huge. "Eric, you can't do that, she's—"

"Shut up, Harlan." Eric looks at me. "You got anything to trade? Anything we can use?"

I'm ready for this. I might not have anything I can give them, but I've still got the most important thing: my skills as a tracer.

"I can run," I say. "Back on Outer Earth I was a tra…I carried packages and messages and things. I can help. I can go wherever you need me to."

But even as I say the words, I'm aware of how pathetic they sound. I'm not even halfway through before Eric is shaking his head. "Don't need any of that," he says. "Time's up. Get out of here. And *don't* come back."

For the second time, he turns and walks away.

"Eric," says Harlan. "Eric, please."

But it's not going to work. Not this time.

So I do the only thing I can.

I've always been quick from a standing start, and I'm on top of

Eric before anyone can stop me. I reach out, spinning him around. In the same movement, I grab the butt of his gun and plant the end of the barrel on my forehead.

That knocks the sour expression off his face—for a moment, real terror shoots across it.

Guns are being pointed at me from a dozen directions, warnings being shouted, but nobody really knows what to do. After all, how can you seriously threaten to shoot someone already holding a gun to her own head?

I've got Eric's weapon with both hands, one under the barrel, the other under the stock. The fever is doubling and tripling my vision, and my thigh is screaming at me.

"I don't get to walk away from this," I say through gritted teeth. "And you don't get to leave me to die slow. Harlan said you could help me, but if you can't, or won't, then do me a favour and kill me now."

Nobody moves. Behind me, Harlan moans.

Eric's finger is just outside the trigger guard. A second's worth of movement, and it's all over. No pain. No more fighting.

No Prakesh, no Carver. No Okwembu, either. Do you really want that? Do you really want to lose that chance?

Eric wrenches the gun away, so quickly that the edge of the barrel scratches my forehead. I hear hurried footsteps behind me, Eric's group closing in, but he raises a hand, and they stop.

I keep my eyes locked on his, breathing hard. Inwardly, I can't believe I just did what I just did. It was like someone else was in control of my body.

"Let me help her, boss," says someone to my left. I can't see who it is.

Eric closes his eyes briefly. "What are you even doing up here, Finkler?"

A man steps into the light. He's Eric's polar opposite—podgy, with rolls of skin under his chin. He has bright, mischievous eyes, and his ears are enormous, sticking out from the side of his head like handles. He wears a torn T-shirt with the words *Yukon Horsepacking* across it, in big, curving letters. His arms are bare, but if the cold bothers him he gives no sign.

"If she's still walking," he says, "then we've still got time. Couple of minutes with the old tweezers, some antibiotics, and she'll be good to go."

"Not going to happen," Eric says, but he sounds less sure now.

Finkler looks at me, tilting his head. "Where'd you get hit?" he says.

I don't want to take my pants off in front of everyone, so instead I point, my finger brushing my inner thigh. I have to make a real effort not to scream—not just at the pain, but at how hot and puffy the flesh feels, even under my pants.

"I took the main piece out," I say, my mouth dry. "But there's still a few shards in there."

"I can handle that." Finkler turns to Eric. "Come on, boss. I need the practice anyway."

For a very long minute, nobody moves. Everybody is looking at Eric. I don't dare speak, don't dare make a single move. I definitely don't try to think about the word *practice*.

"You got spine, I'll give you that," Eric says to me. He looks back at Finkler. "Do it. And stay up top—I don't want her going anywhere she's not supposed to."

"No problem," says Finkler. "I've still got a few supplies up here anyway."

I don't get a chance to thank Eric. He raises a finger, pointing it at me. "But once he's done, you're gone. Both of you."

Without another word, he turns, marching off into the darkness. Harlan tries to follow, but is brought up short behind me, two of Eric's people stepping in to block his path. They're muttering to each other, as if they aren't quite sure what just happened.

"OK then," Finkler says. His voice is high and musical, elated, like Eric just gave him a new toy. "Come with me, and we'll fix you right up."

He ducks through another set of thick double doors. I follow, too stunned to speak.

The interior of the hospital is a wreck. I can see the sky through the lobby ceiling. The corridors leading off it are dark, but Finkler seems to know where he's going. He moves surprisingly fast for a big man, his feet nimble as he skips around a pile of rubble.

I'm still trying to process the last few minutes, and it takes me some time to find my voice. "Thank you," I say.

"Don't sweat it," Finkler says. He smiles at me, his teeth picking up the light from outside. His voice is slightly nasal, like he's speaking through a pinched nose.

"I'm Riley."

"And I," he says, turning mid-stride and pulling off a weird bow, "am Finkler. Pleased to meet you."

He bashes through a set of double doors, sending them swinging wildly. "This way," he says over his shoulder.

I trail behind him. The corridor is almost pitch-black, but it doesn't stop Finkler. He's looking left and right, hunting for something.

"In here," Finkler says, waving me over. He ducks into a room off the corridor, and when I follow him he's lighting an oil lamp, adjusting the light level using the wheel on the side.

The room we're in is so similar to Morgan Knox's surgery that it shakes me a little. It has the same kind of bed, the same wheeled machines and sets of drawers lining the walls, the same instruments laid out on metal trays. But there's a mattress on the bed, ancient and stained, and Finkler is bustling around collecting bottles and meds, lighting more oil lamps. He's whistling to himself—notes that almost form a tune but not quite.

The horror I felt before drips through me like poison. This is going to happen. He's going to cut into me. Right here, right now.

Finkler sees me standing in the doorway. "Come on," he says, patting the bed.

The mattress is scratchy and wet under my hands. I shuck my shoes, and slide my pants down my legs. The air is cold, goose-bumping my skin—I'm self-conscious in my underwear, but Finkler barely notices. He's pulling on rubber gloves that look like they've been used to clean out a septic tank. I lie on my back, head towards the door.

I feel Finkler unwrapping the bandages, and raise my head just in time to see him grimace at the wound. "Yeesh," he says. "Good thing you got here when you did. You say this happened yesterday?"

I nod.

"Hmm. Infection's taken faster than it should have done. Must be the metal in the leg. Nothing some meds won't cure, but it's good you got here when you did. Few more hours, that'd be that."

I decide not to look. I rest my head back down on the mattress, telling myself to breathe.

"I'm going to give you some local anaesthetic, 'kay?" Finkler says. "Some of the fragments look to be buried pretty deep, so I need to cut around them a little. Sorry I can't knock you out or anything. Don't really know how."

"But you *are* a doctor, right?" I say, trying not to let my nerves show in my voice. "You've done this before?"

Finkler smiles, not in the least bit concerned. "Yeah, totally. Air goes in and out, blood goes round and round. Long as that's happening, you got nothing to worry about."

I stare at him.

He sees the expression on my face. "Stop being such a nervous nellie," he says, slipping a syringe into the top of a bottle and drawing the plunger back. "Honey, I learned medicine by doing medicine. Fixing broken legs, digging bullets out of people."

He resumes his whistling, bending over me, and running a hand down my right leg.

"This'll sting a little," he says, then laughs. "I've always wanted to say that. Usually the people I operate on are unconscious, or passed out from blood loss. It'll be nice to have someone to talk to."

The needle goes in. I hiss, without really meaning to. Finkler scoffs. "You big baby," he says.

The needle comes out, and numbness creeps up and down my leg, radiating outwards from my thigh. Finkler is pottering around, lining up instruments—tweezers, a pair of forceps, a scalpel. A memory blindsides me—Morgan Knox's surgery again, waking up after he put the explosives inside me. I shiver, shutting my eyes tight.

"Alrighty," says Finkler. "Here we go."

I feel pain when he cuts, but it's a distant sting, nothing more. I can get through this—it's far from the worst insult my body's suffered. Sweat stings my eyes, and the fever is making it hard to form thoughts. But I'm already thinking ahead, to what'll happen when Finkler is done. Somehow, I need to work out how to get to Anchorage. Maybe I can persuade Harlan to come with me...

That's when I hear voices from the corridor. Raised ones, shouting commands back and forth.

"Finkler?" I say, not opening my eyes.

"Yeah?"

"Everything OK out there?"

"What? Oh yeah, yeah, fine, they're probably just—"

The door behind me bangs open. The volume of the voices increases, and I look up to see Eric leaning over me. His face is upside down, but there's no mistaking the fury on it.

"You led them right to us," he says. A fleck of saliva hits me on the cheek, and I have to resist the urge to brush it off.

"Led who?" I say. I twist my shoulders around without thinking, looking back at the door—Finkler has to put a hand on my leg to stop me. I can feel pressure in the wound—he's still got an instrument in it, nestled inside.

There's the sound of running feet in the corridor, and I see Harlan in the doorway, his face pale with fear. "You and him," Eric says, jabbing a finger at Harlan. "Nomads."

"How many?" Finkler says. He doesn't move his hand from the wound.

"Lots." He looks back at me. "They must have been tracking you, and now you *brought 'em right here*."

I don't know what to say to that, but I'm saved when Finkler speaks up. "Scouts said they'd left the area," he says. It's impossible to miss the worry in his voice.

"Guess they got it wrong. And now it's coming down on top of us."

He doesn't wait for me to respond. "Finkler," he says. "Get below. Right now."

"You got it," Finkler says, and I feel him slowly withdrawing the scalpel. "Sorry about this, but we're gonna have to postpone—"

He stops speaking, and that's when I notice a different sensation in my leg. Not pain, exactly—it's more a feeling of tension, like how my muscles feel after a long run.

"Oh, fuck," says Finkler quietly.

I lift my head. He's got the scalpel in the wound—I can just see his fingers wrapped around the handle—and there's a *lot* of blood. It's spattering his gloves, dotting the skin on his forearms. Eric is staring at him, his eyes wide.

"It's OK," Finkler says. "I just...I think I might have nicked your femoral artery."

"*What?*" Harlan and I say at the same time.

"Leave it," says Eric, striding over to Finkler, trying to pull him away.

He shakes Eric off. "No way," he says. "Gotta fix this."

"*Finkler.*"

"If I don't, she'll bleed out."

"Not our problem. I can lose her, but I can't lose you. Get below, right now."

I thump my head back down on the mattress. This is not happening. *This is not happening.*

"I'm not leaving her," Finkler says. There's a note of steel in his voice, one I haven't heard before now. "She stays, I stay."

"No."

"You can't just leave me here," I say, horrified. I'm feeling strangely lightheaded now, and I recognise the sensation—this isn't the first time I've lost blood.

Eric ignores me, speaking to Finkler. "Don't be stupid. You're putting everyone in danger."

"What's the matter, boss?" he replies. "Can't handle a few Nomads?"

He sees Eric about to explode, and speaks quickly. "She's my patient. I screwed up, and I have to handle this. Boss, I *have* to. I've got clamps and sutures—it won't take me long."

There are a few seconds when I think Eric is going to win. He's going to drag Finkler away, and leave me to die. But then something passes between them, a look I can't even begin to decode. Eric swears loudly, turning and running for the door. I see him grab Harlan, pushing him out into the corridor. "We'll hold them off as long as we can," he shouts back at us. "Just hurry."

"You'll be OK," Harlan says. "He knows what he's doing."

Finkler starts whistling again, and I hear the first gunshot echoing down the corridor.

37

Riley

I lay my head back, trying to remember to breathe. I tell myself that there's nothing I can do, that I have to let Finkler work.

"Goddamn it," he says, talking more to himself than to me. "Stupid thing. Keeps slipping."

More gunshots ring out, closer this time, like they're coming from *inside* the hospital. "Please hurry," I say, clenching my teeth so hard that my jaw twinges. It helps keep the lightness in my head at bay.

"Sorry. Never done this before. Artery, I mean."

I hear running footsteps, and tilt my head back to see people sprinting past the door, yelling at each other. A face appears in the doorway. Eric. His eyes are dancing, alive with the heat of battle.

"How're we doing?" Finkler says, without looking up.

In response, Eric swings away from the door, letting off a round of shots at someone we can't see.

A moment later, he strides into the room, then reaches around behind his back and pulls out a handgun.

I'm so wired that, for a moment, I'm convinced he's going to shoot me. But he just holds it out to Finkler, who gestures at him to put it on the table.

"They're coming in from all sides," Eric says. "We have to split our defences. You see anybody come in that's not us, shoot them."

"Got it."

"There are too many of them. They must have been lying low, camped somewhere we couldn't see."

"Got it."

"We're going to hold this corridor, but they're coming in from everywhere, and we don't have nearly enough people. If we—"

"I said I got it, Eric! I'm working here!" Finkler waves him away.

Eric vanishes, exploding out of the door, loosing off another volley of shots.

Finkler keeps operating. He's working with stitches now—I can feel the thread jerking through my artery. I try not to imagine what it looks like. The anaesthetic is still there, but the pain is winning, hot and sharp, shooting up from the wound.

It isn't enough to hold off the fogginess in my mind.

There's a shout from the doorway. My eyes fly open to see Finkler grabbing the gun, loosing off two quick shots. The bangs are enormous, and the shots ricochet off the corridor wall. I have just enough time to see a shadow there before it vanishes, ducking out of sight.

"Yeah!" Finkler shouts. I look over to him, in time to see a fresh spurt of blood jet up from the wound.

He sees it, too, and his brow furrows. "Here," he says, holding the gun out to me.

I take it in one shaking hand. It's heavier than the stingers we had on Outer Earth, the surface slimy with oil.

"You've got to be kidding me," I say.

"It's easy," he says, raising a scalpel. "You point it at someone and pull the trigger. Bang."

"I know how a *damn gun works*!" I say, shouting the last three words as the anaesthetic gives way, a shrieking pain blasting up from my thigh.

"Sorry," Finkler mutters. He doesn't stop, using his teeth to hold the end of the thread. His arms are soaked in my blood. I don't know how much I've lost already, and I *really* don't want to think about it.

I keep my eyes on the door. I have to tilt my head back to look at it, so it's upside down. "How will I know who to shoot?" I say, tasting sweat.

"What?" Finkler is barely listening.

"What if I shoot one of your guys?"

A second later, a Nomad comes through the door, and I realise that that's not a mistake I'm going to make.

The man is tall, with pale skin and lank dreadlocks. He wears a sleeveless T-shirt and torn pants. At first, I think his face is scarred, but then I see that it's paint: long slashes of it, red and grey, curving around his nose and mouth.

He has a gun, long-barrelled, battle-scarred, around his neck on a sling. He leads with it, kicking open the door and flying into the operating theatre. For a second, he's brought up short, not expecting to find an operation in progress.

One second is all I need.

I raise the gun and fire, not thinking, not *wanting* to think. I pull the trigger again and again. The kick from the weapon nearly takes my head off. My view is upside down, and my wooziness makes it tough to aim: two bullets go wide, but the third finds its mark, tearing away half of the man's neck. He goes down, full ragdoll, spinning as he hits the floor.

"Jesus!"

Finkler ducked when I fired, pulling the scalpel out of the wound. The pain rockets through me, delayed by my adrenaline but finally shooting home, and I let loose an animal cry. The air is thick with the smell of gunpowder.

Finkler gets back up, wiping his forehead, staring down at the wound. "Shit. I think I sliced a muscle."

"*What?*" The word is almost a shriek.

"No, hang on. It's fine. I just have to be careful." I feel Finkler's fingers in the wound, opening it further. "Hang on... got it. There. Artery's patched up. No harm done. We're fine."

He's barely finished speaking when another Nomad bursts into the room. This one is even more terrifying—his head is shaven, and the paint goes right over the top of his skull, as if his head is some kind of ancient totem. He's bare-chested, and he's already raising his gun.

I raise mine faster. I fire once. Twice. Both bullets go wide. I pull the trigger again, and the gun clicks empty.

The Nomad grins, takes a step forward. His eyes move from me to Finkler. He lets his gun drop, and takes a wicked-looking knife out of his belt. Its blade is long, slightly curved, the edge notched and gouged. *Smart*, I think, not wanting to but doing it anyway. *He doesn't want to waste ammo.*

I hurl the gun at the Nomad. It's a last-ditch move, awkward from my position, and it doesn't even come close to hitting him. Finkler cries out—a high, warbling yell. But he doesn't move away from the table. Instead, he moves around it, trying to shield me.

The Nomad smiles, sauntering towards us, taking his time.

The room swims in front of me. I blink, and there's something around the man's neck. It's a rifle, and behind it is Harlan, yanking it backwards, pulling tight.

The Nomad grunts, tries to fight him off. He's strong, and when he wrenches his body to the side, Harlan is lifted clean off his feet. He screams, but refuses to let go, pulling the top of the rifle into the man's throat.

I will myself to move, but it's as if my mind is no longer attached to my body. I don't know if it's the fever or the blood loss. I can't do anything but watch.

The Nomad reaches behind him, slamming his fist into the side of Harlan's head, who lets go, tumbling away. But the Nomad is focused on Harlan, and he doesn't see Finkler lunge forward, doesn't even realise he's there until the scalpel is buried in the side of his neck.

His knife clatters to the floor. It's the last thing I hear before I sink into oblivion.

38

Prakesh

Everything hurts.

The ache in Prakesh's legs radiates upwards through his spine. His arms are in agony. It's his shoulders that hurt the most—every time he takes a step, the enormous bag of soil presses down on them.

He concentrates on putting one foot in front of the other, blinking away the sweat dripping into his eyes. Then he's at the mustering point, the other bags of soil appearing in his field of view. With a groan, he rolls the bag he's carrying off his shoulders. It thumps on top of the rest, starts to slide back. For a horrible moment, Prakesh thinks it's going to slide right off—he'll have to pick it up, and that means crouching down, which he's not sure he can do at that moment.

The bag comes to a quivering halt. Prakesh straightens up, tries to ignore the pain in his upper body. He places his hands at the small of his back, rolls his neck.

"Move it," the guard says.

He's sitting on a nearby crate, elbows on his knees, and his voice has a high-pitched, needling quality to it that Prakesh has already learned to hate. The guard has told him to *move it* every time Prakesh has brought another bag of soil, and he doesn't vary his tone no matter how quickly Prakesh heads back to the other side of the hangar.

Out of the corner of his eye, Prakesh sees another prisoner stumbling towards him, almost collapsing under the weight of the bag of soil. Prakesh sidesteps smartly, but something under his shoe causes him to slide, a slick of oil, maybe, and he overbalances. His windmilling left hand brushes the bag on the worker's shoulders, and he has to stop himself from grabbing hold. He finds his balance, exhaling hard. The worker glances at him as he offloads the bag. He looks brittle, like his bones are made of thin glass. Every prisoner is like that, moving as if each step will make their shins crumble.

"Move it."

Prakesh walks back across the hangar, past the line of trudging workers, back towards the dwindling pile of soil bags. He's counted twenty-eight prisoners here besides him, plus six guards spaced around the hangar. He wonders how many people are actually on this ship, the ratio of prisoners to guards, but then realises he's too tired to care. The gruel they ate a couple of hours ago barely registered inside his body, and his throat is screaming for water.

The hangar is in the centre of the ship, and it's enormous—not as big as the Air Lab, but still a couple of hundred feet from end to end. It's baking hot, shimmering with a wet, sticky heat. There are stacks of crates everywhere, rusted together, their tops and sides ripped off in places. A disused forklift is parked near the wall, missing two of its wheels. There's even a plane in a corner of the hangar, hulking and silent, covered with frayed netting like a captured animal.

Most of the floor space is given over to huge troughs, filled with soil, running wall to wall. The troughs are badly made, little more than sheet metal clumsily welded together. The soil is poor quality. The few living plants that Prakesh can see are wilted, feeble things: tomatoes and beans and cabbage and squash.

The irony is, there are a dozen ways he could improve the yield: space the plants properly, introduce interplanting, create better fertiliser. He tries to think about the procedures, hoping to distract himself, but he's just too damn tired.

Prakesh reaches the first pile of soil sacks. He focuses on the one he has to pick up—the pile is low to the ground now, and the sack is at knee level. Like the others, it's made of thin brown fabric, harsh on the hands, with grains of dirt leaking out between the fibres. He's going to have to crouch after all.

Move it, Prakesh thinks, and bends to pick up the sack.

There's movement in front of him, flickering at the edge of his vision. He looks up to see one of the prisoners fall—a woman so thin that her collarbone appears to be holding up her body like scaffolding.

The woman hits the ground with a staggered thump, her arms splayed out on either side of her. She gives a thin, rattling breath, then falls still.

Prakesh tries to cry out, but his throat won't cooperate. He takes a step towards the woman, reaches out to her—

A hand lands on his chest, pushes him back. One of the guards, her face utterly bored. She has long hair running down her back, deep red in colour.

"Back to work," she says.

Prakesh stares at her. "She—"

"I *said*, back to work."

And Prakesh knows that the woman is dead. Knows it down to his bones. Is he really the only one who sees this? He looks over his shoulder—the other prisoners are looking at him, glancing up as they trudge, but nobody is coming to help. Not a single person.

The scene swims in front of him, and a burst of nausea propels itself up from his stomach. He reels in place, bent double, aware that he has to throw up and not sure how to stop himself.

The guard doesn't tell him again. She doesn't wait for a response. Prakesh senses that she's raised her rifle, that she's turning it in her hands. Any moment now, the butt is going to crash into him, and that'll be that. If she hits him, he's not getting up. Not that he can do anything about it.

At least I'll see Mom and Dad, he thinks. *Maybe Riley, too.* He's aware that he's trembling, but he doesn't know how to stop.

"No!" It's a different voice, high and reedy. The speaker steps between Prakesh and the guard. "He's n- he's n-"

Whoever it is gulps, two quick sounds, then says, "He's n-n-new. He d-d-doesn't kn-kn-know how it w-works, that's all."

There's a pause. The guard's rifle doesn't crash into him.

A canteen appears, raised by a thin, grimy arm. Somehow, Prakesh gets hold of it, and manages to drink. It's a few seconds before his throat responds, and then it's almost too much, like he's trying to drink the ocean.

Somehow, he manages to keep it down. When he lowers the empty canteen, he sees the kid with the freckles staring back at him. He's just as emaciated as the others, but his eyes are alive. The guard, the one with the tattered boots, is standing off to one side, looking sour. The woman's body is still there. Two of the guards are bending down for it. (*Her*, Prakesh thinks. *Not it.*) The man holding the wrists says something Prakesh can't hear, and his partner actually laughs.

The kid with the stutter bends down, and with a grunt, hoists a sack of soil. Prakesh does the same, trying hard not to look at the body, trying not to think about what he just saw. The thoughts come anyway. *How long before you end up like that? How long before they work you to death? A month? A week?*

He and the kid trudge back to the empty troughs in silence. It's only when they're halfway there, when no guards are nearby, that that kid speaks.

"J-J-J-" he says, scrunching up his face, trying to get the word out without raising his voice. "Jojo. My n-n-n-name's J-J-Jojo."

"Prakesh."

They reach the second pile of soil bags, and heave their loads onto it. A puff of dirt shoots up from the pile, the motes floating in the air in front of them. As Prakesh looks up, he sees that the two nearby guards are turned away, muttering to each other.

Prakesh speaks as quietly as possible, keeping his head down, aware of the guards. The water is having an effect, and his head is starting to clear. "How many guards?"

"Wh-what?"

Prakesh gestures to the nearest one, then raises a questioning eyebrow.

Jojo bows his head, hunches his shoulders. He starts walking a little faster, and Prakesh has to up his pace to stay level. Jojo shakes his head—a quick, almost imperceptible movement—then his mouth forms a single word.

Later.

39

Okwembu

Prophet leads Okwembu down through the vessel, through endless corridors and T-junctions, walking for so long that she's given up trying to keep track.

They're below the waterline now. They must be close to the outer hull—she can hear the ocean lapping at the walls, the echoing sound of the metal creaking in the cold water. Okwembu's clothes are still damp, and she shivers as they walk, rubbing her arms. Prophet hasn't said a word since they left his quarters, hasn't even looked at her.

Eventually, they come to what looks like a dead end in the corridor. No—not a dead end. The lights in the ceiling have burned out, and as they get closer Okwembu can see a massive set of double doors. A track runs down the centre of the corridor, with a single wide rail set into it. Chunks of the rail have rusted away—when this ship was still in service it must have been used to transport heavy equipment.

There are three guards outside the door. Two leaning against it, and one sitting up against the corridor wall, spooning food into his mouth from a can. All three are heavily built, camouflage tight across their shoulders, and all three carry rifles. The two standing men stiffen as Prophet and Okwembu approach, fingers just touching their trigger guards.

The man on the floor stops eating, his spoon halfway to his mouth, eyes tracking between them. He gets to his feet, dusting himself off.

"Brothers," Prophet says, spreading his arms wide. He sees where the men are looking. "She is under my purview, for now." He gestures to the door. "Open her up."

The other men keep looking at Okwembu, not moving. She meets their eyes, her face expressionless.

"I said, open it." Prophet's voice has become very soft.

The two guards by the door look at each other. The one on the left nods almost imperceptibly, and his partner fishes a key out of his uniform. The key isn't like anything Okwembu has seen before: it's long and flat, the metal scored with a line of precise circles.

There's a slot in the left door, at ground level, and the guard has to crouch down to insert the key. He grunts as he turns it, and within the door a locking mechanism clicks back.

Prophet watches, his arms folded, as the two men haul the doors apart. Metal screeches on metal, and a shiver of rust falls from the top of the doors, flakes drifting to the ground. Okwembu peers into the space beyond, but there's nothing but darkness. What little light there is from the corridor reveals a grated metal surface.

"Thank you, brothers," says Prophet, walking past them. As he does so, one of the men mutters to himself.

Prophet whirls, getting in the man's face. "You say something?"

Okwembu expects the man to quail, to protest. He doesn't. Above his trim black beard, his eyes are cold.

After a moment, he shakes his head. "No, Prophet."

"You got anything to say to me, you can say it to my face. Or I'll see you taken to the stern, Engine's my witness."

The man breaks his gaze, looking away. "Nothing, Prophet."

She expects Prophet to persist, but he just turns and strides past the doors. "Kyle. Vladimir," he says over his shoulder. "Lock it behind us."

"Yes, Prophet."

"Yes, Sir."

Curious, Okwembu thinks, as she falls in behind him. Perhaps Prophet's control isn't as iron-clad as she thought. That's good. It could make things easier.

Prophet turns the lights on. Okwembu's mouth falls open.

They're standing on a platform above a hangar, as wide as one of the galleries on Outer Earth. Banks of high-power lights are clicking on in the ceiling, one after the other. On the floor of the hangar are several massive containers—Okwembu counts twelve, stretching to the back wall. They remind her of the vats in the Recycler Plants on Outer Earth, the ones that treated human waste. It's as if an entire plant's worth of vats have been laid on their side, placed end to end.

She leans on the platform's railing, looking closely at the nearest container. It's been made in the past few years—there's very little rust. The seals have been badly done, as if each one was put together from spare parts. There's a hole cut in the top of each container, as wide as three men. Okwembu glances up: there are half a dozen thick pipes hanging down from the roof, their ribbed surfaces crinkling as they gently sway in place. The pipes disappear into the mess of girders in the ceiling.

And there's the smell of fuel. It fills the air, thick and oily.

"Why are you showing me this?" she says.

"We came to this ship ten years ago," Prophet says, and there's something in his voice that wasn't there before. The bright tone he had while taking about the Engine has disappeared. There's a set of metal stairs leading to the floor, and he marches down them, his hands clasped behind his back. "We were tired. Tired of living underground. The elders told us that the whole world was dust, but we decided to see for ourselves."

They reach the floor, and Prophet idly trails a hand along the vertical pleats of a giant container. "We thought if we went east, the land would be different. So we got as many air filters and supplies as we could, and made the crossing. The journey was... well. We were tested."

He pauses, as if gathering himself. "We were hugging the coast, and found this ship out in the bay. There'd been some sort of battle. We don't know who they were or what they were fighting over, but none of them survived. There *was* a fusion reactor, broken, beyond our capability to repair. And they had this fuel stored down here. Enough to last us a while."

He taps a container, and a boom echoes off the walls. It's the sound of an empty vessel.

Okwembu waits for the echoes to vanish. "But not long enough," she says.

"We could always use more fuel, hence the radio message," says Prophet. "Survivors provide that, and more. They provide their hands, their labour. This is a big ship, and we can only do so much."

He smiles. "Do you have faith, Janice Okwembu?"

She knows enough to stay silent, letting him fill in the gap. He obliges. "We all do. Even in the worst of the Alaskan winter, where the wind would take your mind if you let it, we had faith. Even when we had to burrow down into the dirt, wait out the dust storms, we had faith. We would be provided for. And we were."

He raises his hands to the ceiling. "Not just with the *Ramona*. Not just with the fuel. But with the *Engine*."

He shakes his head. "It took us a little while to get it working. We had to figure out how to run it on the fuel we had. But once it did, it smiled down on us. It changed the air, allowed us to go outside without masks. It raised the temperature, brought the trees back. It gave us the land, and we used it. No more hiding under the dirt, scared of the world above."

"Wait," Okwembu says, shaking her head. "I don't understand. The Engine... you're using gasoline to run a fusion reactor? That isn't possible."

Prophet ignores her. "We are running low on fuel, Janice Okwembu. I am a man of faith, but even I know that miracles are most often based in reality. There are fewer and fewer survivors coming in, and when they do, they bring less and less fuel. We have barely enough to last one more winter. If we run out of fuel, this ship will die. And the Engine will die with it."

He raises his eyes to the ceiling. "Some of my men think we should let it. That we should stop feeding the Engine with fuel, and let the land starve. The climate here is so fragile—even a year without the Engine's influence would destroy it."

Abruptly, Prophet turns and stalks away, striding down a line of containers bigger than he is. Okwembu follows, her mind reeling. "Prophet, wait," she says.

"You asked why I'm showing you this. It's to illustrate the consequences of lying to me." He doesn't turn to look at her, but Okwembu can hear the razor edge in his voice. "We need that reactor. We need it to keep the Engine alive, and to free us from our dependence on this."

He taps the container again. There's a thin line of fuel running down from one of the containers, dripping out of a microfracture in the metal. Prophet runs his finger along it, the liquid coating his skin.

"You're right," he says. "I'm not going to torture you into retrieving that data. I'm going to torture you if you *can't* retrieve it. And once it starts, there'll be nothing you can do to make it stop."

Okwembu makes herself speak. "Prophet, I don't understand this at all. *What is the Engine?* If it's not the fusion reactor…"

Prophet's smile grows wider.

And he tells Janice Okwembu what the Engine really is.

40

Riley

When I awake, I'm still lying face up on the bed, and my thigh is bandaged tight. Finkler is in a chair, leaning against the wall, fast asleep. His mouth is open, with a thin slick of drool on his chin, and he's snoring gently, snuffling through his nose. His arms hang by his side, and I see that he still has his gloves on.

I try to sit up, but something pulls at my right arm. A drip, the needle buried in the vein. The fluid bag is suspended on a slightly rusty pole, and it's almost empty, with only a half-inch of yellow liquid remaining. Wincing, I slowly pull the drip out. There's a tiny spurt of blood, but that's all.

The events of the night before come back to me. When I look around the room, I see an enormous patch of blood on the floor, parts of it still liquid. I'm still a little fuzzy, and it takes me a minute to remember what happened. The Nomad bursting through the door, Harlan fighting him off, Finkler stabbing him through the neck.

I give my leg an experimental flex. It hurts like hell, but it's not as bad as I thought it would be. I swing my legs off the bed, take a deep breath, and stand up, moving even more slowly than when I pulled the needle out. My thigh groans, but it can handle the weight. I take one step, and then another. The floor is freezing cold, but I don't mind. I can walk.

I think about waking Finkler to ask him if he has some pain-killers, but I don't. He saved my life. He even treated the wolf bite on my leg—it's bandaged, too, with yellow disinfectant leaking through. The least I can do is let him sleep.

I pull my pants back on, slipping them over cold skin, taking it very gently. There's a bottle of water balanced on top of one of the shelves, almost full. I drain half the bottle before I realise that it might not have been for me, and I put it back, feeling a little guilty.

The water wakes my stomach up. There are still some plants in the pocket of my jacket, and I chew on one as I walk down the hospital corridor. It's cattail, I think—Harlan showed which parts I could eat, the white centres at the base of the leaves. The taste is fresh and sharp. I follow it up with the last of the meat strips, savouring them.

The hospital looks different in the daylight. There's no telling what time it is, but the parts of sky I can see through the shattered ceiling make me think that it's early morning; the clouds are lightening, their dark grey fading away. I make it to the entrance, seeing things I didn't see the night before. Plants have grown across the floor, as well as the desk at the back of the room. The old signs are still up on the wall, still legible after all this time: OBSTETRICS, GYNAECOLOGY, OUT-PATIENTS.

And there are bodies, stacked in the corner.

They're all Nomads, from what I can tell. Maybe six of them. A mess of limbs and ugly paint. I don't see any of Eric's people, but that doesn't mean they weren't hurt, or that they don't keep the bodies somewhere else. For a horrible moment, I could swear that I see Syria among them, but it's just my mind playing tricks.

The bodies are being tended by a man and a woman, who are dragging another one across. Neither of them glance at me as I walk past them. I think about talking to them, saying something, but realise I don't want to. Not now.

Every atom in me wants to go, to head right out of the front door, keep going, and not stop until I get to Anchorage. But it's not hard to picture Carver, picture him shaking his head, telling me that I need a plan first.

He's right.

There are stairs on the other side of the entrance hall. I climb them slowly, knowing that my leg can take the pressure but not wanting to push it too hard just yet. The pain has settled down to a low throb. I'll have to wait until Finkler is awake to know if there's any lasting damage, but from the feel of things, I should be OK.

I don't really know where I'm going. Right now, just moving is enough.

The stairs take a ninety-degree turn to the left, leading out onto a corridor on the second floor. It's a mess. There are a couple of upturned stretchers, and the floor is covered in dead leaves and plant roots. The only light comes from an open door a little way down. As I get closer, I hear voices.

It's Harlan. "...suffered enough," he's saying. "I'm out there, by myself, with nobody to help me. I survived for over a year in those mountains."

"Oh, don't make out like you're some kind of hero." Eric's voice is sharp and hard. "After what you did? You think you have any right to come back here?"

"Eric—"

"And bringing *her*...what, did you think we'd just open our arms? It's a cheap trick, Harlan. You know it, I know it."

"I saved her. I did. You can't take that away from me. She told you herself. That has to mean something, whatever you say about it."

"Fuck you, Harlan. You need to leave. Not tomorrow. Not later today. Now."

The space outside the doorway is a balcony—a wide rooftop space, empty except for a single plastic chair by the waist-high railing. Puddles of foul water dot the gravelly surface. I can see out across the river, across the low buildings of Whitehorse to the mountains beyond. There's a gap in the clouds, just a tiny one, and the rising sun has turned it to a gorgeous, burning orange slash. It reflects off the surface of the river. The space before the bridge is clogged with debris, but the water runs clear downstream of it, the river growing larger as it filters into a lake.

For the first time, I find I can look at the sky without my vision going weird. Maybe Harlan was right—up until yesterday, the largest space I'd been in was outside the station, and that was only for a few minutes. My body's slowly adjusting to having a horizon, getting used to not being enclosed in a tiny metal ring.

Harlan and Eric haven't noticed me. They're standing over by the balcony, facing each other, close enough to touch. They're wearing the same clothes they were the night before. Eric's airforce jacket is dark in places, crusted with dried blood, and Harlan's ankle is wrapped in a bulky bandage.

"You think I'm kidding?" Eric says, jabbing a finger in Harlan's chest. "You play games with me on this, and I'll shoot you myself."

"You'd like that, wouldn't you? Then you wouldn't have to think about me."

I shouldn't be here. I'm intruding on something very private. I try to remember why I came up here in the first place, and find that I can't. I turn to go, automatically shifting onto the balls of my feet, and that's when Harlan says, "Oh, hey—you're up."

I close my eyes briefly, then turn. They're both looking at me, silhouetted slightly by the burning sky. Harlan is smiling, relieved, but the look on Eric's face is thunderous.

May as well make the most of it. I look up at Eric. "I wanted to say thank you," I say, stumbling over the words a little. "I don't know how I can pay you back, but..."

Eric crosses the space between us in three long strides, and slaps me across the face.

It's a backhand hit, not as hard as a punch but still strong. I raise my hand to block it, but I'm not fast enough. It takes me across the mouth, and my teeth cut into my top lip. I taste blood, harsh and salty.

"Eric!" Harlan says.

My first instinct is to hit back, to take a swing at him, but I don't. I just stand there, watching his shoulders heaving.

"I don't know what happened to you," Eric says, "and I don't care. I want you gone."

The slap has brought the anger back, instantly, like it was waiting to happen. And that awful voice again, bitter and strident: *You hit me again, I'll break your arm.*

With an effort of will, I bring myself under control. Eric must see something on my face, because he takes a step back.

"I'm sorry," I say, picking my words carefully. "I didn't have a choice. There was no one else who could help me."

Eric stalks away before I'm finished, coming to a stop by the railing, leaning on it like he's admiring the sunrise. My cheek is throbbing, and I can taste blood in my mouth.

Harlan shuffles over. "You OK?"

"Fine," I say.

"Don't mind Eric. He'll come round. Nomad attack wasn't too bad—couple of his folks got hurt, but nothing serious."

I look down at my feet, then back up, into his eyes. Before he can do anything, I pull him into a hug. He's taller than me, and I have to stand on tiptoe to put my head next to his.

"Then thank *you*," I say. "For everything."

"It's OK," he says, laughing a little, patting my back, as if he's not quite sure how to take this. I pull away, and he nods, two quick dips of the head.

"I'm going to head out," I say. "The sooner I get moving, the better."

A dark expression crosses Harlan's face. "Come on now. You aren't still talking about—"

"They're out there," I say, thinking of Prakesh, and Carver. *And Okwembu.* "I have to find them."

"You got nothing between those ears of yours?" he says, tapping his forehead. "You. Won't. Make. It. Nobody would. Even the Nomads don't go that far west."

He pats the air, like he's trying to calm the situation. "Listen. Listen, now. Why don't you just come with me? You can make a life out here for yourself. Plenty of people have. There aren't a lot of us, but we do all right. It's better than dying out *there*, when you don't even know if your friends are alive or—"

"Stop," I say.

Harlan doesn't. "It's suicide," he says, angry now. "It's insanity. You almost got dead from that infection, and now you want to walk to *Anchorage*?"

"Anchorage?" Eric is still angry—I can see it in the way his mouth is set—but he's confused, too. "What the hell is she going to Anchorage for? Doesn't she know what happens out there?"

"I *told* her!" Harlan's eyebrows skyrocket. "She won't listen."

"I'll be fine," I say, but neither of them is paying attention to me now.

"We can't let her go, Eric. She'll die out there."

"That's on her," Eric says. "And you, since apparently you didn't do a good enough job of telling her how bad an idea it is."

"But she'll—"

I stick two fingers in my mouth, and whistle. The piercing sound explodes across the rooftop before drifting off into the cold morning air. It brings both of them up short.

"I'm going, OK?" I say. I turn to Eric. "You won't see me again, I promise. Just let me say goodbye to Finkler, and I'll be on my way."

Eric nods. "Good. Listen to Harlan, though. You're insane, thinking you'll make it to Anchorage."

I've managed to contain my anger so far, holding it back with an effort of will, but Eric's words almost make that will fail completely. I want to grab him, shout at him, *make* him understand.

In my last months on Outer Earth, I was scared. All the time. Scared of people who want to hurt me, scared of losing the people I love, scared of getting someone killed. I thought I could do it—I thought I could live with it. But it didn't matter. I ended up losing them anyway. And in the process, everything I know was ripped away.

So I'm done being scared. I'm sick of it. Eric thinks I'm insane? No. It would be insane to not go, to *not* try and get my friends back. If I don't, I'll spend the rest of my life wondering if they're still out there. I'll spend the rest of my life knowing that I had a chance to track down Okwembu, and didn't.

I don't say any of this. Somehow, I get that anger back under control. Because Eric doesn't deserve it—not after I put him and his people in danger. Not after they helped me.

"OK, Eric, listen," Harlan says. "If she's gonna be hard-headed about it, then at least help her out with some supplies. A better coat or something. I saw your people wearing some pretty heavy gear, and I know Marla's still got a full storage locker, saw it when I was down there."

Eric says nothing. When Harlan speaks again, he sounds like he's panicking. "What about the seaplane?" he says, pointing. "That one, in the river? I know it's rusted all to shit, but we could fix it up!"

"Good luck with that. Believe me, we tried. Thing's shot to shit. You'd be better off asking the Nomads for theirs." He turns, looking Harlan dead in the eyes. "You want the one out front? You're welcome to it. Just get the hell out."

He turns and stalks past me, almost shoving me out of the way. I jump back just in time.

"Wait a second," Harlan says, jogging after him. "The Nomads have a seaplane? Since when did that happen?"

Seaplane...

As Harlan and Eric vanish down the passage, I jog over to the railings, doing it without thinking, pleased to feel my leg take the speed. From up here, I can see across to the river, clogged with trash and debris. The dilapidated boats bob in the current. I notice the one that caught my eye the night before—the enormous white cylinder, supported by two pontoons, bobbing on the water's surface.

I know what a plane does, although I haven't needed to think about it until this moment. It's not exactly the kind of thing worth teaching people who live on a space station. That thing must be able to fly—or did, a very long time ago. Right now, I'm amazed it's even able to float.

And the Nomads have one. One that sounds like it's still working.

I don't give myself a chance to consider the flaws in the idea. I push off the railing, and start jogging after Eric and Harlan.

41

Prakesh

They sleep ten to a room, curled up on the floor. There used to be bunk beds on the walls—Prakesh saw the places where cots were bolted on—but they're long gone. There's no light in the ceiling, and when the door behind them is banged shut the room is in total darkness. The bodies inside it quickly raise the temperature, and the smell of sweat mixes with the coppery tang of dried urine.

At least the room is large enough for all the workers. They huddle in small groups, sitting against the wall or trying to stretch out on the hard floor. Prakesh tries to find a spot, tripping over outstretched feet more than once.

He's too tired to sleep, and too wired to do anything but sit and stare into the darkness. The last few hours passed in an exhausted blur: more soil bags, another dose of slop in that mess hall, some water, a chance to use the bathroom. Then this... *hole*. He saw Jojo come in with them, caught a glimpse of his face before the door was shut, but he doesn't know if he should call out for him.

He keeps seeing Carver, vanishing under a hail of feet and fists.

Keeps seeing the look on his face. Prakesh curls his hand into a fist of his own.

Jojo's voice comes out of the darkness, so close that Prakesh nearly jumps. "Hey. Y-y-you…uh, awake?"

The kid is right next to him, his mouth by his ear, but Prakesh can't see a thing. "Yeah," he says, keeping his voice low.

Jojo's stutter seems to be less prominent, as if the fact that it's too dark to see him means he finds it easier to speak. "W-we can talk now, if y-y-you want. W-what's it like?"

His question catches Prakesh off guard. "What do you mean?"

"Outside the sh-ship."

Prakesh tries to marshal his thoughts. It's hard to even know where to start. "We weren't out there long," he says. "We got picked up by Ray and Nessa."

"I hate them. R-R-Ray 'sssssspecially. So w-where are you from? I'm f-f-from Denali, up north, or I w-was before my p-p-p-" He stops, and makes two of those gulping sounds again. "Parents brought me here. Th-th-they n-named me J-Joseph, but th-they always called m-m-me Jojo. Everyone d-d-does."

"Where are your parents now?"

"D-d-dead." He says it without regret, like it's a simple fact, and that alone is enough to make Prakesh's stomach clench. It's enough to remind him of his own parents, on Outer Earth. Thinking about them is like walking on the edge of a gaping hole. He knows he'll never see them again, but even trying to comprehend that fact is like leaning out over the hole, daring gravity to take him.

"B-b-but I'm g-gonna get back there," Jojo says. "My uncle st-stayed b-b-behind. He's w-waiting fffff-for me. I know he is."

Prakesh nods, knowing Jojo can't see him, but not sure what else to say.

Jojo saves him the trouble. "So w-where *are* you from?"

Prakesh takes a breath. "Outer Earth."

"Like the ssss-space station?" Jojo says. It's impossible to miss the excitement in his voice.

"That's right."

"But that's a m-m-million m-miles away! W-why did you come down here?"

Because I unleashed a virus that destroyed the station. Because we couldn't stop people from leaving. Because no matter how hard I tried, I couldn't do the right thing.

"Doesn't matter," Prakesh says. "We're here now, and that's all there is."

Jojo pauses, as if turning this over in his mind. Prakesh takes the moment. "Jojo," he says, leaning in closer. "How many people on this ship? How many prisoners?"

Jojo shrugs—Prakesh can feel it, feel Jojo's shoulders brushing his. "Th-thirty of us in the farm. M-m-m-maybe another thirty somewhere else?"

"What about the guards?"

"Twenty-f-f-five, I think? B-but they got all the guns and they never let us near them and th-th-they—" He stops, and takes a couple of hitching breaths.

"How long have you been here?" Prakesh says.

Another shrug. "A c-c-couple years. I d-d-don't r-really know. L-lost time. But P-P-Prophet says we have to w-work for the—"

He stops, coughing, like he hasn't talked this much in years, and isn't used to it. "Engine," he says eventually, without a single hitch in the word. "The Engine."

"And what *is* the Engine?" Prakesh says.

"W-we don't know. It's b-b-below decks, and they d-d-don't l-let us go there."

"You've never been?"

Jojo makes a negative sound. "Th-they keep their f-f-f-f-f-*fuel* down there, right at the bottom of the sh-sh-ship. Th-th-they won't l-let anyone near it." A note of excitement creeps into his voice. "One day w-w-we're gonna burn this place down. All of it. G-go off and f-f-f-find a suh-spot of our own."

Prakesh hears movement—someone scrabbling across the floor in front of them. He feels hot breath on his face. "You two shut up. Shut up right now."

"We were just—" Prakesh says.

The man cuts him off. "I don't give a shit. I don't want our rations taken away because you felt like a conversation."

"Hey *f-f-f-f-f-*" Jojo says in a harsh whisper, not quite managing to get the curse out. He swallows loudly. "I'll talk if I w-want. Just 'cos you got n-n-nothin' good to say..."

He trails off. For a moment, Prakesh wonders if the other man is going to retaliate, but then the hot breath on his face vanishes and he hears the man withdrawing to the other wall.

Jojo shifts his body a little. "F-f-fraid he's right. We shouldn't r-r-really be talking. I'll s-s-s-s-s-see you tomorrow."

He turns away. Someone snores loudly, groaning in their sleep.

Prakesh sits in the darkness, thinking hard. And the more he thinks the angrier he gets.

He's been on the edge of a long drop before, only that time it was for real. After Riley brought him the news about Resin, that it was his genetic experiments that caused it, Prakesh almost took his own life. The grief and despair was almost too much to take. He stood on the roof of the Air Lab control room, seconds away from stepping off. It was only a last-second thought that stopped him.

He was going to save as many people as possible. It didn't matter where they ended up, whether they stayed on the station or came to the planet below: he was going to dedicate the rest of his life to that goal. It was the only way to atone for what he'd done.

It's what he thought he was doing, when he helped stop Riley from destroying the *Shinso Maru*'s fusion reactor. *Saving lives.*

But it didn't work. Everybody he tried to help is either dead, or trapped here. His colleagues, his friends, his parents—another clench of his stomach muscles, an involuntary reaction. And Riley—gods, even the thought of what happened to Riley is enough to make him want to pound the walls, scream and roar until they come in and knock his head right off his shoulders.

What would Riley do? If she were here right now?

That's when Prakesh has a thought that is as clear and sharp as the one he had on the control room roof. *She'd fight. She'd do whatever it took to get to safety. She'd never give up, never, no matter how bad things got.*

As sleep finally takes him, Prakesh has time to think one last thing. He's going to escape. No, not just escape. He's going to do what he promised himself, and get the rest of these people off this ship.

42

Riley

I put on an extra burst of speed, coming alongside Harlan as he reaches the stairs. My legs grumble, but I ignore them.

Harlan is still shouting at Eric. "There's a working seaplane out there, E? And you haven't gone to check it out? Are you crazy? That's what you've always wanted!"

We've reached the lobby. Eric ignores us, striding right past the desk at the back, not looking at the pile of bodies stacked in the far corner. He glances up at the mezzanine, where a guard is staring into the distance, half hidden behind a pillar, his rifle held at ease on his shoulder.

"Eric, wait up a second," I say, aware of his short temper but not caring.

"Jesus," Eric mutters, not breaking stride. "Finkler!" he shouts, bellowing down the passage where Finkler has his surgery. When there's no response, he starts striding towards it, only to be brought up short when the guard on the mezzanine speaks.

"He ain't there," the guard says. "Went below."

Eric's face twists in irritation. He turns on his heel, heading deeper into the hospital. "Come," he says to me. "I'll let Finkler look you over once more, and then you get the hell out."

I lag behind him and Harlan, my mind moving at light speed. I don't have the faintest idea how I'm going to get to the seaplane, but I am damn well going to try.

We head deeper into the hospital. It's not until we've actually gone down the second flight of stairs that I realise we're underground. It's quiet down here, and warmer. What was it that Eric told Finkler, before the Nomads arrived? *Stay up top.*

The corridor we're in is dark, but there's a dim glow coming from round a corner. As we turn it, I see a small door set into a dead end, with a glimmering fluorescent light above it. There are two guards outside, both wearing thick, bulky black jackets. They spring to attention when they see Eric, dropping their rifles.

Eric nods to them, and pushes open the door.

It's the sound I notice first. It's like the noise of a gallery on Outer Earth—the hum of people, the almost subsonic rumble of machines, the clanking of old metal. In the galleries, the lights were set far above the floor—here, they're just above our heads, intensely bright. I have to squint to see.

We've come out onto a small metal platform in the top corner of a huge open space. After the closed-in passages, the size of it is startling. The floor below us has been cordoned off into discrete sections: a vegetable garden here, a common area there, an enormous section with cots and mattresses scattered around it. Wood panels separate each section. A group of children sit cross-legged on the floor in one corner, with two adults showing them something on a board that's been stuck to the wall. It's as if the entirety of Outer Earth has been condensed down into a space around half the size of the station dock.

There's a narrow metal stairway leading down from our platform. Eric descends, not bothering to check if we're following.

As we get closer to the ground, I see that the space isn't as regular as I first thought. Jagged sections of concrete jut out of the wall, flat on top, with bent metal bars poking out of the sides like stray hairs on skin. Previous floors, perhaps, long since fallen away, opening the space up. And there's an even stranger structure diagonally across from us: a curving ramp, also made of concrete, with a high lip around its outer edge. It rises from the floor, bending back on itself. It must have been used for vehicles, like the ones Harlan and I saw on the road.

It stops before it reaches its highest point, ending in an explosion of metal rods. There's a depression in the wall beyond it, what looks like an exit to the outside world, now completely bricked up.

The moment Eric hits the floor, he's besieged on all sides, asked a thousand questions, his input begged for, his attention needed. The people—*his* people—are all thin, all dressed in threadbare clothing. Plenty of them are missing hands, or arms, or legs. He has a few seconds for each one, never lingering, giving clipped, direct answers to every question thrown at him.

Some of the people glance at me, with a few of the glances lingering longer than I'd like. I feel my face going red, a hot flush creeping under the skin. When I brought the Nomads to their door last night, I didn't know I was risking... *this.*

"They used to put cars here."

Harlan is standing next to me, gazing around the space with pride. "Not that there's been a car down here for a thousand years. There used to be whole floors of 'em, just lined up next to each other. That'd be quite something, wouldn't it?"

I nod, more stunned than I'd like to admit. "How do the Nomads not know about this place?" I say.

"Eric's smart. It's why I married him. He—"

"Wait, you and Eric were married?"

"Sure. Twenty years and counting."

He flashes me a smile. I decide not to mention the fact that Eric apparently doesn't want him around any more.

"Anyway," he says. "Eric keeps scouts in the field. They get food, supplies, report back whenever Nomads move through the area. They get close, Eric locks the hospital down. Haven't been discovered yet."

He sees my expression of disbelief. "Oh, they've been in the building plenty of times, but they never managed to get into the basement."

I shudder. I had to get the wound in my thigh cleaned, didn't have a choice, but I'm appalled at the destruction I nearly brought down on Eric and his people. No wonder he wants me out of here.

Eric leads us to the far end. There's a tiny space, in the shadow of the giant concrete ramp, separated from the rest of the floor by scarred metal plates that look as if they were cut from something much larger, then propped up so they form a vertical barrier. There's a gap in the plates, guarded by another man with another gun. He starts when he sees us, but Eric waves us through and he relaxes.

I take in the space. A bent and twisted table, its surface empty, balanced on wobbly legs. Two straight-backed metal chairs. A duffel bag squats under the table, clothes spilling out of a half-open zip.

There's a cot in the corner, a faded mattress on top of it. No blanket or pillow. The only decoration is on one of the walls: a map, like Harlan's, but in even worse condition. It doesn't show as much land mass, just what looks like the surrounding area. Printed on the map, running in large, spaced-out letters, are the words: THE YUKON.

"Stay here," Eric says. "Both of you. I'll get Finkler."

He steps out through the gap between the plates, and I see the guard slide into place, blocking off the exit.

"Harlan," I say. "Where would this seaplane be? The working one?"

"Goddamn fool," Harlan says, staring at the door. "Always was stubborn. That's what I liked about him. Even back when—"

"*Harlan.*"

"Kind of hard to say." He saunters up to the map, running his finger along it. After a moment, he taps a segment on it where the brown land gives way to a splodge of blue. "My guess is Fish Lake."

I blink. It takes me a second to dredge up the meaning of the word *lake*. The idea of a body of water that size is almost impossible to imagine.

"I was on the north shore few months ago, spotted smoke," he says. "Got a look through my binocs—seemed like they set up a camp of some kind." He shrugs. "Weren't no seaplane there, though. Not then, anyway."

"I thought you said the Nomads moved around?" I say.

"They do. Camp might've been temporary. But if I was a Nomad with a seaplane around these parts, Fish Lake'd be the place I'd land it."

"OK," I say, studying the map. I spot Whitehorse, and nearly scream with joy—it's close to the lake, no more than a few miles on the map. I could get there soon. I could get there *today*.

"And they can get to Anchorage?" I say, trying to stay calm, tracing across the map with my finger. The paper feels slightly damp under my fingertip. "They can fly that far?"

"Range-wise? Sure. Assuming they've got enough fuel. And assuming they're even there in the first place. Nomads aren't exactly predictable."

My finger touches the edge of the map, right on the border with Alaska—and that's when my heart sinks.

I need someone to fly the plane. It's all too easy to picture it coming down on the water—if the angle's off, even a little bit, it would flip right over the second it touched the surface.

"The Nomads'll have a pilot, right?" I say, more to myself than to anyone else. Of course they'll have one—they couldn't fly the plane otherwise. I'll have to get hold of that pilot, convince them to get me airborne. I don't have the first clue how I'm going to do that, but it's a start.

Eric returns, entering the room without looking at us. "Where's Finkler?" I say.

"He'll be here in a minute," Eric says, crossing around the other side of the table, dropping heavily onto one of the chairs. The metal frame protests, scraping across the concrete floor.

Harlan shakes his head, incredulous. "You know, I can't believe you, E," says Harlan. "You've been wanting to get in the air your whole life, and you just leave a damn seaplane *sitting there*?"

"What?" I say, turning away from the map. Surely I didn't hear that right. "You can fly a plane?"

Harlan and Eric glance at each other, for just a split second, and something passes between them. I don't even think they know they've done it.

"I can't fly a plane," Eric says.

"Sure you can," says Harlan. He turns to me. "We grew up in the same bunker together. I always remember he had this book—about how planes work? Engine diagrams, things like that. He read it a thousand times, always talking about how he was gonna learn to fly one day."

"Harlan, if you say one more word—"

"Well, sorry, E, but it's kind of obvious now, isn't it?" Harlan says, annoyed. My eyes drift to the logo on Eric's jacket. ROYAL CANADIAN AIRFORCE.

Eric sees me looking. "You want to know why I haven't gone up there?" he says. "Because I'd just get myself and my people killed. We're doing just fine here, and we *don't* need to risk everything we've built for a goddamn seaplane."

I turn back to the map, studying it, buying myself some time to think.

Assuming the plane is still there, then somehow convincing a Nomad pilot to help me without getting captured or killed—when I don't know the terrain and all I have is Harlan's rifle and no bullets—is going to be next to impossible. There's an easier way, and he's sitting right in front of me, still arguing with Harlan.

Except it isn't easier. Because even if Eric has enough knowledge to fly a plane, I don't have the faintest idea how I'm going to convince him to help me. I don't have a single thing to offer him. Asking for more, after what happened last night? I might as well demand that Harlan pull a teleportation device out of his back pocket.

And that's when the anger comes back. I know what I'm asking is too much, but it doesn't stop me from wanting to scream at Eric, to grab him and *make* him take me to the plane. The existence of the seaplane ignited a bright, burning hope inside me, but now that hope is fading, and the anger is in its place, dark and hot. With it comes the voice inside me, speaking quietly, insistently, telling me what I have to do.

There's only one way I'm going to convince Eric to help me. And I don't like it one bit.

I close my eyes. Then I turn back to Eric, folding my arms. "I'm going to Fish Lake. I'm taking that seaplane. If you're too scared to come with me, that's fine."

Eric is shrugging off his coat, pulling on a tattered sweater. I catch a knowing smile just before he pulls it over his head. "Nice try," he says, when he re-emerges.

I take a step closer. "Because you *are* scared, aren't you? That's why you're in here, right? That's why you hide every time the Nomads come by. You don't want to fight them."

"Careful," Eric says. But he doesn't look at me when he says it, and I hear the voice again: *keep pushing*.

"Must be nice," I say, and the spite in my voice shocks me. "Hiding out here while the rest of the world goes to shit."

"Come on, that is not—" Harlan says.

I cut him off. "This is a sweet hole in the ground," I say, spreading my arms wide. "But it's still just a hole. At least the Nomads have the guts to survive on the outside."

Eric's eyes flash with anger. "I'm here to keep my people alive. This little hole in the ground kept *you* alive, last night. Or did you forget that?"

That almost derails me. I don't have any right to say these things. Not even a little bit. But I can't let that stop me.

I cup my hands to my mouth. "Can anyone else here fly a plane?" I shout, and that's when Eric grabs me. He wraps his hands around the lapels of my jacket and pulls me close, looking right into my eyes.

He speaks very softly. "Get. Out."

I smile. Because I *wanted* that anger, that naked, white-hot fury.

"I would have hidden too," I say. "I would have kept my people around me, and kept it just us."

I can't help but think of the Devil Dancers, of the Nest. Of Amira.

"But here's the thing, Eric," I say. "The world doesn't care. It will take your friends from you no matter what you do. Now you can get angry at me—" I drop my voice a little "—or you can get angry at the Nomads. You can take the fight to them. Take the seaplane for yourselves."

Harlan is staring at me, confusion on his face. I don't recognise the words coming out of my mouth. Whoever owns the voice at the back of my mind is speaking for me. It's like I'm jamming a blade into a tiny crack, twisting, finding the place where I can lever it open.

I reach up, and slowly pull Eric's hands from my jacket, clasping them firmly.

"You know I'm right," I say, whispering now.

And then a voice, from over by the entrance. "She kind of is, you know."

Finkler. He looks as if he hasn't slept: his hair is a mess, his skin sallow, and there are giant sweat stains under his armpits. He walks over to me, and without waiting for an invitation tries to pull my pants down.

"Hey!" I say, letting go of Eric, twisting away.

"Come on," says Finkler. "Either you can pull them down, or I can, but I gotta see."

He waves at Harlan and Eric. "You two turn around. Give the lady some privacy."

Eric stares at me for a long moment, then turns to face the wall, along with Harlan. Blushing slightly, I work my pants down until the waistband is just above my knees.

Finkler runs his finger along the stitched-up cut. "Good, good, good. Okey-dokey. Any pain? I'm guessing you're walking OK?"

"Yeah. Thanks to you."

"Excellent," he says, motioning at me to pull up my pants. His belly is peeking out below the hem of his T-shirt, and I see the fat wobbling slightly. "Keep it clean, drink lots of water. You'll be fine. We caught it in time. I'd tell you to rest, but I'm pretty sure you'd just ignore me." He shouts over his shoulder. "OK, now we can talk about going to get this seaplane."

"Finkler..." Eric says. He sounds more tired than angry now.

"No, listen," he says. "I'll admit, last night was a bit of a clusterfuck, but it doesn't stop her being right. We've known about that plane for months, and we haven't done a damn thing about it. Now I know you're in charge, man, but you know how everyone feels about this."

"You're serious," says Eric. "You actually want us to go out there? Risk everything we've built?"

Finkler snorts. "I think it's a terrible idea. But the Nomads know we're here now. Even if we move the bodies somewhere, they'll figure it out. If we strike back, let 'em know we won't just lie down—"

"That's—"

"*Plus*, maybe we get a seaplane out of it. Maybe we get whatever's *in* the seaplane. Our medical supplies could use a restock, for one thing." He glances at me, then back at Eric. "So is it *really* that terrible? There's plenty of water to land it on. We can figure out how to disable it, too, if any Nomads do come looking. Just take a few crucial pieces out the engine."

He doesn't give them a chance to answer. "I'm going with her. If nothing else, it'll be a fun day trip."

"*You* could die," Eric says. "You ever think about that, Finkler?"

He pauses a second before answering. "Yup. And you wouldn't want to send your only real medic out there with nothing but *her* for protection now, would you?" He jerks a finger at me.

I could hug Finkler. Instead, I flash him a warm smile, then look back at Eric, raising my chin slightly.

I desperately want to take back everything I just said. I hate having to do this, hate having to manipulate people to get what I want. That's what Amira would have done, or Okwembu. It's not me, and it never has been. I tell myself that I only did it because Eric left me no choice, but no matter how hard I try, I can't convince myself.

I try to ignore my thumping heart. Eric could still say no. He could still send us away. I don't know if I'd blame him.

"Hell," Harlan says. "If you're really doing this, then I'm in. I'm no coward."

He's looking at me when he says it, but there's no mistaking who he's directing it at. Slowly, Eric raises his eyes.

"OK," he says. "We'll go."

Before I can speak, he raises a finger. "It's a scouting mission *only*. The four of us, and that's it. I'm not risking anybody else on this."

I take a deep, shaky breath. "That's all I ask."

Eric calls Harlan and Finkler over. I turn back to the map, my eyes on Fish Lake.

The voice inside me is silent, the anger turned down low. But I can feel it, just below the surface. It was so easy to tap into, like a vein of energy I'd always had inside me but never knew about. I tell myself that I won't let it happen again, that I won't let that be who I am. But the quiet voice inside me knows better. If it helps get me to Anchorage, then I'll use it.

No matter what.

43

Anna

Anna finds Dax Schmidt on the stairwell that leads to the main Apex control room. He's with Doctor Arroway, their heads close together, conferring in low voices.

She moves in quietly, on the balls of her feet, and neither of them realise she's there until she puts a hand on Arroway's shoulder, spins him around and slams him against the wall.

Arroway shouts in protest, shoving her away. He's stronger than she is, but he isn't ready for what Anna does next, which is to grab his hand and twist. Hard.

He grunts, the force bringing him to his knees, his arm twisted up at an awkward angle. Anna's used the move a few times before, usually on whoever tried to jack her cargo. She knows how painful this little hold is—and from here, a further twist coupled with a strike to the elbow will snap Arroway's arm. She doesn't do that. She needs him talking, not screaming.

"You're going to tell me what's going on," she says. "And you're going to tell me right now."

Arroway looks at Dax, as if pleading for help. Anna adds a little more torque to the twist, making sure Dax sees it, making sure he knows not to come any closer. "He can't help you. Start talking."

Fury crosses Dax's face. "Let him go."

Anna actually smiles. "There's an astronaut outside the station—I don't know how they got out there, but they did. And *you*." She spits the word at Arroway. "You're packing your bags, like you've won the lottery already. What do you know that we don't?"

Neither of them respond. Arroway is still squirming a little, but the stairway is silent, save for the hum of the station.

"Anna," Dax says again. "Let the doctor go, and I'll tell you."

Anna hadn't realised she was breathing so hard. She makes a conscious effort to slow down, but doesn't let go of Arroway's wrist.

"Please," Dax says.

After a moment, Anna lets the doctor go. He staggers to his feet, trembling. Anna looks at Dax, folding her arms and raising her eyebrows questioningly. He looks over one shoulder, as if to check that they really are alone.

"You're right, OK?" he says, leaning in and lowering his voice. "We sent one of our men outside."

"Dax," Arroway says, hissing the word.

"Shut up, Elijah." Dax holds Anna's gaze. "He took one of the escape pods. Once he was outside the station, he put on one of the pod's space suits, then he did an EVA."

Anna frowns, not understanding. Why launch yourself in a pod if you were just going to climb out of it?

Dax sees her confusion. "We had him use the thrusters on his suit to manoeuvre the pod back inside its launch bay. Nobody would know it had ever been launched, and we'd have a man outside the station."

"What about the fire? Was that part of it?"

"We had to get people out of the gallery area."

Anna stares at him in disbelief, as much for his candour as anything else. "You could have got everybody killed."

"Well, we didn't. We were always going to put the fire out. That wasn't the issue."

"What did you do? Turn off the suppression systems or something?"

"Just for long enough to get our man where he needed to be."

Anna closes her eyes, remembering the tech on the night of the fire. No wonder he was cursing. He must have been wondering why chemicals weren't spraying out, when the system was perfectly configured. That must have been why he tried to get into the power boxes, thinking the fault was inside.

"OK," she says. "Where is he now? Your astronaut?"

Dax takes a shaky breath. "We sent him to the dock. Or what's left of it. His mission was to secure one of the tug ships. Each one has plenty of emergency rations, plus a water reclaimer, so he can live out there for quite a while if he needs to."

"A tug?" Anna says, frowning. That doesn't make any sense.

"We think—" Dax says. "I mean, my advisers tell me that there's a way to construct a rudimentary heat shield on one of the tugs. Something that would ablate the heat of re-entry."

Arroway groans. Anna just keeps staring at Dax. This wasn't the confession she was expecting—although, in hindsight, she's not sure *what* she was expecting.

"But this is good," she says, after a moment. "If we can put heat shields on the tugs, then more people can escape. Right?"

"There's only enough heat-shield material for one tug," Dax says. "We made it out of epoxy and a type of copper alloy. We still had some in one of the labs."

"Then just hold the lottery now," Anna says, hating the pleading sound in her voice, hating how young it makes her feel. "If there's a way to escape, we should take it before the reactor..."

She trails off, her eyes wide. How could she have missed it? Why didn't she see it before?

She shut her eyes, screwing them tightly together. "There isn't going to be a lottery, is there?"

Dax's voice is quiet, gentle. "What would you do if you were in my position?"

Anna opens her mouth to speak, but no words come out.

"We've picked engineers, Air Lab techs, doctors." He glances at Arroway. "The best and the brightest. We're giving ourselves the best possible chance of surviving once we reach the ground. Something like this..."

He pauses, tries again. "It's too important to be left to a selection of random people. We're talking about the survival of our species."

Anna raises her eyes to meet his. "And council members?"

"What?"

"You're going, too. Aren't you?"

He shrugs. "Someone has to lead. We're going to need structure and order down there."

For a long moment none of them moves. Anna wishes she wasn't seeing things so clearly, wishes she wasn't filling in the gaps. They'll take the escape pods—all of them. Jordan is probably in on it—probably the one who started the fire. Dax and his friends will need the suits, after all, to transfer to the modified tug. Everybody else will be left behind. Even if they're still alive by the time the *Tenshi* gets there, they won't have any way to make it on board.

Eventually, Dax says, "We can try and get you a space on the tug, if that's what you want."

It's his solicitousness, his reasonable tone, that finally kicks Anna back into action. She almost snarls, backing away from them. "I'm going to tell everyone," she says. "They're all going to hear what you're doing."

She regrets the words the instant they are out of her mouth. She's still alone with the two of them. What if Dax has a gun? What if he tries to stop her?

"If you put a hand on me, I'll break every bone in your body," she says.

"Gods, Anna. No," Dax says, horrified. "Who do you think I am? Oren Darnell? Nobody's going to touch you."

"Doesn't mean I'm going to keep this a secret." Anna is already thinking ahead. She's still going to run, as fast as she can, right to the main amphitheatre. Her dad. She needs to find her dad. He'll know what to do.

"You're free to tell whoever you want," Dax says. "But understand this. If you let everyone know that we've got the means to escape now, there'll be anarchy. Complete breakdown. People will die."

"Yeah. Like you."

"Yes," Dax says simply. "But then what happens? You think things will go back to normal? You think this will be resolved *peacefully*?"

It's impossible for Anna not to think of Achala Kumar. Of her desperation to reach her son.

Dax smiles sadly. He walks past her, gesturing for Arroway to follow him. The doctor looks back at her, fear crossing his face.

"Think about it," Dax says. "It's up to you. But you'd better be sure you're making the right decision."

He and Arroway walk away, leaving Anna alone in the silence of the stairwell.

44

Riley

The howl stops us in our tracks.

For a moment, nobody moves. Harlan raises his face to the sky, head tilted very slightly.

The sound fades, and he visibly relaxes. "That's miles away. My guess is they don't know we're here."

He gives me a toothy smile. I try to smile back, don't quite manage it.

Eric seats his gun more comfortably in his arms. Harlan sees, shakes his head. "Doubt we'll need it. They might be aggressive, but there's easier prey than four folks with guns."

"Depends how hungry they are," says Eric, more to himself than to us. Without another word, he starts walking again.

My dark green jacket feels tight across my shoulders, padded out by the extra layers that Finkler insisted I wear. The grimy backpack on my shoulders keeps catching on branches. It's heavy with supplies: food, water, blankets, flares. *What I wouldn't give for my old tracer pack*, I think.

It's hard going. The ground is flat, but it's boggy and uneven, with plenty of frozen puddles ready to catch an ankle. There are trees, but they're spaced widely apart. Above our heads, the sky is low and grey, and there's no sound but the crunch–snap of our footsteps.

I've had some more time to think about what I baited Eric into, and it's not looking any better. It's all very well heading for a seaplane with someone who might be able to fly it, but that doesn't mean we're going to be able to walk in and take it. Harlan and Eric have a couple of those ancient rifles, now with some ammunition, but it's hard to imagine using them to take out a group of Nomads.

"Hey."

I hadn't noticed Finkler falling into step beside me. He hops over a patch of boggy ground, its surface speckled with ice, and lands with both feet. Despite his size, he seems to be doing better than all of us, even though he's wearing a bulky grey coat that makes him look even larger than he is. The ground has started to slope upwards, and there are more trees now, their bare branches reaching to the sky.

"How's the leg holding up?" he says. "Not that I'm worried or anything."

I smile, then look away into the distance. "Hurts a little, but I can handle it."

"I'm sure you can."

There are two fallen trees blocking our path, their branches standing straight up, their trunks caked with brittle moss. Finkler helps me over them, or tries to, holding out a hand to me even as he's struggling to keep his own balance. I wave him off, clambering over the trunks and hopping down on the other side. When I look up, I see that Harlan and Eric have reached the top of the slope, silhouetted against the sky.

"So what's the deal with them?" I say.

Finkler hits the ground behind me with a thud. He nearly topples over, and I have to steady him, holding his shoulder as he finds his feet.

"Who?" he says, dusting himself off. "Harlan and Eric?"

"I get that they used to be together, but why doesn't Harlan live with the rest of you?"

Finkler doesn't answer for a minute. As we trudge in silence up the hill, I start thinking that I've gone too far, but then he says, "They had a kid, you know."

"Had?" I raise my eyes to the figure of Harlan, gazing about him at the top of the ridge. Eric is swigging from a bottle of water, shivering slightly in the cold.

"She'd be about your age now," Finkler says. "Name of Samantha. Nomads killed her parents down in Utah on a raid when she was a baby. Eric saved her life, and he and Harlan took her in."

"What happened to her?" My throat is dry, and it's not because I'm thirsty. I dig in my pocket, hardly aware I'm doing it, and stick a cattail leaf into my mouth, chewing hard. My legs are burning from the climb, my upper back aching from the weight of the pack.

"They loved that kid. We all did. She had this smile like... Anyway, she was out hunting with Harlan one day, and they startled a bear."

"Gods," I say, more to myself than to him. I can fill in the blanks myself. I've never seen a bear, but I've seen pictures of one. Fur and teeth and muscle and claws.

"Eric had told Harlan not to take her, but that wasn't going to happen. Harlan doted on Samantha. He wanted to show her everything."

Finkler speaks in a matter-of-fact tone, which makes his words so much worse.

"The bear went for Samantha first. Harlan couldn't stop it. He tried to fight it off, but if he hadn't run when he did, he'd be dead too."

Ahead of me, Harlan laughs at something Eric said. Apparently it wasn't meant to be funny, because Eric meets it with a scowl.

"After Harlan came back," Finkler says, "Eric went out by himself."

The tooth. On the string around Eric's neck.

"Eric told him to get the hell out," Finkler says, and gives a bitter laugh. "Last night's the first time I've seen him in three years."

Harlan's face comes back to me, that night in the cave. It feels like decades ago. I remember the expression on his face—the sheer desperation. *You gotta tell 'em I helped you. You gotta tell 'em I looked after you, all right? Made sure you were OK.*

We crest the ridge. There's a flat part, an open plateau with tufts of grass sticking up through the mud. The forest sweeps away below us, and we begin picking our way down the slope. It's hard going; the ground is still slippery, and the rocks embedded in the slope aren't tight enough to hold onto. Harlan and Eric have already reached the bottom.

"Tell me something," Finkler says. "What happened to you up there?"

"What do you mean?"

He jabs a finger at the sky. "You tumble into my operating room, claiming that you crash-landed after escaping from a space station. That must be quite a story."

I open my mouth to tell him—but how do I even start? Janice Okwembu, Amira, my father, Morgan Knox, Resin, the mad escape from the dock, all of it. It's like a hunk of metal, with layers and layers of rust, the oxidation building on itself until you can't see the original shape underneath, the whole thing ugly and misshapen, with sharp edges that you have to be careful around.

"It's OK," Finkler says. He has a weird, crooked smile on his face. "I don't mean to pry."

"No, it's just—"

"But listen. You need to deal with that anger, and you need to deal with it soon."

His words stun me, although I'm careful not to show it. I shrug, but it's an unnatural motion, as if I have to instruct each individual muscle to move. "I just want to find my friends."

We've reached a steep part of the slope, and he has to watch his footing as he climbs down it. "Post." He takes a step. "Traumatic." Another, pausing to catch his balance. "Stress. Disorder."

He stops and looks at me, his eyes narrowed, breathing hard. "You think I haven't seen this a dozen times before? I've dug enough bullets out of people, done plenty of amputations. Even read a couple of books. I'm no psychologist, but I'm not stupid. How are the hallucinations?"

"What you talking about?"

"Please. I mean, don't get me wrong, I've had plenty of hallucinations myself, but they're usually self-induced? If you get my meaning? I'm not sure I want the ones you're having."

"I'm *not* hallucinating." But I can't help thinking of how I thought Eric was Amira. Such a small thing, so small I'd almost forgotten about it. And the voice inside me. Quiet, calm, insistent. Like part of my mind has decided to take over.

He goes on as if I hadn't spoken. "OK. You're not hallucinating. There's no anger in you. No aggression. You don't feel guilty that your friends might be dead, and you're a completely well-adjusted person with absolutely no fixation on a completely impossible task."

He purses his lips. "What do you want, Riley?"

"What do you mean?"

"When this is all over. After you and your buddies are back together. What are you going to do?"

I stare at him. Because, right then, I realise I don't know. So far, all I've thought about is getting to Alaska. Finding Carver and Prakesh, confronting Okwembu. I haven't even considered what'll happen after that.

I have a better idea of what I *don't* want. I don't want to be scared. I don't want to be cold, or hungry, and I don't want to keep fighting people who want to hurt me.

I don't want to be alone. And at this moment I don't know whether I want Prakesh or Carver to be with me. As long as someone is.

My thoughts are interrupted as Eric's voice reaches us. "*Finkler.*"

He and Harlan have stopped dead, crouching down on top of a huge spear rock jutting out of the hill. Without looking back, he motions for us to get down. I drop to a crouch, then all fours, letting my pack slip off my shoulders. Moving as quickly as I can, I scoot across the ground until I'm level with Harlan. There's an icy wind slicing through the trees, cutting through my jacket like it isn't there.

What I see takes my breath away.

We're perhaps a hundred feet up on the hillside, with Fish Lake stretching below us. It's more water than I've ever seen in one place, more water than I could ever imagine. It goes on forever, miles long. Under the low-hanging clouds, the water is the colour of burnished metal. The surface isn't still: I can see the water forming into waves with white caps, battering against the shore. The waves look tiny, as if I could rub them out with a finger.

The forest goes right up to the shore on all sides, the trees hanging down, reaching for the water. I can see right into the distance, right to the icy mountains with their peaks shrouded in the clouds.

Finkler is cursing and grumbling behind me as he tries to come up on our viewpoint. Harlan beckons me over, and points to a spot on the shore below.

Not just one seaplane, but two. Parked nose to tail, bobbing up and down as the waves hit them. Unlike the one in Whitehorse, these have wings, each one holding a single engine and a spiky propeller. They're just offshore, next to a simple floating platform, cobbled together from barrels and misshapen wooden planks.

There's a figure standing on the platform, hefting a tank. I can't make out the details, but it looks as if he's fuelling the plane, pouring liquid into the engine.

Harlan points again, and I see the tents, their grey fabric surfaces just visible through the trees. I can see the glint and glimmer of a fire, and there's a wisp of smoke snaking through the branches.

Eric has a pair of binoculars out, gunmetal grey, the lenses chipped. He's scanning the shoreline.

"How many?" says Harlan.

"Can't say," Eric says.

Eric crawls backwards off the rock, then slips into the trees. After a confused moment, the rest of us follow.

Once we're back in cover, we stand up. My legs are freezing, my toes almost completely numb. "OK," I say, thinking hard, reaching for my abandoned pack. "If we can—"

"No."

Eric isn't even looking at me. He's shouldering his own pack, making as if to leave.

Worry fills me, like an expanding bubble, pushing up through my body. "We can take them," I say, trying to keep the desperation out of my voice. "We just need a plan."

"We don't know how many there are down there," Eric says. "But two seaplanes? That means way too many Nomads."

"OK," I say again. "We wait until it's dark. They can't shoot what they can't see, right? And we can get closer, get numbers. Maybe even sneak past, take a plane."

"You don't know much, do you?" Eric says, scorn dripping from his voice. "You know how much noise a plane makes when you turn it on?"

Finkler brightens. "What about starting a fire? We could burn them out." He grins. "That'd be a lot of fun, actually."

Harlan looks around him. "Wood's too wet. No way we'd get it big enough. Even if we did, how are you planning on controlling it?"

Finkler's shoulders sag. I close my eyes, almost groaning in frustration. *There's got to be a way.* What if we could push a plane out into the lake? Start it away from the shore? No—the Nomads still have guns, and they'd still be able to shoot at the plane. We'd be a static target.

"So we come back with more people," I say. I'm grasping at ideas now, desperately trying to find *something* that will work. "We go back to Whitehorse and—"

"Wrong." Eric's voice has hardened again. "I can't ask my men to risk their lives because *you* want a seaplane. We're done."

He turns to go. Harlan and Finkler are getting ready, too, putting on their packs in silence. In the silence, another wolf howl drifts across the forest. It sounds as if it's a little closer.

"Harlan," I say.

"He's right," Harlan says. He won't meet my eyes. "I'm sorry, but we have to—"

"Tell me again," I say. "About the wolves. About how they track their prey." I keep my voice quiet and even. A tiny spark of an idea is flickering in my mind.

Harlan's brow furrows in confusion. "Well, it's like I said, they've been getting more aggressive every year. Chances are they still got a little bit of our scent, but we'll be back in Whitehorse long before they…"

He stops when he sees the expression on my face. I'm barely listening. The spark has ignited a fire, and the idea itself is flaring brightly. Finkler looks back and forth between us, puzzled.

"No," Harlan says, his eyes wide. "Oh no. No. That's *suicide*."

He's right. It doesn't stop a smile from spreading across my face.

45

Riley

I concentrate on my breathing.

I don't know how long I've been out here. I gave up keeping

track hours ago. The night is bitterly cold, and there's nothing for me to do but try and keep my attention on the forest around me, watching for movement in the trees. My eyes are adjusted to the darkness now, and I can make out white vapour, curling in front of me with every breath.

I'm a hundred yards or so up the slope from the Nomads' camp. I can see the glimmer of their fire through the trees. I picked this spot carefully: there's a slight depression in the slope, shielded from the wind, and there's a relatively straight path through the trees to the camp. I scouted it out as the last of the daylight faded. I also made sure to test my leg, doing a couple of sprints in a clearing a short distance away. It hurts, and the cold makes the pain worse, but running won't be a problem.

Harlan begged me not to do this. So did Finkler. Even Eric was surprised that I was considering it—he told me it was the craziest thing he'd ever heard. He's probably right, but I think that's also why he and Finkler haven't left yet. The risk is all on me. If I mess this up, I die. Eric and the others can walk away, slipping back through the forest. If I don't, then Eric gets his seaplane—and this particular group of Nomads won't bother him and his people any more.

I told them to get as close to the camp as they could, and be ready to go. All they could do was insist I wear extra clothing: a thicker jacket, a scarf, a thin beanie. It helps, but only a little. I have my hands jammed deep in the pockets of the jacket, and every so often I windmill my arms to keep my body temperature up.

Around me, the forest is silent.

I breathe in, closing my eyes. I feel exhausted, but my mind is working in overdrive.

I've had time to think about what I said to Eric, how I convinced him to come out here. On one hand, it's hard to forgive myself for it—what I said was horrible. But at the same time I can't help thinking that it's the only choice I had. That's what I keep coming back to. The anger I feel—that hot, burning rage—is what's keeping me alive down here. In the end, getting to Prakesh and Carver is going to be about how hard I fight. I don't have to give in to the anger, but I can use it as a fuel, powering me all the way to Anchorage.

But the problem with those thoughts is that suddenly the voice is there, whispering in my ear. *It's not Prakesh and Carver. It's Okwembu. You want to find her. You want to make her pay.*

And that's the problem. I can tell myself I don't have to let the anger control me, but what's going to happen when I find Okwembu? When I'm face to face with her?

I exhale, and open my eyes. The moon has come out, spreading its light through a tiny gap in the clouds.

The wolf is right in front of me.

It's the leader, the small one. Its head is tilted slightly to one side, studying me, as if asking why I would be stupid enough to be alone in a forest at night.

I meet its bright eyes, just for a second. Looking into them drives a spike of terror into my chest. I look away, and that's when I see the rest of them, moving silently between the trees. Giant tongues pass across gleaming teeth. Clawed feet paw at the ground. There are too many of them to count.

"Thought you'd never get here," I say. It comes out as a harsh whisper.

Harlan was right. The wolves might be aggressive, but they're still animals. They'll go for the easy prey: a single target over a big group. They must have smelled us from miles away, tracked us here, urged on by their rumbling stomachs.

This is going to be the most dangerous thing I've ever done. Worse than running the Core on Outer Earth, worse than defending the dock. Because there is zero room for error. One mistake, no matter how small, and they'll have me.

But there's no going back. Not now.

My hands grip the flare in my jacket pocket. Slowly, oh so slowly, I pull it out.

It's a thin tube, ten inches long, the writing on it long since worn away. Eric gave me two of them. I considered using one in each hand, but I wouldn't be able to light them quickly enough.

It's only when the flare is fully out of my pocket that the wolf in front of me growls. The sound is so low it's almost subsonic. It opens its mouth, long tongue dropping from its lips.

How long before they attack? I don't even know if it'll come from the lead wolf. It could come from behind me, or from either side. I can hear them, padding through the trees.

In one movement, I reach up, grip the tab on the bottom of the flare, and pull. The tab comes out, jerking away from the body.

Nothing happens.

The wolf cocks its head to the other side. I try to keep breathing, thinking ahead, getting ready to drop the flare I'm holding and go for the second one.

With a gushing hiss, the first flare ignites. There's a white-hot flash at the end of the tube, and thick orange smoke begins pouring out. The smoke is lit from within by a cone of fire and sparks, and it turns the forest into a scene from hell.

The wolves go crazy. They bark and snap, clawing at the dirt, darting back and forth. Only the leader doesn't move. But I see his ears flatten against his head, see the orange light reflected in his eyes.

I take one last breath, sucking in the scent of the burning flare.

And then I run.

I explode outwards, my arms pumping, running at full speed towards the lead wolf. It jumps back, scared of the fire, just like I thought it would be. It's fast, but it doesn't get back far enough, not willing to give up that easily. With a yell, I swing the flare upwards, slashing it across the wolf's face. It yelps in pain, twisting away from me.

Behind me, the pack gives chase.

I'm reacting to things before I even register that they're in front, leaping over rocks, ducking under incoming branches. The wolves are on me in seconds, coming in from both sides so fast that I nearly lose my footing out of pure terror. The speed of the creatures is appalling. They're not just coming from the sides now—they're sprinting ahead of me, turning back, legs scrabbling in the dirt as they try to change momentum for an attack.

I keep going, swinging the flare behind me. The burning tip smacks into soft fur, and there's an agonised howl.

You can't outrun wolves. Harlan was right about that, too. But they've never hunted prey armed with a flame burning at 750°C. Over a longer sprint, they'd take me—Harlan said that the flame only lasts for about fifteen seconds. But fifteen seconds is all I need.

There's a steep drop in the slope ahead, a few feet, no more. I see the drop less than two seconds before I hit it, but I react instantly, slashing the flare across my left side to clear some space. Then I jump.

In the sputtering light from the flare, all I can see are teeth and eyes. Jumping doesn't make me move any faster, but being in the air means I'm out of the way of the wolves—the longer I can stay airborne, the better.

I bend my knees, ready to take the landing, to roll if I have to. It's not enough. I hit the ground badly, and my ankle twists.

The movement sends a shocking, agonising bolt of pain up through my leg. A single word blares in my mind, endlessly, like a siren: *No, no, no, no*.

A set of jaws snaps shut around my arm.

I react on instinct, jamming the flare right into the wolf's face. It lets go with a yelp, and I'm up on my feet before I can think about it. Another wolf snaps at my leg, but I'm too far away, and its jaws close on nothing but air. My ankle is screaming at me. The terror blocks out everything, even sound: all I can hear is a thin ringing in my ears.

I look up, and there's a Nomad ten feet away.

He's young—my age maybe, no more. He hasn't raised his gun, which is held slack across his chest. He's staring at me, at the wolves, completely confused.

I have half a second to pick out the details: the dried scraps of face paint, the torn jacket hanging on his slender frame. Then I'm sprinting past him, and he's raising his gun, yelling at me to stop. But he's much too late, and the wolves take him, knocking him to the ground. His gun goes off, but I can't tell if it found its mark. I don't dare stop. Not for a second.

I get flashes of activity as I run through the camp. Bodies springing out of tents, shouting in confusion. An oil lamp knocked over, spreading fire across the ground. The wolves are darting back and forth, snarling, growling, unsure of what to do with such a large group of humans but driven on by hunger.

It's what I was counting on. The only way through the camp, the only way to get past the men with guns, is to make the biggest, most insane entrance possible.

Two wolves have attacked a Nomad. I see him, blood spurting from his neck as he tries to push them away. On my left, a rifle is going off, the shooter repeatedly pulling the trigger. One wolf, more determined and focused than the rest, darts ahead of me, trying to cut me off. The flare is spent, and I hurl it at the wolf. It buys me just enough time to get ahead of it.

And I can see the seaplanes. They're floating a few feet off the shore, just beyond the makeshift wooden platform. Their white surfaces glimmer in the light of the spreading fire. The door on the leftmost plane is open, exposing the dark interior.

There's a Nomad in front of them, a scrawny stick of a man. He's got his gun up, tracking me as I run towards him. I spring forward as he fires, tucking into a roll, my knees scraping across the platform as the bullet splits the air above me.

Then I'm up, leading with my shoulder, charging full speed into the man's stomach.

He topples backwards with a surprised *ooof*, the gun whirling away, bouncing off the side of the seaplane. I feel his hands on my jacket, hunting for a hold. Then we're tumbling into the seaplane, my body on top of his, my legs hanging out the side.

I don't wait for him to get his breath back. I twist around and punch him, fist connecting with his jaw. He grunts, trying to buck me off.

I push myself upwards, and that's when the lead wolf lands on top of me.

46

Riley

It's jumped the gap, launching itself right into the plane, the back of its body hanging out of the door. Its mouth is drawn back in an enormous snarl.

I jerk away, and a second later its jaws snap shut right where my head was. I'm still on top of the Nomad, my knee in his throat. The wolf lunges again, biting, snarling, moving in a fury. I try to get my feet underneath it, try to tuck them to my chest so I can kick it off, but I can't get enough space.

The wolf rears back, its front legs straight, its head silhouetted against the light from the camp. Its eyes are alive with the hunt, its mouth open, flecks of saliva flying as it bares jagged teeth. It's smart, backing off a little, giving it a bit more space to jump. This time, its teeth are going into my throat.

I don't see Harlan coming. All I see are his hands, wrapped around the wolf's midsection. With a terrified roar, he hurls the wriggling wolf right into the lake.

This wasn't the plan. They were supposed to come when the platform was clear. I thought that the Nomads would occupy the pack, letting us steal away in the plane as the camp dissolved in chaos. I didn't count on one of the wolves following me. Not that I have time to complain—Harlan saved my life. Eric and Finkler are pounding up the shore behind him, leaping onto the platform.

I don't have time to be relieved to see them. Harlan shoves me back into the plane, scrambling in after me, and then Eric and Finkler are there and my hands are shaking and I can barely breathe.

They grab the Nomad I punched, taking him by the arms. My punch was hard enough to break his jaw, which is already beginning to swell. I'm dimly aware of my hand aching, of a feeling of wetness as blood runs down from my knuckles.

The Nomad groans as they pull him up. "Can you fly this thing?" Eric shouts at him. The fire on the shore makes the sweat on his face glisten. When the Nomad doesn't answer, Eric sticks a rifle barrel in his face, jamming it against the man's undamaged cheek. "*Can you?*"

The Nomad nods, his eyes squeezed shut. Without another word, Eric pulls him towards the cockpit.

The interior of the plane is cramped, with a bare metal floor and straps hanging from the walls. Finkler is up against the wall next to me, hyperventilating. The camp is a nightmare. Dark shapes fly across the ground, flames lick at the sky. Screams and gunfire echo across the lake.

Impact

"The plane! They've got the plane!"

The shout comes from the shore, where two Nomads are running towards us. Their bodies are dark shapes against the flames.

Harlan swings the rifle around, and fires. His first shot goes wide, and he rips the bolt back, chambering another round. This one takes a Nomad in the shoulder, sending him spinning off the wooden platform and into the water. Harlan fumbles with the gun, his fingers slipping on the bolt, and then the second Nomad reaches the plane.

He's big, with square shoulders and jagged red paint above an unkempt beard. He doesn't have a gun, but he plants his hands on either side of the door, and starts to haul himself in. Harlan swings the gun around, but the Nomad just grabs the barrel.

I lash out, hammering my elbow into him. He's not expecting an attack from the side, and it knocks him off balance just enough for his one hand to slip off the doorframe. He tries to stay on, so I grab hold of his fingers, ripping them away. He goes down, falling out of sight.

The engines start, the propellers on either side of us whirling to life. The noise is so loud that I have to clap my hands over my ears. It's like being inside the belly of a roaring monster. I can see into the cockpit, up at the front. The Nomad's hands are moving like lightning, flicking switches and pulling levers. Eric is seated on the right, head low, gun trained on the pilot.

The plane starts to move, juddering beneath us. I can just see the shore slipping sideways through one of the windows.

We're moving way too slowly. Another burst of gunfire rakes the side of the plane. Finkler grabs me and pulls me down, just in time, almost slamming my head into the bare metal.

The plane lifts, just for a second, then hammers back down onto the water. This time I do knock my head on the floor and stars explode across my vision. Finkler's hand finds mine, squeezing tight.

We lift upwards for a second time. And stay there.

My stomach is rolling, not used to the sensation of take-off. Finkler's face is split in a massive grin. He pumps the air, cheering, then grabs my shoulders and pulls my face close to his. I can see his lips moving, see him shouting something, but I can barely hear the words over the noise of the engines and the rushing air from the open door. Harlan is there, too, down on one knee, breathing hard.

I sit back against the wall, feeling the vibrations travel through me. We have a seaplane. *And we're flying.*

The relief is exquisite, so powerful that I have to close my eyes for a second, fight the tears back. We did it. I can get to Anchorage.

The feeling lasts all of three seconds. Another window shatters, the bullet burying itself in the far wall.

The second seaplane comes into view, flying alongside us.

47

Riley

For a long, frozen second, it looks like their plane is going to crash right into ours.

I can just see it through the broken window. It's coming in off our left wing, rising up from below. I can't see into the cockpit, but the door in the side of the plane is open, and one of the Nomads is leaning out. He has a rifle, and he's trying to get a bead on us again, trying to steady his shot against the buffeting air.

He fires. The bullet goes wide, and the plane drops out of sight.

"It's OK," Harlan shouts, his mouth next to my ear. "First shot was lucky. Son of a bitch'll never—"

The second seaplane collides with us.

The bang feels like the world tearing apart. My stomach plummets as our plane lists to the left, tilting sideways. It's all I can do to keep my balance. With a roar, the second plane appears on the right, its wingtip only just missing ours.

Whoever is flying that plane is insane. He'll take both of us out at once. A hit in the right place will damage an engine, shear off a wing.

Impact

The other plane drifts away, as if it's taking a run-up. Then it banks towards us, filling the windows.

There's an angry shout from our cockpit. Eric is leaning across, hands wrapped around the control yoke, pushing the Nomad pilot aside. We tilt again, the nose dropping, and the incoming plane roars above us.

The Nomad in the cockpit grabs Eric's head by a fistful of hair, smashing him into the yoke. Eric is in an exposed position, bent over, and he can't reach around to stop the attack.

I launch myself up the body of the plane. Finkler is just behind me, almost rolling across the wall. I can't do anything about the attacking plane, but I can do something about the Nomad in the cockpit.

I reach through the gap between the two front seats, and wrap my arm around the man's throat.

He tries to fight me, tries to push me off. But I brace my knees against the back of the seat, and pull. He can't stop himself being hauled upwards, even as his fingernails rake across my cheek.

I twist my body sideways, dragging the man through the gap between the seats and into the body of the plane. I can just see the other seaplane through the cockpit glass—it's coming up from below us, trying to find an angle. Eric is trying to haul himself into the pilot's seat, trying to grab the yoke.

The attention slip costs me. The Nomad lands a blow on my eye socket, setting off a burst of stars in my vision. He's wriggling out of my grip, his chin pushing against my arm.

Finkler and Harlan are grabbing his arms and legs, trying to hold him down. But we're all awkwardly balanced, the confined interior of the plane not letting us move around. The Nomad takes the advantage. With a sudden burst of strength, he rips out of my grip, his body swinging sideways. He nearly falls out of the open door, but manages to grab on, his fingers snagging the edge.

His eyes meet mine, and I can see him getting ready to move, getting ready to throw himself back inside. The second seaplane is in view, moving in from behind us, coming in fast, a white ghost against the dark sky.

I don't think. I just move. My foot slams into the Nomad's chest.

He swings sideways, his fingers ripped from the edge of the door, just like the one who tried to climb in off the platform. Except this time there's nothing to break his fall.

The shock and anger on his face are unbelievable. Then he's falling, tumbling out. Slamming into the other plane.

Its wing takes him at his waist. For an instant, he just hangs there, stuck fast by the rushing air. Then he slips sideways, his upper body dropping right onto the whirling propeller.

There's a grinding bang. The propeller knocks the Nomad sideways, his body spinning out of view. The engine starts to tear itself apart. Grey smoke billows out of it as the housing comes apart in shreds, the propeller curved inward now, starting to tear up the wing itself.

The plane tilts, as if the mangled engine is pulling it to the ground. Then it's gone.

For a moment, I'm perfectly balanced in the plane's unstable interior, hands just touching the wall. I'm reliving the Nomad's expression again—that horrified shock as he realised he was falling. That was me. I did that.

I don't feel anything. Not a thing. And for the first time, that doesn't bother me.

"Eric!" Harlan shouts.

The sound drags me out of my thoughts. I turn to see Harlan leaning into the space at the back of the cockpit. Just past him, I can see Eric in the pilot's seat, hands on the controls. He's gripping them so hard that his skin has turned white.

He's never flown a plane before—never even been inside one, for all I know. He might have the knowledge, gleaned from books, but that's all he's got. And now he's at the controls, a thousand feet up. The plane starts to tilt, its nose pointing towards the ground.

I stagger up towards the cockpit, squeezing through the opening and slipping into the seat on Eric's right. It used to be fabric and foam padding, but it's been worn down to a bare skeleton, and the struts jam into my back. There's a second stick in front of me, moving in tandem with Eric's. I can just make out the dark shapes of mountains through the smeared cockpit glass.

The plane levels out a little. We're still descending, but more slowly now. Eric is staring straight ahead, mouth open. Sweat drips from his chin, landing on his vice-grip hands.

I say his name, but it gets lost in the roar of the engines. When I reach out to grab him, I find that he's trembling, his shoulder vibrating under my hand.

Finkler shoves his way through the opening, hunting for something. He reaches up behind me and jams something over my head. A pair of headphones, huge and bulbous, catching my hair and trapping it against my scalp. I adjust them, pulling the microphone stalk down as Finkler puts another pair on Eric's head.

The sound of the engine is muffled now. I feel on the stalk for the transmit switch, clicking it into place. A thin crackle of static emerges over the engine.

"Eric," I say. I have to repeat his name before he looks at me, and, when he does, there's naked terror in his eyes. This isn't the commander I saw back at the hospital. This is someone who is coming face to face with his worst fear.

I see his lips moving, but I can't hear him. I point to the stalk, and after some fumbling his voice comes across the channel: "—do it. Can't do it."

"Yes, you can," I say.

He shakes his head, letting go of the control yoke and gripping the mic stalk with both hands. The plane dips even further, sliding me forward in my seat. I grab my own control yoke, moving more on instinct than anything else, pulling it backwards. We start rising, but I've pushed it too far, overcorrecting the movement. The yoke feels heavy in my hands, the plane both sluggish and impossibly sensitive.

"Eric, listen to me," I say. "I can't do this by myself. I don't know how."

"You think I do?"

"You've read the books. You know how this thing works. Eric, *please*."

"No." He's shaking his head. "We need to go back to Whitehorse. We'll find someone else."

It would be so easy to get angry, to scream at him. It's not just that I could—I *want* to. But getting angry isn't going to work—not this time. I don't have the first clue what I'm doing. Eric needs to figure out how to fly this thing, and soon, or we're going to crash. I have to help him understand that he can do it.

A memory tugs at me. Carver, back on the station. We'd been captured by Mikhail's Earthers, and to escape I'd taken a little girl hostage. Ivy, her name was. I held her round the throat, used her to buy us some time. Carver gave me hell for it, told me that I was trying to handle everything myself, acting before my friends could help me.

I reach out, grabbing his hands, pulling them gently off the stalk. Then I place them on the control yoke, holding them tight, before returning my hands to my own controls.

My eyes meet his. "We're going to do it together," I say. "We'll pull it up. All right?"

The terrified expression hasn't left his face. But after a long moment, he nods.

"Here we go," I say. Together, we pull back on our control yokes.

The plane levels out, and then slowly begins to climb.

48

Anna

Anna Beck leans over the control panel, her mouth inches from the mic set into the edge of the touchscreen.

She opens her mouth to speak, then stops.

It takes her several attempts to form the words. "*Shinso Maru*, please respond. This is Outer Earth. Do you copy?"

Nothing. Just static, ebbing and flowing.

"*Shinso Maru*, can you hear me?"

Her voice breaks on the last word, and she sits back, head bowed. This isn't the first time she's been in the Apex control room, and it's not the first time she's tried to find a sign that the asteroid catcher survived. Why should now be any different? She's not going to hear from the *Shinso*. She's not going to hear from anyone. Earth is silent—the last time any signal was picked up was decades ago. One by one, they all winked out.

Anna Beck doesn't cry. She hasn't shed a single tear, and she's not going to now.

The Apex control room is a long and narrow space, with banks of screens bordering a thin strip of metal flooring. Most of the screens are dead. The few chairs that remain are battered and worn. Anna is sitting in one of them, elbows on her knees, staring at nothing.

Nobody comes here any more, mostly because there's no point—most of the technicians who used the systems are dead, and what's left is running on automatic, humming away while they wait for the reactor to die. The control room is the one place that Anna can virtually guarantee that she'll be alone. She's afraid that if she runs into anyone she won't be able to keep Dax's plan to herself. And she can't tell anyone about it. Not yet.

Because it might be the wrong choice.

Anna laughs. There's no humour in the sound. She's thinking about the people she killed during the siege in the dock, when she squatted behind a barricade with her long gun and fired again and again and again. She's thought about them a lot in the past few days. Why shouldn't she? Nobody should have to take a life, let alone five or six of them, one after the other.

And yet, it doesn't bother her. Not as much as it should have. The choice to do it was cut and dried. Those people—the Earthers—were coming to hurt her and her friends. They wanted out, and they didn't care what was in their path. She did the right thing—no, she did the *only* thing.

This isn't so simple.

Objectively, Dax is right. That's the worst part. It *does* make sense to send the people who give them the best chance of survival. That doesn't stop it from being completely insane, a plan that takes the chance of life away from almost everyone on the station, without their consent.

Anna could let it happen. She could let them die, and give humanity the best possible chance. Or she could tell everyone, and accept that in the chaos that comes afterwards—and Anna knows it'll be chaos, knows it in her bones—there might still be deaths.

Every time she thinks she's made her decision, every time she starts to rise from her chair, she falters. This isn't just a group of people in a thought experiment. This is her parents. Achala and Ravi Kumar. Marcus, and Ivy, and the rest of the kids. These are people she knows.

Which ones will die, and which ones will live?

Without really realising she's doing it, Anna leans forward, idly trailing her hand along the onscreen frequency band. "This is Outer Earth," she whispers, not expecting an answer but not sure what else to do. "I need help. Please. If anyone can hear me, this is station control for Outer Earth. Please respond."

49

Riley

Finkler's voice comes through the channel. "Can you hear us up there?"

I twist round, looking through the gap in the seats. As I do so, I get a better look at the plane's interior. It's old—ancient, actually. The walls are caked with rust, and the floor is a mess of struts and hinges, the seats they once held long since removed. There are a few battered plastic crates scattered across the floor of the plane, and, at the back, there's a loose mesh netting hanging from floor to ceiling, with more crates stacked tightly behind it. Finkler and Harlan have found headphones of their own, pulled down from brackets mounted on the wall.

Eric is staring straight ahead. "Yeah, I hear you," he says, barely moving his lips. He seems…not calm, exactly, but a little more focused. We're not going to crash, at least not right away.

"How much fuel do we have?" I say.

His eyes don't leave the windshield. "We're lucky. They'd filled her up. Probably getting ready to head out in the morning." He glances at me, and his face hardens. "Before you say anything: yes, I'll take you to Anchorage."

I don't know *what* to say. Despite everything that's happened, he's still got every right to turn this plane around and return to Whitehorse. He'd be putting his people's needs above mine, and I wouldn't be able to fault him for it.

He sees my confusion. "That plan of yours was the stupidest, most insane thing I've ever heard. It should have got you killed, and you know it. But you went out there anyway. That counts for something, at least to me."

There's a long pause.

"Thank you." It's all I can think to say.

"But let's get it straight," he says, and I can hear the strength coming back into his voice. "We're not sticking around. Once we get you there, you're on your own. I'm taking this thing back home. That's assuming I don't mess up the landing and kill us all."

"Fair enough."

There's a square screen to his left, full of strange shapes, and he taps it with a fingernail. "The plane's got some working nav software on it. We'll head for…" He checks the screen. "Cook Inlet. It's just up past Anchorage. If we get down safe, we can get you onto the shoreline. We should have enough fuel to make it back OK."

I sink back against the seat. The plane is rocking gently from side to side, steadily climbing, and Finkler and Harlan are talking in excited bursts as they dig through the containers at the back of the plane.

Eric looks around for a long minute, hunting across the control panel. "Hit that button there," he says, pointing to a spot on my side, where there's a bank of toggle switches. I reach over and grab the one I think he's pointing to, on the far left.

"No, that's the—" Eric says, and then I flip the switch and our headphones explode with noise.

My eardrums feel like they're tearing in two, like every frequency in the spectrum is trying to jam itself inside my head. I grab my headphones, trying to rip them off, but one of them is caught on my ear. Eric launches across the space between us, scrambling for the switch.

At the last second, just before he turns the switch off and kills the radio, I hear something.

Something that shouldn't be there.

"Jesus," Eric says, shaking his head as he sits back in his seat. He yanks the control stick downwards, jerking the plane back up. "That was the radio. The one I was *pointing to* is the autopilot switch, so if you could—"

"Turn it back on," I say.

"What?"

"Turn it back on. Right now." I don't wait for him to do it. I reach forward, and flip the switch. Eric stares at me, wincing at the noise. Then he grabs a dial just under the bank of switches, and twists it all the way to the left.

The sound is still a jumble of noise, but it's softer now, almost inaudible. Eric is staring at me like I've gone mad.

Slowly, very slowly, I turn the volume up. A little at time. My eyes are closed, as if it'll help me find the signal in the noise.

Nothing.

I must have imagined it. My shoulders sag. For a second there, I thought—

The voice comes across the transmission, almost buried by the noise, split in two by the static: "—anyone hear me?"

Eric is staring at me, confused. "So some kid's got hold of a transmitter. So what?"

"We have to respond," I say, my voice curiously breathless. I'm hunting the panel for a transmit button, but I can hardly make sense of the labels: DOPPLR and TFREQ, RFREQ and OFFSET.

"Finkler!" Eric shouts, not bothering to use his headset. I hear clunking footfalls, and then Finkler's flushed face pokes into the space between Eric and me.

"Mind giving us a little warning before you mess with the radio?" he shouts.

I grab his shoulder, jamming my headphones back on. "I have to transmit," I say. "Outside the plane."

"Hey, whoa," Finkler says, his face serious. "I mean, I don't know if—"

"Please."

"Do it," Eric says.

Finkler shakes his head, his eyes wide, but leans forward until he's on all fours, half in and half out of the cockpit. He toggles some switches and adjusts some knobs, his tongue sticking a little out of his mouth.

"Hurry," I say.

The voice comes again, and my heart almost explodes out of my chest. The sound is fainter this time: "—Control on Outer Earth transmitting. If there's—out there—"

"My God," Eric says, staring at the radio.

Finkler twists a knob, and reaches over to flick a second switch, his arm nearly colliding with my face. Then he leans back, and touches a button on the centre console.

The static vanishes.

For a second, I think we've lost her, but then Finkler gestures at me to speak.

"Anna?" I say. "This is Riley. Come back."

Finkler releases the button. The static returns. There are more artefacts in the noise now, strange blips and clicks, as if my words have disturbed a strange god, slowly coming to life.

Then, almost inaudible, I hear Anna Beck's stunned voice. "Riley?"

Finkler and Eric are staring at me in shock. Harlan has arrived, too, his face visible above Finkler's back.

"I can hear you!" I say.

Anna's reply is fractured "—shit, you're alive! How—others, are you—"

"Anna, what about everybody up there? Is Outer Earth OK?"

"—dying. The reactor's cut out, and—"

"Anna, say again?"

"—send a ship back to Earth, but we don't know—"

"It has to be passing right overhead," says Finkler, as Anna's voice cracks apart in the static. "That's the only way this is happening." He grabs my shoulder. "You've probably got about fifteen seconds, maybe less."

Hearing Anna's voice, knowing she's alive, after the breach in the dock, is almost too much to take. I hit the button again. "Anna, listen to me carefully. If you can make it back to Earth, aim for a place called Whitehorse, in the Yukon. We'll be waiting for you." I don't know what Eric might say about that, and right then I couldn't care less.

Her voice is even fainter now. "—ley, I copy, we'll come—you. As soon as I—"

And then she's gone. There's nothing but static

"You have to tune it," I say, pointing to the radio. "Get her back."

"She's out of range," says Finkler, giving a helpless shrug.

"There's gotta be something we can do."

He reaches forward and adjusts the dial marked DOPPLR. The squelches and clicks mutate, lengthening and twisting into new sounds. He grunts in frustration, turning his attention to TFREQ, then RFREQ. After a long moment, he drops his hand.

"Nada," he says. "Doppler offset didn't catch her. She's out of range."

He looks genuinely distraught, like he's let someone die. I reach up and put a hand on his, squeezing tight.

"Were we just talking to someone in space?" Harlan says.

"Who was she?" Eric says. "And did you just seriously invite *more people* to live with us in Whitehorse?"

I don't have a chance to answer. At that moment, another voice cuts across the static.

"—broadcasting from a secure location in what used to be Anchorage, Alaska. There are at least a hundred of us here, and we have managed to establish a colony. We have food, water and shelter. The—"

I flick the radio off.

50

Anna

Riley is alive.

The implications cascade through Anna's mind as she sprints across the sector. The *Shinso Maru* made it down. The plan to use the asteroid as a heat shield actually worked. And what was that Riley said? *We'll be waiting for you.*

She barrels around a corner in the corridor, slamming into the wall but pushing off it, sprinting even faster. She doesn't have to make the choice any more. If there are people down there already, then Dax's decision—to take only *the best and the brightest*—doesn't have to be made. She doesn't have to play his game.

Riley made it. Maybe Aaron Carver, too, and Prakesh. She has to tell her dad. She has to tell the Kumars. Hell, she has to tell everyone. She runs faster, pumping her arms, and this time she opens her mouth and let loose an ear-splitting whoop of joy. It occurs to her that she could have used the station comms, which are operated from the control room. Then again, she thinks, that would deny her the opportunity of seeing the look on Dax's face.

She doesn't slow down as she approaches the amphitheatre. The door is open, slid away into the wall, and she can hear the crowd as she gets close. She can hear—

Angry shouts.

She hesitates, and that hesitation nearly kills her. She's going too fast, and the pause shifts her centre of gravity slightly, tilting her forward. Her feet try to compensate, stutter-stepping, and then she slams into the edge of the door. It takes her in the shoulder, and a starburst of pain explodes on her collarbone.

She comes to a halt, leaning against it, and finally sees inside the amphitheatre.

Everyone is on their feet, screaming at each other, giant knots of people hurling accusations. Her father is standing on one of the chairs at the front, his hands around his mouth, yelling at everybody to stay calm. An empty food container flies through the air, bouncing down the centre steps.

There's a woman coming out of the amphitheatre, a grim look on her face. Anna pushes past the pain, and grabs her. "What's going on?" she says.

"You haven't heard?"

Anna manages to controls herself. "Tell me."

The woman shakes her head. "The escape pods launched," she says, speaking as if she can't believe the words herself.

Anna stares at her, eyes wide. "How many?"

The woman doesn't answer. She shakes Anna off, then jogs away down the corridor.

Dax.

He wasn't giving her a choice. He was just buying himself time, taking her out of the equation so she wouldn't warn anyone before he could make his escape. How could she have been so stupid?

Anna's shoulder is on fire. She ignores it. She takes one last look at her dad, down in the amphitheatre.

Then she turns, and runs.

51

Riley

"We're getting close," Eric says.

His words jerk me awake. Until that moment, I hadn't even been aware that I was sleeping, but the vibration of the plane and the whirr of the engines made me drift off. My back is kinked from the hard chair, and, despite the meat strips I ate a couple of hours ago, my stomach feels hollow and tight.

I raise myself up a little, looking out of the cockpit glass. I can't see a damn thing. Dawn is starting to glimmer behind us, but I can still barely tell the difference between the ground and the sky. It's hard to believe that Eric knows where he's going.

"Shouldn't we be seeing lights?" I say.

"We don't know what we should be seeing," says Eric. He sounds more subdued than before, a note of worry creeping into his voice. Not surprising—soon he'll have to land the plane, one way or another.

"Don't you worry about Eric," says Harlan, his voice coming crystal-clear over the headset. "He'll fly us right. Hey, Riley—come back here for a second, would you?"

I stretch briefly, kneeling on the seat. Then I clamber out into the main body of the plane, leaving my headset behind. Eric is making a gentle right turn, and it nearly throws me off balance, but I manage to keep one hand on the side.

Harlan and Finkler have turned the place inside out. Boxes lie everywhere, their contents upended and scattered across the metal floor: scrap metal, spare parts, tools, pieces of foam rubber, articles of clothing so threadbare that it's a wonder they don't fall apart when I look at them. Finkler is on all fours, picking through a pile of seemingly identical screws. Bandages and bottles are stacked on his right. A single dim bulb, set into the ceiling, is the only light.

Harlan waves me over. He passes me an extra set of headphones, the cable running into a box bolted to the roof.

"Here," he says, bending down, once I've got them in place. There's a backpack by his feet, covered in lurid red and green stripes, the fabric torn in places. By the way he grunts as he lifts it up, it's clear that the pack is heavy.

"Food, some extra clothing, odds and ends that you might need," he says. "There's a gun in there, too, although we can't find any ammo. Still, might come in handy. Oh, and here."

He passes me a piece of clothing—his coat. When he sees my expression, he shrugs. "It's thick, you know? Thicker'n the one you got on, anyway. You'll need to keep warm."

I tell him thanks, pulling off my coat and exchanging it for Harlan's. He's right. It's scratchy and uncomfortable, but it's also warm. The fabric smells of smoke. The pockets are stuffed full—I decide not to pull everything out now, where it could roll around the plane. I'll check on it later.

"I still think we should give her those socks," says Finkler, from his position on the floor.

Harlan rolls his eyes. "They're more hole than sock."

"I'm just saying."

"She'd be better off wrapping her feet in marsh grass."

"Fine. Then I'll keep them. I like socks."

I try to smile at Finkler's words, and don't quite manage it. The thought of going out there by myself, of leaving them, is almost too much to take.

I crouch down to Finkler's level, putting an arm around his shoulders. He stops picking through his pile of screws, letting his hand rest on the cold metal floor. "Just get back to Whitehorse safe."

I reach over and grip Harlan's shoulder. "You too, all right? You'd better be around when I get back."

He nods, not looking at me. "The terrain down there isn't going to be what you've seen before," he says. "Alaska's a bad place."

"Bad? Like how?"

"It's tougher for things to grow. The land isn't *honest*. It plays tricks on your feet. It's all bog and swamp, especially this close to the shore. You watch yourself."

"Thought you'd never been to Anchorage."

"I ain't. But I've been a little ways west. I've seen how it gets."

Eric's voice comes over the headphones, crisp and cold. "We're coming up on Fire Island, which means Anchorage is north of us. I'll go a little way past it, down the inlet. I don't want to put this bird down in Anchorage, not when I don't know what's out there."

"Fire Island?" I say.

Harlan points to the window, and I bend down to look through it. There's more light in the sky now, enough for me to see the vast ocean stretching away from us, a thousand times bigger than Fish Lake. I try to take it all in, but the sheer size of it makes me blink with astonishment.

At the very bottom of the view, peeking over the edge of the window, is a black strip of land. Water pushes in on it from all sides. We're coming in low over the ocean, and I can just make out scrubby plants on the shoreline. Water laps against the rocks.

Almost there.

Finkler stands up, resting one hand on the wall for balance. He puts his head close to mine, gazing at the view out of the window, and whistles softly. "You keep that incision clean, you hear me?" he says after a moment. "Don't wreck my beautiful stitches."

"Wouldn't dream of it."

"Good. Because if I find out you picked up *another* infection, I'm never going to let you forget it."

And that's when the sky explodes.

It's like we've flown into a meteor shower. The plane shudders as objects pelt it from all sides, too many to count. And the noise. All at once, I'm back on the *Shinso* as it plunged down through the atmosphere, tearing itself apart.

Eric banks the plane sharply, shouting over the headset. Harlan is thrown to the floor, and Finkler and I nearly land on top of him. At the last second, I manage to grab one of the headphone brackets on the wall, and stop myself falling. But the plane rocks from side to side, shaking to pieces as the storm gets more intense. My fingers slip loose, and my knee slams into Harlan's shoulder. Finkler is on his feet, whirling his arms, desperately trying to keep his balance.

A window detonates, glass raining inwards. Something is burning, and I smell the sharp stench of fuel, shooting upwards into the cabin from an unseen puncture. It's like we've flown into some insane weather pattern, a localised storm that—

Gunfire. It's gunfire. We're being shot at, by what feels like a million stingers going off at once.

We lurch to the side, tilting almost ninety degrees. Finkler slams into me, knocking me off Harlan. I feel his arm wrapping around me, like he's drawing me into a protective embrace.

We're heading right for a closed door in the side of the plane. The thoughts come in split-second bursts: *It slides open sideways, it'll hold us, it has to.*

Finkler takes the full force of the impact. I feel the bang, and it's so powerful that it rips the door off the wall.

I don't know if the metal is too old or the rails it's on are too fragile, but one second we're in the body of the plane and the next there's nothing but open sky above us. My headphones are yanked right off my head.

The tracer part of me kicks into overdrive, adrenaline and instinct overwhelming everything. I see the plane's pontoon and grab it in the same instant, wrapping my forearm around it. With my other arm, I reach for Finkler, already bracing to take the weight.

I get one last look at him, at the raw shock on his face. Then my hand closes on empty air and Finkler is gone.

Bullets are whizzing by me like angry insects, and the roaring chatter of the gun is everywhere, coming in quick bursts now, like whoever is firing is trying to save ammo. The plane took fewer hits than I thought, but it's still holed in a dozen places, gushing black smoke.

Harlan is above me, spreadeagled in the doorway, trying to get a better grip. He sees me, shouts my name, but then Eric swings the plane back the other way.

For a moment, I'm weightless, the motion of the plane cancelling gravity out. I can see the ocean below me. The white caps on the waves look as if they're frozen solid. We're seventy feet up, maybe more.

Harlan reaches out from the doorway, desperately trying to find my hand.

Another bullet hits us. I feel the plane tilt, and my arm rips free from the pontoon.

52

Riley

I thought I knew real panic. Not even close. As I plummet towards the water, the panic that surges through me is knife-point sharp.

Impact

I'm face up, windmilling my arms. Harlan is still leaning out of the plane, still reaching for me, as if his arm is going to extend and catch me. Then I'm falling, and I find that my mind is capable of only one thought, repeating over and over, Harlan's voice in my head. *Water that cold, it'll shut your body down in thirty seconds.*

I have to stabilise myself, brace for landing, do *something*. But my tracer instinct, so strong a few moments before, has vanished.

When I hit the water, it's with a thud so loud that it feels like it cracks my skull open.

It's as if someone has flicked the switch, turning out all the light in the world. I try to breath, and suck in a mouthful of seawater. It's foul, as cold as space itself, but forcing it back out is almost impossible. Somewhere, very distant, the muscles in my back are screaming at me. My lungs are on fire. I'm panicking, thrashing in place. I don't even know which direction to swim in.

Light. A tiny glimmer, no more. It takes me a good three seconds to get my muscles to push me in the right direction. My chest has turned into a supernova, and with every foot I swim, my vision gets smaller, shrinking down to a tiny circle.

My sight is almost gone when I break the surface.

I breathe too soon, before I'm fully out. I suck in a mouthful of water, coughing and spluttering. My eyes open so wide that it feels like they're going to tear right off my face.

The water is so cold that it's as if it's burning me, scourging my skin. It's slate-grey, spattered with white foam, hissing like an angry monster. There's a black shape rising out of it, an uneven jumble of contours.

Fire Island. I have to get there, and I have to get there *now*.

It takes every ounce of effort I have to keep my body above the icy water, but I manage it, kicking hard to stay afloat. More than once, the panic grips me, like a tentacle threatening to pull me under. I have to fight it off, willing myself to keep kicking, using my hands and forearms to push through the water.

I'm not going to last much longer. The muscles in my back are dull and useless, and the cold is shutting my body down, robbing me of energy. A chemical reaction in my cells. Prakesh would know…

The thought of him makes me force my exhausted arms to keep going. Prakesh is just over the horizon, and Carver, and Okwembu, and I did *not* come all this way just to drown here.

Kick, stroke, breathe. Kick, stroke, breathe.

Soon, the only sensation I can feel are my trembling lips. I can hear the teeth behind them chattering, my tongue a dead slab of flesh in my mouth.

And then something changes. I try to make a stroke, and my hand bounces back at me.

I keep going. My forearms slam into dirt, and I'm raised up on my knees. I start crawling, and when I fall, face crunching into the dirt, I pull myself along with my hands.

I don't know how long it is before I stop moving. But I can feel another sensation now: grains of sand, rubbing against my lips.

I'm out of the water. I'm on land. Wonderful, amazing, solid land.

I blink. Or I try to, anyway. The second I close my eyes, I discover that I don't want to open them again. They feel like they're welded shut, and what's behind them is too sweet to turn away from.

Don't.

It's the voice—the one at the back of my mind, the angry one, except this time it's not angry. It's distraught, crazy with fear, pleading with me. *You have to get up.*

It's like waking from a deep sleep, where you've stayed in one position all night and your arm or leg has gone dead. I have to focus on my fingers, slowly clenching them into a fist, then pull backwards until I'm resting on the forearm.

I raise my head. A muscle in my shoulder twinges, sending a sharp, shooting pain down my back. I push a clenched, angry noise through gritted teeth and open my eyes.

Black sand gives way to jagged rocks, sloping steeply away from me. I can see plants pushing up between the rocks, but they're withered and stunted, barely alive. There are a few trees further inland, their branches bare. The sky beyond them is ash-grey, and the only sound is the pounding of the ocean, the steady swish of water around my ankles.

My clothes are soaked. Streams of water fall off me, soaking into the sand. The wind has picked up, and it's like a blast from an open freezer, chilling me to the bone.

I look at the rocks again. There's something there, something splayed across them.

Finkler's neck is broken, his arms twisted at unnatural angles. The shocked expression is still on his face.

53

Okwembu

Okwembu's eyes fly open. She sits bolt upright, so quickly that she nearly hits her head on the underside of the bunk above her.

She listens hard. There: distant, humming bursts of gunfire. The Phalanx gun.

Okwembu kicks the thin blanket off her legs and slides off the bed. She's been given her own room, a tiny space on one of the upper levels of the ship, with low ceilings and a bunk bed bolted to the wall. She has to hammer on the door three times before the guard outside unlocks it. Okwembu ducks under his arm and strides down the corridor, only stopping when he grabs her above the elbow.

"What do you think you're doing?" the guard says. He's in his thirties, with blond hair and an angular, almost blocky face. His voice is alert, but Okwembu can see the fog of sleep in his eyes.

She shrugs him off. "I'm going up to the bridge," she says.

"Get back inside, right now."

Okwembu has a sudden, surprising urge to reach out and wrap her hands around his throat, to squeeze until that bright voice is extinguished. She shakes it off. "I'm going up to the bridge," she says again, her voice cold. "Touch me, and you'll have to answer to Prophet."

Another burst of muted gunfire rumbles down through the ship. The guard must see something in her eyes, because he stays rooted to the spot. She starts walking again, not looking back. He follows, but at a discreet distance, and after a few steps she forgets that he's even there.

The bridge is at the top of a central tower on the deck of the ship. Okwembu pushes herself up the last flight of stairs, ignoring her protesting legs, and pushes open the door.

The space reminds her of the main control room on Outer Earth. It's longer, and wider, but it has the same banks of screens and uncomfortable wheeled chairs, the same sickly fluorescent lighting. There are three large tables in the centre of the room, spread with yellowing maps and charts. Floor-to-ceiling windows line the wall to her right, looking out across the deck of the ship to the ocean beyond. Through the glass she can see the first faint glimmerings of dawn.

The bridge is packed with people, most of them still blurry with sleep. She picks out the alert ones instantly. They're the ones holding rifles, the ones who were on nightshift, or whatever these people call it. She can feel their eyes on her, hear their whispered, angry mutterings. Ray and Iluk are there, hunched over one of the tables. Ray's eyebrows almost touch his hairline when he sees her.

She spots Prophet immediately, standing before one of the windows. He's holding something up to his face, using both hands—some kind of binoculars, black and bulky. It's still dark outside, so Okwembu supposes they must have some kind of night vision.

She strides around the bank of screens, ignoring the suspicious stares. "What's going on?" she says, when she's standing next to Prophet.

He glances at her, irritation slipping on and off his face in a microsecond. "You should be sleeping."

"Just tell me."

He doesn't speak. She's about to ask again when he says, "An aircraft came in over the water. Our gunner caught it."

"Aircraft?" Okwembu squints, looking out over the water.

"Seaplane. Haven't seen one of them in years. Could be Nomads."

"Did you shoot them down?"

"Not sure. Definitely hit 'em, though, Engine be praised."

The words are taken up by the others on the bridge, rippling out from Prophet. Just as before, Okwembu can't help but notice a few people who conspicuously fail to praise the Engine.

She turns back to the window. "Who were they? Do you know?"

"Prophet." The voice comes from one of his men, standing off to their right. He has an identical pair of binoculars, and he's leaning forward, resting them on the window glass. "Got something."

"Where?" Prophet raises his own lenses again.

"Over by the island."

The murmuring on the bridge drops even lower. Prophet scans the horizon, tracking right to left.

He shakes his head, lowering the binoculars. "I don't see anything."

"Could have sworn," the other man says. "Right around the rocks on the western point."

"Nothing could have survived a fall from that plane," Prophet says, more to himself than to anyone else. "Not even if they hit the water."

He falls silent, still holding the binoculars at chest level, staring out across the water.

Janice Okwembu has always trusted her instincts. Sometimes, she thinks that they are all that has kept her alive. They've led her here, up to the bridge, and now she understands why. Despite the belief in the Engine, despite the military uniforms and the rudimentary chain of command, Prophet and his followers aren't good at reacting to the unknown. They're fine as long as new workers keep coming in, as long as there's a constant stream of supplies. She's an anomaly: a potential worker who somehow managed to avoid her fate, to position herself next to the ship's leader. That seaplane is an anomaly, too. It's upset the balance, disrupted the status quo.

Which gives her the perfect opportunity.

"You need to send some men out there," she says, careful to address herself to Prophet—she's not at the stage of giving orders. *Not yet.*

Prophet looks at her, his eyes wide. "You forget your place."

She pushes on. "You need to be sure. If there's someone on that island, they might be able to tell you about where the plane came from."

"She calling the shots now, Prophet?" says someone from behind her. Prophet's eyes are dark, but Okwembu holds his gaze. *Strength over weakness.*

After a moment, he turns away. "The Engine has brought her to us for a reason. We'll take her advice, for now. Ray: take Iluk and get out there. Bring Koji with you—if there's any debris, I want him to take a look at it first."

Okwembu turns back to the window, looking back out into the darkness.

54

Riley

Crying or screaming isn't enough. I want to turn and go back into the ocean, stop swimming, let myself sink into the blackness.

He saved my life. He helped get me to the Nomads' camp. He got me all the way here, and now he's dead. Just like Amira, and my father, and Syria, and everyone else. I can't save any of them.

My legs stop supporting me. I drop to my knees, bent over, digging furrows in the dirt with numb fingers. The tears finally come.

Maybe I shouldn't try to find Prakesh and Carver. They're not safe around me. Maybe I should just…vanish.

Listen, says the voice inside me.

And I do. I listen as it tells me what I need to do next. Because, right then, I realise that it's something that will never let me down. It'll help me, and it'll keep me alive. As long as I trust it. As long as I pay attention to it.

What was it Finkler said? Post-traumatic stress disorder. The result of bottling everything up, pretending that these horrible things never happened. Not any more. I'm not going to bottle this up. Finkler isn't going to have died for nothing. I'm not going to die. I'm going to find Prakesh and Carver, I'm going to take out Okwembu, and I'm going to make sure that this *never* happens again.

Somehow, I manage to get to my feet. I stumble over to the rocks, retching and coughing. When I'm a few feet away, my legs give out again. I go to one knee in the sand, breathing hard. I make myself get up, make myself pull Finkler's body off the rocks. It takes almost all the strength I have to do it, and when I feel that there's still body heat under the clothing, it nearly stops me in my tracks.

I pull Finkler's clothes off him, working his pants down around his ankles, rolling him over to get to his jacket sleeves. What I'm doing is awful, like spitting in his face, but I do it anyway, because I don't have a choice. I need dry clothes.

I strip naked, right there on the beach. The tips of my fingers have gone blue, and it takes everything I have just to stay upright. The enormous grey coat, and the shirt and sweater underneath it, almost swallow me whole. The pants balloon around my waist. My skin is still wet, and the remaining water makes the clothes a little damp, but I barely notice.

His boots are far too big. My feet slide around in them, threatening to slip out at any moment. In the end, I have to wear my own shoes. They're soaked, and the water bites through the dry socks instantly, but it's better than nothing.

I stand up, shivering in the wind, clutching my arms around me with my hands jammed in my armpits. I'm still far too cold, my thoughts coming in sluggish waves.

Harlan and Eric.

My eyes go wide. How could I not have thought about them? It was as if what happened to Finkler took up all the space in my mind. I scan the sky, hunting for the plane, listening hard for the noise of the engine. Several times I think I spot it, a black dot against the clouds, but then I blink and it's gone. *They're* gone.

I try to tell myself that they stayed in the air, try to make myself believe that they're OK. But how can they be, after that barrage? I squeeze my eyes shut, fighting off the despair.

There's nothing you can do for them, the voice says. *You need fire.*

That's what Harlan said, too. Clothes, shelter, fire. Whatever happened to him, he'd want me to keep going.

Finding shelter here isn't an option—it's rocks and sand and scrub as far as the eye can see. Fire it is. But how? Harlan never showed me how to make it. Back on Outer Earth, we'd use fuel oil, drenching rags with it and igniting it all with a lighter…

I jog over to the discarded jacket. It feels frozen solid when I pick it up, but I manage to keep hold of it, turning it the right way up and digging in the pockets. I feel something, pull it out. It's the bear spray, the one Harlan gave me. I growl in frustration, stuffing the spray into the pocket of Finkler's jacket, then keep digging. There are a couple of meat strips, a spare scarf, also soaked through, and a folded-up map. I shake it out, but it's too wet to even think about using as kindling.

There's something else in the pockets, something round and solid. A flare. Harlan was the one who gave me two of them to use on the wolves—he must have kept one for himself.

It's soaked, what's left of the label peeling off. Shivering hard, I clamber up the rocks towards the trees. I'm finding it more difficult to flex my fingers, and it's tough to get a good grip on the rocks, but somehow I manage it. I don't dare strike the flare until I have something to light it with. I try not to think about what will happen to me if this doesn't work.

The trees are spaced widely apart, pushing their way out of the uneven ground. They're tilted at odd angles, as if they've been frozen in the act of trying to escape. It takes me a few minutes to find some old man's beard. I let out a harsh, ragged cry of joy when I find some, and one of my fingernails breaks as I scrape it off the bark. It's a tiny amount, no larger than my palm, but it will have to do.

Harlan didn't explain how to keep a fire going after you start one, but that's not hard to work out. I dump the flare and the old man's beard in a clearing, and start collecting twigs. The ground is frosty beneath my shoes, and my feet have gone completely numb, but I keep going.

It seems like hours before I have enough. I crouch in the clearing, back aching, and squash the old man's beard into an uneven lump. I reach out for the flare, but it's not there any more. My fingers scramble at the ground in horror. Have I lost it? Did I take it with me? The cold is making it hard to focus. My mind keeps drifting, and it's hard to pull it back.

Then I spot the flare, a little way behind me, and grab it as if it's a lifeline. With shaking fingers, I turn it upright, and pull the tab. If it doesn't work…

It hisses like an angry animal, burning bright. It happens so quickly that it burns my eyes. I snap them shut, feeling the heat bake onto my hand, then jam the flare onto the old man's beard.

Nothing. There's smoke, lots of it, and some pieces of moss start to catch, but it's not working. The moss is too damp, too—

Flames. Shooting upwards. With a cry of triumph, I jam the flare deeper into the moss, and start piling sticks on the fire.

The smoke is unbelievable now, acrid and hot. The flames start to lick upwards as I add more twigs, little by little, and it's not long before the fire is a foot high. I get as close as I can to it, hugging my knees, letting the heat bake onto my face. The wind has grown worse, but I just manage to shield the fire from it with my body, kicking off my wet shoes and propping them as close to the heat as I dare.

I don't know how long I'm out for, but when I wake up the fire has burned down to cinders, and it's daylight—or what passes for it, under the grey clouds. Slowly, I pull my shoes on. They're still damp, but much less than before. The wind has died down, and I'm not quite as cold.

The faces of Harlan and Finkler and Eric swim to the surface of my mind. I push them away. I can't mourn for them now, not if I want to make it through this.

I try to picture Fire Island as I saw it from the air. It didn't look too big—I can probably make it to the far shore in a few minutes. I stand up on shaking legs, and start walking.

The pain in my back has settled into two burning rods at my

shoulder blades, but I make good time, pushing through the scrub and stumbling onto the rocky beach. The ocean in front of me is enormous. It's become choppier, the waves slamming onto the sand. I can just make out the land on the horizon, a dark line above the water, reflecting the grey sky.

There's something else there, too. A black shape, separate from the line of the land. I squint, putting a hand up to my eyes, but I can't figure out what it is. It's too far away.

My shoulders sag. It doesn't matter what it is. I have to get across this expanse of water, and I don't have the first clue how to do it. If Carver were here, he'd—

Voices.

I stop, listening hard, then hear them again, coming from further down the beach. I react fast, hurling myself to the ground. Sand scratches against my palms as I crawl behind a nearby rock. I put my back against it, trying to ignore the pain in my shoulders.

The voices are coming closer. I can't make out the words yet, but I can hear that the speakers are male. Their footsteps crunch on the sand.

"...the whole damn island," I hear one of them say. His voice is gruff.

Another one speaks. He's using a language I've never heard before, all elongated vowels.

"There's nothing here," says a third. "We would've found them by now."

"In the water, you think?"

"Then what about the dead guy? What happened to his clothes? Unless you're telling me they stripped him, *then* threw him out of the plane."

Finkler. They know about him, which means they know I'm here. Any second now, they're going to come round the side of the rock. I have no weapons, and I can't even imagine fighting three people in this cold. I close my eyes, trying to stay as still as possible.

"You're sure you saw—"

"*Yes*, Koji, I'm damn sure. Two of 'em, clear through the binocs."

There's a pause. The footsteps stop.

"Let's get back to the boat," the first one says.

When the reply comes, it's in an angry burst of that strange language.

"Tell you what, Iluk. *You* can stay here and double-check. Me, I'm going back to my booze and my bed. Only thing the *Ramona*'s good for any more."

I lick my lips. These people, whoever they are, have a way off this rock. I can't let that slip away.

But the second the thought occurs, so does every problem with it. I can't fight them—not in my current state, with no weapons.

I could follow them, track them across the island. I've done it before, on Outer Earth, when I followed a psychotic killer named Arthur Gray onto the monorail tracks. But this isn't Outer Earth—here, the ground is uneven, littered with rocks and branches, and staying silent will be difficult. I could try and get ahead of them, make it to the boat before they do, but I don't even know where it is.

There's another way, the voice says.

I stand up, turning to face the men, my legs burning as I push up off the sand. Then I cup my hands to my mouth and yell, "Hey!"

55

Prakesh

This time, Prakesh pays more attention.

He hardly got any sleep, but even a little is better than nothing. He's more alert now, looking for anything that he can use.

They're back in the farm, carrying the last of the soil sacks to their new position. Some of the workers have already begun filling the troughs, and the hangar is alive with the thumping, scratchy sound of dirt on metal. As Prakesh drops a sack on the pile, he takes a closer look at the guards.

It isn't hard to see how they've kept control. The workers might outnumber them three to one, but they've got all the guns. And they're smart about their positioning, too, spacing themselves out around the edges of the room, always keeping the workers in view. It would be easy to see a coordinated attack coming—and even if it succeeded there's no telling how many workers would die in the attempt.

Prakesh looks back at the troughs. They stretch all the way from the middle of the hangar to the far wall. Each one is waist-height, around forty feet long. *Easy enough for a man to hide behind.* If he could slip out of view, he could find a way out. And once he's out into the ship…

But there's no way he'll be able to get to a hiding place before being cut down. It would take an extraordinary amount of luck. For a moment, he entertains the idea that the guards have set movement patterns, but then discards it. They aren't robots.

Frustrated, he starts walking back the other way, his shoulders groaning under the heavy sack. Jojo passes him on the right, not looking at him. He hasn't said a word to Prakesh since the night before, as if the act of talking as much as he did has exhausted him. Prakesh can't help thinking of their conversation—how Jojo shut down the man who tried to stop them talking. He may have a stutter, may not even be out of his teens yet, but the other workers respect him.

The sack slips a little, sliding down Prakesh's shoulder onto his upper arm. He stops, shifting it back, and that's when the idea comes.

It's not just what Riley would do in this situation. It's what Aaron Carver would do, too. Carver, whose first response to any situation was to use a gadget or a tool, to use something he'd made. Carver, who was (*is*, he tells himself) always looking for new equipment.

Carver wouldn't just rely on what was here. Carver would be looking to see what he could do with it.

Prakesh stands there for a moment too long, and one of the guards shouts at him to get moving. He bobs his head in apology, hefting the sack as he starts walking.

He can't take out the guards individually. None of them can. But what if he could take them all out in one go?

They move to the troughs, all of them unloading the soil now, dumping it in and mixing it with fertiliser. The stuff comes in foul-smelling buckets, the white granules gritty and slightly slimy. There's insecticide, too: yellowish dust that Prakesh recognises as sulphur. He spotted it earlier, off to one side in a pair of grimy containers. It stains his hands and prickles the inside of his nose. You're supposed to handle this stuff with gloves—it can irritate the skin, causing blisters if you use a lot of it.

Jojo is next to him, head bent, patting the soil down. Prakesh doesn't look at him. Keeping his voice low, he says, "Jojo."

No response.

"Jojo," he hisses, a little louder. Out of the corner of his eye, he sees Jojo's hand flick the air twice. *No. Not now.*

"Then don't talk, just listen," Prakesh says.

It doesn't take him long to explain his plan. Jojo does nothing, doesn't even register that he's heard, but Prakesh isn't worried. *He wants this more than you do,* he thinks, pushing a handful of fertiliser under the soil.

When Prakesh is finished, Jojo doesn't respond for a long minute. Then his right hand forms a quick thumbs up.

It takes a long time for Jojo to tell the rest of the workers the plan. He has to be careful, changing places only when the guards' attention wanders, conferring with them in an almost inaudible voice. Eventually, he makes his way back to Prakesh, and flashes another thumbs up, more emphatic this time.

Prakesh lifts his hands out of the soil. He can feel the other workers watching him. There's a guard close by, a stick-thin woman with a shorn head, and Prakesh slowly starts to walk towards her.

The guard sees him coming before he gets within twenty feet. Her rifle goes up instantly, finger in the trigger guard. "Stop right there."

Prakesh can feel the other rifles on him, like needles sticking into his back. For a moment, it's as if all activity on the floor has stopped. He can't hear anything but the roaring of blood in his ears.

"Back in the line," the guard says, jerking her rifle. "We'll take a break in an hour. You can piss then."

"I don't need a piss. I need to ask you something."

"I said, *back in the line.*"

Prakesh looks over his shoulder, gestures to the troughs. "I can make your fertiliser better."

The guard's eyes narrow. "What?"

"Fertiliser. I used to be a plant technician, a biologist—"

He feels the bullet before he hears the gunshot. It *spangs* off the floor a few feet away, the gunshot echoing around the hangar. Prakesh jumps, and the workers hit the deck, throwing themselves to the floor.

"Move away!" shouts a voice. One of the other guards. "If she doesn't shoot you, I will."

Prakesh puts his hands above his head. He speaks as loudly and clearly as he can. "I can make it so everything grows faster. OK? Faster and stronger. I can make you a new batch of fertiliser. We can grow new plants—tomatoes, fruit, whatever you want. I just need a few things to do it."

Silence. The guard still has her gun on him. He tenses, sure that at any second a bullet is going to slam right through him.

But he guessed right. A grow-op like this won't give them a lot of variety in their diet. He's offering them some new tastes, and he can see them looking at each other, thinking it over.

One of the guard's colleagues wanders over, and they have a whispered conversation. Prakesh watches, not wanting to move, not wanting to give the others any reason to shoot.

Eventually, the first guard looks over at him. "I'll pass it up the chain," she says. "Keep working."

56

Riley

The three men stand frozen, staring at me like I'm a ghost.

One of them is young, still in his twenties, with a round face and tiny bud of a mouth. The man on his left is enormous, a neat goatee covering his chin, the skin above it lined and scarred. The one on the right has a hooked nose and prominent chin that look like they've been carved from stone. Somehow, I know he's Iluk—he looks like his name sounds. The one with the round face must be Koji.

All three are wearing thick jackets, and all three have rifles. I have just enough time to take this in, and then I'm face down in the dirt, my arms twisted behind me. The ice-cold tip of a gun barrel is shoved into the back of my neck, and I can feel grains of sand digging into my cheek.

All three men are shouting—two in English, and one in that strange language. The man with the rifle shouts at the others to shut up, digging it harder into the back of my neck.

I have to tell myself to breathe. This is the only way. If I want to get off this island, I have to go with them. I don't know what happens after that, but I'll figure it out. Somehow.

"You alone out here?" the man says. When I don't answer immediately, he shoves the back of my head. I feel sand in my mouth, rough against my tongue. "Answer me."

"I'm alone," I say, the words muffled.

"You sure you're telling the truth there, girl?" I feel the gun barrel shift, as if the man holding it is getting a better grip on the trigger. "Because if you're not..."

I raise my head, just enough to get my mouth out of the sand. "I'm the only survivor."

"Now I know you're lying. There were more people in that plane of yours. It was still flying, even after Curtis shot 'em full of holes."

The pressure comes off my back, and the man flips me over. I try to get an elbow underneath me, but then the gun is in my face. It's hard to look anywhere but the huge black barrel in front of me.

"Where'd you come from?"

There's no point lying to him. Unless they've got planes of their own, they're not getting to Eric's people. "Whitehorse," I say.

He laughs. "That so? Long way to come. You want to tell me why you're all the way out here?"

To find my friends. To kill someone.

While I'm trying to think of something to say, he lifts his foot and slams it down on my stomach.

I curl into a ball. I don't have a choice. The pain is hot and feverish, radiating up from my abdomen in long waves. I feel Ray digging through my pockets, pulling out the contents, grunting as he stuffs them into his jacket.

"Jesus, Ray!" says Koji. Iluk spits a sentence I can't understand—I don't know if he's angry with Ray, or goading him on.

"You want to come back with us?" Ray's mouth is inches from my ear. "Fine. But you're going to wish you'd stayed here."

57

Riley

My hands are bound behind me, held in place by rusty metal cuffs. The edges are worn and jagged, and I have to keep my hands as still as I can to avoid cutting the skin. The floor of the boat is hard plastic, cold and wet under my cheek.

It goes against everything I am to lie still. I want to take these people down, one by one, take that rifle away and shove it in their faces, listen to them beg. But the voice tells me to be calm, and I'm learning to listen to it.

Ray sees me looking up at him, and shakes his head. "The second you come off that floor, I'll put a bullet in your kneecap."

The sides of the boat are large tubes made of grainy rubber, tapering to a point at the front. A wave slaps the side, its tip launching over the tube, spraying me in the face. There's a motor at the back of the boat, which Iluk controls using a long handle.

We crest another wave, and the engine coughs and splutters, threatening to give out. Iluk says something back in that strange language, irritated. Ray stands up, moving to help him. "Watch her," he says, jamming the rifle into Koji's hands.

I clear my throat, looking up at Koji. He seems calmer than Ray, less likely to lash out. "Where are we going?" I say.

No response.

"Am I the only new person?" I say. "Or are there others like me?"

Koji looks down, then back up at me. For the second time, I see something in his eyes, something I can't quite read.

The engine starts up again. Ray straightens, satisfied, then glares at me. "You speak when spoken to, you hear?"

I fall silent, desperate to know more, but aware of how fragile my position is. Underneath me, my bound hands are in agony.

And then all at once, there's something above us. Sliding into view, impossibly huge. It's like a mountain decided to shoot up from underwater. I squint up at it, trying to work out what it is.

This was what I saw from the island—that strange shape against the skyline. It's man-made, built from giant metal plates, leaning over us at a sharp angle. The plates are discoloured for a few feet above the water, painted with green fungus and brown rust. Over our heads, I see the letters A-11 marked on the metal. Each letter is white, outlined in thick grey paint, and each one has to be four times the size of a man.

There's a wide rectangular gap in the plates, twenty feet above the waterline. Faces peer down from it. Iluk cuts the motor, and one of them shouts, the words lost in the rush of the ocean. Ray cups his hand to his mouth and yells back. "Nah, just the one. Throw us the ladder."

The face vanishes. A second later, a rope ladder unfurls, clanking against the hull and splashing into the water. Koji reaches out for it, pulling it towards us, while Ray secures the boat. There's an upright piece of metal that's been welded to the hull, sticking out from it, and Ray ties the boat to it with a thick, wet length of rope.

Iluk's face appears above me, upside down. He grabs me by the shoulders and hauls me to my feet. The rocking motion of the boat nearly topples me over, and he has to grab me by the scruff of my jacket, only just stopping me from falling in.

"How's she gonna climb?" says Koji.

"What?" says Ray.

"Her hands are tied."

Ray makes an annoyed sound, then grabs hold of me, spinning me around. The cuffs snap off my wrists, and I resist the urge to cry out as the blood rushes back, pins and needles digging deep into my hands.

He brings me back the other way, pulling my hands together and cuffing them in front. This time, the cuffs aren't quite as tight.

"Climb," he says, jerking his thumb upwards.

It takes one or two tries to grab the swaying ladder. The sides are rope, but the rungs are made of rough wood, and splinters bite into my palms as I move. The cuffs make the climb even more awkward. Halfway up, I glance back over my shoulder. Fire Island is there, and the impossibly empty sea beyond it. I look for the seaplane, but it's nowhere to be found.

"Keep moving," Ray says from below me.

As I reach the top of the ladder, strong hands pull me over the edge. I roll onto the deck, my heart pumping. The people standing above me are all variations of Ray, with beards and grimy skin and dark, angry eyes.

I look past them, to the space we're in. It's huge—big enough to park two seaplanes across, wingtip to wingtip. The walls are made of ribbed metal, with curved struts every couple of feet. Oversized fluorescent lights criss-cross the ceiling.

"This is all you came back with?" one of the men says, prodding my shoulder with the tip of his boot. "Doesn't look like much."

"We'll let Prophet decide that," Ray says. Now that he's in here, his voice is quieter, as if shouting won't be tolerated. He and Koji lift me to my feet, and the crowd parts in front of us.

I'm hustled through a door into a narrow corridor—so narrow that we have to walk single file: Iluk and Ray in front, Koji behind. The corridor has heavy, ribbed walls, like the entranceway. The lights are sparse, one every twenty feet or so, each one covered by a wire cage. There are enormous pipes running along the ceiling, cocooned in thick, silver insulation.

There's no chance of escape here, nowhere to go, no door that isn't sealed tight. Frustration starts to build—Carver and Prakesh are somewhere on this ship, they have to be, but I can't see any way I can escape.

And there's something behind the frustration. It takes me a moment to pinpoint it. A weird sense of déjà vu, like I should recognise my surroundings. Like I've been here before.

I close my eyes, irritated with myself. My mind's playing tricks on me, just like it did when I looked at the sky for the first time. I breathe deep, letting the frustration fade, letting it be replaced with anger. I have to trust that anger—it's kept me alive so far, and it's going to keep me alive now.

The passage opens up a little. There's a stairway leading up to the next level: impossibly steep, with steps even narrower than the corridor. Ray and Iluk are already climbing it, and Koji gives me a push from behind, his hand on the small of my back.

Another door, with a valve handle. When Iluk cranks it back, bright daylight shoots into the corridor. I try to raise a hand to my eyes, forgetting for a moment that I'm cuffed. Ray reaches for me, pulling me through the door.

We're outside, on a long balcony bordered by waist-high railings. Below us is the deck of the ship: a massive space, bigger than any gallery on Outer Earth. Its surface is covered with strange markings, yellow chevrons, white stripes, warnings in huge lettering.

There are a dozen planes, lined up in rows along the deck. They aren't like the seaplane: they're sleek, predatory, with needle-like noses and enormous tail fins. But as I look closer, I see that their surfaces are caked in rust. The surface of their wheels has rotted away, and several of them list to one side.

We move along the balcony. My shoulder blades are hurting a little less now, and it's getting easier to move. I keep sneaking glances at the deck. There are things I missed the first time round, like the metal plates angled at forty-five degrees to the deck. There's a strange structure on the edge, too: a massive cylinder, capped by a dome.

Ray sees me looking, claps a hand on my shoulder. For a moment, he sounds almost jovial. "That's the Phalanx gun. Still got plenty of ammo left. But you and your friends in the plane figured that out already, right?"

As I watch, the gun gives out a metallic whirring noise, turning a few degrees to the right. Its barrel comes into view, sticking out at right angles to the cylinder.

A moment later, we duck through a door, coming out into another narrow stairway. There's more light here, and it's a little quieter than down below.

Another set of stairs. Then another. And then Ray is cranking open a door, much larger than the others, and he and Iluk pull me through.

We're in a control room of some kind, not much larger than the one in Apex on Outer Earth. The layout is immediately familiar: banks of screens, chaotic groups of chairs, low lighting. There are large windows overlooking the deck, and I can see the fog just starting to lift.

The room is packed with people. Some of them are gathered around screens, while others are off to one side, talking in small groups. Several of them have rifles, slung across their chests or hanging down their backs. I feel their eyes on me, sizing me up, taking in my mismatched clothing and bound hands.

My gaze falls on a table in the middle of the room. There's a map spread across it, like the one Harlan showed me, only much larger. Alaska, the Yukon, other areas I can't name.

Ray reaches into his jacket, pulling out the items he took from me: the scarf, the bear spray, the meat strips. He lines them up on the table in front of him, then clears his throat. "Prophet."

One of the men clustered around the table raises his head to look at us. He wears a stiff, brown jacket over a dark shirt, and one of his eyes is gone, sewn closed with ugly, amateurish stitches.

And sitting behind him, bent over a computer screen: Janice Okwembu.

58

Okwembu

Before Okwembu can do anything, Hale somehow gets away from the men holding her.

One moment she's being held by her arms, the next she's twisted free. Her hands are still cuffed in front of her, but it's as if she barely notices. She's at the table in two strides, launching herself across it. Her left foot lands squarely on the map, planting itself on the border between Alaska and Canada, crumpling the paper, and then she's diving for Okwembu.

Prophet's forearm takes Hale on the collarbone. Okwembu has just enough time to step to the side before Hale crashes across the floor.

Everyone on the bridge is on their feet, racking the bolts on their rifles. Ray plants a foot on Hale's stomach, forcing her to stay down.

Okwembu finds her eyes, holds them. She may not know how Hale managed to get here, to escape the *Shinso* and make it all the way to Alaska, but it doesn't matter. Her shock is starting to give way to anger, to pure righteous fury. She holds her ground, breathing hard, keeping her expression neutral.

Hale is a mess. Her clothing is ragged, mismatched, soaked from sea spray. She has a cut on her cheek, and dark rivulets of blood have dried on her face. She's struggling, spitting mad, her eyes never leaving Okwembu's. "You," she says. "You. You. Y—"

Ray hits her, driving a foot into her stomach, and her body shakes from the impact. Okwembu's hand strays to the data stick, still hanging round her neck. She was about to take it off when Hale attacked her. If it had been damaged…

Prophet looks at Ray. He's deeply rattled, his lip shaking with fury. "What in the name of the Engine did you bring her up here for?"

"She's from the plane," Ray says, giving Hale a shake. "Her friend didn't make it."

Prophet walks over, lifting Hale's chin.

"Now why would the Engine send you?" he says. His expression hardens. "Let's start with the aircraft. Where did you take off from?"

Hale tries to get loose again, wrenching her shoulders back and forth. She doesn't succeed, and this time Ray hits her across the face, his fist landing with a sound like a gun firing. Hale falls limp, blood dripping from her mouth, pattering softly on the floor.

Prophet leans in close to her. "I'll ask again," he says. "Where did the plane come from?"

Hale says nothing, flexing her jaw left and right, eyes squeezed shut. When she speaks, it's to Okwembu, not Prophet. "Where are they?" she says. The aggression in her voice is like an open wound. She's speaking around the blood, and more of it drips between her lips, coating her teeth. "Prakesh. Carver. Are they here?"

"Now you listen," Prophet says, grabbing Hale's chin and turning her head towards him. "That plane. Are there others like it? How many people were with you?"

Hale stares at him, like he's speaking another language. After a long moment, she swallows hard, then says, "Out of Whitehorse. Just the one plane."

"Good. How many of you were there?"

"... Four."

"And why did you—"

Hale cuts him off, speaking to him but looking directly at Okwembu. "I hope you realise who you've got on your ship. Whatever she's told you, it's a lie. That's what she does. She lies. You let me walk out of here with her, and—"

Iluk grabs Hale's hair and yanks her head back. She barks a cry of fury, and he spits something at her in Inuktuk.

Okwembu can feel Prophet looking at her, his eyes searching. She ignores him, looking right back at Hale. *Get control of the situation.*

"She's the one who isn't being honest," she says. "I know her from Outer Earth. She's responsible for the virus that nearly wiped us out."

Hale tries to speak. It earns her another punch, snapping her head sideways and sending dots of blood onto one of the screens.

"Then why did she attack you?" Prophet says.

Okwembu shrugs. "She disagreed with some of the decisions I made."

Silence. Okwembu keeps her eyes on Prophet. She suppresses the urge to elaborate, letting the seconds tick by.

"Should I take her downstairs, Prophet?" Ray says. "We lost another one yesterday. They could probably use the extra hands."

Prophet shakes his head, looking Hale up and down. "She's violent, this one. Something tells me she won't be so comfortable serving the Engine."

He turns away. "Take her to the stern."

59

Anna

By the time Anna reaches the gallery, her shock has turned into a righteous, roaring fury. Every stride she takes feels like it drives an electric bolt of anger through her body.

She skids to a halt on the Level 1 catwalk above the gallery floor. There's a muted alarm blaring somewhere, along with the recorded voice advising evacuation. The escape pod bay doors are still closed, with nothing but darkness through their viewports.

For a moment, Anna is confused. Where were the stompers? Why didn't they stop Dax and his group from...

That's when she sees them. Two bodies, clad in grey stomper jumpsuits, sprawled face down on the floor. It's impossible to miss the blood pooling under them.

Another electric bolt shoots up through her, and she pounds

her fist on the railing in frustration. Jordan. That must have been her price. Places in the escape pods for her and her buddies. Did the two dead stompers refuse? Did they try to stop them?

A strange sound pulls her out of her thoughts. It takes a second to place it: someone is crying. No—not just someone. A child.

Anna launches herself over the catwalk railing, turning one-eighty degrees in mid-air, using a hand on the railing as a fulcrum. She comes down with her toes in between the railings and her heels hanging out over the edge. She relaxes into the landing, then pushes herself off the catwalk.

It's not far down—ten feet, maybe, no more. She lands with a thud, not bothering to roll, staggering a little on impact. The crying is coming from her left, and she turns her head, hunting for the source.

Ivy.

She must've been here when it all went down. She's huddled by the wall, sitting with her back against it, her hands wrapped around her knees. Anna sprints to her, pulling the trembling girl into an embrace.

"It's all right," Anna says. She says it again, then a third time, as if she needs to convince herself.

There's nothing she can do. She should take Ivy back, find somebody to look after her. She gets to her feet, cradling the girl. Ivy is still crying, but the sobs are silent now, and she snuggles into Anna's shoulder.

That's when Anna notices the last airlock.

The viewpoints in almost all the airlocks are dark, but the last one is different. There's the faintest glimmer inside it, so faint that at first Anna is sure she's imagined it.

She crosses the floor, avoiding the two dead stompers. As she reaches the bay door, she sees that the viewport is just out of her reach. But she didn't imagine the light—it's a little clearer now, like the glow cast from a tab screen.

Her heart beating faster, she drops to one knee, whispering in Ivy's ear. "I have to put you down, OK? Just for a second."

Ivy doesn't move. Slowly, Anna disengages the girl's hands from around her neck, and places her gently on the floor, making sure she's not looking at the stompers. Then she gets on tiptoe, straining to get as high as she can, and looks into the viewport.

The escape pod is still there.

Anna doesn't know why they didn't take it. Maybe someone got cold feet. Maybe they left so quickly that there wasn't time to inform everybody. It doesn't matter. Not now.

She crouches down, putting her hand on Ivy's cheek, feeling still-warm tears as her fingers touch the skin. The girl's face is deathly pale.

"Ivy? Honey?" she says. "I want you to do something for me."

Ivy starts to answer, glancing at the stompers.

"No," Anna says. "Don't look at them. They can't hurt you. I promise. Now, what I want you to do is run. Fast as you can, far as you can, until you find a grown-up. Can you do that for me?"

Ivy stares at her. Anna is about to repeat herself when the girl nods. Her enormous brown eyes prickle with fresh tears.

"Good," Anna says, forcing a smile onto her face. She hugs Ivy one more time. "Go. Now."

Ivy skims across the floor, her oversized red sweater trailing out behind her. She only looks back once. Anna stays put, anticipating the look, and even manages a wave. Then Ivy is into the corridor, and out of sight.

Anna turns back to the pod. Her fingers brush the release catch next to the door. "Oh, this is a very bad idea," she mutters to herself.

She clambers into the airlock, pulling open the door of the escape pod inside it. The pod itself is tiny. There are three soft-backed seats arranged in a triangular formation at the front. A transparent locker on one side holds three space suits. Anna can't see a thing through the cockpit viewport, which stretches around the seats. The only light comes from the controls themselves, from the multiple touchscreens on the U-shaped line of controls around the front seat.

I shouldn't be doing this, Anna thinks. But then she's clambering over the seats, dropping into the foremost one, fumbling with the safety belt. There are straps, clicking into place at her sternum. Three touchscreens in front of her, black and silent. There's a single joystick beneath them, with two thick plastic buttons—one on the top, one on the front.

She doesn't know that much about Outer Earth's escape pods. She remembers being told once that they're relatively simple to operate—they have to be, given the situations they might be used in. But how do you turn them on? How do you launch them?

Breathing fast, she gives the nearest touchscreen an experimental tap. Somewhere behind her, she hears an engine kick into action, rumbling through the little craft. The airlock around the pod comes to life. A rotating light near the ceiling comes on, and the door to the station seals shut behind her with a grinding noise.

A dozen readouts appear on the screens: fuel capacity, estimated range, attitude, thruster locations. Anna stares at them, horrified. A half-second later the displays dim, and a message appears on the centre display. LAUNCH?

Anna raises a finger. Stops.

She is out of her depth. The fear is setting in now, crawling out of her nightmares and tearing its way into the real world. *You're going to die out there*, she thinks, and it's almost enough to send her flying out of the chair, back into the station, back to her parents. *There has to be someone else who can do this.*

And then, before she can stop herself, her finger touches the screen.

60

Prakesh

It takes a while for the guard to return. She strides over to Prakesh, rifle swinging. "Higher-ups say to do it. Get going."

He doesn't waste time getting to work, already aware of what he needs. The ammonium sulphate is easy. Prakesh can get that from the slippery white fertiliser pellets. Same with the sulphur—that's the yellow insecticide. They give him a plastic cup to use as a scoop, but some still gets on his hands, prickling at his skin.

The calcium hydroxide is the tricky part. He needs calcium oxide first, and the usual source of that would be a stick of chalk. The guard assigned to watch him just stares blankly when Prakesh asks for some.

He tries to keep the frustration off his face. "What about shells?"

"Shells?" the guard says slowly. He's not much older than Prakesh, with dark brown skin and a shaggy mess of black hair, but he holds his rifle like it's an extension of his arm. Like it would be the work of a single thought to bring it up and pull the trigger.

"Yeah, like—" Prakesh can feel the word, dancing on the tip of his tongue. *What the hell are those things called?* The name snaps to the front of his mind. "Barnacles. They'd be stuck to the ship? Right at the waterline. I just need two or three."

He takes a step forward, moving without thinking, and is brought up short by a rifle barrel in his face.

"You don't move," says the guard. "I'll get them."

Slowly, he lowers the rifle, then calls one of the others over to spot for him. He stalks off, his boots tapping on the metal floor of the farm.

They've got Prakesh in one corner of the hangar, set up with a couple of old tables. There's a portable gas ring, purloined from the mess hall. Fresh water sloshes in a big metal drum. They've even managed to find him some tongs, their metal surface blackened with age.

It's not even close to perfect. The chemistry he's about to perform is unbelievably inefficient, the kind of procedure that would make his old Air Lab colleagues burst out laughing. But it's all Prakesh has.

He waits, hands on the table, head bent. Jojo and the others are still at the troughs, working on the soil. Every few minutes, a guard will pull some of them away, letting them take a piss break.

Please let this work.

The guard returns with a handful of barnacles: lumpy, misshapen things with jagged white shells. He dumps them onto the table.

"Ruined my knife getting these off," he says, tapping a chipped blade hanging from his belt.

"Sorry," Prakesh mutters, gathering the shells.

He gets both hands under one of the metal drums, lifts it up, then smashes it down on the shells. They're hard, weather-worn, and it takes a few hits before they begin to crack.

The gas burner is tricky to get going—Prakesh can't stop his hands from shaking, and he keeps fumbling the butane lighter. Eventually, he does it, and a scorching blue flame rises up from the plate.

Prakesh holds the smashed shells over the flames until they smoulder and crumble, kicking off a thin white smoke. He catches the fragments in one of the plastic beakers. He can feel the heat singeing the skin on his fingers, and bites his lip, pushing through it. Soon, the beaker is full of clumpy, off-white powder. Calcium oxide, or something close to it.

He dumps it in the water-filled drum, using the tongs to stir it. There. Calcium hydroxide.

The guard leans in. "So how does it work?"

"Huh?"

"This chemistry shit." He gestures at the drum.

"Oh," says Prakesh. "Well…calcium hydroxide from the shells will react with the existing fertiliser, and it should make it more potent, so…"

"Right." The guard's actually interested, his gun lowered, tilting his head to one side as he regards the drum. "My mom showed me this stuff in a book once. Didn't really know how it all worked but I always wanted to try it."

The drum goes on top of the burner. Prakesh has to get the guard to help, which he does willingly, handing his rifle off to one of the others. Even then, they nearly send the entire mess flying when the guard's fingers slip. Prakesh pulls it back at the last moment, exhaling a shaky breath.

"There," says the guard, dusting off his hands. "What's next?"

Prakesh's mind goes blank for a moment, surprised at having such an eager lab assistant. "Uh…the sulphur. Right over there."

"Yeah, you got it."

The guard brings it over. Working quickly, Prakesh dumps several scoops of the sulphur into the pot, then stirs it all together. The ammonium sulphate fertiliser goes in last, followed by a thick sheet of scrap metal as a makeshift lid.

"So shouldn't there be some sort of, what's it called, reaction now?" the guard says.

Prakesh shrugs, trying to ignore how much his shoulders hurt. "It'll take a little time, but sure."

"Nice," says the guard, hands on his hips. "Guess you'd better get back to work." He sounds genuinely apologetic.

Prakesh walks with his head down, sliding in next to Jojo. The kid says nothing, doesn't even look at him.

Prakesh digs his hands into the soil, and tries not to look at the metal drum.

61

Riley

They carry me off the bridge. I try and stop them, kicking and thrashing, screaming at them to let me go. It doesn't do any good. My hands are still cuffed, and while Ray holds my upper body, Iluk wraps his huge arms around my legs, pinning them together. My eyes keep being drawn back to Okwembu, like light getting sucked into a black hole.

Iluk lets go when we reach the bottom of the stairs. Ray lifts me up, spins me around and slams me back against the wall. I bang my head, sending flickering sparks across the edge of my vision. My face is numb, and the ache in my stomach is rolling up through my body.

"You got a choice," Ray says. "You can go to the stern as you are, or you can go there with broken arms. Your call."

I stop struggling. There's got to be a way out of this, there must be, but I won't be able to act on it if I'm crippled. After a few moments, I raise my chin then give Ray a tight nod.

"All right then," he says.

Ray drags me down the corridors, Iluk and Koji following behind us, down more flights of stairs, until eventually we reach another rectangular opening in the side of the ship. I can see white clouds through it, hanging low over the gently whispering ocean. Unlike the way we came in, there's no one else here. The space is completely empty.

Ray and Iluk drop me on the metal floor, right on the edge. There's nothing between me and the world outside.

"Maybe we shouldn't do this," Koji says.

"One more word, Koji," Ray says. "Just one."

I look back, and see that Ray has a new gun.

I don't know where he got it from. It's a rifle, the wooden stock polished to a high sheen. He's loading it carefully, almost tenderly. Iluk stands with his arms folded. Koji is cowering behind him, as if he's being forced to watch.

Ray sees me looking. "Sorry. Prophet says you're gone, you're gone." He racks the bolt. "You can die on your feet, or on your knees. I don't much care which."

I barely register his words. There's a taste of copper in my mouth, the metallic tang of fear. My hands are shaking. The whole way down here, I was looking for anything I could use, and got nothing. Even if I somehow managed to escape, I'd still be stuck on the ship, trapped in the narrow corridors. And in the next few seconds Ray is going to put a bullet through me.

But the anger I feel is stronger than the fear. Even after everything I've been through, there's one thing that will never change. I'm a tracer—no, more than that, I'm a *Devil Dancer*, and I've come too far and fought too hard to let it end here.

Slowly, I get to one knee. Ray glances down at the gun again, and that's when I act.

I launch myself forwards, head down, leading with my shoulder. Ray sees me coming, raises the gun, but I'm moving way too fast for him. My shoulder bends his body in two, the air leaving him in an explosive rush.

Iluk is there, his hands on me, trying to push me to the floor. He's strong, much stronger than I am, and if I let him get ahold of me I'll be a static target for Ray to aim at. So I throw my head back, and feel bone shatter as it crunches against Iluk's nose.

Ray jerks the gun around, snapping the side of the barrel against my cheek. It's a glancing blow, but it's enough to knock me off balance, sending me to my knees. I twist to one side, and the gun goes off, right by my head—I feel the kick power through me, the bang slamming my ears shut.

Ray's hand goes to the bolt again, starts to pull it back. That makes him vulnerable. I use the tiny window of time it gives me, and throw myself towards him.

My hands are still cuffed in front of me. I lift them high, then bring them down on the other side of Ray's head. It looks like I'm embracing him. I rock backwards, the handcuffs digging into the back of his neck, pulling with every ounce of strength I have.

He grunts, trying to plant his feet. For a horrifying instant he feels too heavy, and I don't know if I'll be able to throw him off balance. But I'm faster than he is, and his centre of gravity is way too high. As I roll backwards, he comes with me, his weight pressing down.

His hands pull at my jacket, but I've got momentum on my side. I keep the roll going, using my thighs and abdominal muscles to transfer the energy to him. He somersaults, landing flat on his back. I look back, the world upside down suddenly, and I can see that his feet are hanging over the edge.

I roll over, pushing myself upwards with my bound hands. Koji is backing away, terrified, and Iluk is lying face down on the floor. There's a pool of blood spreading out from around his head. One of his hands is tucked under his neck, as if trying to seal the bullet wound.

Ray is up on one knee. Somehow, he's still holding the gun. He pulls the trigger, but there's no bullet in the chamber—he never got a chance to pull the bolt back before I threw him over.

Tough luck, Ray.

He curses, hands flying to the bolt. I sprint towards him, and drive my fist into his temple.

I can almost see the pressure waves moving through his flesh. He doesn't fall, but his head snaps to the side, and I feel a burst of bitter pleasure as I regain my balance. My hearing is coming back, and Ray's moan of pain is crystal-clear.

I snatch the gun away, gripping it by the top of the barrel. Then I lean back, and kick Ray in the chest.

The move disrupts my own centre of gravity, and I fall flat on my ass. It doesn't matter. Ray is in mid-air, his eyes wide with terror. A half-second later he's gone.

No time. There's still one more.

I can feel the prolonged effects of adrenaline starting to take hold, making my hands shake and my vision blur. I rock forward, launching my body upright. I'm holding the gun wrong, my hands around the barrel—and it's a big gun, heavy, my wrists already aching from keeping it up. It's useless in this position, unless I want to use it as a club. If Koji's got a weapon of his own, that decision might cost me.

There's only one thing I can do. I launch myself into a sprint, heading for one side of the opening, the gun held out in front of me. I feel the shock wave as the stock slams into the wall, but I'm ready for it, letting my hands travel down the body, twisting sideways to let the barrel slide past me. It works. My fingers find the bolt, and I have just enough grip to swing the gun, letting the stock seat itself in my stomach.

I'm already thinking ahead—I have to draw the bolt back, chamber a round, reseat my hands so I can pull the trigger, draw a bead on Koji, and fire. It's going to have to be perfect. One mistake, and he'll do to me what I did to Ray.

My hands turn sideways, catching the bolt, snapping it backwards. I feel a round enter the chamber, and I'm already hunting for the trigger guard when Koji yells out, "Wait! Don't shoot!"

I look up. He's standing a few feet away, his hands up, terror on his face. "Don't shoot," he says again.

My finger finds the trigger. My skin is soaked with sweat, and a drop falls into my eye, blurring my vision, stinging with salt. *Aim. Aim now, while he's standing still.*

"I knew John Hale," he says. "Your father. I knew him."

62

Prakesh

The liquid in the drum is bubbling, the metal lid clanking up and down. The sound scratches at Prakesh's eardrums.

It's taking too long. He should be smelling something by now. They all should. But there's just the loamy, thick fug of the soil, accentuated by the tang of the fertiliser.

Prakesh tells himself not to look, but does anyway. The guard is hovering near the drum, watching the reaction.

Prakesh looks back down. *It didn't work. They're going to figure it out. It's over.*

At that moment, he hears the guard shouting at him.

The guard doesn't know his name. He's just shouting, "Chemistry guy!" Prakesh looks up, feeling all the blood drain from his face.

"Is it meant to smell that bad?" the guard shouts.

Slowly, Prakesh walks over. Every step feels awkward, every motion forced.

The guard watches him approach. He bangs the drum with the butt of his rifle, and it wobbles slightly on its perch. "Starting to stink. Worse than before. Is that supposed to happen?"

And that's when Prakesh smells it. The makeshift lid has kept most of it inside, but some has escaped, and it scours the inside of his nostrils.

"Let me see," he says, stepping behind the table. His heart is pounding.

"I gotta say, though," says the guard, "this is by far the most interesting shift I've had in a long time." He claps Prakesh on the back. "Can't wait to eat those first tomatoes. I had one once, when I was a kid."

Prakesh forces a smile, bending over the barrel, trying to hold his breath.

"So?" says the guard. He looks more eager than ever, almost

excited, like a child getting a toy. Prakesh actually feels a little bad for what he's about to do.

"It's ready," he says.

Then he puts a hand on the side of the drum and shoves it off the table.

The barrel crashes to the floor, spilling its contents everywhere: pale green slurry, with slimy lumps floating in it. A second later, the full force of the smell hits Prakesh.

It's as if boiling acid has been forced into his lungs. He bends double, trying to raise a hand to his nose, not quite getting there before his stomach reacts. He vomits, the liquid forcing its way out of his lungs, spraying across the floor.

The guard is vomiting, too. He was right next to the barrel, and got a full dose of the fumes.

Sulphur, ammonium sulphate, calcium hydroxide. Water. Heat.

Clunky, but effective.

Prakesh has enough presence of mind to pull himself behind a nearby crate. He gets there half a second before the shooting starts. Bullets explode off the metal floor around him. One hits the gas canister, which flies off across the floor, whirling like a child's toy.

The smell is spreading. The hangar is big, but the stench is powerful enough to penetrate every corner of it. Prakesh can hear the other guards coughing, hear them starting to heave. That sets him off again. He retches, spilling more slime onto the floor by his head. The smell is so strong that he feels like it's a living creature clamped onto his face, forcing itself down his throat.

There's nothing more he can do. He curls into a ball, his hands over his mouth and nose, and waits for it to be over.

It takes him a few moments to realise that the shooting has stopped. His ears are ringing, but the hangar is silent. No—not silent. He can hear voices now, muffled, shouting orders to one another. And soft thuds, like boots being driven into flesh.

He gets to his knees, dry-heaving. The smell has ebbed, just a little, but it's still enough to set off a coughing fit. When he looks up, wiping gunk from his lips, Jojo is standing over him, holding the bottom of his shirt to his face. The shirt is wet, soaked with urine, blocking out the smell. Prakesh sees that every other worker did the same thing, clamping wet fabric over their noses and mouths. It gave them just enough time to take down the incapacitated guards.

And all of them are dead. Prakesh can see that. Or, if they're not dead, they will be soon. His eyes fall on the one who helped him. The man's eyes are staring at nothing, blood leaking out of a massive head wound. Prakesh feels an odd sense of loss, a feeling he doesn't quite understand.

"Nnnn-" Jojo gulps twice, the wet fabric across his mouth muffling the sound. He helps Prakesh to his feet. "Not bad."

Prakesh finds it hard to keep his balance, especially when the other workers start slapping him on the back and pulling him into massive bear hugs. Someone passes him a soaked strip of cloth—it's revolting, having to hold it up to his mouth, but it's a million times better than the smell.

For a long moment, nobody moves. The workers are looking around them, unsure, cradling the guns.

Jojo breaks the silence. "S-s-see that?" he says, pointing upwards. Prakesh follows his finger, landing on a clunky security camera bolted onto the wall. "W-we gotta mmmm-move f-fast."

Prakesh groans, irritated that he didn't see it before. Their revolt will be noticed—assuming the camera works, there'll be reinforcements arriving at any moment.

"Y-you two—generator room," Jojo says, pointing at the other workers. His words are muffled by the fabric. "Heard the g-g-guards t-talking about it earlier. It w-w-won't be too heavily g-g-guarded. D-D-Devi, t-take a few p-p-people w-with you and g-go and secure the b-b-b-boats."

The workers split off from the group, charging away across the hangar.

"What's in the generator room?" Prakesh says.

"Th-th-th-the other workers. W-w-we're n-n-not gonna l-leave them here."

Prakesh's head snaps up. *Other workers. Carver.* If he's still alive, that's where he'd be. But the moment the thought occurs, so does the memory of those fists and feet raining down on him. Prakesh desperately wants to believe he's still alive, but he knows the odds aren't good.

"What about the rest of us?" says a man behind Prakesh. "I say we take the bridge."

"We'll never get near it," someone else says. "Not unless our man's got another batch of those chemicals somewhere."

"N-n-no," says Jojo. "We c-c-c-c-can't go to the b-b-bridge. It's t-t-too heavily guarded."

"So then what do we do?" It comes from an older woman. She's holding one of the rifles like a newborn baby.

Jojo gulps twice. "W-we blow it up."

There's a stunned silence. "What, the bridge? Or the ship?" says the woman.

"The shhhhh-ship. We hit the f-f-f-fuel hangar, lllll-light it up. T-torch the p-p-place."

"Jojo, that's crazy," the woman says.

Jojo talks over her. "We g-g-get in, t-take some f-f-fuel for ourselves, then burn the r-r-rest."

Prakesh finally finds his voice. "What about the other workers? The ones you just sent off? Shouldn't we warn them?"

"They know how to get to the b-boats," Jojo says, barely glancing at him, excitement chasing away most of his stammer. "W-w-we won't leave without 'em. D-don't w-worry."

"What do we do about weapons?" Prakesh says.

But Jojo and the rest of the workers are already heading for the hangar doors. A couple of them loose shots into the ceiling, ignoring Jojo's stuttered shouts to save ammo. Prakesh has no choice but to follow them.

63

Riley

There's no way Koji just said what I think he said. I keep the gun pointed at him. The only sound is my breathing, harsh and hot.

"I knew your father," he says. "I was with John Hale on the *Akua Maru*. I—"

"Shut up."

I get to my feet slowly, keeping a very, very tight grip on the gun.

"Look," Koji says, spreading his hands slowly. "My name is Koji Yamamoto. I was born on Outer Earth, in Tzevya. I was a junior officer on John Hale's crew. We crash-landed in eastern Russia eight years ago."

This isn't possible. The *Akua Maru* was thought destroyed, lost forever. It wasn't. My father was still on Earth, and with Janice Okwembu's help, he managed to repair the ship, intending to use it to destroy a station he thought had abandoned him. We thought the rest of the ship's crew were dead.

"You're lying," I say. But is he? How could he know any of this? How else would he know the names *John Hale* and *Akua Maru*? Could Okwembu have told him? But why would she?

"How do you know who I am?" I say.

Koji lowers his eyes. "You look just like him."

I lift the gun a little higher, and he starts speaking more quickly. "I knew he had a daughter, but I never thought…you have his eyes. You *are* his daughter, right? Riley?"

"The *Akua* landed in eastern Russia," I say. "That's a long, long way from here."

He nods. "Kamchatka. Some of us survived the crash. We decided to head east, see if we could find anything. We crossed the Bering Strait, ended up here."

"Why tell me this now? Why not say anything before?"

A pained expression crosses his face. "I was scared. All right? They would have killed me if I tried to help you." He points to Iluk's body.

"So you wait until I'm the one with the gun," I say. "Convenient."

"I'm telling the truth, I swear." He's trembling now, overcome with emotion. "I don't know what happened to your father—he wanted to stay with the ship, but if you—"

"Shut up," I say for the second time. I have to calm my racing mind. I have to think.

Right now, it doesn't matter who Koji is, or where he came from. What matters is that he might be the only person here who could help me. There's no chance of taking Okwembu down yet—not with one gun, not when she's on the ship's bridge. But she's not the only reason I'm here.

"Uncuff me," I say.

He gives a helpless shrug. "Ray had the key. I'm sorry."

I bite back the frustration. Nothing I can do—I'll just have to live with it. "I'm looking for two people," I say. "Their names are Aaron Carver and Prakesh Kumar." I have to assume that they're alive—I almost physically recoil from the alternative.

Koji shakes his head, and I feel my stomach drop a couple of inches. "We've had some new people," he says. "I don't know their names."

"Tell me about these arrivals. What happens to them?"

"They get put to work. All across the ship."

"Where?"

Sweat is trickling down his face. "All over. Depends on what needs doing. But the closest is probably the generator room. We've been having some power problems, so—"

"Take me there," I say. "Right now."

I make him go first, keeping my gun up, ignoring the burn in my cuffed hands. We're almost at the corridor entrance when he says, "Wait. You need to give me the gun."

"Are you serious?"

"You don't understand," he says, licking his lips. "What do you think is going to happen if someone sees you marching *me* at gunpoint?"

"They'll do nothing. Because if they do, I'll shoot you." The words sound hollow, even to me.

"You think they care?" Koji shakes his head. "If we're going to find your friends, then you're going to have to trust me."

"Why should I?" I say.

"Because—" He stops, looks away. "Because I owe your father. I owe him everything."

I don't move.

"Please," he says.

My finger tightens on the trigger.

Then slowly, very slowly, I pass him the gun. I'm already visualising the angles, anticipating what he'll do. The moment he brings the gun around, I can swing my hands into the side of the barrel, knock it away, then shoulder-charge him, which should—

But he holds the gun as if it's an unexploded bomb, keeping it pointed at the floor. He tries a smile, but it's gone before it can fully form.

We resume our walk down the corridor. Every so often, Koji will tell me to turn left or right, directing me deeper into the ship. He's visibly trembling, trying to look everywhere at once. It's hard to imagine someone like him surviving in this place.

"How did you end up here, anyway?" I say.

"Me and two of the crew—Dominguez and Rogers," Koji says. "We left the crash site. Rogers, she…she didn't make it."

He goes silent for a moment. Then he says, "There was this radio message. Talking about food and shelter."

"I've heard it."

"It was a lie. Obviously. I got put to work like everyone else."

"But you're not a worker any more."

"No. I figured out what the Engine—"

At that moment, a shape blocks out the light from the passage above us. Koji swears quietly, not looking up. I keep my gaze on the corridor ahead.

Footsteps descend the stairs behind us. "Hey," a voice calls out.

Neither of us responds—I'm waiting for Koji to say something, but he stays silent.

"Hey," says the voice again, louder this time, and now it's accompanied by heavy footsteps, clumping down the corridor behind us.

Koji looks round. "Just bringing her to the work detail at the generators," he says, nodding at me.

I keep my eyes on the floor. The man is wearing thick work boots, much too big for him, as if he took them from somebody else.

"Where's Ray?" says the man, his voice gruff.

Koji shrugs. "Probably with Iluk somewhere."

"Go find them. Something's happened in the farm, we need every available…"

He trails off. I flick my eyes upwards, and that's when I recognise him. Sandy hair, red face. He was on the bridge when I was brought in, and I can see recognition sparking to life in his eyes, see the yell forming on his lips.

64

Prakesh

The cleaner air outside the hangar is like a splash of cold water. Prakesh takes a huge breath, letting the strip of urine-soaked cloth fall to the floor.

The workers push through a door ahead of him, exploding out of the corridor into a larger space. It's an old weapons bay—there are empty racks everywhere, running floor to ceiling, some of them still carrying ancient ordnance, their labels cracked and faded. Computers line the wall, the screens black and dead.

By the time Prakesh gets there, the gunfire has started.

There are at least two guards, firing from behind one of the racks. Prakesh hits the ground, going down hard. He has no weapon, nothing to protect him. All he can do is stay down. The gunshots are deafening.

One of the workers takes a bullet, his arm almost torn from his shoulder. He collapses onto the floor, twitching, and Prakesh sees that it's the man who wanted to take the bridge. He pushes himself away, rolling across the floor.

The shooting stops. There's a split second where Prakesh thinks they've lost, that one of the guards is about to come round the corner and put a bullet through him. But then he hears Jojo's voice. "L-l-let's go!"

The rest of the workers roar in agreement, and he feels feet pounding on the metal surface. He tries to get up, but as he does so his hand slips in the blood pooled on the floor, and he crashes back down, knocking his chin on the metal plating.

Jojo pulls him up. He's surprisingly strong. He and Prakesh stumble to the exit, and that's when one of the racks gives way.

Its supports are riddled with bullet holes. It gives off a metallic screech as it comes down, collapsing in on itself, kicking up clouds of dust as it goes, spewing its cargo across the floor. Prakesh pulls Jojo back just in time.

The sounds of the crash die away, replaced by Prakesh's ragged breathing. Their way to the passage beyond is blocked. A woman, the one who told Jojo that it was crazy to hit the fuel hangar, is staring at them through a gap in the debris, her eyes wide. Her lank hair hangs down her forehead in streaks of wet grey.

Prakesh moves to climb the wreckage, but Jojo grabs his shoulder. "There's an-n-n-nother way r-round," he says.

He doesn't give him a chance to respond—just plunges back the way they came, ducking into the passage. Prakesh takes one last look at the woman, and then follows.

Prakesh struggles to keep up with Jojo. He moves at a brisk pace, the rifle swinging back and forth. There's an alarm blaring somewhere, distant but urgent, and he swears he can hear more gunfire, as if the ship has finally woken up to the threat inside it. At each junction and stairway, Jojo pauses for a split second before picking a path and heading down it. Within minutes, Prakesh is lost—he knows they're heading deeper into the ship, but he has no clue where they are.

Eventually, he catches up to Jojo at the top of a set of narrow stairs, where he pauses a little longer than normal. "Hang on a second," he says, gasping out the words.

"Gotta k-k-keep g-going," Jojo says, starting down the stairs.

A few minutes later, they reach a T-junction in the corridor, marked by a rotating yellow light that casts strange shadows across the walls. Jojo stops, peering around the side of the junction, as if he senses something up ahead.

Prakesh stumbles to a halt, hands on his knees, blood pounding in his ears.

"Jojo," he says.

"J-j-just g-gimme me a s-s-second." He starts down the passage, then abruptly turns, heading back in the other direction.

Prakesh raises his head, and Jojo glances back at him. "I haven't b-b-been d-down here b-before. B-b-but I th-think this is—"

"Wait," says Prakesh. "How do we get out after we torch the fuel?"

"I t-t-told you. W-we g-get to the b-b-boats."

"What if there aren't enough? What if we get ambushed again?"

"W-w-won't happen." Jojo's eyes are alive. "I b-b-been planning th-this for a l-long t-time. I'm g-gonna g-g-g-get out, and th-then I'm g-g-going back to D—to D—" His voice cuts off, and he swallows hard: "...Denali. Up n-n-n-north."

"We can't—"

"*No.*" Jojo's tone of voice is almost pleading, as if he's trying to make Prakesh understand. "I have to g-g-get out. M-m-my uncle c-c-can't s-s-survive if I'm n-n-not there. He's g-g-g-got a b-b-bad leg. I g-g-gotta find him."

Prakesh puts a hand on the wall, breathing hard, forcing oxygen into his lungs. *This is all happening too fast*, he thinks. He assumed Jojo had a coherent plan, latched onto it, desperate to get out of this place. It's a mistake that might get him killed. There'll be no ordered exit, no regimented attack on their captors. Jojo doesn't even know where he's going. The whole thing has already gone to shit, and there'll be more deaths by the time it's done. He can't let that happen. He won't.

Jojo tilts his head. "Th-that was p-p-pretty clever b-b-back there," he says, glancing down at the rifle. "W-w-w-with the sssss-st-st-stinker."

"Thanks." Prakesh doesn't know what else to say.

Jojo grins, hefting the rifle and stepping into the corridor. "OK. I th-think I know w-where we are. Let's—"

The bullet takes him in the side of the neck.

Impact

65

Riley

I'm on the guard in two steps, aiming a knee right for his groin. He sees it coming, manages to half turn, but he's not even close to fast enough. My knee crunches into him, and he doubles over, wheezing. I shove him sideways, and his head bangs off the corridor floor.

"Shit," Koji says, his voice curiously breathy.

"No choice," I say as I get to my feet. I'm amazed that I can speak, even more amazed that he hears me over the blood pounding in my ears. But if he'd used the gun, it would have brought others running.

"No, I mean, shit!" Koji is pointing down the corridor. I look up—and that's when the bullet buries itself in the wall next to me.

There are two more guards by the stairway. One of them is already turning, using the rail to swing himself around, shouting for help. The second is raising his gun again, taking careful aim.

I don't turn to see where the bullet ended up. I run with my head and shoulders tucked in, zigzagging in the narrow corridor, presenting as small a target as possible. I can hear Koji behind me, hear his panicked breathing and stumbling footsteps. Another gunshot: this time, the bullet ripples the air above my head.

"Go right! Go right!" Koji shouts. Another corridor branches off the one we're in, and I have to dig into the turn hard to stop myself from crashing into the wall. I scrape my shoulder along it, barely feeling it through the thick coat.

We crash down another steep stairway, tumbling into the corridor beyond. "Where's the generator room?" I shout.

"Just ahead," Koji says. He can barely get the words out.

Another left. Another right. The pumping noise is louder now, coming from all directions. But then another sound eclipses it. Gunfire. And it's coming from in *front* of us, from further down the corridor.

"There," Koji says. The corridor ahead of us opens up into a larger space, terminating in a vertical drop of a few feet. The floor is slightly curved where it meets the wall, the metal racks of equipment stretching beyond my field of view. I can smell engine oil, and, over it, the sharp stench of gunpowder.

There are two guards hugging the door on either side, their backs to us. One of them is blind-firing into the room, but the other—a man with powerful upper arms and thick dreadlocks hanging down his back—is picking his targets, aiming carefully. He squeezes off a shot, and there's a howl of pain from inside the room.

These guards aren't shooting at us. They don't even know we're here. What is this?

I don't waste time trying to find out. If that's the generator room, then it means the guards are firing on the workers. I don't know why, or why it's happening now, but something tells me I've got a much better chance with the people in that room than I have on my own.

The two guards haven't seen us yet. I go faster, sprinting right for the entrance, pumping my arms from side to side, head down, eyes up, muscles on fire.

Dreadlocks whips his head round, finally noticing us. There's no time for finesse here. I stutter-step, closing the distance, and launch myself towards him.

The first thought is to lead with my elbow, or my knee. But I launched a little too late, with no time in the air to line up the strike. The man's head collides with my torso, the impact spasming through me, and then he and I are tangled up in a confusing embrace, everything spinning, my leg knocking into the door, smacking my head on the ground, trying to tuck into a roll, not quite doing it. I come to a stop, skidding on my back in icy water

The floor is under an inch of it, foaming with muck, and it immediately soaks through my clothes. The air above me is full of gunfire and angry shouts and screams of pain. I try to get up, propping myself on one elbow, then have to throw myself down again as a gun goes off. In the dim light, the other people in the room are nothing but silhouettes.

The gunfire has stopped, and now people are shouting, talking over each other. I can't see Koji at all. What I can see is the other guard, the one who was blind-firing. He's slumped over the edge of the door, blood trickling into the water.

"Get the door! Shut it!"

"Can we lock it from the inside?"

"Anybody hurt?"

"They'll be more coming. Hurry."

We're in a chamber with rusted walls, bare bulbs hanging from the ceiling. Generators squat on low tables, looking like alien artefacts, all black piping and tarnished silver blocks. Tools are half-submerged in the water, spinning in place: wrenches, screwdrivers, welding goggles, something that looks like a primitive plasma cutter.

I look from face to face: men and women, less than a dozen, all dirty, all thin. Workers—have to be. I don't see Carver, or Prakesh. I spot Koji—he's managed to get inside, but whoever these people are, they've identified him as a guard. They've got him pinned to a wall, an elbow at his throat.

"No no no!" I shout, forcing myself to my feet. I can't have them shoot Koji. I still need him. "He's here to help."

The workers look between me and Koji, suspicious, not sure how to proceed. I open my mouth to speak, and then feel a hand on my shoulder.

I'm still too wired from the run, and I spin round, my body moving before I can stop it, bringing my arms up, ready to fight.

Aaron Carver puts his hands on top of mine, and slowly pushes them down. There's the strangest expression on his face—like he's expecting me to vanish, like I'm a dream that he's about to wake up from. His face is mottled with bruises, his lip split. A dried crust of blood marks his forehead like warpaint.

He reaches out, his fingertips brushing my face.

He's going to say something smart, like he always does. He's going to make a crack about always having to save my ass, or about me making an entrance. He's going to—

Then he pulls me towards him, wrapping his arms around me. And just for a second, I'm safe.

66

Okwembu

Prophet is hunched over a bank of screens, staring down at the scenes unfolding on them. His eyes flick back and forth, terror on his face. Gunshots flare on the screens, washing out the cameras.

Riley Hale is there. Okwembu saw her moving through the corridors, saw her take out one of the guards. *She's still alive.*

She looks around the bridge. It's packed with people, all of them watching Prophet, all of them waiting for an order. On one of the screens, something explodes, sending another flare of white light across Prophet's pale skin. His lips are moving, but no words come out.

"Sir?" says one of the men, standing by the map table. He's older than Prophet, more grizzled, but it's impossible not to see the fear in his eyes.

Okwembu looks at him, then back at Prophet. He doesn't react to the question, his eyes locked on the screen.

"Prophet?" the man says, more urgently this time.

Okwembu doesn't hesitate. Prophet's thin veneer of control is cracking open, and she's not going to let the opportunity pass.

"You, you and you," she says, pointing. "Lead your men down there and provide support. Get word to the gunner: if anybody tries to get off this ship, blow them out of the water. It'll stop anyone else from trying to leave."

She ignores the surprise on their faces. "You three," she says, turning to face the others. "When they're gone, you lock this bridge down."

The man by the map table sneers, disgust winning out over fear. "I don't take orders from *you*."

For the first time since she killed Mikhail, Okwembu loses it. "*I don't care who you take orders from.* If you don't stop this right now, you lose control of the ship."

She jabs a finger at Prophet, who hasn't reacted to the outburst. "It's exactly what he'd order you to do if he was thinking straight. Now get moving."

A dart of worry shoots through her, but she ignores it. She's lived through revolutions before—usually, all it takes is a few deaths, and then the instigators stop fighting. They should be able to keep the majority of the *Ramona*'s workforce.

A ripple of emotion travels around the room, borne on glances and nods. The ones at the back move first, hefting their guns, then jogging for the doors.

"One thing," Okwembu says, talking over the rising tide of voices. "The woman who Ray and Iluk brought in earlier. If you find her, I want her alive. Bring her to me."

Prophet is finally looking at her, but she ignores him. She drops her head and closes her eyes, just for a moment.

Okwembu is tired. Tired of trying to keep people safe. She's sick of it. She has tried, over and over, but no matter what she does, it never works. She has suffered, been imprisoned, nearly tortured. Whenever she has found supporters, they've been snatched away. And now, just as she finally finds a place she can keep safe, a place of order which she can control, Riley Hale comes along.

A woman she respected. A woman she had high hopes for. A woman who hates her, and wants to destroy everything she would build.

On some level, Okwembu understands Riley's hate. She knows she deserves it, after what happened to the *Akua Maru*. But Hale is about to destroy the one thing she has left, and Okwembu will not stand for it. Not this time.

She is going to kill Hale herself.

67

Anna

All Anna Beck can see is stars.

There was no sound when the pod ejected. No roar of rocket engines. The airlock is designed to open completely in a fraction of a second, letting the vacuum shoot the pod away from the station. Anna's heart has climbed up her throat and into her mouth—she's struggling to breathe, as if she can't push the air around its mass. The G-forces have welded her to the chair.

The touchscreen displays are alight, each one incomprehensible, as if the craft is daring her to take control. The pod is spinning, the stars give way to Outer Earth's massive hull, moving from the top of the viewport to the bottom, vanishing before she can pick out any details. Three seconds later, it appears again, and Anna is sure she's going to smash into it.

The feeling passes. Her hand is still locked tight around the joystick, and she makes herself push the top button. An engine bursts into life behind her, rumbling up into her spine. The pod tilts on its axis, the stars yawing to the right. A million tiny pinpricks, more than she could ever have imagined. The sun flashes into view, filling the cockpit with an awful glare.

Anna pulls the stick towards her—gently, almost tentatively. A different sensation this time, as boosters on the side of the pod fire. Dimly, Anna realises that she's weightless. There's a ripple of nausea in her stomach, and her sinuses feel strange, like they're slowly filling with mucous.

With a tiny rasp of fabric, her beanie comes loose from her head. It was dislodged by the launch, and now gravity floats it above her eyeline, mocking her. She grabs it, pulling it back on.

"Fuck," Anna says, the sound more of a breath than a word, horrifyingly loud in the silence.

Slowly, carefully, she stops the pod from moving. Outer Earth is no longer appearing in the cockpit viewport, and she has no idea where she is in space, but the stars have stopped moving. That's good enough for now.

Tiny movements are best. Little flicks on the stick, no more. The two buttons control her thrust—the top one sends her forward, and the one on the front of the stick causes a burst of white smoke to shoot from a nozzle on the front of the craft, out of sight below the cockpit.

Outer Earth comes back into view. She nearly loses it, brings it back, and holds it.

For a few seconds she can't tear her eyes away. Outer Earth is a monolith: a scarred, grey, ancient relic, hanging in the black void. The sun is behind the escape pod, and its light picks out the station perfectly.

The dock is easy to spot. It's as if a giant monster locked its jaws around the station, and tore away a huge chunk. The wound is marked by a haze of debris, glittering in the vacuum.

Anna doesn't know exactly where the tug will be—Dax didn't tell her—but the dock's her best bet. Pushing back the fear, she thumbs the thruster. The pod responds, and Outer Earth begins to get larger. It's hard to control—the station keeps sliding away, only for Anna to overcorrect and send it veering in the other direction. How much fuel does she have? She doesn't dare look down at the gauges to find out—if she does that, she feels like she'll never be able to look away. The thought of being lost out here, trapped in the void forever, is enough to send her heart back into her mouth.

The hull looms in front of her, and she brings the pod around so that the nose is pointing towards the dock. It's a little further along the station's curve, but she can see the debris. Slowly, ever so slowly, she heads towards it, keeping a close eye on the nearby hull.

The debris takes shape. A crate here, a destroyed tug there. Half of the dock's smashed airlock door. The mag rails that pulled the tugs inside the station are twisted and torn, spinning gently, as if they weighed no more than a human hair.

There's an urgent beep, and one of the displays flashing a warning. PROXIMITY ALERT.

The hull. It's too close, swallowing the right half of the viewport. She jerks the stick, and the pod drifts to the left, silencing the alarm.

There. She sees the other pods, just inside the destroyed dock. They're widely spaced, rotating on their individual axes. Their doors are open—Anna can see inside one of them, right out of the viewport on the other side. Dax and the others have got their space suits on. They'll be transferring to the tug, clambering aboard, getting ready to depart.

Anna thinks hard, picturing the dock as she remembers it. A huge hangar, packed with tugs and equipment. If she can manoeuvre her pod inside, if she can spot Dax's tug, she can ram it. If it's damaged, they won't be able to use it, which means their only option will be to return to Outer Earth.

Except...*shit*. She's not wearing a space suit. She didn't even think to put one on yet. An awful image comes to her mind: the escape pod hitting the tug, cracking down the middle. She's heard stories about what happens to a body in space—everybody on the station has.

There's no time. She's coming up on the debris. Anna pulls the stick, trying to steer her way through. Something scratches across the roof of the pod, and she yelps in fear.

She can see the tug. It's hanging right in the middle of the dock, facing outwards. It dwarfs her escape pod: a bulbous, misshapen thing, with a prominent nose and small fins on the sides. There's something on its underside, just out of view, something gold-coloured and thin. The heat shield.

Anna steers herself between two escape pods. *Almost there*, she thinks. Maybe she can come to a stop, let herself drift while she straps into a suit.

For a second time, the proximity alarm explodes to life. Anna's head snaps to the side, expecting to see the wall of the dock creeping up on her. But there's nothing—she's through the pods, past the debris, so what—

She has half a second to register the man in the space suit, half a second to see the horrified expression on his face. Then he slams into the viewport with a bang that shakes the tiny escape pod.

68

Riley

I don't try to process what I'm feeling: the relief, and joy, and fear, all tangled up in a big knot. I just let Carver hold me.

It's a full minute before he lets me go. By then, the fabric of his overalls is wet from my tears, and my face is red and puffy.

He cracks a smile. One of his teeth is gone. "Nice of you to join us," he says.

I smile back, wiping away more tears. "Not like I had anything better to do."

There's splashing ahead of us, and we turn to see a worker lifting one of the guards' rifles from the water. He's painfully thin, with lank hair and a gaunt, scarred face, but his hands are sure as he checks the gun. Another worker is at the door, a woman with a closely shorn head and a nasty scar across the back of her neck. "Does anyone know how to lock this?" she shouts over her shoulder.

"Riley, I don't..." Carver stops, shaking his head. "How are you even here?"

I open my mouth to tell him, but then I realise that explaining everything that happened to me would take longer than we have. Instead, it's Prakesh who jumps to the front of my mind. I look around again, certain that I'll see him among the other workers, but he isn't there.

"I'll tell you later," I say. "Promise."

"Seriously, what—"

"Right now, we need to get Prakesh, and then we're going to find Okwembu. Where is he? Was he with you?"

"I can't lock this," the woman by the door shouts. A couple of workers respond, wading over to help out.

Carver looks at me. "We got separated. I sort of maybe mouthed off to the guards."

He sees my expression. "Yeah, I know. Not smart. Ended up

getting the shit beaten out of me. Bastards still put me to work, though—yesterday we were cleaning out the guards' quarters, and today it was here." He gestures around the dank space. "Water was leaking in and fried some of their generators. They put us to work repairing them."

I point at the worker with the rifle. "But if you were working, then what happened with—"

"Beats me. One minute we were fixing holes in the hull, then the next a bunch of other workers burst in here and start shooting. Took the guards by surprise."

He pauses, looking over at the man checking the rifle. "At least, I think they're workers. We haven't really had a chance to get to know each other."

"We're workers, all right," the man says. He finally decides the rifle isn't worth using—water-damaged, probably, and throws it aside, disgusted. "We were in the farm. The new guy did something—had us all soak our shirts in piss, then knocked out the guards with…hell, I don't know *what* it was. Some kind of chemical stuff. Never seen anything like it."

Carver raises an eyebrow. "Oh yeah. That makes total sense. Thanks."

Chemicals. Prakesh.

Before I can say anything else, there's a panicked yell from behind us. We turn to see one of the workers standing over Koji, a hand wrapped in his jacket at the scruff of his neck. He has a gun in one hand, one that doesn't look like it hit the water.

I get between them. "Don't even think about it," I say. Koji is on his knees, shaking in fear.

The man stares at me. "He's one of *them*."

"I *told* you. He can help us."

"Who are you?" the man says, glancing at my cuffs. "What are you even doing here?"

Carver steps between us. "Back up, Adam," he says.

The man—Adam—spits, his saliva plopping into the water. He jerks his head at Koji. "These people don't deserve to live."

"This one does," I say.

Adam holds my gaze a moment longer, then turns away, disgusted.

"What's his deal?" says Carver, nodding to Koji.

"Long story," I say. "But I need him."

"Come on," says the gaunt worker from behind Adam. "Jojo said to get to the boats."

"The hell is Jojo?" Carver says.

"Forget the boats," Adam says. He points to the body of one of the guards, face down in the water. "We leave without taking care of the rest of 'em, they'll come after us. Hunt us down."

"You're gonna get yourself killed, man," says Carver. "You and everyone else."

"He's right," Koji says, and everybody turns to look at him. "Believe me, you aren't getting to the bridge. It's too heavily guarded."

Adam tries to speak, but the gaunt worker talks over him. "Then we get as many weapons as we can," he says. He looks over his shoulder, raising his voice. "Find 'em, bring 'em here. I'll check 'em for any water damage."

As the workers start to move, Carver looks down at my hands, frowning as he takes in the cuffs.

"Hang on," he says, casting about him. He spots what he's looking for, and holds up the old-fashioned cutter. It's acetylene, not plasma, and he aims it at the metal join between the two cuffs. I wince as the torch singes my skin. But within a second my hands spring apart. I badly want to get the actual cuffs off my wrists, but a cutting torch isn't the way to do it.

The voice inside me speaks, reminding me that Prakesh isn't the only reason I'm here. "Carver, was Okwembu with you? What happened to her?"

"Gods know," he says, running his fingers along the cuff on my right wrist. "Lost her when they took me and Prakesh." He sees me about to protest, and talks over me. "I know you probably want to throw her off the side of the ship right now, but it's too dangerous. Let's just get out of here."

"Hold on," says the woman by the door. "There's—"

She doesn't get a chance to finish. The door flies open, smashed from the other side, knocking her and the others aside.

Gunfire deafens me. Adam flies backwards, his arms stretched over his head, like he's calling out for his own personal god. I feel blood speckle my face, and then his body slaps the surface of the water.

A split second later, something else comes through the door—a small cylinder, squat and black. I get a momentary glimpse of it before it vanishes under the surface, bumping up against Adam's body.

Koji moves faster than I would have thought he could, grabbing me and Carver, pulling us down. "Flash-bang!" he shouts.

Everything goes white.

69

Prakesh

Prakesh squeezes himself against the wall. He can't take his eyes off Jojo's body, sprawled across the floor in the corridor junction. Half of the boy's neck is torn away.

"Got him!" someone shouts, speaking over the noise of the fading gunshot. The voice is shockingly close.

"See any others?" says another voice.

Prakesh starts to edge away from the T-junction, moving as quickly and quietly as he can. He glances to his right—there's a turn ten feet behind him in the corridor, with a corner he can slip around.

Bam.

Another gunshot. Prakesh snaps his head around, half convinced that he's hit. But whoever shot Jojo is blind-firing, the barrel of the rifle pointed around the corner. Another shot comes, the report deafening in the cramped space.

It feels like all the blood in Prakesh's body is rushing to his head. But he keeps moving, sliding along the wall. The turn is three feet away. Two.

Prakesh slips around the corner. At the very last second, he sees movement out of the corner of his eye. A head, poking round the edge of the junction.

They've seen me. There's no way they didn't.

Jojo's blood is still speckled across his face, slowly going tacky. It loosens the muscles in his legs, and he has to work very hard to stay upright, pushing himself against the wall. He realises he didn't know how old Jojo was, if he had a last name, anything about him except for the fact that he came from somewhere called Denali and he wanted to get off this ship more than anything else in the world.

He pauses, his knees bent, trying very hard not to breathe.

The voice comes again. "Nobody here. Guess he was the only one."

"I don't buy it, man. Why come down here by yourself?"

"Doesn't matter now." There's a muffled thump, and it takes Prakesh a second to realise that it's the sound of a boot colliding with Jojo's body. He has to fight down a wave of nausea. Could he keep moving? Slip away silently? He tells himself to move, but he's frozen to the spot.

Another pause. Then the sound of metal scraping on metal—Jojo's gun, being lifted off the floor. The sound is followed by footsteps, trailing off into nothingness.

Prakesh counts to ten. Then twenty. Silently mouthing the words, telling himself to move. It's only when he gets to thirty that his legs kick into gear.

He peeks around the corner.

Deserted.

In ten steps, he's crossed to the T-junction. He pauses, holding his breath. There's more distant gunfire, quick bursts of it, but the area around him is silent.

He glances down at Jojo's body, immediately looks away. There's nothing he can do. He can't even take the body with him—not if he wants to get out of here alive. And he has to make it out, otherwise Jojo died for nothing.

He should try and find the fuel hangar. Link up with the others. He keeps walking, listening hard for any footsteps coming his way, keenly aware that he doesn't have anything to defend himself with.

The corridor opens up into a wider hub area, with various passages leading off from it. There's a sign bolted to the wall, but the letters are rusted over, faded with age. Prakesh can just make out the words AIRCRAFT ELEVATORS, but the rest of the sign is illegible.

The boats must be on a lower level, surely, so all he has to do is—

What is that?

There's a subsonic hum, almost inaudible. He has to focus to hear it, and focus even harder to work out where it's coming from. It's emanating from his left, down a corridor that's even narrower than the others.

Prakesh hasn't been on the *Ramona* long, but he's become familiar with the sounds of the ship, the rumbles and clanks and bangs that echo through its rusted body. This is different. This is something he hasn't heard before.

Jojo told him the Engine was below decks. He said they didn't let the workers get close to it. His curiosity overwhelms him, and before he can stop himself, he's walking down the corridor, treading as quietly as he can.

A light flickers in the ceiling as Prakesh makes his way down it, the buzzing and clicking accenting the machine hum. He's holding his breath, and has to force himself to exhale. There aren't any more guards that he can see, but he still proceeds carefully.

The passage turns right, then left, and then Prakesh is in a high-ceilinged, brightly lit storeroom. The walls are lined with racks, just like the one that nearly took him and Jojo out. The shelves are brimming with equipment, a hodgepodge of frayed wires and oversized batteries and rusted cutting torches, nestled up against machinery whose use Prakesh can only guess at.

He focuses. There's a set of double doors in front of him, shut tight, with two folding chairs off to one side. The two who killed Jojo must have been guarding it. For a few moments, Prakesh wonders why they abandoned their post. They must have decided to join the fighting on the upper levels.

The doors are twice his size, as if heavy equipment needs to be moved in and out. A metal plaque is bolted to the door, faded words picked out on it in black lettering. *HAARP MOBILE UNIT 2769X-B8 AUTHORISED ACCESS ONLY.*

Prakesh takes in the letters. The split in the doors bisects the B in *MOBILE*, and the first C in *ACCESS*.

HAARP.

He knows what that is. He's sure of it. But it's like something glimpsed out of the corner of an eye, vanishing the moment you turn to look at it.

Prakesh knows he has to get to the boats, knows that it won't be long before the other workers escape. But it's as if his feet have stopped listening to his mind. He looks around, then walks towards the door. There's a chunky keypad on the wall by the door, but as he gets closer he sees that it's dead, its digital display blank. And the doors aren't sealed completely. There's the tiniest gap.

The hum rumbles in Prakesh's stomach.

He puts his fingers in the gap, braces his arms, and pulls.

The doors resist for a moment, then give way, moving so fast that they almost knock Prakesh off balance. The hum is even more powerful now. He steadies himself, then raises his head and looks inside.

Nothing but darkness. Prakesh is on a metal grate, and he can feel empty space below him. He moves along it, hands touching the wall. A line of switches slides under his fingers, plasticky to the touch. Taking a deep breath, he flicks them up.

Banks of lights begin to click on, one after the other. Huge spotlights in the ceiling spring to life, making Prakesh blink, chasing away the shadows.

He's standing above another hangar—this one slightly smaller than the others. Most of the space is taken up by four enormous cubes, at least fifty feet on all sides, their surfaces dull grey metal. There's a thin passage below him, running between the cubes. The floor is covered with thickly insulated cables, tangled up in each other, running up the walls of the cubes and into them via giant connectors. Some of the cables go higher, vanishing into the ceiling. Prakesh's nostrils haven't recovered from the chemicals he cooked up, but he can still pick out the sharp stench of ozone.

He puts a hand on the railing, trying to work out what he's seeing. Again the word tugs at his mind. *HAARP.*

There's a ladder hanging off the end of the platform he's standing on. He swings himself onto it, climbing down, wincing as the noise of his feet on the rungs echoes across the hangar. He's more careful as he hops off onto the grated floor and walks between two of the cubes.

He keeps walking, running his hand along the side of the cube. It vibrates ever so slightly under his fingers. The hum is loud now, so loud that Prakesh wonders why the whole room isn't shaking. There must be some kind of inertial dampening, shock mounts built into the floor and ceiling...

He looks up as he comes round the corner of the cube. There's a rectangular, rusted metal plaque, mounted on the side of the next cube along. Prakesh moves closer, reaching out to touch it. At the top of the plaque is a triangle with an exclamation point inside it, its bright yellow turned ochre with age. There's a litany of warnings underneath it—Prakesh's mouth moves as he scrolls down it. "Unauthorised personnel...risk of electric shock...safety equipment..."

He reaches the bottom. There's a set of barcodes, slightly raised off the metal surface. Underneath them are the words *Mobile High-frequency Active Auroral Research Program—Installation 2769X-B8.*

HAARP.

Prakesh's heart starts beating faster. This is the Engine, he's sure of it, but why can't he remember what it does? He knows he's heard the word HAARP before, somewhere on Outer Earth—a lesson in a schoolroom, a snatched conversation somewhere, an archived article on a tab screen.

He starts walking faster down the passage. At the very end, near the wall, is a screen built into the side of the cube on his right. It's dusty, and as Prakesh wipes it off, it springs to life, flickering under his fingers.

The screen is old. Prakesh can see plenty of dead pixels, and there's a crack that extends almost all the way across it. But he can still read the information displayed. He flicks across it with his finger, scrolling faster and faster. It's data—complex scientific data. An analysis of radio frequencies, breaking them down by different values.

He moves further along. The second screen doesn't work—the touch function has degraded, and it's glitched out. But the third, which he finds at the back of the room, shows something different.

It's displaying complicated electrical diagrams, each one showing the flow of current.

Prakesh taps one, and a new window appears, displaying a separate graph. The lettering at the top of the window reads, *Fluxgate Magnetometer Data File Reviewer*.

He frowns. A fluxgate magnetometer measures the Earth's magnetic field. But why would—

The puzzle pieces slot into place, and Prakesh's eyes go wide.

HAARP. It's weather control. A way of altering the make-up of the ionosphere to control climate.

Before the war, Earth's governments tried to get various HAARP projects off the ground, but they didn't manage to do it before the missiles fell. Except this HAARP unit is here. And it's working. Prakesh puts his hand flat on the side of the cube, feeling the vibration travel up his arm.

This is why the area has become habitable. Why humans have been able to establish themselves here. This is the sacred Engine, the life-giver, the reason Prophet and his followers have thrived. Prakesh can't believe something like this still exists, can't believe that Prophet worked out how to get it running. It's *beyond* belief.

And the workers are going to burn the fuel supplies. They're going to sink the ship. And when they do, whatever this HAARP unit is doing to the climate will stop. It'll be lost at the bottom of the ocean. This part of the planet will go back to the way it was before: a frozen wasteland. It'll never recover.

Prakesh turns, and runs.

70

Riley

I close my eyes a split second too late.

The flash jabs hot needles into my retinas. The bang finishes the job, slamming my ears closed, filling them with an awful, high-pitched whine. A spray of water splashes across my face.

It feels like a whole minute before I can open my eyes. When I do, the generator room is exploding around me. I see a worker go down, his head snapping backwards as he takes a bullet. A guard is out of ammo, using his gun like a club, swinging it back and forth as two workers dodge out of range. A generator tips over, sparks flying as it lands on top of a prone guard, pushing her under the surface of the water.

Carver helps me, pulling me to my feet. Somehow, he's got hold of one of the rifles, and is trying to load it, yanking at the bolt. The mechanism is jammed, stuck halfway. He gives up, swinging it at an approaching guard. The butt takes the man in the face, and he spits a thick gout of blood as he topples sideways, crashing against the wall.

The impact from the hit travels up Carver's arm, knocking the rifle out of his hands and into the water. I don't wait for him to retrieve it. I just grab him and go, heading for the corridor. He pulls me back at the last second, just as another volley of bullets explodes past the door.

"We'll never make it!" he screams. I can barely hear him. Koji appears behind him, hyperventilating, hardly able to stand upright.

He's right. That corridor is a death trap—a couple of guards hanging back will be able to cut down anyone coming out of here. I cast around for something to use, and that's when I see the man Carver took down. More importantly, I see what's on his belt.

A squat cylinder, just like the one that came through the door. What did Koji call it? *Flash-bang.*

I sprint over to him, skidding onto my knees in the water, grabbing the cylinder. It crosses my mind that the water might have damaged it, but there's no time to check. We lose nothing by trying.

"Koji!" I shout. I can't tell how loud my own voice is. It hums in my ears, sounding as if it's coming through thick padding. He looks over to me, and I toss him the grenade.

He catches it with two hands, almost fumbling it, but then he reaches up and pulls a pin out of the cylinder. He spins around, hurling it underhand into the corridor.

Impact

The bang is just as loud, but this time we're prepared for it, hands over our ears, our eyes closed. And a second after it goes off, Carver and I rocket out of the door.

For a moment, it's almost like we're tracers again, running through Outer Earth. I can feel him behind me, hear his feet pounding the metal, like we're sprinting through a sector with me on point. The corridor is filled with thick smoke, stinking of gunpowder. A guard appears in front of me, on his feet but unsteady. I barely pause as I knock him aside, elbowing him in the ribcage.

"This way!"

It's Koji, pointing at a turn-off from the corridor. Somehow, he's managed to stay with us. I'm closest, and I skid to a halt alongside it, quickly peeking my head round. Deserted.

The surviving workers clamber out of the generator room, coughing and blinking. We can't leave them here—not after everything they've been through. I motion them to follow us, and they accept the order without comment. Two of them, I see, have managed to retrieve rifles. I almost ask them to test-fire the guns, check if they work, but decide not to. Last thing we need is someone getting hit with a ricochet in the tight corridors.

We keep moving. There's no telling how far this little worker rebellion has spread—not without a way to communicate with Prakesh's group. An alarm is blaring somewhere, harsh and guttural, but there's no more gunfire. I make Koji take the lead—the bowels of the ship are impossible to figure out, every corridor identical, with the same ribbed walls and recessed doors.

I'd give anything to have Harlan and Eric here. The seaplane could give us a way out. But thinking about them hurts too much, and I make myself stop. Even if they're alive, they have no way of knowing what's happening on the ship.

Ahead of us, the corridor opens up into a mezzanine level, with railings on the left. I can see a set of stairs leading down from the railings a few feet into the room, but it's only when we sprint through the entrance that we see what's in there.

It's some kind of storage hangar. Planes—the same as the ones on the ship's deck—are parked wingtip to wingtip, with their noses angled diagonally towards us. Close-up, they're enormous, at least fifty feet long, with cockpits like huge eyes. Puddles of old oil and grimy tyre tracks dot the floor beneath them. Huge rolling pallets rest up against the plane wheels.

There's an enormous roller door on the far wall of the hangar; it's hard to imagine these planes flying in here, so there must be an elevator platform beyond it, something to get them to the deck. The railing on my left has a thick coating of dust on it, and the whole place looks like it hasn't been touched in years.

"Over there," says Koji, pointing. I can make out the opposite end of the hangar, six planes away. It's identical to ours, with its own mezzanine.

"That get us to the boats?" says one of the workers. It's the woman who was trying to lock the door—somehow, she survived the assault. Even scored herself a rifle.

"Quickest way," Koji says, resting his hand on the railing. "Once we get there, we need to—"

The bullet ricochets off the railing next to his hand, burying itself in the wall. Another goes wide, pinging off the wall below us. The workers scatter. The woman with the rifle tries to fire back, then hurls it away when nothing happens.

I can see figures running across the floor, using the planes as cover. There's nowhere for us to hide—not up here, exposed, with nothing but railings between us and guards. Carver and I share a split-second glance, then in one movement, he and I hurdle the railing, bringing our legs up to our chests. We land on the closest wing with an enormous bang, hitting it so hard that the plane rocks in place, tilting on its three wheels.

They want to use the planes as cover? Then so will we.

The jump to the wing wasn't high enough to need a roll. I take a second to catch my balance, centring myself on the metal surface. Then I take off, sprinting up the plane's body. There was no time to explain what we were doing to Koji and the other workers. I look back over my shoulder, and, as I do so, I hear the voice in my mind again, speaking the same words it did when Harlan and I were hanging off that cliff near Whitehorse. *Leave them. They'll just slow you down.*

But Koji has already jumped, crashing onto the wing, sending shock waves through the metal. Two of the others follow. I keep moving, pushing into a full sprint, leaping over the plane's body. The gap between the first and the second plane is no more than five feet, and I land easily, momentum carrying me forward. I see a guard, his face hidden by the body of his rifle, and only just leap across to the third plane when he fires.

The bullet passes above me, but I can't stop myself ducking. The movement pushes me off balance, and it happens right when I hurdle the plane's body. I land awkwardly, try to correct it, nearly manage, and then my feet tangle and I crash onto my side onto the third plane's wing.

At the last second, I turn my body so I'm sliding feet first. It's just enough. I tuck my body as I come off the wing, rolling, smacking my shoulder on the floor. But the momentum's on my side now, and I use it, angling my body forward as I come up to my feet, going from a roll to a sprint in half a second. Somewhere, deep inside me, my heart is pounding hard enough to shatter my ribcage.

Another gunshot. No telling where the round went, or where any of the others are. I start zigzagging—it slows me down, but that's better than a bullet in the back. There aren't any guards on the floor in front of me, and I don't dare risk looking over my shoulder.

I spread the zigzag, sprinting between cover on the floor, using the tool pallets and wheel struts as cover. I'm at the fifth plane when one of the guards, smarter than the others or maybe just more controlled, gets a real bead on me.

He must have been tracking my movements, looking for where I'm going to be instead of where I am. I dive, skidding on my stomach across the floor into cover, just as the space above me fills itself with gunfire.

"Riley!"

Carver has made it to the other end of the hangar. He's got hold of one of the wheeled pallets, and is pushing it towards me, using it as mobile cover. I flatten myself to the floor, crawling towards him. We meet at the edge of the fifth plane, and I squirm into position behind the box. There's no telling where Koji is—he could be on the planes, or he could be bleeding out somewhere.

"I'll go left, you go right," I say to Carver. "Now!"

Open floor. Gunfire. Shouts. Stairs. Railings. Mezzanines. Stumbling. Almost falling. Running. Koji has made it—he's standing in the door, waving us in. I get there half a second before Carver, skidding into the passage, and then Koji slams the door shut. He and Carver spin the valve, locking it tight.

The noise from the plane hangar vanishes, replaced by the thrumming sound of the ship. Carver leans against the wall, breathing hard. Koji looks like he's about to throw up—his face is ash-grey.

"What about the others?" Carver asks.

He shakes his head, and Carver kicks the corridor wall in a fury.

The corridor we're in is wider than the others. It's a hub, with several other passages branching off from it. The choking smell of gunpowder has made it out here, and I can see dust motes caught in the light from the bulbs in the ceiling.

"We need to keep moving," I say, turning to go. "We don't know if they can open the door from the other—"

The guard is fifteen feet away, calm and ready, squinting down the barrel of a rifle. It's pointing right at me, and I can see him starting to squeeze the trigger.

I can't close the distance between us. Not fifteen feet, not before he squeezes the trigger. I don't have a single thing I could use as a weapon.

Then I see Prakesh, sprinting out of one of the side passages.

He's wearing a ragged pair of overalls, identical to Carver's, and there's blood streaming down his face from a cut below his eye. He looks exhausted and terrified but in that instant I don't care because *he's alive.*

I see him look towards me, see the disbelief on his face, see his mouth start to form words.

I see the guard's surprise, see him swing his gun around, hunting for the movement.

I don't see him pull the trigger. But I hear the shot. And I see Prakesh stumble, his hands reaching out towards me. Then he's on the ground and I can see blood and all I can do is scream.

Impact

71

Riley

Carver crosses the fifteen feet in an instant, driving a fist into the guard's face.

The man crumples, his legs collapsing under him, his gun clattering to the floor. I barely notice. I'm already past Carver, skidding to my knees next to Prakesh.

I can't see the bullet hole. There's too much blood. Prakesh looks at me—there's a momentary flare of recognition, and then his eyes close, and they don't open again.

I fumble for his hand, gripping it hard, *willing* him to squeeze back. Nothing. I can hear footsteps around me, more than just Carver and Koji, and the corridor is suddenly filled with voices. But I can't look up. Carver has his hands on Prakesh's chest, hunting for the wound, trying to put pressure on it.

And that's when the voice inside me speaks.

I don't want to listen. But the voice is everywhere now, filling me with white-hot light, the anger burning away everything else.

This isn't just about the man who shot him, it says. *It isn't about the people on this ship. It's about the chain of events that led you here, to this exact spot. There's someone at the start of that chain of events. She's responsible—for everything. And it's time for her to pay. Not tomorrow. Not later on. Now.*

Slowly, I get to my feet.

"Riley, what are you doing?" Carver says. I glance down at him. His arms are red from fingertips to elbows, pushing down on Prakesh's chest. I should help him. Prakesh is dying in front of me, and I'm standing here, just looking at him.

You can't save him. Just like you couldn't save Amira, or your father, or Royo or Kev or Yao. You can't save anyone. The only thing you can do is avenge them.

The corridor is packed with people. Three of them are locked in an argument with Koji. The others are in a loose circle around us—other workers, wearing the same threadbare overalls. I recognise some of them as the ones who followed us from the generator room, but there are others I haven't seen before. The new arrivals have guns, rifles that they must have taken from the guards. And they've got supplies: containers of fuel, food, water canteens, as if they grabbed whatever they could on their way here.

I look past them, and that's when I find the source of the strange feeling: the déjà vu I had when I first arrived on the ship.

I know these corridors. I've spent my entire life moving through ones just like them, using their walls and ceilings and angles and obstacles to craft the fastest, most efficient routes. That's what I do. I'm a tracer—nothing more, nothing less.

I don't know why I didn't see it before. The guards might run this place, they might have weapons and they might have numbers. But in this environment? In this warren of corridors and right angles and hard surfaces? I'm in control. I am the single most dangerous person on this ship.

"Ry, you have to help me," Carver says.

"Get him out of here," I say. My voice is as calm as still water. "Get to the boats, get off the ship. Keep him safe."

And before anyone can say anything, I start running.

72

Prakesh

Everything comes in flashes.

Prakesh is awake, being dragged down one of the *Ramona*'s corridors. Something is wrong with his chest. It's like his ribs are made of hot coals. Every time he tries to breathe, they flare up, searing him with impossible pain. He can hear someone screaming. By the time he realises it's him, he's falling back into darkness.

Another flash. He's outside, looking at the sky. No: not quite outside. The hull of the *Ramona* curves above him, a black mass blotting out the clouds. He's in one of the ovular entrances in the ship's side, lying on his back.

"How many boats down there?" It's Carver's voice. *He's alive.*

"Three. Should be enough for us and the supplies both," says someone else.

He saw Riley. He's sure of it. Where is she? Is she here? He tries to speak, but he can't get enough air into his lungs. He was shot. Why was he shot? He was on his way to find the other workers, to stop them from…

He doesn't know. He almost has it, but holding onto the memory is almost impossible.

Carver appears, leaning into view above Prakesh, arguing with one of the workers. His arms are soaked in blood, streaked up to the elbows. Dimly, Prakesh realises that it's his blood.

"You did *what*?" Carver is staring at the man, his eyes wide.

"There's enough time," the worker says. Sweat is pouring down his face, and a cut on his cheek spills blood down his jawline. "We put down a long trail of fuel. It'll take a while to really catch."

"No way," Carver says, jabbing a finger at the ceiling. "Riley's still up there. I'm not leaving without her."

"Fine," the man says. "Then stay. But we can't come back for you."

Carver turns away, on the verge of leaving. Prakesh struggles to speak, desperate to remember. But it's too much effort, and he feels his eyes starting to close again.

HAARP.

Prakesh's eyes fly open. He has to find a way to tell them. If they let that fuel catch, the detonation will sink the ship. There's got to be a way to stop it.

His throat is dry as old bone. He tries again, and this time sound escapes. It's a moan, low and weak, but it's enough. Carver looks down at him, just for a second.

Please, Prakesh thinks. And somehow, he finds the strength to form words.

"HAARP," he says. It's a rough bark, barely a word.

"You're going to be OK," Carver says, squeezing his shoulder. He's getting ready to leave.

"HAARP," Prakesh says again.

This time, his voice is stronger. Carver glances at him again, and there must be something on Prakesh's face, because he drops to one knee next to him, concern on his face. "What's that?"

"There's a HAARP," Prakesh says. He tries to keep going, but his voice gives out, and he coughs. Pain envelopes him, and he blinks away hot tears.

"A *what*?"

Prakesh doesn't have much left. He can already feel himself slipping back into unconsciousness. He gives it one last try. "There's a HAARP unit," he says. "On this ship. Climate control. Weather. You can't let it burn."

It'll have to be enough. There's nothing left.

"What the hell is—" Carver says, and stops. His eyes go huge.

It was all Prakesh could do to provide the information he did, but he can see that Carver has put it all together. He understands. They're both scientists. He grows things, and Carver builds things, but they still come from the same place.

The worker appears in Prakesh's field of vision. "What's he saying?"

"You stupid, *stupid* son of a bitch." Carver rockets to his feet, so suddenly that the man has to jump back. "This ship—it's got bulkhead doors, right? Where's the closest door to the fuel stash?"

"Door 6 on C deck, I think, but—"

"How do I close them? *Tell me.*"

Good, Prakesh thinks. *That's good.*

And he sinks into oblivion.

73

Riley

The fastest a human being can run is twenty-six miles an hour. Thirty-eight feet per second.

Back on Outer Earth, the other Devil Dancers and I used to argue about whether anybody would ever break that record. I was sure someone would do it someday, even hoped I might do it myself. Yao and Carver insisted that it was impossible.

I don't know how fast I'm going. But right now, it feels like I've taken that record and doubled it. *Tripled* it. My legs are a blur. White-hot fury is exploding through me, acting like rocket fuel, propelling me through the corridors.

I have never moved this fast, or this cleanly. There's a T-junction ahead of me, and I barely slow down, leaping towards the wall, hardly aware of my own movements. I use my left foot to cushion the impact, then push myself to the side, zero momentum lost, the air roaring in my ears, my heart thundering in my chest.

It doesn't matter that I don't know the way. I just have to keep moving upwards, to the bridge. Okwembu will still be there. I'm sure of it. It's the safest place on the ship. It'll be heavily guarded, but I can figure that out when I get there. Right now, I feel like I could blow past them before they even raise their weapons.

I fly up a stairway, my feet hammering on the steps, four at a time. The anger inside me, the sheer *rage*, is like a miniature fusion reactor all on its own. An endless source of energy.

Two guards appear in the corridor, running towards me, guns up. One fires just as I jump, and the bullet scorches the air on my right as I jump towards the wall. I use the tic-tac to push myself higher, scalp scraping the ceiling, foot landing on the opposite wall, then pushing off again and driving my knee into the first one's face. I roll over him, taking out the second guard at the knees, and all the while the voice inside me is screaming. *Faster. Go faster.*

My lungs are burning, but I take that burn and use it, pushing myself harder. At one point, the access to the level above me is gone, the stairs ripped out. I don't even slow down. I angle my run and tic-tac off the wall again, grabbing the ledge, ignoring the jagged metal biting into my skin. The momentum I have swings my body, and I pull it back, using it to launch myself upwards. I get an elbow on the ledge, then two, and then I'm up and running.

There's an entrance ahead of me, like the one leading into the generator room. The room beyond it is flooded with natural light—there's an opening in the wall on my right, another rectangular entrance port. The hangar itself is empty, an open space big enough to hold another six planes. I lean into the run, pushing myself harder. Okwembu can't be far, two more levels, then—

The door at the far end starts to slide open. It's big and heavy, moving on screeching metal rollers. There are shapes behind it in the darkness. Guards.

There's half a second when I think about running towards them. But even at the speed I'm moving, I won't reach it before the guards burst through. They can blanket the hangar with gunfire. I can't dodge bullets, no matter how fast I'm going.

I skid to a halt, back-pedalling, then lunge for the only cover I can see: the rectangular opening. I stop myself just in time, my foot skidding over the edge. There's nothing below me but cold sea. I can see Fire Island in the distance, dark and brooding under the cloudy sky.

The frame of the door is two feet wide—just enough to hide my body. I'm cursing the loss of momentum, but the anger is quickly replaced by fear. There's nowhere else to go. I can hear them, moving across the hangar, and I can tell by their voices that it's a big group of them. And then I realise—they're not sweeping through the hangar. They're heading towards the opening. I sneak a look, just peeking my head around the side of the frame. They're coming right towards me, guns low.

I thought I could get past them, wait until they'd cleared out, then keep moving. But it doesn't matter how much adrenaline I have, or how confident I am—they're going to find me. They'll be on me in seconds.

I look out at Fire Island, and realise that I know where I am. I can place myself on the ship. And at the same time, Koji's words come back to me. *We'd need a lot more guns to even think about getting to the bridge.*

Maybe we don't need a lot more guns.

Maybe we just need one.

74

Riley

I lean out over the edge, and crane my neck upwards. The frame of the opening extends a foot or so beyond the wall, and the deck is thirty feet above my head. At first, I see nothing but smooth metal, and fear rises up inside me, a black spot in the angry, white heat. But then I see the rivets, each the size of my closed fist. There are small openings in the hull, too—miniature ovals, with ancient, rotted cables hanging out of them like tongues.

You can do this.

The voices of the guards are getting closer. I take two quick breaths, then make my move.

I don't have time to be scared. I don't have time for anything. I reach for the nearest cable, fingers snagging, jerking it sideways. Then I swing myself off the edge.

I slide down the cable, burning the skin on my hands. My foot catches something, a rivet, and it brings me to a jerking halt, with one leg cocked at an awkward angle. The air is cold on my face, the wind wicking sweat from my forehead.

I start climbing, moving as fast as I can. My muscles scream as I haul myself up the cable, lunging for the ovular opening. I get a hand in it, then thrust upwards, hunting for a second one. My body moves faster than my mind, and I jam myself against the other side of the frame, out of sight. I nearly fall, my foot slipping on the surface. I have to be still. For five seconds, I don't dare move.

I can hear the guards in the doorway. If one of them looks around the frame, they'll have a clear shot. The only thing protecting me is the illogical nature of what I just did. Nobody in their right mind would try to climb up the side of the ship.

"Did she jump?"

"I don't see her."

"Forget it. If she's in the water, she's dead anyway. Let's go."

The voices fade. I wait five seconds, then five more. It lets the guards get out of earshot, but it gives me a chance to consider where I am. I make the mistake of looking down and out, and the sea feels like it's rushing towards me, as if I'm already falling. The clouds reflect off the surface, the glare bright enough to make me squint.

Grunting, I turn myself until I'm face up against the wall, and start climbing again. One hand at a time, focusing on planting my feet. The rivets are evenly spaced—I use them to hold my feet up while I hunt for handholds. I can feel the wall starting to curve, tilting me outwards, but I just push my torso into it, refusing to let it defeat me. The sound of gunfire inside the ship reaches me, elongated and warped.

Then, suddenly, there are no more handholds. The section of hull above me is completely smooth. Worse than that: the curve is more prominent, jutting out above me as the deck extends over the water. I keep my breathing deep and even, cheek flat against the surface. The metal is freezing cold, damp with condensation and sea spray, speckled with gritty rust. I have to find a way. I can't stay here, and the thought of climbing back down is enough to make my stomach lurch.

I look to my right. There's platform bolted onto the edge of the deck—a metal grate, five feet wide and ten long. It has a pair of antennae hanging vertically off the bottom, spaced maybe four feet apart. Each of the thin metal tubes has a fist-sized bubble at the end, and they're swaying in the breeze, the metal creaking gently. They must be radio antennae—maybe they're even the ones that broadcast the message.

Impact

Suddenly, I'm back in the Yukon, trapped on that clifftop by the wolves, preparing to jump to the branch jutting out of the rock. That was nothing compared to what I'm about to do. Here, I have to jump sideways, with no gravity to help me on distance.

My foot slips off one of the rivets. I cry out, my fingers aching as my foot flails at the air. Somehow, I manage to get it back on, manage to get myself flat against the wall again. Wind whips at my clothes. I can't stay up here. I either jump now, or I fall.

I lean to my left, as far as I can go. Then, in one movement, I throw myself the other way, towards the closest antenna.

My world shrinks down to my forearms, my hands, the tips of my fingers. I touch metal, my fingers wrapping around the cylinder, and then my hands slam into the top of the bubble. I can feel the antenna straining, reaching its limit. If I swing too far, it'll snap right off.

I lift my legs up, gritting my teeth, controlling my swing. I come to a stop, hanging with my arms extended, my numb fingers wrapped around the antenna. Instantly, I realise my mistake. I should have used my swing, channelling the momentum into an upwards lunge. Nothing for it: I'm going to have to do this ugly.

I can't pull my entire body up the antenna. My arms won't take it. I need something to take the weight, and that means I need to get my ankles wrapped around the second antenna.

I throw my legs up, trying to snag it. My first attempt is a failure, and I feel my fingers slip a little. The pain in my arms is getting worse. My muscles are taut cables, stretched almost to breaking point.

I try again. This time, I make it. I'm face up, my hands wrapped around the first antenna, my ankles gripping the second. It'll take some weight off, give me some leverage. I close my eyes, ask my arms to do this one last thing for me, and start pulling myself up the first antenna. I tense the muscles in my legs and my core, teasing out every bit of leverage I can.

More than once, I slip, sliding down the pole, the metal biting into my hands where they got scorched on the cable. I tighten the muscles in my legs, gasping as I keep pulling myself up.

It feels like it takes hours. Eventually, I'm standing upright, my feet perched on the bubble at the bottom of the second antenna, my fingers gripping the edge of the platform. I take a breath, then climb onto it, forcing my body upwards, letting my arms take the weight.

I roll onto my back, my tortured fingers clenching, my lungs and arms on fire. I'm on dangerous ground: rage might keep me going, but my body can only take so much of this.

I let myself lie there for a full thirty seconds. There's plenty of noise—the howling of the wind, the creaking of the hull, the smack of waves against metal, far below me.

And bursts of gunfire from the Phalanx gun.

It's targeting the boats, firing out into the ocean. Whoever is operating it doesn't know I'm here yet. I roll onto my stomach, then prop myself up on my elbows and look around the deck. There's no one around. The old, silent fighter jets are lined up in front of me. The bridge itself is on my right, a tower at the edge of the deck. Its windows reflect the white clouds.

Get up, Riley.

I clamber to my feet and start moving, going from a walk to a jog to a sprint, staying as low as I can.

75

Prakesh

The voice comes from a long way away. "Hang in there."

It takes Prakesh a full minute to work out what's happening. He's lying in one of the boats, propped up against the prow. The boat is full of people and equipment, and Prakesh can see that they're speeding across the water. He can hear the roar of the boat's engine, feel it buck as it climbs the waves. There are three other boats, moving alongside, all of them packed with workers.

Another sound explodes across the water—a guttural roar, ripping through the frigid air. One of the boats tears in two, its surface shredding before Prakesh's eyes. Its crew spill into the water, the surface churning with froth and blood.

Prakesh's boat reacts instantly, veering to one side. Someone collapses on top of him, and that's when the pain in his chest *really* wakes up. He tries to scream, but can't get enough air into his lungs. There is something very, very wrong down there.

The boat changes direction again, digging into the water. The roar is coming in bursts now, seconds apart.

"Hold on!"

"Goddamn Phalanx gun—"

"It's gonna cut us apart."

"Turn. *Turn!*"

Prakesh hears the motor throttle up another octave, its pilot pushing it to the limit. But it's not going to be enough. They won't be able to outrun bullets.

He opens his eyes, and sees one of the other boats running straight towards them. Its pilot is panicking, turning the boat hard, desperately trying to get away from the hailstorm of bullets. Pain explodes through Prakesh as the boat collides with theirs. He feels the floor tilt underneath him, then it slams back down onto the water.

The bullets are sending up spikes of white froth, getting closer by the second. Prakesh can't look away.

76

Okwembu

The *Ramona* has been torn apart from the inside out.

The screens on the bridge are still displaying camera views, and each one shows nothing but fire and smoke and spitting sparks.

The bridge itself is locked down tight—its doors barred, the men and women inside all armed with rifles. But that doesn't stop worry from churning at Okwembu's gut. It's all slipping away from her, all of it.

The people on the *Ramona* should have planned for this. Their setup—spacing their people, never letting the workers get hold of weapons—was clever. But they didn't think it through. They didn't think about what would happen if things went wrong. They were stupid. Sloppy. She won't let that happen again.

Prophet is still standing over the control panel, still in a mute trance. Okwembu looks across the screens, hunting for something she can use. She can't even tell if there are any workers left on board, and there's no way to see if the Phalanx gun is hitting its targets. She's already thinking ahead—should they give chase? Round up any stragglers?

"How many boats do we have left?" she says, not looking away from the screens.

She hears the guards shifting behind her, and lowers her voice to a growl. "How many?"

"One or two," says a voice. "There should still be some left on the C deck ramp."

"Go and secure them."

There's no movement behind her, and she doesn't have to turn around to picture the guards—to picture the lazy, slow expressions on their faces. She closes her eyes for a moment, then turns to Prophet. If she can just get him to—

But as she does so, she gets a look out of the window.

There's a figure on the deck, sprinting across it, running between the line of disused planes. It's heading right for the Phalanx gun. Okwembu stops, her eyes narrowing. In an instant, the figure is gone, covered by the wing of a plane. But Okwembu saw the dark hair, recognised the body shape.

"Hale," she whispers.

And then raw terror floods through her.

She doesn't waste another second. She walks over to Prophet, grabbing him by both shoulders and turning him towards her. "You have to talk to the gun operator."

He stares at her as if he doesn't know who she is. "Curtis?" he says, after a long moment.

Okwembu has to work very hard to keep her voice level. She desperately wants Hale alive, but she doesn't have a choice now. "Yes. Curtis. We need to talk to him."

Moving slowly, way too slowly, Prophet bends over a bank of screens. There's a radio, attached to the edge of one of the screens on a coiled cable, and he unhooks it and pulls it towards him.

"Curtis, are you there?" he says.

Okwembu snatches it away from him, hammering the transmit button. "You've got a runner heading towards you on the deck. Take her out. *Take her out now.*"

77

Riley

I can feel my body starting to rebel. The muscles in my shoulders and upper back are roaring in pain, and my arms hurt from my climb up the side of the ship. But I have to keep going. I *have* to get to that gun.

Somewhere in the back of my mind, I realise that it's stopped firing. Has it run out of ammo? Are Prakesh and Carver out of range? I sneak a glance to my left, off the edge of the deck, but I can't see any boats from where I am.

I keep running. The body of the planes are too low for me to move between the wheel struts, but there's just enough room for me under the wings. I'll need to stay in cover—I'll be too exposed out on the open deck.

Ahead of me, one of the planes is tilted sideways. One of its wheel struts is missing, and the tip of its wing scrapes the surface of the deck. I tilt my body, leaning into the turn, already plotting my angle of attack.

There's a roar of gunfire, and the plane in front of me rips apart.

Great gouges appear in the body. The cockpit glass shatters, raining down on me, and one of the wings almost shears off. If I hadn't started to turn, if I wasn't in the process of running around it, I would have gone right into the bullets.

I switch direction, adjusting my angle, sprinting away from the planes—onto the open deck.

There's no choice. Behind me, the line of planes is being ripped apart. The noise is unbelievable. Something explodes—a missile, a fuel tank, no way to tell. I keep my head down, my feet hammering the deck.

The gun stops firing, just for a second. Under the ringing in my ears, there's a thin mechanical whine. The barrel is tracking me, turning in my direction, trying to aim ahead of me.

I can't outrun bullets. But I can outrun that barrel.

The gun starts firing again. Bullets dig divots out of the deck behind me, so close that metal shrapnel bites through the leg of my pants. The fragments are tiny, nothing like the one that buried itself in my leg when we crashed the escape pod, so I ignore them. Acrid smoke stings my throat, but I ignore that, too. I couldn't stop, even if I wanted to.

The bridge tower is on my right. For an instant, the bullets stop coming, the person inside the gun not wanting to shoot the tower itself. I seize the advantage, pushing myself harder, hurdling a chevron-striped ramp. But the gun is still tracking me, and, a moment later, whoever is inside hits the trigger. Bullets split the air behind me. Gods, how many does he *have*?

I'm ahead of the barrel's targeting line—no more than a few feet, but it's enough. I'm getting closer, leaning into the turn, coming up on the gun. A cry bursts out of me as I sprint the final few feet, and then I'm out of the line of fire, under the barrel itself. The bullets stop coming, the barrel shuttling left and right, hunting for a target.

The gun looks even more menacing up close. It's foundation is a metal box with rivets on it as big as the ones on the side of the ship. There's a mess of machinery above the box: a rotating platform, with two wings bracketing a curving chain of bullets, each one the size of my ring finger. The gun barrel itself is like something out of hell, blacker than space itself, longer than I am tall.

I move to the seaward side of the gun. At first, I think I've made a mistake—that the gun is controlled from the bridge. But then I see the door, set into the side of the platform, its surface caked with rust. There's lettering across the door, in stencilled capital letters: PHALANX CLOSE-IN WEAPONS SYSTEM AUTHORISED PERSONNEL ONLY.

There's no valve lock—just a simple handle. The door is slightly open, and as I move towards it I see movement. Someone behind the door, trying to close it, lock me out.

Not today.

I sprint to the door, dropping my shoulder, driving hard. It slams backwards—whoever is behind it shouts in surprise, almost knocked off balance. They recover quickly, try to close it again, but they're not fast enough. My follow-up kick almost knocks the door off its hinges.

A man lunges at me. He's pale from lack of sunlight, his lank hair hanging down his face in thick, gungy strands. He throws a clumsy punch, aiming for my face. It's the work of half a second to grab his arm, turn the strike against him. I shove him backwards, then come in after him.

I see screens leaking green light into the gun's interior. There's the most awful smell—stale sweat and rotting food, mixed into a horrible miasma. I try to ignore it, dodging another of the man's punches. He's off balance, and I take the gap, grabbing the back of his head and smashing it into the wall.

He mewls in pain, but his hand keeps moving. I look to the side, and see a rifle on a nearby chair—one he's hunting for, feeling his way towards it. I stop him, gripping his arm, turning him around in one move and twisting it behind his back. The mewling noise becomes a yell, deafening in the tiny space. I make a fist with my other hand, then slam it into the pressure point on the back of his neck.

I give him a shove. His body sprawls across the floor, his head thumping off it. He's twitching slightly, his eyes rolled back in his head, but I barely notice. All my attention switches to the screens.

Some of them are radar displays, others internal readings from the gun. One of them shows the deck, where the gun is currently pointing, and there's a complicated target reticle overlaid on top.

I slide into the chair. The seat underneath me is still warm. My hands slide over the control panel, stopping when I find a small joystick with a prominent button on it. I give it an experimental push. The body of the gun vibrates around me as the motor kicks in, and the view on the screen changes, moving to the left. Slowly, the bridge slides into view.

"OK," I say to myself. "Here we go."

78

Okwembu

Okwembu can't see Hale any more. The tracer vanished when her path took her along the wall of the bridge tower. It doesn't help that the deck is shrouded in drifting smoke, obscuring the Phalanx gun. Half of the planes are on fire, their fuselages hanging in shreds.

The bridge behind her is silent. No one speaks. They're all staring out of the windows, their faces illuminated by flickering screens.

Okwembu tries to control her breathing. *There's no way Hale survived that. Nobody could. Not even a tracer would be able to outrun—*

The gun starts to move again.

The barrel raises itself in short jerks, as if the operator isn't quite sure of the equipment, still trying to get the hang of it. Prophet is muttering under his breath. "Engine's gonna save us," he says, more to himself than to anyone else. "The Engine will keep us safe."

Okwembu reaches out, gripping his arm. "You have to shut the gun down. Right now."

He stares at her blankly, as if he doesn't know who she is.

"The Phalanx gun," she says. *"How do we shut it off?"*

He shakes his head. "It's manual control," he says. "Only Curtis can do that."

Okwembu looks back out of the window. The Phalanx gun is turning in a slow circle, the barrel moving upwards.

Aiming for the bridge.

"Get out!" Okwembu shouts. She throws Prophet to the side, launching herself towards the doors. "We have to get out now!"

And Riley Hale opens up.

79

Riley

The bridge *implodes*.

That's the only word for it. The structure folds inwards, its struts bending and snapping under the barrage. Part of the roof caves in. In seconds, the entire bridge is wreathed in smoke, glitchy and pixelated on my screen. It's like the bullets brought a black hole to the bridge.

The whole gun shakes around me, the vibrations travelling up through my chair. I laugh, and my laughter vanishes under the roar of the gunfire.

I keep my finger on the trigger until the ammo counter on the screen blinks a big fat zero.

The only sound is my breathing, close in the cramped space. There's a water canteen off to one side, balanced on the control panel. It's half full. I drain most of it in one go, then tip the rest over my head, soaking my hair and neck. I take one last look at the smoking, sputtering wreck of the bridge, then step over the unconscious gunner and push my way out of the door.

The harsh daylight makes me blink, the smoke worming its way into my lungs. My body chooses that moment to really wake up, my muscles burning, protesting against everything I put them through. A sudden wave of nausea rolls through me, and I drop to one knee on the deck, retching.

My shoulder blades are twisted rods of red-hot steel, and there's something wrong with the muscles on my right side. Every movement sends a sharp arc of pain up into my armpit. It's like a stitch that's got out of control, taking on a life of its own. I'm pushing my body to a level it hasn't gone to before, and if I'm not careful I won't make it out the other side.

You're not done yet, says the voice.

I look over my shoulder at the bridge. It's a smoking ruin. There's no way anybody survived that. But I can't walk away, not until I see Janice Okwembu's body, not until I know she's paid for everything she's done.

It's hard to get moving again, but I do it. Each step hurts, and I have to grit my teeth to keep going, gripping my right side as if I can massage the pain away. I hear a bang, and look up. Something on the bridge has exploded, gushing even more fire and smoke.

There's a buzzing sound, growing by the second, and a shape explodes out of the smoke. No—not out of it. *Above it.* It takes me a moment to realise what I'm seeing.

The seaplane.

I stare at it, open-mouthed, as it soars above me. I can just see Harlan through the blown-off door, hanging on for dear life. The plane's body is damaged in a hundred places, bullet holes standing out like acne scars. It banks, descending towards the sea, vanishing past the edge of the deck.

How did they survive? Did they land somewhere? No way to tell—and they don't dare land on the deck, not without wheels. It doesn't matter. They're alive. *They made it.*

The knowledge makes me want to punch the air and throw up, all at once. I hadn't realised how much it was weighing on me. Ever since I saw Finkler, lying broken on the rocks of Fire Island, I thought they were gone. I told myself that I didn't know for sure, but I never really believed it.

If I can get to them afterwards, we can get back to Whitehorse. Carver and Prakesh and I can…

Prakesh. My good feeling vanishes. My stomach gives another sickening lurch, and I squeeze my eyes shut. When I open them again, the buzz of the seaplane has faded, and I'm looking back up at the bridge.

Later. That can all come later. You've got a job to do first.

It takes me a few minutes to find an entrance. I have to go nearly all the way round the bridge structure, to the far side of the ship. I hesitate for a moment, not wanting to enter the pitch darkness of the interior again.

But there's no choice. Not this time. I take a deep breath of cold ocean air, then step inside.

80

Anna

Anna can't get control of the escape pod.

She's wrestling with the stick, willing it to do what she wants, but every time she tries to correct her course she overcompensates, sending the pod into a flat spin. The destroyed dock revolves around her, tugs and debris orbiting like miniature planets.

With an enormous bang, Anna's pod collides with the wall of the dock.

It hits rear-first. Anna lurches forward in her seat, and that's when she sees the crack.

It's spreading slowly across the cockpit viewport, moving in tiny jerks, growing larger and larger. She can't take her eyes off it, can't focus on anything else.

She doesn't know whether the crack came from the impact on the wall or when she collided with the astronaut. Doesn't matter.

Her fingers scrabble at her seat belt, digging into the catch. It snaps back, and she floats upwards, feeling a fresh wave of nausea roll through her. The crack is bigger now, almost to the other edge of the viewport.

Space suit. I have to get to a space suit.

She pulls herself to the back of the craft, hammering on the suit locker's release button. She has no idea of the right way to put on one of these suits, and there's no time to find out.

An alarm starts beeping on the escape pod's console. It's not like the proximity alarm—this is the harsh cry of a machine that knows it's dying. Anna ignores it, pulling the suit out of the locker. It's made of tough, rubber-like material, with the seam running down the torso. She forces it open, then tries to spin her body so she can jam a leg inside it. She misses the first time, her foot grazing the outside of the suit. She's breathing too hard, using up too much oxygen, unable to think of anything but zero gravity, of being lost in space, floating forever.

One leg. Then the other. Then the arms. It's like being entombed. The material holds her body fast, and she has to make an effort even to move her fingers inside the gloves. Anna knows enough about these suits to be aware that the helmet is integrated—all she has to do is activate it.

There's a control panel on her wrist. Slowly, she moves her other hand around, pushing at the large buttons. A second later, there's a hiss, and the faceplate slides up and over her head, using the rigid arches on the suit's shoulders to guide itself, locking into place with a heavy click. The heads-up display winks to life in front of her. Oxygen, power levels, a thousand other things she can only guess at.

She doesn't hear the cockpit viewport give way. The first she knows about it, she's tumbling out the front of the escape pod, sucked out by the pressure loss, rolling end over end. The fear is potent now, like a toxic gas that she's sucking deep into her lungs with every breath.

A piece of debris heaves into view, a piece of a mechanical arm, and Anna smashes into it before she can stop herself. It knocks her sideways. Fingers fumble at her wrist controls, fat and useless.

Impact

With a thud that jars her body inside the suit, Anna comes to a stop. It takes a confused few seconds to understand what happened. She's ended up in one of the top corners of the dock—somehow, she's wedged in it, as if the oxygen pack on the back of her suit is being held by the walls as they join up.

She can see the tug. The heat shield is hanging off the bottom of the vessel. It's a thin sheet, dull gold in colour, wrinkled and malformed. It's been joined to the main body by a series of ugly-looking welds.

The rear ramp of the tug is open, surrounded by space-suited figures. A few of them are looking in her direction, although they're too far away for her to see their faces. She has to get to them. She has to *stop* them.

But how? What exactly is she supposed to do? Drag each one of them out of the tug? It's absurd.

What if she could talk to them? Persuade them not to do it? It's a million-to-one shot, but it's the only one she has. She prods at the wrist control. Seconds tick by before she works out which one turns on the radio—she hesitates half a dozen times, unsure about what each button does.

Static swells in her helmet, and then voices penetrate, coming over the suit radio.

"—anybody see that?" It's Arroway, sounding more panicky than ever.

"Jordan's gone."

"We've got someone else in a suit out here. Who is that?"

And then Dax: "Identify yourself."

Anna can't help it. She screams Dax's name, the sound reverberating inside her helmet. It's only when he doesn't respond, when the chatter continues, that she realises she doesn't have her transmit button activated. It takes her another few seconds to find it.

"Dax," she says, quieter now, but still determined. "Don't do this."

"*Anna?*" he says. "What are you doing out here?"

"I can't let you leave." Her voice is husky, her throat tight with anger.

"I don't—"

The words cut off. She has a horrible moment where she thinks her suit radio has died on her, but then the static returns, fizzing in her ear.

"Say again?" she says.

"I don't see how you're going to stop us."

Arroway cuts in "Dax, maybe we should—"

"No, Anna. You come with us. You've earned that much."

What would Riley do?

Easy. She'd find something. She'd *make* it work.

Anna makes herself stay calm. She lowers her breathing, pushes back against the fear, and starts looking around the dock.

"Anna," Dax says. "Come with us or stay, but we're gone in three minutes."

She sees nothing but debris. Torn metal, bullet casings, strands of broken mag rail. The mechanical arm she smashed into. Bodies, too: frozen, twisted, curled in on themselves. *Keep looking. There's got to be something.*

Anna's eyes track along the far wall of the dock, and come to a sudden halt.

There's no way. It's not possible.

But it is. It's right there, caught on a ceiling support.

The long gun.

Her rifle. The one she used during the siege of the dock. She thought it was lost. She thought she'd never see it again. But there it is. Anna doesn't know if guns work in space, if the gunpowder will even ignite, but she has to try.

Slowly, she brings her wrist control to her face. The moment she pushes the THRUST button, her suit springs to life. She feels pressure in her shoulder blades and at the base of the spine, like she's being punched from multiple angles, and the suit launches forward. The heads-up display changes, displaying a diagram of the suit with six thruster points highlighted. She senses mechanical movement at her stomach, and when she brings her right hand there, she finds a joystick has popped out from the suit's midsection.

"Anna, be reasonable," says Dax. "We're offering you a way out. It's more than anyone else on this station will get."

Impact

It takes more than a few false starts to get the hang of it. Anna goes into a spin more than once, aware that she's attracting more attention from the tug, aware that a couple of the suited figures are moving towards her. But she's too far ahead of them, and within a minute she's at the gun. She can pick out the details: the thin black barrel, the fake-wood-grain stock. The scope, perched on top. It's wedged into the wall, at the bottom of the triangle formed by the roof support. She reaches out for it, fingers questing.

Too fast. You're coming in too fast—

Anna slams into the wall, so hard that her head bounces off the back of the helmet. The gun is knocked away, spinning out into the void.

Anna grips the joystick at her stomach, propels herself off the wall. She's running out of time. The rest of Dax's group have given up on her—they're heading back to the tug. If she can't grab that rifle soon, it's over.

She boosts herself towards it. Three yards. Two.

"I'm sorry, Anna." Dax sounds almost regretful.

Her hand touches the barrel. She clenches her fingers, gritting her teeth as her skin scrapes against the inside of the suit glove. But she's got hold of the rifle.

She's still moving, heading towards the gaping mouth of the dock. No time. She turns the rifle round, welding the stock to her shoulder and using her right hand to steady the barrel. She jams the finger of her left hand in the trigger guard. It is a tight fit, almost too tight, and her stomach lurches again when she realises that she didn't even think about that. If she hadn't been able to pull the trigger…

The rifle is bolt-action, but the bolt itself is gone, sheared off. She won't be able to load another round.

Sighting down the barrel is impossible. She can't move her head. She's going to have to do this on instinct, trusting her arm to find the aim.

She finds the tug, then the heat shield, glimmering in the light from the sun. Slowly, she brings the gun towards it.

81

Okwembu

Janice Okwembu picks herself up off the floor of the bridge.

As the bullets tore through the walls, she threw herself behind the thick map table, skidding across the floor. There was nothing she could do but put her hands over her ears, and wait for it to be over.

Slowly, she gets to her feet. She's unsteady, her ears ringing. She isn't injured—the table was thick enough and low enough to protect her—but her face and the backs of her hands are scratched and bloody.

The interior of the bridge is a sparking, smoking mess, as if what they saw on the cameras earlier has come through the screens, exploding into life around them. The windows are gone, smashed apart. Part of the roof has collapsed, opening the bridge up to the sky. The banks of screens have disappeared. There's thick, white smoke everywhere, and the wall behind Okwembu is completely shredded.

But not as shredded as the bodies.

Mercifully, most of the men and women on the bridge are dead. But there are still a few moaning in pain, pulling themselves across the floor, their camouflage fatigues stained black with blood. Okwembu sees Prophet, lying face down. His left arm is almost gone, ripped off at the shoulder. As Okwembu watches, his body twitches slightly.

She tells herself to help him. But there's no point—he's dead, whatever she does. Instead, she finds herself stumbling over to the space where the windows used to be, pushing her way past the destroyed screens. A part of her knows she should stay behind cover. Hale might have more bullets, might be waiting for her to show herself.

She ignores the impulse, reaching the gap, looking out across the deck. The Phalanx gun is still shrouded with thick smoke, and several small fires have started among the ruins of the planes.

There's a flash of movement. Okwembu looks down, just in time to see Riley Hale sprinting towards the base of the bridge tower. In an instant, she's gone.

Anger, hot and bright, fills every space in Okwembu's body.

She turns, and almost immediately sees what she's looking for. There's a narrow metal support, up against the wall. It's been blown in half: a four-foot segment has come loose, attached to the bottom part of the support by a tiny shred of metal. It reminds her of Prophet's arm, but she doesn't dwell on the thought.

With a strength she didn't know she had, Okwembu grabs the displaced segment, trying to wrench it loose. But she can't get it free from the strand connecting it to the main body. She casts around, finds another chunk of metal, something hot and misshapen, and hammers it against the support. It snaps free, the metal giving a tortured shriek.

Okwembu discards the debris, then hefts the support, testing its weight. She strides over to the door, positioning herself along the wall to its left, and waits for Riley Hale to walk through.

82

Anna

The long gun's recoil knocks Anna sideways.

There's no sound, but she feels the kick, feels the butt slamming its way past her right side. It sends her spinning again. She fumbles with the joystick, tries to right herself, but every move makes the spin worse.

The wall of the dock rushes towards her. She hits it faceplate first, the heads-up display shuddering and fracturing as the transparent material takes the impact. The material holds, and Anna finds herself moving away from the wall, still turning in that sickening spin. Somehow, she brings herself to a halt. Her fingers are trembling inside the gloves, holding the stick tight, but she's not spinning any more.

Slowly, Anna raises her head and looks for the tug. She doesn't want to know. If she missed, then she won't be able to stop them from leaving.

The tug's heat shield is torn in two.

It may be strong enough to withstand the intense, even heat of re-entry, but the direct, shearing impact of the bullet sliced right through it. The two halves are still rigid, but there's a gaping hole in the crinkly golden material, the edges bending slightly in the vacuum. It's beyond repair—even if they managed to patch the two sides back together, the heat of re-entry would worm its way through.

The tug itself is spinning slightly from the impact, and as the gold heat shield angles towards her, as it picks up the light from the sun, Anna can't help smiling. *Guess guns do work in space, after all.*

The suit's radio is going insane: a dozen confused voices, all clamouring for attention. Dax cuts through them. "What's happening?" he shouts. "We—"

The radio cuts off again, stays silent for a few seconds, then roars back.

"Some sort of impact. I can't see it."

"Hey, Dax," Anna says, keying the transmit button. "How's that heat shield looking?"

She doesn't wait for him to respond. Moving as carefully as she can, she turns herself until she's facing the mouth of the dock, then uses the thrusters to steer herself out. She keeps each burst short, aware that her supplies are limited. Still, it should be enough to get her back to the pod bay.

Dax is swearing at her over the suit radio. She turns it off, almost absent-mindedly.

She feels drained. But it's a good feeling. She survived. It didn't matter how young she was—she made the right call. She saved the station, just like Riley did. That's enough.

Anna doesn't know if the people in Dax's group will be able to make it back inside, but there's nothing she can do about that. They don't have a choice—if they don't make it back, they'll die.

She's outside the dock now, moving along the curve of the station. She's gone past most of the debris, gently spinning, letting herself drift. She sees the others start to make their way out of the dock, moving in short bursts, close to the station's hull.

She's drifting too far away. As she activates the thrusters to correct her course, Anna sees the curve of the Earth below her.

She stares for a moment, mesmerised. The planet is brightly lit, the clouds swirling, scraps of brown land only just visible. It looks alien, forbidding. And yet, somehow, it's the most beautiful thing she's ever seen.

Riley is down there. Waiting for her.

Anna makes herself focus. She can see the pod bays now, just dimpling the hull at the point where it starts curving away from her. She angles herself towards it—she's really got the hang of this now. The nausea is still there, but she feels it at a remove, as if it belongs to someone else. There's a readout on her display—a vertical bar, decreasing every time she hits the thrusters. She's still got a third of her fuel left: more than enough to take her right into the pod bay. *Almost home.*

Something smashes into her from behind.

In the half-second available to her, Anna thinks it must be a piece of debris—something she missed. But whatever it is is *holding* her, pulling her tight to itself. She's spinning out of control, the station whirling away from her.

Dax's face slides into view, inches from her own. Behind the transparent helmet, his face is contorted with hate.

83

Riley

The smoke sears the back of my throat, scratching my eyes. It gets thicker the higher I climb, and I have to pull the top of my shirt over my mouth and nose. It's damp and sticky with sweat and dirt, but it's better than nothing.

Most of the lights are dead. There's an alarm blaring, and I can smell fire. A sprinkler springs to life above me, soaking me with a short spray of cold water before sputtering out.

As I get closer to the bridge, I see that part of the stairway has collapsed. There's a gaping hole in the wall, the metal shredded and torn. The Phalanx gun's barrage ripped the stairs away. I allow myself a small smile. *Should have aimed a little more carefully.*

I climb up, hauling myself onto the remaining steps. This time, getting up is harder, the muscles in my right side clenching in pain.

I've come up onto the bridge level in the same corridor that Ray and Iluk used to bring me in. The door to the bridge is firmly shut, although the wall to its right is pocked with bullet holes. I grip the valve lock hard, and wrench it down, pushing the door inwards.

I can barely see a thing. The smoke is a solid white wall, pushing me back. I hold my shirt fabric tight around my mouth, and step inside. The windows of the bridge have been blown away, and daylight is leaking in from the massive holes. Sparks from destroyed electronics shower the floor.

There are bodies everywhere.

They lie sprawled across the floor, collapsed across chairs. Some of them still have their rifles, their fingers locked around the triggers. The floor is a sticky mess of blood and bone fragments. Prophet is there, too. One of the bullets caught him in the shoulder, almost tearing his arm off.

All dead. Because of me.

I should feel something. Remorse, guilt, anything. But I'm done with that. I've felt all of those things before, and they didn't help. They didn't bring the dead back to life. All I've got is an emptiness, like I've given out all the emotion I have, and there's nothing left inside. I just want to do what I came to do, and get out of here.

Movement. Behind me. Janice Okwembu. She has a metal pole, and before I can react, she smashes it into my side.

84

Okwembu

Riley Hale goes down in silence.

Okwembu can see her screaming, howling in pain as she clutches her side. But she can't hear a thing. Even the ringing in her ears has disappeared.

It's the strangest sensation, like she's standing outside herself, watching her body lift the metal support over her head.

In that instant, she doesn't even feel anger. She feels nothing but a quiet satisfaction.

And yet Hale is still alive. She rolls away across the floor, and for an instant Janice Okwembu loses her in the billowing smoke. But only for an instant—Hale is injured, struggling to get to her feet, and in two steps Okwembu is on her. She brings the support down. It's more a diagonal hit than a vertical one, the weight robbing it of momentum. But it still hurts, crushing into the small of Hale's back.

This time, Okwembu does hear her scream.

The girl is writhing on the ground, her legs kicking. She throws an arm out, tries to catch Okwembu in the ankle, misses. Okwembu didn't hit her nearly as hard as she should have—she was hoping for a crushed vertebra, at the very least. It's a cold, clean, satisfying thought.

Why is she bothering with trying to maim Hale? Why is she

waiting? She should have aimed for Hale's head, or better yet, retrieved a rifle from one of Prophet's men. She's not in her right mind, not thinking straight. It's the same mistake Amira Al-Hassan made, when she was under orders to kill the girl. She talked, and stalled, and Hale made her pay for it. Okwembu made the same mistake, months ago, after Hale had destroyed her father's ship. She should have killed her then—no talk, no waiting. Just a bullet in the head.

It's not a mistake she will make again.

Hale is trying to crawl away, her legs useless. Her hair has fallen to one side, leaving the back of her neck exposed. Okwembu watches herself step forward, planting her feet just so, lifting the heavy metal support in a high arc.

85

Riley

I feel the pole coming before it hits.

I don't know if it's a change in air pressure, or the sound of the metal as it plunges downwards. But I know it's coming.

I react, throwing myself to one side, only just managing to get out of the way. I feel the edge of the pole catch my shoulder—it's a glancing blow, but it spasms up into my neck. I can barely feel my legs. My back and side are sending up shocks of frantic, agonised pain.

I get a momentary glimpse of Okwembu through the smoke. She's a mess—her jumpsuit is sweat-stained, torn and ragged, and there's a cut on her face, below her right eye. The blood looks like warpaint.

There's no time to be angry with myself. I can't stop moving. Not for a second. Okwembu brings the pole down again, smashing it into the floor. It's heavy, far too heavy for her to use effectively, but it won't be long before it hits me in a way I won't be able to come back from.

I try to rise, trying to get my legs underneath me. Too late, I realise that I've pushed myself up against a body. I sprawl against it, then have to wrench myself out of the way as Okwembu attacks.

She screams in fury, lifting the pole for another strike. Could I stop it somehow? Grab it as she swings it towards me? No chance—the pole is heavy, almost too heavy for her to hold. If I try and stop it, it'll crush my hands.

I lift my leg, lash out at her. No good. She starts moving sideways—this time, instead of lifting the pole, she lets it drag along the ground behind her, getting ready to line up an overhead strike.

My hands stretch out, hunting for anything I can use. A rifle? I'll still have to aim it, still have to check the safety and bring it around…

My fingers close on metal—but not the textured metal of a rifle. It's a fat tube, cool against my hand, familiar somehow. Behind me, I hear Okwembu lift the pole off the floor. I expect her to say something, to laugh, but she's deathly silent. Intent on what she's doing.

I focus on the object in my hand.

The bear spray.

The one Ray took when he frisked me, the one he placed on the table in front of Prophet.

My finger finds the trigger on the top of the canister. Putting every last shred of energy I have into the movement, I twist my body around, and empty the spray into Okwembu's face.

86

Okwembu

At the very last second, Okwembu turns her head sideways.

Not fast enough.

It's like a million needles, driving into her eyes and throat. She howls in pain, her hands flying to her face, dropping the metal support. The needles give way to a rolling wall of fire, stinging and burning, like a blowtorch held to her face.

And yet a part of her mind is still working. Hale might be down, but Okwembu isn't her equal in a fight—and Hale just took away her ability to see. She can feel the pole resting against her foot, but reaching for it would mean taking her hands away from her face, and that's almost too horrible to think about.

Get out. Get out now.

She hates herself for running, for leaving Hale where she is. But she doesn't have a choice, not if she wants to live. She turns and runs, stumbling across the bridge. Something takes her in the knee, the edge of a bank of screens, and she almost falls. The pain has got even worse—her throat is swelling up, her nose clogged. Every breath feels like she's forcing it through layers of gauze.

Her foot knocks into a body, and this time she does fall, sprawling across the floor. To get to her feet, she has to take her hands away from her eyes—it's the only way. When she does, the needles come back, hammering through her skull directly into her brain. The pain blots out all other thoughts. She's reduced to a simple set of instructions. *Go. Run. Move.*

Tears are streaming down her cheeks, and the world doubles and triples as she looks at it. She is at the opposite side of the bridge to where she first waited for Hale, coming up on one of the locked doors. She reaches for it, manages to get her hands around the valve lock, turns it with every ounce of strength she can muster. She's coughing now, each breath shredding her chest.

But then she's through, stumbling down the passage, moving with no thought but to get as far away as possible. A set of stairs appears in front of her, and she comes very close to falling right over the edge. She stops herself, gripping the railings, swaying in place.

One step. Two. Her throat still burning, but opening up a little more now, yes, she can feel it...

There's a distant thud, like a mountain collapsing on the horizon, felt more than heard. Okwembu barely notices it until the ship lurches sideways, tilting down at a crazy angle. She cries out as she loses her balance, throwing out her hands. The stairs rush up towards her, doubled by the tears in her eyes. When she hits them, it feels like the end of the world.

87

Riley

The ship starts to tilt.

At first, I think it's the smoke messing with my head. But I heard the bang, felt it rumble up from below me. Something deep in the ship has detonated.

I let the bear spray fall from my hand, and it rolls away across the floor. My eyes are streaming, itchy and sore, but I only caught a little of the spray. I have to get after Okwembu. I didn't come this far, go through this much, to let her escape.

I try to get up. I make it all the way to one knee before the world starts shaking in front of me. I list sideways, unable to stop myself, then topple to the floor.

I could lie here for a while. Just close my eyes and just drift away. Everything hurts. My back, my shoulders, my throat, the palms of my hands. Smoke forces stinging tears out of my eyes.

Get up, says the voice. But it's coming from a very long way away. I want to listen to it, want more than anything else in the world, but I'm drifting off into a warm darkness where it doesn't seem important at all.

"Riley, get up."

I'm imagining the voice. I have to be. It sounds like Carver. But I know he isn't here. He's with Prakesh.

There's a pressure on my chest. I try to ignore it, but it doesn't go away.

"Riley!"

My eyes open. The deck is tilting so much I can barely stay in one place. Objects and bodies are sliding everywhere, clattering to the floor and rolling away.

And Carver is there.

He doesn't give me a choice about getting up. The second he sees I'm awake, he hauls me to my feet, pulling me into an embrace. I get the same feeling as before, when I first saw him in the generator room. A massive wave of relief and joy and fear, all blended into one.

"How did you find me?" I say. My voice sounds like it's coming from someone else's throat.

"Easy. I just followed the screams and explosions. Led me right to you."

He's a mess, bloody and sweat-soaked. We both are. "What the hell did you do?" he says as we pull apart.

"Long story. Prakesh—Carver, is he—"

He nods. "Last I checked. He'll be fine."

His eyes say otherwise. I want to push him, make him tell me more, but there isn't time. As much as I desperately want to, I can't go after Okwembu—not if we want to make it out of here alive.

"We have to get off the ship," I say. "Right now."

He shakes his head. "No."

"Carver, there's got to be a way. We'll just jump off the side if we have—"

"No, I mean, we can't get off the ship. We have to stop it from sinking."

"*What?*"

"The fuel supplies have gone up. Prakesh's friends did it. And my guess is there's a big-ass hole in the side of the ship. If we can seal the bulkhead doors from the bridge—"

"What are you talking about?" It takes everything I have not to bolt, right then and there. He's gone insane.

"You don't understand," Carver says, his eyes wide. "If this ship goes down, the Earth goes down with it."

The deck beneath me gives a sudden shudder, nearly knocking me off my feet. I have to hold onto the bank of controls, my shredded palms screaming in pain.

"You have to trust me," says Carver. "Normally I wouldn't say this, but there's *really* not enough time to explain it all."

He looks around. "Is there a control for the ship bulkheads here?"

The world swims in front of me. "Bulkheads?"

"They're doors that seal sections of the ship off in case of a leak. They're supposed to work automatically, but my guess is that isn't happening. You should be able to operate them from here."

I look around the destroyed bridge. It's hopeless. Most of the electronics here are completely destroyed, riddled with bullet holes. Even if we could figure out which one of these dozens of screens operates the bulkhead doors, there's no guarantee it would still be working.

Carver sees it, too. "Ah, shit," he says. "OK. We'll need to do it manually. On-site. It's the only way."

"How would we even know which doors to close?" The floor gives another sickening lurch, and I have to scramble to stay where I am, planting my feet. My body is in agony.

"Door 6 on C deck should do the trick. It should be above the waterline, and it'll seal the compartments below it. That should stop the ship from sinking. Any further along and there'll be too many compartments flooded to hold the ship up."

He sees my expression. "Riley, we have to do this."

I don't want to go down there. I want to get off this ship. I'm tired of running. Every muscle in my body is screaming for rest. I want to be with my friends, and get far away from here, and only stop when I'm in a place that is safe. I just want it all to be over.

And why shouldn't I want that? How much have I sacrificed so that other people could live? I've lost so many friends. I sacrificed my own *father* so that Outer Earth could carry on. And all it brought me was more pain.

When my dad was on a collision course out of Earth, ready to drive his ship into us, to tear the station apart, I told him he had a choice. He could give me the override code that would let me destroy his ship, or he could kill me. He made his choice. And I can make mine. I don't have to suffer any more. I can say no. I can let someone else do it.

"Ry?" Carver says. "I can't do it alone. We don't know if anyone's still down there, and if I get taken out...Please tell me you understand what I'm saying."

I don't. Not even a little bit. I don't understand why I have to do this.

But I also know that Carver would never lie to me. Not ever. He wouldn't ask me to do this if there was another option. If he says that this ship is the key to humanity's survival, if he says he's sure, then I have to believe him.

"Is this really the only way?" I say.

He nods.

I take a deep breath. "Then let's go."

88

Anna

Dax's mouth is moving, but the radio link is inactive. Anna can't hear the words. They're spinning out of control, away from the station, and it's all happening in complete silence. There should be noise, shouts, raw anger. Instead, there's nothing.

Dax puts a hand on her faceplate, as if he can grab it in his fingers and tear it off her head. She reaches up to push him off, but he's too strong, elbowing her arm out of the way. The fear is back, digging its claws into her shoulders. Nausea comes with it, accented by the end-over-end spin.

Her thrust meter has started to blink red. She's got a little under a third left, but if she doesn't get free soon, she might not have enough to make it home.

The Earth and the station spin around them, as if she and Dax are the centre of the universe. With a terrified cry, Anna tries to push him away, planting a gloved hand directly on his chest. But it's like her dream—the movement feels slow and soft, and she's barely able to get enough force into her arms.

Dax doesn't seem to be aware of what he's doing. His face is barely human now, his helmet misting up with his breath. He's still shouting, and she can't hear a thing. She raises her knees, trying to get between them.

The spin intensifies, each movement adding to their momentum. And—*oh gods*—Dax has activated his suit's plasma cutter. It's sparking from his wrist, firing in short bursts, blinding her. Any second now, he's going to slice a hole right through her suit.

The sight shocks her into action. Anna pulls her leg up and kicks it out towards Dax's mid-section.

It's just enough. They fly apart, and the plasma cutter misses her by six inches. She grabs the joystick, firing her thrusters to get even further away from him. She burns through almost half her remaining fuel before she manages to raise her finger off the thruster control.

Outer Earth is behind her. With a little luck, she can coast right towards it on her current momentum. She'll do it backwards, keeping an eye on Dax. If he tries to make another run at her, she'll be ready.

Dax has managed to stabilise himself, but, as she watches, the exhaust from his thruster ports changes. It's thinner now, less substantial, as if...

She switches her radio back on. Dax's voice comes through immediately. "—anybody hear me? I've got no fuel!"

"Negative." It's one of the others—Anna can just see them in her peripheral vision, still drifting along the curve of the station. "We're too far away."

"No!" Dax shouts, and this time fear creeps into his voice. "You can't leave me here."

Anna keys her transmit button. "Dax."

He reaches his hands out towards her, as if beseeching her. "Anna. Help me!" He's gripping his own joystick, squeezing the controls, but his thruster fuel is completely exhausted.

She should turn and leave. He doesn't deserve to live.

But he doesn't deserve to die either. Not like this. Not even after he nearly killed them both.

The others are too far away. There's nobody else but her.

Anna closes her eyes, then thumbs her own thruster control. The meter is blinking faster now, down to its last eighth. She uses the thrust in short bursts, aware that she's going to have to time this *very* carefully.

"Thank gods," says Dax, whimpering. "Thank gods."

Anna is fifty feet away. "Burn off your plasma cutter," she says.

"What?"

"*Do it*. Or I turn around and go home."

"It's already gone. It uses the same fuel as the thrusters do..."

"Show me."

"OK." He thumbs his wrist control pad. The cutter flame briefly springs to life, then shrinks and dies, the very last of his fuel burning off.

Anna corrects her course slightly, prompting her meter to blink even faster. If she hits Dax too hard, she'll send them both into a spin. They'll have to use another thruster boost to correct their course, and she doesn't have any fuel to spare.

She's coming in from above him. "Grab my legs," she says.

She slows herself down as she reaches him, and he manages to get his fingers around her ankles. They start spinning, but it's a gentle spin, and Anna knows she can compensate for it.

Dax is sobbing now. Anna suppresses the urge to shout at him, concentrating on her movement, using incremental thruster bursts to turn them around. A warning flashes up in her helmet. *THRUST FUEL CRITICAL.*

No shit, she thinks. With a push on the stick, she sends them moving back towards the station.

They're two hundred feet away. Anna can't see the others, but she can see the escape pod airlocks, like little black pockmarks in the station's surface.

They need to head for the airlocks, but when Anna tries to correct for it, her thrust meter vanishes completely. Another set of words appears on her heads-up.

THRUST DEPLETED.

Anna keys her transmit button, doing everything she can to fight the panic rippling through her. "We're out."

Dax gives a long, horrified moan. Anna can't take her eyes off Outer Earth. On their current course, they're not going to get anywhere near the hull. They'll sweep right over the curve of the station, and then past it, out into space.

"Anna!" It's Arroway, loud and clear over the suit radio. "I can—"

And then her radio dies again.

Anna can hear nothing but her breathing and heartbeat—both too fast, both impossibly loud inside the helmet. Another meter has started flashing—her O2. She's burning through it too fast, just like the thruster fuel.

No. Please, no.

She's trying to look around, but all she can see is the station hull, stretching below her. A hundred feet away, but it may as well be a million.

And then another space-suited figure collides with them, roaring in from below, grabbing her around the waist. The figure's thrusters are firing, quick bursts, left and right, stabilising them.

There's a burst of static, and then Arroway says, "Got you!"

89

Okwembu

The corridor itself is tilting, sliding to one side, like the world itself has gone wrong. Okwembu forces herself to keep moving, leaning on the wall. She's still coughing, and her nose is still plugged and sore, but her eyes have stopped streaming.

The ship is going down. Okwembu knows this, knows it in her bones, and it's all she can do not to start slamming her fists into the corridor wall.

The light changes. She looks up—without realising it, she's come out onto one of the loading platforms in the side of the ship. There are a few discarded crates and tarpaulins, piled in one corner. Daylight is streaming through the opening, and she can see the ocean stretching beyond.

And there's a boat, hanging on the wall.

It's barely worthy of the name—a tiny dinghy, its tubes flat and deflated. The bottom of the boat is punctured in several places, and the whole thing looks like it's about to fall apart.

Okwembu stumbles to the drop. Her legs are starting to ache from the effort of staying upright on the tilted floor. She slows as she approaches, wanting to recoil from the edge.

But where else is she going to go?

She could try and find another dock, but the chances are that the boats will be gone, taken by the escaped workers. There's no point finding somewhere to hide—whatever just happened, the *Ramona* is sinking, and fast. What about Hale? Could she go back and finish what she started? She shakes her head, the frustration bitter in her mouth. There's no way she'd get the drop on the girl again.

She leans out over the edge, then immediately pulls back. It's thirty feet to the ocean below, right into the slate-grey water. Okwembu can't help but think of when their escape pod smashed into Eklutna Lake—how cold the water was, how it felt like it was draining her strength.

She'll have to take the boat. With its tube walls deflated, there's a chance it might not stay afloat, but it's the only chance she's got.

The ship lurches underneath her, almost knocking her off her feet, and Janice Okwembu raises her head to the ceiling and roars.

The sound trails off, and she stands there, silent, her shoulders rising and falling.

She stumbles to the wall. It takes almost all her strength to lift the boat off its storage hooks and drag it to the edge. She pushes it over, and it smashes into the water, bobbing in the swell and bumping up against the hull.

Okwembu takes one last look over her shoulder. *It's not too late. I could go back, find Hale.*

The thought barely has a chance to form, and then she steps off the edge. She screams all the way down.

Impact

90

Riley

The ship has turned into a nightmare.

When I ran through it, after Prakesh was shot, the corridors felt like the ones on Outer Earth. I could navigate them, move through them at high speed. No chance of that now. Every corridor is tilting at a crazy angle, and anything not strapped down has piled itself up along the bottom. Doors that weren't locked shut hang open, creating low-hanging obstacles that we have to duck under. Fire alarms have activated across the ship. Most of the sprinkler systems aren't working, but a few are, and soon I'm drenched in chemical spray.

I don't know how I'm still moving. Somehow, I've managed to access one last reservoir of energy. I'm in agony: the worst of it, even worse than the insistent pain in my side and upper back, is at the bottom of my spine. The place where Okwembu hit me. Every single movement sends bolts of electricity shooting out from it.

The corridors are all but deserted. Once, rounding a corner, Carver and I see people in the distance, sprinting away from us. I can't tell if they're guards or workers. It doesn't matter. I don't dare stop moving, not even for a second.

The stairs have tilted along with the corridors, showing off their own weird geometry. We have to slow down at every stairwell, use the railings on the side of the stairs, take them in a weird bow-legged gait. I'm coming up on the stairway between B deck and C deck, getting ready to take it, picking my footholds.

It's hard going. Halfway down, my fingers come loose from a handhold. I let myself fall, knowing I'm only a few feet up, but it doesn't stop me gasping when I hit the water rushing through the C deck corridor.

Everything below my knees soaks right through. The water is

a churning mass of dirt and debris, so cold that I gasp. Running isn't even a possibility now. Carver drops down behind me, and we start wading, the water sloshing up our legs.

I try to be as careful as I can—I can't afford to fall. I do that, and the cold will sap what little energy I have left. But as we reach the junction, I realise that the water is getting higher. It's snuck up over my knees to mid-thigh. Soon, it'll be at my waist, then my chest.

The lights are starting to fail. The bulbs in the ceiling are flickering, casting strange shadows across the walls. A door flies open as I walk past it, nearly smacking me in the face. I dodge back, knocking my elbow on the wall of the passage as a spew of debris splashes into the water. I take a deep breath, then keep going.

It's impossible to miss the bulkhead doors. They're larger than the others, built more solidly. They drop down from the ceiling—I can just see the edge of the door below the roof, marked with more yellow and black chevrons. There's a lever, flat against the wall. A big steel rod half my height, with a rubber grip at the top, ready to be pulled down and outwards. There's an identical one on the other side of the door.

I don't know how many compartments have flooded already. If too much water gets through too many compartments, the ship won't be able to stay afloat. We have to seal this door, or it all goes down. And if Carver is right, then whatever is keeping this part of the planet alive goes down with it.

The water's at my waist now. I step in behind Carver, gripping the lever with my hands just underneath his. Then we summon every last bit of strength we have left, and pull.

Nothing happens. The lever doesn't move an inch.

I try not to think of the words *rusted* and *seized*. I don't let myself dwell on the possibilities. We try again, putting all our weight into pulling the lever back. As we do so, it moves, just a little, and I let out a cry of triumph.

My hands are wet—wet enough to slip free of the rubber grip, and I fall backwards into the water. My clothes protect me for no more than an instant. I'm fully submerged, shocked into immobility by the cold. I feel Carver's hand brushing my shoulder, and then he pulls me upright.

I splash over to the lever again, shivering, furious with myself. This time, I can't get a good grip. My wet, numb hands can't hold onto it. Carver steps in front of me, motions me off. He pulls the lever back, the muscles in his neck standing out like thick cords. "Come on!" he shouts.

It's working. It's working! I can see the lever starting to move. Any second now, it's going to go all the way. We can shut this door, then get the hell off this ship.

A gunshot echoes down the corridor, the bullet ripping past us.

I look round, and that's when I see a ghost.

Prophet.

He's wading down the corridor. White teeth gleam on his blood-soaked face. His left shoulder is in tatters, his arm hanging on by a shred of skin and muscle.

If I'm in bad shape, he's worse. I don't even know how it's possible for him to have followed us down here. Then I remember Oren Darnell. His mid-section was crushed in a massive door, his organs turned to pulp, but he kept on coming. He wouldn't let himself die.

Prophet's the same. He isn't going to be alive for much longer, but whatever energy is fuelling him, it hasn't run out yet. He must have overheard us on the bridge, talking about what we were going to do.

He raises his pistol, fires again, the bullet slicing the water a few feet from us. There's only one spot of available cover: the bulkhead doorframe. We swing ourselves around it, pressing up against the wall on the other side. Prophet takes another shot, and it ricochets off the frame.

The water is above my waist now. Despite the cold, despite the soaked clothes against my skin, I feel sweat break out across my forehead. We've got nowhere to go. All he has to do is come a little closer, and he'll have a point-blank shot.

The lever. The one on this side of the door. It's right between us.

"Help me with this," I say, wrapping my hands around the top of the lever, keeping my body as flat against the wall as I can. Prophet has stopped shooting. Smart. He's saving his shots, waiting until he gets closer.

"No," says Carver. "You'll trap us inside."

"You got a better idea?"

Carver groans in frustration, then leans over and wraps his hands around the lever. We're on either side of it, and we're going to have to pull it outwards for this to work.

"OK!" I shout, and we both lean into it, trying to force the lever away from the wall. But it's exactly like the one on the other side. It barely moves, budging only a fraction, and we don't have enough leverage to push it out from our position. We can't lean out—that would mean exposing ourselves in the doorway.

Prophet is getting closer, wading down the passage towards us. It might be my imagination, but I swear I can hear him breathing, harsh and ragged.

Carver lets go of the lever. "No dice. We're going to have to lean out."

Inspiration hits. "We both do it in one move, OK?"

Carver shakes his head. But he too reseats his grip, tensing his shoulders, bracing himself against the wall. He knows we don't have a choice.

"The Engine will have its revenge!" Prophet shouts. He doesn't sound human.

Carver and I throw ourselves forwards, moving in unison, pulling the lever out and down as hard as we can.

91

Riley

The lever gives an agonising squeal, and jerks down. Carver and I fall backwards into the icy water.

There's a split second where I get a good look at Prophet. He's almost done, barely able to keep himself upright. His eyes find mine. He might be chest-deep in freezing water, but the hatred in those eyes is hotter than the surface of the sun.

Then the bulkhead door drops, slamming into the passage with a giant boom, sending a wave of water slapping against my face.

"Can he get through?" says Carver. He puts his feet on the bottom, doing his best to hold his arms above the water. Not that it matters. We're both soaked.

"I don't think so," I say. I'm slurring my words. "If it took two of us to work that lever, there's no way he's doing it on his own."

We may have saved the ship, but we're trapped. The realisation is starting to sink in. I'm already looking around the corridor, hunting for an exit. This side of the door, the water is still climbing fast. The corridor tilts away from us, the water lapping at the ceiling a few yards away.

Could we wait it out? Wait for Prophet to die, and then open the door? Carver sees where I'm looking. "There's no way we're getting that door open again," he says.

I wade over to him, trying to keep my arms above the water. It's a struggle to get the words out. "So we swim out of here."

"You're crazy."

"There's a hole from the explosion, right? We make our way along the passage, and we find it."

He laughs, shaking his head. "Oh, man. Oh, shit."

I can see the terror on his face, and feel it in my heart. Everything below our chests is frozen, and there's no telling how long we'll last if we're completely submerged. Even if we make it out, we'll be a mile from shore, floating in open water.

"All right," he says, steeling himself. "Here we go." He takes two quick breaths, his hand finding mine. We'll go under together.

"Wait," I say.

"There's no time."

"I have to say this."

And I do. I should have said it a long time ago. I've known it ever since I kissed Carver, back on Outer Earth. I've tried to tell myself that I wanted to be with Prakesh, that it would be wrong *not* to be with him, after everything we've been through.

But I've been through just as much with Carver. He understands me in a way Prakesh couldn't. I've tried to ignore it, tried to run from it, but that doesn't stop it being true. Prakesh is one of the best men I know, but Carver is the one who's always been there for me. He's never let me down.

And I knew this, even before we came down here to try and save the ship. I knew it back on the bridge, when he was telling me about the bulkhead doors. He didn't need me—I could have let him do it himself. He's just as capable as I am.

But that would have meant letting him go. It would have meant being apart from him. And I'm not going to let that happen again. Not ever.

I look into his eyes. "You remember back on the *Shinso*? I told you I still loved Prakesh? You asked me who you had left."

"Riley, I don't—"

"I was wrong, Aaron," I say, barely able to get the words out. "I love you. You have me, and you'll always have me."

It doesn't matter that *always* may only be a few minutes more. It's the truth. No one should ever have to make this choice, but, right now, in the depths of this ship, I'm glad I've made mine.

I don't give him a chance to answer. I wrap my arms around him, and pull him close. Our lips touch, but we're shivering so badly that we can't hold the kiss.

He's got that weird smile on his face, like he can't quite believe what's happening. He runs a finger along my cheek, then leans close, his forehead against mine.

And in that moment, it's as if the water isn't even there. There's nothing but us.

I try to hold it for as long as I can. But the water is almost at our necks. Carver kisses me once more, then says, "Let's get out of here."

I nod. "Yeah."

He holds me tight. "On zero," he says. "Three. Two. One."

"Zero," I whisper, and we sink below the surface of the water.

92

Riley

The cold is everywhere. It's not like ice—it's like fire, scorching me, making my skin bubble and spit.

I feel Carver push away from me, and force my eyes to open. There's still some light from the bulbs above the water, and it's filtering down around us. I can just make out the walls of the passage. Debris floats in front of me, swirling in the current.

I don't know how long I have before the cold sucks my life away. I don't care. I push myself through the water, pumping my arms and legs, not sure if I'm doing right, not caring. I can feel Carver alongside me. I look down, and see that he's using the ribbed metal on the walls to pull himself along. I try the same trick, and find that my fingertips are completely numb.

Globs of fuel float in the water, and I manage to get one of them in my eyes. It forces me to squeeze them closed, blocking out the sting. When I open them, I've lost Carver.

My lungs are already tight, but panic crushes them. I spin in place, hunting for him, but there's hardly any light now. I'm in a black pit, and if I don't get moving again, I'm going to run out of air long before I die from cold.

There he is, just below me, beckoning me on. I thrash my arms—they feel like they've got lead weights tied to them. It's hard to remember what I'm doing. I can't keep my thoughts straight. I find myself thinking of Outer Earth, of the hab Prakesh and I shared. A moment later, I remember my father, right before he went on the Earth Return mission. Why am I thinking of him? I don't want to think at all. I just want to sleep. I close my eyes, just for a second, but that second stretches out into eternity.

Carver is pointing at something. A part of the corridor wall, darker than the rest. A hole. Why is there a hole? It'll let the water in.

Carver grabs me. His grip is incredibly tight. I want to shake him off, but he's insistent, refusing to let go.

His grip makes me focus. I snap back to life, thrashing in the water, then thrust myself towards the hole. There's debris in front of me, floating metal, and I almost scream as I push it out of the way. My lungs are roaring in pain.

There's nothing but darkness beyond the hole. It's as if we're swimming out into deep space.

I push and push and push, but I don't seem to be getting anywhere. It feels as if my lungs are going to pop. There's a crushing weight in my head, pulling everything down with it.

I swear I feel Carver take my hand, but I'm so numb that I can't tell if he's there or not.

93

Riley

Fragments.

Each one is as sharp as a piece of broken glass, lancing into my mind. They only last a moment before vanishing, leaving no trace. No memory. Nothing.

Carver is in front of me in the water. I can just make out his shape, see his arms and legs moving, his hand reaching out for me.

The sky above us, the grey clouds hanging low. *Air.* Searing my lungs, burning a million times worse than the cold water.

The ocean. How could there be this much water in one place? It's unimaginable. Made up. It's a dream I'm having, and any second now it'll be gone.

Something looming up from the water in front of us. The seaplane. Harlan reaching down from it, reaching towards me. How is it here? How did it know how to find us?

Impact

I'm half in, half out of the plane. Harlan has me under the arms, and Carver is pushing me from below.

We're moving over the surface of the water, high above it. I can see the ship, dropping away behind us. And then we're on the ground, surrounded by people. Hands and faces everywhere. Harlan is there, and Eric, but I can't see Prakesh, or Carver. I want to find them so badly. But even keeping my eyes open is beyond me. It's like trying to hold the entire world across my shoulders. I let my head drop, close my eyes.

When I come back, there's something wrapped around me. A blanket, or a coat. It doesn't seem to matter. It's thick and warm, slightly scratchy against my cheek.

"Give her some water."

There's a pressure, under my head. A hand lifts me up, and another one brings the lip of a water canteen to my mouth. The water is tepid, slightly salty, but I drink and drink.

The canteen slips away. I want to tell whoever is holding it to keep it there, but at that moment pins and needles explode across my body. My muscles clench involuntarily, and that just makes it worse.

The pressure on me increases. It's someone lying on top of me.

"Stay still," Eric whispers in my ear, as he squeezes me tight, giving me as much heat as possible.

It's some time before I open my eyes again. Eric is gone. I'm wrapped in a thick, dark brown coat, curled up on the damp ground. My wet clothes have been removed—I've still got my underwear, but that's all. I'm shivering uncontrollably, my teeth clacking together.

There are people everywhere. Workers from the ship. There are dozens of them—they're ragged and worn out, but it's impossible not to see the relief on their faces. They're moving in small groups, shouting orders, marshalling supplies: food and blankets and containers of fuel.

The shore itself is made up of black dirt and jagged rocks. The seaplane floats in the water, a few yards away. There are the strangest things piercing the surface of the sea, and it takes me a minute to realise that they're buildings. Or what used to be buildings, anyway. The hulking *Ramona* is beyond them, a distant black shape.

"Hey."

It's Harlan, crouching down next to me.

I stare at him for the longest time. Then I crawl over, doing my best to keep the coat on my shoulders, and wrap my arms around him. I can't stop shaking.

"How?" I say. It's all I can manage.

He looks perplexed, but then his eyes light up. "Oh, the plane? We got hit, but not nearly as bad as we thought. Eric put her down upriver, up on the Knik Arm. Nearly went into the drink. He bossed me around some when we tried to fix her, but we got the bird up in the air again, no sweat. Eric always was good at that kind of shit. I told you how he read all those books, right? When we were kids?"

"You came back." The words are coming a little more easily now.

He looks guilty. "Almost didn't. We thought you and Finkler were done. But then we took off, and saw that gun tearing up the bridge on the ship. That's...kind of not what we expected to see, so we thought we should get a closer look. And then we saw you running across the deck like your feet were on fire."

It takes me a minute to process his words. I'm still doing it when the memory of what happened to Prakesh broadsides me.

I look round, and this time I find him almost immediately. He's lying on his back, one arm flung out to the side. His face is so pale, his dark walnut skin gone bloodless. There are people on their knees around him, bent over him, and there's too much blood. *Way* too much blood.

I can't describe the sound I make. It's halfway between a moan and a scream. A memory surfaces: Prakesh, kidnapped by Oren Darnell, sprawled out on the floor of a disused storage facility off the Outer Earth monorail tracks. I was in the ventilation system in the ceiling, looking through a gap in the panels. But the panic I felt then is like a cup of water, and what I feel now is an ocean, stretching out in front of me to an endless horizon.

I don't remember getting up. The coat falls from my shoulders, leaving me almost naked, sprinting across the shore. Sharp rocks dig into my feet, slowing me down.

Eric materialises at my elbow, his strong hands falling on my shoulders. I have to make myself pay attention to what he's saying.

"You need to stay warm," he says. "Get back there, wrap yourself up."

I try to push past him, but I'm not strong enough, and he holds me in place.

"We think he'll be OK," Eric says. "One of the people off that ship has some medical training."

He indicates a grey-haired man, his blood-soaked hands pressing down on Prakesh's chest. "Right now, infection is the big worry. We've got supplies in Whitehorse, so we'll get him back there."

I look back at Prakesh, at his blood soaking into the sand. Frustration and helplessness boil inside me, and I try to push past Eric again.

"No," Eric says, blocking me with an arm across my chest. "You'll just be in the way. Let them work."

I can see the *Ramona* in the distance, over his shoulder. The ship is a black, smoking hulk, squatting on the horizon like a bad dream. But it's still there. We saved it. Carver and I.

Carver. I swing my head around, so suddenly that the muscles in my neck creak, sending a fresh wave of pins and needles down my back.

"The man I was with," I say. My throat is parched again, and I swallow, sending razor blades dancing across it. "Where is he?"

Eric says nothing.

"Eric?" I say.

But then I catch sight of something over his shoulder.

A tarpaulin, spread out across the filthy sand. There's a shape underneath it. A person, lying on their back.

I shake my head. "No."

"He pushed you out of the water," Eric says.

"No."

"You were unconscious, and he was still swimming, and he made sure you were in the plane first. Riley, he was already hypothermic—"

"No."

I'm running. Sprinting across the sand. I'm going to tear that tarpaulin off him, shake him, wake him up. He's not dying on me. Not after he came back. Not after I told him that I'd made my choice. Not happening. No way. I won't let it.

But when I get there, my hands have stopped listening to me. The damp tarpaulin is too heavy, and I can't move it. I try to grip the edge, but my fingers keep slipping. And then Eric has his arms around me and I'm trying to get away but I can't, and all I can hear are my screams.

94

Anna

Anna wraps the blanket tighter around herself. It's all the way up to her chin, tucked in around her crossed legs, but she can't stop shivering. She's lost her beanie—she can't even remember it coming off her head. She feels naked without it.

The family's hab is the only quiet space they could find—the only space where a thousand people weren't trying to talk to her, where she wasn't getting bombarded by a million questions on all sides. The door is shut, but she can still hear voices from the corridor. She tries to tune them out, closing her eyes. She knows she won't sleep—she's way too wired for that—but it helps.

Dax and Arroway and the rest of their group are in the sector brig. They all came back into the escape pod airlocks, every one of them—it was either that, or drift in space for the rest of time. Anna doesn't know what'll happen to them. Dax was sobbing when they pulled him out of his suit. He tried to reach for her, but she got away as quickly as she could, not wanting to look at him, at *any* of them.

She made it almost ten steps before collapsing.

The door to the hab slides open. Voices snap into focus. "If we could just see her—"

"No." Frank Beck's voice is thunderous. "She's been through enough. Get out of here."

He doesn't give them a chance to answer—just slams the door shut. Then he stands there for a moment, his shoulders heaving.

Anna slides off the bed, letting the blanket fall to her feet. Cold air pricks the skin on her arms, but she barely notices. She walks over to her dad, wraps her arms around him and pulls him close.

They hold each other for a long moment. "What were you thinking?" Frank says, his voice muffled by her hair.

"I—"

He pulls apart from her, thrusting her to arm's length. *"What were you thinking?"* he bellows into her face, then almost immediately pulls her back into a hug. It's such an absurd, theatrical performance that she wants to call him out on it, make a joke, say something clever. It's his shoulders that stop her. They're trembling, and she feels tears staining her scalp.

So she says nothing. She just holds him.

Eventually, her father gives her a squeeze and they pull apart. He wipes his face, not looking at her, and sits down heavily on the bed. Anna grabs the discarded blanket on the floor, and sits next to him, cross-legged, wrapping it around her legs.

"I'm sorry," she whispers.

He actually laughs—or tries to. "Are you, now?"

"Dad, come on."

He drops his head. "I know."

It's then that she realises she never told him about Riley. About the radio conversation. She does so, and the more she talks, the wider his eyes get.

"Anna, that's..." he leaps up off the bed, pacing the floor. "That's *brilliant*. And they told you where to come down?"

She nods.

"Brilliant," he says again. "I've got to tell everyone. We've got to tell the crew on the *Tenshi*."

He's moving towards the door when Anna says, "What's going to happen?"

"Hmmm?" He looks over his shoulder at her.

"To—you know, to Dax and the rest of them?"

"Oh," her father says, as if it's an irrelevance. "We don't know yet."

"Are they going to be taken out of the lottery?" It's the only outcome she can think of. How could they let any of them have a place on the *Tenshi Maru*?

Her father comes to a halt, staring at the door. After a moment, he makes his way back to the bed, sitting down next to her.

He sighs. "I don't think they should."

"*What?*"

"So do a few others. They'll have to stay in the brig, to be sure, but—"

She shakes her head. "They were going to leave us here. They were going to take the space suits and *leave us*."

"Well—"

"No. Dad, you can't be thinking about letting them go."

He puts a hand on her knee, and she subsides.

"They thought they were better than us," her father says. "That's the whole reason they went in the first place, wasn't it?"

"Yeah…"

"So what better punishment than making them exactly the same as everyone else? By making them take the lottery just like all of us here?"

She opens her mouth to reply—and finds she has nothing.

That's when the full realisation hits her. There's still going to be a lottery. There's still going to be some who go, and some who get left behind. Nothing she did—working out what Dax was planning, contacting Riley, the insane trip through space—none of it changes that. She's not going to be able to save her family, or Ravi and Achala Kumar, or Ivy, or Marcus, or anybody else. It's all going to be left to chance.

And that's the worst thing of all. Because it's the only way to do it.

She reaches over and pulls her dad into a fierce hug. She buries her face in his shoulder, and this time it's her turn to cry.

"It's going to be OK," he says, holding her tight.

Anna wants to believe him. But she's not sure that she can.

95

Riley

I sit on the beach for a long time, staring out at the water.

Someone found me clothes. A threadbare collared shirt made of a stiff, blue material. Black pants. There's even a pair of shoes, scabbed with dirt. The clothes come from someone much larger than me. I don't know who they belong to, but at least they're dry.

I'm dimly aware of the activity on the beach. Harlan is arguing with Eric, saying that they need to bring the workers with them. Eric is saying that they'll never fit them all in the plane, and Harlan responds by telling him that they'll make multiple trips if they have to. He sounds almost jubilant—not surprising. He survived Anchorage.

The workers are talking in a big group. One of them protests loudly, saying that they should retake the ship, that all the guards are dead.

I let it wash over me. I don't know what's going to happen next. It's too big a task, too many people to find homes for, too many loose ends to tie up. I can't even do anything for Prakesh—he's stable now, but unconscious, bundled up inside the plane and being tended to by the man with the grey hair. So I just sit.

It's all I can do.

Someone crouches down next to me. Koji. There's dried blood on his face, crusted under his right eye. His hair hangs in lanky strands on his face, and his overalls are patchy with seawater.

"I can go," he says, "if you'd rather be alone."

I shake my head. I feel like I should want to be by myself right now, but I find I don't care very much.

Koji sits cross-legged on the sand, wincing as he does so. "They don't like me very much," he says, nodding to a group of workers. One of them scowls back at him. "I was hoping you could tell them…I mean, if…"

He trails off, looking embarrassed.

"I think I'd like to hear that story now," I say.

"Story?"

"About my dad."

Koji looks out at the horizon. He's silent for so long that I'm on the verge of prompting him, and then he says, "The *Akua Maru* didn't make it through the atmosphere. There was... an explosion. Something in the reactor went wrong."

"I know," I say.

Koji continues as if I hadn't spoken. "There's no way we should have made it down. We were going thousands of miles an hour. But your dad did it. He pulled it off. Two of us died during the descent, but there were still eight of us who made it down."

He looks at me. "Your dad saved my life."

"What happened? After you landed?"

He shrugs. "The ship was a wreck. Fusion reactor was still intact, just about, but it wasn't working. Everything else was done for. And Kamchatka... we couldn't have come down in a worse area. It was *cold*. Cold enough to freeze your bones inside you."

He attempts a smile. "Your dad kept us going. He organised us. He made sure we got enough to eat, that we stayed warm enough. We wouldn't have lasted a week without him."

When I speak, my voice is as brittle as thin glass. "But you came here."

He continues as if I hadn't spoken. "Your dad was a hero, but he wasn't a miracle worker. We were running out of supplies, so three of us decided to head east, see if there was anything out there. Your father and four others stayed behind. He kept trying to contact Outer Earth. He said they'd send another ship—that it was just a matter of time. Did they? Did Outer Earth ever send a rescue?"

I don't know what to tell him. He sees my dad as a hero, as the man who saved him. How do I tell him that he went insane? That he killed the rest of the crew? He was down there for seven years, and after he finally got the ship going again, he set it on a collision course for Outer Earth, determined to destroy the station he thought had left him there to rot. Even thinking about it is like touching a wound that's only just started to scab over.

"No," I say. "They didn't send anybody."

Koji shakes his head. "Doesn't matter. Two of us made it across the Bering Strait, turned south. We were half dead when the people on the *Ramona* found us. Dominguez died on the way, but they brought me on board. Made me into a slave, like all the others. Until..."

He trails off, as if not sure how to say it.

"Until what?" I say.

"They didn't call it the Sacred Engine at first," he says. "When they took us, it was broken. They had plenty of fuel stored in the ship, and a working fusion reactor, but they couldn't get the Engine working again."

"I don't see how—"

"Don't you understand? I was the *Akua Maru*'s terraforming specialist. Our mission was to make the Earth habitable again. Or to start making it habitable, anyway. Our terraforming equipment was destroyed in the crash. The equipment we had on the *Akua* was a more advanced version of what the Engine was: something called a HAARP unit.

"They developed the HAARP over a hundred years ago. It was supposed to fix the climate by effecting changes in the ionosphere, but they didn't get it off the ground before the nukes came raining down. The one on the *Ramona* was a much smaller version of it. I guess the plan was to deploy a bunch of them around the planet."

I stare at him, my mouth open.

"I knew how to fix it," Koji says. "Took me a long time to convince them to let me try, but I did it. I got the HAARP working again. Even then, Prophet made out like it was all his doing."

He shrugs. "Still, they made me one of them. Problem was, the ship's fusion reactor was dead, so I had to figure out how to run the HAARP using the fuel supplies—*that* took a lot of work. Almost couldn't do it. It wasn't nearly as efficient, and if it had gone on much longer...Where are you going?"

I'm on my feet, arms tightly folded, walking away from him. I can't stop shaking, and this time it has nothing to do with the cold.

When I was in the Outer Earth control room, pleading with my father not to destroy the station, he told me that he had to finish the mission. He spent seven years in Kamchatka, freezing, desperately trying to stay alive so he could reunite with his family. When Janice Okwembu reached him, told him that my mom and I were dead, the only thing he wanted was to take revenge.

But it doesn't matter what he became. He landed his crew safely, and he made it possible for the Earth to recover. The chain of events led Koji here, to the one place where he could make a difference. What Okwembu did set in motion everything that happened to me, and what my father did—bringing that ship down intact—ended up saving the world.

I can never see my dad again. But I'm standing here, on a planet everybody thought was dead and gone, because of what he did.

He finished his mission.

"Dad," I say, and then I feel another wrench of emotion so powerful it doubles me over. My tears fall to the sand.

I walk away, leaving everyone behind. I walk until their voices have faded to a dull murmur over the wind. After a while I stop, looking out at the ocean, at the horizon beyond it. I stand for a long time, doing nothing. My mind is as clear as an empty sky.

Strangely, it's a good feeling—like I can fill my body up with whatever I want. Like I'm finally free to choose what goes inside me.

There's a sound, off to my left. It takes me a second to realise what I'm seeing.

Janice Okwembu is crawling up the beach. Her clothes are sodden, streams of water cascading off her. She's coughing, her fingers clawing the dirt.

And the empty space inside me fills with white-hot rage, expanding outwards at the speed of light.

Impact

96

Okwembu

Okwembu focuses on putting one hand in front of the other. It's the only thing she's capable of doing.

She doesn't know how long she was out in the water. After a while, there was no feeling left in her hands and arms. The boat kept her above the surface, just. Half the time it felt like it was going to pull her down with it. When she got within a few feet of the shore, a swell finally capsized her. By then, she was so cold that it barely made a difference.

But she's *alive.*

One hand, then the other, pulling herself along the sand. She forces herself to think ahead. It's hard, as if the pathways between her synapses have frozen shut. She has to push the thoughts into being, mould them, concentrate to keep them in place.

First, she's going to get to her knees. Then her feet. Then she's going to see if she can stay standing. After that, she'll find a way to get warm. She doesn't know how yet, but, right now, that's all that matters.

She stops, trembling, then gets a knee underneath her. The front of her shirt is caked with sand. She almost falls over, puts a hand out, and winces as her numb fingers take the weight.

The ice in her mind is melting slowly. She'll have to make fire somehow—she remembers a history lesson, in a distant Outer Earth schoolroom, where the instructors talked about their ancestors making fire. How did they do it? Doesn't matter. She'll figure it out. Then, after she's got fire, she'll find food, and water. She still has the data stick—no telling if the saltwater has damaged it, but it's not important right now. The *Ramona* won't be the only civilisation out there, and she knows the remaining workers are somewhere on the shore—she caught a glimpse of them as she came in. Would they accept her? Did they know she was with Prophet? Maybe she could—

Running footsteps, hissing on the sand. Okwembu looks up, and then Riley Hale kicks her in the stomach.

97

Riley

The world disappears.

Okwembu is struggling to get up, one arm clutching her stomach, gasping for air. I don't let her get any. I step back, wind up another kick and drive it hard into her ribs.

The kick overbalances me, and I crash to the ground. Right then, it's as if my muscles just give up on me. The ones in my back constrict, locking in place. I lie next to Okwembu, breathing hard, desperate to get up but unable to do so, fingers clawing at the dirt.

On your feet, says the voice. *You're not finished.*

I roll onto my side, coughing. Okwembu tries to push me away, but she's as weak as I am.

Finally, I struggle up to one knee. Okwembu puts a hand on my leg, trying to pull me down, so I grab her by the front of her shirt and lift her off the ground. My punch snaps her head back. She spits blood and fragments of tooth, cursing now, howling for help.

My second punch shuts her up. My aim is off this time, and I just graze the side of her head. I can't stop my momentum, and I slide forward, falling on top of her.

For a moment, it's as if we're hugging each other, embracing in the dirt. She shoves me off, just managing to get an arm underneath me. I hold on, pulling her with me as I roll onto my back. Then I throw my head forward, smashing my forehead into her face, breaking her nose. She moans, long and low, but refuses to let go.

Is that all? the voice says to me. *Is that everything you have? After what she's done? Pathetic. You can do much better than that. You can show her pain.*

My muscles wake up. I shove Okwembu off me, then stagger to my feet. The sky swims in front of me, and hot sweat trickles into my eyes. I barely notice. I'm going to kill her. I know this as sure as I know my own name. I'm going to send her into the next world with broken bones and torn flesh. I'm going to send her there screaming.

I circle her, watching her try to crawl away. She surprised me before, back on the *Ramona*'s bridge. Almost finished me, too. Not this time. This time, she's all mine.

I rest my foot on her head. "Prakesh," I say, pushing down hard. Okwembu's cheek grinds into the dirt. "Amira," I say, grinding down, until I can see the dirt entering her mouth, milling around her broken teeth. "Kevin. Yao. Royo." *Harder.* "Carver." I lean into it, putting all my weight on her head. "John Abraham *Hale.*"

Just before the last name, I lift my foot off her and slam it into her ribs. This time, I swear I feel one of them break. I fall backwards, landing on my ass in the churned-up sand.

"Please," Okwembu says. The word is mushy, forced through swollen lips.

Enough. Finish it.

I get to my feet again, unsteady, my fine balance shot to pieces. I take one step towards Okwembu. Then another. She's trying to crawl away again, and I almost laugh. *Where are you going? Got somewhere to be?*

I flip her over, onto her back. Then I straddle her, my knees pinning her shoulders to the ground.

I don't know where I find the rock. It's like I put my hand out and it's right there, waiting for me. It's stuck deep into the ground, and it's too big for one hand anyway. I have to lean over to get it, ripping it out of the earth with both hands. It's heavy, caked with clods of dirt.

I lift the rock over my head, holding it high. It takes me a second to understand what I'm feeling. It's not anger now. It's joy. A kind of terrible joy. I look down at Okwembu, one last time. The disbelief and shock in her eyes only makes the joy burn brighter.

"Will it help?"

Eric is standing in front of me, a few feet away.

I don't know how long he's been there, and there's no one else with him. His arms are folded, his head tilted to one side. The expression on his face is completely blank.

The voice is shouting now, a deafening roar that only I can hear. The rock is heavy in my hands.

"Killing her." Eric nods towards the thing on the ground. "Will it help?"

When I don't answer, he says, "You know, I had a daughter. We did. Harlan and I."

As he speaks, he absently pulls the necklace out of his shirt—the bear's tooth, hanging on a piece of tattered string. He rolls the tooth in his fingers.

I lower the rock, holding it at my chest. I want more than anything to finish this, to drive that rock into Okwembu's face, but I can't take my eyes off Eric. It's then that I realise that I'm crying, tears staining my cheeks.

"She was killed," Eric says. "Bear. I went and tracked it down myself, put eight bullets through its face."

He looks at me, a sad smile on his face.

"It didn't bring my Samantha back. And it didn't help. I see her when I go to sleep. Asking me why I couldn't save her." He says this matter-of-factly, like it barely matters. "It was like I hadn't just lost her. I'd lost something else, too. I could never get it back no matter how hard I looked."

"This is different," I say, forcing each word out.

Eric shrugs. "Maybe."

"You can't stop me."

"I won't try. But you'll still see them. Everybody you've lost will always be there, whether you do this or not. It won't change a single thing."

Seconds go by. Eric watches me, his face still completely blank.

It would be so easy. The work of a single movement.

My arms give out. I let the rock drop to my waist, resting on Okwembu's chest. I roll it off, and it thumps onto the ground.

The world comes back. Slowly, one piece at a time. Ocean. Sky. The trees, climbing up from the shoreline. Okwembu coughs, blood dribbling down her cheek, staring up at me in disbelief.

I get to my feet, and, with Eric watching, I walk over to one of the trees. It doesn't have what I'm looking for, so I try a second, then a third. On the fourth tree, I find it: a clump of moss, wispy and threadlike, clinging to the trunk. I tear it off, rolling it in my hands.

I walk back over to Okwembu, and drop it on her chest.

"Old man's beard," I say. "It's a fire starter. You can—" I swallow "—combine it with spruce sap, and it'll burn forever. And there are lowbush cranberries you can eat. Little red berries, near tree roots. Burdock. Cattail. Lady fern…"

I trail off, my voice giving out.

There's something hanging round her neck. A data stick, on a thin lanyard. I reach down and pull, snapping the lanyard in two. Whatever's on that stick, she doesn't need it any more. I take a shaky breath, then turn and walk away.

The voice inside me is gone. Like it never existed.

"We can't leave her here," Eric says. "She's injured."

"She gets some food," I say. "Medical supplies. Water. Let her take what she needs." I see him about to protest, and look him right in the eyes. "But she stays here."

I'll let Okwembu live. But she's going to have to survive out here, by herself. She's never going to manipulate anybody ever again. From now on, everything she gets is going to come from her own two hands.

Eric stares at me for what feels like a whole minute. Then he nods.

I start walking, back towards the others.

98

Prakesh

"You're sure?" Eric says.

Prakesh nods. "There are plenty of reactor schematics on that data stick. I mean, it'll take time, and some of us'll need to live on the *Ramona* for a while, but it's definitely possible."

Eric grimaces. "I don't like it. That ship's barely afloat as it is."

"Yeah, but the HAARP's fuel got destroyed in the explosion. If we want it to keep going, we need that reactor working."

"But you're *sure*?" says Harlan.

They're in the hospital basement in Whitehorse, clustered around the table in Eric's quarters. The space around them is full of noise: low conversations, laughter. The sound of life.

He nods. "We can do it."

Eric leans over the map. The frown hasn't left his face. "It's a shame the other one isn't here. Riley's friend. From what I hear, he was pretty good with machines."

A little bomb goes off in Prakesh's chest, like it always does when someone mentions Aaron Carver. He knows what Eric means—Carver would have had the best idea of how to get the fusion reactor working again, how to get it joined up to the HAARP. He saw things differently, especially machines. Prakesh misses him a lot more than he thought he would. Jojo, too—and he knew him for less than two days. His body, like those of so many others, is still on the *Ramona*.

"We'll make do," he says. "We have to." And they would. They have the astronauts from the *Tenshi Maru*, plenty of whom have technical knowledge. They'll find a way.

They're never going to be able to get the *Ramona* upright. But despite the damage, the HAARP itself made it through. It hasn't had fuel for a while, so it's probably shut itself off, but they should be able to start it up again before any permanent damage is done to the climate.

He doesn't know if they'll have to station people on the *Ramona* permanently, or if that's even possible given the ship's condition. That's all still up in the air. Prakesh has heard Eric and Harlan and some of the others talking it over, late at night, occasionally raising their voices to argue a point. He hasn't joined them yet. *One thing at a time*, he tells himself.

Suddenly, Prakesh doesn't want to be here. It's been like that lately—an urge to move, to walk, no matter what he's doing at the time. It comes out of nowhere, and he knows better than to fight it.

He straightens up, smiles at them. "I'll leave you to it."

"Where are you going?" Harlan says.

"Just, you know."

He ducks out of Eric's quarters, wincing as he does so. The bullet punched right through him, leaving an ugly scar—a round crater of painful, puckered flesh, right below his heart. He still doesn't know how he survived. The first thing he remembers is waking up in Whitehorse, in more pain than he'd ever felt in his life.

Somehow, he got through it. The rest of the workers were there, along with dozens of others he hadn't seen before. Eric brought them all, running back and forth to Anchorage. It took three or four trips to do it.

He walks down the central passageway, hands in his pockets. Over at the end, he can see one of Riley's old tracer unit friends, deep in conversation with someone he thinks is her dad. Anna, that's her name. He hasn't said much to her, but she gives him a friendly wave anyway. He returns it.

He intends to head out of the hospital, maybe take a walk. But as he passes the vegetable garden, he changes course. The garden itself is in an area walled off with hanging plastic sheets, sticky with condensation. He pushes through them, casting a practised eye over the large half-drums, turned on their sides and filled with good soil. His fingers stray to the surface of one, and tiny clumps gather under his fingernails.

He'll get his walk in a minute.

The trowel is just where he left it, and he squats on his haunches.

His scar complains, but he ignores it, working the soil, letting his mind drift. As it so often does, it drifts back to his parents.

He's read the message Anna brought him so often that he has it memorised. It's not difficult, not for something so short. His mother was the one who wrote it, tapping it out on a small tab screen that Anna brought with her. Prakesh has wondered a thousand times why they didn't record a video. The letter doesn't say, and when he asked Anna she said she didn't know.

We don't have long, the message read. *Your father and I want you to know that we won't suffer. Nobody on the station will. They've found a way to make it painless—we'll all just go to sleep.*

He works the soil harder, the words running through his mind.

We know you took responsibility for Resin. We cannot tell you enough that it wasn't your fault. Nobody here thinks so. It was bad luck, and that's the end of it. I know this probably won't change how you feel but please realise that if you hadn't done it, someone else would have. It was inevitable.

We never thought any of us would ever go back to Earth. It hurts that we can't be there with you and see the things you're seeing. But we know you and Riley will be happy. I wish we could have known her better but she means a lot to you and that is enough for us. Take care of her. I want grandchildren!!!

We love you and we are so so very proud of you.

Prakesh props the trowel in the end of the soil bed, running the last line over again in his mind.

This can wait. He needs to get out.

As he heads back down the passage towards the entrance, his thoughts turn to Riley.

She's getting better every day. She smiles more, talks more. She's coming back to him, piece by piece. He wishes it would happen faster, but he knows not to rush things. He's got a long way to go himself.

Where are you? he thinks. He finds himself closing his eyes, as if he can find out where she is by thought alone. Then he opens them, and keeps walking.

Impact

99

Riley

I let the ice-cold water crash over me. It explodes across my head and neck, runs down onto my shoulders, spatters on my chest and thighs. I give it five more seconds, then I step out of the waterfall, shivering, every inch of my skin tingling.

It's an incredible feeling. No matter how many times I step under the waterfall, I never get tired of it. Maybe it's because we never had showers on Outer Earth. I never had the sensation of having water all around me until we came here.

At first I hated it—it's all too easy to remember Fire Island, and the sick, leaden feeling that came with swimming to shore. But as the winter faded away, I started running in the hills above Whitehorse. Eric and Harlan didn't want me to, said it was too dangerous, but they couldn't stop me. And then one day I came across another waterfall—a trickle, really, a stream running off a six-foot drop onto mossy rocks. On a whim, I took my clothes off and stood under it. I screamed with cold at first, gasping, not sure what the hell I was doing, but when I stepped out it felt like I'd been given a brand new body.

The water here is different from the ocean. Just as cold, but brighter somehow. I can't explain it.

I move on shivering tiptoes to the edge of the rocks, shake off the excess water and quickly pull on my clothes. A dark jacket, a faded blue shirt, a rough pair of pants. Thick socks, and light shoes. I keep an ear out for movement in the forest—we haven't seen the Nomads for a while, and the wolves seem to have moved on, too. But I still keep my ears open.

There's pain as I pull my clothes on. I spent most of the winter in a hospital bed, drifting in and out of consciousness. I'd torn muscles in my back, my side. I had cracked ribs. Some of my cuts got infected—Finkler would have been furious. I don't remember a lot about that part of the winter, but as the weather got warmer my body started to come back.

I'm still freezing. The air has a serious chill in it, even though winter is gone. A run will warm me up. I jump once, twice, relishing the almost audible crackle of my shocked skin, then take off into the forest.

After all this time, the rhythm of running still calms me, even when I don't have a direction, even when there's no cargo on my back. *Stride, land, cushion, spring, repeat.* I let the movement take me, block out everything else.

I only come to a stop when I reach the big tree.

It's not much—it's long dead, broken off and weathered away, but its stump still reaches two feet above my head. Its roots are huge, digging out of the earth, stretching in all directions. It should be a bad place, a dead place. But it isn't. It's surrounded by plants: old man's beard and cattail, and little white flowers that bend towards it. I look up, like I always do, and can just see a streak of blue through a gap in the clouds.

Aaron Carver is buried in Anchorage. Before we did it, I tore a strip of fabric from his shirt. I still can't fully explain why I took it. I tucked it inside my pocket, held tight to it, and all through the long winter, when the wind roared and howled and icy rain and snow buffeted the hospital and infection turned my body into a furnace, my hand kept finding it.

I didn't intend to bury the fabric at this tree. Carver would have preferred somewhere with machinery, with a worktop and soldering iron, where he could tinker. But I wanted somewhere private, and I liked how the tree made me feel, so I pushed the fabric down into the earth, nestled it against one of the roots.

I've come up here plenty of times since then. I've cried a lot, but this time, as I sit down with my back against the tree, my face is dry. I feel like I've cried every single tear I have. There's nothing left to give.

"Are you there?" I whisper. I've never worshipped any of Outer Earth's gods. I don't know what happens to us after we die. I'm just doing the only thing I can do.

No answer. Nothing but the wind through the trees.

I sit there for a few minutes, until the cold starts to sink into my muscles. Then I get to my feet, looking in the direction of Whitehorse.

Prakesh will never know what I said to Carver in the depths of the *Ramona*, after we sealed the bulkhead door. He can't know. I won't let the choice I made affect what happens next. We've been through so much together, and while our bond might not be perfect, it's still strong.

One of the lucid thoughts I remember from the long winter is that I never asked Prakesh what he wanted. I was so caught up in how I'd treated Carver, and the decision I made, that I never gave any thought to what he might be feeling. I'm going to change that. He deserves some happiness. I think I can give it to him.

Maybe along the way I'll find some of my own.

But that can come later. There's still two miles between me and Whitehorse, and this is my favourite part of the whole run.

I head downhill through the forest, slowing when I come to the tree line. I can see the shape of the Whitehorse hospital in the distance.

Between us is a field. It's overgrown, the ground uneven, but it's filled with long grass. The grass flickers in shades of yellow and green, teased by the wind.

The clouds have faded a little. More gaps have opened in them, and the sun is just peeking through. I raise my face to it, let it warm my skin. The sky beyond the clouds is so blue that it hurts to look at it.

I start running. I sprint across the field, arms out behind me, pounding the ground, focusing on the in–out, push–pull of my breathing. The sun is warm on the back of my neck, the world falling away behind me as I go faster, and faster, and faster.

Acknowledgments

Writer: Rob Boffard
Editor: Anna Jackson
Agent: Ed Wilson
Copy-Editors: Nick Fawcett, Richard Collins
Omnibus Cover Design: Helen Surman for LBBG
Original Series Cover Designs: Nico Taylor
Scientific Advice: Dr. Barnaby Osborne, Chris Warrick, Prof. Marcel Dicke, Dr. Paul Goulart, Andrew Wyld, Prof. Owen Brian Toon
Medical Advice: Prof. Ken Boffard, Dr. Vee Boffard, Prof. Guy Richards
Psychological Advice: Dr. Joanne Duma
Wilderness Advice: Mandy Johnson, Cameron Feaster
Early Readers: Nicole Simpson, George Kelly, Chris Ellis, Dane Taylor, Rayne Taylor, Ida Horwitz, Rob Long, Ryan Beyer, Werner Schutz, Taryn Arentsen Schutz
Additional Editing: James Long
Orbit Managing Editor: Joanna Kramer
Marketing: Felice Howden
Publicity: Gemma Conley-Smith, Nazia Khatun, Clara Diaz, Ellen Wright
Publisher: Tim Holman
Orbit U.S.: Devi Pillai, Anne Clarke

Thanks to our families and friends. Special thanks to booksellers and reviewers worldwide. Extra special thanks to you.

For access to exclusive stories, artwork and deleted scenes from the Outer Earth universe and beyond (and to score a free audiobook), head to robboffard.com/newsletter.

extras

orbit

meet the author

Photo Credit: Nicole Simpson

ROB BOFFARD is a South African author who splits his time between London, Vancouver and Johannesburg. He has worked as a journalist for over a decade, and has written articles for publications in more than a dozen countries, including the *Guardian* and *Wired* in the UK.

if you enjoyed
OUTER EARTH
look out for
ADRIFT
by
Rob Boffard

In the far reaches of space, a group of tourists board a small vessel for what will be the trip of a lifetime—in more ways than one…

They are embarking on a tour around Sigma Station—a remote mining facility and luxury hotel with stunning views of the Horsehead Nebula.

During the course of the trip, a mysterious ship with devastating advanced technology attacks the Station. Their pilot's quick evasive action means that the tour group escapes with their lives—but as the dust settles, they realize they may be the only survivors.…

Adrift in outer space, out of contact with civilization, and on a vastly under-equipped ship, these passengers are out of their depth. Their chances of getting home are close to none, and with the threat of another attack looming they must act soon—or risk perishing in the endless void of space.

Chapter 1

Rainmaker's heads-up display is a nightmare.

The alerts on it are coming faster than she can dismiss them. Lock indicators. Proximity warnings. Fuel alerts. Created by her neurochip, appearing directly in front of her. The world outside her fighter's cockpit is alive, torn with streaking missiles and twisting ships.

In the distance, a nuke detonates against a frigate, a baby sun tearing its way into life. The Horsehead Nebula glitters behind it.

Rainmaker twists her ship away from the heat wave, making it dance with precise, controlled thoughts. As she does so, she gets a full view of the battle: a thousand Frontier Scorpion fighters, flipping and turning and destroying one another in an arena bordered by the hulking frigates.

The Colony forces thought they could hold the area around Sigma Orionis—they thought they could take control of the jump gate and shut down all movement into this sector. They didn't bank on an early victory at Proxima freeing up a third of the Frontier navy, and now they're backed into a corner, fighting like hell to stay alive.

Maybe this'll be the battle that does it. Maybe this is the one that finally stops the Colonies for good.

Rainmaker's path has taken her away from the main thrust of the battle, out towards the edge of the sector. Her targeting systems find a lone enemy: a black Colony fighter, streaking towards her. Her training takes over, the mental command to fire forming in her mind. But then she stops it, cutting off the thought.

Something's not right.

"Control, this Rainmaker," she says. Despite the chaos around her, her voice is calm. "I have locked on incoming. Why's he alone? Over."

The reply is clipped and urgent. "Rainmaker, this is Frontier Control: evade, evade, evade. *Do not engage.* You have multiple bogies closing in on your six. They're trying to lock the door on you, over."

Rainmaker doesn't bother to respond, snarling an inaudible curse. Her radar systems were damaged earlier in the fight, and she has to rely on Control for the bandits she can't see. She breaks her lock, twisting her craft away as more warnings bloom on her console. "Twin, Blackbird, anybody. I've got multiples inbound, need a pickup, over."

The sarcastic voice of one of her wingmen comes over the comms. "Can't handle 'em yourself? I'm disappointed."

"Not a good time, Omen," she replies, burning her thrusters. "Can you help me or not? Over."

"Negative. Got three customers to deal with over here. Get in line."

A second, older voice comes over her comms. "Rainmaker, this is Blackbird. What's your twenty? Over."

Her neurochip recognises the words, both flashing up the info on her display and automatically sending it to Blackbird's. "Quadrant thirty-one," she says anyway, speaking through gritted teeth.

"Roger," says Blackbird. "I got 'em. Just sit tight. I'll handle it for y—Shit, I'm hit! I—"

"Eric!" Rainmaker shouts Blackbird's real name, her voice so loud it distorts the channel. But he's already gone. An impactor streaks past her, close enough for her to see the launch burns on its surface.

"Control, Rainmaker," she says. "Confirm Blackbird's position, I've lost contact!"

Control doesn't reply. Why would they? They're fighting a thousand fires at once, advising hundreds of Scorpion fighters. Forget the callsigns that command makes them use: Blackbird is a number to them, and so is she, and unless she does something right now, she's going to join him.

She makes the ship dance, forcing the two chasing Colony

fighters to face her head-on. They're a bigger threat than the lone one ahead. Now they're coming in from her eleven and one o'clock, curving towards her, already opening fire. She guns the ship, aiming for the tiny space in the middle, racing to make the gap before their impactors close her out.

"Thread the needle," she whispers. "Come on, thread the needle, thr—"

Everything freezes.

The battle falls silent.

A second later, a blinking red error box appears above one of the missiles.

"Oh. Um." Hannah Elliott's voice cuts through the silence. "Sorry, ladies and gentlemen. One second."

The box goes away—only to reappear a split-second later, like a fly buzzing back to where it was swatted from. This time, the simulation gives a muted *ding*, as if annoyed that Hannah can't grasp the point.

She rips the slim VR goggles from her head. She's not used to them—she forgot to put her lens in after she woke up, which meant she had to rely on the VR room's antiquated backup system. A strand of her long red hair catches on the strap, and she has to yank it loose, looking down at the ancient console in front of her.

"Sorry, ladies and gentlemen," she says again. "Won't be a minute."

She can her see her worried face reflected on the dark screen, her freckles making her look even younger than she is. She uses her finger this time, stabbing at the box's confirm button on the small access terminal on the desk. It comes back with a friend, a second, identical error box superimposed over the first. Beyond it, an impactor sits frozen in Rainmaker's viewport.

"Sorry." *Stop saying sorry*, she thinks, trying and failing to bring up the sim's main menu. "It's my first day."

Stony silence is the only answer. The twenty tourists in the darkened room before her are strapped into reclining motion seats with frayed belts. Most have their eyes closed, their personal lenses still displaying the frozen sim. A few are blinking, looking faintly annoyed. One of them, an older man with a salt-and-pepper beard, catches Hannah's eye with a scowl.

She quickly looks away, back at the error boxes. She can barely make it out the writing on them—the VR's depth of field has made the letters as tiny as the ones on the bottom line of an eye chart.

She should reset the sim. But how? Does that mean it'll start from scratch? Can she fast-forward? The supervisor who showed her the simulation that morning was trying to wrangle about fifteen new tour guides, and the instructions she gave Hannah amounted to watching the volume levels, and making sure none of the tourists threw up when Rainmaker turned too hard.

She gives the screen an experimental tap, and breathes a sigh of relief when a menu pops up: a list of files. There. Now she just has to—

But which one is it? The supervisor turned the sim on, and Hannah doesn't know which file she used. Their names are meaningless.

She taps the first one. Upbeat music explodes from the room's speakers, loud enough to make a couple of the tourists jump. She pulls the goggles back on, to be greeted by an animated, space-suited lizard firing laser beams at a huge, tentacled alien. A booming voice echoes across the music. "Adventurers! Enter the world of Reptar as he saves the galaxy from—"

The voice cuts off as Hannah somehow manages to stop the sim. In the silence that follows, she can feel her cheeks turning red.

She gives the screen a final, helpless look, and leaps to her feet. She'll figure this out. Somehow. They wouldn't have given her this job if they didn't think she could deal with the unexpected.

"OK!" She claps her hands together. "Sorry for the mix-up. I think there's a bit of a glitch in the old sim there."

She tries a laugh, which gets precisely zero reaction. Swallowing, she soldiers on.

"So, as you saw, that was the Battle of Sigma Orionis, which took place fifteen years ago, which would be..." She thinks hard. "2157, in the space around the hotel we're now in. Hopefully our historical sim gave you a good idea of the conditions our pilots faced—it was taken directly from one of their neurochip feeds."

She smiles. "Coincidentally, the battle took place almost exactly a hundred years after we first managed to first send a probe through a wormhole, which, as you... as you probably know already, fuelled the Great Expansion, and led to the permanent, long-range gates, like the one you came in on."

"We know," says the man with the salt-and-pepper beard. He reminds Hannah of a particularly grumpy high school teacher she once had. "It was in the intro you played us."

"Right." Hannah nods, like he's made an excellent point. She'd forgotten about the damn intro video, her jump-lag from the day before fuzzing her memory. All she can remember is a voiceover that was way, way too perky for someone discussing a battle as brutal as Sigma Orionis.

She decides to plunge ahead. "So, the... the Colonies lost that particular fight, but the war actually kept going for five years after the Frontier captured the space around Sigma Orionis."

They know this already, too. Why is she telling them? Heat creeps up her cheeks, a sensation she does her best to ignore.

"Anyway, if... if you've got any questions about the early days of the Expansion, while we were still constructing the jump gates, then I'm your girl. I actually did my dissertation on—"

Movement, behind her. She turns to see one of the other tour guides, a big dude with a tribal tattoo poking out the collar of his red company shirt.

"Oh, thank God," Hannah hisses at him. "Do you know how to fix the sim?"

He ignores her. "OK, folks," he says to the room, smooth and loud. "That concludes our VR demonstration. Hope you enjoyed it, and if you have any questions, I'll be happy to answer them while our next group of guests are getting set up."

Before Hannah can say anything, he turns to her, his smile melting off. "Your sim slot was over five minutes ago. Get out of here."

He bends down, and with an effortless series of commands,

resets the simulator. As the tourists file out, the bearded man glances at her, shaking his head.

Hannah digs in her back pocket, her face still hot and prickly. "Sorry. The sim's really good, and I got kind of wrapped up in it, so..." She tries to say the words with a smile, which fades as the other guide continues to ignore her.

She doesn't even know what she's doing—the sim wasn't good. It was creepy. Learning about a battle was one thing—actually being there, watching people get blown to pieces...

Sighing, she pulls her crumpled tab out of her pocket and unfolds it, which she'd faithfully written out her schedule on, copying it off her lens. It's a habit she's had since she was a kid, when her mom's lens glitched and they missed a swimming trial. "Can you tell me how to get to the dock?"

The other guide glances at the outdated tab, his mouth forming a *moue* of distaste. "There should be a map on your lens."

"Haven't synced it to the station yet." She's a little too embarrassed to tell him that it's still in its solution above the tiny sink in her quarters, and she forgot to go back for it before her shift started.

She would give a kidney to go back now, and not just for the lens. Her staff cabin might be small enough for her to touch all four walls at once without stretching, but it has a bed in it. With *sheets.* They might be scratchy and thin and smell like bleach, but the thought of pulling them over her head and drifting off is intoxicating.

The next group is pushing inside the VR room, clustered in twos and threes, eyeing the somewhat threadbare motion seats. The guide has already forgotten Hannah, striding towards the incoming holidaymakers, clapping his hands and booming a welcome.

"Thanks for your help," Hannah mutters, as she slips out the room.

The dock. She was there yesterday, wasn't she? Coming off the intake shuttle. How hard could it be to find a second time? She turns right out of the VR room, heading for where she thinks the main station atrium is. She's not late, according to her tab, but she picks up her pace all the same.

The wide walkway is dominated by a floor-to-ceiling window taller than the house Hannah grew up in. It's gently curved, and is packed with tourists. Most of them are clustered at the apex, admiring the view dominated by the Horsehead Nebula.

Hannah barely caught a glimpse when they arrived last night, which was filled with safety briefings and room assignments and roster changes and staff canteen conversations that were way too loud. Hannah had sat at a table to one side, both hoping that someone would come talk to her, and hoping they wouldn't.

In the end, with something like relief, she'd managed to slink off for a few hours of disturbed sleep.

The station she's on used to be plain old Sigma XV—a big, boring, industrial mining outpost that the Colony and the Frontier fought over during the war. They still did mining here—helium-3, mostly, for fusion reactors—but it was now also known as the Sigma Hotel and Luxury Resort.

It always amazed Hannah just how quickly it had all happened. It felt like the second the war ended, the tour operators were lobbying the Frontier Senate for franchise rights. Now, Sigma held ten thousand tourists, who streamed in through the big jump gate from a dozen different worlds and moons, excited to finally be able to travel, hoping for a glimpse of the Neb.

Like the war never happened. Like there aren't a hundred different small conflicts and breakaway factions still dotted across both Frontier *and* Colonies. The aftershocks of war, making themselves known.

Not that Sigma Station is the only one in on the action. It's happening everywhere—apparently there's even a tour company out Phobos way that takes people inside a wrecked Colony frigate that hasn't been hauled back for salvage yet.

As much as she feels uncomfortable with the idea of setting up a hotel here, so soon after the fighting, Hannah needs this job. It's the only one her useless history degree would get her, and at least it means that she doesn't have to sit at the table at her parents' house on Titan, listening to her sister talk about how fast her company is growing.

The walkway she's on takes a sharp right, away from the windows, opening up into an airy plaza. The space is enormous, climbing up ten whole levels. A glittering light fixture the size of a truck hangs from the ceiling, and in the centre of the floor, there's a large fountain, fake marble cherubs and dragons spouting water streams that crisscross in midair.

The plaza is packed with more tourists, milling around the fountain or chatting on benches or meandering in and out of the shops and restaurants that line the edges. Hannah has to slow down, sorry-ing and excuse-me-ing her way through.

The wash of sensations almost overwhelms her, and she can't help thinking about the sheets again. White. Cool. Light enough to slide under and—

No. Come on. You need this job.

Does she go left from here, or is it on the other side of the fountain? She tries to recall the station map she looked at while they were jumping, tries to picture it, but it's like trying to decipher something in Sanskrit. Then she sees a sign above one of the paths leading off the plaza. SHIP DOCK B. That's the one.

Three minutes later, she's there. The dock is small, a spartan mustering area with four gangways leading out from the station to the airlock berths. There aren't many people around, although there are still a few people sitting on benches.

One of them has a little girl sleeping on it, curled up with her hands tucked between shoulder and cheek, legs pulled up to her chest. Her mom—or the person Hannah thinks is her mom—sits next to her, blinking at something on her lens.

There are four tour ships visible through the glass, brightly lit against the inky black. Hannah's been on plenty of tours, and she still can't help thinking that every ship she's ever been on is ugly as hell.

if you enjoyed
OUTER EARTH
look out for
PLACES IN THE DARKNESS
by
Chris Brookmyre

Hundreds of miles above Earth, the space station Ciudad de Cielo—the City in the Sky—is a beacon of hope for humanity's expansion into the stars. But not everyone aboard shares such noble ideals.

Bootlegging, booze, and prostitution form a lucrative underground economy for rival gangs, which the authorities are happy to turn a blind eye to until a disassembled corpse is found dancing in the micro-gravity.

In charge of the murder investigation is Nikki "Fix" Freeman, who is not thrilled to have Alice Blake, an uptight government Goody-Two-shoes, riding shotgun. As the bodies pile up, and the partners are forced to question their own memories, Nikki and Alice begin to realize that gang warfare may not be the only cause for the violence.

AWAKENING (I)

"There will be no children."

It is the first thought that flashes into Alice's mind as she slowly approaches consciousness, like a diver rising towards the surface. The words are prompted by a sound: that of children's voices, laughing and shrieking with delight. At first she thinks she is imagining them, but though her eyes are closed she knows the voices are coming from outside her head.

There will be no children. It is one of the things she remembers being told to expect about her first trip to Ciudad de Cielo—CdC—and yet she can hear them, clear as day. Is it a recording?

She opens her eyes. She can only see directly in front, the beige wall of the passenger capsule's interior. Her head is restrained for safety inside a protective cradle, but the brace is not there purely to hold her in position. It also houses sensors monitoring her vital signs, which it streams to her lens, superimposing the data upon her field of vision.

The standard lens system comprises one contact for each eye, transferring data to and from a circular processing unit attached to the wrist. This disc also accommodates a sensor that interprets finger gestures by way of a primary control interface. The rig is completed by a sub-vocal audio relay that integrates so seamlessly with one's hearing that Alice sometimes forgets it's an auxiliary source. It is from this that the children's laughter briefly issues once more before being cut off.

She has been asleep. Or maybe it would be more accurate to say she must have passed out. She does not know for how long. Alice has never felt so disoriented, so brain-scrambled. This must be what it feels like to have a hangover, she thinks, never having experienced one personally. She has consumed alcohol, but only in moderation, strictly within the recommended lower- and upper-limit parameters prescribed for maximum health benefit.

"Dr. Blake?" says a voice, close by this time, not originating from the speakers.

A male face moves into view, the motion strangely fluid, as though gliding. It is further evidence of her wooziness. He seems to float into her field of vision like a figment from a dream. His hand is resting on the outer guard rail around her passenger cradle.

His features are Chinese, but less diluted than hers. He is about her age, either side of thirty. He is smiling, his tone gentle, his accent American.

"You lost consciousness. It sometimes happens during the ascent."

Alice searches for her voice, feeling relief when it comes online.

"How long was I out?"

He smiles in a manner she interprets as intended to be reassuring.

"Precisely two hours, seventeen minutes and twenty-two seconds, but you've been monitored the whole time."

"What caused it?" she asks. She knows that a precipitate loss of consciousness sits on a spectrum bookended by simple fainting and hypoxic brain injury.

Again the patient smile.

"I'm not qualified to interpret the data, but in my experience, most of the time it's a result of cumulative exhaustion brought on by tension and anxiety over the prospect of the ascent, exacerbated if you had a long trip to reach Ocean Terminal. Don't think of it as anything more significant than that you were tired and you fell asleep."

It feels like more than that though, like coming around from anaesthetic or something. Some parts of her mind seem accessible, others clouded. She knows that the platform is one hundred and sixty thousand kilometres above the base. She knows that the ascent takes five hours and fifty-three minutes. She knows all manner of technical data regarding the elevator and its operations, but she has an altogether less crisp recollection of her trip prior to entering this capsule.

"How much longer is the climb?" Alice asks. She can see the current time on her lens, but the formerly animated trip data field is now blank.

"The climb ended twenty minutes ago," he replies, amusement now taking over from reassurance in his tone. "Welcome to Heinlein Halfway Station."

He loosens his grip on the guard rail, which is when she understands that he was not resting on it, but holding it to prevent himself from floating away.

"The other passengers have already disembarked from the capsule. The protocol states that we leave you to come around on your own. Nobody stays out for very long once we hit the top, though you were nudging at the upper end of the scale."

He brushes his fingers against the rail, the action providing enough purchase for him to rise and drift away from her with dreamlike fluidity. It is no dream, though.

"Ladies and gentlemen, we are floating in space," he says.

She wonders why he makes this statement of the obvious, confused further by the absence of passengers who might be the other addressees. She detects a certain self-consciousness to it too.

She searches her memory for secondary levels of significance to the words and he reads her confusion in the blankness of her response.

"It's just something we say, a stupid tradition. Don't know how it started, but it kinda stuck."

Of course. The minute self-consciousness denoted that he was quoting. Like many such frivolous and pointless customs, it was observed for no greater reason than that it has been observed many times before, though its current observers could not explain its origin.

"Don't worry if you're feeling a little disoriented," he assures her. "Again, it's perfectly normal."

Alice stares at his features. She doesn't remember ever seeing this man before, though he must have been with her in the capsule.

No, she recalls. He wasn't. Nobody occupies a passenger position unnecessarily. An escort leaves you at the bottom and another meets you at the top. Every inch of storage space, every gram of weight is carefully accounted for to a precisely budgeted dollar value. The elevator massively reduced the cost of reaching geostationary orbit. Cars run constantly, as many as four simultaneously at different stages of ascent and descent, totalling twenty trips per day. The weight and volume of materials being transported over any given twenty-four-hour period exceeds the cumulative payload weight and volume the human race sent into orbit in its first five decades of space exploration. But nonetheless, nobody is assigned a passenger cradle unless their travel has a demonstrable value—which is what truly confuses her as once again laughter and high-pitched squeals of delight ring through her ears.

"I can hear children."

"Yeah, that's a common-access feed from elsewhere on the platform. You'll be sharing a shuttle with them to CdC. The family came up on an earlier car but they have been taking a tour of the platform before moving on."

"A family?"

"Tourists." He gives her a knowing look. "Every million they spend pushes us a little closer to the stars."

Alice strains to look around, but her head is snugly secured.

"If you feel you're good to go, I'll disengage your restraints. You ready?"

He means is she ready for physical movement and for microgravity, but these are merely physical considerations.

"My body seems fine, but my brain feels like it is still catching up."

"Don't worry, that's perfectly normal too. Do you need any pointers? Like who you are and what you're doing here?"

She realises that this is a joke, though it is uncomfortably close to the truth.

"Probably wouldn't hurt."

It is coming back in waves: articles and fragments of memory washed up like flotsam that she now has to assemble into coherent objects. She hopes this is all an effect of the ascent, and therefore temporary, rather than a result of being in space. Her name is Alice Blake. She is travelling to CdC on behalf of the Federation of National Governments to replace the outgoing Principal of the Security Oversight Executive. She will be here a minimum of six months as long as she doesn't screw up; considerably less if this woolly-headedness proves chronic.

She remembers things about her journey but she isn't sure they are in the right order. The capsule. The elevator. A platform in the ocean.

Logic helps fill in the blanks between specifics like track between stations. There was a long flight in an airplane. Did she fly direct to Ocean Terminal? No. It was too small to land an aircraft that size. She was on a large passenger jet, a long-haul flight. There was a delay, a problem with hydraulics.

She remembers the docks, azure water all around the platform, sparkling in the hot sun as she climbed the gangway. She went there by boat, a hydrofoil. She remembers ships moored at other points on the hexagon, offloading cargo. The shouts of men on the vast floating docks working to prepare the payloads for the elevator, the complex tessellation of pallets and cases in the vast hold beneath the tiny passenger capsule.

There is a soft hum as restraints withdraw from around her body, the head brace folding up and back. She attempts to stand but finds she cannot: one final anchor point at the base of her spine is preventing her from moving.

"Yeah, before I uncouple the last safety bolt, I have to advise you to please let me know if you think you might throw up, in which case I'll guide you to the nearest vacuum sluice. A proportion of people get nauseous in microgravity. We still don't know why: it's been happening since the first rocket crews, though obviously what they brought up was the right stuff."

She doesn't understand what he means, how twentieth-century astronauts' vomitus could somehow be a suitable substance, though from his expression she suspects it was another joke. She does not get it, but responds with a polite smile.

"Just take it slow, see how it feels."

Alice hears the clunk of the maglock disengaging and pushes up with her palms. She recalls her briefings on this but the result is still massively disproportionate to the effort. She rises instantly and at speed, shooting up past her escort before throwing out a hand to stave off impact with the ceiling.

Another childish giggle reverberates in her ears, but this time the source is her own throat.

As the sensation of drifting through the air registers around her body, she experiences the most intense endorphin rush. It is as though the weightlessness extends beyond the physical, a feeling of the purest pleasure, the simplest, most undiluted awareness of mere being. She is lost in the moment, everything beyond it divested of relevance. It only lasts a few seconds, but even as her body thrills, it is as though this purge reboots her mind. Everything comes rushing back in, the fragments assembling themselves into place, properly this time.

He guides her towards a circular hatch in the ceiling, a bladed aperture on a surface ninety degrees from the doorway by which she entered the capsule. It dilates in response to his proximity, granting access to an airlocked passage at the end of which is a second blade-locked circle. She is uncomfortably reminded of an automated device for chopping vegetables that sat in her parents' kitchen, but she obliges as he glides to one side and beckons her to pass through first.

The second aperture swishes quietly open once they are both inside and its counterpart has closed. Again he urges her upwards. She rises into a white-walled corridor, punctuated by panels of black. As she draws closer, she sees that they are not black, but transparent: there are tiny points of light in the darkness. She is looking into space. Then as she floats closer and higher, her elevation affords her a perspective directly down upon the Earth.

She gasps, quite involuntarily, looking round at him as though to say: "Are you seeing this?"

"Yeah. It never gets old."

He looks pleased but there is something knowing about his intonation, something minutely self-conscious, like when he said "we are floating in space."

She does not have enough experience of this individual to get a reliable reading on his microgestures and the subtler nuances of his speech. She can't be sure, but something seems insincere, rehearsed. She searches for a comparison. It prompts a memory of a tour guide, an attendant at a theme park. And, of course, that is all he is. This is not her liaison.

Glancing up again, away from the mesmerising sight of the glowing sphere beneath, Alice looks out into the blackness and observes that the points of light she saw were not stars. They are shuttlecraft, part of a constant traffic between here and her final destination.

"Getting like a freeway out there," her escort tells her. "Our fleet of ion shuttles are the workhorses of modern space. CdC is in an orbit seventy thousand kilometres above us, but these old faithfuls make each round trip burning less energy than it takes to drive a city block."

He beckons her along the passage, leading her upwards at a perpendicular junction. His hair moves like he is underwater, and as it lifts she sees a thin line below the base of his skull, where no new hair will grow: the site of his mesh implant.

She skims the wall with her fingers for propulsion, adjusting the force she exerts following her initial miscalculation. The shaft plunges several storeys beneath her unsupported feet at the perpendicular junction, a drop so dizzying as to make her eerily aware of what would happen should the magic spell wear off and gravity apply as it normally does.

There is another perpendicular turn, before they pass into what a sign above the larger bladed aperture denotes the Passenger Holding Area. It is a cylindrical chamber, with an airlocked doorway to the shuttle bay dominating one side. Along the other, a row of windows looks down into the cavernous interior of the space elevator's upper terminus, formally known as Heinlein Halfway Station.

There are seven people already inside the chamber. Instantly she recognises three of them as the other passengers who had travelled in her capsule. She hadn't spoken much to any of them, though they were all introduced when they boarded the elevator down on Earth. Their names are Kai Roganson, Davis Ikicha and Emmanuelle Deveraux. The other four comprise the family she has been told about: a man, a woman, a girl and a younger boy. The children are spinning in the air, laughing fit to burst.

Their mother warns them to cool it down or they might be sick. A sign on the wall cautions passengers against unnecessary manoeuvres in micro-gravity. Alice is dismayed that neither entreaty appears to be having an impact.

They are small, however. Perhaps the sign is generally more concerned with the greater hazards deriving from the potential of adult collisions.

She has learned that many rules do not apply so rigidly to children, or at least that some discretion may be applied in their enforcement.

The children are wearing miniature versions of the same environment suit as was issued to everyone else. It is designed to create a perfect seal with a rebreather mask in the event of a pressure loss, but in practice it functions principally as a giant diaper, collecting and filtering secretions during what could be an eleven- or twelve-hour journey between gravity-dependent toilet facilities.

Astronaut training used to involve learning to pee through a suction tube (crucially disengaging without spillage). She learned its history by way of background prep for the mission. She thinks of the commitment and determination required simply to enter the selection process, the punishing multidisciplinary programmes and simulations that had to be mastered, the sacrifices and risks driven by an unquenchable desire to reach space.

This triggers a connection in her memory and belatedly, she gets the joke. The right stuff.

She's had plenty of preparation and been briefed exhaustively, but none of it was about making the journey. Like everybody else in this chamber, she got here by stepping into an elevator. None of them was trained for the ascent any more than a commercial airline passenger gets flying lessons.

"Everyone, this is Dr. Alice Blake, as some of you already know. Alice is here with the Federation of National Governments."

He reprises introductions for the three she has already met, then indicates the four she has not.

"Dr. Blake, this is Mr. Sayid Uslam and his wife Arianne. And of course, taking advantage of the environmental conditions over there are their two children Karima and Zack. They are here on a sightseeing vacation."

Alice puts the name and the face together. Uslam is an energy magnate, a riches-to-ultra-riches entrepreneur whose family name has run through the infrastructure of Jadid Alearabia since the days of post-oil and post-war reconstruction.

Mr. Uslam nods and offers the empty smile of someone who knows Alice is not important enough for him to care who she is or why she is here. His wife doesn't even look, instead floating closer to the children who are now bumping their heads against the glass despite signs specifically warning passengers not to touch the windows.

Alice does not believe this is one of those areas where discretion must be exercised.

"What ages are your children?" Alice asks their mother.

"Zack is six and Karima is almost eight."

"Then presumably at least one of them can read the notices regarding contact with the glass."

The woman's eyes flash with barely suppressed outrage. In Alice's experience this is often the emotional response when a person is confronted with dereliction of their responsibilities. In this instance it does not prevent her from making amends.

"Zack, Karima, don't bump the glass or this lady here will have us thrown off the space station," Mrs. Uslam tells them.

This last seems an unnecessary level of threat, but children sometimes require exaggeration in order to make a point.

There ensues a silence in the chamber, an awkwardness that Alice has learned often follows when a person's behavioural shortcomings have been made explicit in the company of others.

The individual most uncomfortable in the aftermath appears to be the escort, which is when it occurs to her that the one person he has not introduced is himself. People are often welcoming of a distraction at such moments, so she decides to offer one.

"Forgive me, but I don't believe you told me your name."

"Oh, my apologies. I'm pretty sure I did, but I'm forgetting you were a little woozy."

He is mistaken. Her memory is functioning perfectly now, and she only ever has to be told someone's name once.

"Also, on CdC you get used to people's names showing up on your lens, so we can be a little lax about introductions. I'm Tony Chu. I am the Uslam family's official guide on their trip, but up here, we're all about efficiency so everybody doubles up on tasks to avoid any unnecessary redundancy. I'm to make sure you get to CdC and are met by your official liaison. There was a flight delay from New York, I believe?"

"Yes. I was supposed to be meeting up with a delegation before we took the hydrofoil, but I didn't make it. I believe they are already on CdC."

"As will you be, soon enough. You're halfway there, after all."

He smiles again, indicating a plaque above the shuttle bay door. This time she more quickly identifies the note of tour-guide insincerity.

The plaque reads:

> Once you get to earth orbit, you're halfway to anywhere in the solar system.
>
> —Robert A Heinlein

"What are they doing?" asks the little girl, staring down into the expansive vault that is the core of the facility.

"They are unloading the freight compartments of the elevator car that these other passengers just arrived on," Chu replies. "That's why you're having such fun floating around."

He turns to address the adults. "We don't have any centripetal gravity systems here on Heinlein because principally this place is about processing heavy cargo. We've got the strongest stevedores in human history: one person can move a forklift load with their pinkie."

Alice glances into the cargo bay. She counts six shuttle docks, three either side of an octagonal chamber.

"The freight is broken down into smaller loads and sent to different destinations around CdC."

"Are any of them androids?" asks the little boy.

"Remember, sweetie, we spoke about this already," his mother reminds him; not for the first time if the weariness in her tone is anything to go by.

"We have some of the most advanced automated systems known to man," Chu replies with professionally cheery indulgence. "But if you mean robots or cyborgs like in the simworlds you may have seen, then I'm afraid not."

The kid looks crestfallen, like he had been hoping his spoilsport mom was lying or misinformed.

Chu reads it and responds with cheerful mock-incredulity.

"You saying space isn't cool enough?"

The boy blushes, shaking his head bashfully.

Alice thinks of the stuttering history of AI, the intoxication of the early days when a few leaps in progress made people believe this was the beginning of an exponential acceleration. In fact, the sum of what those leaps achieved was merely to educate scientists as to the true complexity of what they were trying to comprehend.

Someone once described it as like building a tower to the moon. Every year they congratulated themselves on how much higher the tower was, but they weren't getting much closer to their target. In fact, the higher they built, the more they were able to appreciate its true distance. To Alice, the significance of this could not be underlined more firmly than by the fact that she has just ascended a tower to space, an engineering feat that proved considerably easier to achieve than the artificial replication of human intelligence.

"There are no androids here," the kid's mother affirms. "And when we get to CdC, there will be no androids there either."

Her tone is final, but her words remind Alice that she was assured there would be no children.

As the shuttle-bay lights come on, indicating the arrival of their transport, it is a timely reminder that she has no more first-hand knowledge than this child regarding what awaits her when she finally reaches Ciudad de Cielo, the City in the Sky.